THE CLOISTER AND THE HEARTH

THE CLOISTER
AND THE HEARTH

By

CHARLES READE

With critical and biographical material by

BRADFORD A. BOOTH

New York

HARPER & BROTHERS, PUBLISHERS

Library of Congress catalog card number: 61-7310

CONTENTS

BIOGRAPHICAL NOTE

The author of *The Cloister and the Hearth,* who with Charles Dickens and Wilkie Collins made up the triumvirate of foremost Victorian "sensation" novelists, was born near Oxford, England, on June 8, 1814. He was the youngest of the ten children born to a university-educated country squire and a rather domineering woman with strong Evangelical interests. In 1831, after an uneventful childhood and private tutoring, Reade entered Oxford, where he made a reputation as a somewhat eccentric aesthete. In due course he was graduated with third-class honors, disappointing his mother's ambitions for a higher rank because, characteristically, he chose to pursue only those studies which interested him.

Immediately following his graduation in 1835 occurred an event which, in effect, determined the course of his life: he was elected a probationary fellow of Magdalen College. The young man was already developing literary aspirations and had little stomach for academic life, but his father made it clear that he could not support him through an apprentice period as a writer. Reade had therefore no choice but to accept the college appointment. To hold it, however, it was necessary to be ordained in the church. Unable to face taking orders, Reade applied for and was granted permission by the college to enter the legal profession. He was entered at Lincoln's Inn and began to read law in chambers with Samuel Warren, later the author of the celebrated *Ten*

Thousand a Year but already a novelist of growing reputation. When complications developed because Reade had not yet taken his M.A. degree, he decided to study medicine. But a brief experience at the University of Edinburgh taught this sensitive young man that he could not endure even to see a patient bled, let alone take part in operating and dissecting procedures. In despair, he returned to law and was finally admitted to the bar in 1842. Like Sir Walter Scott, Wilkie Collins, Robert Louis Stevenson, and other notable English novelists, Reade never practiced. Cut off from other income he was forced to maintain his Oxford connection, becoming successively Junior Dean of Arts, Bursar, and finally Vice President at Magdalen.

Another harassing complication of his academic post was the Magdalen statute which demanded celibacy of its fellows. Reade's resentment against this rule later drew him to the subject of *The Cloister and the Hearth,* where in a footnote, as you will see, he describes enforced celibacy of the clergy as "an invention truly fiendish." Because he dared not give up his post, however, Reade never married. But before being called to the bar he fell in love with a Scottish girl, apparently of lower social rank, and there ensued an irregular "Scottish marriage," much like that of Gerard and Margaret in *The Cloister and the Hearth,* and a son, whom Reade did not acknowledge until shortly before his death. The immediate literary result was a play *Christie Johnstone,* later reworked into a novel, the action of which is based upon the author's own unhappy situation.

While he was in London studying law, Reade became fascinated by the theater, particularly French melodrama, the exaggerations of which are prominent in all his work. After one or two experimental failures he produced, in collaboration with the well-known dramatist Tom Taylor, his great theatrical success *Masks and Faces* (1852), which he immediately rewrote as a novel under the title of *Peg Woffington.* The popularity of these two works launched Reade on his long career in the two media, which he felt were closely related. His novels are so highly dramatic that he found it relatively easy to adapt most of them for the stage.

In 1856 Reade interrupted a period of dramatic activity and theatrical management to publish another major novel, *It Is Never Too Late to Mend,* the first of a group in which he employed fiction to attack social abuses, in this case the brutalities of the English prison system. This was followed in 1861 by *The Cloister and the Hearth* and in 1863 by *Hard Cash,* the best known of his propaganda novels. *Hard Cash* gives such a terrifying picture of conditions in lunatic asylums that Reade was deluged by protests. Not one to shun an argument (he was, in fact, a very contentious fellow), he carried the battle to his opponents with a flurry of letters and articles in which he showed that he had, as always, documentary evidence for his charges.

Reade's next novel, *Griffith Gaunt* (1866), dealing with a priest's love for a married woman, whose husband in revenge contracts a bigamous marriage, is certainly not pleasant, but with equal certainty it is not immoral, as widely and vociferously charged. *Foul Play* (1869) involves the scuttling in the Pacific of a ship supposed to be carrying a consignment of gold, the object being to defraud the underwriters. *Put Yourself in His Place* (1870) describes a form of terrorism developed by trades-unions called "rattening"; that is, stealing tools or destroying machinery. And *A Terrible Temptation* (1871), the last of the major novels, is concerned with the efforts of an unscrupulous ne'er-do-well to defraud his cousin of an inheritance, which include locking up the innocent man in an insane asylum. One of the principal characters is a kept woman, and some of the details were considered in such bad taste that the critics flayed the author with a severity that now seems ludicrous, one of them dismissing the book as "brothel garbage." In consequence, of course, the novel was a great financial success, particularly in the United States.

Reade was by this time tired of controversy, however, and in his last years he devoted himself chiefly to short stories and to the theater, making a hit with *Drink,* an adaptation of Zola's *L'Assommoir,* and taking Ellen Terry and Forbes-Robertson on tour. He suffered a deep spiritual loss in 1879 in the death of the actress Laura Seymour, with whom he had a long, close, but platonic friendship. By 1882 his health was permanently broken, and he died quietly on February 11, 1884.

CHAPTER I

NOT a day passes over the earth, but men and women of no note do great deeds, speak great words, and suffer noble sorrows. Of these obscure heroes, philosophers, and martyrs, the greater part will never be known till that hour, when many that are great shall be small, and the small great; but of others the world's knowledge may be said to sleep: their lives and characters lie hidden from nations in the annals that record them. The general reader cannot feel them, they are presented so curtly and coldly: they are not like breathing stories appealing to his heart, but little historic hailstones striking him but to glance off his bosom: nor can he understand them; for epitomes are not narratives, as skeletons are not human figures.

Thus records of prime truths remain a dead letter to plain folk; the writers have left so much to the imagination, and imagination is so rare a gift. Here, then, the writer of fiction may be of use to the public—as an interpreter.

There is a musty chronicle, written in tolerable Latin, and in it a chapter where every sentence holds a fact. Here is told, with harsh brevity, the strange history of a pair, who lived untrumpeted, and died unsung, four hundred years ago; and lie now, as unpitied, in that stern page, as fossils in a rock. Thus, living or dead, Fate is still unjust to them. For if I can but show you what lies below that dry chronicler's words, methinks you will correct the indifference of centuries, and give those two sore tried souls a place in your heart—for a day.

It was past the middle of the fifteenth century, Louis XI. was sovereign of France; Edward IV. was wrongful King of England; and Philip "the Good," having by force and cunning dispossessed his cousin Jacqueline, and broken her heart, reigned undisturbed this many years in Holland, where our tale begins.

Elias, and Catherine his wife, lived in the little town of Tergou.

The Cloister and the Hearth

He traded, wholesale and retail, in cloth, silk, brown holland, and, above all, in curried leather, a material highly valued by the middling people, because it would stand twenty years' wear, and turn an ordinary knife, no small virtue in a jerkin of that century, in which folk were so liberal of their steel; even at dinner a man would leave his meat awhile, and carve you his neighbour, on a very moderate difference of opinion.

The couple were well to do, and would have been free from all earthly care, but for nine children. When these were coming into the world, one per annum, each was hailed with rejoicings, and the saints were thanked, not expostulated with; and when parents and children were all young together, the latter were looked upon as lovely little playthings invented by Heaven for the amusement, joy, and evening solace of people in business.

But as the olive-branches shot up, and the parents grew older, and saw with their own eyes the fate of large families, misgivings and care mingled with their love. They belonged to a singularly wise and provident people: in Holland reckless parents were as rare as disobedient children. So now when the huge loaf came in on a gigantic trencher, looking like a fortress in its moat, and, the tour of the table once made, seemed to have melted away, Elias and Catherine would look at one another and say, "Who is to find bread for them all when we are gone?"

At this observation the younger ones needed all their filial respect to keep their little Dutch countenances; for in their opinion dinner and supper came by nature like sunrise and sunset, and, so long as that luminary should travel round the earth, so long *must* the brown loaf go round their family circle, and set in their stomachs only to rise again in the family oven. But the remark awakened the national thoughtfulness of the elder boys, and being often repeated, set several of the family thinking, some of them good thoughts, some ill thoughts, according to the nature of the thinkers.

"Kate, the children grow so, this table will soon be too small."

"We cannot afford it, Eli," replied Catherine, answering not his words, but his thought, after the manner of women.

Their anxiety for the future took at times a less dismal but more mortifying turn. The free burghers had their pride as well as the

2

nobles; and these two could not bear that any of their blood should go down in the burgh after their decease.

So by prudence and self-denial they managed to clothe all the little bodies, and feed all the great mouths, and yet put by a small hoard to meet the future; and, as it grew, and grew, they felt a pleasure the miser hoarding for himself knows not.

One day the eldest boy but one, aged nineteen, came to his mother, and with that outward composure which has so misled some persons as to the real nature of this people begged her to intercede with his father to send him to Amsterdam, and place him with a merchant. "It is the way of life that likes me; merchants are wealthy; I am good at numbers; prithee, good mother, take my part in this, and I shall ever be, as I am now, your debtor."

Catherine threw up her hands with dismay and incredulity. "What leave Tergou!"

"What is one street to me more than another? If I can leave the folk of Tergou, I can surely leave the stones."

"What! quit your poor father now he is no longer young?"

"Mother, if I can leave you, I can leave him."

"What leave your poor brothers and sisters, that love you so dear?"

"There are enough in the house without me."

"What mean you, Richart? Who is more thought of than you? Stay, have I spoken sharp to you? Have I been unkind to you?"

"Never that I know of; and if you had, you should never hear of it from me. Mother," said Richart gravely, but the tear was in his eye, "it all lies in a word. And nothing can change my mind. There will be one mouth less for you to feed."

"There now, see what my tongue has done," said Catherine, and the next moment she began to cry. For she saw her first young bird on the edge of the nest trying his wings, to fly into the world. Richart had a calm, strong will, and she knew he never wasted a word.

It ended as nature has willed all such discourse shall end: young Richart went to Amsterdam with a face so long and sad as it had never been seen before, and a heart like granite.

That afternoon at supper there was one mouth less. Catherine looked at Richart's chair and wept bitterly. On this Elias shouted roughly and angrily to the children "sit wider! Can't ye: sit wider!" and turned his head away over the back of his seat awhile, and was silent.

Richart was launched; and never cost them another penny: but to fit him out and place him in the house of Vander Stegen the merchant took all the little hoard but one gold crown. They began again. Two years passed, Richart found a niche in commerce for his brother Jacob, and Jacob left Tergou directly after dinner, which was at eleven in the forenoon. At supper that day Elias remembered what had happened the last time; so it was in a low whisper he said, "sit wider, dears!" Now until that moment, Catherine *would* not see the gap at table, for her daughter Catherine had besought her not to grieve to-night, and she had said, "No, sweetheart, I promise I will not, since it vexes my children." But when Elias whispered "Sit wider!" says she, "Ay! the table will soon be too big for the children: and you thought it would be too small:" and having delivered this with forced calmness, she put up her apron the next moment, and wept sore.

" 'Tis the best that leave us," sobbed she, "that is the cruel part."

"Nay! nay!" said Elias, "our children are good children, and all are dear to us alike. Heed her not! What God takes from us still seems better than what he spares to us: that is to say, men are by nature unthankful—and women silly."

"And I say Richart and Jacob were the flower of the flock," sobbed Catherine.

The little coffer was empty again, and to fill it they gathered like ants. In those days speculation was pretty much confined to the card-and-dice business. Elias knew no way to wealth but the slow and sure one. "A penny saved is a penny gained," was his humble creed. All that was not required for the business, and the necessaries of life, went into the little coffer with steel bands and florid key. They denied themselves in turn the humblest luxuries, and then, catching one another's looks, smiled; perhaps with a greater joy than self-indulgence has to bestow. And so in three years more they had gleaned enough to set up their fourth son as a master tailor, and their eldest daughter as a robe-maker, in Tergou. Here were two more provided for: their own trade would enable them to throw work into the hands of this pair. But the coffer was drained to the dregs, and this time the shop too bled a little in goods if not in coin.

4

The Cloister and the Hearth

Alas! there remained on hand two that were unable to get their bread, and two that were unwilling. The unable ones were 1, Giles, a dwarf, of the wrong sort, half stupidity, half malice, all head and claws and voice, run from by dogs and unprejudiced females, and sided with through thick and thin by his mother; 2, Little Catherine, a poor little girl that could only move on crutches. She lived in pain, but smiled through it, with her marble face and violet eyes and long silky lashes: and fretful or repining word never came from her lips. The unwilling ones were Sybrandt, the youngest, a ne'er-do-weel, too much in love with play to work, and Cornelis, the eldest, who had made calculations, and stuck to the hearth, waiting for dead men's shoes. Almost worn out by their repeated efforts, and above all dispirited by the moral and physical infirmities of those that now remained on hand, the anxious couple would often say, "What will become of all these when we shall be no longer here to take care of them?" But when they had said this a good many times, suddenly the domestic horizon cleared, and then they used still to say it, because a habit is a habit, but they uttered it half mechanically now, and added brightly and cheerfully, "but thanks to St. Bavon and all the saints, there's Gerard."

Young Gerard was for many years of his life a son apart and distinct; object of no fears and no great hopes. No fears; for he was going into the Church; and the Church could always maintain her children by hook or by crook in those days: no great hopes, because his family had no interest with the great to get him a benefice, and the young man's own habits were frivolous, and indeed, such as our cloth merchant would not have put up with in any one but a clerk that was to be. His trivialities were reading and penmanship, and he was so wrapt up in them that often he could hardly be got away to his meals. The day was never long enough for him: and he carried ever a tinder-box and brimstone matches, and begged ends of candles of the neighbors, which he lighted at unreasonable hours—ay, even at eight of the clock at night in winter, when the very burgomaster was abed. Endured at home, his practices were encouraged by the monks of a neighboring convent. They had taught him penmanship, and continued to teach him, until one day they discovered, in the middle of a lesson, that he was teaching them. They pointed this out to him in a merry way: he hung his

5

head and blushed: he had suspected as much himself, but mistrusted his judgment in so delicate a matter. "But, my son," said the elderly monk, "how is it that you, to whom God has given an eye so true, a hand so subtle yet firm, and a heart to love these beautiful crafts, how is it you do not colour as well as write? a scroll looks but barren unless a border of fruit, and leaves, and rich arabesques, surround the good words, and charm the sense as those do the soul and understanding; to say nothing of the pictures of holy men and women departed, with which the several chapters should be adorned, and not alone the eye soothed with the brave and sweetly blended colours, but the heart lifted by effigies of the saints in glory. Answer me, my son."

At this Gerard was confused, and muttered that he had made several trials at illuminating, but had not succeeded well; and thus the matter rested.

Soon after this a fellow-enthusiast came on the scene in the unwonted form of an old lady. Margaret, sister and survivor of the brothers Van Eyck, left Flanders, and came to end her days in her native country. She bought a small house near Tergou. In course of time she heard of Gerard, and saw some of his handiwork: it pleased her so well that she sent her female servant, Reicht Heynes, to ask him to come to her. This led to an acquaintance: it could hardly be otherwise, for little Tergou had never held so many as two zealots of this sort before. At first the old lady damped Gerard's courage terribly. At each visit she fished out of holes and corners drawings and paintings, some of them by her own hand, that seemed to him unapproachable: but if the artist overpowered him, the woman kept his heart up. She and Reicht soon turned him inside out like a glove: among other things, they drew from him what the good monks had failed to hit upon, the reason why he did not illuminate, viz., that he could not afford the gold, the blue, and the red, but only the cheap earths; and that he was afraid to ask his mother to buy the choice colours, and was sure he should ask her in vain. Then Margaret Van Eyck gave him a little brush-gold, and some vermilion, and ultramarine, and a piece of good vellum to lay them on. He almost adored her. As he left the house Reicht ran after him with a candle and two quarters: he quite kissed her. But better even than the gold and lapis lazuli to the illuminator was the sympathy to the isolated enthusiast. That sympathy was always ready, and, as he returned it, an affection sprung up between the old painter and the young caligrapher that was doubly characteristic of the time. For this was a century in which the fine arts and the higher mechanical arts were not separated by any distinct boundary, nor were those who practised them: and it was an age in which artists sought out and loved one another. Should this last statement stagger a painter or writer of our day, let me remind him that even Christians loved one another at first starting.

Backed by an acquaintance so venerable, and strengthened by female sympathy, Gerard advanced in learning and skill. His spirits, too, rose visibly: he still looked behind him when dragged to dinner in the middle of an initial G; but once seated showed great social qualities: likewise a gay humour, that had hitherto but peeped in him, shone out, and often he set the table in a roar, and kept it there, sometimes with his own wit, sometimes with jests which were glossy new to his family, being drawn from antiquity.

As a return for all he owed his friends the monks, he made them exquisite copies from two of their choicest MSS., viz., the life of their founder, and their Comedies of Terence, the monastery finding the vellum.

The high and puissant Prince, Philip "the Good," Duke of Burgundy, Luxemburg, and Brabant, Earl of Holland and Zealand, Lord of Friesland, Count of Flanders, Artois, and Hainault, Lord of Salins and Macklyn—was versatile.

He could fight as well as any king going; and he could lie as well as any, except the King of France. He was a mighty hunter, and could read and write. His tastes were wide and ardent. He loved jewels like a woman, and gorgeous apparel. He dearly loved maids of honour, and indeed paintings generally; in proof of which he ennobled Jan Van Eyck. He had also a rage for giants, dwarfs, and Turks. These last stood ever planted about him, turbaned, and blazing with jewels. His agents inveigled them from Istamboul with fair promises: but, the moment he had got them, he baptized them by brute force in a large tub; and, this done, let them squat with their faces toward Mecca, and invoke Mahound as much as they pleased, laughing in his sleeve at their simplicity in fancying they were still infidels. He had lions in cages, and fleet leopards trained by Orientals to run down hares and deer. In short, he relished all rarities except the humdrum virtues. For anything singularly pretty, or diabolically ugly, this was your customer. The best of him was, he was open-handed to the poor; and the next best was, he fostered the arts in earnest: whereof he now gave a signal proof. He offered prizes for the best specimens of "orfèvrerie" in two kinds, religious and secular; item for the best paintings in white of egg, oils and tempera; these to be on panel, silk, or metal, as the artists chose: item for the best transparent painting on glass: item for the best illuminating and border painting on vellum: item for the fairest writing on vellum. The burgomasters of the several towns were commanded to aid all the poorer competitors by receiving their specimens and sending them with due care to Rotterdam at the expense of their several burghs. When this was cried by the bellman through the streets of Tergou, a thousand mouths opened, and one heart beat—Gerard's. He told his family timidly he should try for two of those prizes. They stared in silence, for their breath was gone at his audacity: but one horrid laugh exploded on the floor like a petard. Gerard looked down, and there was the dwarf, slit and fanged from ear to ear at his expense, and laughing like a lion. Nature relenting at having made Giles so small, had given him as a set-off the biggest voice on record. His very whisper was a bassoon. He was like those stunted wide-mouthed pieces of ordnance we see on fortifications; more like a flower-pot than a cannon; but ods tympana how they bellow!

Gerard turned red with anger, the more so as the others began to titter. White Catherine saw, and a pink tinge came on her cheek. She said softly, "Why do you laugh? Is it because he is our brother you think he cannot be capable? Yes, Gerard, try with the rest. Many say you are skilful; and mother and I will pray the Virgin to guide your hand."

"Thank you, little Kate. You shall pray to our Lady, and our mother shall buy me vellum and the colours to illuminate with."

"What will they cost, my lad?"

"Two gold crowns" (about three shillings and fourpence English money).

"What?" screamed the housewife; "when the bushel of rye costs but a groat! What! me spend a month's meal and meat and fire on such vanity as that: the lightning from Heaven would fall on me and my children would all be beggars."

"Mother!" sighed little Catherine imploringly.

"Oh! it is in vain, Kate," said Gerard, with a sigh. "I shall have to give it up, or ask the dame Van Eyck. She would give it me, but I think shame to be for ever taking from her."

"It is not her affair," said Catherine, very sharply; "what has she to do coming between me and my son?" And she left the room with a red face. Little Catherine smiled. Presently the housewife returned with a gracious affectionate air, and two little gold pieces in her hand.

"There, sweetheart," said she, "you won't have to trouble dame or demoiselle for two paltry crowns."

But on this Gerard fell a-thinking how he could spare her purse.

"One will do, mother. I will ask the good monks to let me send my copy of their 'Terence:' it is on snowy vellum, and I can write no better: so then I shall only need six sheets of vellum for my borders and miniatures, and gold for my ground, and prime colours—one crown will do."

"Never tyne the ship for want of a bit of tar, Gerard," said this changeable mother. But she added, "Well, there, I will put the crown in my pocket. That won't be like putting it back in the box. Going to the box to take out instead of putting in, it is like going to my heart with a knife for so many drops of blood. You will be sure to want it, Gerard. The house is never built for less than the builder counted on."

Sure enough, when the time came, Gerard longed to go to Rotterdam and see the duke, and above all to see the work of his competitors, and so get a lesson from defeat. And the crown came out of the housewife's pocket with a very good grace. Gerard would soon be a priest. It seemed hard if he might not enjoy the world a little before separating himself from it for life.

The night before he went, Margaret Van Eyck asked him to take a letter for her, and when he came to look at it, to his surprise he found it was addressed to the Princess Marie, at the Stadthouse, in Rotterdam.

The day before the prizes were to be distributed, Gerard started for Rotterdam in his holiday suit, to wit, a doublet of silver-grey cloth with sleeves, and a jerkin of the same over it, but without sleeves. From his waist to his heels he was clad in a pair of tight-fitting buckskin hose fastened by laces (called points) to his doublet.

His shoes were pointed, in moderation, and secured by a strap that passed under the hollow of his foot. On his head and the back of his neck he wore his flowing hair, and pinned to his back between his shoulders was his hat: it was further secured by a purple silk ribbon little Kate had passed round him from the sides of the hat, and knotted neatly on his breast; below his hat, attached to the upper rim of his broad waist-belt, was his leathern wallet. When he got within a league of Rotterdam he was pretty tired, but he soon fell in with a pair that was more so. He found an old man sitting by the roadside quite worn out, and a comely young woman holding his hand, with a face brimful of concern. The country people trudged by and noticed nothing amiss: but Gerard, as he passed drew conclusions. Even dress tells a tale to those who study it so closely as he did, being an illuminator. The old man wore a gown, and a fur tippet, and a velvet cap, sure signs of dignity: but the triangular purse at his girdle was lean, the gown rusty, the fur worn, sure signs of poverty. The young woman was dressed in plain russet cloth: yet snow-white lawn covered that part of her neck the gown left visible, and ended half way up her white throat in a little band of gold embroidery: and her head-dress was new to Gerard; instead of hiding her hair in a pile of linen or lawn, she wore an open net-work of silver cord with silver spangles at the interstices: in this her glossy auburn hair was rolled in front into two solid waves, and supported behind in a luxurious and shapely mass. His quick eye took in all this, and the old man's pallor, and the tears in the young woman's eyes. So when he had passed them a few yards, he reflected, and turned back, and came towards them bashfully.

"Father, I fear you are tired."

"Indeed, my son, I am," replied the old man; "and faint for lack of food."

Gerard's address did not appear so agreeable to the girl as to the old man. She seemed ashamed, and with much reserve in her manner said, that it was her fault; she had underrated the distance, and imprudently allowed her father to start too late in the day.

"No! no!" said the old man; "it is not the distance, it is the want of nourishment."

The girl put her arms round his neck, with tender concern, but took that opportunity of whispering, "Father, a stranger—a young man!"

But it was too late. Gerard, with simplicity, and quite as a matter of course, fell to gathering sticks with great expedition. This done, he took down his wallet, out with the manchet of bread and the iron flask his careful mother had put up, and his everlasting tinder-box; lighted a match, then a candle end, then the sticks; and put his iron flask on it. Then down he went on his stomach and took a good blow: then looking up, he saw the girl's face had thawed, and she was looking down at him and his energy with a demure smile. He laughed back to her: "Mind the pot," said he, "and don't let it spill, for Heaven's sake: there's a cleft stick to hold it safe with;" and with this he set off running towards a corn-field at some distance.

Whilst he was gone, there came by, on a mule with rich purple housings, an old man redolent of wealth. The purse at his girdle was plethoric, the fur on his tippet was ermine, broad and new. It was Ghysbrecht Van Swieten, the burgomaster of Tergou. He was old, and his face furrowed. He was a notorious miser, and looked one generally. But the idea of supping with the duke raised him just now into manifest complacency. Yet at the sight of the faded old man and his bright daughter sitting by a fire of sticks, the smile died out of his face, and he wore a strange look of pain and uneasiness. He reined in his mule. "Why, Peter,—Margaret—" said he almost fiercely. "what mummery is this!" Peter was going to answer, but Margaret interposed hastily, and said: "My father was exhausted, so I am warming something to give him strength before we go on." "What, reduced to feed by the roadside like the Bohemians," said Ghysbrecht, and his hand went into his purse: but it did not seem at home there; it fumbled uncertainly, afraid too large a coin might stick to a finger and come out.

At this moment who should come bounding up but Gerard. He had two straws in his hand, and he threw himself down by the fire, and relieved Margaret of the cooking part: then suddenly recognizing the burgomaster, he coloured all over. Ghysbrecht Van Swieten started and glared at him, and took his hand out of his purse. "Oh," said he bitterly, "I am not wanted:" and went slowly on, casting a long look of suspicion on Margaret, and hostility on Gerard, that was not very intelligible. However, there was something about it that Margaret could read enough to blush at, and almost toss her head. Gerard only stared with surprise. "By St. Bavon, I think the old miser grudges us three our quart of soup," said he. When the young man put that interpretation on Ghysbrecht's strange and meaning look, Margaret was greatly relieved, and smiled gaily on the speaker.

Meantime Ghysbrecht plodded on, more wretched in his wealth than these in their poverty. And the curious thing is that the mule, the purple housings, and one half the coin in that plethoric purse, belonged not to Ghysbrecht Van Swieten, but to that faded old man and that comely girl, who sat by the road-side fire to be fed by a stranger. They did not know this, but Ghysbrecht knew it, and carried in his heart a scorpion of his own begetting. That scorpion is remorse; the remorse, that, not being penitence, is incurable, and ready for fresh misdeeds upon a fresh temptation.

Twenty years ago, when Ghysbrecht was a hard and honest man, the touchstone opportunity came to him, and he did an act of heartless roguery. It seemed a safe one. It had hitherto proved a safe one, though he had never felt safe. To-day he has seen youth, enterprise, and above all, knowledge, seated by fair Margaret and her father on terms that look familiar and loving.

And the fiends are at his ear again.

CHAPTER II

"THE soup is hot," said Gerard.

"But how are we to get it to our mouths?" inquired the senior, despondingly.

"Father, the young man has brought us straws." And Margaret smiled slily.

"Ay, ay!" said the old man: "but my poor bones are stiff, and indeed the fire is too hot for a body to kneel over with these short straws. St. John the Baptist, but the young man is adroit!"

For, while he stated his difficulty, Gerard removed it. He untied in a moment the knot on his breast, took his hat off, put a stone in each corner of it, then wrapping his hand in the tail of his jerkin, whipped the flask off the fire, wedged it in between the stones, and put the hat under the old man's nose with a merry smile. The other tremulously inserted the pipe of rye-straw and sucked. Lo and behold his wan, drawn face was seen to light up more and more, till it quite glowed; and, as soon as he had drawn a long breath:

"Hippocrates and Galen!" he cried, " 'tis a soupe au vin—the restorative of restoratives. Blessed be the nation that invented it, and the woman that made it, and the young man who brings it to fainting folk. Have a suck, my girl, while I relate to our young host the history and virtues of this his sovereign compound. This corroborative, young sir, was unknown to the ancients: we find it neither in their treatises of medicine, nor in those popular narratives, which reveal many of their remedies, both in chirurgery and medicine proper. Hector, in the Ilias, if my memory does not play me false,—"

Margaret. "Alas! he's off."

"—was invited by one of the ladies of the poem to drink a draught of wine; but he declined, on the plea that he was just going into battle, and must not take aught to weaken his powers. Now, if the 'soupe au vin' had been known in Troy, it is clear that in declining 'vinum merum' upon that score, he would have added in the next hexameter. 'But a "soupe au vin," madam, I will degust, and gratefully.' Not only would this have been but common civility—a virtue no perfect commander is wanting in—but not to have done it would have proved him a shallow and improvident person, unfit to be trusted with the conduct of a war; for men going into a battle need sustenance and all the possible support, as is proved by this, that foolish generals, bringing hungry soldiers to blows with full ones, have been defeated, in all ages, by inferior numbers. The Romans lost a great battle in the north of Italy to Hannibal the Carthaginian, by this neglect alone. Now, this divine elixir gives in one moment force to the limbs and ardour to the spirits; and taken into Hector's body at the nick of time, would, by the aid of Phœbus, Venus, and the blessed saints, have most likely procured the Greeks a defeat. For, note how faint and weary and heart-sick I was a minute ago; well, I suck this celestial cordial, and now behold me brave as Achilles and strong as an eagle."

"Oh father, now? an eagle; alack!"

"Girl, I defy thee and all the world. Ready, I say, like a foaming charger, to devour the space between this and Rotterdam, and strong to combat the ills of life, even poverty and old age, which last philosophers have called the 'summum malum.' Negatur; unless the man's life has been ill-spent—which, by the by, it generally has. Now for the moderns."

"Father! dear father!"

"Fear me not, girl, I will be brief, unreasonably and unseasonably brief. The 'soupe au vin' occurs not in modern science; but this is only one proof more, if proof were needed, that for the last few hundred years physicians have been idiots, with their chicken broth and their decoction of gold, whereby they attribute the highest qualities to that meat which has the least juice of any meat, and to that metal which has less chemical qualities than all the metals; mountebanks! dunces! homicides! Since, then, from these no light is to be gathered, go we to the chroniclers; and first we find that Duguesclin, a French knight, being about to join battle with the English—masters, at that time, of half France, and sturdy strikers by sea and land—drank, not one, but three, 'soupes au vin,' in honour of the Blessed Trinity. This done, he charged the islanders; and as might have been foretold, killed a multitude, and drove the rest into the sea. But he was only the first of a long list of holy and hard-hitting ones who have, by this divine restorative, been sustentated, fortified, corroborated, and consoled."

"Dear father, prithee add thyself to that venerable company ere the soup cools." And Margaret held the hat imploringly in both hands till he inserted the straw once more.

This spared them the "modern instances," and gave Gerard an opportunity of telling Margaret how proud his mother would be her soup had profited a man of learning.

"Ay! but," said Margaret, "it would like her ill to see her son give all and take none himself. Why brought you but two straws?"

"Fair mistress, I hoped you would let me put my lips to your straw, there being but two."

Margaret smiled, and blushed. "Never beg that you may command," said she. "The straw is not mine, 'tis yours: you cut it in yonder field."

"I cut it, and that made it mine; but, after that, your lip touched it, and that made it yours."

"Did it? Then I will lend it you. There—now it is yours again: your lip has touched it."

"No, it belongs to us both now. Let us divide it."

"By all means; you have a knife."

"No, I will not cut it—that would be unlucky. I'll bite it. There. I shall keep my half: you will burn yours, once you get home, I doubt."

"You know me not. I waste nothing. It is odds but I make a hair-pin of it, or something."

This answer dashed the novice Gerard instead of provoking him to fresh efforts, and he was silent. And now, the bread and soup being disposed of, the old scholar prepared to continue his journey. Then came a little difficulty: Gerard the adroit could not tie his ribbon again as Catherine had tied it. Margaret, after slily eyeing his efforts for some time, offered to help him; for at her age girls love to be coy and tender, saucy and gentle, by turns, and she saw she had put him out of countenance but now. Then a fair head, with its stately crown of auburn hair, glossy and glowing through silver, bowed sweetly towards him; and, while it ravished his eye, two white supple hands played delicately upon the stubborn ribbon, and moulded it with soft and airy touches. Then a heavenly thrill ran through the innocent young man, and vague glimpses of a new world of feeling and sentiment opened on him. And these new and exquisite sensations Margaret unwittingly prolonged: it is not natural to her sex to hurry aught that pertains to the sacred toilet. Nay, when the taper fingers had at last subjugated the ends of the knot, her mind was not quite easy, till, by a manœuvre peculiar to the female hand, she had made her palm convex, and so applied it with a gentle pressure to the centre of the knot—a sweet little coaxing hand-kiss, as much as to say, "Now be a good knot, and stay so." The palm-kiss was bestowed on the ribbon, but the wearer's heart leaped to meet it.

"There, that is how it was," said Margaret, and drew back to take one last keen survey of her work; then, looking up for simple approval of her skill, received full in her eyes a longing gaze of such ardent adoration, as made her lower them quickly and colour all over. An indescribable tremor seized her, and she retreated with downcast lashes and tell-tale cheeks, and took her father's arm on the opposite side. Gerard, blushing at having scared her away with his eyes, took the other arm; and so the two young things went downcast and conscious, and propped the eagle along in silence.

They entered Rotterdam by the Schiedamze Poort; and, as Gerard was unacquainted with the town, Peter directed him the way to the Hoog Straet, in which the Stadthouse was. He himself was going with Margaret to his cousin, in the Ooster-Waagen Straet, so, almost on entering the gate, their roads lay apart. They bade each other a friendly adieu, and Gerard dived into the great town. A profound sense of solitude fell upon him, yet the streets were crowded. Then he lamented too late that, out of delicacy, he had not asked his late companions who they were and where they lived.

"Beshrew my shamefacedness!" said he. "But their words and their breeding were above their means, and something did whisper me they would not be known. I shall never see her more. Oh! weary world, I hate you and your ways. To think I must meet beauty and goodness and learning— three pearls of price,—and never see them more!"

Falling into this sad reverie, and letting his body go where it would, he lost his way; but presently meeting a crowd of persons all moving in one direction, he mingled with them, for he argued they must be making for the Stadthouse. Soon the noisy troop that contained the moody Gerard emerged, not upon the Stadthouse, but upon a large meadow by the side of the Maas; and then the attraction was revealed. Games of all sorts were going on: wrestling, the game of palm, the quintain, legerdemain, archery, tumbling, in which art, I blush to say, women as well as men performed, to the great delectation of the company. There was also a trained bear, who stood on his head, and marched upright, and bowed with prodigious gravity to his master; and a hare that beat a drum, and a cock that strutted on little stilts disdainfully. These things made Gerard laugh now and then; but the gay scene could not really enliven it, for his heart was not in tune with it. So, hearing a young man say to his fellow that the duke had been in the meadow, but was gone to the Stadthouse to entertain the burgomasters and aldermen and the competitors for the prizes, and their friends, he suddenly remembered he was hungry, and should like to sup with a prince. He left the river-side, and this time he found the Hoog Straet, and it speedily led him to the Stadthouse. But when he got there he was refused, first at one door, then at another, till he came to the great gate of the court-yard. It was kept by soldiers, and superintended by a pompous major-domo, glittering in an embroidered collar and a gold chain of office, and holding a white staff with a gold knob. There was a crowd of persons at the gate endeavoring to soften this official rock. They came up in turn like ripples, and retired as such in turn. It cost Gerard a struggle to get near him, and when he was within four heads of the gate, he saw something that made his heart beat: there was Peter, with Margaret on his arm, soliciting humbly for entrance.

"My cousin the alderman is not at home. They say he is here."

"What is that to me, old man?"

"If you will not let us pass in to him, at least take this leaf from my tablet to my cousin. See I have written his name: he will come out to us."

"For what do you take me? I carry no messages. I keep the gate."

He then bawled, in a stentorian voice, inexorably:

"No strangers enter here but the competitors and their companies."

"Come, old man," cried a voice in the crowd, "you have gotten your answer; make way."

Margaret turned half round imploringly:

"Good people, we are come from far, and my father is old; and my cousin has a new servant that knows us not, and would not let us sit in our cousin's house."

At this the crowd laughed hoarsely. Margaret shrank as if they had struck her. At that moment a hand grasped hers—a magic grasp: it felt like heart meeting heart, or magnet steel. She turned quickly around at it, and it was Gerard. Such a little cry of joy and appeal came from her bosom, and she began to whimper prettily.

They had hustled her and frightened her for one thing; and her cousin's thoughtlessness, in not even telling his servant they were coming, was cruel; and the servant's caution, however wise and faithful to her master, was bitterly mortifying to her father and her. And to her so mortified, and anxious and jostled, came suddenly this kind hand and face. "Hinc illæ lacrimæ."

"All is well now," remarked a coarse humourist; "she hath gotten her sweetheart."

"Haw! haw! haw!" went the crowd.

She dropped Gerard's hand directly, and turned round, with eyes flashing through her tears:

"I have no sweetheart, you rude men. But I am friendless in your boorish town, and this is a friend; and one who knows, what you know not, how to treat the aged and the weak."

The crowd was dead silent. They had only been thoughtless,

17

and now felt the rebuke, though severe, was just. The silence
enabled Gerard to treat with the porter.

"I am a competitor, sir."

"What is your name?" and the man eyed him suspiciously.

"Gerard, the son of Elias."

The janitor inspected the slip of parchment he held in his hand:
"Gerard Eliassoen can enter."

"With my company; these two?"

"Nay; those are not your company: they came before you."

"What matter? they are my friends, and without them I go not
in."

"Stay without, then."

"That will I not."

"That we will see."

"We will, and speedily." And with this, Gerard raised a voice
of astounding volume and power, and shouted, so that the whole
street rang:

"Ho! PHILIP EARL OF HOLLAND!"

"Are you mad?" cried the porter.

"HERE IS ONE OF YOUR VARLETS DEFIES YOU."

"Hush, Hush!"

"AND WILL NOT LET YOUR GUESTS PASS IN."

"Hush! murder! The duke's there. I'm dead," cried the janitor,
quaking.

Then suddenly trying to overpower Gerard's thunder, he shouted,
with all his lungs:

"OPEN THE GATE, YE KNAVES! WAY THERE FOR GERARD ELIAS-
SOEN AND HIS COMPANY! (the fiends go with him!)"

The gate swung open as by magic. Eight soldiers lowered their
pikes half way, and made an arch, under which the victorious
three marched in triumphant. The moment they had passed, the
pikes clashed together horizontally to bar the gateway, and all but
pinned an abdominal citizen that sought to wedge in along with them.

Once passed the guarded portal, a few steps brought the trio upon
a scene of Oriental luxury. The court-yard was laid out in tables
loaded with rich meats, and piled with gorgeous plate. Guests in
rich and various costumes sat beneath a leafy canopy of fresh cut
branches fastened tastefully to golden, silver, and blue silken cords
that traversed the area; and fruits of many hues, including some

artificial ones of gold, silver, and wax, hung pendent, or peeped like fair eyes among the green leaves of plane-trees and lime-trees. The duke's minstrels swept their lutes at intervals, and a fountain played red Burgundy in six jets that met and battled in the air. The evening sun darted its fires through those bright and purple wine spouts, making them jets and cascades of molten rubies, then passing on, tinged with the blood of the grape, shed crimson glories here and there on fair faces, snowy beards, velvet, satin, jewelled hilts, glowing gold, gleaming silver, and sparkling glass. Gerard and his friends stood dazzled, spell bound. Presently a whisper buzzed around them, "Salute the duke! Salute the duke!" They looked up, and there on high, under the dais, was their sovereign, bidding them welcome with a kindly wave of the hand. The men bowed low, and Margaret curtsied with a deep and graceful obeisance. The duke's hand being up, he gave it another turn, and pointed the newcomers out to a knot of valets. Instantly seven of his people, with an obedient start, went headlong at our friends, seated them at a table, and put fifteen many coloured soups before them, in little silver bowls, and as many wines in crystal vases.

"Nay, father, let us not eat until we have thanked our good friend," said Margaret, now first recovering from all this bustle.

"Girl, he is our guardian angel."

Gerard put his face into his hands.

"Tell me when you have done," said he, "and I will reappear and have my supper, for I am hungry. I know which of us three is the happiest at meeting again."

"Me?" inquired Margaret.

"No: guess again."

"Father?"

"No."

"Then I have no guess which it can be;" and she gave a little crow of happiness and gaiety. The soup was tasted, and vanished in a twirl of fourteen hands, and fish came on the table in a dozen forms, with patties of lobster and almonds mixed, and of almonds and cream, and an immense variety of "brouets," known to us as "rissoles." The next trifle was a wild boar, which smelt divine. Why, then, did Margaret start away from it with two shrieks of dismay, and pinch so good a friend as Gerard? Because the duke's "cuisinier" had been too clever; had made this excellent dish too captivating to the

19

sight as well as taste. He had restored to the animal, by elaborate mimicry with burnt sugar and other edible colours, the hair and bristles he had robbed him of by fire and water. To make him still more enticing, the huge tusks were carefully preserved in the brute's jaw, and gave his mouth the winning smile that comes of tusk in man or beast: and two eyes of coloured sugar glowed in his head. St. Argus! what eyes! so bright, so blood-shot, so threatening—they followed a man and every movement of his knife and spoon. But, indeed, I need the pencil of Granville or Tenniel to make you see the two gilt valets on the opposite side of the table putting the monster down before our friends, with a smiling, self-satisfied, benevolent obsequiousness—for this ghastly monster was the flower of all comestibles—old Peter clasping both hands in pious admiration of it; Margaret wheeling round with horror-stricken eyes and her hand on Gerard's shoulder, squeaking and pinching; his face of unwise delight at being pinched, the grizzly brute glaring sulkily on all, and the guests grinning from ear to ear.

"What's to do?" shouted the duke, hearing the signals of female distress. Seven of his people with a zealous start went headlong and told him. He laughed and said, "Give her of the beef-stuffing, then, and bring me Sir Boar." Benevolent monarch! The beef-stuffing was his own private dish. On these grand occasions an ox was roasted whole, and reserved for the poor. But this wise as well as charitable prince had discovered, that whatever venison, hares, lamb, poultry, &c., you skewered into that beef cavern, got cooked to perfection, retaining their own juices and receiving those of the reeking ox. These he called his beef-stuffing, and took delight therein, as did now our trio; for, at his word, seven of his people went headlong, and drove silver tridents into the steaming cave at random, and speared a kid, a cygnet, and a flock of wild fowl. These presently smoked before Gerard and company; and Peter's face sad and slightly morose at the loss of the savage hog, expanded and shone. After this, twenty different tarts of fruits and herbs, and last of all, confectionery on a Titanic scale; cathedrals of sugar, all gilt and painted in the interstices of the bas-reliefs; castles with their moats, and ditches, imitated to the life; elephants, camels, toads; knights on horseback, jousting; kings and princesses looking on; trumpeters blowing; and all these personages delicious eating, and their veins filled with sweet-scented juices: works of art made to be destroyed. The guests breached a bastion, crunched a crusader and his horse and lance, or cracked a bishop, cope, chasuble, crosier and all, as remorselessly as we do a caraway comfit; sipping, meanwhile, hippocras and other spiced drinks, and Greek and Corsican wines, while every now and then little Turkish boys, turbaned, spangled, jewelled, and gilt, came offering on bended knee golden troughs of rose-water and orange-water to keep the guests' hands cool and per-fumed.

But long before our party arrived at this final stage, appetite had succumbed, and Gerard had suddenly remembered he was the bearer of a letter to the Princess Marie, and, in an undertone, had asked one of the servants if he would undertake to deliver it. The man took it with a deep obeisance: "He could not deliver it himself, but would instantly give it one of the princess's suite, several of whom were about."

It may be remembered that Peter and Margaret came here not to dine, but to find their cousin. Well, the old gentleman ate heartily, and being much fatigued dropped asleep, and forgot all about his cousin. Margaret did not remind him, we shall hear why.

Meantime, that cousin was seated within a few feet of them, at their backs, and discovered them when Margaret turned round and screamed at the boar. But he forbore to speak to them, for municipal reasons. Margaret was very plainly dressed and Peter inclined to threadbare. So the alderman said to himself,

"'Twill be time to make up to them when the sun sets and the company disperses: then I will take my poor relations to my house, and none will be the wiser."

Half the courses were lost on Gerard and Margaret. They were no great eaters, and just now were feeding on sweet thoughts that have ever been unfavourable to appetite. But there is a delicate kind of sensuality, to whose influence these two were perhaps more sensitive than any other pair in that assembly; the delights of colour, music, and perfume, all of which blended so fascinatingly here.

Margaret leaned back and half closed her eyes, and murmured to Gerard: "What a lovely scene! the warm sun, the green shade,

the rich dresses, the bright music of the lutes and the cool music of
the fountain, and all faces so happy and gay! and then, it is to
you we owe it."

Gerard was silent all but his eyes; observing which—

"Now, speak not to me," said Margaret languidly; "let me
listen to the fountain: what are you a competitor for?"

He told her.

"Very well! You will gain one prize, at least."

"Which? Which? Have you seen any of my work?"

"I? no. But you will gain a prize."

"I hope so: but what makes you think so?"

"Because you were so good to my father."

Gerard smiled at the feminine logic, and hung his head at the
sweet praise, and was silent.

"Speak not," murmured Margaret. "They say this is a world
of sin and misery. Can that be? What is your opinion?"

"No! that is all a silly old song," explained Gerard. "'Tis a
byword our elders keep repeating, out of custom: it is not true."

"How can you know? you are but a child," said Margaret, with
pensive dignity.

"Why only look round! And then I thought I had lost you for
ever; and you are by my side: and now the minstrels are going
to play again. Sin and misery? Stuff and nonsense!"

The lutes burst out. The court-yard rang again with their delicate harmony.

"What do you admire most of all these beautiful things, Gerard?"

"You know my name? How is that?"

"White magic. I am a witch."

"Angels are never witches. But I can't think how you—"

"Foolish boy! was it not cried at the gate loud enough to deave
one?"

"So it was. Where is my head? What do I admire most? If
you will sit a little more that way, I'll tell you."

"This way?"

"Yes; so that the light may fall on you. There. I see many
fair things here, fairer than I could have conceived; but the bravest
of all to my eye, is your lovely hair in its silver frame, and the
setting sun kissing it. It reminds me of what the Vulgate praises

for beauty, *'an apple of gold in a network of silver,'* and, O what a pity I did not know you before I sent in my poor endeavours at illuminating! I could illuminate so much better now. I could do everything better. There, now the sun is full on it, it is like an aureole. So our Lady looked, and none since her until to-day."

"O fie! it is wicked to talk so. Compare a poor, coarse-favoured girl like me with the Queen of Heaven? O Gerard! I thought you were a good young man." And Margaret was shocked apparently.

Gerard tried to explain. "I am no worse than the rest: but how can I help having eyes; and a heart—Margaret!"

"Gerard?"

"Be not angry now!"

"Now, is it likely?"

"I love you."

"O for shame! you must not say that to me," and Margaret coloured furiously at this sudden assault.

"I can't help it. I love you. I love you."

"Hush, hush! for pity's sake! I must not listen to such words from a stranger. I am ungrateful to call you a stranger. O how one may be mistaken! If I had known you were so bold—" And Margaret's bosom began to heave, and her cheeks were covered with blushes, and she looked towards her sleeping father, very much like a timid thing that meditates actual flight.

Then Gerard was frightened at the alarm he caused. "Forgive me," said he imploringly. "How could any one help loving you?"

"Well, sir, I will *try* and forgive you—you are so good in other respects; but then you must promise me never to say you—to say *that* again."

"Give me your hand then, or you don't forgive me."

She hesitated; but eventually put out her hand a very little way, very slowly, and with seeming reluctance. He took it, and held it prisoner. When she thought it had been there long enough, she tried gently to draw it away. He held it tight: it submitted quite patiently to force. What *is* the use resisting force? She turned her head away, and her long eyelashes drooped sweetly. Gerard lost nothing by his promise. Words were not heeded here: and silence was more eloquent. Nature was in that day what she is in ours; but manners were somewhat freer. Then, as now, virgins drew back alarmed at the first words of love; but of prudery and artificial coquetry there was little, and the young soon read one another's hearts. Everything was on Gerard's side: his good looks, her belief in his goodness, her gratitude; and opportunity: for at the duke's banquet this mellow summer eve, all things disposed the female nature to tenderness: the avenues to the heart lay open; the senses were so soothed and subdued with lovely colours gentle sounds, and delicate odours; the sun gently sinking the warm air, the green canopy, the cool music of the now violet fountain.

Gerard and Margaret sat hand in hand in silence: and Gerard's eyes sought hers lovingly; and hers now and then turned on him timidly and imploringly: and presently two sweet unreasonable tears rolled down her cheeks, and she smiled deliciously while they were drying: yet they did not take long.

And the sun declined; and the air cooled, and the fountain plashed more gently; and the pair throbbed in unison, and silence, and this weary world looked heaven to them.

CHAPTER III

A GRAVE white-haired seneschal came to their table, and inquired courteously whether Gerard Eliassoen was of their company. Upon Gerard's answer, he said:

"The Princess Marie would confer with you, young sir; I am to conduct you to her presence."

Instantly all faces within hearing turned sharp round, and were bent with curiosity and envy on the man that was to go to a princess.

Gerard rose to obey.

"I wager we shall not see you again," said Margaret, calmly, but colouring a little.

"That will you." was the reply: then he whispered in her ear: "This is my good princess; but you are my queen." He added aloud: "Wait for me, I pray you, I will presently return."

"Ay, ay!" said Peter awaking and speaking at one and the same moment.

The Cloister and the Hearth

Gerard gone, the pair whose dress was so homely, yet they were with the man whom the princess sent for, became "the cynosure of neighbouring eyes;" observing which, William Johnson came forward, acted surprise, and claimed his relations:

"And to think that there was I at your backs, and you saw me not."

"Nay, cousin Johnson, I saw you long syne," said Margaret, coldly.

"You saw me, and spoke not to me?"

"Cousin, it was for you to welcome us to Rotterdam, as it is for us to welcome you at Sevenbergen. Your servant denied us a seat in your house."

"The idiot!"

"And I had a mind to see whether it was 'like maid like master:' for there is sooth in bywords."

William Johnson blushed purple. He saw Margaret was keen, and suspected him. He did the wisest thing under the circumstances, trusted to deeds not words. He insisted on their coming home with him at once, and he would show them whether they were welcome to Rotterdam or not.

"Who doubts it, cousin? Who doubts it?" said the scholar.

Margaret thanked him graciously, but demurred to go just now: said she wanted to hear the minstrels again. In about a quarter of an hour Johnson renewed his proposal, and bade her observe that many of the guests had left. Then her real reason came out.

"It were ill manners to our friend: and he will lose us. He knows not where we lodge in Rotterdam, and the city is large, and we have parted company once already."

"Oh!" said Johnson, "we will provide for that. My young man, ahem! I mean my secretary, shall sit here and wait, and bring him on to my house: he shall lodge with me and with no other."

"Cousin, we shall be too burdensome."

"Nay, nay; you shall see whether you are welcome, or not, you and your friends, and your friends' friends if need be: and I shall hear what the princess would with him."

Margaret felt a thrill of joy that Gerard should be lodged under the same roof with her; then she had a slight misgiving. "But if your young man should be thoughtless, and go play, and Gerard miss him?"

"He go play? He leave that spot where I put him? and bid him stay? Ho! Stand forth, Hans Cloterman."

A figure clad in black serge and dark violet hose arose, and took two steps and stood before them without moving a muscle: a solemn, precise young man, the very statue of gravity and starched propriety. At his aspect Margaret, being very happy, could hardly keep her countenance. But she whispered Johnson, "I would put my hand in the fire for him. We are at your command, cousin, as soon as you have given him his orders."

Hans was then instructed to sit at the table and wait for Gerard, and conduct him to Ooster-Waagen Straet. He replied, not in words, but by calmly taking the seat indicated, and Margaret, Peter, and William Johnson went away together.

"And, indeed, it is time you were abed, father, after all your travel," said Margaret. This had been in her mind all along.

Hans Cloterman sat waiting for Gerard, solemn and business-like. The minutes flew by, but excited no impatience in that perfect young man. Johnson did him no more than justice when he laughed to scorn the idea of his secretary leaving his post, or neglecting his duty, in pursuit of sport or out of youthful hilarity and frivolity.

As Gerard was long in coming, the patient Hans—his employer's eye being no longer on him—improved the time by quaffing solemnly, silently, and at short but accurately measured intervals, goblets of Corsican wine. The wine was strong, so was Cloterman's head: and Gerard had been gone a good hour ere the model secretary imbibed the notion that Creation expected Cloterman to drink the health of all good fellows, and "nommément" of the Duke of Burgundy there present. With this view he filled bumper nine, and rose gingerly but solemnly and slowly. Having reached his full height, he instantly rolled upon the grass, goblet in hand, spilling the cold liquor on more than one ankle—whose owners frisked—but not disturbing a muscle in his own long face, which, in the total eclipse of reason, retained its gravity, primness, and infallibility.

The seneschal led Gerard through several passages to the door of the pavilion, where some young noblemen, embroidered and feathered, sat sentinel, guarding the heir-apparent, and playing cards by the red light of torches their servants held. A whisper from the seneschal, and one of them rose reluctantly, stared at Gerard with haughty surprise, and entered the pavilion. He presently returned, and, beckoning the pair, led them through a passage or two and landed them in an ante-chamber, where sat three more young gentlemen, feathered, furred, and embroidered like pieces of fancy work, and deep in that instructive and edifying branch of learning, dice.

"You can't see the princess—it is too late," said one.

Another followed suit:—

"She passed this way but now with her nurse. She is gone to bed, doll and all. Deuce-ace again!"

Gerard prepared to retire. The seneschal, with an incredulous smile, replied:—

"The young man is here by the countess's orders; be so good as conduct him to her ladies."

On this a superb Adonis rose, with an injured look, and led Gerard into a room where sat or lolloped eleven ladies, chattering like magpies. Two, more industrious than the rest, were playing cat's-cradle with fingers as nimble as their tongues. At the sight of a stranger all the tongues stopped like one piece of complicated machinery, and all the eyes turned on Gerard, as if the same string that checked the tongues had turned the eyes on. Gerard was ill at ease before, but this battery of eyes discountenanced him, and down went *his* eyes on the ground. Then the cowards finding, like the hare who ran by the pond and the frogs scuttled into the water, that there was a creature they could frighten, giggled and enjoyed their prowess. Then a duenna said, severely, "Mesdames!" and they were all abashed at once as though a modesty string had been pulled. This same duenna took Gerard, and marched before him in solemn silence. The young man's heart sank, and he had half a mind to turn and run out of the place. "What must princes be," he thought, "when their courtiers are so freezing? Doubtless they take their breeding from him they serve." These reflections were interrupted by the duenna suddenly introducing him into a room where three ladies sat working, and a pretty little girl tuning a lute. The ladies were richly but not showily dressed, and the duenna went up to the one who was hemming a kerchief, and said a few words in a low tone. This lady then turned towards Gerard, with a smile, and beckoned him to come near her. She did not rise, but she laid aside her work, and her manner of turning towards him, slight as the movement was, was full of grace and ease and courtesy. She began a conversation at once.

"Margaret Van Eyck is an old friend of mine, sir, and I am right glad to have a letter from her hand, and thankful to you, sir, for bringing it to me safely. Marie, my love, this is the young gentleman who brought you that pretty miniature."

"Sir, I thank you a thousand times," said the young lady.

"I am glad you feel her debtor, sweetheart, for our friend could have us to do him a little service in return."

"I will do anything on earth for him," replied the young lady with ardour.

"Anything on earth is nothing in the world," said the Countess of Charolois, quietly.

"Well, then, I will—— What would you have me to do, sir?"

Gerard had just found out what high society he was in. "My sovereign demoiselle," said he, gently and a little tremulously, "where there have been no pains there needs no reward."

"But we must obey mamma. All the world must obey mamma."

"That is true. Then, our demoiselle, reward me, if you will, by letting me hear the stave you were going to sing and I did interrupt it."

"What, you love music, sir?"

"I adore it."

The little princess looked inquiringly at her mother, and received a smile of assent. She then took her lute and sang a romaunt of the day. Although but twelve years old, she was a well-taught and painstaking musician. Her little claw swept the chords with courage and precision, and struck out the notes of the arpeggio clear, and distinct, and bright, like twinkling stars; but the main charm was her voice. It was not mighty, but it was round, clear, full, and ringing like a bell. She sang with a certain modest eloquence, though she knew none of the tricks of feeling. She was too young to be theatrical, or even sentimental, so nothing was forced—all gushed. Her little mouth seemed the mouth of Nature. The ditty, too, was as pure as its utterance. As there were none of those false divisions—those whining slurs, which are now sold so dear by Italian songsters, though every jackal in India delivers them gratis to his customers all night, and sometimes gets shot for them, and always deserve it—so there were no cadences and fiorituri, the trite, turgid, and feeble expletives of song, the skim milk, with which mindless musicians and mindless writers quench fire, wash out colour, and drown melody and meaning dead.

While the pure and tender strain was flowing from the pure young throat, Gerard's eyes filled. The countess watched him with interest, for it was usual to applaud the princess loudly, but not with cheek and eye. So when the voice ceased, and the glasses left off ringing, she asked demurely, "Was he content?"

Gerard gave a little start; the spoken voice broke the charm, and brought him back to earth.

"Oh, madam!" he cried, "surely it is thus that cherubs and seraphs sing, and charm the saints in heaven."

"I am somewhat of your opinion, my young friend," said the countess, with emotion; and she bent a look of love and gentle pride upon her girl: a heavenly look, such as, they say, is given to the eye of the short-lived resting on the short-lived.

The countess resumed:

"My old friend requests me to be serviceable to you. It is the first favour she has done us the honour of asking us, and the request is sacred. You are in holy orders, sir?"

Gerard bowed.

"I fear you are not a priest, you look too young."

"Oh no, madam; I am not even a sub-deacon. I am only a lector; but next month I shall be an exorcist; and before long an acolyth."

"Well, Monsieur Gerard, with your accomplishments you can soon pass through the inferior orders. And let me beg you to do so. For the day after you have said your first mass I shall have the pleasure of appointing you to a benefice."

"Oh, madam!"

"And, Marie, remember I make this promise in your name as well as my own."

"Fear not mamma: I will not forget. But if he will take my advice, what he will be is Bishop of Liége. The Bishop of Liége is a beautiful bishop. What! do you not remember him, mamma, that day we were at Liége? he was braver than grandpa himself. He had on a crown, a high one, and it was cut in the middle, and it was full of oh! such beautiful jewels: and his gown stiff with gold; and his mantle, too; and it had a broad border, all pictures: but, above all, his gloves; you have no such gloves, mamma. They were embroidered and covered with jewels, and scented with such lovely scent; I smelt them all the time he was giving me his blessing on my head with them. Dear old man! I dare say he will die soon —most old people do—and then, sir, you can be bishop, you know, and wear—"

"Gently, Marie, gently: bishoprics are for old gentlemen; and this is a young gentleman."

"Mamma! he is not so very young."

"Not compared with you, Marie, eh?"

"He is a good bigth, dear mamma; and I am sure he is *good* enough for a bishop."

"Alas, mademoiselle! you are mistaken."

"I know not that, Monsieur Gerard; but I am a little puzzled to know on what grounds mademoiselle there pronounces your character so boldly."

"Alas, mamma!" said the princess, "you have not looked at his face, then;" and she raised her eyebrows at her mother's simplicity.

"I beg your pardon," said the countess, "I have. Well, sir, if I cannot go quite so fast as my daughter, attribute it to my age, not to a want of interest in your welfare. A benefice will do to begin your career with; and I must take care it is not too far from —what call you the place?"

"Tergou, madam."

"A priest gives up much," continued the countess; "often, I fear, he learns too late how much:" and her woman's eye rested a moment on Gerard with mild pity and half surprise at his resigning her sex, and all the heaven they can bestow, and the great parental joys: "at least you shall be near your friends. Have you a mother?"

"Yes, madam; thanks be to God!"

"Good! You shall have a church near Tergou. She will thank me. And now, sir, we must not detain you too long from those who have a better claim on your society than we have. Duchess, oblige me by bidding one of the pages conduct him to the hall of banquet; the way is hard to find."

The Cloister and the Hearth

Gerard bowed low to the countess and the princess, and backed towards the door.

"I hope it will be a nice benefice," said the princess to him, with a pretty smile, as he was going out; then, shaking her head with an air of solemn misgiving, "but you had better have been Bishop of Liége."

Gerard followed his new conductor, his heart warm with gratitude: but ere he reached the banquet-hall a chill came over him. The mind of one who has led a quiet, uneventful life is not apt to take in contradictory feelings at the same moment and balance them, but rather to be overpowered by each in turn. While Gerard was with the countess, the excitement of so new a situation, the unlooked for promise, the joy and pride it would cause at home, possessed him wholly: but now it was passion's turn to be heard again. What, give up Margaret, whose soft hand he still felt in his, and her deep eyes in his heart? resign her and all the world of love and joy she had opened on him to-day? The revulsion, when it did come, was so strong, that he hastily resolved to say nothing at home about the offered benefice. "The countess is so good," thought he, "she has a hundred ways of aiding a young man's fortune: she will not compel me to be a priest when she shall learn I love one of her sex: one would almost think she does know it, for she cast a strange look on me and said, 'A priest gives up much, too much.' I dare say she will give me a place about the palace." And with this hopeful reflection his mind was eased, and, being now at the entrance of the banqueting-hall, he thanked his conductor, and ran hastily with joyful eyes to Margaret. He came in sight of her table—she was gone. Peter was gone too. Nobody was at the table at all: only a citizen in sober garments had just tumbled under it dead drunk, and several persons were raising him to carry him away. Gerard never guessed how important this solemn drunkard was to him: he was looking for "Beauty," and let the "Beast" lie. He ran wildly round the hall, which was now comparatively empty. She was not there. He left the palace: outside he found a crowd gaping at two great fanlights just lighted over the gate. He asked them earnestly if they had seen an old man in a gown, and a lovely girl pass out. They laughed at the question. "They were staring at these new lights that turn night into day. They didn't trouble their heads about old men and young wenches, every-day sights."

The Cloister and the Hearth

From another group he learned there was a Mystery being played under canvas hard by, and all the world gone to see it. This revived his hopes, and he went and saw the Mystery. In this representation divine personages, too sacred for me to name here, came clumsily down from heaven to talk sophistry with the cardinal Virtues, the nine Muses, and the seven deadly Sins, all present in human shape, and not unlike one another. To enliven which weary stuff in rattled the Prince of the power of the air, and an imp that kept molesting him and buffeting him with a bladder, at each thwack of which the crowd were in ecstasies. When the Vices had uttered good store of obscenity and the Virtues twaddle, the celestials, including the nine Muses, went gingerly back to heaven one by one; for there was but one cloud; and two artisans worked it up with its supernatural freight, and worked it down with a winch, in full sight of the audience. These disposed of, the bottomless pit opened and flamed in the centre of the stage; the carpenters and Virtues shoved the Vices in, and the Virtues and Beelzebub and his tormentor danced merrily round the place of eternal torture to the fife and tabor.

This entertainment was writ by the Bishop of Ghent for the diffusion of religious sentiment by the aid of the senses, and was an average specimen of theatrical exhibitions so long as they were in the hands of the clergy. But, in course of time, the laity conducted plays, and so the theatre, I learn from the pulpit, has become profane.

Margaret was nowhere in the crowd, and Gerard could not enjoy the performance: he actually went away in Act 2, in the midst of a much-admired piece of dialogue, in which Justice out-quibbled Satan. He walked through many streets, but could not find her he sought. At last, fairly worn out, he went to a hostelry and slept till daybreak. All that day, heavy and heartsick, he sought her, but could never fall in with her or her father, nor ever obtain the slightest clue. Then he felt she was false or had changed her mind. He was irritated now, as well as sad. More good fortune fell on him: he almost hated it. At last, on the third day, after he had once more been through every street, he said "She is not in the town, and I shall never see her again. I will go home." He started for Tergou with a royal favour promised, with fifteen golden angels in his purse, a golden medal on his bosom and a heart like a lump of lead.

CHAPTER IV

IT was near four o'clock in the afternoon. Eli was in the shop. His eldest and youngest sons were abroad. Catherine and her little crippled daughter had long been anxious about Gerard, and now they were gone a little way down the road, to see if by good luck he might be visible in the distance; and Giles was alone in the sitting-room, which I will sketch, furniture and dwarf included.

The Hollanders were always an original and leading people. They claim to have invented printing (wooden type), oil-painting, liberty, banking, gardening, &c. Above all, years before my tale, they invented cleanliness. So while the English gentry, in velvet jerkins, and chicken-toed shoes, trode floors of stale rushes, foul receptacle of bones, decomposing morsels, spittle, dogs' eggs, and all abominations, this hosier's sitting-room at Tergou was floored with Dutch tiles, so highly glazed and constantly washed, that you could eat off them. There was one large window; the cross stone-work in the centre of it was very massive, and stood in relief, looking like an actual cross to the inmates, and was eyed as such in their devotions. The panes were very small and lozenge-shaped, and soldered to one another with strips of lead: the like you may see to this day in our rural cottages. The chairs were rude and primitive, all but the arm-chair, whose back, at right angles with its seat, was so high that the sitter's head stopped two feet short of the top. This chair was of oak and carved at the summit. There was a copper pail, that went in at the waist, holding holy water; and a little hand-besom to sprinkle it far and wide; and a long, narrow but massive oak table, and a dwarf sticking to its rim by his teeth, his eyes glaring, and his claws in the air like a pouncing vampire. Nature, it would seem, did not make Giles a dwarf out of malice prepense: she constructed a head and torso with her usual care: but just then her attention was distracted, and she left the rest to chance; the result was a human wedge, an inverted cone. He might justly have taken her to task in the terms of Horace:—

Amphora cœpit
Institui; currente rotâ cur urceus exit?

33

His centre was anything but his centre of gravity. Bisected, upper Giles would have outweighed three lower Giles. But this very disproportion enabled him to do feats that would have baffled Milo. His brawny arms had no weight to draw after them; so he could go up a vertical pole like a squirrel, and hang for hours from a bough by one hand like a cherry by its stalk. If he could have made a vacuum with his hands, as the lizard is said to do with its feet, he would have gone along a ceiling. Now, this pocket athlete was insanely fond of gripping the dinner-table with both hands, and so swinging; and then—climax of delight!—he would seize it with his teeth, and taking off his hands, hold on like grim death by his huge ivories.

But all our joys, however elevating, suffer interruption. Little Kate caught Sampsonet in this posture, and stood aghast. She was her mother's daughter, and her heart was with the furniture, not with the 12mo. gymnast.

"Oh, Giles! how can you? Mother is at hand. It dents the table."

"Go and tell her, little talebearer," snarled Giles. "You are the one for making mischief."

"Am I?" inquired Kate, calmly; "that is news to me."

"The biggest in Tergou," growled Giles, fastening on again.

"Oh, indeed?" said Kate drily.

This piece of unwonted satire launched, and Giles not visibly blasted, she sat down quietly and cried.

Her mother came in almost at that moment, and Giles hurled himself under the table, and there glared.

"What is to do now?" said the dame, sharply. Then turning her experienced eye from Kate to Giles, and observing the position he had taken up, and a sheepish expression, she hinted at cuffing of ears.

"Nay, mother," said the girl; "it was but a foolish word Giles spoke. I had not noticed it at another time; but I was tired and in care for Gerard, you know."

"Let no one be in care for me," said a faint voice at the door, and in tottered Gerard, pale dusty, and worn out; and amidst uplifted hands and cries of delight, curiosity, and anxiety, mingled, dropped exhausted into the nearest chair.

Beating Rotterdam, like a covert, for Margaret, and the long journey afterwards, had fairly knocked Gerard up. But elastic youth soon revived, and behold him the centre of an eager circle. First of all they must hear about the prizes. Then Gerard told them he had been admitted to see the competitors' works all laid out in an enormous hall before the judges pronounced. "Oh, mother! oh Kate; when I saw the goldsmith's work, I had like to have fallen on the floor. I had thought not all the goldsmiths on earth had so much gold, silver, jewels, and craft of design and facture. But, in sooth, all the arts are divine."

Then to please the females, he described to them the reliquaries, feretories, calices, crosiers, crosses, pyxes, monstrances, and other wonders ecclesiastical, and the goblets, hanaps, watches, clocks, chains, brooches, &c., so that their mouths watered.

"But Kate, when I came to the illuminated work from Ghent and Bruges, my heart sank. Mine was dirt by the side of it. For the first minute I could almost have cried; but I prayed for a better spirit, and presently I was able to enjoy them, and thank God for those lovely works, and for those skilful, patient craftsmen, whom I own my masters. Well, the coloured work was so beautiful I forgot all about the black and white. But, next day, when all the other prizes had been given, they came to the writing, and whose name think you was called first?"

"Yours," said Kate.

The others laughed her to scorn.

"You may well laugh," said Gerard, "but for all that Gerard Eliassoen of Tergou was the name the herald shouted. I stood stupid; they thrust me forward. Everything swam before my eyes. I found myself kneeling on a cushion at the feet of the duke. He said something to me, but I was so fluttered I could not answer him. So then he put his hand to his side and did not draw a glaive and cut off my dull head, but gave me a gold medal, and there it is." There was a yell and almost a scramble. "And then he gave me fifteen great bright golden angels. I had seen one before, but I never handled one. Here they are."

"Oh Gerard! oh Gerard!"

"There is one for you, our eldest; and one for you, Sybrandt, and for you, Little Mischief; and two for thee, Little Lily, because God hath afflicted thee; and one for myself to buy colours and vellum; and nine for her that nursed us all, and risked the two crowns upon poor Gerard's hand."

The gold drew out their characters. Cornelis and Sybrandt clutched each his coin with one glare of greediness and another glare of envy at Kate who had got two pieces. Giles seized his and rolled it along the floor and gambolled after it. Kate put down her crutches and sat down, and held out her little arms to Gerard with a heavenly gesture of love and tenderness, and the mother, fairly benumbed at first by the shower of gold that fell on her apron, now cried out, "Leave kissing him, Kate, he is my son, not yours. Ah, Gerard, my boy! I have not loved you as you deserved."

Then Gerard threw himself on his knees beside her, and she flung her arms round him and wept for joy and pride, upon his neck.

"Good lad! good lad!" cried the hosier, with some emotion. "I must go and tell the neighbors. Lend me the medal, Gerard, I'll show it my good friend, Peter Buyskens; he is ever regaling me with how his son Jorian won the tin mug a shooting at the butts."

"Ay, do my man; and show Peter Buyskens one of the angels. Tell him there are fourteen more where that came from. Mind you bring it me back!"

"Stay a minute, father, there is better news behind," said Gerard, flushing with joy at the joy he caused.

"Better! Better than this?"

Then Gerard told his interview with the countess, and the house rang with joy.

"Now God bless the good lady and bless the Dame Van Eyck! A benefice? our son! My cares are at an end. Eli, my good friend and master, now we two can die happy whenever our time comes. This dear boy will take our place, and none of these loved ones will want a home or a friend."

From that hour Gerard was looked upon as the stay of the family. He was a son apart, but in another sense. He was always in the right, and nothing was too good for him. Cornelis and Sybrandt became more and more jealous of him, and longed for the day he should go to his benefice: they would get rid of the favourite, and his reverence's purse would be open to them. With these views he co-operated. The wound love had given him, throbbed duller and duller. His success and the affection and admiration of his parents, made him think more highly of himself, and resent with more spirit Margaret's ingratitude and discourtesy. For all that, she had power to cool him towards the rest of her sex, and now for every reason he wished to be ordained priest as soon as he could pass the intermediate orders. He knew the Vulgate already better than most of the clergy, and studied the rubric and the dogmas of the Church with his friends the monks; and, the first time the bishop came that way, he applied to be admitted "exorcist," the third step in holy orders. The bishop questioned him, and ordained him at once. He had to kneel, and after a short prayer, the bishop delivered to him a little MS. full of exorcisms, and said: "Take this, Gerard, and have power to lay hands on the possessed, whether baptized or catechumens!" and he took it reverently, and went home invested by the Church with power to cast out demons.

Returning home from the church, he was met by little Kate on her crutches.

"Oh, Gerard! who think you, hath sent to our house seeking you?—the burgomaster himself."

"Ghysbrecht Van Swieten? What would he with me?"

"Nay, Gerard, I know not. But he seems urgent to see you. You are to go to his house on the instant."

"Well, he is the burgomaster: I will go: but it likes me not. Kate, I have seen him cast such a look on me as no friend casts. No matter; such looks forewarn the wise. To be sure, he knows—"

"Knows what, Gerard?"

"Nothing."

"Nothing?"

"Kate, I'll go."

CHAPTER V

GHYSBRECHT VAN SWIETEN was an artful man. He opened on the novice with something quite wide of the mark he was really aiming at. "The town records," said he, "are crabbedly written, and the ink rusty with age." He offered Gerard the honour of transcribing them fair.

Gerard inquired what he was to be paid.

Ghysbrecht offered a sum that would have just purchased the pens, ink, and parchment.

"But, burgomaster, my labour? Here is a year's work."

"Your labour? Call you marking parchment labour? Little sweat goes to that, I trow."

" 'Tis labour, and skilled labour to boot: and that is better paid in all crafts than rude labour, sweat or no sweat. Beside, there's my time."

"Your time? Why what is time to you, at two-and-twenty?" Then fixing his eyes keenly on Gerard, to mark the effect of his words, he said: "Say rather, you are idle grown. You are in love. Your body is with these chanting monks, but your heart is with Peter Brandt and his red-haired girl."

"I know no Peter Brandt."

"This denial confirmed Ghysbrecht's suspicion that the caster-out of demons was playing a deep game.

"Ye lie!" he shouted. "Did I not find you at her elbow, on the road to Rotterdam?"

"Ah!"

"Ah. And you were seen at Sevenbergen but t'other day."

"Was I?"

"Ay; and at Peter's house."

"At Sevenbergen?"

"Ay, at Sevenbergen."

Now, this was what in modern days is called a draw. It was a guess, put boldly forth as fact, to elicit by the young man's answer, whether he had been there lately or not.

The result of the artifice surprised the crafty one. Gerard started up in a strange state of nervous excitement.

"Burgomaster," said he, with trembling voice, "I have not been at Sevenbergen this three years, and I knew not the name of those you saw me with, nor where they dwelt; but as my time is precious, though you value it not, give you good day." And he darted out with his eyes sparkling.

Ghysbrecht started up in huge ire; but he sank into his chair again.

"He fears me not. He knows something if not all."

Then he called hastily to his trusty servant, and almost dragged him to a window.

"See you yon man?" he cried. "Haste! Follow him! But let him not see you. He is young, but old in craft. Keep him in sight all day. Let me know whither he goes and what he does."

It was night when the servant returned.

"Well? well?" cried Van Swieten, eagerly.

"Master, the young man went from you to Sevenbergen."
Ghysbrecht groaned.

"To the house of Peter the Magician."

CHAPTER VI

"LOOK into your own heart and write!" said Herr Cant; and earth's cuckoos echoed the cry. Look into the Rhine where it is deepest, and the Thames where it is thickest, and paint the bottom. Lower a bucket into a well of self-deception, and what comes up must be immortal truth, mustn't it? Now, in the first place no son of Adam ever reads his own heart at all, except by the habit acquired, and the light gained, from some years' perusal of other hearts; and even then, with his acquired sagacity and reflected light, he can but spell and decipher his own heart, not read it fluently. Half way to Sevenbergen Gerard looked into his own heart, and asked it why he was going to Sevenbergen. His heart replied without a moment's hesitation. "We are going out of curiosity, to know why she jilted us, and to show her it has not broken our hearts, and that we are quite content with our honours and our benefice in prospectu, and don't want her nor any of her fickle sex."

He soon found out Peter Brandt's cottage; and there sat a girl in the doorway, plying her needle, and a stalwart figure leaned on a long bow and talked to her. Gerard felt an unaccountable pang at the sight of him. However, the man turned out to be past fifty years of age, an old soldier, whom Gerard remembered to have seen shoot at the butts with admirable force and skill. Another minute and the youth stood before them. Margaret looked up and dropped her work, and uttered a faint cry, and was white and red by turns. But these signs of emotion were swiftly dismissed, and she turned far more chill and indifferent than she would if she had not betrayed this agitation.

"What! is it you, Master Gerard? What on earth brings you here, I wonder?"

"I was passing by and saw you; so I thought I would give you good day and ask after your father."

39

"My father is well. He will be here anon."

"Then I may as well stay till he comes."

"As you will. Good Martin, step into the village and tell my father here is a friend of his."

"And not of yours?"

"My father's friends are mine."

"That is doubtful. It was not like a friend to promise to wait for me, and then make off the moment my back was turned. Cruel Margaret! you little know how I searched the town for you; how for want of you nothing was pleasant to me."

"These are idle words; if you had desired my father's company, or mine, you would have come back. There I had a bed laid for you, sir, at my cousin's, and he would have made much of you, and, who knows, I might have made much of you too. I was in the humour that day. You will not catch me in the same mind again, neither you nor any young man, I warrant me."

"Margaret, I came back the moment the countess let me go; but you were not there."

"Nay, you did not, or you had seen Hans Cloterman at our table; we left him to bring you on."

"I saw no one there, but only a drunken man that had just tumbled down."

"At our table? How was he clad?"

"Nay, I took little heed: in sad coloured garb."

At this Margaret's face gradually warmed; but presently, assuming incredulity and severity, she put many shrewd questions, all of which Gerard answered most loyally. Finally, the clouds cleared, and they guessed how the misunderstanding had come about. Then came a revulsion of tenderness, all the more powerful that they had done each other wrong; and then, more dangerous still, came mutual confessions. Neither had been happy since, neither ever would have been happy but for this fortunate meeting.

And Gerard found a MS. Vulgate lying open on the table, and pounced upon it like a hawk. MSS. were his delight; but before he could get to it two white hands quickly came flat upon the page, and a red face over them.

"Nay, take away your hands, Margaret, that I may see where you are reading, and I will read there too at home; so shall my soul meet yours in the sacred page. You will not? Nay, then, I must kiss them away." And he kissed them so often, that for very shame they were fain to withdraw, and, lo! the sacred book lay open at

An apple of gold in a network of silver.

"There, now," said she, "I had been hunting for it ever so long, and found it but even now—and to be caught!" and with a touch of inconsistency she pointed it out to Gerard with her white finger.

"Ay," said he, "but to-day it is all hidden in that great cap."

"It is a comely cap, I'm told by some."

"Maybe: but what it hides is beautiful."

"It is not: it is hideous."

"Well, it was beautiful at Rotterdam."

"Ay, everything was beautiful that day" (with a little sigh).

And now Peter came in, and welcomed Gerard cordially, and would have him stay to supper. And Margaret disappeared; and Gerard had a nice learned chat with Peter; and Margaret reappeared with her hair in a silver net, and shot a glance half arch half coy, and glided about them, and spread supper, and beamed bright with gaiety and happiness. And in the cool evening Gerard coaxed her out, and she objected, and came; and coaxed her on to the road to Tergou and she declined, and came, and there they strolled up and down, hand in hand; and when he must go they pledged each other never to quarrel or misunderstand one another again; and they sealed the promise with a long loving kiss, and Gerard went home on wings.

From that day Gerard spent most of his evenings with Margaret, and the attachment deepened and deepened on both sides till the hours they spent together were the hours they lived; the rest they counted and underwent. And at the outset of this deep attachment all went smoothly; obstacles there were, but they seemed distant and small to the eyes of hope, youth and love. The feelings and passions of so many persons, that this attachment would thwart, gave no warning smoke to show their volcanic nature and power. The course of true love ran smoothly, placidly, until it had drawn these two young hearts into its current for ever.

And then—

The Cloister and the Hearth

ONE bright morning unwonted velvet shone, unwonted feathers waved, and horses' hoofs glinted and rang through the streets of Tergou, and the windows and balconies were studded with wondering faces. The French ambassador was riding through to sport in the neighbouring forest.

Besides his own suite he was attended by several servants of the Duke of Bergundy, lent to do him honour and minister to his pleasure. The duke's tumbler rode before him with a grave, sedate majesty that made his more noble companions seem light, frivolous persons. But ever and anon, when respect and awe neared the oppressive, he rolled off his horse so ignobly and funnily that even the ambassador was fain to burst out laughing. He also climbed up again by the tail in a way provocative of mirth, and so he played his part. Towards the rear of the pageant rode one that excited more attention still—the duke's leopard. A huntsman mounted on a Flemish horse of prodigious size and power, carried a long box fastened to the rider's loins by straps curiously contrived, and on this box sat a bright leopard crouching. She was chained to the huntsman. The people admired her glossy hide and spots, and pressed near, and one or two were for feeling her, and pulling her tail; then the huntsman shouted in a terrible voice, "Beware! At Antwerp one did but throw a handful of dust at her, and the duke made dust of him."

"Gramercy!"

"I speak sooth. The good duke shut him up in prison, in a cell under ground, and the rats cleaned the flesh off his bones in a night. Served him right for molesting the poor thing." There was a murmur of fear, and the Tergovians shrank from tickling the leopard of their sovereign.

But an incident followed that raised their spirits again. The duke's giant, a Hungarian seven feet four inches high, brought up the rear. This enormous creature had, like some other giants, a treble, fluty voice of little power. He was a vain fellow, and not conscious of this nor any defect. Now it happened he caught sight of Giles sitting on top of the balcony; so he stopped and began to make fun of him.

The Cloister and the Hearth

"Hallo! brother!" squeaked he, "I had nearly passed without seeing thee."

"*You* are plain enough to see," bellowed Giles, in his bass tones.

"Come on my shoulder, brother," squeaked Titan, and held out a shoulder of mutton fist to help him down.

"If I do I'll cuff your ears," roared the dwarf.

The giant saw the homuncule was irascible, and played upon him, being encouraged thereto by the shouts of laughter. For he did not see that the people were laughing not at his wit, but at the ridiculous incongruity of the two voices—the gigantic feeble fife, and the petty, deep, loud drum, the mountain delivered of a squeak and the mole-hill belching thunder.

The singular duet came to as singular an end. Giles lost all patience and self-command, and being a creature devoid of fear, and in a rage to boot, he actually dropped upon the giant's neck, seized his hair with one hand, and punched his head with the other. The giant's first impulse was to laugh, but the weight and rapidity of the blows soon corrected that inclination.

"He! he! Ah! ha! hallo! oh! oh! Holy saints! here! help! or I must throttle the imp. I can't! I'll split your skull against the——" and he made a wild run backwards at the balcony. Giles saw his danger, seized the balcony in time with both hands, and whipped over it just as the giant's head came against it with a stunning crack. The people roared with laughter and exultation at the address of their little champion. The indignant giant seized two of the laughers, knocked them together like dumb-bells, shook them and strewed them flat—(Catherine shrieked and threw her apron over Giles)—then strode wrathfully away after the party. This incident had consequences no one then present foresaw. Its immediate results were agreeable. The Tergovians turned proud of Giles, and listened with more affability to his prayers for parchment. For he drove a regular trade with his brother Gerard in this article. Went about and begged it gratis, and Gerard gave him coppers for it.

On the afternoon of the same day, Catherine and her daughter were chatting together about their favourite theme, Gerard, his goodness, his benefice, and the brightened prospects of the whole family.

Their good luck had come to them in the very shape they would have chosen; besides the advantages of a benefice such as the Countess Charolois would not disdain to give, there was the feminine delight

43

at having a priest, a holy man, in their own family. "He will marry Cornelis, and Sybrandt: for they can wed (good housewives), now if they will. Gerard will take care of you and Giles, when we are gone."

"Yes mother, and we can confess to him instead of to a stranger," said Kate.

"Ay, girl! and he can give the sacred oil to your father and me, and close our eyes when our time comes."

"Oh, mother! not for many, many years I do pray Heaven. Pray speak not of that, it always makes me sad. I hope to go before you, mother dear. No; let us be gay to-day. I am out of pain; mother, quite out of all pain; it does seem so strange; and I feel so bright and happy, that—mother, can you keep a secret?"

"Nobody better, child. Why, you know I can."

"Then I will show you something so beautiful. You never saw the like, I trow. Only Gerard must never know; for sure he means to surprise us with; he covers it up so, and sometimes he carries it away altogether."

Kate took her crutches, and moved slowly away, leaving her mother in an exalted state of curiosity. She soon returned with something in a cloth, uncovered it, and there was a lovely picture of the Virgin, with all her insignia, and wearing her tiara over a wealth of beautiful hair, which flowed loose over her shoulders. Catherine, at first was struck with awe.

"It is herself," she cried; "it is the Queen of Heaven. I never saw one like her to my mind before."

"And her eyes, mother: lifted to the sky, as if they belonged there, and not to a mortal creature. And her beautiful hair of burning gold."

"And to think I have a son that can make the saints live again upon a piece of wood!"

"The reason is, he is a young saint himself, mother. He is too good for this world; he is here to portray the blessed, and then to go away and be with them for ever."

Ere they had half done admiring it, a strange voice was heard at the door. By one of the furtive instincts of their sex they hastily hid the picture in the cloth, though there was no need. And the next moment in came, casting his eyes furtively around, a man that had not entered the house this ten years—Ghysbrecht Van Swieten.

The two women were so taken by surprise, that they merely stared at him and at one another, and said, "The Burgomaster!" in a tone so expressive, that Ghysbrecht felt compelled to answer it.

"Yes! I own, the last time I came here was not on a friendly errand. Men love their own interest—Eli's and mine were contrary. Well, let this visit atone for the last. To-day I come on your business, and none of mine." Catherine and her daughter exchanged a swift glance of contemptuous incredulity. They knew the man better than he thought.

"It is about your son Gerard."

"Ay! ay! you want him to work for the town all for nothing. He told us."

"I come on no such errand. It is to let you know he has fallen into bad hands."

"Now Heaven and the saints forbid! Man, torture not a mother! Speak out, and quickly: speak ere you have time to coin a falsehood: we know thee."

Ghysbrecht turned pale at this affront, and spite mingled with the other motives that brought him here. "Thus it is, then," said he, grinding his teeth, and speaking very fast. "Your son Gerard is more like to be the father of a family than a priest: he is for ever with Margaret, Peter Brandt's red-haired girl, and he loves her like a cow her calf."

Mother and daughter both burst out laughing. Ghysbrecht stared at them.

"What, you knew it?"

"Carry this tale to those who know not my son Gerard. Women are nought to him."

"Other women, mayhap. But this one is the apple of his eye to him or will be, if you part them not, and soon. Come, dame, make me not waste time and friendly counsel: my servant has seen them together a score of times, handed, and reading babies in one another's eyes like—you know, dame—you have been young too.

"Girl, I am ill at ease. Yea I have been young, and know how blind and foolish the young are. My heart! He has turned me sick in a moment. Kate, if it should be true."

"Nay, nay!" cried Kate, eagerly. "Gerard might love a young woman: all young men do: I can't find what they see in them to love so: but if he did he would let us know; he would not deceive us.

You wicked man! No, dear mother look not so! Gerard is too good to love a creature of earth. His love is for our Lady and the saints. Ah! I will show you the picture—there: if his heart was earthly could he paint the Queen of Heaven like that—look! look!" and she held the picture out triumphantly, and more radiant and beautiful in this moment of enthusiasm than ever dead picture was or will be, overpowered the burgomaster with her eloquence and her feminine proof of Gerard's purity. His eyes and mouth opened, and remained open: in which state they kept turning face and all, as if on a pivot, from the picture to the women, and from the women to the picture.

"Why, it is herself," he gasped.

"Isn't it?" cried Kate, and her hostility was softened. "You admire it? I forgive you for frightening us."

"Am I in a mad-house?" said Ghysbrecht Van Swieten, thoroughly puzzled. "You show me a picture of the girl; and you say he painted it; and that is proof he cannot love her. Why they all paint their sweethearts, painters do."

"A picture of the girl?" exclaimed Kate, shocked. "Fie! this is no girl; this is our blessed Lady."

"No; no, it is Margaret Brandt."

"Oh blind! It is the Queen of Heaven."

"No; only of Sevenbergen village."

"Profane man! behold her crown!"

"Silly child! look at her red hair! Would the Virgin be seen in red hair? She who had the pick of all the colours ten thousand years before the world began."

At this moment an anxious face was insinuated round the edge of the open door: it was their neighbour Peter Buyskens.

"What is to do?" said he in a cautious whisper. "We can hear you all across the street. What on earth is to do?"

"O, neighbour! What is to do? Why here is the burgomaster blackening our Gerard."

"Stop!" cried Van Swieten. "Peter Buyskens is come in the nick of time. He knows father and daughter both. They cast their glamour on him."

"What is she a witch, too?"

"Else the egg takes not after the bird. Why is her father called the magician? I tell you they bewitched this very Peter here; they cast unholy spells on him, and cured him of the colic: now, Peter, look and tell me who is that? and you be silent, women, for a moment, if you can; who is it, Peter?"

"Well to be sure!" said Peter in reply: and his eye seemed fascinated by the picture.

"Who is it?" repeated Ghysbrecht, impetuously.

Peter Buyskens smiled. "Why you know as well as I do; but what have they put a crown on her for, I never saw her in a crown, for my part."

"Man alive! Can't you open your great jaws, and just speak a wench's name plain out to oblige three people?"

"I'd do a great deal more to oblige one of you than that, burgomaster. If it isn't as natural as life!"

"Curse the man! he won't, he won't—curse him!"

"Why, what have I done, now?"

"Oh, sir!" said little Kate, "for pity's sake tell us; are these the features of a living woman, of—of—Margaret Brandt?"

"A mirror is not truer, my little maid."

"But is it she, sir, for very certain?"

"Why, who else should it be?"

"Now, why couldn't you say so at once?" snarled Ghysbrecht.

"I did say so, as plain as I could speak," snapped Peter; and they growled over this small bone of contention so zealously, that they did not see Catherine and her daughter had thrown their aprons over their heads, and were rocking to and fro in deep distress. The next moment Elias came in from the shop, and stood aghast. Catherine, though her face was covered, knew his footstep.

"That is my poor man," she sobbed. "Tell him, good Peter Buyskens, for I have not the courage."

Elias turned pale. The presence of the burgomaster in his house, after so many years of coolness, coupled with his wife's and daughter's distress, made him fear some heavy misfortune.

"Richart! Jacob!" he gasped.

"No! no! said the burgomaster; "it is nearer home, and nobody is dead or dying, old friend."

"God bless you, burgomaster! Ah! something is gone off my breast that was like to choke me. Now, what is the matter?"

Ghysbrecht then told him all that he told the women, and showed the picture in evidence.

"Is that all?" said Eli, profoundly relieved. "What are ye roaring and bellowing for? It is vexing, it is angering, but it is not like death nor even sickness. Boys will be boys. He will outgrow that disease: 'tis but skin deep.'

But when Ghysbrecht told him that Margaret was a girl of good character; that it was not to be supposed she would be so intimate if marriage had not been spoken of between them, his brow darkened.

"Marriage? that shall never be," said he, sternly. "I'll stay that, ay, by force if need be, as I would his hand lifted to cut his throat. I'd do what old John Koestein did t'other day."

"And what is that, in Heaven's name?" asked the mother, suddenly removing her apron.

It was the burgomaster who replied:

"He made me shut young Albert Koestein up in the prison of the Stadthouse till he knocked under: it was not long. Forty-eight hours, all alone, on bread and water, cooled his hot stomach. 'Tell my father I am his humble servant,' says he, 'and let me into the sun once more—the sun is worth all the wenches in the world.'"

"Oh the cruelty of men!" sighed Catherine.

"As to that, the burgomaster has no choice: it is the law. And if a father says, 'Burgomaster, lock up my son,' he must do it. A fine thing it would be if a father might not lock up his own son."

"Well, well! it won't come to that with me and my son. He never disobeyed me in his life: he never shall. Where is he? It is past supper-time. Where is he, Kate?"

"Alas, I know not, father."

"I know," said Ghysbrecht; "he is at Sevenbergen. My servant met him on the road."

Supper passed in gloomy silence. Evening descended—no Gerard: eight o'clock came—no Gerard. Then the father sent all to bed except Catherine.

"You and I will walk abroad, wife, and talk over this new care."

"Abroad, my man, at this time? Whither?"

"Why on the road to Sevenbergen."

"Oh no, no hasty words, father. Poor Gerard! he never vexed you before."

"Fear me not. But it must end; and I am not one that trusts tomorrow with to-day's work."

The old pair walked hand in hand; for strange as it may appear to

48

some of my readers, the use of the elbow to couples walking was not discovered in Europe till centuries after this. They sauntered on a long time in silence. The night was clear and balmy. Such nights, calm and silent, recall the past from the dead.

"It is a many years since we walked so late, my man," said Catherine, softly.

"Ay, sweetheart, more than we shall see again (Is he never coming, I wonder?")

"Not since our courting days, Eli."

"No. Ay, you were a buxom lass then."

"And you were a comely lad, as ever a girl's eye stole a look at. I do suppose Gerard is with her now, as you used to be with me. Nature is strong, and the same in all our generations."

"Nay, I hope he has left her by now, confound her, or we shall be here all night."

"Eli!"

"Well, Kate?"

"I have been happy with you sweetheart, for all our rubs,—much happier, I trow, than if I had—been—a—a—nun. You won't speak harshly to the poor child? One can be firm without being harsh."

"Surely."

"Have you been happy with me, my poor Eli?"

"Why, you know I have. Friends I have known, but none like thee. Buss me, wife!"

"A heart to share joy and grief with is a great comfort to man or woman. Isn't it, Eli?"

"It is so, my lass."

> 'It doth joy double,
> And halveth trouble,'

runs the byword. And so I have found it, sweetheart. Ah! here comes the young fool."

Catherine trembled and held her husband's hand tight. The moon was bright, but they were in the shadow of some trees, and their son did not see them. He came singing in the moonlight, and his face shining.

CHAPTER VIII

WHILE the burgomaster was exposing Gerard at Tergou, Margaret had a trouble of her own at Sevenbergen. It was a housewife's distress, but deeper than we can well conceive. She came to Martin Wittenhaagen, the old soldier, with tears in her eyes.

"Martin, there's nothing in the house, and Gerard is coming, and he is so thoughtless. He forgets to sup at home. When he gives over work then he runs to me straight, poor soul: and often he comes quite faint. And to think I have nothing to set before my servant that loves me so dear."

Martin scratched his head. "What can I do?"

"It is Thursday: it is your day to shoot,—sooth to say, I counted on you to-day."

"Nay," said the soldier, "I may not shoot when the duke or his friends are at the chace; read else. I am no scholar." And he took out of his pouch a parchment with a grand seal. It purported to be a stipend and a licence given by Philip Duke of Burgundy to Martin Wittenhaagen, one of his archers, in return for services in the wars, and for a wound received at the duke's side. The stipend was four marks yearly to be paid by the Duke's almoner and the licence was to shoot three arrows once a week, viz., on Thursday, and no other day, in any of the Duke's forests in Holland, at any game but a seven-year-old buck or a doe carrying fawn, proviso, that the duke should not be hunting on that day, or any of his friends. In this case Martin was not to go and disturb the woods on peril of his salary, and his head, and a fine of a penny.

Margaret sighed and was silent.

"Come, cheer up, mistress," said he, "for your sake I'll peril my carcass; I have done that for many a one that was not worth your forefinger. It is no such mighty risk either. I'll but step into the skirts of the forest, here. It is odds but they drive a hare or a fawn within reach of my arrow."

"Well, if I let you go you must promise me not to go far, and not to be seen: far better Gerard went supperless than ill should come to you, faithful Martin."

The Cloister and the Hearth

The required promise given, Martin took his bow and three arrows, and stole cautiously into the wood: it was scarce a furlong distant. The horns were heard faintly in the distance, and all the game was afoot. "Come," thought Martin, "I shall soon fill the pot and no one be the wiser." He took his stand behind a thick oak that commanded a view of an open glade, and strung his bow, a truly formidable weapon. It was of English yew, six feet two inches high, and thick in proportion: and Martin, broad chested, with arms all iron and cord, and used to the bow from infancy, could draw a three-foot arrow to the head, and, when it flew, the eye could scarce follow it, and the bowstring twanged as musical as a harp. This bow had laid many a stout soldier low in the wars of the Hoecks and Cabbel-jaws. In those days a battle-field was not a cloud of smoke; the combatants were few but the deaths many; for they saw what they were about, and fewer bloodless arrows flew than bloodless bullets now. A hare came cantering, then sat sprightly, and her ears made a capital V. Martin levelled his tremendous weapon at her: the arrow flew, the string twanged: but Martin had been in a hurry to pot her, and lost her by an inch: the arrow seemed to hit her, but it struck the ground close to her, and passed under her belly like a flash, and hissed along the short grass and disappeared. She jumped three feet perpendicular, and away at the top of her speed. "Bungler!" said Martin. A sure proof he was not an habitual bungler, or he would have blamed the hare. He had scarcely fitted another arrow to his string when a wood-pigeon settled on the very tree he stood under.

"Aha!" thought he, "you are small, but dainty." This time he took more pains; drew his arrow carefully, loosed it smoothly, and saw it, to all appearance, go clean through the bird, carrying feathers skyward like dust. Instead of falling at his feet, the bird, whose breast was torn, not fairly pierced, fluttered feebly away, and, by a great effort rose above the trees, flew some fifty yards, and fell dead at last; but where, he could not see for the thick foliage.

"Luck is against me," said he, despondingly. But he fitted another arrow, and eyed the glade keenly. Presently he heard a bustle behind him, and turned round just in time to see a noble buck cross the open, but too late to shoot at him. He dashed his bow down with an imprecation. At that moment a long, spotted animal glided swiftly across after the deer; its belly seemed to touch the ground as it went.

Martin took up his bow hastily: he recognized the duke's leopard. "The hunters will not be far from her," said he, "and I must not be seen. Gerard must go supperless this night."

He plunged into the wood, following the buck and leopard, for that was his way home. He had not gone far when he heard an unusual sound ahead of him—leaves rustling violently, and the ground trampled. He hurried in the direction. He found the leopard on the buck's back, tearing him with teeth and claw, and the buck running in a circle and bounding convulsively, with the blood pouring down his hide. Then Martin formed a desperate resolution to have the venison for Margaret. He drew his arrow to the head and buried it in the deer, who, spite of the creature on his back, bounded high into the air, and fell dead. The leopard went on tearing him as if nothing had happened.

Martin hoped that the creature would gorge itself with blood, and then let him take the meat. He waited some minutes, then walked resolutely up, and laid his hand on the buck's leg. The leopard gave a frightful growl, and left off sucking blood. She saw Martin's game, and was sulky and on her guard. What was to be done? Martin had heard that wild creatures cannot stand the human eye. Accordingly he stood erect and fixed his on the leopard; the leopard returned a savage glance, and never took her eye off Martin. Then Martin continuing to look the beast down, the leopard, brutally ignorant of natural history, flew at his head with a frightful yell, flaming eyes, and jaws and claws distended. He had but just time to catch her by the throat, before her teeth could crush his face; one of her claws seized his shoulder and rent it, the other aimed at his cheek, would have been more deadly still, but Martin was old fashioned, and wore no hat, but a scapulary of the same stuff as his jerkin, and this scapulary he had brought over his head like a hood; the brute's claw caught in the loose leather. Martin kept her teeth off his face with great difficulty, and gripped her throat fiercely, and she kept rending his shoulder. It was like blunt reaping-hooks grinding and tearing. The pain was fearful: but, instead of cowing the old soldier, it put his blood up, and he gnashed his teeth with rage almost as fierce as hers, and squeezed her neck with iron force. The two pairs of eyes flared at one another—and now the man's were almost as furious as the brute's. She found he was throttling her, and made a wild attempt to free herself, in which she dragged his cowl all over his face and blinded him, and tore her claw out of his shoulder, flesh and all: but still he throttled her with hand and arm of iron. Presently her long tail, that was high in the air, went down. "Aha!" cried Martin, joyfully, and gripped her like death; next, her body lost its elasticity, and he held a choked and powerless thing: he gripped it till all motion ceased, then dashed it to the earth; then, panting, removed his cowl: the leopard lay mute at his feet with tongue protruding and bloody paw; and for the first time terror fell on Martin. "I am a dead man: I have slain the duke's leopard." He hastily seized a few handfuls of leaves and threw them over her; then shouldered the buck and staggered away, leaving a trail of blood all the way—his own and the buck's. He burst into Peter's house a horrible figure, bleeding and blood-stained, and flung the deer's carcass down.

"There, no questions" said he, "but broil me a steak on't; for I am faint."

Margaret did not see he was wounded: she thought the blood was all from the deer.

She busied herself at the fire, and the stout soldier stanched and bound his own wound apart, and soon he and Gerard and Margaret were supping royally on broiled venison.

They were very merry; and Gerard, with wonderful thoughtfulness, had brought a flask of Schiedam, and under its influence Martin revived, and told them how the venison was got; and they all made merry over the exploit.

Their mirth was strangely interrupted. Margaret's eye became fixed and fascinated, and her cheek pale with fear. She gasped, and could not speak, but pointed to the window with trembling finger. Their eyes followed hers, and there in the twilight crouched a dark form with eyes like glowworms.

It was the leopard.

While they stood petrified, fascinated by the eyes of green fire, there sounded in the wood a single deep bay. Martin trembled at it.

"They have lost her, and laid muzzled bloodhounds on her scent. They will find her here, and the venison. Good-bye, friends, Martin Wittenhaagen ends here."

Gerard seized his bow, and put it into the soldier's hands.

"Be a man," he cried, "shoot her, and fling her into the wood ere they come up. Who will know?"

More voices of hounds broke out, and nearer.

"Curse her!" cried Martin. "I spared her once; now she must die, or I, or both more likely;" and he reared his bow, and drew his arrow to the head.

"Nay! nay!" cried Margaret, and seized the arrow: it broke in half: the pieces fell on each side of the bow. The air at the same time filled with the tongues of the hound: they were hot upon the scent.

"What have you done, wench? You have put the halter round my throat."

"No!" cried Margaret. "I have saved you: stand back from the window, both! Your knife quick!"

She seized his long-pointed knife, almost tore it out of his girdle, and darted from the room. The house was now surrounded with baying dogs and shouting men.

The glowworm eyes moved not.

CHAPTER IX

MARGARET cut off a huge piece of venison, and ran to the window, and threw it out to the green eyes of fire. They darted on it with a savage snarl: and there was a sound of rending and crunching: at this moment, a hound uttered a bay so near and loud it rang through the house; and the three at the window shrank together. Then the leopard feared for her supper, and glided swiftly and stealthily away with it toward the woods, and the very next moment horses and men and dogs came helter skelter past the window, and followed her full cry. Martin and his companions breathed again: the leopard was swift, and would not be caught within a league of their house. They grasped hands. Margaret seized this opportunity, and cried a little: Gerard kissed the tears away.

To table once more and Gerard drank to woman's wit: "'Tis stronger than man's force," said he.

"Ay," said Margaret, "when those she loves are in danger; not else."

To-night Gerard stayed with her longer than usual, and went home prouder than ever of her, and happy as a prince. Some little distance from home, under the shadow of some trees, he encountered two figures: they almost barred his way.

It was his father and mother.

Out so late: what could be the cause?

A chill fell on him.

He stopped and looked at them: they stood grim and silent. He stammered out some words of inquiry:

"Why ask?" said his father; "you know why we are here."

"Oh, Gerard!" said his mother, with a voice full of reproach and yet of affection.

Gerard's heart quaked: he was silent.

Then his father pitied his confusion, and said to him:

"Nay, you need not to hang your head. You are not the first young fool that has been caught by a red cheek, and a pair of blue eyes."

"Nay, nay!" put in Catherine: "it was witchcraft. Peter the Magician is well known for that."

"Come, Sir Priest," resumed his father, "you know you must not meddle with women-folk. But give us your promise to go no more to Sevenbergen, and here all ends: we won't be hard on you for one fault."

"I cannot promise that, father."

"Not promise it, you young hypocrite."

"Nay, father, miscall me not: I lacked courage to tell you what I knew would vex you: and right grateful am I to that good friend, whoever he be, that has let you wot. 'Tis a load off my mind. Yes, father, I love Margaret: and call me not a priest, for a priest I will never be. I will die sooner."

"That we shall see, young man. Come, gainsay me no more; you will learn what 'tis to disrespect a father."

Gerard held his peace: and the three walked home in gloomy silence, broken only by a deep sigh or two from Catherine.

From that hour the little house at Tergou was no longer the abode of peace. Gerard was taken to task next day before the whole family; and every voice was loud against him, except little Kate's, and the dwarf's, who was apt to take his cue from her without knowing why. As for Cornelis and Sybrandt, they were bitterer than their father. Gerard was dismayed at finding so many enemies, and looked wistfully into his little sister's face:

her eyes were brimming at the harsh words showered on one who but yesterday was the universal pet. But she gave him no encouragement: she turned her head away from him, and said:

"Dear, dear Gerard, pray to Heaven to cure you of this folly!"

"What, are you against me too?" said Gerard, sadly; and he rose with a deep sigh, and left the house, and went to Sevenbergen.

The beginning of a quarrel, where the parties are bound by affection though opposed in interest and sentiment, is comparatively innocent; both are perhaps in the right at first starting, and then it is that a calm, judicious, friend, capable of seeing both sides, is a gift from Heaven. For, the longer the dissension endures, the wider and deeper it grows by the fallibility and irascibility of human nature: these are not confined to either side, and finally the invariable end is reached—both in the wrong.

The combatants were unequally matched: Elias was angry, Cornelis and Sybrandt spiteful; but Gerard, having a larger and more cultivated mind, saw both sides where they saw but one, and had fits of irresolution, and was not wrath, but unhappy. He was lonely too in this struggle. He could open his heart to no one. Margaret was a high-spirited girl: he dared not tell her what he had to endure at home; she was capable of siding with his relations by resigning him, though at the cost of her own happiness. Margaret Van Eyck had been a great comfort to him on another occasion; but now he dared not make her his confidante. Her own history was well known. In early life she had many offers of marriage; but refused them all for the sake of that art, to which a wife's and mother's duties are so fatal: thus she remained single and painted with her brothers. How could he tell her that he declined the benefice she had got him, and declined it for the sake of that, which at his age she had despised and sacrificed so lightly?

Gerard at this period bade fair to succumb. But the other side had a horrible ally in Catherine Senior. This good-hearted but uneducated woman, could not, like her daughter, act quietly and firmly: still less could she act upon a plan. She irritated Gerard at times, and so helped him; for anger is a great sustainer of the courage: at others, she turned round in a moment and made onslaughts on her own forces. To take a single instance out of many: one day they were all at home, Catherine and all, Cornelis said: "Our Gerard wed Margaret Brandt? Why it is hunger marrying thirst."

The Cloister and the Hearth

"And what will it be when you marry?" cried Catherine. "Gerard can paint, Gerard can write, but what can you do to keep a woman, ye lazy loon? Nought but wait for your father's shoon. Oh, we can see why you and Sybrandt would not have the poor boy to marry. You are afraid he will come to us for a share of our substance. And say that he does, and say that we give it him, it isn't yourn we part from, and mayhap never will be."

On these occasions Gerard smiled slily, and picked up heart: and temporary confusion fell on Catherine's unfortunate allies. But at last, after more than six months of irritation, came the climax. The father told the son before the whole family he had ordered the burgomaster to imprison him in the Stadthouse rather than let him marry Margaret. Gerard turned pale with anger at this, but by a great effort held his peace. His father went on to say, "And a priest you shall be before the year is out, nilly-willy."

"Is it so?" cried Gerard. "Then hear me, all. By God and St. Bavon I swear I will never be a priest while Margaret lives. Since force is to decide it, and not love and duty, try force, father; but force shall not serve you, for the day I see the burgomaster come for me, I leave Tergou for ever, and Holland too, and my father's house, where it seems I have been valued all these years, not for myself, but for what is to be got out of me."

And he flung out of the room white with anger and desperation.

"There!" cried Catherine, "that comes of driving young folk too hard. But men are crueller than tigers, even to their own flesh and blood. Now, Heaven forbid he should ever leave us, married or single."

As Gerard came out of the house, his cheeks pale and his heart panting, he met Reicht Heynes: she had a message for him: Margaret Van Eyck desired to see him. He found the old lady seated grim as a judge. She wasted no time in preliminaries, but inquired coldly why he had not visited her of late: but before he could answer, she said in a sarcastic tone, "I thought we had been friends, young sir."

At this Gerard looked the picture of doubt and consternation.

"It is because you never told her you were in love," said Reicht Heynes, pitying his confusion.

"Silence, wench! Why should he tell us his affairs? We are not his friends: we have not deserved his confidence."

"Alas! my second mother," said Gerard, "I did not dare to tell you my folly."

"What folly? It is it folly to love?"

"I am told so every day of my life."

"You need not have been afraid to tell my mistress; she is always kind to true lovers."

"Madam—Reicht,—I was afraid because I was told—"

"Well? you were told—?"

"That in your youth you scorned love, preferring art."

"I did, boy; and what is the end of it? Behold me here a barren stock, while the women of my youth have a troop of children at their side and grandchildren at their knee. I gave up the sweet joys of wifehood and motherhood for what? for my dear brothers. They have gone and left me long ago; for my art. It has all but left me too. I have the knowledge still, but what avails that when the hand trembles. No, Gerard: I look on you as my son. You are good, you are handsome, you are a painter, though not like some I have known. I will not let you throw your youth away as I did mine: you shall marry this Margaret. I have inquired, and she is a good daughter. Reicht here is a gossip. She has told me all about it. But that need not hinder *you* to tell me."

Poor Gerard was overjoyed to be permitted to praise Margaret aloud, and to one who could understand what he loved in her.

Soon there were two pairs of wet eyes over his story; and when the poor boy saw that, there were three.

Women are creatures brimful of courage. Theirs is not exactly the same quality as manly courage; that would never do, hang it all; we should have to give up trampling on them. No; it is a vicarious courage. They never take part in a bull-fight by any chance; but it is remarked that they sit at one unshaken by those tremors, and apprehensions for the combatants, to which the male spectator—feeble-minded wretch!—is subject. Nothing can exceed the resolution with which they have been known to send forth men to battle: as some witty dog says, "Les femmes sont très braves avec le peau d'autrui."

By this trait Gerard now profited. Margaret and Reicht were agreed that *a man* should always take the bull by the horns. Gerard's only course was to marry Margaret Brandt off-hand; the old people would come to after a while, the deed once done. Whereas, the longer this misunderstanding continued on its present footing, the worse for all parties, especially for Gerard.

"See how pale and thin they have made him amongst them."

"Indeed you are, Master Gerard," said Reicht. "It makes a body sad to see a young man so wasted and worn. Mistress, when I met him in the street to-day, I had like to have burst out crying: he was so changed."

"And I'll be bound the others keep their colour; eh, Reicht? such as it is."

"Oh, I see no odds in them."

"Of course not. We painters are no match for boors. We are glass, they are stone. We can't stand the worry, worry, worry of little minds; and it is not for the good of mankind we should be exposed to it. It is hard enough, Heaven knows, to design and paint a masterpiece, without having gnats and flies stinging us to death into the bargain."

Exasperated as Gerard was by his father's threat of violence, he listened to these friendly voices telling him the prudent course was rebellion. But though he listened he was not convinced.

"I do not fear my father's violence," he said, "but I do fear his anger. When it came to the point he would not imprison me. I would marry Margaret to-morrow if that was my only fear. No; he would disown me. I should take Margaret from her father, and give her a poor husband, who would never thrive, weighed down by his parent's curse. Madam! I sometimes think if I could but marry her secretly and then take her away to some country where my craft is better paid than in this; and after a year or two, when the storm had blown over, you know, could come back with money in my purse, and say 'My dear parents, we do not seek your substance, we but ask you to love us once more as you used, and as we have never ceased to love you'—but alas! I shall be told these are the dreams of an inexperienced young man."

The old lady's eyes sparkled.

"It is no dream, but a piece of wonderful common sense in a boy; it remains to be seen whether you have spirit to carry out your own thought. There is a country, Gerard, where certain fortune awaits you at this moment. Here the arts freeze, but there they flourish, as they never yet flourished in any age or land."

"It is Italy!" cried Gerard. "It is Italy!"

The Cloister and the Hearth

"Ay, Italy! where painters are honoured like princes, and scribes are paid three hundred crowns for copying a single manuscript. Know you not that his Holiness the Pope has written to every land for skilful scribes to copy the hundreds of precious manuscripts that are pouring into that favoured land from Constantinople, whence learning and learned men are driven by the barbarian Turks?"

"Nay, I know not that; but it has been the dream and hope of my life to visit Italy, the queen of all the arts; oh, madam. But the journey, and we are all so poor."

"Find you the heart to go, I'll find the means. I know where to lay my hand on ten golden angels: they will take you to Rome; and the girl with you if she loves you as she ought."

They sat till midnight over this theme. And, after that day, Gerard recovered his spirits, and seemed to carry a secret talisman against all the gibes and the harsh words that flew about his ears at home.

Besides the money she procured him for the journey, Margaret Van Eyck gave him money's worth. Said she, "I will tell you secrets that I learned from masters that are gone from me, and have left no fellow behind. Even the Italians know them not; and what I tell you now in Tergou you shall sell dear in Florence. Note my brother Jan's pictures: time, which fades all other paintings, leaves his colours bright as the day they left the easel. The reason is, he did nothing blindly, nothing in a hurry. He trusted to no hireling to grind his colours; he did it himself, or saw it done. His panel was prepared, and prepared again—I will show you how—a year before he laid his colour on. Most of them are quite content to have their work sucked up and lost, sooner than not be in a hurry. Bad painters are always in a hurry. Above all, Gerard, I warn you use but little oil, and never boil it; boiling it melts that vegetable dross into its very heart, which it is our business to clear away; for impure oil is death to colour. No; take your oil and pour it into a bottle with water. In a day or two, the water will turn muddy: that is muck from the oil. Pour the dirty water carefully away, and add fresh. When that is poured away, you will fancy the oil is clear. You are mistaken. Reicht, fetch me *that!*" Reicht brought a glass trough with a glass lid fitting tight. "When your oil has been washed in bottle, put it into this trough with water, and put the trough in the sun all day. You will soon see the water turbid again. But mark, you must not carry this game too far, or the sun will turn your oil to varnish. When it is as clear as crystal, not too luscious, drain carefully, and cork it up tight. Grind your own prime colours, and lay them on with this oil, and they shall live. Hubert would put sand or salt in the water to clear the oil quicker. But Jan used to say, 'Water will do it best, give water time.' Jan Van Eyck was never in a hurry, and that is why the world will not forget *him* in a hurry."

This and several other receipts, quæ nunc perscribere longum est, Margaret gave him with sparkling eyes, and Gerard received them like a legacy from Heaven, so interesting are some things that read uninteresting. Thus provided with money and knowledge, Gerard decided to marry, and fly with his wife to Italy. Nothing remained now but to inform Margaret Brandt of his resolution, and to publish the banns as quietly as possible. He went to Sevenbergen earlier than usual on both these errands. He began with Margaret; told her of the Dame Van Eyck's goodness, and the resolution he had come to at last, and invited her co-operation.

She refused it plump.

"No, Gerard; you and I have never spoken of your family, but when you come to marriage—" She stopped, then began again. "I do think your father has no ill will to me more than to another. He told Peter Buyskens as much, and Peter told me. But so long as he is bent on your being a priest (you ought to have told me this instead of I you), I could not marry you, Gerard, dearly as I love you."

Gerard strove in vain to shake this resolution. He found it very easy to make her cry, but impossible to make her yield. Then Gerard was impatient and unjust.

"Very well!" he cried; "then you are on their side, and you will drive me to be a priest, for this must end one way or another. My parents hate me in earnest, but my lover only loves me in jest."

And with this wild, bitter speech, he flung away home again and left Margaret weeping.

When a man misbehaves, the effect is curious on a girl who loves him sincerely. It makes her pity him. This, to some of us males, seems anything but logical. The fault is in our own eye; the logic is too swift for us. The girl argues thus:— "How unhappy, how vexed, poor . . . must be; *him* to misbehave! Poor thing!"

Margaret was full of this sweet womanly pity, when, to her great surprise, scarce an hour and a half after he left her, Gerard came running back to her with the fragments of a picture in his hand, and panting with anger and grief.

"There Margaret! see! see! the wretches! Look at their spite! They have cut your portrait to pieces."

Margaret looked. And, sure enough, some malicious hand had cut her portrait into five pieces. She was a good girl, but she was not ice; she turned red to her very forehead.

"Who did it?"

"Nay, I know not. I dared not ask; for I should hate the hand that did it, ay, till my dying day. My poor Margaret! The butchers, the ruffians. Six months' work cut out of my life, and nothing to show for it now. See, they have hacked through your very face; the sweet face that every one loves who knows it. O, heartless, merciless vipers!"

"Never mind, Gerard," said Margaret, panting. "Since this is how they treat you for my sake— Ye rob him of my portrait, do ye? Well, then he shall have the face itself, such as it is."

"O, Margaret!"

"Yes, Gerard; since they are so cruel, I will be the kinder: forgive me for refusing you. I will be your wife: to-morrow, if it is your pleasure."

Gerard kissed her hands with rapture and then her lips; and in a tumult of joy ran for Peter and Martin. They came and witnessed the betrothal; a solemn ceremony in those days, and indeed for more than a century later, though now abolished.

CHAPTER X

THE banns of marriage had to be read three times, as in our days; with this difference, that they were commonly read on week-days, and the young couple easily persuaded the curé to do the three readings in twenty-four hours: he was new to the place, and their looks spoke volumes in their favour. They were cried on Monday at matins and at vespers; and, to their great delight, nobody from Tergou was in the church. The next morning they were both there palpitating with anxiety, when, to their horror, a stranger stood up and forbade the banns, on the score that the parties were not of age, and their parents not consenting.

Outside the church door, Margaret and Gerard held a trembling and almost despairing consultation; but, before they could settle anything, the man who had done them so ill a turn approached, and gave them to understand that he was very sorry to interfere; that his inclination was to further the happiness of the young: but that in point of fact his only means of getting a living was by forbidding banns: what then? "The young people give me a crown, and I undo my work handsomely; tell the curé I was misinformed; and all goes smoothly."

"A crown? I will give you a golden angel to do this," said Gerard, eagerly. The man consented as eagerly, and went with Gerard to the curé, and told him he had made a ridiculous mistake, which a sight of the parties had rectified. On this the curé agreed to marry the young couple next day at ten: and the professional obstructor of bliss went home with Gerard's angel. Like most of these very clever knaves, he was a fool, and proceeded to drink his angel at a certain hostelry in Tergou, where was a green devoted to archery and the common sports of the day. There, being drunk, he bragged of his day's exploit; and who should be there, imbibing every word, but a great frequenter of the spot, the ne'er-do-weel Sybrandt. Sybrandt ran home to tell his father; his father was not at home; he was gone to Rotterdam to buy cloth of the merchants. Catching his elder brother's eye, he made him a signal to come out, and told him what he had heard.

There are black sheep in nearly every large family: and these two were Gerard's black brothers. Idleness is vitiating: waiting for the death of those we ought to love is vitiating: and these two one-idead curs were ready to tear any one to death who should interfere with that miserable inheritance, which was their thought by day and their dream by night. Their parents' parsimony was a virtue; it was accompanied by industry, and its motive was love of their offspring: but in these perverse and selfish hearts that homely virtue was perverted into avarice, than which no more fruitful source of crimes is to be found in nature.

They put their heads together, and agreed not to tell their mother, whose sentiments were so uncertain, but to go first to the burgomaster. They were cunning enough to see that he was averse to the match, though they could not divine why.

Ghysbrecht Van Swieten saw through them at once; but he took care not to let them see through him. He heard their story; and putting on magisterial dignity and coldness, he said:

"Since the father of the family is not here, his duty falleth on me, who am the father of the town. I know your father's mind; leave all to me: and above all, tell not a woman a word of this, least of all the women that are in your own house: for chattering tongues mar wisest counsels."

So he dismissed them a little superciliously: he was ashamed of his confederates.

On their return home they found their brother Gerard seated on a low stool at their mother's knee: she was caressing his hair with her hand, speaking very kindly to him, and promising to take his part with his father and thwart his love no more. The main cause of this change of mind was characteristic of the woman. She it was who in a moment of female irritation had cut Margaret's picture to pieces. She had watched the effect with some misgivings, and had seen Gerard turn pale as death, and sit motionless like a bereaved creature, with the pieces in his hands, and his eyes fixed on them till tears came and blinded them. Then she was terrified at what she had done; and next her heart smote her bitterly; and she wept sore apart: but, being what she was, dared not own it, but said to herself, "I'll not say a word, but I'll make it up to him." And her bowels yearned over her son, and her feeble violence died a natural death, and she was transferring her fatal alliance to Gerard when the two black sheep came in. Gerard knew nothing of the immediate cause; on the contrary, inexperienced as he was in the ins and outs of females, her kindness made him ashamed of a suspicion he had entertained that she was the depredator; and he kissed her again and again, and went to bed happy as a prince to think his mother was his mother once more at the very crisis of his fate.

The next morning, at ten o'clock, Gerard and Margaret were in the church at Sevenbergen, he radiant with joy, she with blushes. Peter was also there, and Martin Wittenhaagen, but no other friend. Secrecy was everything. Margaret had declined Italy. She could not leave her father; he was too learned and too helpless. But it was settled they should retire into Flanders for a few weeks until the storm should be blown over at Tergou. The curé did not keep them waiting long, though it seemed an age. Presently he stood at the altar, and called them to him. They went hand in hand, the happiest in Holland. The curé opened his book.

But ere he uttered a single word of the sacred rite, a harsh voice cried "Forbear!" And the constables of Tergou came up the aisle and seized Gerard in the name of the law. Martin's long knife flashed out directly.

"Forbear, man!" cried the priest. "What! draw your weapon in a church, and ye who interrupt this holy sacrament, what means this impiety?"

"There is no impiety," said the burgomaster's servant respectfully. "This young man would marry against his father's will, and his father has prayed our burgomaster to deal with him according to the law. Let him deny it if he can."

"Is this so, young man?"

Gerard hung his head.

"We take him to Rotterdam to abide the sentence of the duke."

At this Margaret uttered a cry of despair, and the young creatures, who were so happy a moment ago, fell to sobbing in one another's arms so piteously, that the instruments of oppression drew back a step, and were ashamed; but one of them that was good-natured stepped up under pretence of separating them, and whispered to Margaret:

"Rotterdam? it is a lie. We but take him to our Stadthouse."

They took him away on horseback, on the road to Rotterdam; and, after a dozen halts, and by sly detours, to Tergou. Just outside the town they were met by a rude vehicle covered with canvas. Gerard was put into this, and about five in the evening was secretly conveyed into the prison of the Stadthouse. He was taken up several flights of stairs and thrust into a small room lighted only by a narrow window, with a vertical iron bar. The whole furniture was a huge oak chest.

Imprisonment in that age was one of the highroads to death. It is horrible in its mildest form; but in those days it implied cold, unbroken solitude, torture, starvation, and often poison. Gerard felt he was in the hands of an enemy.

"Oh, the look that man gave me on the road to Rotterdam. There is more here than my father's wrath. I doubt I shall see no more the light of day." And he kneeled down and commended his soul to God.

Presently he rose and sprang at the iron bar of the window and clutched it. This enabled him to look out by pressing his knees against the wall. It was but for a minute; but in that minute, he saw a sight such as none but a captive can appreciate.

Martin Wittenhaagen's back.

Martin was sitting, quietly fishing in the brook near the Stadthouse.

Gerard sprang again at the window, and whistled. Martin instantly showed that he was watching much harder than fishing. He turned hastily round and saw Gerard;—made him a signal, and taking up his line and bow went quickly off.

Gerard saw by this that his friends were not idle: yet he had rather Martin had stayed. The very sight of him was a comfort. He held on, looking at the soldier's retiring form as long as he could, then falling back somewhat heavily, wrenched the rusty iron bar, held only by rusty nails, away from the stone-work just as Ghysbrecht Van Swieten opened the door stealthily behind him. The burgomaster's eye fell instantly on the iron, and then glanced at the window; but he said nothing. The window was a hundred feet from the ground; and if Gerard had a fancy for jumping out, why should he balk it? He brought a brown loaf and a pitcher of water, and set them on the chest in solemn silence. Gerard's first impulse was to brain him with the iron bar, and fly down the stairs; but the burgomaster seeing something wicked in his eye, gave a little cough, and three stout fellows, armed, showed themselves directly at the door.

"My orders are to keep you thus until you shall bind yourself by an oath to leave Margaret Brandt, and return to the Church to which you have belonged from your cradle."

"Death sooner."

"With all my heart." And the burgomaster retired.

Martin went with all speed to Sevenbergen; there he found Margaret pale and agitated, but full of resolution and energy. She was just finishing a letter to the Countess Charolois, appealing to her against the violence and treachery of Ghysbrecht.

"Courage!" cried Martin on entering. "I have found him. He is in the haunted tower; right at the top of it. Ay! I know the place: many a poor fellow has gone up there straight, and come down feet foremost."

He then told them how he had looked up and seen Gerard's face at a window that was like a slit in the wall.

"Oh Martin! how did he look?"

"What mean you? He looked like Gerard Eliassoen."

"But was he pale?"

"A little."

"Looked he anxious? Looked he like one doomed?"

"Nay, nay; as bright as a pewter pot."

"You mock me. Stay! then that must have been at sight of you. He counts on us. Oh! what shall we do? Martin, good friend, take this at once to Rotterdam."

Martin held out his hand for the letter.

Peter had sat silent all this time, but pondering, and yet contrary to custom, keenly attentive to what was going on around him.

"Put not your trust in princes," said he.

"Alas! what else have we to trust in?"

"Knowledge."

"Well-a-day, father! your learning will not serve us here."

"How know you that? Wit has been too strong for iron bars ere to-day."

"Ay, father; but nature is stronger than wit, and she is against us. Think of the height! No ladder in Holland might reach him."

"I need no ladder; what I need is a gold crown."

"Nay. I have money for that matter. I have nine angels. Gerard gave them me to keep; but what do they avail? The burgomaster will not be bribed to let Gerard free."

"What do they avail? Give me but one crown, and the young man shall sup with us this night."

Peter spoke so eagerly and confidently, that for a moment Margaret felt hopeful; but she caught Martin's eye dwelling upon him with an expression of benevolent contempt.

"It passes the powers of man's invention," said she, with a deep sigh.

"Invention?" cried the old man. "A fig for invention. What need we invention at this time of day? Everything has been said that is to be said and done that ever will be done. I shall tell you how a Florentine knight was shut up in a tower higher than Gerard's: yet did his faithful squire stand at the tower foot and get him out, with no other engine than that in your hand, Martin, and certain kickshaws I shall buy for a crown."

Martin looked at his bow, and turned it round in his hand; and seemed to interrogate it. But the examination left him as incredulous as before.

Then Peter told them his story, how the faithful squire got the knight out of a high tower at Brescia. The manœuvre, like most things that are really scientific, was so simple, that now their wonder was they had taken for impossible what was not even difficult.

The letter never went to Rotterdam. They trusted to Peter's learning and their own dexterity.

It was nine o'clock on a clear moonlight night; Gerard, senior, was still away; the rest of his little family had been sometime abed.

A figure stood by the dwarf's bed. It was white, and the moonlight shone on it.

With an unearthly noise, between a yell and a snarl, the gymnast rolled off his bed and under it by a single unbroken movement. A soft voice followed him in his retreat.

"Why, Giles, are you afeard of me?"

At this, Giles's head peeped cautiously up, and he saw it was only his sister Kate.

She put her finger to her lips. "Hush! lest the wicked Cornelis or the wicked Sybrandt hear us." Giles's claws seized the side of the bed, and he returned to his place by one undivided gymnastic.

Kate then revealed to Giles that she had heard Cornelis and Sybrandt mention Gerard's name; and being herself in great anxiety at his not coming home all day, had listened at their door, and had made a fearful discovery. Gerard was in prison, in the haunted tower of the Stadthouse. He was there it seemed by their father's authority. But here must be some treachery; for how could their father have ordered this cruel act? he was at Rotterdam. She ended by entreating Giles to bear her company to the foot of the haunted tower, to say a word of comfort to poor Gerard, and let him know their father was absent, and would be sure to release him on his return.

"Dear Giles, I would go alone, but I am afeard of the spirits that men say do haunt the tower: but with you I shall not be afeard."

"Nor I with you," said Giles. "I don't believe there are any spirits in Tergou. I never saw one. This last was the likest one ever I saw; and it was but you, Kate, after all."

In less than half an hour Giles and Kate opened the house door cautiously and issued forth. She made him carry a lantern though the night was bright. "The lantern gives me more courage against the evil spirits," said she.

The first day of imprisonment is very trying, especially if to the horror of captivity is added the horror of utter solitude. I observe that in our own day a great many persons commit suicide during the first twenty-four hours of the solitary cell. This is doubtless why our Jairi abstain so carefully from the impertinence of watching their little experiment upon the human soul at that particular stage of it.

As the sun declined, Gerard's heart too sank and sank: with the waning light even the embers of hope went out. He was faint, too, with hunger; for he was afraid to eat the food Ghysbrecht had brought him; and hunger alone cows men. He sat upon the chest, his arms and his head drooping before him, a picture of despondency. Suddenly something struck the wall beyond him very sharply. and then rattled on the floor at his feet. It was an arrow; he saw the white feather. A chill ran through him—they meant then to assassinate him from the outside. He crouched. No more missiles came. He crawled on all fours, and took up the arrow: there was no head to it. He uttered a cry of hope: had a friendly hand shot it? He took it up, and felt it all over: he found a soft substance attached to it. Then one of his eccentricities was of grand use to him. His tinder-box enabled him to strike a light: it showed him two things that made his heart bound with delight, none the less thrilling for being somewhat vague. Attached to the arrow was a skein of silk; and on the arrow itself were words written.

How his eyes devoured them, his heart panting the while!

Well beloved, make fast the silk to thy knife and lower to us: but hold thine end fast: then count an hundred and draw up.

Gerard seized the oak chest and with almost superhuman energy dragged it to the window: a moment ago he could not have moved it.

The Cloister and the Hearth

Standing on the chest and looking down he saw figures at the tower foot. They were so indistinct they looked like one huge form. He waved his bonnet to them with trembling hand: then he undid the silk rapidly but carefully, and made one end fast to his knife and lowered it till it ceased to draw. Then he counted a hundred. Then pulled the silk carefully up: it came up a little heavier. At last he came to a large knot, and by that knot a stout whipcord was attached to the silk. What could this mean? While he was puzzling himself, Margaret's voice came up to him, low but clear. "Draw up, Gerard, till you see Liberty." At the word Gerard drew the whipcord line up, and drew and drew till he came to another knot, and found a cord of some thickness take the place of the whipcord. He had no sooner begun to draw this up than he found that he had now a heavy weight to deal with. Then the truth suddenly flashed on him, and he went to work and pulled and pulled till the perspiration rolled down him: the weight got heavier and heavier, and at last he was well nigh exhausted; looking down he saw in the moonlight a sight that revived him: it was as it were a great snake coming up to him out of the deep shadow cast by the tower. He gave a shout of joy, and a score more wild pulls, and lo! a stout new rope touched his hand: he hauled and hauled, and dragged the end into his prison and instantly passed it through both handles of the chest in succession, and knotted it firmly; then sat for moment to recover his breath and collect his courage. The first thing was to make sure that the chest was sound, and capable of resisting his weight poised in mid air. He jumped with all his force upon it. At the third jump the whole side burst open, and out scuttled the contents, a host of parchments.

After the first start and misgiving this gave him, Gerard comprehended that the chest had not burst but opened: he had doubtless jumped upon some secret spring. Still it shook in some degree his confidence in the chest's powers of resistance; so he gave it an ally: he took the iron bar and fastened it with the small rope across the large rope, and across the window. He now mounted the chest, and from the chest put his foot through the window, and sat half in and half out, with one hand on that part of the rope which was inside. In the silent night he heard his own heart beat.

The free air breathed on his face, and gave him the courage to risk what we must all lose one day—for liberty. Many dangers awaited him, but the greatest was the first getting on to the rope outside. Gerard reflected. Finally he put himself in the attitude of a swimmer, his body to the waist being in the prison, his legs outside. Then holding the inside rope with both hands, he felt anxiously with his feet for the outside rope, and when he had got it, he worked it in between the palms of his feet, and kept it there tight: then he uttered a short prayer, and all the calmer for it, put his left hand on the sill and gradually wriggled out. Then he seized the iron bar, and for one fearful moment hung outside from it by his right hand, while his left hand felt for the rope down at his knees; it was too tight against the wall for his fingers to get round it higher up. The moment he had fairly grasped it, he left the bar, and swiftly seized the rope with the right hand too; but in this manœuvre his body necessarily fell about a yard. A stifled cry came up from below. Gerard hung in mid air. He clenched his teeth and nipped the rope tight with his feet and gripped it with his hands, and went down slowly hand below hand. He passed by one huge rough stone after another. He saw there was green moss on one. He looked up and he looked down. The moon shone into his prison window: it seemed very near. The fluttering figures below seemed an awful distance. It made him dizzy to look down: so he fixed his eyes steadily on the wall close to him, and went slowly down, down, down.

He passed a rusty, slimy, streak on the wall: it was some ten feet long. The rope made his hands very hot. He stole another look up.

The prison window was a good way off, now.

Down—down—down—down.

The rope made his hands sore.

He looked up. The window was so distant, he ventured now to turn his eyes downward again: and there, not more than thirty feet below him were Margaret and Martin, their faithful hands upstretched to catch him should he fall. He could see their eyes and their teeth shine in the moon light. For their mouths were open, and they were breathing hard.

"Take care, Gerard! Oh take care! Look not down."

"Fear me not," cried Gerard, joyfully, and eyed the wall, but came down faster.

In another moment his feet were at their hands, They seized

him ere he touched the ground, and all three clung together in one embrace.

"Hush! away in silence, dear one."

They stole along the shadow of the wall.

Now, ere they had gone many yards, suddenly a stream of light shot from an angle of the building, and lay across their path like a barrier of fire, and they heard whispers and footsteps close at hand.

"Back!" hissed Martin. "Keep in the shade."

They hurried back, passed the dangling rope, and made for a little square projecting tower. They had barely rounded it when the light shot trembling past them, and flickered uncertainly into the distance.

"A lantern!" groaned Martin, in a whisper. "They are after us."

"Give me my knife," whispered Gerard. "I'll never be taken alive."

"No, no!" murmured Margaret: "is there no way out where we are?"

"None, none. But I carry six lives at my shoulder:" and, with the word, Martin strung his bow, and fitted an arrow to the string: "in war never wait to be struck: I will kill one or two ere they shall know where their death comes from:" then motioning his companions to be quiet, he began to draw his bow, and, ere the arrow was quite drawn to the head, he glided round the corner ready to loose the string the moment the enemy should offer a mark.

Gerard and Margaret held their breath in horrible expectation: they had never seen a human being killed.

And now a wild hope, but half repressed, thrilled through Gerard, that this watchful enemy might be the burgomaster in person. The soldier, he knew, would send an arrow through a burgher or burgomaster as he would through a boar in a wood.

But who may fortell the future, however near? The bow, instead of remaining firm, and loosing the deadly shaft, was seen to waver first, then shake violently, and the stout soldier staggered back to them, his knees knocking and his cheeks blanched with fear. He let his arrow fall, and clutched Gerard's shoulder.

"Let me feel flesh and blood," he gasped; "the haunted tower! the haunted tower!"

His terror communicated itself to Margaret and Gerard. They gasped, rather than uttered, an inquiry.

"Hush!" he cried, "it will hear you. *Up* the wall! it is going *up* the wall! Its head is on fire. *Up* the wall, as mortal creatures walk upon green sward. If you know a prayer say it! For hell is loose to-night."

"I have power to exorcise spirits," said Gerard, trembling. "I will venture forth."

"Go alone, then!" said Martin. "I have looked on't once and live."

CHAPTER XI

THE strange glance of hatred the burgomaster had cast on Gerard, coupled with his imprisonment, had filled the young man with a persuasion that Ghysbrecht was his enemy to the death: and he glided round the angle of the tower, fully expecting to see no supernatural appearance, but some cruel and treacherous contrivance of a bad man to do him mischief in that prison, his escape from which could hardly be known.

As he stole forth, a soft but brave hand crept into his, and Margaret was by his side to share this new peril.

No sooner was the haunted tower visible, than a sight struck their eyes that benumbed them as they stood. More than half way up the tower, a creature with a fiery head, like an enormous glowworm, was steadily mounting the wall: the body was dark, but its outline visible through the glare from the head, and the whole creature not much less than four feet long.

At the foot of the tower stood a thing in white, that looked exactly like the figure of a female. Gerard and Margaret palpitated with awe.

"The rope, the rope! It is going up the rope," gasped Gerard.

As they gazed, the glowworm disappeared in Gerard's late prison, but its light illuminated the cell inside and reddened the window. The white figure stood motionless below.

Such as can retain their senses after the first prostrating effect of the supernatural, are apt to experience terror in one of its strangest forms, a wild desire to fling themselves upon the terrible

object. It fascinates them as the snake the bird. The great trage-
dian Macready used to render this finely in Macbeth at Banquo's
second appearance. He flung himself with averted head at the horrible shadow. This strange impulse now seized Margaret. She put
down Gerard's hand quietly, and stood bewildered; then, all in a
moment, with a wild cry, darted towards the spectre. Gerard, not
aware of the natural impulse I have spoken of, never doubted
the evil one was drawing her to her perdition. He fell on his
knees.

"Exorcizo vos. In nomine beatæ Mariæ, exorcizo vos."

While the exorcist was shrieking his incantations in extremity of
terror, to his infinite relief he heard the spectre utter a feeble cry
of fear. To find that hell had also its little weaknesses was encouraging. He redoubled his exorcisms and presently he saw the
ghastly shape kneeling at Margaret's knees and heard it praying
piteously for mercy.

Kate and Giles soon reached the haunted tower. Judge their surprise when they found a new rope dangling from the prisoner's
window to the ground.

"I see how it is," said the inferior intelligence, taking facts as
hey came. "Our Gerard has come down this rope. He has got
clear. Up I go, and see."

"No, Giles, no!" said the superior intelligence, blinded by prejudice. See you not this is glamour? This rope is a line the evil
one casts out to wile thee to destruction. He knows the weaknesses
of all our hearts; he has seen how fond you are of going up things.
Where should our Gerard procure a rope? how fasten it in the sky
like this? It is not in nature. Holy saints protect us this night,
for hell is abroad."

"Stuff!" said the dwarf: "the way to hell is down, and this rope
leads up. I never had the luck to go up such a long rope. It may
be years ere I fall in with such a long rope all ready hung for me.
As well be knocked on the head at once as never know happiness."

And he sprung on to the rope with a cry of delight, as a cat jumps
with a mew on to a table where fish is. All the gymnast was on fire;
and the only concession Kate could gain from him was permission
to fasten the lantern on his neck first.

"A light scares the ill spirits," said she.

And so, with his huge arms and his legs like feathers, Giles went up the rope faster than his brother came down it. The light at the nape of his neck made a glowworm of him. His sister watched his progress with trembling anxiety. Suddenly a female figure started out of the solid masonry, and came flying at her with more than mortal velocity.

Kate uttered a feeble cry. It was all she could, for her tongue clove to her palate with terror. Then she dropped her crutches, and sank upon her knees, hiding her face and moaning:

"Take my body, but spare my soul!"

Margaret (panting). "Why it is a woman."

Kate (quivering). "Why it is a woman."

Margaret. "How you scared me."

Kate. "I am scared enough myself. Oh! oh! oh!"

"This is strange. But the fiery-headed thing? Yet it was with you, and you are harmless. But why are you here at this time of night?"

"Nay, why are YOU?"

"Perhaps we are on the same errand? Ah you are his *good* sister, Kate."

"And you are Margaret Brandt."

"Yea."

"All the better. You love him: you are here. Then Giles was right. He has won free."

Gerard came forward, and put the question at rest. But all further explanation was cut short by a horrible, unearthly noise, like a sepulchre ventriloquizing.

"PARCHMENT!—PARCHMENT!—PARCHMENT!"

At each repetition it rose in intensity. They looked up, and there was the dwarf, with his hands full of parchments, and his face, lighted with fiendish joy, and lurid with diabolical fire. The light being at his neck, a more infernal "transparency" never startled mortal eye. With the word the awful imp hurled parchment at the astonished heads below. Down came records, like wounded wild ducks, some collapsed, others fluttering and others spread out and wheeling slowly down in airy circles. They had hardly settled when again the sepulchral roar was heard: "Parchment:—Parchment!" and down pattered and sailed another flock of documents: another followed: they whitened the grass. Finally the fire-headed imp with his light body and horny hands slid down the rope like a falling star and (business before sentiment) proposed to his rescued brother an immediate settlement for the merchandise he had just delivered.

"Hush!" said Gerard; "you speak too loud. Gather them up and follow us to a safer place than this."

"Will you not come home with me, Gerard?" said little Kate.

"I have no home."

"You shall not say so. Who is more welcome than you will be, after this cruel wrong, to your father's house?"

"Father? I have no father," said Gerard sternly. "He that was my father is turned my gaoler. I have escaped from his hands; I will never come within their reach again."

"An enemy did this and not our father."

And she told him what she had overheard Cornelis and Sybrandt say. But the injury was too recent to be soothed. Gerard showed a bitterness of indignation he had hitherto seemed incapable of.

"Cornelis and Sybrandt are two curs that have shown me their teeth and their heart a long while; but they could do no more. My father it is that gave the burgomaster authority, or he durst not have laid a finger on me, that am a free burgher of this town. So be it, then. I was his son. I am his prisoner. He has played his part. I shall play mine. Farewell the burgh where I was born and lived honestly, and was put in prison. While there is another town left in creation, I'll never trouble you again, Tergou."

"Oh, Gerard! Gerard!"

Margaret whispered her:—"Do not gainsay him now. Give his choler time to cool!"

Kate turned quickly towards her. "Let me look at your face!" The inspection was favourable, it seemed, for she whispered:—"It is a comely face, and no mischief-maker's."

"Fear me not," said Margaret, in the same tone. "I could not be happy without your love as well as Gerard's."

"These are comfortable words," sobbed Kate. Then, looking up, she said, "I little thought to like you so well. My heart is willing, but my infirmity will not let me embrace you."

At this hint, Margaret wound gently round Gerard's sister, and kissed her lovingly.

"Often he has spoken of you to me, Kate, and often I longed for this."

"You, too, Gerard," said Kate, "kiss me ere you go, for my heart lies heavy at parting with you this night."

Gerard kissed her, and she went on her crutches home. The last thing they heard of her was a little patient sigh. Then the tears came and stood thick in Margaret's eyes; but Gerard was a man, and noticed not his sister's sigh.

As they turned to go to Sevenbergen, the dwarf nudged Gerard with his bundle of parchments, and held out a concave claw.

Margaret dissuaded Gerard. "Why take what is not ours?"

"Oh! spoil an enemy how you can."

"But may they not make this a handle for fresh violence?"

"How can they? Think you I shall stay in Tergou after this? The burgomaster robbed me of my liberty; I doubt I should take his life for it if I could."

"Oh fie, Gerard!"

"What? Is life worth more than liberty. Well I can't take his life, so I take the first thing that comes to hand."

He gave Giles a few small coins, with which the urchin was gladened, and shuffled after his sister. Margaret and Gerard were speedily joined by Martin, and away to Sevenbergen.

CHAPTER XII

GHYSBRECHT VAN SWIETEN kept the key of Gerard's prison in his pouch. He waited till ten of the clock ere he visited him; for he said to himself, "A little hunger sometimes does well; it breaks 'em." At ten he crept up the stairs with a loaf and pitcher, followed by his trusty servant well armed. Ghysbrecht listened at the door. There was no sound inside. A grim smile stole over his features. "By this time he will be as downhearted as Albert Koestein was," thought he. He opened the door.

No Gerard.

Ghysbrecht stood stupefied.

Although his face was not visible, his body seemed to lose all motion in so peculiar a way, and then after a little he fell a trembling so, that the servant behind him saw there was something amiss, and crept close to him and peeped over his shoulder. At sight of the empty cell and the rope, and iron bar, he uttered a loud exclamation of wonder: but his surprise doubled when his master, disregarding all else suddenly flung himself on his knees before the empty chest, and felt wildly all over it with quivering hands, as if unwilling to trust his eyes in a matter so important.

The servant gazed at him in utter bewilderment.

"Why, master, what is the matter?"

Ghysbrecht's pale lips worked as if he was going to answer; but they uttered no sound: his hands fell by his side, and he stared into the chest.

"Why, master, what avails glaring into that empty box? The lad is not there. See here! Note the cunning of the young rogue; he hath taken out the bar, and—"

"GONE! GONE! GONE!"

"Gone? What is gone? Holy saints! he is planet struck."

"STOP THIEF!' shrieked Ghysbrecht, and suddenly turned on his servant and collared him, and shook him with rage. "D'ye stand there, knave, and see your master robbed? Run! fly! A hundred crowns to him that finds it me again. No, no! 'tis in vain. Oh fool! fool! to leave that in the same room with him. But none ever found the secret spring before. None ever would but he. It was to be. It is to be. Lost! lost!" and his years and infirmity now gained the better of his short-lived frenzy, and he sank on the chest muttering "lost! lost!"

"What is lost, master?" asked the servant kindly.

"House and lands and good name," groaned Ghysbrecht, and wrung his hands feebly.

"WHAT?" cried the servant.

This emphatic word, and the tone of eager curiosity, struck on Ghysbrecht's ear, and revived his natural cunning.

"I have lost the town records," stammered he, and he looked askant at the man like a fox caught near a hen-roost.

"Oh, is that all?"

"Is't not enough? What will the burghers say to me? What will the burgh do?" Then he suddenly burst out again, "A hundred crowns to him who shall recover them; all, mind, all that were in this box. If one be missing, I give nothing."

"'Tis a bargain, master: the hundred crowns are in my pouch. See you not that where Gerard Eliassoen is, there are the pieces of sheepskin you rate so high?"

"That is true; that is true; good Dierich: good faithful Dierich. All, mind, all, that were in the chest."

"Master, I will take the constables to Gerard's house and seize him for the theft."

"The theft? ay! good; very good. It is theft. I forgot that. So, as he is a thief now, we will put him in the dungeons below: where the toads are and the rats. Dierich, that man must never see daylight again. 'Tis his own fault; he must be prying. Quick, quick! ere he has time to talk, you know, time to talk."

In less than half an hour Dierich Brower and four constables entered the hosier's house, and demanded young Gerard of the panic-stricken Catherine.

"Alas! what has he done now?" cried she: "that boy will break my heart."

"Nay, dame, but a trick of youth," said Dierich. "He hath but made off with certain skins of parchment, in a frolic doubtless; but the burgomaster is answerable to the burgh for their safe keeping, so he is in care about them: as for the youth, he will doubtless be quit for a reprimand."

This smooth speech completely imposed on Catherine: but her daughter was more suspicious, and that suspicion was strengthened by the disproportionate anger and disappointment Dierich showed the moment he learned Gerard was not at home, had not been at home that night.

"Come away then," said he roughly. "We are wasting time." He added, vehemently, "I'll find him if he is above ground."

Affection sharpens the wits, and often it has made an innocent person more than a match for the wily. As Dierich was going out, Kate made him a signal she would speak with him privately. He bade his men go on, and waited outside the door. She joined him.

"Hush!" said she, "my mother knows not. Gerard has left Tergou."

"How?"

"I saw him last night."

"Ay? Where?" cried Dierich, eagerly.

"At the foot of the haunted tower."

"How did he get the rope?"

"I know not; but this I know; my brother Gerard bade me there farewell, and he is many leagues from Tergou ere this. The town you know, was always unworthy of him, and, when it imprisoned

The Cloister and the Hearth

him, he vowed never to set foot in it again. Let the burgomaster be content, then. He has imprisoned him, and he has driven him from his birthplace and from his native land. What need now to rob him and us of our good name?"

This might at another moment have struck Dierich as good sense; but he was too mortified at this escape of Gerard and the loss of a hundred crowns.

"What need had he to steal?" retorted he, bitterly.

"Gerard stole not the trash; he but *took* it to spite the burgomaster, who stole his liberty; but he shall answer to the duke for it, he shall. As for these skins of parchment you keep such a coil about, look in the nearest brook, or stye, and 'tis odds but you find them."

"Think ye so, mistress?—think ye so?" And Dierich's eyes flashed. "Mayhap you know 'tis so."

"This I know, that Gerard is too good to steal, and too wise to load himself with rubbish, going a journey."

"Give you good day, then," said Dierich, sharply. "The sheepskin you scorn, I value more than the skin of any he in Tergou."

And he went off hastily on a false scent.

Kate returned into the house and drew Giles aside.

"Giles, my heart misgives me; breathe not to a soul what I say to you. I have told Dirk Brower that Gerard is out of Holland: but much I doubt he is not a league from Tergou."

"Why, where is he, then?"

"Where should he be, but with her he loves? But if so, he must not loiter. These be deep and dark and wicked men that seek him. Giles, I see that in Dirk Brower's eye makes me tremble. Oh! why cannot I fly to Sevenbergen, and bid him away? Why am I not lusty and active like other girls? God forgive me for fretting at His will: but I never felt till now what it is to be lame and weak and useless. But you are strong, dear Giles," added she coaxingly, "you are very strong."

"Yes, I am strong;" thundered Perpusillus: then, catching sight of her meaning, "but I hate to go on foot," he added, sulkily.

"Alas! alas! who will help me if you will not? Dear Giles, do you not love Gerard?"

"Yes I like him best of the lot. I'll go to Sevenbergen on Peter Buyskens his mule. Ask you him, for he won't lend her me."

80

Kate remonstrated. The whole town would follow him. It would be known whither he was gone, and Gerard be in worse danger than before.

Giles parried this by promising to ride out of the town the opposite way, and not turn the mule's head toward Sevenbergen till he had got rid of the curious.

Kate then assented, and borrowed the mule. She charged Giles with a short but meaning message, and made him repeat it after her, over and over, till he could say it word for word.

Giles started on the mule, and little Kate retired, and did the last thing now in her power for her beloved brother; prayed on her knees long and earnestly for his safety.

CHAPTER XIII

GERARD and Margaret went gaily to Sevenbergen in the first flush of recovered liberty, and successful adventure. But these soon yielded to sadder thoughts. Gerard was an escaped prisoner, and liable to be retaken and perhaps punished; and therefore he and Margaret would have to part for a time. Moreover he had conceived a hatred to his native place. Margaret wished him to leave the country for a while, but at the thought of his going to Italy her heart fainted. Gerard, on the contrary, was reconciled to leaving Margaret only by his desire to visit Italy, and his strong conviction that there he should earn money and reputation, and remove every obstacle to their marriage. He had already told her all that the demoiselle Van Eyck had said to him. He repeated it, and reminded Margaret that the gold pieces were only given him to go to Italy with. The journey was clearly for Gerard's interest. He was a craftsman and an artist, lost in this boorish place. In Italy they would know how to value him. On this ground above all the unselfish girl gave her consent: but many tender tears came with it, and at that Gerard, young and loving as herself, cried bitterly with her, and often they asked one another what they had done, that so many different persons should be their enemies, and combine, as it seemed, to part them.

They sat hand in hand till midnight, now deploring their hard fate, now drawing bright and hopeful pictures of the future, in the midst of which Margaret's tears would suddenly flow, and then poor Gerard's eloquence would die away in a sigh.

The morning found them resigned to part, but neither had the courage to say when; and much I doubt whether the hour of parting ever would have struck.

But about three in the afternoon, Giles, who had made a circuit of many miles to avoid suspicion, rode up to the door. They both ran out to him, eager with curiosity.

"Brother Gerard," cried he, in his tremendous tones, "Kate bids you run for your life. They charge you with theft; you have given them a handle. Think not to explain. Hope not for justice in Tergou. The parchments you took they are but a blind. She hath seen your death in the men's eyes: a price is on your head. Fly! For Margaret's sake and all who love you, loiter not life away, but fly!"

It was a thunder-clap, and left two white faces looking at one another, and at the terrible messenger.

Then Giles, who had hitherto but uttered by rote what Catherine bade him, put in a word of his own.

"All the constables were at our house after you, and so was Dirk Brower. Kate is wise, Gerard. Best give ear to her rede, and fly."

"Oh, yes! Gerard," cried Margaret, wildly. "Fly on the instant. Ah! those parchments; my mind misgave me: why did I let you take them?"

"Margaret, they are but a blind: Giles says so: no matter, the old caitiff shall never see them again; I will not go till I have hidden his treasure where he shall never find it." Gerard then, after thanking Giles warmly, bade him farewell, and told him to go back, and tell Kate he was gone. "For I shall be gone, ere you reach home," said he. He then shouted for Martin; and told him what had happened, and begged him to go a little way towards Tergou, and watch the road.

"Ay!" said Martin, "and if I see Dirk Brower, or any of his men, I will shoot an arrow into the oak tree that is in our garden; and on that you must run into the forest hard by, and meet me at the weird hunter's spring. Then I will guide you through the wood."

Surprise thus provided against, Gerard breathed again. He went with Margaret, and, while she watched the oak-tree tremblingly, fearing every moment to see an arrow strike among the branches, Gerard dug a deep hole to bury the parchments in.

He threw them in, one by one. They were nearly all charters and records of the burgh: but one appeared to be a private deed between Floris Brandt, father of Peter, and Ghysbrecht.

"Why this is as much yours as his," said Gerard. "I will read this."

"Oh, not now, Gerard, not now," cried Margaret. "Every moment you lose fills me with fear; and see, large drops of rain are beginning to fall, and the clouds lower."

Gerard yielded to this remonstrance: but he put the deed into his bosom, and threw the earth in over the others, and stamped it down.

While thus employed there came a flash of lightning followed by a peal of distant thunder, and the rain came down heavily. Margaret and Gerard ran into the house, whither they were speedily followed by Martin.

"The road is clear," said he, "and a heavy storm coming on."

His words proved true. The thunder came nearer and nearer till it crashed overhead: the flashes followed one another close, like the strokes of a whip, and the rain fell in torrents. Margaret hid her face not to see the lightning. On this, Gerard put up the rough shutter, and lighted a candle. The lovers consulted together, and Gerard blessed the storm that gave him a few hours more with Margaret. The sun set unperceived, and still the thunder pealed, and the lightning flashed, and the rain poured. Supper was set, but Gerard and Margaret could not eat: the thought that this was the last time they should sup together, choked them. The storm lulled a little. Peter retired to rest. But Gerard was to go at peep of day, and neither he nor Margaret could afford to lose an hour in sleep. Martin sat a while, too: for he was fitting a new string to his bow, a matter in which he was very nice.

The lovers murmured their sorrows and their love beside him.

Suddenly the old man held up his hand to them to be silent.

They were quiet and listened, and heard nothing. But the next moment a footstep crackled faintly upon the autumn leaves that lay strewn in the garden at the back door of the house. To those who had nothing to fear such a step would have said nothing: but to those who had enemies it was terrible. For it was a foot trying to be noiseless.

Martin fitted an arrow to his string, and hastily blew out the candle. At this moment, to their horror, they heard more than one footstep approach the other door of the cottage, not quite so noiselessly as the other, but very stealthily—and then a dead pause.

Their blood froze in their veins.

"Oh! Kate! oh, Kate! You said, fly on the instant." And Margaret moaned and wrung her hands in anguish and terror, and wild remorse for having kept Gerard.

"Hush girl!" said Martin, in a stern whisper.

A heavy knock fell on the door.
And on the hearts within.

CHAPTER XIV

AS if this had been a concerted signal, the back door was struck as rudely the next instant. They were hemmed in. But at these alarming sounds Margaret seemed to recover some share of self-possession. She whispered, "Say he *was* here, but is gone." And with this she seized Gerard and almost dragged him up the rude steps that led to her father's sleeping-room. Her own lay next beyond it.

The blows on the door were repeated.

"Who knocks at this hour?"

"Open, and you will see!"

"I open not to thieves—honest men are all abed now."

"Open to the law, Martin Wittenhaagen, or you shall rue it."

"Why, that is Dirk Brower's voice, I trow. What make you so far from Tergou?"

"Open, and you will know."

Martin drew the bolt, very slowly, and in rushed Dierich and four more. They let in their companion who was at the back door.

"Now, Martin, where is Gerard Eliassoen?"

"Gerard Eliassoen? Why he was here but now?"

"Was here?" Dierich's countenance fell. "And where is he now?"

"They say he has gone to Italy. Why? What is to do?"

"No matter. When did he go? Tell me not that he went in such a storm as this!"

"Here is a coil about Gerard Eliassoen," said Martin contemptuously. Then he lighted the candle, and, seating himself coolly by the fire, proceeded to whip some fine silk round his bow-string at the place where the nick of the arrow frets it. "I'll tell you," said he carelessly. "Know you his brother Giles—a little misbegotten imp all head and arms? Well, he came tearing over here on a mule, and bawled out something. I was too far off to hear the creature's words, but only its noise. Anyway, he started Gerard. For as soon as he was gone, there was such crying and kissing, and then Gerard went away. They do tell me he has gone to Italy—mayhap you know where that is; for I don't."

Dierich's countenance fell lower and lower at this account. There was no flaw in it. A cunninger man than Martin would, perhaps, have told a lie too many, and raised suspicion. But Martin did his task well. He only told the one falsehood he was bade to tell, and of his own head invented nothing.

"Mates," said Dierich, "I doubt he speaks sooth. I told the burgomaster how 'twould be. He met the dwarf galloping Peter Buyskens' mule from Sevenbergen. 'They have sent that imp to Gerard' says he, 'so, then, Gerard is at Sevenbergen.' 'Ah, master!' says I, ''tis too late now. We should have thought of Sevenbergen before, instead of wasting our time hunting all the odd corners of Tergou for those cursed parchments that we shall never find till we find the man that took 'em. If he was at Sevenbergen,' quoth I, 'and they sent the dwarf to him, it must have been to warn him we are after him. He is leagues away by now,' quoth I. Confound that chalk-faced girl! she has out-witted us bearded men: and so I told the burgomaster, but he would not hear to reason. A wet jerkin apiece, that is all we shall get, mates, by this job."

Martin grinned coolly in Dierich's face.

"However," added the latter, "to content the burgomaster, we will search the house."

Martin turned grave directly.

This change of countenance did not escape Dierich. He reflected a moment.

"Watch outside two of you, one on each side of the house, that no one jump from the upper windows. The rest come with me."

And he took the candle and mounted the stairs, followed by three of his comrades.

Martin was left alone.

The stout soldier hung his head. All had gone so well at first: and now this fatal turn! Suddenly it occurred to him that all was not yet lost. Gerard must be either in Peter's room or Margaret's; they were not so very high from the ground. Gerard would leap out. Dierich had left a man below; but what then? For half a minute Gerard and he would be two to one, and in that brief space, what might not be done?

Martin then held the back door ajar and watched. The light shone in Peter's room. "Curse the fool!" said he, "is he going to let them take him like a girl?"

The light now passed into Margaret's bedroom. Still no window was opened. Had Gerard intended to escape that way he would not have waited till the men were in the room. Martin saw that at once, and left the door, and came to the foot-stair and listened. He began to think Gerard must have escaped by the window while all the men were in the house. The longer the silence continued the stronger grew this conviction. But it was suddenly and rudely dissipated.

Faint cries issued from the inner bedroom—Margaret's.

"They have taken him," groaned Martin; "they have got him."

It now flashed across Martin's mind that if they took Gerard away his life was not worth a button; and that, if evil befel him, Margaret's heart would break. He cast his eyes wildly round like some savage beast seeking an escape, and in a twinkling formed a resolution terribly characteristic of those iron times and of a soldier driven to bay. He stepped to each door in turn, and imitating Dirk Bower's voice, said sharply, "Watch the window!" He then quietly closed and bolted both doors. He then took up his bow and six arrows; one he fitted to his string, the others he put into his quiver. His knife he placed upon a chair behind him, the hilt towards him; and there he waited at the foot of the stair with the calm determination to slay those four men, or be slain by them. Two, he knew, he could dispose of by his arrows, ere they could get near him, and Gerard and he must take their chance hand-to-hand, with the remaining pair. Besides, he had seen men panic-stricken by a sudden attack of this sort. Should Brower and his men hesitate but an instant before closing with him, he should shoot three instead of two, and then the odds would be on the right side.

He had not long to wait. The heavy steps sounded in Margaret's room, and came nearer and nearer.

The light also approached, and voices.

Martin's heart, stout as it was, beat hard, to hear men coming thus to their death, and, perhaps to his; more likely so than not; for four is long odds in a battle-field of ten feet square, and Gerard might be bound, perhaps, and powerless to help. But this man, whom we have seen shake in his shoes at a Giles-o'-lanthorn, never wavered in this awful moment of real danger, but stood there, his body all braced for combat, and his eyes glowing, equally ready to take life and lose it. Desperate game! to win which was exile instant and for life, and to lose it was to die that moment upon that floor he stood on.

Dierich Brower and his men found Peter in his first sleep. They opened his cupboards; they ran their knives into an alligator he had nailed to his wall; they looked under his bed: it was a large room, and apparently full of hiding places, but they found no Gerard.

Then they went on to Margaret's room, and the very sight of it was discouraging—it was small and bare, and not a cupboard in it; there was, however, a large fireplace and chimney. Dierich's eye fell on these directly. Here they found the beauty of Sevenbergen sleeping on an old chest, not a foot high, and no attempt made to cover it; but the sheets were snowy white, and so was Margaret's own linen. And there she lay, looking like a lily fallen into a rut.

Presently she awoke, and sat up in the bed, like one amazed; then, seeing the men, began to scream faintly, and pray for mercy.

She made Dierich Brower ashamed of his errand.

"Here is a to-do," said he, a little confused. "We are not going to hurt you, my pretty maid. Lie you still, and shut your eyes, and think of your wedding-night, while I look up this chimney to see if Master Gerard is there."

"Gerard! in my room?"

"Why not? They say that you and he—"

"Cruel; you know they have driven him away from me—driven him from his native place. This is a blind. You are thieves; you are wicked men; you are not men of Sevenbergen, or you would know Margaret Brandt better than to look for her lover in this room of all others in the world. Oh brave! Four great hulking men to come, armed to the teeth, to insult one poor honest girl! The women that live in your own houses must be naught, or you would respect them too much to insult a girl of good character."

"There, come away, before we hear worse," said Dierich, hastily. "He is not in the chimney. Plaster will mend what a cudgel breaks; but a woman's tongue is a double-edged dagger, and a girl is a woman with her mother's milk still in her." And he beat a hasty retreat. "I told the burgomaster how 'twould be."

CHAPTER XV

WHERE is the woman that cannot act a part? Where is she who will not do it, and do it well, to save the man she loves? Nature on these great occasions comes to the aid of the simplest of the sex, and teaches her to throw dust in Solomon's eyes. The men had no sooner retired, than Margaret stepped out of bed, and opened the long chest on which she had been lying down in her skirt and petticoat and stockings, and nightdress over all; and put the lid, bed-clothes and all, against the wall: then glided to the door and listened. The footsteps died away through her father's room, and down the stairs.

Now in that chest there was a peculiarity that it was almost impossible for a stranger to detect. A part of the boarding of the room had been broken, and Gerard being applied to to make it look neater, and being short of materials, had ingeniously sawed away a space sufficient just to admit Margaret's *soi-disant* bed, and with the materials thus acquired he had repaired the whole room. As for the bed or chest it really rested on the rafters a foot below the boards. Consequently it was full two feet deep, though it looked scarce one.

All was quiet. Margaret kneeled and gave thanks to Heaven. Then she glided from the door, and leaned over the chest, and whispered tenderly, "Gerard!"

Gerard did not reply.

She then whispered, a little louder, "Gerard, all is safe, thank Heaven! You may rise; but, oh! be cautious!"

Gerard made no reply.

She laid her hand upon his shoulder—"Gerard!"

No reply.

The Cloister and the Hearth

"Oh! what is this?" she cried, and her hands ran wildly over his face and his bosom. She took him by the shoulders; she shook him; she lifted him; but he escaped from her trembling hands, and fell back not like a man but like a body. A great dread fell on her. The lid had been down. She had lain upon it. The men had been some time in the room. With all the strength of frenzy she tore him out of the chest. She bore him in her arms to the window. She dashed the window open. The sweet air came in. She laid him in it and in the moonlight. His face was the colour of ashes, his body was all limp and motionless. She felt his heart. Horror! it was as still as the rest! Horror of horrors! she had stifled him with her own body.

The mind cannot all at once believe so great and sudden and strange a calamity. Gerard, who had got alive into that chest scarce five minutes ago, how could he be dead?

She called him by all the endearing names that heart could think or tongue could frame. She kissed him and fondled him and coaxed him and implored him to speak to her.

No answer to words of love, such as she had never uttered to him before, nor thought she could utter. Then the poor creature, trembling all over, began to say over that ashy face little foolish things that were at once terrible and pitiable.

"Oh, Gerard! I am very sorry you are dead. I am very sorry I have killed you. Forgive me for not letting the men take you, it would have been better than this. Oh, Gerard! I am very, very sorry for what I have done." Then she began suddenly to rave. "No! no! such things can't be, or there is no God. It is monstrous. How can my Gerard be dead? How can I have killed my Gerard? I love him. Oh, God! you know how I love him. He does not. I never told him. If he knew my heart, he would speak to me, he would not be so deaf to his poor Margaret. It is all a trick to make me cry out and betray him: but, no, I love him too well for that. I'll choke first." And she seized her own throat, to check her wild desire to scream in her terror and anguish.

"If he would but say one word. Oh, Gerard! don't die without a word. Have mercy on me and scold me! but speak to me: if you are angry with me, scold me! curse me! I deserve it: the idiot that killed the man she loved better than herself. Ah! I am a murderess. The worst in all the world. Help, help! I have murdered him. Ah! ah! ah! ah! ah!"

She tore her hair, and uttered shriek after shriek so wild, so piercing, they fell like a knell upon the ears of Dierich Brower and his men. All started to their feet, and looked at one another.

CHAPTER XVI

MARTIN WITTENHAAGEN standing at the foot of the stairs with his arrow drawn nearly to the head and his knife behind him, was struck with amazement to see the men come back without Gerard: he lowered his bow, and looked openmouthed at them. They, for their part, were equally puzzled at the attitude they had caught him in.

"Why, mates, was the old fellow making ready to shoot at *us?*"

"Stuff!" said Martin, recovering his stolid composure, "I was but trying my new string. There, I'll unstring my bow, if you think that."

"Humph!" said Dierich, suspiciously, "there is something more in you than I understand: put a log on, and let us dry our hides a bit, ere we go."

A blazing fire was soon made and the men gathered round it, and their clothes and long hair were soon smoking from the cheerful blaze. Then it was that the shrieks were heard in Margaret's room. They all started up, and one of them seized the candle, and ran up the steps that led to the bedrooms.

Martin rose hastily, too, and being confused by these sudden screams, and apprehending danger from the man's curiosity, tried to prevent him from going there.

At this Dierich threw his arms round him from behind, and called on the others to keep him. The man that had the candle got clear away, and all the rest fell upon Martin, and after a long and fierce struggle, in the course of which they were more than once all rolling on the floor, with Martin in the middle, they succeeded in mastering the old Samson, and binding him hand and foot with a rope they had brought for Gerard.

Martin groaned aloud. He saw the man had made his way to Margaret's room during the struggle, and here was he powerless.

"Ay, grind your teeth, you old rogue," said Dierich, panting with the struggle. "You shan't use them."

"It is my belief, mates, that our lives were scarce safe while this old fellow's bones were free."

"He makes me think this Gerard is not far off," put in another.

"No such luck," replied Dierich. "Hallo, mates. Jorian Ketel is a long time in that girl's bedroom. Best go and see after him, some of us."

The rude laugh caused by this remark had hardly subsided, when hasty footsteps were heard running along overhead.

"Oh! here he comes, at last. Well, Jorian, what is to do now up there?"

CHAPTER XVII

JORIAN KETEL went straight to Margaret's room, and there, to his infinite surprise, he found the man he had been in search of, pale and motionless, his head in Margaret's lap, and she kneeling over him, mute now, and stricken to stone. Her eyes were dilated, yet glazed, and she neither saw the light nor heard the man, nor cared for anything on earth, but the white face in her lap.

Jorian stood awe-struck, the candle shaking in his hand.

"Why, where was he, then, all the time?"

Margaret heeded him not. Jorian went to the empty chest and inspected it. He began to comprehend. The girl's dumb and frozen despair moved him.

"This is a sorry sight," said he: "it is a black night's work: all for a few skins! Better have gone with us than so. She is past answering me, poor wench. Stop—let us try whether—"

He took down a little round mirror, no bigger than his hand, and put it to Gerard's mouth and nostrils, and held it there. When he withdrew it it was dull.

"THERE IS LIFE IN HIM!" said Jorian Ketel to himself.

Margaret caught the words instantly, though only muttered, and it was as if a statue should start into life and passion. She rose and flung her arms round Jorian's neck.

"Oh bless the tongue that tells me so!" and she clasped the great rough fellow again and again, eagerly, almost fiercely.

The Cloister and the Hearth

"There, there! let us lay him warm," said Jorian; and in a moment he raised Gerard, and laid him on the bed-clothes. Then he took out a flask he carried, and filled his hand twice with Schiedamze, and flung it sharply each time in Gerard's face. The pungent liquor co-operated with his recovery—he gave a faint sigh. Oh, never was sound so joyful to human ear! She flew towards him, but then stopped, quivering for fear she should hurt him. She had lost all confidence in herself.

"That is right—let him alone," said Jorian: "don't go cuddling him as you did me, or you'll drive his breath back again. Let him alone: he is sure to come to. 'Tisn't like as if he was an old man."

Gerard sighed deeply, and a faint streak of colour stole to his lips. Jorian made for the door. He had hardly reached it, when he found his legs seized from behind.

It was Margaret! She curled round his knees like a serpent, and kissed his hand, and fawned on him. "You won't tell? You have saved his life; you have not the heart to thrust him back into his grave, to undo your own good work?"

"No, no! It is not the first time I've done you two a good turn; 'twas I told you in the church whither we had to take him. Besides, what is Dirk Brower to me? I'll see him hanged ere I'll tell him. But I wish you'd tell *me* where the parchments are? There are a hundred crowns offered for them. That would be a good windfall for my Joan and the children, you know."

"Ah! they shall have those hundred crowns."

"What! are the things in the house?" asked Jorian, eagerly.

"No; but I know where they are: and, by God and St. Bavon I swear you shall have them to-morrow. Come to me for them when you will, but come alone."

"I were mad, else. What! share the hundred crowns with Dirk Brower? And now may my bones rot in my skin if I let a soul know the poor boy is here."

He then ran off, lest by staying longer he should excite suspicion, and have them all after him. And Margaret knelt, quivering from head to foot, and prayed beside Gerard, and for Gerard.

"What is to do?" replied Jorian, to Dierich Brower's query; "why we have scared the girl out of her wits. She was in a kind of fit."

"We had better all go and doctor her, then."

"Oh yes! and frighten her into the churchyard. Her father is a doctor, and I have roused him, and set him to bring her round. Let us see the fire, will ye?"

His off-hand way disarmed all suspicion. And soon after the party agreed that the kitchen of the "Three Kings" was much warmer than Peter's house, and they departed, having first untied Martin.

"Take note, mate, that I was right, and the burgomaster wrong," said Dierich Brower, at the door: "I said we should be too late to catch him, and we were too late."

Thus Gerard, in one terrible night, grazed the prison and the grave.

And how did he get clear at last? Not by his cunningly contrived hiding-place, nor by Margaret's ready wit; but by a good impulse in one of his captors, by the bit of humanity left in a somewhat reckless fellow's heart, aided by his desire of gain. So mixed and seemingly incongruous are human motives, so short sighted our shrewdest counsels.

They whose moderate natures, or gentle fates, keep them, in life's passage, from the fierce extremes of joy and anguish our nature is capable of, are perhaps the best, and certainly the happiest, of mankind. But to such readers I should try in vain to convey what bliss unspeakable settled now upon these persecuted lovers. Even to those who have joyed greatly, and greatly suffered, my feeble art can present but a pale reflection of Margaret's and Gerard's ecstasy.

To sit and see a beloved face come back from the grave to the world, to health and beauty by swift gradations; to see the roses return to the loved cheek, love's glance to the loved eye, and his words to the loved mouth; this was Margaret's—a joy to balance years of sorrow. It was Gerard's to awake from a trance, and find his head pillowed on Margaret's arm; to hear the woman he adored murmur new words of eloquent love, and shower tears and tender kisses and caresses on him. He never knew, till this sweet moment, how ardently, how tenderly, she loved him. He thanked his enemies. They wreathed their arms sweetly round each other, and trouble and danger seemed a world, an age, behind them. They called each other husband and wife. Were they not solemnly betrothed? And had they not stood before the altar together? Was not the blessing of Holy Church upon their union?—her curse on all who would part them?

But as no woman's nerves can bear with impunity so terrible a strain, presently Margaret turned faint, and sank on Gerard's shoulder, smiling feebly, but quite, quite unstrung. Then Gerard was anxious, and would seek assistance. But she held him with a gentle grasp, and implored him not to leave her for a moment. "While I can lay my hand on you, I feel you are safe, not else. Foolish Gerard! nothing ails me. I am weak, dearest, but happy, oh! so happy."

Then it was Gerard's turn to support that dear head, with its great waves of hair flowing loose over him, and nurse her, and soothe her, quivering on his bosom, with soft encouraging words and murmurs of love, and gentle caresses. Sweetest of all her charms is a woman's weakness to a manly heart.

Poor things! they were happy. To-morrow they must part. But that was nothing to them now. They had seen Death, and all other troubles seemed light as air. While there is life there is hope: while there is hope there is joy. Separation for a year or two, what was it to them, who were so young, and had caught a glimpse of the grave? The future was bright, the present was Heaven: so passed the blissful hours.

Alas! their innocence ran other risks besides the prison and the grave: they were in most danger from their own hearts and their inexperience, now that visible danger there was none.

CHAPTER XVIII

GHYSBRECHT VAN SWIETEN could not sleep all night for anxiety. He was afraid of thunder and lightning: or he would have made one of the party that searched Peter's house. As soon as the storm ceased altogether, he crept down stairs, saddled his mule, and rode to the "Three Kings" at Sevenbergen. There he found his men sleeping, some on chairs, some on the tables, some on the floor. He roused them furiously, and heard the story of their unsuccessful search, interlarded with praises of their zeal.

"Fool! to let you go without me," cried the burgomaster. "My life on't he was there all the time. Looked ye under the girl's bed?"

"No: there was no room for a man there."

"How know ye that, if ye looked not?" snarled Ghysbrecht. "Ye should have looked under her bed and in it, too; and sounded all the panels with your knives. Come, now, get up, and I shall show ye how to search."

Dierich Brower got up, and shook himself: "If you find him, call me a horse and no man."

In a few minutes Peter's house was again surrounded.

The fiery old man left his mule in the hands of Jorian Ketel, and, with Dierich Brower and the others, entered the house.

The house was empty.

Not a creature to be seen, not even Peter. They went up-stairs, and then suddenly one of the men gave a shout, and pointed through Peter's window, which was open. The other looked, and there, at some little distance, walking quietly across the fields with Margaret and Martin, was the man they sought. Ghysbrecht with an exulting yell, descended the stairs, and flung himself on his mule; and he and his men set off in hot pursuit.

CHAPTER XIX

GERARD, warned by recent peril, rose before daybreak, and waked Martin. The old soldier was astonished. He thought Gerard had escaped by the window last night. Being consulted as to the best way for him to leave the country and elude pursuit, he said there was but one road safe. "I must guide you through the great forest to a bridle-road I know of. This will take you speedily to a hostelry, where they will lend you a swift horse: and then a day's gallop will take you out of Holland. But let us start ere the folk here quit their beds."

Peter's house was but a furlong and a half from the forest. They started, Martin with his bow and three arrows, for it was Thursday: Gerard with nothing but a stout oak staff Peter gave him for the journey.

Margaret pinned up her kirtle and farthingale, for the road was wet. Peter went as far as his garden hedge with them, and then, with more emotion than he often bestowed on passing events, gave the young man his blessing.

The sun was peeping above the horizon as they crossed the stony field and made for the wood. They had crossed about half, when Margaret, who kept nervously looking back every now and then, uttered a cry, and, following her instinct, began to run towards the wood, screaming with terror all the way.

The Cloister and the Hearth

Ghysbrecht and his men were in hot pursuit.

Resistance would have been madness. Martin and Gerard followed Margaret's example. The pursuers gained slightly on them; but Martin kept shouting, "Only win the wood! only win the wood!"

They had too good a start for the men on foot, and their hearts bounded with hope at Martin's words, for the great trees seemed now to stretch their branches like friendly arms towards them, and their leaves like a screen.

But an unforeseen danger attacked them. The fiery old burgomaster flung himself on his mule, and, spurring him to a gallop, he headed not his own men only but the fugitives. His object was to cut them off. The old man came galloping in a semicircle, and got on the edge of the wood, right in front of Gerard; the others might escape for ought he cared.

Margaret shrieked and tried to protect Gerard by clasping him; but he shook her off without ceremony.

Ghysbrecht in his ardor forgot that hunted animals turn on the hunter; and that two men can hate, and two can long to kill the thing they hate.

Instead of attempting to dodge him, as the burgomaster made sure he would, Gerard flew right at him with a savage, exulting cry, and struck at him with all his heart and soul and strength. The oak staff came down on Ghysbrecht's face with a frightful crash, and laid him under his mule's tail beating the devil's tattoo with his heels, his face streaming, and his collar spattered with blood.

The next moment, the three were in the wood. The yell of dismay and vengeance that burst from Ghysbrecht's men at that terrible blow which felled their leader, told the fugitives that it was now a race for life or death.

"Why run?" cried Gerard panting. "You have your bow; and I have this:" and he shook his bloody staff.

"Boy!" roared Martin; "The GALLOWS! Follow me!" and he fled into the wood. Soon they heard a cry like a pack of hounds opening on sight of the game. The men were in the wood, and saw them flitting amongst the trees. Margaret moaned and panted, as she ran; and Gerard clenched his teeth, and grasped his staff. The next minute they came to a stiff hazel coppice. Martin dashed into it, and shouldered the young wood aside as if it were standing corn.

Ere they had gone fifty yards in it they came to four blind paths.

The Cloister and the Hearth

Martin took one. "Bend low," said he: and, half creeping, they glided along. Presently their path was again intersected with other little tortuous paths. They took one of them; it seemed to lead back, but it soon took a turn, and after a while brought them to a thick pine grove where the walking was good and hard: there were no paths here and the young fir-trees were so thick you could not see three yards before your nose.

When they had gone some way in this, Martin sat down, and having learned in war to lose all impression of danger with the danger itself took a piece of bread and a slice of ham out of his wallet, and began quietly to eat his breakfast.

The young ones looked at him with dismay. He replied to their looks.

"All Sevenbergen could not find you now; you will lose your purse Gerard long before you get to Italy: is that the way to carry a purse?"

Gerard looked, and there was a large triangular purse, entangled by its chains to the buckle and strap of his wallet.

"This is none of mine," said he. "What is in it, I wonder?" and he tried to detach it: but in passing through the coppice it had become inextricably entangled in his strap and buckle. "It seems loath to leave me," said Gerard, and he had to cut it loose with his knife. The purse, on examination proved to be well provided with silver coins of all sizes, but its bloated appearance was greatly owing to a number of pieces of brown paper folded and doubled. A light burst on Gerard. "Why it must be that old thief's? and see! stuffed with paper to deceive the world!"

The wonder was, how the burgomaster's purse came on Gerard.

They hit at last upon the right solution. The purse must have been at Ghysbrecht's saddle-bow, and Gerard rushing at his enemy, had unconsciously torn it away, thus felling his enemy and robbing him, with a single gesture.

Gerard was delighted at this feat, but Margaret was uneasy.

"Throw it away, Gerard, or let Martin take it back. Already they call you a thief. I cannot bear it."

"Throw it away? give it him back? not a stiver. This is spoil lawfully won in battle from an enemy. Is it not, Martin?"

"Why of course. Send him back the brown paper and you will; but the purse or the coin—that were a sin."

97

The Cloister and the Hearth

"Oh, Gerard!" said Margaret, "you are going to a distant land. We need the good-will of Heaven. How can we hope for that, if we take what is not ours?"

But Gerard saw it in a different light.

"It is Heaven that gives it me by a miracle, and I shall cherish it accordingly," said this pious youth. "Thus the favoured people spoiled the Egyptians, and were blessed."

"Take your own way," said Margaret, humbly, "you are wiser than I am. You are my husband," added she, in a low murmuring voice; "is it for me to gainsay you?"

These humble words from Margaret, who till that day had held the whip hand rather surprised Martin for the moment. They recurred to him some time afterwards, and then they surprised him less.

Gerard kissed her tenderly in return for her wife-like docility, and they pursued their journey hand-in-hand, Martin leading the way, into the depths of the huge forest. The farther they went the more absolutely secure from pursuit they felt. Indeed the townspeople never ventured so far as this into the trackless part of the forest.

Impetuous natures repent quickly. Gerard was no sooner out of all danger, than his conscience began to prick him.

"Martin, would I had not struck quite so hard."

"Whom? Oh! let that pass; he is cheap served."

"Martin, I saw his grey hairs as my stick fell on him. I doubt they will not from my sight this while."

Martin grunted with contempt. "Who spares a badger for his grey hairs? The greyer your enemy is, the older; and the older the craftier; and the craftier the better for a little killing."

"Killing? Killing, Martin? speak not of killing!" And Gerard shook all over.

"I am much mistook if you have not," said Martin cheerfully.

"Now Heaven forbid!"

"The old vagabone's skull cracked like a walnut. Aha!"

"Heaven and the saints forbid it!"

"He rolled off his mule like a stone shot out of a cart. Said I to myself, 'there is one wiped out.' " And the iron old soldier grinned ruthlessly.

Gerard fell on his knees, and began to pray for his enemy's life.

At this Martin lost his patience. "Here's mummery. What, you that set up for learning, know you not that a wise man never strikes his enemy but to kill him? And what is all this coil about killing of old men? If it had been a young one now, with the joys of life waiting for him, wine, women, and pillage? But an old fellow at the edge of the grave, why *not* shove him in? Go he must, to-day or to-morrow; and what better place for greybeards? Now, if ever I should be so mischancy as to last so long as Ghysbrecht did, and have to go on a mule's legs instead of Martin Wittenhaagen's, and a back like this (striking the wood of his bow), instead of this (striking the string), I'll thank and bless any young fellow, who will knock me on the head, as you have done that old shopkeeper; malison on his memory."

"Oh, culpa mea! culpa mea!" cried Gerard, and smote upon his breast.

"Look there," said Martin to Margaret scornfully, *"he is a priest at heart still*: and when he is not in ire, St. Paul, what a milk-sop!"

"Tush, Martin!" cried Margaret reproachfully: then she wreathed her arms round Gerard, and comforted him with the double magic of a woman's sense and a woman's voice.

"Sweetheart!" murmured she, "you forget: you went not a step out of the way to harm him who hunted you to your death. You fled from him. He it was who spurred on you. Then did you strike; but in self-defence and a single blow, and with that which was in your hand. Malice had drawn knife, or struck again and again. How often have men been smitten with staves not one but many blows, yet no lives lost! If then your enemy has fallen, it is through his own malice, not yours, and by the will of God."

"Bless you, Margaret, bless you for thinking so!"

"Yes, but, beloved one; if you have had the *misfortune* to kill that wicked man, the more need is there that you fly with haste from Holland. Oh! let us on."

"Nay, Margaret," said Gerard. "I fear not man's vengeance, thanks to Martin here, and this thick wood: only Him I fear whose eye pierces the forest, and reads the heart of man. If I but struck in self-defence, 'tis well; but if in hate, He may bid the avenger of blood follow me to Italy; to Italy? ay, to earth's remotest bounds."

"Hush!" said Martin, peevishly. "I can't hear for your chat."

"What is it?"

"Do you hear nothing, Margaret? My ears are getting old."

Margaret listened, and presently she heard a tuneful sound, like a single stroke upon a deep ringing bell. She described it so to Martin.

"Nay, I heard it," said he.

"And so did I," said Gerard: "it was beautiful. Ah! there it is again. How sweetly it blends with the air. It is a long way off. It is before us; is it not?"

"No, no! the echoes of this wood confound the ear of a stranger. It comes from the pine grove."

"What the one we passed?"

"The one we passed?"

"Why, Martin, is this *anything?* You look pale."

"Wonderful!" said Martin, with a sickly sneer. "He asks me is it *anything?* Come, on, on! at any rate, let us reach a better place than this.'

"A better place—for what?"

"To stand at bay, Gerard," said Martin gravely: "and die like soldiers, killing three for one."

"What's that sound?"

"IT IS THE AVENGER OF BLOOD."

"Oh, Martin, save him! Oh, Heaven be merciful! What new mysterious peril is this?"

"GIRL, IT'S A BLOODHOUND."

CHAPTER XX

THE courage, like the talent, of common men, runs in a narrow groove. Take them but an inch out of that, and they are done. Martin's courage was perfect as far as it went. He had met and baffled many dangers in the course of his rude life; and these familiar dangers he could face with Spartan fortitude, almost with indifference: but he had never been hunted by a bloodhound; nor had he ever seen that brute's unerring instinct baffled by human cunning. Here then a sense of the supernatural combined with novelty to unsteel his heart. After going a few steps he leaned on his bow, and energy and hope oozed out of him. Gerard, to whom the danger appeared slight in proportion as it was distant, urged him to flight.

"What avails it?" said Martin, sadly; "if we get clear of the wood we shall die cheap; here, hard by, I know a place where we may die dear."

"Alas! good Martin," cried Gerard: "despair not so quickly: there must be some way to escape."

"Oh, Martin!" cried Margaret, "what if we were to part company? Gerard's life alone is forfeit. Is there no way to draw the pursuit on us twain and let him go safe?"

"Girl, you know not the bloodhound's nature. He is not on this man's track or that; he is on the track of blood. My life on't they have taken him to where Ghysbrecht fell, and from the dead man's blood to the man that shed it that cursed hound will lead them, though Gerard should run through an army, or swim the Meuse." And again he leaned upon his bow, and his head sank.

The hound's mellow voice rang through the wood.

> A cry more tunable
> Was never halloed to, nor cheered with horn,
> In Crete, in Sparta, or in Thessaly.

Strange that things beautiful should be terrible and deadly. The eye of the boa-constrictor while fascinating its prey is lovely. No royal crown holds such a jewel; it is a ruby with the emerald's green light playing ever upon it. Yet the deer that sees it, loses all power of motion, and trembles, and awaits his death; and even so, to compare hearing with sight, this sweet and mellow sound seemed to fascinate Martin Wittenhaagen. He stood uncertain, bewildered, and unnerved. Gerard was little better now. Martin's last words had daunted him. He had struck an old man and shed his blood, and, by means of that very blood, blood's four-footed avenger was on his track. Was not the finger of Heaven in this?

Whilst the men were thus benumbed, the woman's brain was all activity. The man she loved was in danger.

"Lend me your knife," said she to Martin. He gave it to her.

"But 'twill be little use in your hands," said he.

Then Margaret did a sly thing. She stepped behind Gerard, and furtively drew the knife across her arm, and made it bleed freely: then stooping, smeared her nose and shoes: and still as the blood trickled she smeared them: but so adroitly that neither Gerard nor Martin saw. Then she seized the soldier's arm.

101

"Come be a man," said she "and let this end. Take us to some thick place, where numbers will not avail our foes."

"I am going," said Martin sulkily. "Hurry avails not: we cannot shun the hound, and the place is hard by;" then turning to the left, he led the way, as men go to execution.

He soon brought them to a thick hazel coppice, like the one that had favoured their escape in the morning.

"There," said he, "this is but a furlong broad, but it will serve our turn."

"What are we to do?"

"Get through this, and wait on the other side: then as they come straggling through, shoot three, knock two on the head, and the rest will kill us."

"Is that all you can think of?" said Gerard.

"That is all."

"Then, Martin Wittenhaagen, I take the lead; for you have lost your head. Come, can you obey so young a man as I am?"

"Oh! yes, Martin," cried Margaret, "do not gainsay Gerard? He is wiser than his years."

Martin yielded a sullen assent.

"Do then as you see me do," said Gerard; and drawing his huge knife, he cut at every step a hazel shoot or two close by the ground, and turning round twisted them breast high behind him among the standing shoots. Martin did the same, but with a dogged hopeless air. When they had thus painfully travelled through the greater part of the coppice, the bloodhound's deep bay came nearer, and nearer, less and less musical, louder, and sterner.

Margaret trembled.

Martin went down on his stomach and listened.

"I hear a horse's feet."

"No," said Gerard. "I doubt it is a mule's. That cursed Ghysbrecht is still alive: none other would follow me up so bitterly."

"Never strike your enemy but to slay him," said Martin, gloomily.

"I'll hit harder this time, if Heaven gives me the chance," said Gerard.

At last they worked through the coppice, and there was an open wood. The trees were large, but far apart, and no escape possible that way.

The Cloister and the Hearth

And now with the hound's bay mingled a score of voices, hooping and hallooing.

"The whole village is out after us," said Martin.

"I care not," said Gerard. "Listen, Martin. I have made the track smooth to the dog, but rough to the men, that we may deal with them apart. Thus the hound will gain on the men, and as soon as he comes out of the coppice we must kill him."

"The hound? There are more than one."

"I hear but one."

"Ay! but one speaks, the others run mute; but let the leading hound lose the scent, then another shall give tongue. There will be two dogs at least, or devils in dogs' hides."

"Then we must kill two instead of one. The moment they are dead, into the coppice again, and go right back."

"That is a good thought, Gerard!" said Martin, plucking up heart.

"Hush! the men are in the wood."

Gerard now gave his orders in a whisper.

"Stand you with your bow by the side of the coppice—there, in the ditch. I will go but a few yards to yon oak-tree, and hide behind it; the dogs will follow me, and, as they come out, shoot as many as you can, the rest will I brain as they come round the tree."

Martin's eye flashed. They took up their places.

The hooping and hallooing came closer and closer, and soon even the rustling of the young wood was heard, and every now and then the unerring bloodhound gave a single bay.

It was terrible! the branches rustling nearer and nearer, and the inevitable struggle for life and death coming on minute by minute, and that death-knell leading it. A trembling hand was laid on Gerard's shoulder. It made him start violently, strung up as he was.

"Martin says if we are forced to part company, make for that high ash-tree we came in by."

"Yes! yes! yes! but go back, for Heaven's sake! don't come here, all out in the open!"

She ran back towards Martin; but, ere she could get to him, suddenly a huge dog burst out of the coppice, and stood erect a moment. Margaret cowered with fear, but he never noticed her.

Scent was to him what sight is to us. He lowered his nose an instant, and the next moment, with an awful yell, sprang straight at Gerard's tree, and rolled head-over-heels dead as a stone, literally spitted by an arrow from the bow that twanged beside the coppice in Martin's hand. That same moment out came another hound and smelt his dead comrade. Gerard rushed out at him; but ere he could use his cudgel, a streak of white lightning seemed to strike the hound, and he grovelled in the dust, wounded desperately, but not killed, and howling piteously.

Gerard had not time to despatch him: the coppice rustled too near: it seemed alive. Pointing wildly to Martin to go back, Gerard ran a few yards to the right, then crept cautiously into the thick coppice just as three men burst out. These had headed their comrades considerably; the rest were following at various distances. Gerard crawled back almost on all fours. Instinct taught Martin and Margaret to do the same upon their line of retreat. Thus, within the distance of a few yards, the pursuers and pursued were passing one another upon opposite tracks.

A loud cry announced the discovery of the dead and wounded hound. Then followed a babble of voices, still swelling as fresh pursuers reached the spot. The hunters, as usual on a surprise, were wasting time, and the hunted ones were making the most of it.

"I hear no more hounds," whispered Martin to Margaret, and he was himself again.

It was Margaret's turn to tremble and despair.

"Oh! why did we part with Gerard? They will kill my Gerard, and I not near him."

"Nay, nay! the head to catch him is not on their shoulders. You bade him meet us at the ash-tree?"

"And so I did. Bless you, Martin, for thinking of that. To the ash-tree!"

"Ay! but with less noise."

They were now nearly at the edge of the coppice, when suddenly they heard hooping and hallooing behind them. The men had satisfied themselves the fugitives were in the coppice; and were beating back.

"No matter," whispered Martin to his trembling companion. "We shall have time to win clear and slip out of sight by hard running.

"Ah!"

The Cloister and the Hearth

He stopped suddenly; for just as he was going to burst out of the brushwood, his eye caught a figure keeping sentinel. It was Ghysbrecht Van Swieten seated on his mule; a bloody bandage was across his nose, the bridge of which was broken; but over this his eyes peered keenly, and it was plain by their expression he had heard the fugitives rustle, and was looking out for them. Martin muttered a terrible oath, and cautiously strung his bow, then with equal caution fitted his last arrow to the string. Margaret put her hands to her face, but said nothing. She saw this man must die or Gerard. After the first impulse she peered through her fingers, her heart panting to her throat.

The bow was raised, and the deadly arrow steadily drawn to its head, when at that moment an active figure leaped on Ghysbrecht from behind so swiftly, it was like a hawk swooping on a pigeon. A kerchief went over the burgomaster, in a turn of the hand his head was muffled in it, and he was whirled from his seat and fell heavily upon the ground, where he lay groaning with terror; and Gerard jumped down after him.

"Hist, Martin! Martin!"

Martin and Margaret came out, the former open-mouthed, crying, "Now fly! fly! while they are all in the thicket; we are saved."

At this crisis, when safety seemed at hand, as fate would have it, Margaret, who had borne up so bravely till now, began to succumb, partly from loss of blood.

"Oh, my beloved! fly!" she gasped. "Leave me, for I am faint."

"No! no!" cried Gerard. "Death together, or safety. Ah! the mule! mount her, you, and I'll run by your side."

In a moment Martin was on Ghysbrecht's mule, and Gerard raised the fainting girl in his arms and placed her on the saddle, and relieved Martin of his bow.

"Help! treason! murder! murder!" shrieked Ghysbrecht, suddenly rising on his hams.

"Silence, cur," roared Gerard, and trode him down again by the throat as men crush an adder.

"Now, have you got her firm? Then fly! for our lives! for our lives!"

But even as the mule, urged suddenly by Martin's heel, scattered the flints with his hind hoofs ere he got into a canter, and even as Gerard withdrew his foot from Ghysbrecht's throat to run, Dierich

Brower and his five men, who had come back for orders, and heard the burgomaster's cries, burst roaring out of the coppice on them.

CHAPTER XXI

SPEECH is the familiar vent of human thoughts: but there are emotions so simple and overpowering, that they rush out not in words, but in eloquent sounds. At such moments man seems to lose his characteristics, and to be merely one of the higher animals; for these, when greatly agitated, ejaculate, though they cannot speak.

There was something terrible and truly animal, both in the roar of triumph with which the pursuers burst out of the thicket on our fugitives, and the sharp cry of terror with which these latter darted away. The pursuers' hands clutched the empty air, scarce two feet behind them, as they fled for life. Confused for a moment, like lions that miss their spring, Dierich and his men let Gerard and the mule put ten yards between them. Then they flew after with uplifted weapons. They were sure of catching them; for this was not the first time the parties had measured speed. In the open ground they had gained visibly on the three this morning, and now, at last, it was a fair race again, to be settled by speed alone. A hundred yards were covered in no time. Yet still there remained these ten yards between the pursuers and the pursued.

This increase of speed since the morning puzzled Dierich Brower. The reason was this. When three run in company, the pace is that of the slowest of the three. From Peter's house to the edge of the forest Gerard ran Margaret's pace; but now he ran his own; for the mule was fleet, and could have left them all far behind. Moreover youth and chaste living began to tell. Daylight grew imperceptibly between the hunted ones and the hunters. Then Dierich made a desperate effort, and gained two yards; but in a few seconds Gerard had stolen them quietly back. The pursuers began to curse.

Martin heard, and his face lighted up. "Courage, Gerard! courage, brave lad! they are straggling."

It was so. Dierich was now headed by one of his men, and another dropped into the rear altogether.

They came to a rising ground, not sharp, but long; and here youth, and grit, and sober living, told more than ever.

Ere he reached the top, Dierich's forty years weighed him down like forty bullets. "Our cake is dough," he gasped. "Take him dead, if you can't alive": and he left running, and followed at a foot's pace. Jorian Ketel tailed off next; and then another, and so, one by one, Gerard ran them all to a standstill, except one who kept on stanch as a bloodhound, though losing ground every minute. His name, if I am not mistaken, was Eric Wouverman. Followed by him, they came to a rise in the wood, shorter, but much steeper than the last.

"Hand on mane!" cried Martin.

Gerard obeyed, and the mule helped him up the hill faster even than he was running before.

At the sight of this manœuvre Dierich's man lost heart, and, being now full eighty yards behind Gerard, and rather more than that in advance of his nearest comrade, he pulled up short, and, in obedience to Dierich's order, took down his crossbow, levelled it deliberately, and just as the trio were sinking out of sight over the crest of the hill, sent the bolt whizzing among them.

There was a cry of dismay; and, next moment, as if a thunderbolt had fallen on them, they were all lying on the ground, mule and all.

CHAPTER XXII

THE effect was so sudden and magical, that the shooter himself was stupefied for an instant. Then he hailed his companions to join him in effecting the capture, and himself set off up the hill: but, ere he had got half way, up rose the figure of Martin Wittenhaagen with a bent bow in his hand. Eric Wouverman no sooner saw him in this attitude, than he darted behind a tree, and made himself as small as possible. Martin's skill with that weapon was well known, and the slain dog was a keen reminder of it.

Wouverman peered round the bark cautiously: there was the arrow's point still aimed at him. He saw it shine. He dared not move from his shelter.

When he had been at peep-bo some minutes, his companions came up in great force.

Then with a scornful laugh, Martin vanished, and presently was heard to ride off on the mule.

All the men ran up together. The high ground commanded a view of a narrow but almost interminable glade.

They saw Gerard and Margaret running along at a prodigious distance; they looked like gnats; and Martin galloping after them *ventre à terre.*

The hunters were outwitted as well as outrun. A few words will explain Martin's conduct. We arrive at causes by noting coincidences: yet, now and then, coincidences are deceitful. As we have all seen a hare tumble over a briar just as the gun went off, and so raise expectations, then dash them to earth by scudding away untouched, so the burgomaster's mule put her foot in a rabbit-hole at or about the time the cross-bow bolt whizzed innocuous over her head: she fell and threw both her riders. Gerard caught Margaret, but was carried down by her weight and impetus; and behold, the soil was strewn with dramatis personæ.

The docile mule was up again directly, and stood trembling. Martin was next, and looking round saw there was but one in pursuit; on this he made the young lovers fly on foot, while he checked the enemy as I have recorded.

He now galloped after his companions, and, when after a long race he caught them, he instantly put Gerard and Margaret on the mule, and ran by their side till his breath failed, then took his turn to ride, and so in rotation. Thus the runner was always fresh, and, long ere they relaxed their speed, all sound and trace of them was hopelessly lost to Dierich and his men. These latter went crest-fallen back to look after their chief, and their winged bloodhound.

CHAPTER XXIII

LIFE and liberty, while safe, are little thought of: for why? they are matters of course. Endangered, they are rated at their real value. In this, too, they are like sunshine, whose beauty men notice not at noon when it is greatest, but towards evening when it lies in flakes of topaz under shady elms. Yet it is

The Cloister and the Hearth

feebler then; but gloom lies beside it, and contrast reveals its fire. Thus Gerard and Margaret, though they started at every leaf that rustled louder than its fellows, glowed all over with joy and thankfulness as they glided among the friendly trees in safety and deep tranquil silence, baying dogs and brutal voices yet ringing in their mind's ears.

But presently Gerard found stains of blood on Margaret's ankles. "Martin! Martin! help! they have wounded her: the crossbow!"

"No, no," said Margaret, smiling to re-assure him. I am not wounded, nor hurt at all."

"But what is it, then, in Heaven's name?" cried Gerard, in great agitation.

"Scold me not then!" and Margaret blushed.

"Did I ever scold you?"

"No, dear Gerard. Well, then, Martin said it was blood those cruel dogs followed; so I thought, if I could but have a little blood on my shoon, the dogs would follow me instead, and let my Gerard wend free. So I scratched my arm with Martin's knife—forgive me! Whose else could I take? Yours, Gerard? Ah, no. You forgive me?" said she beseechingly, and lovingly and fawningly, all in one.

"Let me see this scratch first," said Gerard, choking with emotion. "There, I thought so. A scratch? I call it a cut—a deep terrible, cruel cut."

Gerard shuddered at sight of it.

"She might have done it with her bodkin," said the soldier. "Milksop! that sickens at sight of a scratch and a little blood."

"No, no. I could look on a sea of blood; but not on hers. Oh, Margaret! how could you be so cruel?"

Margaret smiled with love ineffable. "Foolish Gerard," murmured she, "to make so much of nothing." And she flung the guilty arm round his neck. "As if I would not give all the blood in my heart for you, let alone a few drops from my arm." And, with this, under the sense of his recent danger, she wept on his neck for pity and love: and he wept with her.

"And I must part from her," he sobbed, "we two that love so dear—one must be in Holland, one in Italy. Ah me! ah me! ah me!"

At this Margaret wept afresh, but patiently and silently. Instinct

is never off its guard, and with her unselfishness was an instinct
To utter her present thoughts would be to add to Gerard's misery
at parting, so she wept in silence.

Suddenly they emerged upon a beaten path and Martin stopped
"This is the bridle-road I spoke of," said he, hanging his head
"and there away lies the hostelry."

Margaret and Gerard cast a scared look at one another.

"Come a step with me, Martin," whispered Gerard. When he
had drawn him aside, he said to him in a broken voice, "Good Martin
watch over her for me! She is my wife; yet I leave her. See Mar
tin! here is gold—it was for my journey; it is no use my asking her
to take it: she would not; but you will for her, will you not? Oh
Heaven! and is this all I can do for her? Money? But poverty
is a curse. You will not let her want for anything, dear Martin?
The burgomaster's silver is enough for me."

"Thou art a good lad, Gerard. Neither want nor harm shall come
to her. I care more for her little finger than for all the world: and
were she nought to me, even for thy sake would I be a father to her.
Go with a stout heart, and God be with thee going and coming."
And the rough soldier wrung Gerard's hand, and turned his head
away, with unwonted feeling.

After a moment's silence, he was for going back to Margaret; but
Gerard stopped him. "No, good Martin: prithee, stay here behind
this thicket, and turn your head away from us while I— Oh Martin!
Martin!"

By this means Gerard escaped a witness of his anguish at leaving
her he loved, and Martin escaped a piteous sight. He did not see
the poor young things kneel and renew before Heaven those holy
vows cruel men had interrupted. He did not see them cling together
like one, and then try to part and fail, and return to one another,
and cling again, like drowning, despairing creatures. But he heard
Gerard sob, and sob, and Margaret moan.

At last there was a hoarse cry, and feet pattered on the hard road.
He started up, and there was Gerard running wildly, with both
hands clasped above his head, in prayer, and Margaret tottering back
towards him with palms extended piteously, as if for help, and ashy
cheek, and eyes fixed on vacancy.

He caught her in his arms, and spoke words of comfort to her;

but her mind could not take them in; only at the sound of his voice she moaned and held him tight, and trembled violently.

He got her on the mule, and put his arm round her, and so, supporting her frame, which, from being strung like a bow, had now turned all relaxed and powerless, he took her slowly and sadly home.

She did not shed one tear, nor speak one word.

At the edge of the wood he took her off the mule, and bade her go across to her father's house. She did as she was bid.

Martin to Rotterdam. Sevenbergen was too hot for him.

Gerard, severed from her he loved, went like one in a dream. He hired a horse and guide at the little hostelry, and rode swiftly towards the German frontier. But all was mechanical; his senses felt blunted; trees and houses and men moved by him like objects seen through a veil. His companion spoke to him twice, but he did not answer. Only once he cried out savagely, "Shall we never be out of this hateful country?"

After many hours' riding they came to the brow of a steep hill; a small brook ran at the bottom.

"Halt!" cried the guide, and pointed across the valley. "Here is Germany."

"Where?"

"On t'other side of the bourn. No need to ride down the hill, I trow."

Gerard dismounted without a word, and took the burgomaster's purse from his girdle: while he opened it, "You will soon be out of this hateful country," said the guide, half sulkily; "mayhap the one you are going to will like you no better: anyway, though it be a church you have robbed, they cannot take you, once across that bourn."

These words at another time would have earned the speaker an admonition, or a cuff. They fell on Gerard now like idle air. He paid the lad in silence, and descended the hill alone. The brook was silvery: it ran murmuring over little pebbles, that glittered, varnished by the clear water: he sat down and looked stupidly at them. Then he drank of the brook: then he laved his hot feet and hands in it; it was very cold: it waked him. He rose, and taking a run, leaped across it into Germany. Even as he touched the strange land he turned suddenly and looked back. "Farewell, ungrateful country!" he cried. "But for *her* it would cost me nought to leave you for ever, and all my kith and kin, and—the mother that bore me, and—my playmates, and my little native town. Farewell, fatherland—welcome the wide world! omne so—lum for—ti p—p—at—ri—a." And with these brave words in his mouth he drooped suddenly with arms and legs all weak, and sat down and sobbed bitterly upon the foreign soil.

When the young exile had sat a while bowed down, he rose and dashed the tears from his eyes like a man; and, not casting a single glance more behind him to weaken his heart, stepped out into the wide world.

His love and heavy sorrow left no room in him for vulgar mis-givings. Compared with rending himself from Margaret, it seemed a small thing to go on foot to Italy in that rude age.

All nations meet in a convent; so thanks to his good friends the monks, and his own thirst of knowledge, he could speak most of the languages needed on that long road. He said to himself, "I will soon be at Rome: the sooner the better, now."

After walking a good league, he came to a place where four ways met. Being country roads and serpentine, they had puzzled many an inexperienced neighbor passing from village to village. Gerard took out a little dial Peter had given him, and set it in the autumn sun, and by this compass steered unhesitatingly for Rome; inex-perienced as a young swallow flying south, but, unlike the swallow, wandering south alone.

CHAPTER XXIV

NOT far on this road he came upon a little group. Two men in sober suits stood leaning lazily on each side of a horse, talking to one another. The rider, in a silk doublet and bright green jerkin and hose, both of English cloth, glossy as a mole, lay flat on his stomach in the afternoon sun, and looked an enor-mous lizard. His velvet cloak (flaming yellow) was carefully spread over the horse's loins.

"Is aught amiss?" inquired Gerard.

"Not that I wot of," replied one of the servants.

"But your master, he lies like a corpse. Are ye not ashamed to let him grovel on the ground?"

"Go to, the bare ground is the best cure for his disorder. If you get sober in bed it gives you a headache; but you leap up from the hard ground like a lark in spring; eh, Ulric?"

"He speaks sooth, young man," said Ulric, warmly.

"What, is the gentleman drunk?"

The servants burst into a hoarse laugh at the simplicity of Gerard's question. But suddenly Ulric stopped, and eyeing him all over, said very gravely, "Who are you, and where born, that know not the count is ever drunk at this hour?" and Gerard found himself a suspected character.

"I am a stranger," said he, "but a true man, and one that loves knowledge: therefore ask I questions, and not for love of prying."

"If you be a true man," said Ulric, shrewdly, "then give us trinkgeld for the knowledge we have given you."

Gerard looked blank. But putting a good face on it, said, "Trinkgeld you shall have, such as my lean purse can spare, an if you will tell me why ye have ta'en his cloak from the man, and laid it on the beast."

Under the inspiring influence of coming trinkgeld two solutions were instantly offered Gerard at once: the one was, that, should the count come to himself (which, being a seasoned toper, he was apt to do all in a minute), and find his horse standing sweating in the cold, while a cloak lay idle at hand, he would fall to cursing, and peradventure to laying on; the other, more pretentious, was, that a horse is a poor milksop, which drinking nothing but water, has to be cockered up and warmed outside; but a master, being a creature ever filled with good beer, has a store of inward heat that warms him to the skin, and renders a cloak a mere shred of idle vanity.

Each of the speakers fell in love with his theory, and to tell the truth, both had taken a hair or two of the dog that had bitten their master to the brain: so their voices presently rose so high that the green sot began to growl instead of snoring; in their heat they did not notice this.

Ere long the argument took a turn that sooner or later was pretty sure to enliven a discussion in that age. Hans, holding the bridle with his right hand, gave Ulric a sound cuff with his left; Ulric returned it with interest, his right hand being free, and at it they went ding dong over the horse's mane, pommelling one another, and jagging the poor beast, till he ran backward and trode with iron heel upon a promontory of the green lord; he, like the toad stung by Ithuriel's spear, started up howling, with one hand clapped to the smart and the other tugging at his hilt. The servants, amazed with terror, let the horse go; he galloped off whinnying, the men in pursuit of him crying out with fear, and the green noble after them volleying curses, his naked sword in his hand and his body rebounding from hedge to hedge in his headlong but zigzag career down the narrow lane.

"In which hurtling" Gerard turned his back on them all, and went calmly south, glad to have saved the four tin farthings he had got ready for trinkgeld, but far too heavy hearted even to smile at their drunken extravagance.

The sun was nearly setting, and Gerard, who had now for some time been hoping in vain to find an inn by the way, was very ill at ease. To make matters worse, black clouds gathered over the sky.

Gerard quickened his pace almost to a run.

It was in vain: down came the rain in torrents, drenched the bewildered traveller, and seemed to extinguish the very sun; for his rays already fading could not cope with this new assailant. Gerard trudged on, dark, and wet and in an unknown region. "Fool! to leave Margaret," said he.

Presently the darkness thickened.

He was entering a great wood. Huge branches shot across the narrow road, and the benighted stranger groped his way in what seemed an interminable and inky cave with a rugged floor, on which he stumbled and stumbled as he went.

On, and on, and on, with shivering limbs, and empty stomach, and fainting heart, till the wolves rose from their lairs and bayed all round the wood.

His hair bristled; but he grasped his cudgel, and prepared to sell his life dear.

There was no wind; and his excited ear heard light feet patter at times over the newly fallen leaves, and low branches rustled with creatures gliding swiftly past them.

Presently in the sea of ink there was a great fiery star close to the ground. He hailed it as he would his patron saint. "CANDLE! a CANDLE!" he shouted, and tried to run; but the dark and rugged way soon stopped that. The light was more distant than he had thought; but at last in the very heart of the forest he found a house with lighted candles and loud voices inside it. He looked up to see if there was a sign-board. There was none. "Not an inn, after all," said he, sadly. "No matter; what Christian would turn a dog out into the wood to-night?" and with this he made for the door that led to the voices. He opened it slowly, and put his head in timidly. He drew it out abruptly, as if slapped in the face, and recoiled into the rain and darkness.

He had peeped into a large but low room, the middle of which was filled by a huge round stove or clay oven that reached to the ceiling; round this wet clothes were drying, some on lines, and some more compendiously on rustics: these latter habiliments, impregnated with the wet of the day, but the dirt of a life, and lined with what another foot traveller in these parts calls "rammish clowns," evolved rank vapours and compound odours inexpressible, in steaming clouds.

In one corner was a travelling family, a large one: thence flowed into the common stock the peculiar sickly smell of neglected brats. Garlic filled up the interstices of the air. And all this with closed window, and intense heat of the central furnace, and the breath of at least forty persons.

They had just supped.

Now Gerard, like most artists, had sensitive organs, and the potent effluvia struck dismay into him. But the rain lashed him outside, and the light and the fire tempted him in.

He could not force his way all at once through the palpable perfumes; but he returned to the light again and again like the singed moth. At last he discovered that the various smells did not entirely mix, no fiend being there to stir them round. Odour of family predominated in two corners, stewed rustic reigned supreme in the centre, and garlic in the noisy group by the window. He found too, by hasty analysis, that of these the garlic described the smallest aërial orbit, and the scent of reeking rustic darted farthest; a flavour, as if ancient goats or the fathers of all foxes, had been drawn through a river, and were here dried by Nebuchadnezzar.

So Gerard crept into a corner close to the door. But though the solidity of the main fetors isolated them somewhat, the heat and reeking vapours circulated and made the walls drip: and the home-nurtured novice found something like a cold snake wind about his legs, and his head turn to a great lump of lead; and next he felt like choking, sweetly slumbering, and dying, all in one.

The Cloister and the Hearth

He was within an ace of swooning, but recovered to a deep sense of disgust and discouragement, and settled to go back to Holland at peep of day: this resolution formed, he plucked up a little heart, and, being faint with hunger, asked one of the men of garlic whether this was not an inn after all?

"Whence come you who know not 'The Star of the Forest?'" was the reply.

"I am a stranger; and in my country inns have aye a sign."

"Droll country yours! What need of a sign to a public-house, a place that every soul knows?"

Gerard was too tired and faint for the labour of argument: so he turned the conversation, and asked where he could find the landlord.

At this fresh display of ignorance the native's contempt rose too high for words; he pointed to a middle-aged woman seated on the other side of the oven, and, turning to his mates, let them know what an outlandish animal was in the room. Thereat the loud voices stopped one by one, as the information penetrated the mass, and each eye turned as on a pivot, following Gerard, and his every movement, silently and zoologically.

The landlady sat on a chair an inch or two higher than the rest, between two bundles. From the first, a huge heap of feathers and wings, she was taking the downy plumes, and pulling the others from the quills, and so filling bundle two; littering the floor ankle deep, and contributing to the general stock a stuffy little malaria, which might have played a distinguished part in a sweet room, but went for nothing here. Gerard asked her if he could have something to eat.

She opened her eyes with astonishment. "Supper is over this hour and more."

"But I had none of it, good dame."

"Is that my fault? You are welcome to your share for me."

"But I was benighted, and a stranger, and belated sore against my will."

"What have I to do with that? All the world knows 'the Star of the Forest' sups from six till eight. Come before six, ye sup well; come before eight, ye sup as pleases Heaven; come after eight, ye get a clean bed, and a stirrup cup, or a horn of kine's milk at the dawning."

Gerard looked blank. "May I go to bed then, dame?" said he sulkily, "for it is ill sitting up wet and fasting, and the byword saith 'he sups who sleeps.'"

"The beds are not come yet," replied the landlady: "you will sleep when the rest do. Inns are not built for *one*."

It was Gerard's turn to be astonished. "The beds were not come: what in Heaven's name did she mean?" But he was afraid to ask, for every word he had spoken hitherto had amazed the assembly; and zoological eyes were upon him—he felt them. He leaned against the wall and sighed audibly.

At this fresh zoological trait a titter went round the watchful company.

"So this is Germany," thought Gerard, "and Germany is a great country by Holland. Small nations for me."

He consoled himself by reflecting it was to be his last, as well as his first, night in the land. His reverie was interrupted by an elbow driven into his ribs. He turned sharp on his assailant; who pointed across the room. Gerard looked, and a woman in the corner was beckoning him. He went towards her gingerly, being surprised and irresolute, so that to a spectator her beckoning finger seemed to be pulling him across the floor with a gut line. When he had got up to her, "hold the child," said she in a fine hearty voice and in a moment she plumped the bairn into Gerard's arms.

He stood transfixed, jelly of lead in his hands, and sudden horror in his elongated countenance.

At this ruefully expressive face the lynx-eyed conclave laughed loud and long.

"Never heed them," said the woman cheerfully: "they know no better; how should they, bred an' born in a wood?" She was rummaging among her clothes with the two penetrating hands, one of which Gerard had set free. Presently she fished out a small tin plate and a dried pudding, and resuming her child with one arm, held them forth to Gerard with the other, keeping a thumb on the pudding to prevent it from slipping off.

"Put it in the stove," said she, "you are too young to lie down fasting."

Gerard thanked her warmly: but on his way to the stove his eye fell on the landlady. "*May* I dame?" said he beseechingly.

"Why not?" said she.

The question was evidently another surprise, though less startling than its predecessors.

Coming to the stove, Gerard found the oven door obstructed by "the rammish clowns." They did not budge. He hesitated a moment: the landlady saw, calmly put down her work, and coming up pulled a hircine man or two hither, and pushed a hircine man or two thither, with the impassive countenance of a housewife moving her furniture. "Turn about is fair play," she said. "Ye have been dry this ten minutes and better."

Her experienced eye was not deceived; Gorgonii had done stewing, and begun baking. Debarred the stove they trundled home all but one, who stood like a table where the landlady had moved him to like a table, and Gerard baked his pudding, and, getting to the stove, burst into steam.

The door opened, and in flew a bundle of straw.

It was hurled by a hind with a pitchfork; another and another came flying after it till the room was like a clean farm yard. These were then dispersed round the stove in layers like the seats in an arena, and in a moment the company was all on its back.

The beds had come.

Gerard took out his pudding and found it delicious. While he was relishing it, the woman who had given it him, and who was now abed, beckoned him again. He went to her bundle side. "She is waiting for you," whispered the woman. Gerard returned to the stove, and gobbled the rest of his sausage, casting uneasy glances at the landlady seated silent as fate amid the prostrate multitude. The food bolted, he went to her and said, "Thank you kindly, dame, for waiting for me."

"You are welcome," said she calmly, making neither much nor little of the favour; and with that began to gather up the feathers; but Gerard stopped her. "Nay, that is my task;" and he went down on his knees and collected them with ardour. She watched him demurely.

"I wot not whence ye come," said she with a relic of distrust; adding more cordially, "but ye have been well brought up; y' have had a good mother, I'll go bail."

At the door she committed the whole company to Heaven in a formula, and disappeared. Gerard to his straw in the very corner, for the guests lay round the sacred stove by seniority, i. e. priority of arrival.

This punishment was a boon to Gerard, for thus he lay on the shore of odour and stifling heat, instead of in mid ocean.

He was just dropping off, when he was awaked by a noise, and lo!

there was the hind remorselessly shaking and waking guest after guest to ask him whether it was he who had picked up the mistress's feathers.

"It was I," cried Gerard.

"Oh, it was you was it?" said the other, and came striding rapidly over the intermediate sleepers. "She bade me say, 'One good turn deserves another,' and so here's your night-cap," and he thrust a great oaken mug under Gerard's nose.

"I thank her and bless her, here goes—ugh!" and his gratitude ended in a wry face, for the beer was muddy, and had a strange medicinal twang new to the Hollander.

"Trinke aus!" shouted the hind reproachfully.

"Enow is as good as a feast," said the youth, Jesuitically.

The hind cast a look of pity on this stranger who left liquor in his mug. "Ich brings euch," said he and drained it to the bottom.

And now Gerard turned his face to the wall and pulled up two handfuls of the nice clean straw, and bored in them with his finger, and so made a scabbard, and sheathed his nose in it. And soon they were all asleep: men, maids, wives, and children, all lying higgledy-piggledy, and snoring in a dozen keys like an orchestra slowly tuning; and Gerard's body lay on straw in Germany, and his spirit was away to Sevenbergen.

When he woke in the morning he found nearly all his fellow-passengers gone. One or two were waiting for dinner, nine o'clock: it was now six. He paid the landlady her demand, two pfenning, or about an English halfpenny and he of the pitchfork demanded trinkgeld, and getting a trifle more than usual, and seeing Gerard eye a foaming milk-pail he had just brought from the cow, hoisted it up bodily to his lips. "Drink your fill, man," said he, and on Gerard offering to pay for the delicious draught, told him in broad patois, that a man might swallow a skinful of milk, or a breakfast of air, without putting hand to pouch. At the door Gerard found his benefactress of last night, and a huge-chested artisan, her husband.

Gerard thanked her, and in the spirit of the age offered her a creutzer for her pudding.

But she repulsed his hand quietly. "For what do you take me?" said she, colouring faintly; "we are travellers and strangers the same as you, and bound to feel for those in like plight."

Then Gerard blushed in his turn and stammered excuses.

The hulking husband grinned superior to them both.

"Give the vixen a kiss for her pudding, and cry quits," said he with an air impartial, judge-like and Jove-like.

Gerard obeyed the loftly behest, and kissed the wife's cheek. "A blessing go with you both, good people," said he.

"And God speed you, young man!" replied the honest couple: and with that they parted; and never met again in this world.

The sun had just risen: the rain-drops on the leaves glittered like diamonds. The air was fresh and bracing, and Gerard steered south, and did not even remember his resolve of over night.

Eight leagues he walked that day, and in the afternoon came upon a huge building with an enormous arched gateway and a postern by its side.

"A monastery!" cried he joyfully; "I go no further lest I fare worse." He applied at the postern, and, on stating whence he came and whither bound, was instantly admitted and directed to the guest chamber, a large and lofty room, where travellers were fed and lodged gratis by the charity of the monastic orders. Soon the bell tinkled for vespers, and Gerard entered the church of the convent and from his place heard a service sung so exquisitely it seemed the choir of heaven. But one thing was wanting, Margaret was not there to hear it with him, and this made him sigh bitterly amid rapture. At supper, plain but wholesome and abundant food, and good beer, brewed in the convent, were set before him and his fellows, and at an early hour they were ushered into a large dormitory, and, the number being moderate, had each a truckle bed, and for covering sheepskins dressed with the fleece on: but previously to this a monk, struck by his youth and beauty, questioned him, and soon drew out his projects and his heart. When he was found to be convent bred and going alone to Rome, he became a personage, and in the morning they showed him over the convent and made him stay and dine in the refectory. They also pricked him a route on a slip of parchment, and the prior gave him a silver guilden to help him on the road, and advised him to join the first honest company he should fall in with, "and not face alone the manifold perils of the way."

"Perils?" said Gerard to himself.

That evening he came to a small straggling town where was one inn. It had no sign; but being now better versed in the customs of the country he detected it at once by the coats of arms on its walls.

These belonged to the distinguished visitors who had slept in it at different epochs since its foundation, and left these customary tokens of their patronage. At present it looked more like a mausoleum than a hotel. Nothing moved nor sounded either in it, or about it. Gerard hammered on the great oak door: no answer. He hallooed: no reply. After a while he hallooed louder, and at last a little round window or rather hole in the wall, opened, a man's head protruded cautiously, like a tortoise's from its shell, and eyed Gerard stolidly, but never uttered a syllable.

"Is this an inn?" asked Gerard with a covert sneer.

The head seemed to fall into a brown study; eventually it nodded, but lazily.

"Can I have entertainment here?"

Again the head pondered and ended by nodding, but sullenly, and seemed a skull overburdened with catch-penny interrogatories.

"How am I to get within, an't please you?"

At this the head popped in, as if the last question had shot it; and a hand popped out, pointed round the corner of the building, and slammed the window.

Gerard followed the indication, and after some research discovered that the fortification had one vulnerable part, a small, low door on its flank. As for the main entrance, that was used to keep out thieves and customers, except once or twice in a year, when they entered together, *i. e.* when some duke or count arrived in pomp with his train of gaudy ruffians.

Gerard, having penetrated the outer fort, soon found his way to the stove (as the public room was called from the principal article in it), and sat down near the oven, in which were only a few live embers that diffused a mild and grateful heat.

After waiting patiently a long time, he asked a grim old fellow with a long white beard, who stalked solemnly in, and turned the hourglass and then was stalking out—when supper would be. The grisly Ganymede counted the guests on his fingers—"When I see thrice as many here as now." Gerard groaned.

The grisly tyrant resented the rebellious sound. "Inns are not built for one," said he; "if you can't wait for the rest, look out for another lodging."

Gerard sighed.

At this the greybeard frowned.

The Cloister and the Hearth

After a while company trickled steadily in, till full eighty persons of various conditions were congregated, and to our novice the place became a chamber of horrors; for here the mothers got together and compared ringworms, and the men scraped the mud off their shoes with their knives, and left it on the floor, and combed their long hair out, inmates included, and made their toilet, consisting generally of a dry rub. Water, however, was brought in ewers. Gerard pounced on one of these, but at sight of the liquid contents lost his temper and said to the waiter, "Wash you first your water, and then a man may wash his hands withal."

"An it likes you not, seek another inn!"

Gerard said nothing, but went quietly and courteously besought an old traveller to tell him how far it was to the next inn.

"About four leagues."

Then Gerard appreciated the grim pleasantry of th' unbending sire.

That worthy now returned with an armful of wood, and, counting the travellers, put on a log for every six, by which act of raw justice the hotter the room the more heat he added. Poor Gerard noticed this little flaw in the ancient man's logic, but carefully suppressed every symptom of intelligence, lest his feet should have to carry his brains four leagues farther that night.

When perspiration and suffocation were far advanced, they brought in the table-cloths; but oh, so brown, so dirty, and so coarse: they seemed like sacks that had been worn out in agriculture and come down to this, or like shreds from the mainsail of some worn-out ship. The Hollander, who had never seen such linen even in nightmare, uttered a faint cry.

"What is to do?" inquired a traveller. Gerard pointed ruefully to the dirty sackcloth. The other looked at it with lacklustre eye, and comprehended nought.

A Burgundian soldier with his arbalest at his back came peeping over Gerard's shoulder, and, seeing what was amiss, laughed so loud that the room rang again, then slapped him on the back and cried, "Courage! le diable est mort."

Gerard stared: he doubted alike the good tidings and their relevancy: but the tones were so hearty and the arbalestrier's face, notwithstanding a formidable beard, was so gay and genial, that he smiled, and after a pause said drily, "Il a bien fait: avec l'eau et linge du pays on allait le noircir à ne se reconnaître plus."

"Tiens, tiens!" cried the soldier, "v'là qui parle le Français, peu s'en faut," and he seated himself by Gerard, and in a moment was talking volubly of war, women, and pillage, interlarding his discourse with curious oaths, at which Gerard drew away from him more or less.

Presently in came the grisly servant, and counted them all on his fingers superciliously, like Abraham telling sheep, then went out again and returned with a deal trencher and deal spoon to each.

Then there was an interval. Then he brought them a long mug apiece made of glass, and frowned. By and bye he stalked gloomily in with a hunch of bread apiece, and exit with an injured air. Expectation thus raised, the guests sat for nearly an hour balancing the wooden spoons, and with their own knives whittling the bread. Eventually when hope was extinct, patience worn out, and hunger exhausted, a huge vessel was brought in with pomp, the lid was removed, a cloud of steam rolled forth, and behold some thin broth with square pieces of bread floating. This, though not agreeable to the mind, served to distend the body. Slices of Strasbourg ham followed, and pieces of salt fish, both so highly salted that Gerard could hardly swallow a mouthful. Then came a kind of gruel, and, when the repast had lasted an hour and more some hashed meat highly peppered: and the French and Dutch being now full to the brim with the above dainties, and the draughts of beer the salt and spiced meats had provoked, in came roasted kids, most excellent, and carp and trout fresh from the stream. Gerard made an effort and looked angrily at them, but "could no more" as the poets say. The Burgundian swore by the liver and pike-staff of the good centurion, the natives had outwitted him. Then turning to Gerard, he said, "Courage, l'ami, le diable est mort," as loudly as before, but not with the same tone of conviction. The canny natives had kept an internal corner for contingencies, and polished the kids' very bones.

The feast ended with a dish of raw animalcula in a wicker cage. A cheese had been surrounded with little twigs and strings; then a hole made in it and a little sour wine poured in. This speedily bred a small but numerous vermin. When the cheese was so rotten with them that only the twigs and string kept it from tumbling to pieces

The Cloister and the Hearth

and walking off quadrivious, it came to table. By a malicious caprice of fate cage and menagerie were put down right under the Dutchman's organ of self-torture. He recoiled with a loud ejaculation, and hung to the bench by the calves of his legs.

"What is the matter?" said a traveller disdainfully. "Does the good cheese scare ye? Then put it hither, in the name of all the saints!"

"Cheese!" cried Gerard, "I see none. These nauseous reptiles have made away with every bit of it."

"Well," replied another, "It is not gone far. By eating of the mites we eat the cheese to boot."

"Nay, not so," said Gerard. "These reptiles are made like us, and digest their food and turn it to foul flesh even as we do ours to sweet: as well might you think to chew grass by eating of grass-fed beeves, as to eat cheese by swallowing these uncleanly insects."

Gerard raised his voice in uttering this, and the company received the paradox in dead silence, and with a distrustful air, like any other stranger, during which the Burgundian, who understood German but imperfectly, made Gerard Gallicise the discussion. He patted his interpreter on the back. "C'est bien, mon gars: plus fin que toi n'est pas bête," and administered his formula of encouragement; and Gerard edged away from him; for next to ugly sights and ill odours the poor wretch disliked profaneness.

Meantime, though shaken in argument, the raw reptiles were duly eaten and relished by the company, and served to provoke thirst, a principal aim of all the solids in that part of Germany. So now the company drank "garausses" all around, and their tongues were unloosed, and oh the Babel! But above the fierce clamour rose at intervals like some hero's war cry in battle, the trumpet-like voice of the Burgundian soldier shouting lustily "Courage, camarades, le diable est mort!"

Entered grisly Ganymede holding in his hand a wooden dish with circles and semicircles marked on it in chalk. He put it down on the table and stood silent, sad, and sombre, as Charon by Styx waiting for his boat-load of souls. Then pouches and purses were rummaged, and each threw a coin into the dish. Gerard timidly observed that he had drunk next to no beer, and inquired how much less he was to pay than the others.

"What mean you?" said Ganymede roughly. "Whose fault is it

you have not drunken? Are all to suffer because one chooses to be a milksop? You will pay no more than the rest and no less."

Gerard was abashed.

"Courage, petit, le diable est mort," hiccoughed the soldier, and flung Ganymede a coin.

"You are as bad as he is," said the old man peevishly, "you are paying too much;" and the tyrannical old Aristides returned him some coin out of the trencher with a most reproachful countenance. And now the man, whom Gerard had confuted an hour and a half ago, awoke from a brown study, in which he had been ever since, and came to him and said, "Yes: but the honey is none the worse for passing through the bees' bellies."

Gerard stared. The answer had been so long on the road he hadn't an idea what it was an answer to. Seeing him dumbfoundered, the other concluded him confuted, and withdrew calmed.

The bedrooms were upstairs dungeons with not a scrap of furniture except the bed, and a male servant settled inexorably who should sleep with whom. Neither money nor prayers would get a man a bed to himself here: custom forbade it sternly. You might as well have asked to monopolize a see-saw. They assigned to Gerard a man with a great black beard. He was an honest fellow enough; but not perfect; he would *not* go to bed, and *would* sit on the edge of it telling the wretched Gerard by force, and at length, the events of the day, and alternately laughing and crying at the same circumstances, which were not in the smallest degree pathetic or humorous, but only dead trivial. At last Gerard put his fingers in his ears, and lying down in his clothes for the sheets were too dirty for him to undress, contrived to sleep. But in an hour or two he awoke cold, and found that his drunken companion had got all the feather bed; so mighty is instinct. They lay between two beds; the lower one hard and made of straw, the upper soft and filled with feathers light as down. Gerard pulled at it, but the experienced drunkard held it fast mechanically. Gerard tried to twitch it away by surprise; but instinct was too many for him. On this he got out of bed, and, kneeling down on his bed-fellow's unguarded side easily whipped the prize away and rolled with it under the bed, and there lay on one edge of it, and curled the rest round his shoulders. Before he slept he often heard something grumbling and growling above him, which was some little satisfaction. Thus Instinct was outwitted, and victorious Reason lay chuckling on feathers, and not quite choked with dust.

At peep of day Gerard rose, flung the feather bed upon his snoring companion, and went in search of milk and air.

A cheerful voice hailed him in French: "What ho! you are up with the sun, comrade."

"He rises betimes that lies in a dog's lair," answered Gerard, crossly.

"Courage, l'ami! le diable est mort," was the instant reply. The soldier then told him his name was Denys, and he was passing from Flushing in Zealand to the duke's French dominions; a change the more agreeable to him, as he should revisit his native place, and a host of pretty girls who had wept at his departure, and should hear French spoken again. "And who are you, and whither bound?"

"My name is Gerard, and I am going to Rome," said the more reserved Hollander, and in a way that invited no further confidences.

"All the better; we will go together as far as Burgundy."

"That is not my road."

"All roads take to Rome."

"Ay, but the shortest road thither is my way."

"Well, then, it is I who must go out of my way a step for the sake of good company, for thy face likes me, and thou speakest French, or nearly."

"There go two words to that bargain," said Gerard, coldly. "I steer by proverbs too. They do put old heads on young men's shoulders. 'Bon loup mauvais compagnon, dit le brebis:' and a soldier, they say, is near akin to a wolf."

"They lie," said Denys: "besides, if he is, 'les loups nese mangent pas entre eux.'"

"Ay, but, sir soldier, I am not a wolf; and, thou knowest, 'à bien petite occasion se saisit le loup du mouton.'"

"Let us drop wolves and sheep, being men; my meaning is, that a good soldier never pillages—a comrade. Come, young man, too much suspicion becomes not your years. They who travel should learn to read faces; methinks you might see lealty in mine sith I have seen it in yourn. Is it yon fat purse at your girdle you fear for?" (Gerard turned pale.) "Look hither!" and he undid his belt, and poured out of it a double handful of gold pieces, then returned them to their hiding place. "There is a hostage for you," said he; "carry

The Cloister and the Hearth

you that, and let us be comrades," and handed him his belt, gold and all.

Gerard stared. "If I am over prudent, you have not enow." But he flushed and looked pleased at the other's trust in him.

"Bah! I can read faces; and so must you, or you'll never take your four bones safe to Rome."

"Soldier, you would find me a dull companion, for my heart is very heavy," said Gerard, yielding.

"I'll cheer you, mon gars."

"I think you would," said Gerard sweetly; "and sore need have I of a kindly voice in mine ear this day."

"Oh! no soul is sad alongside me. I lift up their poor little hearts with my consigne: 'Courage, tout le monde, le diable est mort.' Ha! ha!"

"So be it then," said Gerard. "But take back your belt, for I could never trust by halves. We will go together as far as Rhine, and God go with us both!"

"Amen!" said Denys, and lifted his cap. "En avant!"

The pair trudged manfully on, and Denys enlivened the weary way. He chattered about battles and sieges, and things which were new to Gerard; and he was one of those who *make* little incidents wherever they go. He passed nobody without addressing him. "They don't understand it, but it wakes them up," said he. But, whenever they fell in with a monk or priest, he pulled a long face, and sought the reverend father's blessing, and fearlessly poured out on him floods of German words in such order as not to produce a single German sentence. He doffed his cap to every woman, high or low, he caught sight of, and with eagle eye discerned her best feature, and complimented her on it in his native tongue, well adapted to such matters: and, at each carrion crow or magpie, down came his cross-bow, and he would go a furlong off the road to circumvent it; and indeed he did shoot one old crow with laudable neatness and despatch, and carried it to the nearest hen-roost, and there slipped in and set it upon a nest. "The good-wife will say, 'Alack, here is Beelzebub a hatching of my eggs.'"

"No, you forget, he is dead," objected Gerard.

"So he is, so he is. But she doesn't know that, not having the luck to be acquainted with me, who carry the good news from city to city, uplifting men's hearts."

Such was Denys in time of peace.

Our travellers towards nightfall reached a village; it was a very small one, but contained a place of entertainment. They searched for it, and found a small house with barn and stables. In the former was the everlasting stove, and the clothes drying round it on lines, and a traveller or two sitting morose. Gerard asked for supper. "Supper? We have no time to cook for travellers; we only provide lodging, good lodging for man and beast. You can have some beer."

"Madman, who, born in Holland, sought other lands!" snorted Gerard in Dutch. The landlady started.

"What gibberish is that?" asked she, and crossed herself with looks of superstitious alarm. "You can buy what you like in the village, and cook it in our oven; but, prithee, mutter no charms nor sorceries here, good man; don't ye now, it do make my flesh creep so."

They scoured the village for food, and ended by supping on roasted eggs and brown bread.

At a very early hour their chambermaid came for them. It was a rosy-cheeked old fellow with a lanthorn.

They followed him. He led them across a dirty farm-yard, where they had much ado to pick their steps, and brought them into a cow-house. There, on each side of every cow, was laid a little clean straw, and a tied bundle of ditto for a pillow. The old man looked down on this his work with paternal pride. Not so Gerard. "What, do you set Christian men to lie among cattle?"

"Well, it is hard upon the poor beasts. They have scarce room to turn."

"Oh! what it is not hard on us then?"

"Where is the hardship? I have lain among them all my life. Look at me! I am four score, and never had a headache in all my born days—all along of lying among the kye. Bless your silly head, kine's breath is ten times sweeter to drink nor Christians'. You try it!" and he slammed the bedroom door.

"Denys, where are you?" whined Gerard.

"Here, on her other side."

"What are you doing?"

"I know not. But, as near as I can guess, I think I must be going to sleep. What are you at?"

"I am saying my prayers."

"Forget me not in them!"

"Is it likely? Denys I shall soon have done: do not go to sleep, I want to talk."

"Despatch then! for I feel—augh—like—like—floating—in the sky—on a warm cloud."

"Denys!"

"Augh! eh! hallo! is it time to get up?"

"Alack, no. There, I hurried my orisons to talk; and look at you, going to sleep! We shall be starved before morning, having no coverlets."

"Well, you know what to do."

"Not I, in sooth."

"Cuddle the cow."

"Thank you."

"Burrow in the straw then. You must be very new to the world, to grumble at this. How would you bear to lie on the field of battle on a frosty night, as I did t'other day, stark naked, with nothing to keep me warm but the carcass of a fellow I had been and helped kill?"

"Horrible! horrible! Tell me all about it! Oh but this is sweet."

"Well, we had a little battle in Brabant, and won a little victory, but it cost us dear: several arbalestriers turned their toes up, and I among them."

"Killed, Denys? come now!"

"Dead as mutton. Stuck full of pike-holes till the blood ran out of me, like the good wine of Mâcon from the trodden grapes. It is right bounteous in me to pour the tale in minstrel phrase for—augh—I am sleepy. Augh—now where was I?"

"Left dead on the field of battle, bleeding like a pig; that is to say like grapes, or something; go on, prithee go on, 'tis a sin to sleep in the midst of a good story."

"Granted. Well, some of those vagabonds, that strip the dead soldier on the field of glory, came and took every rag off me; they wrought me no further ill, because there was no need."

"No: you were dead."

129

The Cloister and the Hearth

"C'est convenu. This must have been at sundown; and with the night came a shrewd frost that barkened the blood on my wounds, and stopped all the rivulets that were running from my heart, and about midnight I awoke as from a trance."

"And thought you were in heaven?" asked Gerard eagerly, being a youth inoculated with monkish tales.

"Too frost bitten for that, mon gars; besides, I heard the wounded groaning on all sides; so I knew I was in the old place. I saw I could not live the night through without cover. I groped about shivering and shivering; at last one did suddenly leave groaning. 'You are sped,' said I, so made up to him, and true enough he was dead, but warm, you know. I took my lord in my arms; but was too weak to carry him: so rolled with him into a ditch hard by: and there my comrades found me in the morning properly stung with nettles and hugging a dead Fleming for the bare life."

Gerard shuddered. "And this is war; this is the chosen theme of poets and troubadours, and Reden Ryckers. Truly was it said by the men of old 'dulce bellum *inexpertis.*' "

"Tu dis?"

"I say,—oh what stout hearts some men have!"

"N'est-ce pas, p'tit? So after that sort—thing—this sort thing is heaven. Soft—warm—good company comradancow—cou'age—diable—m—ornk!"

And the glib tongue was still for some hours.

In the morning Gerard was wakened by a liquid hitting his eye, and it was Denys employing the cow's udder as a squirt.

"Oh fie!" cried Gerard, "to waste the good milk:" and he took a horn out of his wallet. "Fill this! but indeed I see not what right we have to meddle with her milk at all."

"Make your mind easy! Last night la camarade was not nice; but what then, true friendship dispenses with ceremony. To-day we make as free with her."

"Why what did she do, poor thing?"

"Ate my pillow."

"Ha! ha!"

"On waking I had to hunt for my head, and found it down in the stable gutter. She ate our pillow from us, we drink our pillow from her. A votre santé, madame; et sans rancune;" and the dog drank her to her own health.

The Cloister and the Hearth

"The ancient was right though," said Gerard. "Never have I risen so refreshed since I left my native land. Henceforth let us shun great towns, and still lie in a convent or a cow-house; for I'd liever sleep on fresh straw than on linen well washed six months agone; and the breath of kine it is sweeter than that of Christians, let alone the garlic, which men and women folk affect, but cowen abhor from, and so do I, St. Bavon be my witness!"

The soldier eyed him from head to foot: "Now but for that little tuft on your chin I should take you for a girl: and by the finger-nails of St. Luke, no ill-favoured one neither."

These three towns proved types and repeated themselves with slight variations for many a weary league: but, even when he could get neither a convent nor a cow-house, Gerard learned in time to steel himself to the inevitable, and to emulate his comrade, whom he looked on as almost superhuman for hardihood of body and spirit.

There was however a balance to all this veneration.

Denys, like his predecessor Achilles, had his weak part, his very weak part thought Gerard.

His foible was "woman."

Whatever he was saying or doing, he stopped short at sight of a farthingale, and his whole soul became occupied with that garment and its inmate till they had disappeared; and sometimes for a good while after.

He often put Gerard to the blush by talking his amazing German to such females as he caught standing or sitting indoors or out; at which they stared; and when he met a peasant girl on the road, he took off his cap to her and saluted her as if she was a queen. The invariable effect of which was, that she suddenly drew herself up quite stiff like a soldier on parade, and wore a forbidding countenance.

"They drive me to despair," said Denys. "Is that a just return to a civil bonnetade? They are large, they are fair, but stupid as swans."

"What breeding can you expect from women that wear no hose?" inquired Gerard; "and some of them no shoon? They seem to me reserved, and modest, as becomes their sex; and sober, whereas the men are little better than beer-barrels. Would you have them brazen as well as hoseless?"

"A little affability adorns even beauty," sighed Denys.

"Then let them alone, sith they are not to your taste," retorted Gerard. "What, is there no sweet face in Bergundy that would pale to see you so wrapped up in strange women?"

"Half a dozen that would cry their eyes out."

"Well then!"

"But it is a long way to Burgundy."

"Ay, to the foot, but not to the heart. I am there, sleeping and waking, and almost every minute of the day."

"In Burgundy? Why I thought you had never—"

"In Burgundy?" cried Gerard contemptuously. "No, in sweet Sevenbergen. Ah! well-a-day! well-a-day!"

Many such dialogues as this passed between the pair on the long and weary road, and neither could change the other.

One day about noon they reached a town of some pretensions and Gerard was glad, for he wanted to buy a pair of shoes: his own were quite worn out. They soon found a shop that displayed a goodly array and made up to it, and would have entered it; but the shop-keeper sat on the door-step taking a nap, and was so fat as to block up the narrow doorway: the very light could hardly struggle past his "too, too solid flesh," much less a carnal customer.

My fair readers, accustomed, when they go shopping, to be met half way with nods, and becks and wreathed smiles, and waived into a seat, while almost at the same instant an eager shopman flings himself half across the counter in a semicircle to learn their commands, can best appreciate this mediæval Teuton, who kept a shop as a dog keeps a kennel: and sat at the exclusion of custom, snoring like a pig.

Denys and Gerard stood and contemplated this curiosity; emblem, permit me to remark, of the lets and hindrances to commerce that characterized his epoch.

"Jump over him!"

"The door is too low."

"March through him!"

"The man is too thick."

"What is the coil?" inquired a mumbling voice from the interior: apprentice with his mouth full.

"We want to get into your shop."

"What for, in Heaven's name??!!!"

"Shoon; lazy bones!"

The Cloister and the Hearth

The ire of the apprentice began to rise at such an explanation. "And could ye find no hour out of all the twelve to come pestering us for shoon, but the one little, little hour my master takes his nap, and I sit down to my dinner, when all the rest of the world is full long ago?"

Denys heard, but could not follow the sense. "Waste no more time talking their German gibberish," said he; take out thy knife and tickle his fat ribs."

"That will I not," said Gerard.

"Then here goes; I'll prong him with this."

Gerard seized the mad fellow's arm in dismay, for he had been long enough in the country to guess that the whole town would take part in any brawl with the native against a stranger. But Denys twisted away from him, and the cross-bow bolt in his hand was actually on the road to the sleeper's ribs; but at that very moment two females crossed the road towards him; he saw the blissful vision, and instantly forgot what he was about, and awaited their approach with unreasonable joy.

Though companions they were not equals; except in attractiveness to a Burgundian cross-bow man: for one was very tall, the other short, and, by one of those anomalies which society, however primitive, speedily establishes, the long one held up the little one's tail. The tall one wore a plain linen coif on her head, a little grogram cloak over her shoulders, a grey kirtle, and a short farthingale or petticoat of bright red cloth, and feet and legs quite bare, though her arms were veiled in tight linen sleeves.

The other a kirtle broadly trimmed with fur, her arms in double sleeves, whereof the inner of yellow satin clung to the skin; the outer, all befurred, were open at the inside of the elbow, and so the arm passed through and left them dangling. Velvet head-dress, huge purse at girdle, gorgeous train, bare legs. And thus they came on, the citizen's wife strutting, and the maid gliding after, holding her mistress's train devoutly in both hands, and bending and winding her lithe body prettily enough to do it. Imagine (if not pressed for time) a bantam, with a guinea-hen stepping obsequious at its stately heel.

This pageant made straight for the shoemaker's shop. Denys louted low; the worshipful lady nodded graciously, but rapidly, having business on hand, or rather on foot; for in a moment she poked the point of her little shoe into the sleeper, and worked it round in

The Cloister and the Hearth

him like a gimlet, till with a long snarl he woke. The incarnate shutter rising and grumbling vaguely, the lady swept in and deigned him no further notice. He retreated to his neighbor's shop the tailor's, and, sitting on the step, protected it from the impertinence of morning calls. Neighbors should be neighborly.

Denys and Gerard followed the dignity into the shop, where sat the apprentice at dinner; the maid stood outside with her insteps crossed, leaning against the wall, and tapping it with her nails.

"Those, yonder," said the dignity briefly, pointing with an imperious little white hand to some yellow shoes gilded at the toe. While the apprentice stood stock still, neutralized by his dinner and his duty, Denys sprang at the shoes, and brought them to her; she smiled, and calmly seating herself, protruded her foot, shod, but hoseless, and scented. Down went Denys on his knees, and drew off her shoe, and tried the new ones on the white skin devoutly. Finding she had a willing victim, she abused the opportunity, tried first one pair, then another, then the first again, and so on, balancing and hesitating for about half an hour, to Gerard's disgust and Denys's weak delight. At last she was fitted, and handed two pair of yellow and one pair of red shoes out to her servant. Then was heard a sigh. It burst from the owner of the shop: he had risen from slumber, and was now hovering about, like a partridge near her brood in danger. "There go all my coloured shoes?" said he, as they disappeared in the girl's apron.

The lady departed: Gerard fitted himself with a stout pair, asked the price, paid it without a word, and gave his old ones to a beggar in the street, who blessed him in the market-place, and threw them furiously down a well in the suburbs. The comrades left the shop, and in it two melancholy men, that looked, and even talked, as if they had been robbed wholesale.

"My shoon are sore worn," said Denys, grinding his teeth; "but I'll go barefoot till I reach France, ere I'll leave my money with such churls as these."

The Dutchman replied calmly, "They seem indifferent well sewn."

As they drew near the Rhine, they passed through forest after forest, and now for the first time ugly words sounded in travellers' mouths, seated around stoves. "Thieves!" "black gangs!" "cutthroats!" etc.

The very rustics were said to have a custom hereabouts of murdering the unwary traveller in these gloomy woods, whose dark and devious windings enabled those, who were familiar with them, to do deeds of rapine and blood undetected, or, if detected, easily to baffle pursuit.

Certain it was, that every clown they met, carried, whether for offence or defence, a most formidable weapon; a light axe with a short pike at the head, and a long slender handle of ash or yew, well seasoned. These the natives could all throw with singular precision, so as to make the point strike an object at several yards' distance, or could slay a bullock at hand with a stroke of the blade. Gerard bought one and practised with it. Denys quietly filed and ground his bolts sharp, whistling the whilst; and, when they entered a gloomy wood, he would unsling his cross-bow and carry it ready for action; but not so much like a traveller fearing an attack as a sportsman watchful not to miss a snap shot.

One day, being in a forest a few leagues from Dusseldorf, as Gerard was walking like one in a dream, thinking of Margaret, and scarce seeing the road he trode, his companion laid a hand on his shoulder, and strung his cross-bow with glittering eye. "Hush!" said he in a low whisper that startled Gerald more than thunder. Gerard grasped his axe tight, and shook a little: he heard a rustling in the wood hard by, and at the same moment Denys sprang into the wood, and his cross-bow went to his shoulder, even as he jumped. Twang! went the metal string; and after an instant's suspense he roared, "Run forward, guard the road, he is hit! he is hit!"

Gerard darted forward, and, as he ran, a young bear burst out of the wood right upon him: finding itself intercepted, it went up on its hind legs with a snarl, and, though not half grown, opened formidable jaws and long claws. Gerard in a fury of excitement and agitation flung himself on it and delivered a tremendous blow on its nose with his axe, and the creature staggered; another, and it lay grovelling with Gerard hacking it.

"Hallo! stop! you are mad to spoil the meat."

"I took it for a robber," said Gerard panting. "I mean I had made ready for a robber, so I could not hold my hand."

"Ay, these chattering travellers have stuffed your head full of thieves and assassins: they have not got a real live robber in their whole nation. Nay, I'll carry the beast; bear thou my cross-bow."

"We will carry it by turns then," said Gerard, "for 'tis a heavy load: poor thing how its blood drips. Why did we slay it?"

"For supper, and the reward the baillie of the next town shall give us."

"And for that it must die, when it had but just begun to live: and perchance it hath a mother that will miss it sore this night, and loves it as ours love us; more than mine doth me."

"What, know you not that his mother was caught in a pitfall last month, and her skin is now at the tanner's? and his father was stuck full of cloth-yard shafts t'other day, and died like Julius Cæsar, with his hands folded on his bosom, and a dead dog in each of them?"

But Gerard would not view it jestingly: "Why then," said he, "we have killed one of God's creatures that was all alone in the world—as I am this day, in this strange land."

"You young milksop," roared Denys, "these things must not be looked at so, or not another bow would be drawn nor quarel fly in forest nor battle-field. Why, one of your kidney consorting with a troop of pikemen should turn them to a row of milk-pails: it is ended, to Rome thou goest not alone; for never wouldst thou reach the Alps in a whole skin. I take thee to Remiremont, my native place, and there I marry thee to my young sister, she is blooming as a peach. Thou shakest thy head? ah! I forgot; thou lovest elsewhere, and art a one woman man, a creature to me scarce conceivable. Well then, I shall find thee, not a wife, nor a leman, but a friend; some honest Bergundian who shall go with thee as far as Lyons; and much I doubt that honest fellow will be myself, into whose liquor thou hast dropped sundry powders to make me love thee; for erst I endured not doves in doublet and hose. From Lyons, I say, I can trust thee by ship to Italy, which being by all accounts the very stronghold of milksops, thou wilt there be safe: they will hear thy words, and make thee their duke in a twinkling."

Gerard sighed: "In sooth I love not to think of this Dusseldorf where we are to part company, good friend."

They walked silently, each thinking of the separation at hand; the thought checked trifling conversation, and at these moments it is a relief to do something, however insignificant. Gerard asked Denys to lend him a bolt. "I have often shot with a long bow, but never with one of these!"

"Draw thy knife and cut this one out of the cub," said Denys slily.

"Nay, nay, I want a clean one."

Denys gave him three out of his quiver.

Gerard strung the bow, and levelled it at a bough that had fallen into the road at some distance. The power of the instrument surprised him; the short but thick steel bow jarred him to the very heel as it went off, and the swift steel shaft was invisible in its passage; only the dead leaves, with which November had carpeted the narrow road, flew about on the other side of the bough.

"Ye aimed a thought too high," said Denys.

"What a deadly thing! no wonder it is driving out the long-bow,— to Martin's much discontent."

"Ay, lad," said Denys triumphantly, "it gains ground every day, in spite of their laws and their proclamations to keep up the yewen bow, because forsooth their grandsires shot with it, knowing no better. You see, Gerard, war is not pastime. Men will shoot at their enemies with the hittingest arm and the killingest, not with the longest and missingest."

"Then these new engines I hear of will put both bows down; for these, with a pinch of black dust, and a leaden ball, and a child's finger, shall slay you Mars and Goliah, and the Seven Champions."

"Pooh! pooh!" said Denys warmly; "petrone nor harquebuss shall ever put down Sir Arbalest. Why, we can shoot ten times while they are putting their charcoal and their lead into their leathern smoke belchers, and then kindling their matches. All that is too fumbling for the field of battle; there a soldier's weapon needs be ay ready like his heart."

Gerard did not answer; for his ear was attracted by a sound behind them. It was a peculiar sound, too, like something heavy, but not hard, rushing softly over the dead leaves. He turned round with some little curiosity. A colossal creature was coming down the road at about sixty paces distance.

He looked at it in a sort of calm stupor at first; but the next moment he turned ashy pale.

"Denys!" he cried. "Oh God! Denys!"

Denys whirled round.

It was a bear as big as a cart-horse.

It was tearing along with its huge head down, running on a hot scent.

The very moment he saw it Denys said in a sickening whisper: "THE CUB!"

The Cloister and the Hearth

Oh! the concentrated horror of that one word, whispered hoarsely, with dilating eyes! For in that syllable it all flashed upon them both like a sudden stroke of lightning in the dark—the bloody trail, the murdered cub, the mother upon them, *and it*. DEATH.

All this in a moment of time. The next, she saw them. Huge as she was, she seemed to double herself (it was her long hair bristling with rage): she raised her head big as a bull's, her swine-shaped jaws opened wide at them, her eyes turned to blood and flame, and she rushed upon them, scattering the leaves about her like a whirlwind as she came.

"Shoot!" screamed Denys, but Gerard stood shaking from head to foot, useless.

"Shoot, man! ten thousand devils, shoot! too late! Tree! tree!" and he dropped the cub, pushed Gerard across the road, and flew to the first tree and climbed it, Gerard the same on his side; and, as they fled, both men uttered inhuman howls like savage creatures grazed by death.

With all their speed one or other would have been torn to fragments at the foot of his tree; but the bear stopped a moment at the cub.

Without taking her bloodshot eye off those she was hunting, she smelt it all round, and found, how, her Creator only knows, that it was dead, quite dead. She gave a yell such as neither of the hunted ones had ever heard, nor dreamed to be in nature; and flew after Denys. She reared and struck at him as he climbed. He was just out of reach.

Instantly she seized the tree, and with her huge teeth tore a great piece out of it with a crash. Then she reared again, dug her claws deep into the bark, and began to mount it slowly, but as surely as a monkey.

Denys's evil star had led him to a dead tree, a mere shaft, and of no very great height. He climbed faster than his pursuer, and was soon at the top. He looked this way and that for some bough of another tree to spring to. There was none: and, if he jumped down, he knew the bear would be upon him ere he could recover the fall, and make short work of him. Moreover Denys was little used to turning his back on danger, and his blood was rising at being hunted. He turned to bay.

"My hour is come," thought he. "Let me meet death like a man." He kneeled down and grasped a small shoot to steady himself, drew his long knife, and, clenching his teeth, prepared to jab the huge brute as soon as it should mount within reach.

Of this combat the result was not doubtful.

The monster's head and neck were scarce vulnerable for bone and masses of hair. The man was going to sting the bear, and the bear to crack the man like a nut.

Gerard's heart was better than his nerves. He saw his friend's mortal danger, and passed at once from fear to blindish rage. He slipped down his tree in a moment, caught up the cross-bow, which he had dropped in the road, and, running furiously up, sent a bolt into the bear's body with a loud shout. The bear gave a snarl of rage and pain, and turned its head irresolutely.

"Keep aloof!" cried Denys, "or you are a dead man."

"I care not;" and in a moment he had another bolt ready and shot it fiercely into the bear, screaming, "Take that! take that!"

Denys poured a volley of oaths down at him. "Get away, idiot!"

He was right: the bear finding so formidable and noisy a foe behind him, slipped growling down the tree, rending deep furrows in it as she slipped. Gerard ran back to his tree and climbed it swiftly. But while his legs were dangling some eight feet from the ground, the bear came rearing and struck with her fore paw, and out flew a piece of bloody cloth from Gerard's hose. He climbed, and climbed; and presently he heard as it were in the air a voice say, "Go out on the bough!" He looked, and there was a long massive branch before him shooting upwards at a slight angle; he threw his body across it, and by a series of convulsive efforts worked up it to the end.

Then he looked round panting.

The bear was mounting the tree on the other side. He heard her claws scrape, and saw her bulge on both sides of the massive tree. Her eye not being very quick she reached the fork and passed it, mounting the main stem. Gerard drew breath more freely. The bear either heard him, or found by scent she was wrong: she paused; presently she caught sight of him. She eyed him steadily; then quietly descended to the fork.

Slowly and cautiously she stretched out a paw and tried the bough. It was a stiff oak branch, sound as iron. Instinct taught the creature this: it crawled carefully out on the bough, growling savagely as it came.

Gerard looked wildly down. He was forty feet from the ground.

Death below. Death moving slow but sure on him in a still more horrible form. His hair bristled. The sweat poured from him. He sat helpless, fascinated, tongue-tied.

As the fearful monster crawled growling towards him, incongruous thoughts coursed through his mind. Margaret: the Vulgate, where it speaks of the rage of a she-bear robbed of her whelps,—Rome,—Eternity.

The bear crawled on. And now the stupor of death fell on the doomed man; he saw the open jaws and bloodshot eyes coming, but in a mist.

As in a mist he heard a twang: he glanced down; Denys, white and silent as death, was shooting up at the bear. The bear snarled at the twang; but crawled on. Again the cross-bow twanged; and the bear snarled; and came nearer. Again the cross-bow twanged, and the next moment the bear was close upon Gerard, where he sat, with hair standing stiff on end, and eyes starting from their sockets, palsied. The bear opened her jaws like a grave; and hot blood spouted from them upon Gerard as from a pump. The bough rocked. The wounded monster was reeling; it clung, it stuck its sickles of claws deep into the wood; it toppled, its claws held firm, but its body rolled off, and the sudden shock to the branch shook Gerard forward on his stomach with his face upon one of the bear's straining paws. At this, by a convulsive effort, she raised her head up, up, till he felt her hot fetid breath. Then huge teeth snapped together loudly close below him in the air, with a last effort of baffled hate. The ponderous carcass rent the claws out of the bough; then pounded the earth with a tremendous thump. There was a shout of triumph below, and the very next instant a cry of dismay; for Gerard had swooned, and, without an attempt to save himself, rolled headlong from the perilous height.

CHAPTER XXV

DENYS caught at Gerard, and somewhat checked his fall: but it may be doubted whether this alone would have saved him from breaking his neck or a limb. His best friend now was the dying bear, on whose hairy carcass his head and shoulders descended. Denys tore him off her. It was needless. She panted still, and her limbs quivered, but a hare was not so harmless; and soon she breathed her last: and the judicious Denys propped Gerard up against her, being soft, and fanned him. He came to by degrees, but confused, and feeling the bear all around him, rolled away yelling.

"Courage," cried Denys, "le diable est mort."

"Is it dead? quite dead?" inquired Gerard from behind a tree; for his courage was feverish, and the cold fit was on him just now, and had been for some time.

"Behold," said Denys, and pulled the brute's ear playfully, and opened her jaws, and put in his head, with other insulting antics; in the midst of which Gerard was violently sick.

Denys laughed at him.

"What is the matter now?" said he, "also why tumble off your perch just when we had won the day?"

"I swooned, I trow."

"But *why?*"

Not receiving an answer, he continued, "Green girls faint as soon as look at you, but then they choose time and place. What woman ever fainted up a tree?"

"She sent her nasty blood all over me. I think the smell must have overpowered me. Faugh! I hate blood."

"I do believe it potently."

"See what a mess she has made me!"

"But with her blood, not yours. I pity the enemy that strives to satisfy you."

"You need not to brag, Maître Denys; I saw you under the tree, the colour of your shirt."

"Let us distinguish," said Denys colouring: "it is permitted to tremble *for a friend.*"

Gerard for answer, flung his arms round Denys's neck in silence.

"Look here," whined the stout soldier, affected by this little gush of nature and youth, "was ever aught so like a woman? I love thee, little milksop, go to. Good! behold him on his knees now. What new caprice is this?"

"Oh, Denys, ought we not to return thanks to Him who has saved both our lives against such fearful odds?" And Gerard kneeled and prayed aloud. And presently he found Denys kneeling quiet beside him, with his hands across his bosom, after the custom of his nation.

and a face as long as his arm. When they arose Gerard's countenance was beaming.

"Good Denys," said he, "Heaven will reward thy piety."

"Ah, bah! I did it out of politeness," said the Frenchman. "It was to please thee, little one. C'est égal: 'twas well and orderly prayed; and edified me to the core, while it lasted. A bishop had scarce handled the matter better: so now our evensong being sung, and the saints enlisted with us—marchons."

Ere they had taken two steps, he stopped. "By-the-by, the cub!"

"Oh, no, no!" cried Gerard.

"You are right. It is late: we have lost time climbing trees, and tumbling off 'em, and swooning, and vomiting, and praying, and the brute is heavy to carry; and, now I think on't, we shall have papa after it next; these bears make such a coil about an odd cub: what is this? You are wounded! you are wounded!"

"Not I."

"He is wounded, miserable that I am."

"Be calm, Denys. I am not touched, I feel no pain anywhere."

"You? you only feel when another is hurt," cried Denys, with great emotion and throwing himself on his knees he examined Gerard's leg with glistening eyes.

"Quick! quick! before it stiffens," he cried: and hurried him on.

"Who makes the coil about nothing now?" inquired Gerard composedly.

Denys's reply was a very indirect one.

"Be pleased to note," said he, "that I have a bad heart. You were man enough to save my life, yet I must sneer at you, a novice in war; was not I a novice once myself? then you fainted from a wound, and I thought you swooned for fear, and called you a milksop. Briefly, I have a bad tongue and a bad heart."

"Denys!"

"Plait-il?"

"You lie."

"You are very good to say so, little one, and I am eternally obliged to you," mumbled the remorseful Denys.

Ere they had walked many furlongs, the muscles of the wounded leg contracted and stiffened, till presently Gerard could only just put his toe to the ground, and that with great pain.

At last he could bear it no longer.

The Cloister and the Hearth

"Let me lie down and die," he groaned, "for this is intolerable."

Denys represented that it was afternoon, and the nights were now frosty, and cold and hunger ill companions, and that it would be unreasonable to lose heart, a certain great personage being notoriously defunct. So Gerard leaned upon his axe and hobbled on, but presently he gave in all of a sudden, and sank helpless in the road.

Denys drew him aside into the wood, and to his surprise gave him his cross-bow and bolts, enjoining him strictly to lie quiet, and if any ill-looking fellows should find him out and come to him, to bid them keep aloof; and, should they refuse, to shoot them dead at twenty paces. "Honest men keep the path, and, knaves in a wood none but fools do parley with them." With this he snatched up Gerard's axe and set off running, not, as Gerard expected, toward Dusseldorf, but on the road they had come.

Gerard lay aching and smarting, and to him Rome, that seemed so near at starting, looked far, far, off, now that he was two hundred miles nearer it. But soon all his thoughts turned Sevenbergen-wards. How sweet it would be one day to hold Margaret's hand and tell her all he had gone through for her! The very thought of it, and her, soothed him, and in the midst of pain and irritation of the nerves he lay resigned, and sweetly, though faintly, smiling.

He had lain thus more than two hours, when suddenly there were shouts, and the next moment something struck a tree hard by and quivered in it.

He looked, it was an arrow.

He started to his feet. Several missiles rattled among the boughs, and the wood echoed with battle-cries. Whence they came he could not tell, for noises in these huge woods are so reverberated that a stranger is always at fault as to their whereabout; but they seemed to fill the whole air. Presently there was a lull: then he heard the fierce galloping of hoofs; and still louder shouts and cries arose, mingled with shrieks and groans, and above all strange and terrible sounds like fierce claps of thunder, bellowing loud, and then dying off in cracking echoes; and red tongues of flame shot out ever and anon among the trees, and clouds of sulphureous smoke came drifting over his head: and all was still.

Gerard was struck with awe. "What will become of Denys?" he cried. "Oh why did you leave me? Oh Denys, my friend, my friend!"

143

Just before sunset Denys returned, almost sinking under a hairy bundle. It was the bear's skin.

Gerard welcomed him with a burst of joy that astonished him.

"I thought never to see you again, dear Denys: were you in the battle?"

"No. What battle?"

"The bloody battle of men, or fiends, that raged in the wood a while agone;" and with this he described it to the life, and more fully than I have done.

Denys patted him indulgently on the back.

"It is well:" said he, "thou are a good limner; and fever is a great spur to the imagination. One day I lay in a cart-shed with a cracked skull, and saw two hosts manœuvre and fight a good hour on eight feet square, the which I did fairly describe to my comrade in due order, only not so gorgeously as thou, for want of book learning."

"What then you believe me not? when I tell you the arrows whizzed over my head, and the combatants shouted, and—"

"May the foul fiends fly away with me if I believe a word of it."

Gerard took his arm and quietly pointed to a tree close by.

"Why it looks like—it is—a broad arrow as I live:" and he went close and looked up at it.

"It came out of the battle. I heard it, and saw it."

"An English arrow."

"How know you that?"

"Marry, by its length. The English bowmen draw the bow to the ear, others only to the right breast. Hence the English loose a three-foot shaft, and this is one of them, perdition seize them. Well, if this is not glamour there has been a trifle of a battle: and if there has been a battle in so ridiculous a place for a battle as this, why then 'tis no business of mine, for my duke hath no quarrel hereabouts; so let's to bed," said the professional: and with this he scraped together a heap of leaves, and made Gerard lie on it, his axe by his side: he then lay down beside him with one hand on his arbalest, and drew the bearskin over them, hair inward. They were soon as warm as toast and fast asleep.

But long before the dawn Gerard woke his comrade.

"What shall I do, Denys, I die of famine?"

"Do? why go to sleep again incontinent: qui dort dîne."

"But I tell you I am too hungry to sleep," snapped Gerard.

The Cloister and the Hearth

"Let us march then," replied Denys, with paternal indulgence.

He had a brief paroxysm of yawns; then made a small bundle of bears' ears, rolling them up in a strip of the skin, cut for the purpose; and they took the road.

Gerard leaned on his axe, and, propped by Denys on the other side, hobbled along not without sighs.

"I hate pain," said Gerard, viciously.

"Therein you show judgment," replied papa, smoothly.

It was a clear starlight night; and soon the moon rising revealed the end of the wood at no great distance; a pleasant sight, since Dusseldorf they knew was but a short league further.

At the edge of the wood they came upon something so mysterious that they stopped to gaze at it, before going up to it. Two white pillars rose in the air, distant a few paces from each other; and between them stood many figures, that looked like human forms.

"I go no further till I know what this is," said Gerard, in an agitated whisper; "are they effigies of the saints, for men to pray to on the road? or live robbers waiting to shoot down honest travellers? nay, living men they cannot be, for they stand on nothing that I see. Oh! Denys, let us turn back till daybreak: this is no mortal sight."

Denys halted and peered long and keenly. "They are men," said he, at last. Gerard was for turning back all the more.

"But men that will never hurt us, nor we them. Look not to their feet for that they stand on!"

"Where then i' the name of all saints?"

"Look over their heads!" said Denys gravely.

Following this direction, Gerard presently discerned the outline of a dark wooden beam passing from pillar to pillar; and, as the pair got nearer, walking now on tiptoe, one by one dark snakelike cords came out in the moonlight, each pendent from the beam to a dead man, and tight as wire.

Now as they came under this awful monument of crime and wholesale vengeance, a light air swept by; and several of the corpses swung, or gently gyrated, and every rope creaked. Gerard shuddered at this ghastly salute. So thoroughly had the gibbet with its sickening load seized and held their eyes, that it was but now they perceived a fire right underneath, and a living figure sitting huddled over it. His axe lay beside him, the bright blade shining red in the glow. He was asleep.

145

Gerard started, but Denys only whispered. "Courage, comrade, here is a fire."

"Ay! but there is a man at it."

"There will soon be three:" and he began to heap some wood on it that the watcher had prepared; during which the prudent Gerard seized the man's axe, and sat down tight on it grasping his own, and examining the sleeper. There was nothing outwardly distinctive in the man. He wore the dress of the country folk, and the hat of the district, a three-cornered hat called a Brunswicker, stiff enough to turn a sword cut, and with a thick brass hat-band. The weight of the whole thing had turned his ears entirely down, like a fancy rabbit's in our century; but even this, though it spoiled him as a man, was nothing remarkable. They had of late met scores of these dog's-eared rustics. The peculiarity was—this clown watching under a laden gallows. What for?

Denys, if he felt curious, would not show it; he took out two bears' ears from his bundle, and, running sticks through them began to toast them. "'Twill be eating coined money," said he; "for the burgomaster of Dusseldorf had given us a rix-dollar for these ears, as proving the death of their owners; but better a lean purse than a lere stomach."

"Unhappy man!" cried Gerard, "could you eat food *here?*"

"Where the fire is lighted there must the meat roast, and where it roasts there must it be eaten; for nought travels worse than your roasted meat."

"Well, eat thou, Denys, an thou canst! but I am cold and sick; there is no room for hunger in my heart after what mine eyes have seen," and he shuddered over the fire; "oh! how they creak! and who is this man I wonder? what an ill-favoured churl!"

Denys examined him like a connoisseur looking at a picture; and in due course delivered judgment. "I take him to be of the refuse of that company, whereof these (pointing carelessly upward) were the cream, and so ran their heads into danger."

"At that rate, why not stun him before he wakes?" and Gerard fidgeted where he sat.

Denys opened his eyes with humorous surprise. "For one who sets up for a milksop you have the readiest hand. Why should two stun one? tush! he wakes: note now what he says at waking, and tell me."

These last words were hardly whispered when the watcher opened his eyes. At sight of the fire made up, and two strangers eyeing him keenly, he stared, and there was a severe and pretty successful effort to be calm; still a perceptible tremor ran all over him. Soon he manned himself, and said gruffly, "Good morrow." But, at the very moment of saying it, he missed his axe, and saw how Gerard was sitting upon it with his own laid ready to his hand. He lost countenance again directly. Denys smiled grimly at this bit of by-play.

"Good morrow!" said Gerard quietly, keeping his eye on him.

The watcher was now too ill at ease to be silent. "You make free with my fire," said he; but he added in a somewhat faltering voice, "you are welcome."

Denys whispered Gerard. The watcher eyed them askant.

"My comrade says, sith we share your fire, you shall share his meat."

"So be it," said the man, warmly. "I have half a kid hanging on a bush hard by, I'll go fetch it;" and he arose with a cheerful and obliging countenance, and was retiring.

Denys caught up his cross-bow, and levelled it at his head. The man fell on his knees.

Denys lowered his weapon, and pointed him back to his place. He rose and went back slowly and unsteadily, like one disjointed; and sick at heart as the mouse, that the cat lets go a little way, and then darts and replaces.

"Sit down, friend," said Denys grimly, in French.

The man obeyed finger and tone, though he knew not a word of French.

"Tell him the fire is not big enough for more than three. He will take my meaning."

This being communicated by Gerard, the man grinned; ever since Denys spoke he had seemed greatly relieved. "I wist not ye were strangers," said he to Gerard.

Denys cut a piece of bear's ear, and offered it with grace to him he had just levelled cross-bow at.

He took it calmly, and drew a piece of bread from his wallet, and divided it with the pair. Nay, more, he winked and thrust his hand into the heap of leaves he sat on (Gerard grasped his axe ready to brain him) and produced a leathern bottle holding full two gallons.

He put it to his mouth, and drank their healths then handed it to Gerard; he passed it untouched to Denys.

"Mort de ma vie!" cried the soldier "it is Rhenish wine, and fit for the gullet of an archbishop. Here's to thee, thou prince of good fellows, wishing thee a short life and a merry one! Come, Gerard, sup! sup! Pshaw, never heed them, man! they heed not thee. Natheless, did I hang over such a skin of Rhenish as this, and three churls sat beneath a drinking it and offered me not a drop I'd soon be down among them."

"Denys! Denys!"

"My spirit would cut the cord and womp would come my body amongst ye, with a hand on the bottle, and one eye winking, t'other—"

Gerard started up with a cry of horror and his fingers to his ears, and was running from the place, when his eye fell on the watcher's axe. The tangible danger brought him back. He sat down again on the axe with his fingers in his ears.

"Courage, l'ami, le diable est mort!" shouted Denys gaily, and offered him a piece of bear's ear, put it right under his nose as he stopped his ears. Gerard turned his head away with loathing. "Wine!" he gasped. "Heaven knows I have much need of it, with such companions as thee and—"

He took a long draught of the Rhenish wine: it ran glowing through his veins, and warmed and strengthened his heart; but could not check his tremors whenever a gust of wind came. As for Denys and the other, they feasted recklessly, and plied the bottle unceasingly, and drank healths and caroused beneath that creaking sepulchre and its ghastly tenants.

"Ask him how they came here," said Denys with his mouthful, and pointing up without looking.

On this question being interpreted to the watcher, he replied that treason had been their end, diabolical treason and priestcraft. He then, being rendered communicative by drink, delivered a long prosy narrative, the purport of which was as follows. These honest gentlemen who now dangled here so miserably, were all stout men and true, and lived in the forest by their wits. Their independence and thriving state excited the jealousy and hatred of a large portion of mankind; and many attempts were made on their lives and liberties; these the Virgin and their patron saints, coupled with their individual skill and courage, constantly baffled. But yester-eve a party of merchants came slowly on their mules from Dusseldorf. The honest men saw them crawling, and let them penetrate near a league into the forest, then set upon them to make them disgorge a portion of their ill-gotten gains. But, alas! the merchants were no merchants at all, but soldiers of more than one nation, in the pay of the Archbishop of Cologne; haubergeons had they beneath their gowns, and weapons of all sorts at hand; nathless, the honest men fought stoutly, and pressed the traitors hard, when lo! horsemen, that had been planted in ambush many hours before, galloped up, and with these new diabolical engines of war, shot leaden bullets and laid many an honest fellow low, and so quelled the courage of others that they yielded them prisoners. These, being taken red-handed, the victors, who with malice inconceivable had brought cords knotted round their waists, did speedily hang, and by their side the dead ones, to make the gallanter show. "That one at the end was the captain. He never felt the cord. He was riddled with broad arrows and leaden balls or ever they could take him: a worthy man as ever cried 'Stand and deliver!' but a little hasty, not much: stay! I forgot; he is dead. Very hasty, and obstinate as a pig. That one in the buff jerkin is the lieutenant, as good a soul as ever lived; he was hanged alive: This one here, I never could abide; no (not that one; that is Conrad my bosom friend); I mean this one right overhead in the chicken-toed shoon: you were always carrying tales, ye thief, and making mischief; you know you were; and sirs, I am a man that would rather live united in a coppice than in a forest with backbiters and tale-bearers; strangers, I drink to you." And so he went down the whole string, indicating with the neck of the bottle like a showman with his pole and giving a neat description of each, which though pithy was invariably false; for the showman had no real eye for character and had misunderstood every one of these people.

"Enough palaver!" cried Denys. "Marchons! Give me his axe: now tell him he must help you along."

The man's countenance fell, but he saw in Denys's eye that resistance would be dangerous; he submitted. Gerard it was who objected. He said, "Y pensez-vous? to put my hand on a thief, it maketh my flesh creep."

"Childishness! all trades must live. Besides I have my reasons. Be not you wiser than your elder."

"No. Only if I am to lean on him I must have my hand in my bosom, still grasping the haft of my knife."

"It is a new attitude to walk in; but please thyself."

And in that strange and mixed attitude of tender offices and deadly suspicion the trio did walk. I wish I could draw them: I would not trust to the pen.

The light of the watch-tower at Dusseldorf was visible as soon as they cleared the wood; and cheered Gerard. When, after an hour's march, the black outline of the tower itself and other buildings stood out clear to the eye, their companion halted and said gloomily, "You may as well slay me out of hand as take me any nearer the gates of Dusseldorf town."

On this being communicated to Denys, he said at once, "Let him go then, for in sooth his neck will be in jeopardy if he wends much further with us. Gerard acquiesced as a matter of course. His horror of a criminal did not in the least dispose him to active co-operation with the law. But the fact is, that at this epoch no private citizen in any part of Europe ever meddled with criminals but in self-defence, except by-the-by in England, which, behind other nations in some things, was centuries before them all in this.

The man's personal liberty being restored, he asked for his axe. It was given him. To the friends' surprise he still lingered. Was he to have nothing for coming so far out of his way with them?

"Here are two batzen, friend."

"And the wine, the good Rhenish?"

"Did you give aught for it?"

"Ay! the peril of my life."

"Hum! what say you, Denys?"

"I say it was worth its weight in gold. Here, lad, here be silver groshen, one for every acorn on that gallows tree: and here is one more for thee—who wilt doubtless be there in due season."

The man took the coins, but still lingered.

"Well? what now?" cried Gerard, who thought him shamefully overpaid already. "Do'st seek the hide off our bones?"

"Nay, good sirs; but you have seen to-night how parlous a life is mine. Ye be true men, and your prayers avail: give me then a small trifle of a prayer, an't please you; for I know not one."

Gerard's choler began to rise at the egotistical rogue; moreover, ever since his wound he had felt gusts of irritability. However, he bit his lip and said. "There go two words to that bargain; tell me first, is it true what men say of you Rhenish thieves, that ye do murder innocent and unresisting travellers as well as rob them?"

The other answered sulkily, "They you call thieves are not to blame for that; the fault lies with the law."

"Gramercy! so 'tis the law's fault that ill men break it?"

"I mean not so: but the law in this land slays an honest man an if he do but steal. What follows? he would be pitiful, but is discouraged herefrom: pity gains him no pity, and doubles his peril: an he but cut a purse his life is forfeit; therefore cutteth he the throat to boot to save his own neck: dead men tell no tales. Pray then for the poor soul, who by bloody laws is driven to kill or else be slaughtered; were there less of this unreasonable gibbeting on the high road, there should be less enforced cutting of throats in dark woods, my masters."

"Fewer words had served," replied Gerard, coldly; "I asked a question, I am answered," and, suddenly doffing his bonnet,

"'Obsecro Deum omnipotentem, ut, quâ cruce jam pendent isti quin-decim latrones fures et homicidæ, in eâ homicida fur et latro tu pependeris quam citissime, pro publica salute, in honorem justi Dei cui sit gloria, in æternum, Amen.'"

"And so good day."

The greedy outlaw was satisfied at last. "That is Latin," he muttered, "and more than I bargained for." So indeed it was.

And he returned to his business with a mind at ease. The friends pondered in silence the many events of the last few hours.

At last Gerard said, thoughtfully, "That she-bear saved both our lives—by God's will."

"Like enough," replied Denys; "and talking of that, it was lucky we did not dawdle over our supper."

"What mean you?"

"I mean they are not all hanged; I saw a refuse of seven or eight as black as ink around our fire."

"When? when?"

"Ere we had left it five minutes."

"Good heavens! And you said not a word."

"It would but have worried you, and had set our friend a look-ing back, and mayhap tempted him to get his skull split. All other danger was over; they could not see us, we were out of the moonshine and indeed, just turning a corner; ah! there is the sun; and here are the gates of Dusseldorf. Courage, l'ami; le diable est mort."

"My head! my head!" was all poor Gerard could reply.

So many shocks, emotions, perils, horrors, added to the wound, his first, had tried his youthful body and sensitive nature, too severely.

It was noon of the same day.

In a bedroom of "The Silver Lion" the rugged Denys sat anxious, watching his young friend.

And he lay raging with fever, delirious at intervals, and one word for ever on his lips:

"Margaret!—Margaret!—Margaret!"

CHAPTER XXVI

IT was the afternoon of the next day. Gerard was no longer light-headed, but very irritable, and full of fancies; and in one of these he begged Denys to get him a lemon to suck. Denys, who from a rough soldier had been turned by tender friendship into a kind of grandfather, got up hastily, and bidding him set his mind at ease, "lemons he should have in the twinkling of a quart pot," went and ransacked the shops for them.

They were not so common in the North as they are now, and he was absent a long while, and Gerard getting very impatient, when at last the door opened. But it was not Denys. Entered softly an imposing figure; an old gentleman in a long sober gown trimmed with rich fur, cherry-coloured hose, and pointed shoes, with a sword by his side in a morocco scabbard, a ruff round his neck not only starched severely, but treacherously stiffened in furrows by rebatoes, or a little hidden framework of wood; and on his head a four-cornered cap with a fur border; on his chin and bosom a majestic white beard. Gerard was in no doubt as to the vocation of his visitor, for, the sword excepted, this was as familiar to him as the full dress of a physician. Moreover a boy followed at his heels with a basket, where phials, lint and surgical tools rather courted than shunned observation. The old gentleman came softly to the bedside, and said mildly and sotto voce, "How is't with thee, my son?"

Gerard answered gratefully that his wound gave him little pain now; but his throat was parched, and his head heavy.

"A wound? they told me not of that. Let me see it. Ay, ay, a good clean bite. The mastiff had sound teeth that took this out, I warrant me": and the good doctor's sympathy seemed to run off to the quadruped he had conjured; his jackal.

"This must be cauterized forthwith, or we shall have you starting back from water, and turning somersaults in bed under our hands. 'Tis the year for raving curs, and one hath done your business; but we will baffle him yet. Urchin, go heat thine iron."

"But, sir," edged in Gerard, " 'twas no dog, but a bear."

"A bear! young man?" remonstrated the senior severely: "think what you say; 'tis ill jesting with the man of art who brings his grey hairs and long study to heal you. A bear quotha! Had you dissected as many bears as I, or the tithe, and drawn their teeth to keep your hand in, you would know that no bear's jaw ever made this foolish trifling wound. I tell you 'twas a dog, and, since you put me to it, I even deny that it was a dog of magnitude, but neither more nor less than one of these little furious curs that are so rife, and run devious, biting each manly leg, and laying its wearer low, but for me and my learned brethern, who still stay the mischief with knife and cautery."

"Alas sir! when said I 'twas a bear's jaw? I said, 'A bear': it was his paw, now."

"And why didst not tell me that at once?"

"Because you kept telling me instead."

"Never conceal aught from your leech, young man," continued the senior, who was a good talker, but one of the worst listeners in Europe. "Well, it is an ill business. All the horny excrescences of animals, to wit claws of tigers, panthers, badgers, cats, bears, and the like, and horn of deer, and nails of humans, especially children, are imbued with direst poison. Y'had better have been bitten by a cur, *whatever you may say,* than gored by bull or stag, or scratched by bear. However, shalt have a good biting cataplasm for thy leg; meantime keep we the body cool: put out thy tongue!

153

good!—fever. Let me feel thy pulse: good!—fever. I ordain flebotomy and on the instant."

"Flebotomy! that is blood-letting: humph? Well no matter, if 'tis sure to cure me; for I will not lie idle here." The doctor let him know that flebotomy was infallible; especially in this case.

"Hans, go fetch the things needful; and I will entertain the patient meantime with reasons."

The man of art then explained to Gerard that in disease the blood becomes hot and distempered and more or less poisonous: but, a portion of this unhealthy liquid removed, Nature is fain to create a purer fluid to fill its place. Bleeding therefore, being both a cooler and a purifier, was a specific in all diseases for all diseases were febrile, whatever empirics might say.

"But think not," said he warmly, "that it suffices to bleed: any paltry barber can open a vein (though not all can close it again). The art is to know what vein to empty for what disease. T'other day they brought me one tormented with earache. I let him blood in the right thigh and away flew his earache. By-the-by he has died since then. Another came with the toothache. I bled him behind the ear, and relieved him in a giffy. He is also since dead as it happens. I bled our bailiff between the thumb and forefinger for rheumatism. Presently he comes to me with a headache and drumming in the ears, and holds out his hand over the basin; but I smiled at his folly, and bled him in the left ankle sore against his will, and made his head as light as a nut."

Diverging then from the immediate theme after the manner of enthusiasts, the reverend teacher proceeded thus:—

"Know, young man, that two schools of art contend at this moment throughout Europe. The Arabian, whose ancient oracles are Avicenna, Rhazes, Albucazis; and its revivers are Chauliac and Lanfranc; and the Greek school, whose modern champions are Bessarion, Platinus, and Marsilius Ficinus, but whose pristine doctors were medicine's very oracles, Phœbus, Chiron, Æsculapius, and his sons Podalinus and Machaon, Pythagoras, Democritus, Praxagoras who invented the arteries, and Dioctes 'qui primus urinæ animum dedit.' All these taught orally. Then came Hippocrates, the eighteenth from Æsculapius, and of him we have manuscripts; to him we owe 'the vital principle.' He also invented the bandage, and tapped for water on the chest: and above all he dissected; yet only quadrupeds; for the brutal prejudices of the pagan vulgar withheld the human body from the knife of science. Him followed Aristotle, who gave us the aorta, the largest blood-vessel in the human body."

"Surely, sir, the Almighty gave us all that is in our bodies, and not Aristotle, nor any Grecian man," objected Gerard humbly.

"Child! of course He gave us the thing; but Aristotle did more, he gave us the name of the thing. But young men will still be talking. The next great light was Galen; he studied at Alexandria, then the home of science. He, justly malcontent with quadrupeds, dissected apes, as coming nearer to man: and bled like a Trojan. Then came Theophilus, who gave us the nerves, the lacteal vessels, and the pia mater."

This worried Gerard. "I cannot lie still and hear it said that mortal man bestowed the parts which Adam our father took from Him, who made him of the clay, and us his sons."

"Was ever such perversity?" said the doctor, his colour rising. "Who is the real donor of a thing to man? he who plants it secretly in the dark recesses of man's body, or the learned wight who reveals it to his intelligence, and so enriches his mind with the knowledge of it? Comprehension is your only true possession. Are you answered?"

"I am put to silence, sir."

"And that is better still: for garrulous patients are ill to cure, especially in fever: I say then that Eristratus gave us the cerebral nerves and the milk vessels; nay more, he was the inventor of lithotomy, whatever you may say. Then came another whom I forget: you do somewhat perturb me with your petty exceptions. Then came Ammonius the author of lithotrity, and here comes Hans with the basin—to stay your volubility. Blow thy chafer, boy, and hand me the basin; 'tis well. Arabians quotha! What are they but a sect of yesterday, who about the year 1000 did fall in with the writings of those very Greeks, and read them awry, having no concurrent light of their own? for their demigod, and cameldriver, Mahound, impostor in science as in religion, had strictly forbidden them anatomy even of the lower animals, the which he who severeth from medicine, 'tollit solem e mundo,' as Tully quoth. Nay, wonder not at my fervour, good youth. Where the general weal stands in jeopardy, a little warmth is civic, humane, and honourable; now there is settled of late in this town a pestilent Arabist, a mere empiric, who despising anatomy, and scarce knowing Greek from Hebrew, hath yet spirited away half my patients; and I tremble for the rest. Put forth thine ankle; and thou, Hans, breathe on the chafer."

Whilst matters were in this posture, in came Denys with the lemons, and stood surprised. "What sport is toward?" said he, raising his brows.

Gerard coloured a little and told him the learned doctor was going to flebotomize him and cauterize him; that was all.

"Ay! indeed; and yon imp, what bloweth he hot coals for?"

"What should it be for," said the doctor to Gerard, "but to cauterize the vein when opened, and the poisonous blood let free? 'Tis the only safe way. Avicenna indeed recommends a ligature of the vein; but how 'tis to be done he saith not, nor knew he himself I wot, nor any of the spawn of Ishmael. For me, I have no faith in such tricksy expedients: and take this with you for a safe principle! 'whatever an Arab or Arabist says is right, must be wrong.'"

"Oh, I see now what 'tis for," said Denys; "and art thou so simple as to let him put hot iron to thy living flesh? didst ever keep thy little finger but ten moments in a candle? and this will be as many minutes. Art not content to burn in purgatory after thy death? must thou needs buy a foretaste on't here?"

"I never thought of that," said Gerard gravely: "The good doctor spake not of burning, but of cautery; to be sure 'tis all one, but cautery sounds not so fearful as burning."

"Imbecile! That is their art; to confound a plain man with dark words, till his hissing flesh lets him know their meaning. Now listen to what I have seen. When a soldier bleeds from a wound in battle, these leeches say, 'Fever. Blood him!' and so they burn the wick at t'other end too. They bleed the bled. Now at fever's heels comes desperate weakness; then the man needs all his blood to live: but these prickers and burners, having no forethought, reck-ing nought of what is sure to come in a few hours, and seeing like brute beasts only what is under their noses, have meantime robbed him of the very blood his hurt had spared him to battle that weakness withal; and so he dies exhausted: hundreds have I seen so scratched, and pricked, out of the world, Gerard, and tall fellows too: but lo! if they have the luck to be wounded where no doctor can be had, then they live; this too have I seen. Had I ever outlived that field in Brabant but for my most lucky mischance, lack of chirurgery? The frost choked all my bleeding wounds and so I lived. A chirurgeon had pricked yet one more hole in this my body with his lance, and drained my last drop out, and my spirit with it. Seeing them thus distraught in bleeding of the bleeding soldier, I place no trust in them; for what slays a veteran may well lay a milk-and-water bourgeois low."

"This sounds like common sense," sighed Gerard languidly, "but no need to raise your voice so: I was not born deaf, and just now I hear acutely."

"Common sense! very common sense indeed," shouted the bad listener; "why this is a soldier; a brute whose business is to kill men, not cure them." He added in very tolerable French, "Woe be to you, unlearned man, if you come between a physician and his patient, and woe be to you, misguided youth, if you listen to that man of blood."

"Much obliged," said Denys with mock politeness; "but I am a true man, and would rob no man of his name. I do somewhat in the way of blood, but not worth mention in this presence. For one I slay, you slay a score, and for one spoonful of blood I draw, you spill a tubful. The world is still gulled by shows. We soldiers vapour with long swords: and even in war beget two foes for every one we kill; but you smooth gownsmen, with soft phrases and bare bodkins, 'tis you that thin mankind."

"A sick chamber is no place for jesting," cried the physician.

"No, doctor, nor for bawling," said the patient peevishly.

"Come, young man," said the senior kindly; "be reasonable! Cuilibet in suâ arte credendum est. My whole life has been given to this art. I studied at Montpelier; the first school in France and by consequence in Europe. There learned I Dririmancy, Scatomancy, Pathology, Therapeusis, and, greater than them all, Anatomy. For there we disciples of Hippocrates and Galen had opportunities those great ancients never knew. Good-bye, quadrupeds and apes, and Paganism, and Mohammedanism; we bought of the churchwardens, we shook the gallows; we undid the sexton's work o' dark nights, penetrated with love of science and our kind; all the authorities had their orders from Paris to wink; and they winked. Gods of Olympus, how they winked! The gracious king assisted us; he sent us twice a year a living criminal condemned to die, and said 'Deal ye with him as science asks: dissect him alive, if ye think fit.' "

"By the liver of Herod, and Nero's bowels, he'll make me blush for the land that bore me, an if he praises it any more," shouted Denys at the top of his voice.

Gerard gave a little squawk, and put his fingers in his ears; but speedily drew them out and shouted angrily, and as loudly, "You great, roaring, blaspheming, bull of Basan, hold your noisy tongue!"

Denys summoned a contrite look.

"Tush, slight man," said the doctor with calm contempt, and vibrated a hand over him as in this age men make a pointer dog down charge; then flowed majestic on. "We seldom, or never dissected the living criminal, except in part. We mostly inoculated them with such diseases as the barren time afforded, selecting of course the more interesting ones."

"That means the foulest," whispered Denys meekly.

"These we watched through all their stages, to maturity."

"Meaning the death of the poor rogue," whispered Denys meekly.

"And now, my poor sufferer, who best merits your confidence, this honest soldier with his youth, his ignorance, and his prejudices, or a greybeard laden with the gathered wisdom of ages?"

"That is," cried Denys impatiently, "will you believe what a jackdaw in a long gown has heard from a starling in a long gown, who heard it from a jay-pie, who heard it from a magpie, who heard it from a popinjay; or will you believe what I, a man with nought to gain by looking awry, nor speaking false, have seen; not heard with the ears which are given us to gull us, but seen with these sentinels mine eyne, seen, seen; to wit that fevered and blooded men die, that fevered men not blooded live? stay, who sent for this sang-sue? Did you?"

"Not I. I thought you had."

"Nay," explained the doctor, "the good landlord told me one was 'down' in his house: so I said to myself, 'a stranger, and in need of my art'; and came incontinently."

"It was the act of a good Christian, sir."

"Of a good bloodhound," cried Denys contemptuously. "What, art thou so green as not to know that all these landlords are in league with certain of their fellow-citizens, who pay them toll on each

The Cloister and the Hearth

booty? Whatever you pay this ancient for stealing your life blood, of that the landlord takes his third for betraying you to him. Nay, more, as soon as ever your blood goes down the stair in that basin there, the landlord will see it or smell it, and send swiftly to his undertaker and get his third out of that job. For if he waited till the doctor got down stairs, the doctor would be beforehand and bespeak *his* undertaker, and then *he* would get the black thirds. Say I sooth, old Rouge et Noir? dites!"

"Denys, Denys, who taught you to think so ill of man?"

"Mine eyes, that are not to be gulled by what men say, seeing this many a year what they do, in all the lands I travel."

The doctor with some address made use of these last words to escape the personal question. "I too have eyes as well as thou, and go not by tradition only, but by what I have seen, and not only seen but done. I have healed as many men by bleeding, as that interloping Arabist has killed for want of it. 'Twas but t'other day I healed one threatened with leprosy; I but bled him at the tip of the nose. I cured last year a quartan ague: how? bled its forefinger. Our curé lost his memory. I brought it him back on the point of my lance; I bled him behind the ear. I bled a dolt of a boy, and now he is the only one who can tell his right hand from his left in a whole family of idiots. When the plague was here years ago, no sham plague, such as empirics proclaim every six years or so but the good honest Byzantine pest, I blooded an alderman freely, and cauterized the symptomatic buboes, and so pulled him out of the grave: whereas our then chirurgeon, a most pernicious Arabist, caught it himself, and died of it, aha, calling on Rhazes, Avicenna, and Mahound, who, could they have come, had all perished as miserably as himself."

"Oh, my poor ears," sighed Gerard.

"And am I fallen so low that one of your presence and speech rejects my art, and listens to a rude soldier, so far behind even his own miserable trade as to bear an arbalest, a worn-out invention, that German children shoot at pigeons with, but German soldiers mock at since ever arquebusses came and put them down?"

"You foul-mouthed old charlatan," cried Denys, "the arbalest is shouldered by taller men than ever stood in Rhenish hose, and even now it kills as many more than your noisy, stinking arquebuss, as

159

the lancet does than all our toys together. Go to! He was no fool who first called you 'leeches.' Sang-sues! va!"

Gerard groaned. "By the holy virgin, I wish you were both at Jericho, bellowing."

"Thank you, comrade. Then I'll bark no more, but at need I'll bite. If he has a lance, I have a sword; if he bleeds you, I'll bleed him. The moment his lance pricks your skin, little one, my sword-hilt knocks against his ribs; I have said it."

And Denys turned pale, folded his arms, and looked gloomy and dangerous.

Gerard sighed wearily. "Now, as all this is about me, give me leave to say a word."

"Ay! let the young man choose life or death for himself."

Gerard then indirectly rebuked his noisy counsellers by contrast and example. He spoke with unparalleled calmness, sweetness, and gentleness. And these were the words of Gerard the son of Eli. "I doubt not you both mean me well: but you assassinate me between you. Calmness and quiet are everything to me; but you are like two dogs growling over a bone.

"And in sooth, bone I should be, did this uproar last long."

There was a dead silence, broken only by the silvery voice of Gerard, as he lay tranquil, and gazed calmly at the ceiling, and trickled into words.

"First, venerable sir, I thank you for coming to see me, whether from humanity, or in the way of honest gain; all trades must live.

"Your learning, reverend sir, seems great, to me at least, and for your experience, your age voucheth it.

"You say you have bled many, and of these many many have not died thereafter, but lived, and done well. I must needs believe you."

The physician bowed; Denys grunted.

"Others you say you have bled, and—they are dead. I must needs believe you.

"Denys knows few things compared with you, but he knows them well. He is a man not given to conjecture. This I myself have noted. He says he has seen the fevered and blooded for the most part die; the fevered and not blooded live. I must needs believe him.

"Here, then, all is doubt.

"But thus much is certain; if I be bled, I must pay you a fee, and be burnt and excruciated with a hot iron, who am no felon.

"Pay a certain price in money and anguish for a doubtful remedy, that will I never.

"Next to money and ease, peace and quiet are certain goods, above all in a sick-room; but 'twould seem men cannot argue medicine without heat and raised voices; therefore, sir, I will essay a little sleep, and Denys will go forth and gaze on the females of the place, and I will keep you no longer from those who can afford to lay out blood, and money, in flebotomy and cautery."

The old physician had naturally a hot temper; he had often during this battle of words mastered it with difficulty, and now it mastered him. The most dignified course was silence; he saw this, and drew himself up and made loftily for the door, followed close by his little boy and big basket.

But at the door he choked, he swelled, he burst. He whirled and came back open-mouthed, and the little boy and big basket had to whisk semicircularly not to be run down, for de minimis non curat Medicina—even when not in a rage.

"Ah! you reject my skill, you scorn my art. My revenge shall be to leave you to yourself; lost idiot, take your last look at me, and at the sun. Your blood be on your head!" And away he stamped.

But on reaching the door he whirled and came back; his wicker tail twirling round after him like a cat's.

"In twelve hours at furthest you will be in the secondary stage of fever. Your head will split. Your carotids will thump. Aha! And let but a pin fall you will jump to the ceiling. Then send for me: and I'll not come." He departed. But at the door-handle gathered fury, wheeled and came flying, with pale, terror-stricken boy and wicker tail whisking after him. "Next will come—CRAMPS of the STOMACH. Aha!

"Then—BILIOUS VOMIT. Aha!

"Then—COLD SWEAT, and DEADLY STUPOR.

"Then—CONFUSION OF ALL THE SENSES.

"Then—BLOODY VOMIT.

"And after that nothing can save you, not even I: and if I could I would not, and so farewell!"

Even Denys changed colour at threats so fervent and precise;

but Gerard only gnashed his teeth with rage at the noise, and seized his hard bolster with kindling eye.

This added fuel to the fire and brought the insulted ancient back from the impassable door, with his whisking train.

"And after that—MADNESS!

"And after that—BLACK VOMIT!

"And then—CONVULSIONS!

"And then—THAT CESSATION OF ALL VITAL FUNCTIONS THE VULGAR CALL 'DEATH,' for which thank your own Satanic folly and insolence, farewell." He went. He came. He roared, "And think not to be buried in any Christian churchyard; for the bailiff is my good friend, and I shall tell him how and why you died: felo de se! felo de se! Farewell."

Gerard sprang to his feet on the bed by some supernatural gymnastic power excitement lent him, and, seeing him so moved, the vindictive orator came back at him fiercer than ever, to launch some master-threat the world has unhappily lost: for as he came with his whisking train, and shaking his fist, Gerard hurled the bolster furiously in his face, and knocked him down like a shot, the boy's head cracked under his falling master's, and crash went the dumb-strickened orator into the basket; and there sat wedged in an inverted angle, crushing phial after phial. The boy, being light, was strewed afar; but in a squatting posture: so that they sat in a sequence like graduated specimens, the smaller howling. But soon the doctor's face filled with horror, and he uttered a far louder and unearthly screech, and kicked and struggled with wonderful agility for one of his age.

He was sitting on the hot coals.

They had singed the cloth and were now biting the man. Struggling wildly but vainly to get out of the basket, he rolled yelling over with it sideways, and lo! a great hissing: then the humane Gerard ran and wrenched off the tight basket not without a struggle. The doctor lay on his face groaning, handsomely singed with his own chafer, and slaked a moment too late by his own villainous compounds, which however, being as various and even beautiful in colour, as they were odious in taste, had strangely diversified his grey robe and painted it more gaudy than neat.

Gerard and Denys raised him up and consoled him. "Courage,

man, 'tis but cautery; balm of Gilead; why you recommended it but now to my comrade here."

The physician replied only by a look of concentrated spite, and went out in dead silence, thrusting his stomach forth before him in the drollest way. The boy followed him next moment, but in that slight interval he left off whining, burst in a grin, and conveyed to the culprits by an unrefined gesture his accurate comprehension of, and rapturous though compressed joy at, his master's disaster.

CHAPTER XXVII

THE worthy physician went home and told his housekeeper he was in agony from "a bad burn." Those were the words. For in phlogistic, as in other things, we cauterize our neighbour's digits, but burn our own fingers. His housekeeper applied some old woman's remedy mild as milk. He submitted like a lamb to her experience: his sole object in the case of this patient being cure: meantime he made out his bill for broken phials, and took measures to have the travellers imprisoned at once. He made oath before a magistrate that they, being strangers and indebted to him, meditated instant flight from the township.

Alas! it was his unlucky day. His sincere desire, and honest endeavour, to perjure himself, were baffled by a circumstance he had never foreseen nor indeed thought possible.

He had spoken the truth.

And IN AN AFFIDAVIT!

The officers, on reaching the Silver Lion, found the birds were flown.

They went down to the river, and, from intelligence they received there started up the bank in hot pursuit.

This temporary escape the friends owed to Denys's good sense and observation. After a peal of laughter, that it was a cordial to hear, and after venting his watchword three times, he turned short grave, and told Gerard Dusseldorf was no place for them. "That old fellow," said he, "went off unnaturally silent for such a babbler: we are strangers here: *the bailiff is his friend*: in five minutes we

shall lie in a dungeon for assulting a Dusseldorf dignity: are you
strong enough to hobble to the water's edge? it is hard by. Once
there you have but to lie down in a boat instead of a bed: and
what is the odds?"

"The odds? Denys? untold, and all in favour of the boat. I
pine for Rome: for Rome is my road to Sevenbergen: and then we
shall lie in the boat, but on the Rhine, the famous Rhine: the cool,
refreshing Rhine. I feel its breezes coming: the very sight will
cure a little hop-o'-my-thumb fever like mine; away! away!"

Finding his excitable friend in this mood, Denys settled hastily
with the landlord, and they hurried to the river. On inquiry they
found to their dismay that the public boat was gone this half-hour,
and no other would start that day, being afternoon. By dint however of asking a great many questions, and collecting a crowd, they
obtained an offer of a private boat from an old man and his two sons.

This was duly ridiculed by a bystander. "The current is too
strong for three oars."

"Then my comrade and I will help row," said the invalid.

"No need," said the old man. "Bless your silly heart, *he* owns
t'other boat."

There was a powerful breeze right astern; the boatmen set a
broad sail, and, rowing also, went off at a spanking rate.

"Are ye better, lad, for the river breeze?"

"Much better. But indeed the doctor did me good."

"The doctor? Why you would none of his cures."

"No, but I mean—you will say I am nought—but knocking the
old fool down—somehow—it soothed me."

"Amiable dove! how thy little character opens more and more
every day, like a rosebud. I read thee all wrong at first."

"Nay, Denys, mistake me not, neither. I trust I had borne with
his idle threats, though in sooth his voice went through my poor
ears: but he was an infidel, or next door to one, and such I have been
taught to abhor. Did he not as good as say, we owed our inward
parts to men with long Greek names, and not to Him, whose name
is but a syllable, but whose hand is over all the earth? Pagan!"

"So you knocked him down forthwith—like a good Christian."

"Now Denys, you will still be jesting. Take not an ill man's
part! Had it been a thunderbolt from Heaven, he had met but
his due; yet he took but a sorry bolster from this weak arm."

The Cloister and the Hearth

"What weak arm?" inquired Denys with twinkling eyes. "I have lived among arms, and by Samson's hairy pow never saw I one more like a catapult. The bolster wrapped round his nose and the two ends kissed behind his head, and his forehead resounded, and had he been Goliath, or Julius Cæsar, instead of an old quacksalver, down he had gone. St. Denys guard me from such feeble opposites as thou! and above all from their weak arms—thou diabolical young hypocrite."

The river took many turns, and this sometimes brought the wind on their side instead of right astern. Then they all moved to the weather side to prevent the boat heeling over too much; all but a child of about five years old, the grandson of the boatman, and his darling: this urchin had slipped on board at the moment of starting, and being too light to affect the boat's trim was above, or rather below, the laws of navigation.

They sailed merrily on, little conscious that they were pursued by a whole posse of constables armed with the bailiff's writ, and that their pursuers were coming up with them: for, if the wind was strong, so was the current.

And now Gerard suddenly remembered that this was a very good way to Rome but not to Burgundy. "Oh Denys," said he with an almost alarmed look, "this is not your road."

"I know it," said Denys quietly. "But what can I do? I cannot leave thee till the fever leaves thee: and 'tis on thee still; for thou art both red and white by turns; I have watched thee. I must e'en go on to Cologne I doubt, and then strike across."

"Thank Heaven," said Gerard, joyfully. He added eagerly with a little touch of self-deception, "'Twere a sin to be so near Cologne and not see it. Oh man, it is a vast and ancient city, such as I have often dreamed of, but ne'er had the good luck to see. Me miserable, by what hard fortune do I come to it now. Well then, Denys," continued the young man less warmly, "it is old enough to have been founded by a Roman lady in the first century of grace, and sacked by Attila the barbarous, and afterwards sore defaced by the Norman Lothaire. And it has a church for every week in the year, forbye chapels and churches innumerable of convents and nunneries, and above all the stupendous minster yet unfinished, and therein, but in their own chapel, lie the three kings that brought

165

gifts to our Lord, Melchior gold, and Gaspar frankincense, and Balthazar the black king, he brought myrrh: and over their bones stands the shrine the wonder of the world; it is of ever-shining brass brighter than gold, studded with images fairly wrought, and inlaid with exquisite devices, and brave with colours; and two broad stripes run to and fro of jewels so great so rare, each might adorn a crown or ransom its wearer at need: and upon it stand the three kings curiously counterfeited, two in solid silver richly gilt; these be bareheaded; but he of Æthiop ebony, and beareth a golden crown: and in the midst our blessed Lady in virgin silver, with Christ in her arms; and at the corners, in golden branches, four goodly waxen tapers do burn night and day. Holy eyes have watched and renewed that light unceasingly for ages, and holy eyes shall watch them in sæcula. I tell thee, Denys, the oldest song, the oldest Flemish or German legend, found them burning, and they shall light the earth to its grave. And there is St. Ursel's church, a British saint's, where lie her bones and all the other virgins her fellows: eleven thousand were they who died for the faith, being put to the sword by barbarous Moors, on the twenty-third day of October, two hundred and thirty-eight: their bones are piled in the vaults, and many of their skulls are in the church. St. Ursel's is in a thin golden case, and stands on the high altar, but shown to humble Christians only on solemn days."

"Eleven thousand virgins!" cried Denys. "What babies German men must have been in days of yore. Well: would all their bones might turn flesh again, and their skulls sweet faces, as we pass through the gates. 'Tis odds but some of them are wearied of their estate by this time."

"Tush, Denys!" said Gerard; why wilt thou, being good, still make thyself seem evil? If thy wishing-cap be on, pray that we may meet the meanest she of all those wise virgins in the next world: and, to that end, let us reverence their holy dust in this one. And then there is the church of the Maccabees, and the caldron, in which they and their mother Solomona were boiled by a wicked king for refusing to eat swine's flesh."

"O peremptory king! and pig-headed Maccabees! I had eaten bacon with my pork liever than change places at the fire with my meat."

"What scurvy words are these? it was their faith."

The Cloister and the Hearth

"Nay, bridle thy choler, and tell me, are there nought but churches in this thy so vaunted city? For I affect rather Sir Knight than Sir Priest."

"Ay marry, there is an university near a hundred years old; and there is a market place; no fairer in the world: and at the four sides of it houses great as palaces; and there is a stupendious senate-house all covered with images, and at the head of them stands one of stout Herman Gryn, a soldier like thyself, lad."

"Ay. Tell me of him! what feat of arms earned him his niche?"

"A rare one. He slew a lion in fair combat, with nought but his cloak and a short sword. He thrust the cloak in the brute's mouth, and cut his spine in twain, and there is the man's effigy and eke the lion's to prove it. The like was never done but by three more I ween; Samson was one, and Lysimachus of Macedon another, and Benaiah, a captain of David's host."

"Marry! three tall fellows. I would like well to sup with them all to-night."

"So would not I," said Gerard drily.

"But tell me," said Denys, with some surprise, "when wast thou in Cologne?"

"Never, but in the spirit. I prattle with the good monks by the way, and they tell me all the notable things both old and new."

"Ay, ay, have not I seen your nose under their very cowls? But when I speak of matters that are out of sight, my words they are small, and the thing it was big: now thy words be as big or bigger than the things; art a good limner with thy tongue; I have said it: and, for a saint, as ready with hand, or steel, or bolster—as any poor sinner living: and so, shall I tell thee which of all these things thou has described draws me to Cologne?"

"Ay, Denys."

"Thou, and thou only; no dead saint, but my living friend and comrade true; 'tis thou alone draws Denys of Burgundy to Cologne."

Gerard hung his head.

At this juncture one of the younger boatmen suddenly inquired what was amiss with "little turnip-face?"

His young nephew thus described had just come aft grave as a judge, and burst out crying in the midst without more ado. On

167

this phenomenon, so sharply defined, he was subjected to many interrogatories, some coaxingly uttered, some not. Had he hurt himself?
had he over-ate himself? was he frightened? was he cold? was he
sick? was he an idiot?

To all and each he uttered the same reply, which English writers
render thus, oh! oh! oh! and French writers thus, hi! hi! hi! So
fixed are Fiction's phonetics.

"Who can tell what ails the peevish brat?" snarled the young
boatman impatiently. "Rather look this way and tell me whom be
these after!" The old man and his other son looked, and saw four
men walking along the east bank of the river; at the sight they
left rowing awhile, and gathered mysteriously in the stern, whispering and casting glances alternately at their passengers and the pedestrians.

The sequel may show they would have employed speculation better
in trying to fathom the turnip-face mystery: I beg pardon of my age:
I mean "the deep mind of dauntless infancy."

"If 'tis as I doubt," whispered one of the young men, "why not
give them a squeak for their lives; let us make for the west bank."

The old man objected stoutly. "What," said he, "run our heads
into trouble for strangers? are ye mad? Nay, let us rather cross to
the east side: still side with the strong arm! that is my rede. What
say you, Werter?"

"I say, please yourselves."

What age and youth could not decide upon, a puff of wind settled
most impartially. Came a squall and the little vessel heeled over: the
men jumped to windward to trim her: but, to their horror, they saw
in the very boat from stem to stern a ditch of water rushing to lee-
ward, and the next moment they saw nothing, but felt the Rhine: the
cold and rushing Rhine.

"Turnip-face" had drawn the plug.

The officers unwound the cords from their waists.

Gerard could swim like a duck: but the best swimmer, canted out
of a boat capsized, must sink ere he can swim. The dark water
bubbled louder over his head, and then he came up almost blind and
deaf for a moment: the next he saw the black boat bottom uppermost,
and figures clinging to it; he shook his head like a water-dog and
made for it by a sort of unthinking imitation: but ere he reached it

he heard a voice behind him cry not loud but with deep manly distress, "Adieu, comrade, adieu!"

He looked, and there was poor Denys sinking, sinking, weighed down by his wretched arbalest. His face was pale, and his eyes staring wide, and turned despairingly on his dear friend. Gerard uttered a wild cry of love and terror, and made for him, cleaving the water madly; but the next moment Denys was under water.

The next, Gerard was after him.

The officers knotted a rope and threw the end in.

CHAPTER XXVIII

THINGS good and evil balance themselves in a remarkable manner; and almost universally. The steel bow attached to the arbalestrier's back, and carried above his head, had sunk him. That very steel bow, owing to that very position, could not escape Gerard's hands, one of which grasped it, and the other went between the bow and the cord; which was as good. The next moment, Denys, by means of his cross-bow, was hoisted with so eager a jerk that half his body bobbed up out of water.

"Now, grip me not! grip me not!" cried Gerard, in mortal terror of that fatal mistake.

"Pas si bête," gurgled Denys.

Seeing the sort of stuff he had to deal with, Gerard was hopeful and calm directly. "On thy back," said he sharply, and seizing the arbalest and taking a stroke forward he aided the desired movement. "Hand on my shoulder! slap the water with the other hand! No—with a downward motion: so. Do nothing more than I bid thee." Gerard had got hold of Denys's long hair, and twisting it hard, caught the end between his side teeth, and with the strong muscles of his youthful neck easily kept up the soldier's head, and struck out lustily across the current. A moment he had hesitated which side to make for, little knowing the awful importance of that simple decision; then, seeing the west bank a trifle nearest, he made towards it, instead of swimming to jail like a good boy, and so furnishing one a novel incident. Owing to the force of the current they slanted considerably, and, when they had covered near a hundred yards, Denys murmured uneasily, "How much more of it?"

"Courage," mumbled Gerard. "Whatever a duck knows, a Dutchman knows; art safe as in bed."

The next moment, to their surprise, they found themselves in shallow water; and so waded ashore. Once on terra firma, they looked at one another from head to foot as if eyes could devour, then by one impulse flung each an arm round the other's neck, and panted there with hearts too full to speak. And at this sacred moment life was sweet as heaven to both; sweetest perhaps to the poor exiled lover, who had just saved his friend. Oh, joy to whose height what poet has yet soared, or ever tried to soar? To save a human life: and that life a loved one. Such moments are worth living for, ay threescore years and ten. And then, calmer, they took hands, and so walked along the bank hand-in-hand like a pair of sweethearts, scarce knowing or caring whither they went.

The boat people were all safe on the late concave now convex craft. Herr Turnip-face, the "Inverter of things," being in the middle. All this fracas seemed not to have essentially deranged his habits. At least he was greeting when he shot our friends into the Rhine, and greeting when they got out again.

"Shall we wait till they right the boat?"

"No, Denys, our fare is paid; we owe them nought. Let us on, and briskly."

Denys assented, observing that they could walk all the way to Cologne on this bank.

"I fare not to Cologne," was the calm reply.

"Why, whither then?"

"To Burgundy."

"To Burgundy? Ah, no! that is too good to be sooth."

"Sooth 'tis; and sense into the bargain. What matters it to me how I go to Rome."

"Nay, nay; you but say so to pleasure me. The change is too sudden: and think me not so ill hearted as take you at your word. Also did I not see your eyes sparkle at the wonders of Cologne? the churches, the images, the relics—"

"How dull art thou, Denys; that was when we were to enjoy them together. Churches; I shall see plenty, go Romeward how I will. The bones of saints and martyrs; alas! the world is full of them: but a friend like thee, where on earth's face shall I find another? No, I will not turn thee farther from the road that leads to thy dear home, and her that pines for thee. Neither will I rob myself of thee by leaving thee. Since I drew thee out of Rhine I love thee better than I did. Thou art my pearl: I fished thee; and must keep thee. So gainsay me not, or thou wilt bring back my fever; but cry courage, and lead on; and hey for Burgundy!"

Denys gave a joyful caper. "Courage! va pour la Bourgogne. Oh! soyez tranquille! cette fois il est bien décidément mort, ce coquin là." And they turned their backs on the Rhine.

On this decision making itself clear, across the Rhine there was a commotion in the little party that had been watching the discussion, and the friends had not taken many steps, ere a voice came to them over the water. "HALT!"

Gerard turned, and saw one of those four holding out a badge of office and a parchment slip. His heart sank; for he was a good citizen, and used to obey the voice that now bade him turn again to Dusseldorf—the Law's.

Denys did not share his scruples. He was a Frenchman, and despised every other nation, laws, inmates and customs included. He was a soldier, and took a military view of the situation. Superior force opposed; river between; rear open; why, 'twas retreat made easy. He saw at a glance that the boat still drifted in mid stream, and there was no ferry nearer than Dusseldorf. "I shall beat a retreat to that hill," said he, "and then, being out of sight, quick step."

They sauntered off.

"Halt, in the bailiff's name!" cried a voice from the shore.

Denys turned round and ostentatiously snapped his fingers at the bailiff, and proceeded.

"Halt! in the archbishop's name."

Denys snapped his fingers at his grace, and proceeded.

"Halt! in the emperor's name."

Denys snapped his fingers at his majesty, and proceeded.

Gerard saw this needless pantomime with regret, and as soon as they had passed the brow of the hill said, "There is now but one course, we must run to Burgundy instead of walking;" and he set off, and ran the best part of a league without stopping.

Denys was fairly blown, and inquired what on earth had become of Gerard's fever. "I begin to miss it sadly," said he drily.

"I dropped it in Rhine, I trow," was the reply.

Presently they came to a little village, and here Denys purchased a loaf and a huge bottle of Rhenish wine. For he said "we must sleep in some hole or corner. If we lie at an inn we shall be taken in our beds." This was no more than common prudence on the old soldier's part.

The official network for catching law-breakers, especially plebeian ones, was very close in that age; though the co-operation of the public was almost null, at all events upon the Continent. The innkeepers were everywhere under close surveillance as to their travellers, for whose acts they were even in some degree responsible, more so it would seem than for their sufferings.

The friends were both glad when the sun set: and delighted, when after a long trudge under the stars (for the moon, if I remember right, did not rise till about 3 in the morning) they came to a large barn belonging to a house at some distance. A quantity of barley had been lately thrashed: for the heap of straw on one side the thrashing floor was almost as high as the unthrashed corn on the other.

"Here be two royal beds," said Denys, "which shall we lie on, the mow, or the straw?"

"The straw for me," said Gerard.

They sat on the heap, and ate their brown bread, and drank their wine, and then Denys covered his friend up in straw, and heaped it high above him, leaving him only a breathing-hole: "Water they say is death to fevered men; I'll make warm water on't any how."

Gerard bade him make his mind easy. "These few drops from Rhine cannot chill me. I feel heat enough in my body now to parch a kennel, or boil a cloud if I was in one." And with this epigram his consciousness went so rapidly he might really be said to "fall asleep."

Denys, who lay awake awhile, heard that which made him nestle closer. Horses' hoofs came ringing up from Dusseldorf, and the wooden barn vibrated as they rattled past howling in a manner too well known and understood in the 15th century, but as unfamiliar in Europe now as a red Indian's war-whoop.

Denys shook where he lay.

Gerard slept like a top.

It all swept by, and troop and howls died away.

The stout soldier drew a long breath; whistled in a whisper; closed his eyes; and slept like top 2.

In the morning he sat up and put out his hand to wake Gerard. It lighted on the young man's forehead, and found it quite wet. Denys then in his quality of nurse forbore to wake him. "It is ill to check sleep or sweat in a sick man," said he. "I know that far, though I ne'er minced ape nor gallows-bird."

After waiting a good hour, he felt desperately hungry: so he turned and in self-defense went to sleep again.

Poor fellow, in his hard life he had been often driven to this manœuvre. At high noon he was waked by Gerald moving, and found him sitting up with the straw smoking round him like a dunghill. Animal heat versus moisture. Gerard called him "a lazy loon." He quietly grinned.

They set out, and the first thing Denys did was to give Gerard his arbalest, etc., and mount a high tree on the road. "Coast clear to the next village," said he, and on they went.

On drawing near the village Denys halted and suddenly inquired of Gerard how he felt.

"What! can you not see? I feel as if Rome was no further than yon hamlet."

"But thy body, lad; thy skin?"

"Neither hot nor cold: and yesterday t'was hot one while and cold another. But what I cannot get rid of is this tiresome leg."

"Le grand malheur! Many of my comrades have found no such difficulty."

"Ah! there it goes again; itches consumedly."

"Unhappy youth," said Denys solemnly, "the sum of thy troubles is this: thy fever is gone, and thy wound is—healing. Sith so it is," added he indulgently, "I shall tell thee a little piece of news I had otherwise withheld."

"What is't?" asked Gerard sparkling with curiosity.

"THE HUE AND CRY IS OUT AFTER US: AND ON FLEET HORSES."

"Oh!"

CHAPTER XXIX

GERARD was staggered by this sudden communication; and his colour came and went. Then he clenched his teeth with ire. For men of any spirit at all are like the wild boar; he will run from a superior force; owing perhaps to his not being an ass: but if you stick to his heels too long, and too close, and, in short, bore him, he will whirl, and come tearing at a multitude of hunters, and perhaps bore you. Gerard then set his teeth and looked battle. But the next moment his countenance fell and he said plaintively, "And my axe is in Rhine."

They consulted together. Prudence bade them avoid that village: hunger said "buy food."

Hunger spoke loudest. Prudence most convincingly. They settled to strike across the fields.

They halted at a haystack and borrowed two bundles of hay, and lay on them in a dry ditch out of sight, but in nettles.

They sallied out in turn and came back with turnips. These they munched at intervals in their retreat until sunset.

Presently they crept out shivering into the rain and darkness, and got into the road on the other side of the village.

It was a dismal night, dark as pitch and blowing hard. They could neither see, nor hear, nor be seen nor heard: and for aught I know passed like ghosts close to their foes. These they almost forgot in the natural horrors of the black tempestuous night, in which they seemed to grope and hew their way as in black marble. When the moon rose they were many a league from Dusseldorf. But they still trudged on. Presently they came to a huge building.

"Courage!" cried Denys, "I think I know this convent. Ay, it is. We are in the see of Juliers. Cologne has no power here."

The next moment they were safe within the walls.

CHAPTER XXX

HERE Gerard made acquaintance with a monk, who had constructed the great dial in the prior's garden, and a wheel for drawing water, and a winnowing machine for the grain, &c.; and had ever some ingenious mechanism on hand. He had made several psalteries and two dulcimers, and was now attempting a set of regalles, or little organ for the choir.

Now Gerard played the humble psaltery a little: but the monk touched that instrument divinely, and showed him most agreeably what a novice he was in music. He also illuminated finely, but could not write so beautifully as Gerard. Comparing their acquirements with the earnestness and simplicity of an age in which accomplishments implied a true natural bent, Youth and Age soon became like brothers, and Gerard was pressed hard to stay that night. He consulted Denys, who assented with a rueful shrug.

Gerard told his old new friend whither he was going, and described their late adventures, softening down the bolster.

"Alack!" said the good old man, "I have been a great traveller in my day: but none molested me." He then told him to avoid inns; they were always haunted by rogues and roysterers, whence his soul might take harm even did his body escape; and to manage each day's journey so as to lie at some peaceful monastery; then suddenly breaking off and looking as sharp as a needle at Gerard, he asked him how long since he had been shriven? Gerard coloured up and replied feebly—

"Better than a fortnight."

"And thou an exorcist! No wonder perils have overtaken thee. Come, thou must be assoiled out of hand."

"Yes, father," said Gerard, "and with all mine heart;" and was sinking down to his knees, with his hands joined; but the monk stopped him half fretfully—

"Not to me! not to me! not to me! I am as full of the world as thou or any he that lives in't. My whole soul it is in these wooden pipes, and sorry leathern stops, which shall perish—with them whose minds are fixed on suchlike vanities."

"Dear father," said Gerard, "they are for the use of the Church, and surely that sanctifies the pains and labour spent on them?"

The Cloister and the Hearth

"That is just what the devil has been whispering in mine ear this while," said the monk, putting one hand behind his back and shaking his finger half threateningly, half playfully, at Gerard: "he was even so kind and thoughtful as to mind me that Solomon built the Lord a house with rare hangings, and that this in him was counted gracious and no sin. Oh! he can quote Scripture rarely. But I am not so simple a monk as you think, my lad," cried the good father with sudden defiance, addressing not Gerard but—Vacancy. "This one toy finished, vigils, fasts, and prayers for me; prayers standing, prayers lying on the chapel floor, and prayers in a right good tub of cold water." He nudged Gerard and winked his eye knowingly. "Nothing he hates and dreads like seeing us monks at our orisons up to our chins in cold water. For corpus domat aqua. So now go confess thy little trumpery sins, pardonable in youth and secularity, and leave me to mine, sweet to me as honey, and to be expiated in proportion."

Gerard bowed his head, but could not help saying, "Where shall I find a confessor more holy and clement?"

"In each of these cells," replied the monk, simply (they were now in the corridor): "there go to Brother Anselm, yonder."

Gerard followed the monk's direction and made for a cell; but the doors were pretty close to one another, and it seems he mistook: for just as he was about to tap, he heard his old friend crying to him in an agitated whisper, "Nay! nay! nay!" He turned, and there was the monk at his celldoor in a strange state of anxiety, going up and down and beating the air double-handed, like a bottom sawyer. Gerard really thought the cell he was at must be inhabited by some dangerous wild beast, if not by that personage, whose presence in the convent had been so distinctly proclaimed. He looked back inquiringly and went on to the next door. Then his old friend nodded his head rapidly, bursting in a moment into a comparatively blissful expression of face, and shot back into his den. He took his hourglass, turned it, and went to work on his regalles: and often he looked up, and said to himself, "Well-a-day, the sands how swift they run when the man is bent over earthly toys."

Father Anselm was a venerable monk, with an ample head, and a face all dignity and love. Therefore Gerard in confessing to him, and replying to his gentle though searching questions, could not help thinking, "here is a head!—Oh dear! oh dear! I wonder whether you will let me draw it when I have done confessing." And so his own head got confused, and he forgot a crime or two. However he did not lower the bolstering this time: nor was he so uncandid as to detract from the pagan character of the bolstered.

The penance inflicted was this: he was to enter the convent church, and prostrating himself, kiss the lowest step of the altar three times: then kneeling on the floor, to say three paternosters and a credo: "this done come back to me on the instant."

Accordingly, his short mortification performed, Gerard returned and found Father Anselm spreading plaster.

"After the soul the body," said he; "know that I am the chirurgeon here, for want of a better. This is going on thy leg; to cool it, not to burn it, the saints forbid."

During the operation, the monastic leech, who had naturally been interested by the Dusseldorf branch of Gerard's confession, rather sided with Denys upon "bleeding." "We Dominicans seldom let blood now-a-days; the lay leeches say 'tis from timidity and want of skill; but, in sooth, we have long found that simples will cure most of the ills that can be cured at all. Besides they never kill in capable hands; and other remedies slay like thunderbolts. As for the blood, the Vulgate saith expressly it is 'the life of a man.' And in medicine or law, as in divinity, to be wiser than the All-wise is to be a fool. Moreover, simples are mighty. The little four-footed creature that kills the poisonous snake, if bitten herself finds an herb powerful enough to quell that poison, though stronger and of swifter operation than any mortal malady; and we, taught by her wisdom, and our own traditions, still search and try the virtues of those plants the good Goth hath strewed this earth with some to feed men's bodies, some to heal them. Only in desperate ills we mix heavenly with earthly virtue. We steep the hair or the bones of some dead saint in the medicine, and thus work marvellous cures."

"Think you, father, it is along of the reliques? for Peter a Floris, a learned leech and no pagan, denies it stoutly."

"What knows Peter a Floris? And what know I? I take not on me to say we can command the saints, and, will they nill they, can draw corporal virtue from their blest remains. But I see that the patient drinking thus in faith is often bettered as by a charm. Doubtless faith in the recipient is for much in all these cures. But, so 'twas ever. A sick woman, that all the Jewish leeches failed to cure, did but touch Christ's garment and was healed in a moment. Had she not touched that sacred piece of cloth she had never been healed. Had she without faith not touched it only, but worn it to her grave, I trow she had been none the better for 't. But we do ill to search these things too curiously. All we see around us calls for faith. Have then a little patience! We shall soon know all. Meantime, I, thy confessor for the nonce, do strictly forbid thee on thy soul's health to hearken learned lay folk on things religious. Arrogance is their bane; with it they shut heaven's open door in their own faces. Mind I say learned laics. Unlearned ones have often been my masters in humility, and may be thine. Thy wound is cared for; in three days 'twill be but a scar. And now God speed thee, and the saints make thee as good, and as happy, as thou art beautiful and gracious." Gerard hoped there was no need to part yet; for he was to dine in the refectory. But Father Anselm told him, with a shade of regret just perceptible and no more, that he did not leave his cell this week, being himself in penitence, and, with this he took Gerard's head delicately in both hands, and kissed him on the brow: and almost before the cell door had closed on him, was back to his pious offices. Gerard went away chilled to the heart by the isolation of the monastic life: and saddened too. "Alas!" he thought, "here is a kind face I must never look to see again on earth; a kind voice gone from mine ear and my heart forever. There is nothing but meeting and parting in this sorrowful world. Well-a-day! well-a-day!" This pensive mood was interrupted by a young monk who came for him and took him to the refectory; there he found several monks seated at a table, and Denys standing like a poker, being examined as to the towns he should pass through: the friars then clubbed their knowledge, and marked out the route, noting all the religious houses on or near that road; and this they gave Gerard. Then supper, and after it the old monk carried Gerard to his cell, and they had an eager chat, and the friar incidentally revealed the cause of his pantomime in the corridor. "Ye had well-nigh fallen into Brother Jerome's clutches. Yon was his cell."

"Is Father Jerome an ill man, then?"

"An ill man?" and the friar crossed himself; "a saint, an anchorite, the very pillar of this house! He had sent ye barefoot to Lo-

The Cloister and the Hearth

retto. Nay, I forgot, y'are bound for Italy: the spiteful old—saint upon earth, had sent ye to Canterbory or Compostella. But Jerome was born old and with a cowl; Anselm and I were boys once; and wicked beyond anything you can imagine" (Gerard wore a somewhat incredulous look), "this keeps us humble more or less, and makes us reasonably lenient to youth and hot blood."

Then, at Gerard's earnest request, one more heavenly strain upon the psalterion, and so to bed, the troubled spirit calmed, and the sore heart soothed.

I have described in full this day, marked only by contrast, a day that came like oil on waves after so many passions and perils—because it must stand in this narrative as the representative of many such days which now succeeded to it. For our travellers on their weary way experienced that, which most of my readers will find in the longer journey of life, viz., that stirring events are not evenly distributed over the whole road, but come by fits and starts, and, as it were, in clusters. To some extent this may be because they draw one another by links more or less subtle. But there is more in it than that. It happens so. Life is an intermittent fever. Now all narrators whether of history or fiction, are compelled to slur these barren portions of time—or else line trunks. The practice however tends to give the unguarded reader a wrong arithmetical impression, which there is a particular reason for avoiding in these pages as far as possible. I invite therefore your intelligence to my aid, and ask you to try and realize that, although there were no more vivid adventures for a long while, one day's march succeeded another; one monastery after another fed and lodged them gratis with a welcome always charitable, sometimes genial; and, though they met no enemy but winter and rough weather, antagonist not always contemptible, yet they trudged over a much larger tract of territory than that, their passage through which I have described so minutely. And so the pair, Gerard bronzed in the face and travel-stained from head to foot, and Denys with his shoes in tatters, stiff and footsore both of them, drew near the Burgundian frontier.

CHAPTER XXXI

GERALD was almost as eager for this promised land as Denys; for the latter constantly chanted its praises, and at every little annoyance showed him "they did things better in Burgundy"; and above all played on his foible by guaranteeing clean bed-clothes at the inns of that polished nation. "I ask no more," the Hollander would say; "to think that I have not lain once in a naked bed since I left home! When I look at their linen, instead of doffing habit and hose, it is mine eyes and nose I would fain be shut of."

Denys carried his love of country so far as to walk twenty leagues in shoes that had exploded, rather than buy of a German churl, who would throw all manner of obstacles in a customer's way, his incivility, his dinner, his body.

Towards sunset they found themselves at equal distances from a little town and a monastery: only the latter was off the road. Denys was for the inn, Gerard for the convent. Denys gave way, but on condition that, once in Burgundy, they should always stop at an inn. Gerard consented to this the more readily that his chart with its list of convents ended here. So they turned off the road. And now Gerard asked with surprise hence this sudden aversion to places, that had fed and lodged them gratis so often. The soldier hemm'd and hawed at first; but at last his wrongs burst forth. It came out that this was no sudden aversion, but an ancient and abiding horror, which he had suppressed till now, but with infinite difficulty, and out of politeness: "I saw they had put powder in your drink," said he. "So I forbore them. However, being the last, why not ease my mind? Know then I have been like a fish out of water in all those great dungeons. You straightway levant with some old shaveling: so you see not my purgatory."

"Forgive me! I have been selfish."

"Ay, ay, I forgive thee, little one: 'tis not thy fault: art not the first fool that has been priest-rid, and monk-bit. But I'll not forgive *them* my misery." Then, about a century before Henry VIII.'s commissioners, he delivered his indictment. These gloomy piles were all built alike. Inns differed, but here all was monotony. Great gate, little gate, so many steps and then a gloomy cloister. Here the dortour, there the great cold refectory, where you must sit mumchance, or at least inaudible, he who liked to speak his mind out: "and then," said he, "nobody is a man here, but all are slaves, and of what? of a peevish, tinkling bell, that never sleeps. An 'twere a trumpet now, aye sounding alarums, 'twouldn't freeze a man's heart so. Tinkle, tinkle, tinkle, and you must sit to meat with maybe no stomach for food. Ere your meat settles in your stomach, tinkle, tinkle, and ye must to church with maybe no stomach for devotion: I am not a hog at prayers, for one. Tinkle, tinkle! and now you must to bed with your eyes open. Well, by then you have contrived to shut them, some uneasy imp of darkness has got to the bell-rope, and tinkle, tinkle, it behoves you to say a prayer in the dark, whether you know one or not. If they heard the sort of prayers I mutter when they break my rest with their tinkle! Well, you drop off again and get about an eyeful of sleep; lo, it is tinkle, tinkle, for matins."

"And the only clapper you love is a woman's," put in Gerard half contemptuously.

"Because there is some music in that even when it scolds," was the stout reply. "And then to be always checked. If I do but put my finger in the salt-cellar, straightway I hear, 'Have you no knife that you finger the salt?' And if I but wipe my knife on the cloth to save time, then 'tis, 'Wipe thy knife dirty on the bread, and clean upon the cloth!' Oh small of soul! these little peevish pedantries fall chill upon good fellowship like wee icicles a-melting down from strawen eaves."

"I hold cleanliness no pedantry," said Gerard. "Shouldst learn better manners once for all."

"Nay. 'Tis they who lack manners. They stop a fellow's mouth at every word."

"At every other word you mean; every obscene or blasphemous one."

"Exaggerator, go to! Why, at the very last of these dungeons, I found the poor travellers sitting all chilled and mute round one shaveling, like rogues awaiting their turn to be hanged: so to cheer them up, I did but cry out, 'Courage, tout le monde, le dia—'"

"Connu! what befell?"

"Marry, this. 'Blaspheme not!' quo' the bourreau. 'Plait-il,' say I. Doesn't he wheel and wyte on me in a sort of Alsatian French, turning all the 'P's' into 'B's.' I had much ado not to laugh in his face."

"Being thyself unable to speak ten words of *his* language without a fault."

"Well, all the world ought to speak French. What avail so many jargons except to put a frontier atwixt men's hearts?"

"But what said he."

"What signifies it what a fool says?"

"Oh, not all the words of a fool are folly: or I should not listen to you."

"Well, then, he said, 'such as begin by making free with the devil's name, aye end by doing it with all the names in heaven.' 'Father,' said I, 'I am a soldier, and this is but my "consigne" or watchword.' 'Oh, then, it is just a custom?' said he. I not divining the old fox, and thinking to clear myself, said, 'Ay, it was.' 'Then that is ten times worse,' said he. ' 'Twill bring him about your ears one of these days. He still comes where he hears his name often called.' Observe! no gratitude for the tidings which neither his missals nor his breviary had ever let him know. Then he was so good as to tell me, soldiers do commonly the crimes for which all other men are broke on the wheel; 'à savoir' murder, rape, and pillage."

"And is't not true?"

"True or not, it was ill manners," replied Denys, guardedly. "And so says this courteous host of mine, 'being the foes of mankind, why make enemies of good spirits into the bargain, by still shouting the names of evil ones?' and a lot more stuff."

"Well, but Denys, whether you hearken his rede, or slight it, wherefore blame a man for raising his voice to save your soul?"

"How can his voice save my soul, when a keeps turning of his 'P's' into 'B's'?"

Gerard was staggered: ere he could recover at this thunderbolt of Gallicism, Denys went triumphant off at a tangent, and stigmatized all monks as hypocrites. "Do but look at them, how they creep about and cannot eye you like honest men."

"Nay," said Gerard, eagerly, "that modest downcast gaze is part of their discipline, 'tis 'custodia oculorum.' "

"Cussed toads eating hoc hac horum? No such thing; just so

looks a cut-purse. Can't meet a true man's eye. Doff cowl, monk; and behold, a thief: don cowl thief, and lo, a monk. Tell me not they will ever be able to look God Almighty in the face, when they can't even look a true man in the face down here. Ah, here it is, black as ink! into the well we go, comrade. Miséricorde, there goes the tinkle already. 'Tis the best of tinkles though; 'tis for dinner: stay, listen! I thought so; the wolf in my stomach cried 'Amen!'" This last statement he confirmed with two oaths, and marched like a victorious gamecock into the convent, thinking by Gerard's silence he had convinced him, and not dreaming how profoundly he had disgusted him.

CHAPTER XXXII

IN the refectory allusion was made, at the table where Gerard sat, to the sudden death of the monk, who had undertaken to write out fresh copies of the charter of the monastery, and the rule, etc.

Gerard caught this, and timidly offered his services. There was a hesitation which he mistook. "Nay, not for hire, my lords, but for love, and as a trifling return for many a good night's lodging the brethren of your order have bestowed on me a poor wayfarer."

A monk smiled approvingly; but hinted that the late brother was an excellent penman, and his work could not be continued but by a master. Gerard, on this, drew from his wallet with some trepidation a vellum deed, the back of which he had cleaned and written upon by way of specimen. The monk gave quite a start at sight of it, and very hastily went up the hall to the high table, and bending his knee so as just to touch in passing the fifth step and the tenth, or last, presented it to the prior with comments. Instantly a dozen knowing eyes were fixed on it: and a buzz of voices was heard; and soon Gerard saw the prior point more than once, and the monk came back, looking as proud as Punch, with a savory crustade ryal, or game pie gravied and spiced, for Gerard, and a silver grace cup full of rich pimentum. This latter Gerard took, and bowing low, first to the distant prior, then to his own company, quaffed, and circulated the cup.

Instantly, to his surprise, the whole table hailed him as a brother:

"Art convent bred, deny it not?" He acknowledged it, and gave Heaven thanks for it, for otherwise he had been as rude and ignorant as his brothers, Sybrandt and Cornelis. "But, 'tis passing strange how you could know," said he.

"You drank with the cup in both hands," said two monks, speaking together.

The voices had for some time been loudish round a table at the bottom of the hall: but presently came a burst of mirth so obstreperous and prolonged, that the prior sent the very sub-prior all down the hall to check it, and inflict penance on every monk at the table. And Gerard's cheek burned with shame: for in the heart of the unruly merriment his ear had caught the word "courage!" and the trumpet tones of Denys of Burgundy.

Soon Gerard was installed in feu Werter's cell, with wax lights, and a little frame that could be set at any angle, and all the materials of caligraphy. The work however was too much for one evening. Then came the question, how could he ask Denys, the monk-hater, to stay longer? However he told him, and offered to abide by his decision. He was agreeably surprised when Denys said, graciously, "A day's rest will do neither of us harm. Write thou, and I'll pass the time as I may."

Gerard's work was vastly admired; they agreed that the records of the monastery had gained by poor Werter's death. The sub-prior forced a rix-dollar on Gerard, and several brushes and colours out of the convent stock, which was very large. He resumed his march warm at heart: for this was of good omen; since it was on the pen he relied to make his fortune and recover his well-beloved. "Come, Denys," said he, good humouredly, "see what the good monks have given me: now, do try to be fairer to them; for to be round with you, it chilled my friendship for a moment to hear even you call my benefactors 'hypocrites.'"

"I recant," said Denys.

"Thank you! thank you! Good Denys."

"I was a scurrilous vagabond."

"Nay, nay, say not so, neither!"

"But we soldiers are rude and hasty. I give myself the lie, and I offer those I misunderstood all my esteem. 'Tis unjust that thousands should be defamed for the hypocrisy of a few."

"Now are you reasonable. You have pondered what I said?"

"Nay, it is their own doing."

Gerard crowed a little, we all like to be proved in the right; and was all attention when Denys offered to relate how his conversion was effected.

"Well then, at dinner the first day, a young monk beside me did open his jaws and laughed right out most musically. 'Good,' said I, 'at last I have fallen on a man and not a shorn ape.' So, to sound him further, I slapped his broad back and administered my consigne. 'Heaven forbid!' says he. I stared. For the dog looked as sad as Solomon: a better mime saw you never, even at a Mystery. 'I see war is no sharpener of the wits,' said he. 'What are the clergy for but to fight the foul fiend? and what else are monks for?

> "The fiend being dead,
> The friars are sped."

You may plough up the convents and we poor monks shall have nought to do—but turn soldiers, and so bring him to life again.' Then there was a great laugh at my expense. 'Well, you are the monk for me,' said I. 'And you are the cross-bow-man for me,' quo' he. 'And I'll be bound you could tell us tales of the war should make our hair stand on end.' 'Excusez the barber has put that out of question,' quoth I, and then I had the laugh."

"What wretched ribaldry!" observed Gerard pensively.

The candid Denys at once admitted he had seen merrier jests hatched with less cackle. " 'Twas a great matter to have got rid of hypocrisy. 'So,' said I, 'I can give you the chare de poule, if that may content ye.' 'That we will see,' was the cry, and a signal went round."

Denys then related, bursting with glee, how at bedtime he had been taken to a cell instead of the great dortour, and strictly forbidden to sleep; and, to aid his vigil, a book had been lent him of pictures representing a hundred merry adventures of monks in pursuit of the female laity: and how in due course he had been taken out barefooted and down to the parlour, where was a supper fit for the duke, and at it twelve jolly friars, the roaringest boys he had ever met in peace or war. How the story, the toast, the jest, the wine cup had gone round, and some had played cards with a gorgeous pack, where Saint Theresa, and Saint Catharine, etc., bedizened with gold, stood for the four queens; and black, white, grey, and crutched friars for

the four knaves; and had staked their very rosaries, swearing like
troopers when they lost. And how about midnight a sly monk had
stolen out, but had by him and others been as cannily followed into
the garden, and seen to thrust his hand into the ivy and out with
a ropeladder. With this he had run up on the wall, which was ten
feet broad, yet not so nimbly but what a russet kirtle had popped up
from the outer world as quick as he: and so to billing and cooing:
that this situation had struck him as rather feline than ecclesiastical,
and drawn from him the appropriate comment of a "mew!" The
monks had joined the mewsical chorus, and the lay visitor shrieked
and been sore discomforted; but Abelard only cried "What, are ye
there, ye jealous miauling knaves? ye shall caterwaul to some tune
to-morrow night. I'll fit every manjack of ye with a fardingale."
That this brutal threat had reconciled him to stay another day—
at Gerard's request.

Gerard groaned.

Meantime, unable to disconcert so brazen a monk, and the demoiselle beginning to whimper, they had danced caterwauling in a circle, then bestowed a solemn benediction on the two wallflowers, and
off to the parlour, where they found a pair lying dead drunk, and
the other two affectionate to tears. That they had straightway carried off the inanimate, and dragged off the loving and lachrymose,
kicked them all merrily each into his cell,

> "And so shut up in measureless content"

Gerard was disgusted: and said so.

Denys chuckled, and proceeded to tell him how the next day he
and the young monks had drawn the fish-ponds and secreted much
pike, carp, tench, and eel for their own use: and how in the dead
of night he had been taken shoeless by crooked ways into the chapel,
a ghostlike place, being dark, and then down some steps into a
crypt below the chapel floor, where suddenly paradise had burst on
him.

"'Tis there the holy fathers retire to pray," put in Gerard.

"Not always," said Denys: "wax candles by the dozen were
lighted, and princely cheer; fifteen soups maigre, with marvellous
twangs of venison, grouse, and hare in them, and twenty different
fishes (being Friday), cooked with wondrous art, and each he between two buxom lasses, and each lass between two lads with a

cowl; all but me: and to think I had to woo by interpreter. I doubt the knave put in three words for himself and one for me: if he didn't, hang him for a fool. And some of the weaker vessels were novices, and not wont to hold good wine: had to be coaxed ere they would put it to their white teeth: mais elles s'y faisaient; and the story, and the jest, and the cup went round (by-the-by they had flagons made to simulate breviaries): and a monk touched the cittern, and sang ditties with a voice tuneable as a lark in spring. The posies did turn the faces of the women-folk bright red at first: but elles s'y faisaient." Here Gerard exploded.

"Miserable wretches! Corrupters of youth! Perverters of innocence! but for you being there, Denys, who have been taught no better, oh, would God the church had fallen on the whole gang. Impious, abominable, hypocrites!"

"Hypocrites?" cried Denys with unfeigned surprise. "Why that is what I clept them ere I knew them: and you withstood me. Nay, they are sinners; all good fellows are that: but, by St. Denys his helmeted skull, no hypocrites, but right jolly roaring blades."

"Denys," said Gerard solemnly; "you little know the peril you ran that night. That church you defiled amongst you is haunted: I had it from one of the elder monks. The dead walk there, their light feet have been heard to patter o'er the stones.

"Miséricorde!" whispered Denys.

"Ay, more," said Gerard, lowering his voice almost to a whisper, "celestial sounds have issued from the purlieus of that very crypt you turned into a tavern. Voices of the dead holding unearthly communion have chilled the ear of midnight, and at times, Denys, the faithful in their nightly watches have even heard music from dead lips; and chords, made by no mortal finger, swept by no mortal hand, have rung faintly, like echoes, deep among the dead in those sacred vaults."

Denys wore a look of dismay. "Ugh! if I had known, mules and wain-ropes had not hauled me thither; and so" (with a sigh) "I had lost a merry time."

Whether further discussion might have thrown any more light upon these ghostly sounds who can tell? for up came a "bearded brother" from the monastery, spurring his mule, and waving a piece of vellum in his hand. It was the deed between Ghysbrecht and Floris Brandt. Gerard valued it deeply as a remembrance of home:

he turned pale at first but to think he had so nearly lost it, and to Deny's infinite amusement not only gave a piece of money to the lay brother, but kissed the mule's nose.

"I'll read you now," said Gerard "were you twice as ill written; and—to make sure of never losing you"—here he sat down and taking out needle and thread sewed it with feminine dexterity to his doublet, and his mind, and heart, and soul were away to Sevenbergen.

They reached the promised land, and Denys, who was in high spirits, doffed his bonnet to all the females; who curtsied and smiled in return; fired his consigne at most of the men; at which some stared, some grinned, some both; and finally landed his friend at one of the long-promised Burgundian inns.

"It is a little one," said he, "but I know it of old for a good one; 'Les Trois Poissons.' But what is this writ up? I mind not this:" and he pointed to an inscription that ran across the whole building in a single line of huge letters. "Oh I see. 'Ici on loge à pied et à cheval,'" said Denys going minutely through the inscription, and looking bumptious when he had effected it.

Gerard did look, and the sentence in question ran thus—

"ON NE LOGE CÉANS À CRÉDIT: CE BONHOMME EST MORT, LES MAUVAIS PAIEURS L'ONT TUÉ."

CHAPTER XXXIII

THEY met the landlord in the passage.

"Welcome, messieurs," said he taking off his cap with a low bow.

"Come, we are not in Germany," said Gerard.

In the public room they found the mistress, a buxom woman of forty. She curtsied to them and smiled right cordially. "Give yourself the trouble of sitting ye down, fair sir," said she to Gerard, and dusted two chairs with her apron, not that they needed it.

"Thank you, dame," said Gerard. "Well," thought he, "this *is* a polite nation: the trouble of sitting down? That will I with singular patience; and presently the labour of eating, also the toil of digestion, and finally, by Hercules his aid, the strain of going to bed, and the struggle of sinking fast asleep."

"Why, Denys, what are you doing? ordering supper for only two?"

"Why not?"

"What can we sup without waiting for forty more? Burgundy for ever!"

"Aha! Courage, camarade. Le dia—"

"C'est convenu."

The salique law seemed not to have penetrated to French inns. In this one at least wimple and kirtle reigned supreme; doublets and hose were few in number and feeble in act. The landlord himself wandered objectless, eternally taking off his cap to folk for want of thought; and the women, as they passed him in turn, thrust him quietly aside without looking at him, as we remove a live twig in bustling through a wood.

A maid brought in supper, and the mistress followed her empty handed.

"Fall to, my masters," said she cheerily, "y'have but one enemy here; and he lies under your knife." (I shrewdly suspect this of formula.)

They fell to. The mistress drew her chair a little towards the table; and provided company as well as meat; gossiped genially with them like old acquaintances: but, this form gone through, the busy dame was soon off and sent in her daughter, a beautiful young woman of about twenty, who took the vacant seat. She was not quite so broad and genial as the elder, but gentle and cheerful, and showed a womanly tenderness for Gerard on learning the distance the poor boy had come, and had to go. She stayed nearly half an hour, and, when she left them, Gerard said, "This an inn? Why it is like home."

"Qui fit François il fit courtois," said Denys bursting with gratified pride.

"Courteous? nay, Christian; to welcome us like home guests and old friends, us vagrants, here to-day and gone to-morrow. But indeed who better merits pity and kindness than the worn traveller far from his folk? Hola! here's another."

The new comer was the chambermaid, a woman of about twenty-five, with a cocked nose, a large laughing mouth, and a sparkling black eye: and a bare arm very stout but not very shapely.

The moment she came in, one of the travellers passed a somewhat

The Cloister and the Hearth

free jest on her, the next the whole company were roaring at his expense, so swiftly had her practised tongue done his business. Even as, in a passage of arms between a novice and a master of fence, foils clash—novice pinked. On this another, and then another, must break a lance with her: but Marion stuck her great arms upon her haunches, and held the whole room in play. This country girl possessed in perfection that rude and ready humour, which looks mean and vulgar on paper but carries all before it spoken: not wit's rapier; its bludgeon. Nature had done much for her in this way, and daily practice in an inn the rest.

Yet shall she not be photographed by me, but feebly indicated: for it was just four hundred years ago, the raillery was coarse, she returned every stroke in kind, and, though a virtuous woman, said things without winking, which no decent man of our day would say even among men.

Gerard sat gaping with astonishment. This was to him almost a new variety of "that interesting species," homo. He whispered Denys, "Now I see why you Frenchmen say 'a woman's tongue is her sword'": just then she levelled another assailant; and the chivalrous Denys to console and support "the weaker vessel," the iron kettle among the clay pots, administered his consigne, "Courage, ma mie, le—" etc.

She turned on him directly. "How can *he* be dead as long as there is an archer left alive?" (General laughter at her ally's expense.)

"It is 'washing day' my masters," said she with sudden gravity.

"Après? We travellers cannot strip and go bare while you wash our clothes," objected a peevish old fellow by the fireside, who had kept mumchance during the raillery, but crept out into the sunshine of commonplaces.

"I aimed not your way, ancient man," replied Marion superciliously. "But, *since you ask me*" (here she scanned him slowly from head to foot), "I trow you might take a turn in the tub, clothes and all, and no harm done" (laughter). "But what I spoke for, I thought—this young sire—might like his beard starched."

Poor Gerard's turn had come: his chin crop was thin and silky.

The loudest of all the laughters this time was the traitor Denys, whose beard was of a good length, and singularly stiff and bristly:

The Cloister and the Hearth

so that Shakespeare, though he never saw him, hit him in the bull's
eye.

> "Full of strange oaths and bearded like the pard."
> *As You Like It.*

Gerard bore the Amazonian satire mighty calmly. He had little
personal vanity. "Nay, 'chambrière'" said he with a smile,
"mine is all unworthy your pains: take you this fair growth in
hand!" and he pointed to Denys's vegetable.

"Oh, time for that, when I starch the besoms."

Whilst they were all shouting over this palpable hit, the mistress
returned, and, in no more time than it took her to cross the threshold,
did our Amazon turn to a seeming Madonna meek and mild.

Mistresses are wonderful subjugators. Their like I think
breathes not on the globe. Housemaids, decide! It was a waste of
histrionic ability though; for the landlady had heard, and did not
at heart disapprove, the peals of laughter.

"Ah, Marion, lass," said she, good-humouredly, "If you laid me
an egg every time you cackle, 'Les Trois Poissons' would never lack
an omelet."

"Now, dame," said Gerard, "what is to pay?"

"What for?"

"Our supper."

"Where is the hurry? cannot you be content to pay when you
go? lose the guest, find the money, is the rule of 'The Three
Fish.'"

"But, dame, outside 'The Three Fish' it is thus written—'Ici—
on ne loge—'"

"Bah! Let that flea stick on the wall! Look hither," and she
pointed to the smoky ceiling, which was covered with hieroglyphics.
These were accounts, vulgo scores; intelligible to this dame and her
daughter, who wrote them at need by simply mounting a low stool,
and scratching with a knife so as to show lines of ceiling through
the deposit of smoke. The dame explained that the writing on the
wall was put there to frighten moneyless folk from the inn altogether,
or to be acted on at odd times when a nonpaying face should come
in and insist on being served. "We can't refuse them plump, you
know. The law forbids us."

"And how know you mine is not such a face?"

"Out, fie! it is the best face that has entered 'The Three Fish' this autumn."

"And mine, dame?" said Denys; "dost see no knavery here?"

She eyed him calmly. "Not such a good one as the lad's: nor ever will be. But it is the face of a true man. For all that," added she drily, "an I were ten years younger, I'd as lieve not meet that face on a dark night too far from home."

Gerard stared. Denys laughed. "Why, dame, I would but sip the night dew off the flower; and you needn't take ten years off, nor ten days, to be worth risking a scratched face for."

"There, our mistress," said Marion, who had just come in, "said I not t'other day, you could make a fool of them still, an if you were properly minded?"

"I dare say ye did: it sounds like some daft wench's speech."

"Dame," said Gerard, "this is wonderful."

"What? Oh: no, no, that is no wonder at all. Why, I have been here all my life: and reading faces is the first thing a girl picks up in an inn."

Marion.] "And frying eggs the second; no, telling lies; frying eggs is the third, though."

The Mistress.] "And holding her tongue the last, and modesty the day after never at all."

Marion.] "Alack! Talk of *my* tongue. But I say no more. She, under whose wing I live, now deals the blow. I'm sped— 'tis but a chambermaid gone. Catch what's left on't," and she staggered and sank backwards on to the handsomest fellow in the room, which happened to be Gerard.

"Tic! tic!" cried he, peevishly, "there, don't be stupid! that is too heavy a jest for me. See you not I am talking to the mistress?"

Marion resumed her elasticity with a grimace; made two little bounds into the middle of the floor and there turned a pirouette. "There, mistress," said she, "I give in, 'tis you that reigns supreme with the men; leastways with male children."

"Young man," said the mistress, "this girl is not so stupid as her deportment: in reading of faces, and frying of omelets, there we are great. 'Twould be hard if we failed at these arts, since they are about all we do know."

"You do not quite take me, dame," said Gerard. "That honesty in a face should shine forth to your experienced eye, that seems rea-

192

The Cloister and the Hearth

sonable: but how by looking on Denys here could you learn his one little foible, his insanity, his miserable mulierosity?" Poor Gerard got angrier the more he thought of it.

"His mule—his what?" (crossing herself with superstitious awe at the polysyllable).

"Nay, 'tis but the word I was fain to invent for him."

"Invent? What can a child like you make other words than grow in Burgundy by nature? Take heed what ye do! why we are over-run with them already, especially bad ones. Lord, these be times. I look to hear of a new thistle invented next."

"But, dame, I found language too poor to paint him. I was fain to invent. You know Necessity is the mother of—"

"Ay! ay, that is old enough, o' conscience."

"Well then, dame, mulierose—that means wrapped up, body and soul, in women. So prithee tell me; how did you ever detect the noodle's mulierosity?"

"Alas! good youth, you make a mountain of a molehill. We that are women be notice-takers; and out of the tail of our eye see more than most men can, glaring through a prospect glass. Whiles I move to and fro doing this and that, my glance is still on my guests, and I did notice that this soldier's eyes were never off the women-folk: my daughter, or Marion, or even an old woman like me, all was gold to him: and there a sat glowering; oh you foolish, foolish, man! Now *you* still turned to the speaker, her or him, and that is common sense."

Denys burst into a hoarse laugh. "You never were more out. Why this silky smooth-faced companion is a very Turk—all but his beard. He is what d'ye call 'em oser than ere an archer in the duke's body guard. He is more wrapped up in one single Dutch lass called Margaret than I am in the whole bundle of ye brown and fair."

"Man alive, that is just the contrary," said the hostess. "Yourn is the bane, and hisn the cure. Cling you still to Margaret, my dear. I hope she is an honest girl."

"Dame, she is an angel."

"Ay, ay, they are all that till better acquainted. I'd as lieve have her no more than honest, and then she will serve to keep you out of worse company. As for you, soldier, there is trouble in store for you. Your eyes were never made for the good of your soul."

"Nor of his pouch either," said Marion striking in, "and his lips they will sip the dew, as he calls it, off many a bramble bush."

"Overmuch clack! Marion; overmuch clack."

"Ods bodikins, mistress; ye didn't hire me to be one o' your three fishes, did ye?" and Marion sulked thirty seconds.

"Is that the way to speak to our mistress?" remonstrated the landlord, who had slipped in.

"Hold your whisht," said his wife sharply, "it is not your business to check the girl, she is a good servant to you."

"What is the cock never to crow, and the hens at it all day?"

"You can crow as loud as you like, my man—out o' doors. But the hen means to rule the roost."

"I know a byword to that tune," said Gerard.

"Do ye now? out wi't then."

> " 'Femme veut en toute saison,
> Estre dame en sa maison.' "

"I never heard it afore: but 'tis as sooth as gospel. Ay they that set these bywords a rolling had eyes and tongues, and tongues and eyes. Before all the world give me an old saw."

"And me a young husband," said Marion. "Now there was a chance for you all, and nobody spoke. Oh! it is too late now. I've changed my mind."

"All the better for some poor fellow," suggested Denys.

And now the arrival of the young mistress, or, as she was called, the little mistress, was the signal for them all to draw round the fire, like one happy family, travellers, host, hostess, and even servants in the outer ring, and tell stories till bedtime. And Gerard in his turn told a tremendous one out of his repertory, a MS. collection of "acts of the saints," and made them all shudder deliciously; but soon after began to nod; exhausted by the effort I should say. The young mistress saw, and gave Marion a look. She instantly lighted a rush, and laying her hand on Gerard's shoulder invited him to follow her. She showed him a room where were two nice white beds, and bade him choose. "Either is paradise," said he. "I'll take this one. Do you know, I have not lain in a naked bed once since I left my home in Holland."

"Alack! poor soul!" said she; "well then the sooner my flax and your down (he! he!) come together, the better; so—allons!" and she held out her cheek as business-like as if it had been her hand for a fee.

"Allons? what does that mean?"

"It means 'good-night.' Ahem! What don't they salute the chambermaid in your part?"

"Not all in a moment."

"What, do they make a business on't?"

"Nay, perverter of words, I mean we make not so free with strange women."

"They must be strange women if they do not think you strange fools then. Here is a coil. Why all the old greasy greybeards, that lie at our inn, do kiss us chambermaids; faugh! and what have we poor wretches to set on t'other side the compt, but now and then a nice young—? Alack! time flies, chambermaids can't be spared long in the nursery; so how is't to be?"

"An't please you arrange with my comrade for both. He is mulierose; I am not."

"Nay 'tis the curb he will want, not the spur. Well! well! you shall to bed without paying the usual toll; and oh but 'tis sweet to fall in with a young man, who can withstand these ancient ill customs, and gainsay brazen hussies. Shalt have thy reward."

"Thank you! But what are you doing with my bed?"

"Me? oh only taking off these sheets, and going to put on the pair the drunken miller slept in last night."

"Oh no! no! You cruel, black-hearted thing! There! there!"

"A la bonne heure! What will not perseverance effect? But note now the frowardness of a mad wench! I cared not for't a button. I am dead sick of that sport this five years. But you denied me: so then forthwith I behoved to have it; belike had gone through fire and water for't. Alas, young sir, we women are kittle cattle; poor perverse toads: excuse us: and keep us in our place, savoir, at arm's length! and so good-night!"

At the door she turned and said with a complete change of tone and manner: "The Virgin guard thy head, and the Holy Evangelists watch the bed where lies a poor young wanderer far from home! Amen!"

And the next moment he heard her run tearing down the stairs,

The Cloister and the Hearth

and soon a peal of laughter from the salle betrayed her whereabouts.

"Now that is a character," said Gerard profoundly; and yawned over the discovery.

In a very few minutes he was in a dry bath of cold, clean, linen, inexpressibly refreshing to him after so long disuse: then came a delicious glow: and then—Sevenbergen.

In the morning Gerard awoke infinitely refreshed, and was for rising, but found himself a close prisoner. His linen had vanished. Now this was paralysis; for the night-gown is a recent institution. In Gerard's century, and indeed long after, men did not play fast and loose with clean sheets (when they could get them), but crept into them clothed with—their innocence, like Adam: out of bed they seem to have taken most after his eldest son.

Gerard bewailed his captivity to Denys; but that instant the door opened, and in sailed Marion with their linen, newly washed and ironed, on her two arms, and set it down on the table.

"Oh you good girl," cried Gerard.

"Alack, have you found me out at last?"

"Yes indeed. Is this another *custom?*"

"Nay, not to take them unbidden: but at night we aye question travellers, are they for linen washed. So I came in to you: but you were both sound. Then said I to the little mistress, 'La! where is the sense of waking wearied men, t'ask them is Charles the Great dead, and would they liever carry foul linen or clean, especially this one with a skin like cream.' 'And so he has, I declare,' said the young mistress."

"That was me," remarked Denys with the air of a commentator.

"Guess once more, and you'll hit the mark."

"Notice him not, Marion; he is an impudent fellow; and I am sure we cannot be grateful enough for your goodness, and I am sorry I ever refused you—anything you fancied you should like."

"Oh, are ye there," said l'espiègle. "I take that to mean you would fain brush the morning dew off, as your bashful companion calls it; well then, excuse me, 'tis *customary,* but not prudent. I decline. Quits with you, lad."

"Stop! stop!" cried Denys as she was making off victorious, I am curious to know how many of ye were here last night a-feasting your eyes on us twain.'"

" 'Twas so satisfactory a feast as we weren't half a minute o'er't. Who? why the big mistress, the little mistress, Janet and me, and the whole posse comitatus, on tiptoe. We mostly make our rounds, the last thing not to get burned down; and in prodigious numbers. Somehow that maketh us bolder, especially where archers lie scattered about."

"Why did not you tell me? I'd have lain awake."

"Beau sire, the saying goes that the good and the ill are all one while their lids are closed. So we said 'Here is one, who will serve God best asleep. Break not his rest!' "

"She is funny," said Gerard dictatorially.

"I must be either that or knavish."

"How so?"

"Because 'The Three Fish' pay me to be funny. You will eat before you part? Good! then I'll go see the meat be fit for such worshipful teeth."

"Denys!"

"What is your will?"

"I wish that was a great boy, and going along with us, to keep us cheery."

"So do not I. But I wish it was going along with us as it is."

"Now Heaven forfend! A fine fool you would make of yourself."

They broke their fast, settled their score, and said farewell. Then it was they found Marion had not exaggerated the "custom of the country." The three principal women took and kissed them right heartily, and they kissed the three principal women. The landlord took and kissed them, and they kissed the landlord; and the cry was "Come back, the sooner the better!"   !

"Never pass 'The Three Fish;' should your purses be void, bring yourselves: 'le sieur crédit' is not dead for you."

And they took the road again.

They came to a little town, and Denys went to buy shoes. The shopkeeper was in the doorway, but wide awake, He received Denys with a bow down to the ground. The customer was soon fitted, and followed to the street, and dismissed with graceful salutes from the doorstep.

The friends agreed it was Elysium to deal with such a shoemaker as this. "Not but what my German shoes have lasted well enough," said Gerard the just.

Outside the town was a pebbled walk.

"This is to keep the burghers' feet dry, a-walking o' Sundays with their wives and daughters," said Denys.

Those simple words of Denys, one stroke of a careless tongue, painted "home" in Gerard's heart. "Oh! how sweet," said he. "Mercy! what is this? A gibbet; and ugh, two skeletons thereon! Oh, Denys, what a sorry sight to woo by!"

"Nay," said Denys, "a comfortable sight; for every rogue i' the air there is one the less a-foot."

A little farther on they came to two pillars, and between these was a huge wheel closely studded with iron prongs; and entangled in these were bones and fragments of cloth miserably dispersed over the wheel.

Gerard hid his face in his hands. "Oh to think those patches and bones are all that is left of a man! Of one who was what we are now."

"Excusez! a thing that went on two legs and stole; are we no more than that?"

"How know ye he stole? Have true men never suffered death and torture too?"

"None of my kith ever found the way to the gibbet, I know."

"The better their luck. Prithee how died the saints?"

"Hard. But not in Burgundy."

"Ye massacred them wholesale at Lyons, and that is on Burgundy's threshold. To you the gibbet proves the crime; because you read not story. Alas! had you stood on Calvary that bloody day we sigh for to this hour, I tremble to think you had perhaps shouted for joy at the gibbet builded there; for the cross was but the Roman gallows, Father Martin says."

"The blaspheming old hound!"

"Oh fie! fie! a holy and a book-learned man. Ay, Denys, y'had read them, that suffered there, by the bare light of the gibbet. 'Drive in the nails!' y'had cried: 'drive in the spear! Here be three malefactors. Three "roués."' Yet of those little three one was the first Christian saint, and another was the Saviour of the world which gibbeted him."

Denys assured him on his honour they managed things better in Burgundy. He added too after profound reflection, that the horrors Gerard had alluded to had more than once made him curse and swear with rage when told by the good curé in his native village at Easter-tide; "but they chanced in an outlandish nation; and near a thousand years agone. Mort de ma vie, let us hope it is not true: or at least sore exaggerated. Do but see how all tales gather as they roll!"

Then he reflected again, and all in a moment turned red with ire. "Do ye not blush to play with your book-craft on your unlettered friend, and throw dust in his eyes, evening the saints with these reptiles?"

Then suddenly he recovered his good humour. "Since your heart beats for vermin, feel for the carrion crows! they be as good vermin as these: would ye send them to bed supperless, poor pretty poppets? Why, these be their larder: the pangs of hunger would gnaw them dead, but for cold cutpurse hung up here and there."

Gerard, who had for some time maintained a dead silence, informed him the subject was closed between them and for ever. "There are things," said he, "in which our hearts seem wide as the poles asunder, and eke our heads. But I love thee dearly all the same," he added with infinite grace and tenderness.

Towards afternoon they heard a faint wailing noise on ahead: it grew distincter as they proceeded. Being fast walkers they soon came up with its cause: a score of pikemen, accompanied by several constables, were marching along, and in advance of them was a herd of animals they were driving. These creatures, in number rather more than a hundred, were of various ages, only very few were downright old: the males were downcast and silent. It was the females from whom all the outcry came. In other words the animals thus driven along at the law's point were men and women.

"Good Heaven!" cried Gerard. "What a band of them! But stay, surely all those children cannot be thieves: why there are some in arms. What on earth is this, Denys?"

Denys advised him to ask that "bourgeois" with the badge. "This is Burgundy: here a civil question ever draws a civil reply."

Gerard went up to the officer and removing his cap, a civility which was immediately returned, said, "For our Lady's sake, sir, what do ye with these poor folk?"

"Nay, what is that to you, my lad?" replied the functionary suspiciously.

"Master, I'm a stranger, and athirst for knowledge."

"That is another matter. What are we doing? ahem. Why we —Dost hear, Jacques? Here is a stranger seeks to know what we are doing," and the two machines were tickled that there should be a man who did not know something they happened to know. In all ages this has tickled. However the chuckle was brief, and moderated by their native courtesy, and the official turned to Gerard again. "What we are doing? hum!" and now he hesitated not from any doubt as to what he was doing, but because he was hunting for a single word that should convey the matter.

"Ce que nous faisons, mon gars?—Mais—dam—NOUS TRANSVASONS."

"You decant? that should mean you pour from one vessel to another."

"Precisely." He explained that last year the town of Charmes had been sore thinned by a pestilence, whole houses emptied and trades short of hands. Much ado to get in the rye; and the flax half spoiled. So the bailiff and aldermen had written to the duke's secretary; and the duke he sent far and wide to know what town was too full. "That are we," had the baillie of Toul writ back. "Then send four or five score of your townsfolk," was the order. "Was not this to decant the full town into the empty, and is not the good duke the father of his people, and will not let the duchy be weakened, nor its fair towns laid waste, by sword nor pestilence; but meets the one with pike, and arbalest (touching his cap to the sergeant and Denys alternately), and t'other with policy? LONG LIVE THE DUKE!"

The pikemen of course were not to be outdone in loyalty: so they shouted with stentorian lungs "LONG LIVE THE DUKE!" Then the decanted ones, partly because loyalty was a nonreasoning sentiment in those days, partly perhaps because they feared some further ill consequence should they alone be mute, raised a feeble tremulous shout "Long live the Duke!"

But, at this, insulted nature rebelled. Perhaps indeed the sham sentiment drew out the real, for, on the very heels of that loyal noise, a loud and piercing wail burst from every woman's bosom and a deep groan from every man's; oh! the air filled in a moment with womanly and manly anguish. Judge what it must have been when the rude pikemen halted unbidden, all confused; as if a wall of sorrow had started up before them.

"En avant," roared the sergeant, and they marched again, but muttering and cursing.

"Ah the ugly sound," said the civilian, wincing. "Les malheureux!" cried he ruefully: for where is the single man can hear the sudden agony of a multitude and not be moved? "Les ingrats! They are going whence they were de trop to where they will be welcome: from starvation to plenty—and they object. They even make dismal noises. One would think we were thrusting them forth from Burgundy."

"Come away," whispered Gerard, trembling; "come away," and the friends strode forward.

When they passed the head of the column, and saw the men walk with their eyes bent in bitter gloom upon the ground, and the women, some carrying, some leading, little children, and weeping as they went, and the poor bairns, some frolicking, some weeping because "their mammies" wept, Gerard tried hard to say a word of comfort, but choked and could utter nothing to the mourners; but gasped: "Come on, Denys. I cannot mock such sorrow with little words of comfort." And now, artist-like, all his aim was to get swiftly out of the grief he could not soothe. He almost ran not to hear these sighs and sobs.

"Why, mate," said Denys, "art the colour of a lemon. Man alive, take not other folks' troubles to heart! not one of those whining milksops there but would see thee, a stranger, hanged without winking."

Gerard scarce listened to him.

"Decant them?" he groaned: "ay, if blood were no thicker than wine. Princes, ye are wolves. Poor things! Poor things! Ah, Denys! Denys! with looking on their grief mine own comes home to me. Well-a-day. Ah, well-a-day!"

"Ay, now you talk reason. That you, poor lad, should be driven all the way from Holland to Rome, is pitiful indeed. But these snivelling curs, where is their hurt? There is six score of 'em to keep one another company: besides they are not going out of Burgundy."

"Better for them if they had never been in it."

The Cloister and the Hearth

"Méchant, va! they are but going from one village to another, a mule's journey! whilst thou—there, no more. Courage, camarade, le diable est mort."

Gerard shook his head very doubtfully, but kept silence for about a mile, and then he said thoughtfully, "Ay, Denys, but then I am sustained by book-learning. These are simple folk that likely thought their village was the world: now what is this? more weeping. Oh! 'tis a sweet world. Humph? A little girl that hath broke her pipkin. Now may I hang on one of your gibbets but I'll dry somebody's tears:" and he pounced savagely upon this little martyr, like a kite on a chick, but with more generous intentions. It was a pretty little lass of about twelve: the tears were raining down her two peaches, and her palms lifted to heaven in that utter, though temporary, desolation, which attends calamity at twelve; and at her feet the fatal cause, a broken pot, worth, say the fifth of a modern farthing.

"What, hast broken thy pot, little one?" said Gerard, acting intensest sympathy.

"Hélas! bel gars; as you behold;" and the hands came down from the sky and both pointed at the fragments. A statuette of adversity.

"And you weep so for that?"

"Needs I must, bel gars. My mammy will massacre me. Do they not already" (with a fresh burst of woe) "c-c-call me J-J-Jean-net-on C-c-casse tout? It wanted but this; that I should break my poor pot. Hélas! fallait-il donc, mère de Dieu?"

"Courage, little love," said Gerard: 'tis not thy heart lies broken; money will soon mend pots. See now, here is a piece of silver, and there, scarce a stone's throw off, is a potter; take the bit of silver to him, and buy another pot, and the copper the potter will give thee keep that to play with thy comrades."

The little mind took in all this, and smiles began to struggle with the tears: but spasms are like waves, they cannot go down the very moment the wind of trouble is lulled. So Denys thought well to bring up his reserve of consolation. "Courage, ma mie, le diable est mort!" cried that inventive warrior gaily. Gerard shrugged his shoulders at such a way of cheering a little girl.

> "What a fine thing
> Is a lute with one string,"

said he.

The little girl's face broke into warm sunshine.

"Oh, the good news! oh, the good news!" she sang out with such heartfelt joy, it went off into a honeyed whine; even as our gay old tunes have a pathos underneath. "So then," said she, "they will no longer be able to threaten us little girls with him, MAKING OUR LIVES A BURDEN!" And she bounded off "to tell Nanette," she said.

There is a theory that everything has its counterpart; if true, Denys it would seem had found the mind his consigne fitted.

While he was roaring with laughter at its unexpected success and Gerard's amazement, a little hand pulled his jerkin and a little face peeped round his waist. Curiosity was now the dominant passion in that small but vivid countenance.

"Est-ce toi qui l'a tué, beau soldat?"

"Oui, ma mie," said Denys, as gruffly as ever he could, rightly deeming this would smack of supernatural puissance to owners of bell-like trebles. "C'est moi. Çà vaut une petite embrassade— pas?"

"Je crois ben. Aie! aie!"

"Qu'as-tu?"

"Çà pique! Çà pique!"

"Quel dommage! je vais la couper."

"Nenni, ce n'est rien; et pisque t'as tué ce méchant. T'es fièrement beau, tout d' même, toi; t'es ben miex que ma grande sœur."

"Will you not kiss me too, ma mie?" said Gerard.

"Je ne demande par miex. Tiens, tiens, tiens! c'est doulce celle-ci. Ah, que j'aimons les hommes! Des fames, çà ne m'aurait jamais donné l'arjan blanc, plutôt çà m'aurait ri au nez. C'est si peu de chose, les fames. Serviteur, beaulx sires! Bon voiage; et n'oubliez point la Jeanneton!"

"Adieu, petit cœur," said Gerard, and on they marched: but presently looking back they saw the contemner of women in the middle of the road, making them a reverence, and blowing them kisses with little May morning face.

"Come on," cried Gerard lustily. "I shall win to Rome yet. Holy St. Bavon, what a sunbeam of innocence hath shot across our bloodthirsty road! Forget thee, little Jeanneton? not likely, amidst all this slobbering, and gibbeting, and decanting. Come on, thou laggard! forward!"

"Dost call this marching?" remonstrated Denys: "why we shall walk o'er Christmas-day and never see it."

At the next town they came to, suddenly an arbalestrier ran out of a tavern after them, and in a moment his beard and Denys's were like two brushes stuck together. It was a comrade. He insisted on their coming into the tavern with him, and breaking a bottle of wine. In course of conversation, he told Denys there was an insurrection in the duke's Flemish provinces, and soldiers were ordered thither from all parts of Burgundy. "Indeed I marvelled to see thy face turned this way."

"I go to embrace my folk that I have not seen these three years. Ye can quell a bit of a rising without me I trow."

Suddenly Denys gave a start. "Dost hear, Gerard? this comrade is bound for Holland."

"What then? ah, a letter! a letter to Margaret! but will he be so good, so kind?"

The soldier with a torrent of blasphemy informed him he would not only take it, but go a league or two out of his way to do it.

In an instant out came inkhorn and paper from Gerard's wallet; and he wrote a long letter to Margaret, and told her briefly what I fear I have spun too tediously; dwelt most on the bear, and the plunge in the Rhine, and the character of Denys, whom he painted to the life. And with many endearing expressions bade her be of good cheer; some trouble and peril there had been, but all that was over now, and his only grief left was that he could not hope to have a word from her hand till he should reach Rome. He ended with comforting her again as hard as he could. And so absorbed was he in his love and his work, that he did not see all the people in the room were standing peeping, to watch the nimble and true finger execute such rare penmanship.

Denys, proud of his friend's skill, let him alone, till presently the writer's face worked, and soon the scalding tears began to run down his young cheeks, one after another, on the paper where he was then writing comfort, comfort. Then Denys rudely repulsed the curious, and asked his comrade with a faltering voice whether he had the heart to let so sweet a love letter miscarry? The other swore by the face of St. Luke he would lose the forefinger of his right hand sooner.

Seeing him so ready, Gerard charged him also with a short, cold letter to his parents; and in it he drew hastily with his pen two hands grasping each other, to signify farewell. By-the-by, one drop of bitterness found its way into his letter to Margaret. "I write to thee alone, and to those who love thee. If my flesh and blood care to hear news of me, they must be kind to thee and then thou mayst read my letter to them. But not else, and even then let this not out of thy hand or thou lovest me not. I know what I ask of thee. and why I ask it. Thou knowest not. I am older now by many years than thou art, and I was a month agone. Therefore obey me in this one thing, dear heart, or thou wilt make me a worse wife than I hope to make thee a husband, God willing."

On second thoughts I believe there was something more than bitterness in this. For his mind, young but intense, had been bent many hours in every day upon Sevenbergen and Tergou, and speculated on every change of feeling and circumstance that his exile might bring about.

Gerard now offered money to the soldier. He hesitated, but declined it. "No, no! art comrade of my comrade; and may"—— (etc.)——"but thy love for the wench touches me. I'll break another bottle at thy charge an thou wilt, and so cry quits."

"Well said, comrade," cried Denys. "Hadst taken money, I had invited thee to walk in the court-yard and cross swords with me."

"Whereupon I had cut thy comb for thee," retorted the other.

"Hadst done thy endeavour, drôle, I doubt not."

They drank the new bottle, shook hands, adhered to custom, and parted on opposite routes.

This delay however somewhat put out Denys's calculations, and evening surprised them ere they reached a little town he was making for, where was a famous hotel. However, they fell in with a roadside auberge, and Denys, seeing a buxom girl at the door, said, "This seems a decent inn," and led the way into the kitchen. They ordered supper, to which no objection was raised, only the landlord requested them to pay for it beforehand. It was not an uncommon proposal in any part of the world. Still it was not universal, and Denys was nettled, and dashed his hand somewhat ostentatiously into his purse and pulled out a gold angel. "Count me the change, and speedily," said he. "You tavern-keepers are more likely to rob me than I you."

While the supper was preparing, Denys disappeared, and was eventually found by Gerard in the yard, helping Manon, his plump but not bright decoy duck, to draw water, and pouring extravagant compliments into her dullish ear. Gerard grunted and returned to table, but Denys did not come in for a good quarter of an hour.

"Up-hill work at the end of a march," said he shrugging his shoulders.

"What matters that to you?" said Gerard, drily. "The mad dog bites all the world."

"Exaggerator. You know I bite but the fairer half. Well, here comes supper; that is better worth biting."

During supper the girl kept constantly coming in and out, and looking point-blank at them, especially at Denys; and at last in leaning over him to remove a dish, dropped a word in his ear; and he replied with a nod.

As soon as supper was cleared away, Denys rose and strolled to the door, telling Gerard the sullen fair had relented, and given him a little rendezvous in the stable yard.

Gerard suggested that the cow-house would have been a more appropriate locality. "I shall go to bed, then," said he, a little crossly. "Where is the landlord? out at this time of night? no matter. I know our room. Shall you be long, pray?"

"Not I. I grudge leaving the fire and thee. But what can I do? There are two sorts of invitations a Burgundian never declines."

Denys found a figure seated by the well. It was Manon; but instead of receiving him as he thought he had a right to expect, coming by invitation, all she did was to sob. He asked her what ailed her? She sobbed. Could he do anything for her? She sobbed.

The good-natured Denys, driven to his wits' end, which was no great distance, proffered the custom of the country by way of consolation. She repulsed him roughly, "Is it a time for fooling?" said she, and sobbed.

"You seem to think so," said Denys, waxing wroth. But the next moment he added, tenderly, "and I who could never bear to see beauty in distress."

"It is not for myself."

"Who then? your sweetheart?"

"Oh, que nenni. My sweetheart is not on earth now: and to think I have not an écu to buy masses for his soul;" and in this shallow nature the grief seemed now to be all turned in another direction.

"Come, come," said Denys, "shalt have money to buy masses for thy dead lad; I swear it. Meantime tell me why you weep."

"For you."

"For me? Art mad?"

"No. I am not mad. 'Tis you that were mad to open your purse before him."

The mystery seemed to thicken, and Denys wearied of stirring up the mud by questions, held his peace to see if it would not clear of itself. Then the girl finding herself no longer questioned seemed to go through some internal combat. At last she said, doggedly and aloud, "I will. The Virgin give me courage! What matters it if they kill me, since he is dead? Soldier, the landlord is out."

"Oh, is he?"

"What, do landlords leave their taverns at this time of night? also see what a tempest! We are sheltered here, but t'other side it blows a hurricane."

Denys said nothing.

"He is gone to fetch the band."

"The band! what band?"

"Those who will cut your throat and take your gold. Wretched man; to go and shake gold in an innkeeper's face!"

The blow came so unexpectedly it staggered even Denys, accustomed as he was to sudden perils. He muttered a single word, but in it a volume.

"Gerard!"

"Gerard! What is that? Oh, 'tis thy comrade's name, poor lad. Get him out quick ere they come; and fly to the next town."

"And thou?"

"They will kill me."

"That shall they not. Fly with us."

" 'Twill avail me nought; one of the band will be sent to kill me. They are sworn to slay all who betray them."

"I'll take thee to my native place full thirty leagues from hence, and put thee under my own mother's wing, ere they shall hurt a hair o' thy head. But first Gerard. Stay thou here whilst I fetch him!"

As he was darting off, the girl seized him convulsively, and with all the iron strength excitement lends to women. "Stay me not! for pity's sake," he cried; " 'tis life or death."

"Sh!—sh!" whispered the girl, shutting his mouth hard with her hand, and putting her pale lips close to him, and her eyes, that seemed to turn backwards, straining towards some indistinct sound.

He listened.

He heard footsteps, many footsteps: and no voices. She whispered in his ear "They are come."

And trembled like a leaf.

Denys felt it was so. Travellers in that number would never have come in dead silence.

The feet were now at the very door.

"How many?" said he in a hollow whisper.

"Hush!" and she put her mouth to his very ear.

And who, that had seen this man and woman in that attitude, would have guessed what freezing hearts were theirs, and what terrible whispers passed between them?"

"Seven."

"How armed?"

"Sword and dagger: and the giant with his axe. They call him the Abbot."

"And my comrade?"

"Nothing can save him. Better lose one life than two. Fly!"

Denys's blood froze at this cynical advice. "Poor creature, you know not a soldier's heart."

He put his head in his hands a moment, and a hundred thoughts of dangers baffled whirled through his brain.

"Listen, girl! There is one chance for our lives, if thou wilt but be true to us. Run to the town; to the nearest tavern, and tell the first soldier there, that a soldier here is sore beset, but armed, and his life to be saved if they will but run. Then to the bailiff. But first to the soldiers. Nay, not a word, but buss me, good lass, and fly! men's lives hang on thy heels."

She kilted up her gown to run. He came round to the road with her; saw her cross the road cringing with fear, then glide away, then turn into an erect shadow, then melt away in the storm.

And now he must get to Gerard. But how? He had to run the gauntlet of the whole band. He asked himself, what was the worst thing they could do? for he had learned in war that an enemy does, not what you hope he will do, but what you hope he will not do. "Attack me as I enter the kitchen! Then I must not give them time."

Just as he drew near to the latch, a terrible thought crossed him.

"Suppose they had already dealt with Gerard. Why, then," thought he, "nought is left but to kill, and be killed;" and he strung his bow, and walked rapidly into the kitchen. There were seven hideous faces seated round the fire, and the landlord pouring them out neat brandy, blood's forerunner in every age.

"What? company!" cried Denys, gaily: "one minute, my lads, and I'll be with you;" and he snatched up a lighted candle off the table, opened the door that led to the staircase, and went up it hallooing. "What, Gerard! whither hast thou skulked to?" There was no answer. He hallooed louder, "Gerard, where art thou?"

After a moment in which Denys lived an hour of agony, a peevish half-inarticulate noise issued from the room at the head of the little stairs. Denys burst in, and there was Gerard asleep.

"Thank God!" he said, in a choking voice, then began to sing loud, untuneful ditties. Gerard put his fingers into his ears; but presently he saw in Denys's face a horror that contrasted strangely with this sudden merriment.

"What ails thee?" said he, sitting up and staring.

"Hush!" said Denys, and his hand spoke even more plainly than his lips. "Listen to me."

Denys then pointing significantly to the door, to show Gerard sharp ears were listening hard by, continued his song aloud, but under cover of it threw in short muttered syllables.

"(Our lives are in peril.)

"(Thieves.)

"(Thy doublet.)

"(Thy sword.)

"Aid.

"Coming.

"Put off time." Then aloud.

"Well, now, wilt have t'other bottle? say Nay."

"No, not I."

"But I tell thee, there are half a dozen jolly fellows. Tired."

"Ay, but I am too wearied," said Gerard. "Go thou."

"Nay, nay!" Then he went to the door and called out cheerfully, "Landlord, the young milksop will not rise. Give those honest fellows t'other bottle. I will pay for't in the morning."

He heard a brutal and fierce chuckle.

Having thus by observation made sure the kitchen door was shut, and the miscreants were not actually listening, he examined the chamber door closely: then quietly shut it, but did not bolt it: and went and inspected the window.

It was too small to get out of, and yet a thick bar of iron had been let in the stone to make it smaller; and, just as he made this chilling discovery, the outer door of the house was bolted with a loud clang.

Denys groaned "The beasts are in the shambles."

But would the thieves attack them while they were awake? Probably not.

Not to throw away this their best chance the poor souls now made a series of desperate efforts to converse, as if discussing ordinary matters; and by this means Gerard learned all that had passed, and that the girl was gone for aid.

"Pray Heaven, she may not lose heart by the way," said Denys, sorrowfully.

And Denys begged Gerard's forgiveness for bringing him out of his way for this.

Gerard forgave him.

"I would fear them less, Gerard, but for one they call the Abbot. I picked him out at once. Taller than you, bigger than us both put together. Fights with an axe. Gerard, a man to lead a herd of deer to battle. I shall kill that man to-night, or he will kill me. I think somehow 'tis he will kill me."

"Saints forbid! Shoot him at the door! What avails his strength against your weapon?"

"I shall pick him out: but, if it comes to hand fighting, run swiftly under his guard, or you are a dead man. I tell thee neither of us may stand a blow of that axe: thou never sawest such a body of a man."

Gerard was for bolting the door; but Denys with a sigh showed him that half the door-post turned outward on a hinge, and the great bolt was little more than a blind. "I have forborne to bolt it," said he, "that they may think us the less suspicious."

Near an hour rolled away thus. It seemed an age. Yet it was but a little hour: and the town was a league distant. And some of the voices in the kitchen became angry and impatient.

The Cloister and the Hearth

"They will not wait much longer," said Denys, "and we have no chance at all unless we surprise them."

"I will do whate'er you bid," said Gerard meekly.

There was a cupboard on the same side as the door; but between it and the window. It reached nearly to the ground, but not quite. Denys opened the cupboard door and placed Gerard on a chair behind it. "If they run for the bed, strike at the napes of their necks! a sword cut there always kills or disables." He then arranged the bolsters and their shoes in the bed so as to deceive a person peeping from a distance, and drew the short curtains at the head.

Meantime Gerard was on his knees. Denys looked round and saw him.

"Ah!" said Denys, "above all pray them to forgive me for bringing you into this guetapens!"

And now they grasped hands and looked in one another's eyes; oh, such a look! Denys's hand was cold, and Gerard's warm.

They took their posts.

Denys blew out the candle.

"We must keep silence now."

But in the terrible tension of their nerves and very souls they found they could hear a whisper fainter than any man could catch at all outside that door. They could hear each other's heart thump at times.

"Good news!" breathed Denys, listening at the door.

"They are casting lots."

"Pray that it may be the Abbot."

"Yes. Why?"

"If he comes alone I can make sure of him."

"Denys!"

"Ay!"

"I fear I shall go mad, if they do not come soon."

"Shall I feign sleep? Shall I snore?"

"Will that—?"

"Perhaps."

"Do then, and God have mercy on us!"

Denys snored at intervals.

There was a scuffling of feet heard in the kitchen, and then all was still.

Denys snored again. Then took up his position behind the door.

But he, or they, who had drawn the lot, seemed determined to run no foolish risks. Nothing was attempted in a hurry.

When they were almost starved with cold, and waiting for the attack, the door on the stairs opened softly and closed again. Nothing more.

There was another harrowing silence.

Then a single light footstep on the stair; and nothing more.

Then a light crept under the door: and nothing more.

Presently there was a gentle scratching, not half so loud as a mouse's, and the false door-post opened by degrees and left a perpendicular space through which the light streamed in. The door, had it been bolted, would now have hung by the bare tip of the bolt, which went into the real door-post, but, as it was, it swung gently open of itself. It opened inwards, so Denys did not raise his crossbow from the ground, but merely grasped his dagger.

The candle was held up, and shaded from behind by a man's hand.

He was inspecting the beds from the threshold, satisfied that his victims were both in bed.

The man glided into the apartment. But at the first step something in the position of the cupboard and chair made him uneasy. He ventured no further, but put the candle on the floor and stooped to peer under the chair; but, as he stooped, an iron hand grasped his shoulder, and a dagger was driven so fiercely through his neck that the point came out at his gullet. There was a terrible hiccough, but no cry; and half a dozen silent strokes followed in swift succession, each a death-blow, and the assassin was laid noiselessly on the floor.

Denys closed the door; bolted it gently; drew the post to, and even while he was doing it whispered Gerard to bring a chair. It was done.

"Help me set him up.

"Dead?"

"Parbleu."

"What for?"

"Frighten them! Gain time."

The Cloister and the Hearth

Even while saying this, Denys had whipped a piece of string round the dead man's neck, and tied him to the chair, and there the ghastly figure sat fronting the door.

"Denys, I can do better. Saints forgive me!"
"What? Be quick then, we have not many moments."
And Denys got his cross-bow ready, and, tearing off his straw mattress, reared it before him and prepared to shoot the moment the door should open, for he had no hope any more would come singly, when they found the first did not return.

While thus employed, Gerard was busy about the seated corpse, and, to his amazement, Denys saw a luminous glow spreading rapidly over the white face.

Gerard blew out the candle. And on this the corpse's face shone still more like a glowworm's head.

Denys shook in his shoes, and his teeth chattered.

"What in Heaven's name is this?" he whispered.

"Hush! 'tis but phosphorus. But 'twill serve."

"Away! they will surprise thee."

In fact uneasy mutterings were heard below, and at last a deep voice said, "What makes him so long? is the drôle rifling them?"

It was their comrade they suspected then, not the enemy. Soon a step came softly but rapidly up the stairs: the door was gently tried.

When this resisted, which was clearly not expected, the sham post was very cautiously moved, and an eye no doubt peeped through the aperture: for there was a howl of dismay, and the man was heard to stumble back and burst into the kitchen, where a babel of voices rose directly on his return.

Gerard ran to the dead thief and began to work on him again.

"Back, madman!" whispered Denys.

"Nay, nay. I know these ignorant brutes. They will not venture here awhile. I can make him ten times more fearful."

"At least close that opening! Let them not see you at your devilish work."

Gerard closed the sham post, and in half a minute his brush made the dead head a sight to strike any man with dismay. He put his art to a strange use, and one unparalleled perhaps in the history of mankind. He illuminated his dead enemy's face to frighten his living foe: the staring eyeballs he made globes of fire; the teeth he left white, for so they were more terrible by the contrast, but the palate and tongue he tipped with fire, and made one lurid cavern of the red depths the chap-fallen jaw revealed: and on the brow he wrote in burning letters "LA MORT." And, while he was doing it, the stout Denys was quaking, and fearing the vengeance of Heaven; for one man's courage is not another's; and the band of miscreants below were quarrelling and disputing loudly, and now without disguise.

The steps that led down to the kitchen were fifteen, but they were nearly perpendicular: there was therefore in point of fact no distance between the besiegers and besieged, and the latter now caught almost every word. At last one was heard to cry out "I tell ye the devil has got him and branded him with hell-fire. I am more like to leave this cursed house than go again into a room that is full of fiends."

"Art drunk? or mad? or a coward?" said another.

"Call me a coward, I'll give thee my dagger's point, and send thee where Pierre sits o' fire for ever."

"Come, no quarrelling when work is afoot," roared a tremendous diapason, "or I'll brain ye both with my fist, and send ye where we shall all go soon or late."

"The Abbot," whispered Denys, gravely.

He felt the voice he had just heard could belong to no man but the colossus he had seen in passing through the kitchen. It made the place vibrate. The quarrelling continued some time, and then there was a dead silence.

"Look out, Gerard."

"Ay. What will they do next?"

"We shall soon know."

"Shall I wait for you, or cut down the first that opens the door?"

"Wait for me, lest we strike the same and waste a blow. Alas! we cannot afford that."

Dead silence.

Sudden came into the room a thing that made them start and their hearts quiver.

And what was it? A moonbeam.

Even so can this machine, the body, by the soul's action be strung up to start and quiver. The sudden ray shot keen and pure into that shamble.

Its calm, cold, silvery soul traversed the apartment in a stream of no great volume; for the window was narrow.

After the first tremor Gerard whispered, "Courage, Denys! God's eye is on us even here." And he fell upon his knees with his face turned towards the window.

Ay it was like a holy eye opening suddenly on human crime and human passions. Many a scene of blood and crime that pure cold eye has rested on; but on few more ghastly than this, where two men, with a lighted corpse between them, waited panting, to kill or be killed. Nor did the moonlight deaden that horrible corpse-light. If anything it added to its ghastliness: for the body sat at the edge of the moonbeam, which cut sharp across the shoulder and the ear, and seemed blue and ghastly and unnatural by the side of that lurid glow in which the face and eyes and teeth shone horribly. But Denys dared not look that way.

The moon drew a broad stripe of light across the door, and on that his eyes were glued. Presently he whispered, "Gerard!"

Gerard looked and raised his sword.

Acutely as they had listened they had heard of late no sound on the stair. Yet there—on the door-post, at the edge of the stream of moonlight, were the tips of the fingers of a hand.

The nails glistened.

Presently they began to crawl, and crawl, down towards the bolt, but with infinite slowness and caution. In so doing they crept into the moonlight. The actual motion was imperceptible, but slowly, slowly, the fingers came out whiter and whiter: but the hand between the main knuckles and the wrist remained dark. Denys slowly raised his crossbow.

He levelled it. He took a long steady aim.

Gerard palpitated. At last the crossbow twanged. The hand was instantly nailed, with a stern jar, to the quivering doorpost. There was a scream of anguish. "Cut," whispered Denys eagerly, and Gerard's uplifted sword descended and severed the wrist with two swift blows. A body sank down moaning outside.

The hand remained inside, immovable, with blood trickling from it down the wall. The fierce bolt slightly barbed had gone through it, and deep into the real door-post.

"Two," said Denys, with terrible cynicism.

He strung his crossbow, and kneeled behind his cover again.

"The next will be the Abbot."

The wounded man moved, and presently crawled down to his companions on the stairs, and the kitchen door was shut.

There nothing was heard now but low muttering. The last incident had revealed the mortal character of the weapons used by the besieged.

"I begin to think the Abbot's stomach is not so great as his body," said Denys.

The words were scarcely out of his mouth, when the following events happened all in a couple of seconds. The kitchen door was opened roughly, a heavy but active man darted up the steps without any manner of disguise, and a single ponderous blow sent the door not only off its hinges, but right across the room on to Denys's fortification, which it struck so rudely as nearly to lay him flat. And in the doorway stood a colossus with a glittering axe.

He saw the dead man with the moon's blue light on half his face, and the red light on the other half and inside his chapfallen jaws: he stared, his arms fell, his knees knocked together, and he crouched with terror.

"LA MORT!" he cried in tones of terror, and turned and fled. In which act Denys started up and shot him through both jaws. He sprang with one bound into the kitchen, and there leaned on his axe, spitting blood and teeth and curses.

Denys strung his bow and put his hand into his breast.

He drew it out dismayed.

"My last bolt is gone," he groaned.

"But we have our swords, and you have slain the giant."

"No, Gerard," said Denys gravely: "I have not. And the worst is I have wounded him. Fool! to shoot at a retreating lion. He had never faced thy handiwork again, but for my meddling."

"Ha! to your guard! I hear them open the door."

Then Denys, depressed by the one error he had committed in all this fearful night, felt convinced his last hour had come. He drew his sword, but like one doomed. But what is this? a red light flickers on the ceiling. Gerard flew to the window and looked out. There were men with torches, and breastplates gleaming red. "We are saved! Armed men!" And he dashed his sword through the window shouting "Quick! quick! we are sore pressed."

"Back!" yelled Denys; "they come! strike none but him!"

That very moment the Abbot and two men with naked weapons rushed into the room. Even as they came, the outer door was hammered fiercely, and the Abbot's comrades hearing it, and seeing the torchlight, turned and fled. Not so the terrible Abbot: wild with rage and pain, he spurned his dead comrade, chair and all, across the room, then, as the men faced him on each side with kindling eyeballs, he waved his tremendous axe like a feather right and left, and cleared a space, then lifted it to hew them both in pieces.

His antagonists were inferior in strength, but not in swiftness and daring, and above all they had settled how to attack him. The moment he reared his axe, they flew at him like cats. and both together. If he struck a full blow with his weapon he would most likely kill one, but the other would certainly kill him: he saw this, and intelligent as well as powerful, he thrust the handle fiercely in Denys's face, and, turning, jabbed with the steel at Gerard. Denys went staggering back covered with blood. Gerard had rushed in like lightning, and, just as the axe turned to descend on him, drove his sword so fiercely through the giant's body, that the very hilt sounded on his ribs like the blow of a pugilist, and Denys, staggering back to help his friend, saw a steel point come out of the Abbot behind.

The stricken giant bellowed like a bull, dropped his axe, and clutching Gerard's throat tremendously, shook him like a child. Then Denys with a fierce snarl drove his sword into the giant's back. "Stand firm now!" and he pushed the cold steel through and through the giant and out at his breast.

Thus horribly spitted on both sides, the Abbot, gave a violent shudder, and his heels hammered the ground convulsively. His lips, fast turning blue, opened wide and deep, and he cried "LA MORT! —LA MORT!—LA MORT!!" The first time in a roar of despair, and then twice in a horror-stricken whisper never to be forgotten.

Just then the street door was forced.

Suddenly the Abbot's arms whirled like windmills, and his huge body wrenched wildly and carried them to the doorway, twisting their wrists and nearly throwing them off their legs. "He'll win clear yet," cried Denys: "out steel! and in again!" They tore out their smoking swords, but, ere they could stab again, the Abbot leaped full five feet high, and fell with a tremendous crash against the door below, carrying it away with him like a sheet of paper, and through the aperture the glare of torches burst on the awe struck faces above, half blinding them.

The thieves at the first alarm had made for the back door, but driven thence by a strong guard ran back to the kitchen, just in time to see the lock forced out of the socket, and half a dozen mailed archers burst in upon them. On these in pure despair they drew their swords.

But ere a blow was struck on either side, the staircase door behind them was battered into their midst with one ponderous blow, and with it the Abbot's body came flying, hurled, as they thought by no mortal hand, and rolled on the floor spouting blood from back and bosom in two furious jets, and quivered, but breathed no more.

The thieves smitten with dismay fell on their knees directly, and the archers bound them, while, above, the rescued ones still stood like statues rooted to the spot, their dripping swords extended in the red torchlight, expecting their indomitable enemy to leap back on them as wonderfully as he had gone.

CHAPTER XXXIV

"WHERE be the true men?"

"Here be we. God bless you all! God bless you!"

There was a rush to the stairs, and half a dozen hard but friendly hands were held out and grasped them warmly. "Y'have saved our lives, lads," cried Denys, "y'have saved our lives this night."

A wild sight met the eyes of the rescued pair. The room flaring with torches, the glittering breastplates of the archers, their bronzed faces, the white cheeks of the bound thieves, and the bleeding giant, whose dead body these hard men left lying there in its own gore.

Gerard went round the archers and took them each by the hand with glistening eyes, and on this they all kissed him; and this time he kissed them in return. Then he said to one handsome archer of his own age, "Prithee, good soldier, have an eye to me. A strange drowsiness overcomes me. Let no one cut my throat while I sleep —for pity's sake."

The archer promised with a laugh; for he thought Gerard was jesting: and the latter went off into a deep sleep almost immediately.

Denys was surprised at this: but did not interfere; for it suited his immediate purpose. A couple of archers were inspecting the Abbot's body, turning it half over with their feet, and inquiring, "Which of the two had flung this enormous rogue down from an upper story like that; they would fain have the trick of his arm."

Denys at first pished and pshawed, but he dared not play the braggart, for he said to himself "That young vagabond will break in and say 'twas the finger of Heaven, and no mortal arm, or some such stuff, and make me look like a fool." But now, seeing Gerard unconscious, he suddenly gave this required information:

"Well, then, you see, comrades, I had run my sword through this one up to the hilt; and one or two more of 'em came buzzing about me; so it behoved me have my sword or die: so I just put my foot against his stomach, gave a tug with my hand and a spring with my foot, and sent him flying to kingdom come! He died in the air, and his carrion rolled in amongst you without ceremony: made you jump I warrant me. But pikestaves and pillage! what avails prattling of these trifles once they are gone by? buvons, camarades, buvons."

The archers remarked that it was easy to say "buvons" where no liquor was, but not so easy to do it.

"Nay, I'll soon find ye liquor. My nose hath a natural alacrity at scenting out the wine. You follow me: and I my nose: bring a torch!" And they left the room, and, finding a short flight of stone steps, descended them and entered a large, low, damp cellar.

It smelt close and dank: and the walls were encrusted here and there with what seemed cobwebs; but proved to be saltpetre that had oozed out of the damp stones, and crystallized.

"Oh! the fine mouldy smell," said Denys. "In such placen still lurks the good wine: advance thy torch. Diable! what is that in the corner? A pile of rags? No: 'tis a man."

They gathered round with the torch, and lo! a figure crouched on a heap in the corner, pale as ashes and shivering.

"Why, it is the landlord," said Denys.

"Get up, thou craven heart!" shouted one of the archers.

"Why, man, the thieves are bound, and we are dry, that bound them. Up! and show us thy wine; for no bottles see I here."

"What, be the rascals bound?" stammered the pale landlord; "good news. W—w—wine? that will I, honest sirs."

And he rose with unsure joints and offered to lead the way to the wine cellar. But Denys interposed. "You are all in the dark, comrades. He is in league with the thieves."

"Alack, good soldier, me in league with the accursed robbers! Is that reasonable?"

"The girl said so any way."

"The girl! What girl? Ah! Curse her, traitress!"

"Well," interposed the other archer; "the girl is not here, but gone on to the bailiff. So let the burghers settle whether this craven be guilty or no: for we caught him not in the act: and let him draw us our wine."

"One moment," said Denys, shrewdly. "Why cursed he the girl? If he be a true man, he should bless her as we do."

"Alas, sir!" said the landlord, "I have but my good name to live by, and I cursed her to you, because you said she had belied me."

"Humph! I trow thou art a thief, and where is the thief that cannot lie with a smooth face? Therefore hold him, comrades: a prisoner can draw wine an if his hands be not bound."

The landlord offered no objection; but on the contrary said he would with pleasure show them where his little stock of wine was, but hoped they would pay for what they should drink, for his rent was due this two months.

The archers smiled grimly at his simplicity as they thought it; one of them laid a hand quietly but firmly on his shoulder, the other led on with the torch.

They had reached the threshold when Denys cried "Halt!"

"What is't?"

"Here be bottles in this corner; advance thy light."

The torch-bearer went towards him. He had just taken off his scabbard and was probing the heap the landlord had just been crouched upon.

"Nay, nay," cried the landlord, "the wine is in the next cellar. There is nothing *there*."

The Cloister and the Hearth

"Nothing is mighty hard, then," said Denys, and drew out something with his hand from the heap.

It proved to be only a bone.

Denys threw it on the floor: it rattled.

"There is nought there but the bones of the house," said the landlord.

"Just now 'twas nothing. Now that we have found something 'tis nothing but bones. Here's another. Humph? look at this one, comrade; and you come too and look at it, and bring yon smooth knave along."

The archer with the torch, whose name was Philippe, held the bone to the light and turned it round and round.

"Well?" said Denys.

"Well, if this was a field of battle I should say 'twas the shankbone of a man! no more, no less. But 'tisn't a battle field, nor a churchyard; 'tis an inn."

"True, mate: but yon knave's ashy face is as good a light to me as a field of battle. I read the bone by it. Bring yon face nearer, I say. When the chine is amissing, and the house dog can't look at you without his tail creeping between his legs, who was the thief? Good brothers mine, my mind it doth misgive me. The deeper I thrust the more there be. Mayhap if these bones could tell their tale they would make true men's flesh creep that heard it."

"Alas! young man, what hideous fancies are these! The bones are bones of beeves, and sheep, and kids, and not, as you think, of men and women. Holy saints preserve us!"

"Hold thy peace! thy words are air. Thou hast not got burghers by the ear, that know not a veal knuckle from their grandsire's ribs; but soldiers—men that have gone to look for their dear comrades, and found their bones picked as clean by the crows, as these I doubt have been by thee and thy mates. Men and women, saidst thou? And prithee, when spake I a word of women's bones? Wouldst make a child suspect thee. Field of battle, comrade! Was not this house a field of battle half an hour agone? Drag him close to me, let me read his face; now then, what is this, thou knave?' and he thrust a small object suddenly in his face.

"Alas! I know not."

"Well, I would not swear neither: but it is too like the thumb

221

bone of a man's hand; mates, my flesh it creeps. Churchyard! how know I this is not one?"

And he now drew his sword out of the scabbard and began to rake the heap of earth and broken crockery and bones out on the floor.

The landlord assured him he but wasted his time. "We poor inn-keepers are sinners," said he, "we give short measure and baptize the wine; we are fain to do these things; the laws are so unjust to us; but we are not assassins. How could we afford to kill our customers? May Heaven's lightning strike me dead if there be any bones there but such as have been used for meat. 'Tis the kitchen wench flings them here; I swear by God's holy mother, by holy Paul, by holy Dominic, and Denys my patron saint——ah!"

Denys held out a bone under his eye in dead silence. It was a bone no man however ignorant, however lying, could confound with those of sheep or oxen. The sight of it shut the lying lips, and palsied the heartless heart.

The landlord's hair rose visibly on his head like spikes, and his knees gave way as if his limbs had been struck from under him. But the archers dragged him fiercely up, and kept him erect under the torch staring fascinated at the dead skull which, white as the living cheek opposed, but no whiter, glared back again at its murderer, whose pale lips now opened, and opened, but could utter no sound.

"Ah!" said Denys, solemnly, and trembling now with rage, "look on the sockets out of which thou hast picked the eyes, and let them blast thine eyes, that crows shall pick out ere this week shall end. Now, hold thou that while I search on. Hold it, I say, or here I rob the gallows——" and he threatened the quaking wretch with his naked sword, till with a groan he took the skull and held it, almost fainting.

Oh! that every murderer, and contriver of murder, could see him, sick, and staggering with terror, and with his hair on end holding the cold skull, and feeling that his own head would soon be like it. And soon the heap was scattered, and, alas! not one nor two, but many skulls were brought to light, the culprit moaning at each discovery.

Suddenly Denys uttered a strange cry of distress to come from so bold and hard a man; and held up to the torch a mass of human hair. It was long, glossy, and golden. A woman's beautiful hair. At sight of it the archers instinctively shook the craven wretch in their hands: and he whined.

"I have a little sister with hair just so fair and shining as this," gulped Denys. "Jesu! if it should be hers! There quick, take my sword and dagger, and keep them from my hand, lest I strike him dead and wrong the gibbet. And thou, poor innocent victim, on whose head this most lovely hair did grow, hear me swear thus, on bended knee, never to leave this man till I see him broken to pieces on the wheel even for thy sake."

He rose from his knee. "Ay, had he as many lives as here be hairs, I'd have them all, by God." And he put the hair into his bosom. Then in a sudden fury seized the landlord fiercely by the neck, and forced him to his knees; and foot on head ground his face savagely among the bones of his victims, where they lay thickest: and the assassin first yelled, then whined and whimpered, just as a dog first yells, then whines, when his nose is so forced into some leveret or other innocent he has killed.

"Now lend me thy bowstring, Philippe!" He passed it through the eyes of a skull alternately, and hung the ghastly relic of mortality and crime round the man's neck; then pulled him up and kicked him industriously into the kitchen, where one of the aldermen of the burgh had arrived with constables, and was even now taking an archer's deposition.

The grave burgher was much startled at sight of the landlord driven in bleeding from a dozen scratches inflicted by the bones of his own victims, and carrying his horrible collar. But Denys came panting after, and in a few fiery words soon made all clear.

"Bind him like the rest," said the alderman sternly. "I count him the blackest of them all."

While his hands were being bound, the poor wretch begged piteously that "the skull might be taken from him."

"Humph!" said the alderman. "Certes I had not ordered such a thing to be put on mortal man. Yet being there I will not lift voice nor finger to doff it. Methinks it fits thee truly, thou bloody dog. 'Tis thy ensign, and hangs well above a heart so foul as thine."

He then inquired of Denys if he thought they had secured the whole gang or but a part.

"Your worship," said Denys, " there are but seven of them, and this landlord. One we slew upstairs, one we tumbled down dead, the rest are bound before you."

"Good! go fetch the dead one from upstairs, and lay him beside him I caused to be removed."

Here a voice like a guinea-fowl's broke peevishly in. "Now, now, now, where is the hand? that is what I want to see." The speaker was a little pettifogging clerk.

"You will find it above, nailed to the door-post by a cross-bow bolt."

"Good!" said the clerk. He whispered his master, "What a godly show will the 'pièces de conviction' make!" and with this he wrote them down, enumerating them in separate squeaks as he penned them. Skulls,—Bones,—A woman's hair,—A thief's hand, —1 axe—2 carcases,—1 cross-bow bolt. This done he itched to search the cellar himself: there might be other invaluable morsels of evidence, an ear, or even an earring. The alderman assenting he caught up a torch and was hurrying thither, when an accident stopped him, and indeed carried him a step or two in the opposite direction.

The constables had gone up the stair in single file.

But the head constable no sooner saw the phosphorescent corpse seated by the bedside, than he stood stupefied: and next he began to shake like one in an ague, and, terror gaining on him more and more, he uttered a sort of howl and recoiled swiftly. Forgetting the steps, in his recoil, he tumbled over backward on his nearest companion: but *he,* shaken by the shout of dismay, and catching a glimpse of something horrid, was already staggering back, and in no condition to sustain the head constable, who, like most head constables was a ponderous man. The two carried away the third, and the three the fourth, and they streamed into the kitchen, and settled on the floor, overlapping each other like a sequence laid out on a card-table. The clerk coming hastily with his torch ran an involuntary tilt again the fourth man, who, sharing the momentum of the mass, knocked him instantly on his back, the ace of that fair quint: and there he lay kicking and waving his torch, apparently in triumph, but really in convulsion; sense and wind being driven out together by the concussion.

"What is to do now, in Heaven's name?" cried the alderman, starting up with considerable alarm. But Denys explained, and

offered to accompany his worship. "So be it," said the latter.
His men picked themselves ruefully up, and the alderman put
himself at their head and examined the premises above and below.
As for the prisoners, their interrogatory was postponed till they
could be confronted with the servant.

Before dawn, the thieves, alive and dead, and all the relics and
evidences of crime and retribution, were swept away into the law's
net, and the inn was silent and almost deserted. There remained
but one constable, and Denys and Gerard, the latter still sleeping
heavily.

CHAPTER XXXV

GERARD awoke, and found Denys watching him with some
anxiety.

"It is you for sleeping! Why, 'tis high noon."

"It was a blessed sleep," said Gerard, "methinks Heaven sent
it me. It hath put as it were a veil between me and that awful
night. To think that you and I sit here alive and well. How
terrible a dream I seem to have had!"

"Ay, lad, that is the wise way to look at these things, when once
they are past, why they are dreams, shadows. Break thy fast,
and then thou wilt think no more on't. Moreover I promised to
bring thee on to the town by noon, and take thee to his worship."

"What for?"

"He would put questions to thee; by the same when he was
for waking thee to that end, but I withstood him earnestly, and
vowed to bring thee to him in the morning."

"Thou shalt not break troth for me."

Gerard then sopped some rye bread in red wine and ate it to break
his fast: then went with Denys over the scene of combat, and came
back shuddering, and finally took the road with his friend, and kept
peering through the hedges and expecting sudden attacks unreasonably, till they reached the little town. Denys took him to "The
White Hart."

"No fear of cut-throats here," said he. "I know the landlord
this many a year. He is a burgess, and looks to be bailiff.

'Tis here I was making for yestreen. But we lost time, and night o'ertook us—and—"

"And you saw a woman at the door, and would be wiser than la Jeanneton; she told us they were nought."

"Why, what saved our lives if not a woman? Ay, and risked her own to do it."

"That is true, Denys, and though women are nothing to me, I long to thank this poor girl, and reward her, ay though I share every doit in my purse with her. Do not you?"

"Parbleu."

"Where shall we find her?"

"Mayhap the alderman will tell us. We must go to him first."

The alderman received them with the most singular and inexplicable expression of countenance. However, after a moment's reflection, he wore a grim smile, and finally proceeded to put interrogatories to Gerard, and took down the answers. This done he told them that they must stay in the town until the thieves were tried, and be at hand to give evidence, on peril of fine and imprisonment. They looked very blank at this.

"However," said he, " 'twill not be long, the culprits having been taken red handed." He added, "and you know in any case you could not leave the place this week."

Denys stared at this remark, and Gerard smiled at what he thought the simplicity of the old gentleman in dreaming that a provincial town of Burgundy had attraction to detain him from Rome and Margaret.

He now went to that which was nearest both their hearts. "Your worship," said he, "we cannot find our benefactress in the town."

"Nay, but who is your benefactress?"

"Who? why the good girl that came to you by night and saved our lives at peril of her own. Oh sir, our hearts burn within us to thank and bless her: where is she?"

"Oh, *she* is in prison."

CHAPTER XXXVI

"IN prison, sir; good lack, for what misdeed?"

"Well, she is a witness, and may be a necessary one."

"Why, Messire Bailiff," put in Denys, "you lay not all your witnesses by the heels I trow."

The alderman, pleased at being called bailiff, became communicative. "In a case of blood we detain all testimony that is like to give us leg bail, and so defeat Justice, and that is why we still keep the womenfolk. For a man at odd times bides a week in one mind, but a woman, if she do her duty to the realm o' Friday, she shall undo it afore Sunday, or try. Could you see yon wench now, you should find her a blubbering at having betrayed five males to the gallows. Had they been females, we might have trusted to a subpœna. For they despise one another. And there they show some sense. But now I think on't, there were other reasons for laying this one by the heels. Hand me those depositions, young sir." And he put on his glasses. "Ay! she was implicated: she was one of the band."

A loud disclaimer burst from Denys and Gerard at once.

"No need to deave me," said the alderman. "Here 'tis in black and white. 'Jean Hardy (that is one of the thieves), being questioned confessed that,'—humph? Ay, here 'tis. 'And that the girl Manon was the decoy, and her sweetheart was Georges Vipont, one of the band; and hanged last month: and that she had been deject ever since, and had openly blamed the band for his death, saying, if they had not been rank cowards, he had never been taken, and it is his opinion she did but betray them out of very spite, and—'"

"His opinion," cried Gerard indignantly, "what signifies the opinion of a cut-throat, burning to be revenged on her who has delivered him to justice? And an you go to that what avails his testimony? Is a thief never a liar? Is he not aye a liar? and here a motive to lie? Revenge, why 'tis the strongest of all the passions. And oh, sir, what madness to question a detected felon and listen to him lying away an honest life—as if he were a true man swearing in open day, with his true hand on the Gospel laid!"

"Young man," said the alderman, "restrain thy heat in presence of authority! I find by your tongue you are a stranger. Know then that in this land we question all the world. We are not so weak as to hope to get at the truth by shutting either our left ear or our right."

"And so you would listen to Satan belying the saints!"

"Ta! ta! The law meddles but with men and women, and these cannot utter a story all lies, let them try ever so. Wherefore we shut not the barn-door (as the saying is) against any man's grain. Only having taken it in we do winnow and sift it. And who told you I had swallowed the thief's story whole like fair water? Not so. I did but credit so much on't as was borne out by better proof."

"Better proof?" and Gerard looked blank. "Why who but the thieves would breathe a word against her?"

"Marry, herself."

"Herself, sir? what did you question her too?"

"I tell you we question all the world. Here is her deposition, can you read?—Read it yourself then."

Gerard looked at Denys and read him

MANON'S DEPOSITION

"I am a native of Epinal. I left my native place two years ago because I was unfortunate: I could not like the man they bade me. So my father beat me. I ran away from my father. I went to service. I left service because the mistress was jealous of me. The reason they gave for turning me off was, because I was saucy. Last year I stood in the market-place to be hired with other girls. The landlord of 'The Fair Star' hired me. I was eleven months with him. A young man courted me. I loved him. I found out that travellers came and never went away again. I told my lover. He bade me hold my peace. He threatened me. I found my lover was one of a band of thieves. When travellers were to be robbed the landlord went out and told the band to come. Then I wept and prayed for the travellers' souls. I never told. A month ago my lover died.

"The soldier put me in mind of my lover. He was bearded like him I had lost. I cannot tell whether I should have interfered, if he had had no beard. I am sorry I told now."

The paper almost dropped from Gerard's hands. Now for the first time he saw that Manon's life was in mortal danger. He knew the dogged law, and the dogged men that executed it. He threw himself suddenly on his knees at the alderman's feet. "Oh, sir! think of the difference between those cruel men and this poor weak woman! Could you have the heart to send her to the same death with them; could you have the heart to condemn us to look on and see her slaughtered, who, but that she risked her life for ours, had not now been in jeopardy? Alas, sir! show me and my comrade some pity, if you have none for her, poor soul. Denys and I be true men, and you will rend our hearts if you kill that poor simple girl. What can we do? What is left for us to do then but cut our throats at her gallow's foot?"

The alderman was tough but mortal; the prayers and agitation of Gerard first astounded, then touched him. He showed it in a curious way. He became peevish and fretful. "There get up, do," said he. "I doubt whether anybody would say as many words for me. What ho, Daniel! go fetch the town clerk." And, on that functionary entering from an adjoining room, "Here is a foolish lad fretting about yon girl. Can we stretch a point? say we admit her to bear witness, and question her favorably."

The town clerk was one of your "impossibility" men.

"Nay, sir, we cannot do that: she was not concerned in this business. Had she been accessory, we might have offered her a pardon to bear witness."

Gerard burst in. "But she did better. Instead of being accessory, she stayed the crime; and she proffered herself as witness by running hither with the tale."

"Tush, young man, 'tis a matter of law." The alderman and the clerk then had a long discussion, the one maintaining, the other denying, that she stood as fair in law, as if she had been accessory to the attempt on our travellers' lives. And this was lucky for Manon: for the alderman, irritated by the clerk reiterating that he could not do this and could not that, and could not do t'other, said "he would show him he *could* do anything he chose." And he had Manon out, and, upon the landlord of the "White Hart" being her bondsman, and Denys depositing five gold pieces with him, and the girl promising, not without some coaxing from Denys, to attend as a witness, he liberated her, but eased his conscience by telling her in his own terms his reason for this leniency.

"The town had to buy a new rope for everybody hanged, and present it to the bourreau, or else compound with him in money: and she was not in his opinion worth this municipal expense; whereas decided characters like her late confederates, were." And so Denys and Gerard carried her off, Gerard dancing round her for joy, Denys keeping up her heart by assuring her of the demise of a troublesome personage, and she weeping inauspiciously. However, on the road to the "White Hart" the public found her out, and having heard the whole story from the archers, who naturally told it warmly in her favour, followed her hurrahing and encouraging her, till finding herself backed by numbers she plucked up heart. The landlord too saw at a glance that her presence in the inn would draw custom, and received her politely and assigned her an upper chamber: here she buried herself, and being alone rained tears again.

Poor little mind, it was like a ripple, up and down, down and up, up and down. Bidding the landlord be very kind to her, and keep her a prisoner without letting her feel it, the friends went out: and lo! as they stepped into the street they saw two processions coming towards them from opposite sides. One was a large one attended with noise and howls and those indescribable cries, by which rude natures reveal at odd times that relationship to the beasts of the field and forest, which at other times we succeed in hiding. The other, very thinly attended by a few nuns and friars, came slow and silent.

The prisoners going to exposure in the market-place. The gathered bones of the victims coming to the churchyard.

And the two met in the narrow street nearly at the inn door, and could not pass each other for a long time, and the bier, that bore the relics of mortality, got wedged against the cart that carried the men, who had made those bones what they were, and in a few hours must die for it themselves. The mob had not the quick intelligence to be at once struck with this stern meeting: but at last a woman cried "Look at your work, ye dogs!" and the crowd took it like wildfire, and there was a horrible yell, and the culprits groaned and tried to hide their heads upon their bosoms, but could not, their hands being tied. And there they stood images of pale, hollow-eyed despair, and oh how they looked on the bier, and envied those whom they had sent before them on the dark road they were going upon themselves! And the two men who were the cause of both processions, stood and looked gravely on, and even Manon, hearing the disturbance, crept to the window, and, hiding her face, peeped trembling through her fingers as women will.

This strange meeting parted Denys and Gerard. The former yielded to curiosity and revenge, the latter doffed his bonnet, and piously followed the poor remains of those whose fate had so nearly been his own. For some time he was the one lay mourner: but when they had reached the suburbs, a long way from the greater attraction that was filling the market-place, more than one artisan threw down his tools, and more than one shopman left his shop, and touched with pity, or a sense of our common humanity, and perhaps decided somewhat by the example of Gerard, followed the bones bare headed, and saw them deposited with the prayers of the Church in hallowed ground.

After the funeral rites Gerard stepped respectfully up to the curé, and offered to buy a mass for their souls.

Gerard, son of Catherine, always looked at two sides of a penny: and he tried to purchase this mass a trifle under the usual terms, on account of the pitiable circumstances. But the good curé gently but adroitly parried his ingenuity, and blandly screwed him up to the market price.

In the course of the business they discovered a similarity of sentiments. Piety and worldy prudence are not very rare companions: still it is unusual to carry both so far as these two men did. Their collision in the prayer market led to mutual esteem, as when knight encountered knight worthy of his steel. Moreover the good curé loved a bit of gossip, and finding his customer was one of those who had fought the thieves at Domfront, would have him into his parlour and hear the whole from his own lips. And his heart warmed to Gerard and he said, "God was good to thee. I thank him for't, with all my soul. Thou art a good lad." He added drily, "shouldst have told me this tale in the churchyard. I doubt I had given thee the mass for love. However," said he (the thermometer suddenly falling) "'tis ill-luck to go back upon a bargain. But I'll broach a bottle of my old Medoc for thee: and few be the guests I would do that for." The curé went to his cupboard and, while he groped for the choice bottle, he muttered to himself, "At their old tricks again!"

"Plait-il?" said Gerard.

"I said nought. Ay, here 'tis."

"Nay, your reverence. You surely spoke: you said 'At their old tricks again!'"

"Said I so in sooth?" and his reverence smiled. He then proceeded to broach the wine, and filled a cup for each. Then he put a log of wood on the fire, for stoves were none in Burgundy. "And so I said 'At their old tricks!' did I? Come, sip the good wine, and, whilst it lasts, story for story, I care not if I tell you a little tale."

Gerard's eyes sparkled.

"Thou lovest a story?"

"As my life."

"Nay, but raise not thine expectations too high, neither. 'Tis but a foolish trifle compared with thine adventures."

THE CURÉ'S TALE

"Once upon a time, then, in the kingdom of France, and in the Duchy of Burgundy, and not a day's journey from the town, where now we sit a sipping of old Medoc, there lived—a curé. I say he lived; but barely. The parish was small, the parishioners greedy; and never gave their curé a doit more than he could compel. The nearer they brought him to a disembodied spirit by meagre diet, the holier should be his prayers in their behalf. I know not if this was their creed, but their practice gave it colour.

"At last he pickled a rod for them.

"One day the richest farmer in the place had twins to baptize. The curé was had to the christening dinner as usual; but, ere he would baptize the children, he demanded, not the christening fees only, but the burial fees. 'Saints defend us, parson,' cried the mother; 'talk not of burying! I did never see children liker to live.' 'Nor I,' said the curé, 'the praise be to God. Natheless, they are sure to die; being sons of Adam, as well as of thee, dame. But, die when they will, 'twill cost them nothing; the burial fees being paid and entered in this book.' 'For all that, 'twill cost them something,' quoth the miller, the greatest wag in the place, and as big a knave as any; for which was the biggest God knoweth, but no mortal

232

man, not even the hangman. "Miller, I tell thee nay, quo the curé. 'Parson, I tell you ay,' quo the miller. ' 'Twill cost them their lives.' At which millstone conceit was a great laugh; and in the general mirth the fees were paid and the Christians made.

"But when the next parishioner's child, and the next after, and all, had to pay each his burial fee, or lose his place in heaven, discontent did secretly rankle in the parish. Well, one fine day they met in secret, and sent a churchwarden with a complaint to the bishop, and a thunderbolt fell on the poor curé. Came to him at dinner-time a summons to the episcopal palace, to bring the parish books and answer certain charges. Then the curé guessed where the shoe pinched. He left his food on the board; for small his appetite now; and took the parish books and went quaking.

"The bishop entertained him with a frown, and exposed the plaint. 'Monseigneur,' said the curé right humbly, 'doth the parish allege many things against me, or this one only?' 'In sooth, but this one,' said the bishop; and softened a little. 'First, monseigneur, I acknowledge the fact.' ' 'Tis well,' quoth the bishop; 'that saves time and trouble. Now to your excuse, if excuse there be.' 'Monseigneur, I have been curé of that parish seven years, and fifty children have I baptized, and buried not five. At first I used to say, "Heaven be praised, the air of this village is main healthy," but on searching the register book I found 'twas always so, and on probing the matter, it came out that of those born at Domfront, all, but here and there one, did go and get hanged at Aix. But this was to defraud not their curé only, but the entire Church of her dues: since "pendards" pay no funeral fees, being buried in air. Thereupon, knowing by sad experience their greed, and how they grudge the Church every sou, I laid a trap to keep them from hanging: for, greed against greed, there be of them that will die in their beds like true men, ere the Church shall gain those funeral fees for nought.' Then the bishop laughed till the tears ran down, and questioned the churchwarden, and he was fain to confess that too many of the parish did come to that unlucky end at Aix. 'Then,' said the bishop, 'I do approve the act, for myself and my successors; and so be it ever, till they mend their manners and die in their beds.' And the next day came the ringleaders crest-fallen to the curé, and said, 'Parson, ye were ever good to us, barring this untoward matter: prithee let there be no ill blood anent so trivial a thing.' And the curé said, 'My children, I were unworthy to be your pastor could I not forgive a wrong; go in peace, and get me as many children as may be, that by the double fees the curé you love may miss starvation.'

"And the bishop often told the story, and it kept his memory of the curé alive, and at last he shifted him to a decent parish, where he can offer a glass of old Medoc to such as are worthy of it. Their name it is not legion."

A light broke in upon Gerard, his countenance showed it.

"Ay!" said his host, "I am that curé: so now thou canst guess why I said 'At their old tricks.' My life on't they have wheedled my successor into remitting those funeral fees. You are well out of that parish. And so am I."

The curé's little niece burst in, "Uncle, the weighing:—la! a stranger!" And burst out.

The curé rose directly, but would not part with Gerard.

"Wet thy beard once more, and come with me."

In the church porch they found the sexton with a huge pair of scales, and weights of all sizes. Several humble persons were standing by, and soon a woman stepped forward with a sickly child and said, "Be it heavy, be it light, I vow, in rye meal of the best, whate'er this child shall weigh, and the same will duly pay to holy Church, an if he shall cast his trouble. Pray, good people, for this child, and for me his mother hither come in dole and care!"

The child was weighed, and yelled as if the scale had been the font.

"Courage! dame," cried Gerard. "This is a good sign. There is plenty of life here to battle its trouble."

"Now, blest be the tongue that tells me so," said the poor woman. She hushed her ponderling against her bosom, and stood aloof watching, whilst another woman brought her child to scale.

But presently a loud, dictatorial voice was heard. "Way there, make way for the seigneur!"

The small folk parted on both sides like waves ploughed by a lordly galley, and in marched in gorgeous attire, his cap adorned by a feather with a topaz at its root, his jerkin richly furred, satin doublet, red hose, shoes like skates, diamond-hilted sword in velvet scabbard, and hawk on his wrist, "the lord of the manor." He flung himself into the scales as if he was lord of the zodiac as well as the manor; whereat the hawk balanced and flapped; but stuck: then winked.

While the sexton heaved in the great weights, the curé told Gerard: "My lord had been sick unto death, and vowed his weight in bread and cheese to the poor, the Church taking her tenth."

"Permit me, my lord; if your lordship continues to press with your lordship's staff on the other scale, you will disturb the balance."

His lordship grinned and removed his staff, and leaned on it. The curé politely but firmly objected to that too.

"Mille diables! what am I to do with it, then?" cried the other.

"Deign to hold it out so, my lord, wide of both scales."

When my lord did this, and so fell into the trap he had laid for holy Church, the good curé whispered to Gerard, "Cretensis incidit in Cretensem!" which I take to mean, "Diamond cut diamond." He then said with an obsequious air, "If that your lordship grudges Heaven full weight, you might set the hawk on your lacquey, and so save a pound."

"Gramercy for thy rede, curé," cried the great man, reproachfully. "Shall I for one sorry pound grudge my poor fowl the benefit of holy Church? I'd as lieve the devil should have me and all my house as her, any day i' the year."

"Sweet is affection," whispered the curé.

"Between a bird and a brute," whispered Gerard.

"Tush!" and the curé looked terrified.

The seigneur's weight was booked, and Heaven I trust and believe did not weigh his gratitude in the balance of the sanctuary.

For my unlearned reader is not to suppose there was anything the least eccentric in the man, or his gratitude to the Giver of health and all good gifts. Men look forward to death, and back upon past sickness, with different eyes. Item, when men drive a bargain, they strive to get the sunny side of it; it matters not one straw whether it is with man or Heaven they are bargaining. In this respect we are the same now, at bottom, as we were four hundred years ago: only in those days we did it a grain or two more naïvely, and that naïveté shone out more palpably, because, in that rude age, body prevailing over mind, all sentiments took material forms. Man repented with scourges, prayed by bead, bribed the saints with wax tapers, put fish into the body to sanctify the soul, sojourned in cold water for empire over the emotions, and thanked God for returning health in 1 cwt. 2 stone 7 lb. 3 oz. 1 dwt. of bread and cheese.

The Cloister and the Hearth

Whilst I have been preaching, who preach so rarely and so ill, the good curé has been soliciting the lord of the manor to step into the church, and give order what shall be done with his great-great-grandfather.

"Ods bodikins! what, have you dug him up?"

"Nay, my lord, he never was buried."

"What, the old dict was true after all?"

"So true that the workmen this very day found a skeleton erect in the pillar they are repairing. I had sent to my lord at once, but I knew he would be here."

"It is he! 'Tis he!" said his descendant, quickening his pace. "Let us go see the old boy. This youth is a stranger I think."

Gerard bowed.

"Know then that my great-great-grandfather held his head high, and, being on the point of death, revolted against lying under the aisle with his forbears for mean folk to pass over. So, as the tradition goes, he swore his son (my great-grandfather) to bury him erect in one of the pillars of the church" (here they entered the porch). " 'For,' quoth he, 'NO BASE MAN SHALL PASS OVER MY STOMACH.' Peste!" and, even while speaking, his lordship parried adroitly with his stick a skull that came hopping at him, bowled by a boy in the middle of the aisle, who took to his heels yelling with fear the moment he saw what he had done. His lordship hurled the skull furiously after him as he ran, at which the curé gave a shout of dismay and put forth his arm to hinder him, but was too late.

The curé groaned aloud. And, as if this had evoked spirits of mischief, up started a whole pack of children from some ambuscade, and unseen, but heard loud enough, clattered out of the church like a covey rising in a thick wood.

"Oh! these pernicious brats," cried the curé. "The workmen cannot go to their nonemete but the church is rife with them. Pray Heaven they have not found his late lordship; nay, I mind, I hid his lordship under a workman's jerkin, and—saints defend us! the jerkin has been moved."

The poor curé's worst misgivings were realized: the rising generation of plebeians had played the mischief with the haughty old noble. "The little ones had jockeyed for the bones oh" and pocketed such of them as seemed adapted for certain primitive games then in vogue amongst them.

"I'll excommunicate them," roared the curate, "and all their race."

"Never heed," said the scapegrace lord: and stroked his hawk; "there is enough of him to swear by. Put him back! put him back!"

"Surely, my lord, 'tis your will his bones be laid in hallowed earth, and masses said for his poor prideful soul?"

The noble stroked his hawk.

"Are ye there, Master Curé?" said he. "Nay, the business is too old: he is out of purgatory by this time, *up or down*. I shall not draw my pursestrings for him. Every dog his day. Adieu, Messires, adieu, ancestor:" and he sauntered off whistling to his hawk and caressing it.

His reverence looked ruefully after him.

"Cretensis incidit in Cretensem," said he sorrowfully. "I thought I had him safe for a dozen masses. Yet I blame him not, but that young ne'er-do-weel which did trundle his ancestor's skull at us: for who could venerate his great-great-grandsire and play football with his head? Well it behoves us to be better Christians than he is." So they gathered the bones reverently, and the curé locked them up and forbade the workmen, who now entered the church, to close up the pillar, till he should recover by threats of the Church's wrath every atom of my lord. And he showed Gerard a famous shrine in the church. Before it were the usual gifts of tapers, &c. There was also a wax image of a falcon, most curiously moulded and coloured to the life, eyes and all. Gerard's eye fell at once on this, and he expressed the liveliest admiration. The curé assented. Then Gerard asked "Could the saint have loved hawking?"

The curé laughed at his simplicity. "Nay, 'tis but a statuary hawk. When they have a bird of gentle breed they cannot train they make his image, and send it to this shrine with a present, and pray the saint to work upon the stubborn mind of the original, and make it ductile as wax: that is the notion, and methinks a reasonable one, too."

Gerard assented. "But alack, reverend sir, were I a saint, methinks I should side with the innocent dove, rather than with the cruel hawk that rends her."

"By St. Denys you are right," said the curé. "But, que voulez-vous? the saints are débonair, and have been flesh themselves, and know man's frailty and absurdity. 'Tis the Bishop of Avignon sent this one."

"What do bishops hawk in this country?"

"One and all. Every noble person hawks, and lives with hawk on wrist. Why my lord abbot hard by, and his lordship that has just parted from us, had a two years' feud as to where they should put their hawks down on that very altar there. Each claimed the right hand of the altar for his bird."

"What desecration!"

"Nay! nay! thou knowest we make them doff both glove and hawk to take the blessed eucharist. Their jewelled gloves will they give to a servant or simple Christian to hold: but their beloved hawks they will put down on no place less than the altar."

Gerard inquired how the battle of the hawks ended.

"Why, the abbot he yielded, as the Church yields to laymen. He searched ancient books, and found that the left hand was the more honourable, being in truth the right hand, since the altar is east, but looks westward. So he gave my lord the soi-disant right hand, and contented himself with the real right hand, and even so may the Church still outwit the lay nobles and their arrogance, saving your presence."

"Nay, sir, I honour the Church. I am convent bred, and owe all I have and am to holy Church."

"Ah, that accounts for my sudden liking to thee. Art a gracious youth. Come and see me whenever thou wilt."

Gerard took this as a hint that he might go now. It jumped with his own wish, for he was curious to hear what Denys had seen and done all this time. He made his reverence and walked out of the church; but was no sooner clear of it than he set off to run with all his might: and, tearing round a corner, ran into a large stomach, whose owner clutched him, to keep himself steady under the shock; but did not release his hold on regaining his equilibrium.

"Let go, man," said Gerard.

"Not so. You are my prisoner."

"Prisoner?"

"Ay."

"What for in heaven's name?"

"What for? Why sorcery."

"SORCERY?"

"Sorcery."

CHAPTER XXXVII

THE culprits were condemned to stand pinioned in the market-place for two hours, that should any persons recognize them or any of them as guilty of other crimes, they might depose to that effect at the trial.

They stood however the whole period, and no one advanced anything fresh against them. This was the less remarkable that they were night birds, vampires who preyed in the dark on weary travellers, mostly strangers.

But, just as they were being taken down, a fearful scream was heard in the crowd, and a woman pointed at one of them, with eyes almost starting from their sockets: but ere she could speak she fainted away.

Then men and women crowded round her partly to aid her, partly from curiosity. When she began to recover they fell to conjectures.

" 'Twas at him she pointed."

"Nay, 'twas at this one."

"Nay, nay," said another, " 'twas at yon hangdog with the hair hung round his neck."

All further conjecture was cut short. The poor creature no sooner recovered her senses than she flew at the landlord like a lioness. "My child! Man! man! Give me back my child." And she seized the glossy golden hair that the officers had hung round his neck, and tore it from his neck, and covered it with kisses: then, her poor confused mind clearing, she saw even by this token that her lost girl was dead, and sank suddenly down shrieking and sobbing so over the poor hair, that the crowd rushed on the assassin with one savage growl. His life had ended then and speedily, for in those days all carried death at their girdles. But Denys drew his sword directly, and shouting "A moi, camarades!" kept the mob at bay. "Who lays a finger on him dies." Other archers backed him, and with some difficulty they kept him uninjured, while Denys appealed to those who shouted for his blood.

"What sort of vengeance is this? would you be so mad as rob the wheel, and give the vermin an easy death?"

The Cloister and the Hearth

The mob was kept passive by the archers' steel rather than by Denys's words, and growled at intervals with flashing eyes. The municipal officers seeing this, collected round, and with the archers made a guard, and prudently carried the accused back to gaol.

The mob hooted them, and the prisoners, indiscriminately. Denys saw the latter safely lodged, then made for the "White Hart," where he expected to find Gerard.

On the way he saw two girls working at a first floor window. He saluted them. They smiled. He entered into conversation. Their manners were easy, their complexion high.

He invited them to a repast at the "White Hart." They objected. He acquiesced in their refusal. They consented. And in this charming society he forgot all about poor Gerard, who meantime was carried off to gaol; but on the way suddenly stopped, having now somewhat recovered his presence of mind and, demanded to know by whose authority he was arrested. "By the vice-baillie's," said the constable.

"The vice-baillie! Alas! what have I a stranger done to offend a vice-ballie? For this charge of sorcery must be a blind. No sorcerer am I: but a poor true lad far from his home."

This vague shift disgusted the officer. "Show him the capias, Jacques," said he.

Jacques held out the writ in both hands about a yard and a half from Gerard's eye; and at the same moment the large constable suddenly pinned him; both officers were on tenter-hooks lest the prisoner should grab the document, to which they attached a superstitious importance.

But the poor prisoner had no such thought. Query whether he would have touched it with the tongs. He just craned out his neck and read it, and, to his infinite surprise, found the vice-bailiff who had signed the writ was the friendly alderman. He took courage and assured his captor there was some error. But finding he made no impression, demanded to be taken before the alderman.

"What say you to that, Jacques?"

"Impossible. We have no orders to take him before his worship. Read the writ!"

"Nay, but good kind fellows, what harm can it be? I will give ye each an écu."

"Jacques, what say you to that?"

"Humph? I say we have no orders not to take him to his worship. Read the writ!"

"Then say we take him to prison round by his worship."

It was agreed. They got the money: and bade Gerard observe they were doing him a favour. He saw they wanted a little gratitude as well as much silver. He tried to satisfy *this* cupidity, but it stuck in his throat. Feigning was not his forte.

He entered the alderman's presence with his heart in his mouth, and begged with faltering voice to know what he had done to offend since he left that very room with Manon and Denys.

"Nought that I know of," said the alderman.

On the writ being shown him, he told Gerard he had signed it at daybreak. "I get old and my memory faileth me: a discussing of the girl I quite forgot your own offence: but I remember now. All is well. You are he I committed for sorcery. Stay! ere you go to gaol, you shall hear what your accuser says: run and fetch him, you."

The man could not find the accuser all at once. So the alderman, getting impatient, told Gerard the main charge was that he had set a dead body a burning with diabolical fire, that flamed, but did not consume. "And if 'tis true, young man, I'm sorry for thee, for thou wilt assuredly burn with fire of good pine logs in the marketplace of Neufchasteau."

"Oh, sir, for pity's sake let me have speech with his reverence the curé."

The alderman advised Gerard against it. "The Church was harder upon sorcerers than was the corporation."

"But, sir, I am innocent," said Gerard, between snarling and whining.

"Oh; if *you—think—*you are *innocent—*officer, go with him to the curé! but see he 'scape you not. Innocent quotha?"

They found the curé in his doublet repairing a wheelbarrow. Gerard told him all, and appealed piteously to him. "Just for using a little phosphorus—in self-defence—against cut-throats they are going to hang."

It was lucky for our magician that he had already told his tale in full to the curé: for thus that shrewd personage had hold of the stick at the right end. The corporation held it by the ferule. His reverence looked exceedingly grave and said, "I must question you privately on this untoward business." He took him into a private room and bade the officer stand outside and guard the door, and be ready to come if called. The big constable stood outside the door, quaking, and expecting to see the room fly away and leave a stink of brimstone. Instantly they were alone the curé unlocked his countenance and was himself again.

"Show me the trick on't," said he, all curiosity.

"I cannot, sir, unless the room be darkened."

The curé speedily closed out the light with a wooden shutter. "Now then."

"But on what shall I put it?" said Gerard. "Here is no dead face. 'Twas that made it look so dire." The curé groped about the room. "Good: here is an image: 'tis my patron saint."

"Heaven forbid! That were profanation."

"Pshaw! 'twill rub off, will't not?"

"Ay, but it goes against me to take such liberty with a saint," objected the sorcerer.

"Fiddlestick!" said the divine.

"To be sure my putting it on his holiness will show your reverence it is no Satanic art."

"Mayhap 'twas for that I did propose it," said the curé subtly.

Thus encouraged Gerard fired the eyes and nostrils of the image and made the curé jump. Then lighted up the hair in patches: and set the whole face shining like a glowworm's.

"By'r Lady," shouted the curé, " 'tis strange, and small my wonder that they took you for a magician, seeing a dead face thus fired. Now come thy ways with me!"

He put on his grey gown and great hat, and in a few minutes they found themselves in presence of the alderman. By his side, poisoning his mind, stood the accuser, a singular figure in red hose and red shoes, a black gown with blue bands, and a cocked hat.

After saluting the alderman, the curé turned to this personage and said good-humouredly, "So, Mangis, at thy work again, babbling away honest men's lives! Come, your worship, this is the old tale; two of a trade can ne'er agree. Here is Mangis, who professes sorcery, and would sell himself to Satan to-night, but that Satan is not so weak as to buy what he can have gratis, this Mangis, who would be a sorcerer, but is only a quacksalver, accuses of magic a true lad, who did but use in self-defence a secret of chemistry well known to me and to all churchmen."

"But he is no churchman to dabble in such mysteries," objected the alderman.

"He is more churchman than layman, being convent bred, and in the lesser orders," said the ready curé. "Therefore, sorcerer, withdraw thy plaint without more words!"

"That will I not, your reverence," replied Mangis stoutly. "A sorcerer I am, but a white one, not a black one. I make no pact with Satan, but on the contrary still battle him with lawful and necessary arts. I ne'er profane the sacraments, as do the black sorcerers, nor turn myself into a cat and go sucking infants' blood, nor e'en their breath, nor set dead men o' fire. I but tell the peasants when their cattle and their hens are possessed, and at what time of the moon to plant rye, and what days in each month are lucky for wooing of women and selling of bullocks, and so forth: above all, it is my art and my trade to detect the black magicians, as I did that whole tribe of them who were burnt at Dol but last year."

"Ay, Mangis. And what is the upshot of that famous fire thy tongue did kindle?"

"Why, their ashes were cast to the wind."

"Ay. But the true end of thy comedy is this. The parliament of Dijon hath since sifted the matter, and found they were no sorcerers, but good and peaceful citizens; and but last week did order masses to be said for their souls, and expiatory farces and mysteries to be played for them in seven towns of Burgundy; all which will not of those cinders make men and women again. Now 'tis our custom in this land, when we have slain the innocent by hearkening to false knaves like thee, not to blame our credulous ears, but the false tongue that gulled them. Wherefore bethink thee that, at a word from me to my lord bishop, thou wilt smell burning pine nearer than e'er knave smelt it and lived, and wilt travel on a smoky cloud to him whose heart thou bearest (for the word devil in the Latin it meaneth 'false accuser'), and whose livery thou wearest."

And the curé pointed at Mangis with his staff.

"That is true i'fegs," said the alderman, "for red and black be the foul fiendys colours."

By this time the white sorcerer's cheek was as colourless as his dress was fiery. Indeed the contrast amounted to pictorial. He stammered out "I respect holy Church and her will; he shall fire the churchyard, and all in it, for me: I do withdraw the plaint."

"Then withdraw thyself," said the vice-bailiff.

The moment he was gone, the curé took the conversational tone, and told the alderman courteously that the accused had received the chemical substance from holy Church, and had restored it her, by giving it all to him.

"Then 'tis in good hands," was the reply; "young man, you are free. Let me have your reverence's prayers."

"Doubt it not! Humph? Vice-baillie, the town owes me four silver franks, this three months and more."

"They shall be paid, curé, ay, ere the week be out."

On this good understanding Church and State parted. As soon as he was in the street Gerard caught the priest's hand, and kissed it.

"Oh, sir! Oh, your reverence. You have saved me from the fiery stake. What can I say, what do? what—"

"Nought, foolish lad. Bounty rewards itself. Natheless— Humph?—I wish I had done't without leasing. It ill becomes my function to utter falsehoods."

"Falsehood, sir?" Gerard was mystified.

"Didst not hear me say thou hadst given me that same phosphorus? 'Twill cost me a fortnight's penance, that light word." The curé sighed, and his eye twinkled cunningly.

"Nay, nay," cried Gerard eagerly. "Now Heaven forbid! That was no falsehood, father: well you knew the phosphorus was yours, is yours." And he thrust the bottle into the curé's hand; "But alas, 'tis too poor a gift: will you not take from my purse somewhat for holy Church?" and now he held out his purse with glistening eyes.

"Nay," said the other brusquely, and put his hands quickly behind him: "not a doit. Fie! fie! art pauper et exul. Come thou rather each day at noon and take thy diet with me; for my heart warms to thee;" and he went off abruptly with his hands behind him.

They itched.

But they itched in vain.

Where there's a heart there's a Rubicon.

Gerard went hastily to the inn to relieve Denys of the anxiety so long and mysterious an absence must have caused him. He found him seated at his ease, playing dice with two young ladies whose manners were unreserved, and complexion high.

Gerard was hurt. "N'oubliez point la Jeanneton!" said he, colouring up.

"What of her?" said Denys gaily rattling the dice.

"She said 'le peu que sont les femmes.'"

"Oh did she? and what say you to that, mesdemoiselles?"

"We say that none run women down, but such as are too old or too ill-favoured, or too witless, to please them."

"Witless, quotha. Wise men have not folly enough to please them, nor madness enough to desire to please them," said Gerard loftily: "but 'tis to my comrade I speak, not to you, you brazen toads, that make so free with a man at first sight."

"Preach away, comrade. Fling a byword or two at our heads. Know, girls, that he is a very Solomon for bywords. Methinks he was brought up by hand on 'em."

"Be thy friendship a byword!" retorted Gerard. "The friendship that melts to nought at sight of a farthingale."

"Malheureux!" cried Denys, "I speak but pellets, and thou answerest daggers."

"Would I could," was the reply. "Adieu."

"What a little savage!" said one of the girls.

Gerard opened the door and put in his head. "I have thought of a byword," said he spitefully,

> " 'Qui hante femmes et dez
> Il mourra en pauvretez.'

There." And having delivered this thunderbolt of antique wisdom he slammed the door viciously ere any of them could retort.

And now, being somewhat exhausted by his anxieties, he went to the bar for a morsel of bread and a cup of wine. The landlord would sell nothing less than a pint bottle. Well then he would have a bottle: but, when he came to compare the contents of the bottle with its size, great was the discrepancy: on this he examined the bottle keenly, and found that the glass was thin where the bottle tapered, but towards the bottom unnaturally thick. He pointed this out at once.

The landlord answered superciliously that he did not make bottles: and was nowise accountable for their shape.

The Cloister and the Hearth

"That we will see presently," said Gerard. "I will take this thy pint to the vice-bailiff."

"Nay, nay, for Heaven's sake," cried the landlord changing his tone at once. "I love to content my customers. If, by chance this pint be short, we will charge it and its fellow three sous, instead of two sous each."

"So be it. But much I admire that you, the host of so fair an inn, should practise thus. The wine too smacketh strongly of spring water."

"Young sir," said the landlord, "we cut no travellers' throats at this inn, as they do at most. However, you know all about that. The 'White Hart' is no lion, nor bear. Whatever masterful robbery is done here, is done upon the poor host. How then could he live at all if he dealt not a little crooked with the few who pay?"

Gerard objected to this system root and branch. Honest trade was small profits, quick returns; and neither to cheat nor be cheated.

The landlord sighed at this picture. "So might one keep an inn in heaven, but not in Burgundy. When foot soldiers going to the wars are quartered on me, how can I but lose by their custom? Two sous per day is their pay, and they eat two sous' worth, and drink into the bargain. The pardoners are my good friends, but palmers and pilgrims, what think you I gain by them? marry, a loss. Minstrels and jongleurs draw custom, and so claim to pay no score, except for liquor. By the secular monks I neither gain nor lose, but the black and grey friars have made vow of poverty, but not of famine; eat like wolves and give the poor host nought but their prayers; and mayhap not them: how can he tell? In my father's day we had the weddings: but now the great gentry let their houses and their plates, their mugs, and their spoons, to any honest couple that want to wed, and thither the very mechanics go with their brides and bridal train. They come not to us: indeed we could not find seats and vessels for such a crowd as eat and drink and dance the week out at the homeliest wedding now. In my father's day the great gentry sold wine by the barrel only; but now they have leave to cry it, and sell it by the galopin, in the very market-place. How can we vie with them? They grow it. We buy it of the grower. The coroner's quests we have still, and these would bring goodly profit, but the meat is aye gone ere the mouths be full."

The Cloister and the Hearth

"You should make better provision," suggested his hearer.

"The law will not let us. We are forbidden to go into the market for the first hour. So, when we arrive, the burghers have bought all but the refuse. Besides the law forbids us to buy more than three bushels of meal at a time: yet market day comes but once a week. As for the butchers, they will not kill for us unless we bribe them."

"Courage!" said Gerard kindly, "the shoe pinches every trader somewhere."

"Ay: but not as it pinches us. Our shoe is trode all o' one side as well as pinches us lame. A savoir, if we pay not the merchants we buy meal, meat, and wine of, they can cast us into prison and keep us there till we pay or die. But we cannot cast into prison those who buy those very victuals of us. A traveller's horse we may keep for his debt; but where in Heaven's name? In our own stable, eating his head off at our cost. Nay, we may keep the traveller himself, but where? In gaol? Nay, in our own good house, and there must we lodge and feed him gratis. And so fling good silver after bad? merci; no: let him go with a wanion. Our honestest customers are the thieves. Would to Heaven there were more of them. They look not too close into the shape of the canakin, nor into the host's reckoning: with them and with their purses 'tis lightly come, and lightly go. Also they spend freely, not knowing but each carouse may be their last. But the thief-takers, instead of profiting by this fair example, are for ever robbing the poor host. When noble or honest travellers descend at our door, come the provost's men pretending to suspect them, and demanding to search them and their papers. To save which offence the host must bleed wine and meat. Then come the excise to examine all your weights and measures. You must stop their mouths with meat and wine. Town excise. Royal excise. Parliament excise. A swarm of them, and all with a wolf in their stomachs and a sponge in their gullets. Monks, friars, pilgrims, palmers, soldiers, excisemen, provost-marshals and men, and mere bad debtors, how can the 'White Hart' butt against all these? Cutting no throats in self-defence as do your 'Swans' and 'Roses' and 'Boar's Heads' and 'Red Lions' and 'Eagles,' your 'Moons,' 'Stars,' and 'Moors,' how can the 'White Hart' give a pint of wine for a pint? And everything risen so. Why, lad, not a pound of bread I sell but costs me three

247

good copper deniers, twelve to the sou; and each pint of wine, bought by the tun, costs me four deniers; every sack of charcoal two sous, and gone in a day. A pair of partridges five sous. What think you of that? Heard one ever the like? five sous for two little beasts all bone and feather? A pair of pigeons, thirty deniers. 'Tis ruination!!! For we may not raise *our* pricen with the market. Oh no. I tell thee the shoe is trod all o' one side as well as pinches the water into our eyn. We may charge nought for mustard, pepper, salt, or firewood. Think you we get them for nought? Candle it is a sou the pound. Salt five sous the stone, pepper four sous the pound, mustard twenty deniers the pint: and raw meat, dwindleth it on the spit with no cost to me but loss of weight? Why what think you I pay my cook? But you shall never guess. A HUNDRED SOUS A YEAR AS I AM A LIVING SINNER.

"And my waiter thirty sous, besides his perquisites. He is a hantle richer than I am. And then to be insulted as well as pillaged. Last Sunday I went to church, It is a place I trouble not often. Didn't the curé lash the hotel-keepers? I grant you he hit all the trades, except the one that is a byword for looseness, and pride, and sloth, to wit the clergy. But, mind you, he stripeit the other lay estates with a feather, but us hotel-keepers with a neat's pizzle: godless for this, godless for that, and most godless of all for opening our doors during mass. Why the law forces us to open at all hours to travellers from another town, stopping, halting, or passing: those be the words. They can fine us before the bailiff if we refuse them, mass or no mass: and, say a townsman should creep in with the true travellers, are we to blame? They all vow they are tired wayfarers; and can I ken every face in a great town like this? So if we respect the law our poor souls are to suffer, and if we respect it not, our poor lank purses must bleed at two holes, fine and loss of custom."

A man speaking of himself in general, is "a babbling brook;" of his wrongs, "a shining river."

"Labitur et labetur in omne volubilis ævum."

So luckily for my readers, though not for all concerned, this injured orator was arrested in mid career. Another man burst in upon his wrongs with all the advantage of a recent wrong; a wrong red hot. It was Denys cursing and swearing and crying that he was robbed.

"Did those hussies pass this way? who are they? where do they bide? They have ta'en my purse and fifteen golden pieces: raise the hue and cry! ah! traitresses! vipers! These inns are all guet-apens."

"There now," cried the landlord to Gerard.

Gerard implored him to be calm and say how it had befallen.

"First one went out on some pretence: then after a while the other went to fetch her back, and, neither returning, I clapped hand to purse and found it empty: the ungrateful creatures, I was letting them win it in a gallop: but loaded dice were not quick enough; they must claw it all in a lump."

Gerard was for going at once to the alderman and setting the officers to find them.

"Not I," said Denys. "I hate the law. No: as it came so let it go."

Gerard would not give it up so.

At a hint from the landlord he forced Denys along with him to the provost-marshal. That dignitary shook his head. "We have no clue to occasional thieves, that work honestly at their needles, till some gull comes and tempts them with an easy booty, and then they pluck him."

"Come away," cried Denys furiously. "I knew what use a bourgeois would be to me at a pinch:" and he marched off in a rage.

"They are clear of the town ere this," said Gerard.

"Speak no more on't if you prize my friendship. I have five pieces with the bailiff, and ten I left with Marion, luckily: or these traitresses had feathered their nest with my last plume. What dost gape for so? Nay, I do ill to vent my choler on thee: I'll tell thee all. Art wiser than I. What saidst thou at the door? No matter. Well then I did offer marriage to that Marion."

Gerard was dumbfoundered.

"What? you offered her what?"

"Marriage. Is that such a mighty strange thing to offer a wench?"

"'Tis a strange thing to offer to a strange girl in passing."

"Nay, I am not such a sot as you opine. I saw the corn in all that chaff. I knew I could not get her by fair means, so I was fain to try foul. 'Mademoiselle,' said I, 'marriage is not one of my habits, but struck by your qualities I make an exception: deign to bestow this hand on me.'"

"And she bestowed it on thine ear."

"Not so. On the contrary she— Art a disrespectful young monkey. Know that here, not being Holland or any other barbarous state, courtesy begets courtesy. Says she a colouring like a rose, 'Soldier, you are too late. He is not a patch on you for looks, but then—he has loved me a long time.'

"'He? who?'

"'T'other.'

"'What other?'

"'Why he that was not too late.' Oh, that is the way they all speak, the loves; the she-wolves. Their little minds go in leaps. Think you they marshal their words in order of battle? their tongues are in too great a hurry. Says she, 'I love him not; not to say love him: but he does me, and dearly: and for that reason I'd sooner die than cause him grief, I would.'"

"Now I believe she did love him."

"Who doubts that? Why she said so, round about, as they always say these things, and with 'nay' for 'ay'. 'I hope you will be happy together,' said I.

"Well one thing led to another, and at last as she could not give me her hand, she gave me a piece of advice, and that was to leave part of my money with the young mistress. Then, when bad company had cleaned me out, I should have some to travel back with, said she. I said I would better her advice, and leave it with her. Her face got red. Says she, 'Think what you do. Chambermaids have an ill name for honesty.' 'Oh, the devil is not so black as he is painted,' said I. 'I'll risk it;' and I left fifteen gold pieces with her."

Gerard sighed. "I wish you may ever see them again. It is wondrous in what esteem you do hold this sex, to trust so to the first comer. For my part I know little about them; I never saw but one I could love as well as I love thee. But the ancients must surely know; and they held women cheap. 'Levius quid fœminâ,' said they, which is but la Jeanneton's tune in Latin, 'Le peu que sont les femmes.' Also do but see how the greybeards of our own day speak of them, being no longer blinded by desire: this alderman to wit."

"Oh novice of novices," cried Denys, "not to have seen why that old fool rails so on the poor things! One day, out of the millions of women he blackens one did prefer some other man to him: for which solitary piece of bad taste, and ten to one 'twas good taste, he doth bespatter creation's fairer half, thereby proving what? le peu que sont les hommes."

"I see women have a shrewd champion in thee," said Gerard, with a smile. But the next moment inquired gravely why he had not told him all this before.,

Denys grinned. "Had the girl said 'Ay,' why then I had told thee straight. But 'tis a rule with us soldiers never to publish our defeats: 'tis much if after each check we claim not a victory."

"Now that is true," said Gerard, "Young as I am, I have seen this: that after every great battle the generals on both sides go to the nearest church and sing each a Te Deum for the victory: methinks a Te Martem, or Te Bellonam, or Te Mercurium, Mercury being the god of lies, were more fitting."

"Pas si bête," said Denys, approvingly. "Hast a good eye: canst see a steeple by daylight. So now tell me how thou hast fared in this town all day."

"Come," said Gerard, " 'tis well thou hast asked me: for else I had never told thee." He then related in full how he had been arrested, and by what a providential circumstance he had escaped long imprisonment or speedy conflagration.

His narrative produced an effect he had little expected or desired. "I am a traitor," cried Denys. "I left thee in a strange place to fight thine own battles, while I shook the dice with those jades. Now take thou this sword and pass it through my body forthwith."

"What for in Heaven's name?" inquired Gerard.

"For an example," roared Denys. "For a warning to all false loons that profess friendship, and disgrace it."

"Oh, very well," said Gerard. "Yes. Not a bad notion. Where will you have it?"

"Here, through my heart; that is, where other men have a heart, but I none, or a satanic false one."

Gerard made a motion to run him through, and flung his arms

round his neck instead. "I know no way to thy heart but this,
thou great silly thing."

Denys uttered an exclamation, then hugged him warmly,—and,
quite overcome by this sudden turn of youthful affection and native
grace, gulped out in a broken voice "Railest on women—and art
—like them—with thy pretty ways. Thy mother's milk is in thee
still. Satan would love thee, or—le bon Dieu would kick him out
of hell for shaming it. Give me thy hand! Give me thy hand!
May" (a tremendous oath) "if I let thee out of my sight till Italy."

And so the stanch friends were more than reconciled after their
short tiff.

The next day the thieves were tried. The pièces de conviction
were reduced in number, to the great chagrin of the little clerk, by
the interment of the bones. But there was still a pretty show. A
thief's hand struck off flagrante delicto; a murdered woman's hair;
the Abbot's axe, and other tools of crime. The skulls &c. were sworn
to by the constables who had found them. Evidence was lax in that
age and place. They all confessed but the landlord. And Manon
was called to bring the crime home to him. Her evidence was con-
clusive. He made a vain attempt to shake her credibility by drawing from her that her own sweetheart had been one of the gang, and
that she had held her tongue so long as he was alive. The public
prosecutor came to the aid of his witness, and elicited that a knife
had been held to her throat, and her own sweetheart had sworn with
solemn oaths to kill her should she betray them, and that this
terrible threat, and not the mere fear of death, had glued her lips.

The other thieves were condemned to be hanged, and the landlord
to be broken on the wheel. He uttered a piercing cry when his
sentence was pronounced.

As for poor Manon she became the subject of universal criticism.
Nor did opinion any longer run dead in her favour; it divided into
two broad currents. And, strange to relate, the majority of her
own sex took her part, and the males were but equally divided;
which hardly happens once in a hundred years. Perhaps some lady
will explain the phenomenon. As for me, I am a little shy of ex-
plaining things I don't understand. It has become so common.
Meantime, had she been a lover of notoriety, she would have been
happy, for the town talked of nothing but her. The poor girl however had but one wish; to escape the crowd that followed her, and

hide her head somewhere where she could cry over her "pendard," whom all these proceedings brought vividly back to her affectionate remembrance. Before he was hanged he had threatened her life: but she was not one of your fastidious girls, who love their male divinities any the less for beating them, kicking them, or killing them, but rather the better, provided these attentions are interspersed with occasional caresses; so it would have been odd indeed had she taken offence at a mere threat of that sort. He had never threatened her with a rival. She sobbed single-mindedly.

Meantime the inn was filled with thirsters for a sight of her, who feasted and drank, to pass away the time till she should deign to appear. When she had been sobbing some time, there was a tap at her door, and the landlord entered with a proposal. "Nay, weep not, good lass, your fortune it is made an you like. Say the word, and you are chambermaid of the 'White Hart.'"

"Nay, nay," said Manon with a fresh burst of grief. "Never more will I be a servant in an inn. I'll go to my mother."

The landlord consoled and coaxed her: and she became calmer, but none the less determined against his proposal.

The landlord left her. But ere long he returned and made her another proposal. Would she be his wife, and landlady of the "White Hart?"

"You do ill to mock me," said she sorrowfully.

"Nay, sweetheart. I mock thee not. I am too old for sorry jests. Say you the word, and you are my partner for better for worse."

She looked at him, and saw he was in earnest: on this she suddenly rained hard to the memory of "le pendard:" the tears came in a torrent being the last; and she gave her hand to the landlord of the "White Hart," and broke a gold crown with him in sign of plighted troth.

"We will keep it dark till the house is quiet," said the landlord.

"Ay," said she: "but meantime prithee give me linen to hem, or work to do: for the time hangs on me like lead."

Her betrothed's eye brightened at this house-wifely request, and he brought her up two dozen flagons of various sizes to clean and polish.

She gathered complacency as she reflected that by a strange turn of fortune all this bright pewter was to be hers.

The Cloister and the Hearth

And this mighty furbishing up of pewter reminds me that justice requires me to do a stroke of the same work.

Well then, the deposition, read out in the alderman's room as Manon's, was not so exact as such things ought to be. The alderman had condensed her evidence. Now there are in every great nation about three persons capable of condensing evidence without falsifying it: but this alderman was not one of that small band. In the first part of the deposition he left out as unimportant these words "my mother advised me to keep out of his way till his wrath should cool."

Between the words "jealous of me" and "the reason" Manon had said "My master was aye at my heels: so I told my mistress, and said I would rather go than be cause of mischief." This the alderman suppressed as mere babel: whereas it was a worthy trait. He also let slip the word "afterwards" in the next sentence. Manon had said the reason they gave *afterwards, i. e.,* "when I was no longer there to contradict them." And so on all through the deposition.

Sometimes the deponent suffered as many a one does now-a-days, in the newspaper and other reports, by the mere suppression of the question. For instance this is what actually was said:—

The Alderman. "Come now, should you have interfered if this soldier had had no beard?"

Manon. "How can I tell what I *should* have done?"

Now this was merely a sensible answer to a monstrous question no magistrate had a right to put. But, under the condensing process, behold her saddled with a volunteer statement of a very damaging character.

Finally she had said, "I am sorry I told, if I am to be hanged for it."

This the old boy condensed ut supra, p. 136, anticipating as far as possible the tuneful Sinclair.*

* Sinclair was a singer; and complained to the manager that in the operatic play of Rob Roy he had a multitude of mere words to utter between the songs. 'Cut, my boy, cut!' said the manager. On this vox et p. n. cut Scott, and doubtless many of his cuts would not have discredited the condensers of evidence. But only one of his master-strokes has reached posterity. His melodious organs had been taxed with this sentence: "Rashleigh is my cousin; but, for what reason I cannot divine, he is my bitterest enemy." This he condensed and delivered thus:—"Rashleigh is my cousin, but for what reason I cannot divine."

254

The Cloister and the Hearth

Whilst Manon and I were cleaning, she her coming, I my parting, pewter, the landlord went down stairs and falling in with our friends drew them aside into the bar.

He then addressed Denys with considerable solemnity. "We are old acquaintances, and you want not for sagacity: now advise me in a strait. My custom is somewhat declining: this girl Manon is the talk of the town; see how full the inn is to-night. She doth refuse to be my chambermaid. I have half a mind to marry her. What think you? shall I say the word?"

Denys in reply merely opened his eyes wide with amazement.

The landlord turned to Gerard with a half-inquiring look.

"Nay, sir," said Gerard. "I am too young to advise my seniors and betters."

"No matter. Let us hear your thought."

"Well, sir, it was said of a good wife by the ancients 'bene quæ latuit, bene vixit,' that is, she is the best wife that is least talked of: but here 'male quæ patuit' were as near the mark. Therefore, an you bear the lass good-will, why not club purses with Denys and me and convey her safe home with a dowry? Then mayhap some rustical person in her own place may be brought to wive her."

"Why so many words?" said Denys. "This old fox is not the ass he affects to be."

"Oh! that is your advice is it?" said the landlord testily. "Well then we shall soon know who is the fool, you or me, for I have spoken to her as it happens; and what is more she has said Ay, and she is polishing the flagons at this moment."

"Oho!" said Denys drily, "'twas an ambuscade. Well, in that case, my advice is, run for the notary, tie the noose, and let us three drink the bride's health, till we see six sots a-tippling."

"And shall. Ay, now you utter sense."

In ten minutes a civil marriage was effected upstairs before a notary and his clerk and our two friends.

In ten minutes more the white hind, dead sick of seclusion, had taken her place within the bar, and was serving out liquids, and bustling, and her color rising a little.

In six minutes more she soundly rated a careless servant-girl for carrying a nipperkin of wine awry and spilling good liquor.

During the evening she received across the bar eight offers of marriage, some of them from respectable burghers. Now the

255

landlord and our two friends had in perfect innocence ensconced themselves behind a screen to drink at their ease the new couple's health. The above comedy was thrown in for their entertainment by bounteous fate. They heard the proposals made one after another, and uninventive Manon's invariable answer—"Serviteur; you are a day after the fair." The landlord chuckled and looked good-natured superiority at both his late advisers, with their traditional notions that men shun a woman "quæ patuit," *i. e.*, who has become the town talk.

But Denys scarce noticed the spouse's triumph over him, he was so occupied with his own over Gerard. At each munic pal tender of undying affection, he turned almost purple with the effort it cost him not to roar with glee; and driving his elbow into the deep-meditating and much-puzzled pupil of antiquity, whispered "le peu que sont les hommes."

The next morning Gerard was eager to start, but Denys was under a vow to see the murderers of the golden-haired girl executed.

Gerard respected his vow, but avoided his example.

He went to bid the curé farewell instead, and sought and received his blessing. About noon the travellers got clear of the town. Just outside the south gate they passed the gallows; it had eight tenants: the skeleton of Manon's late wept, and now being fast forgotten, lover, and the bodies of those who had so nearly taken our travellers' lives. A hand was nailed to the beam. And hard by on a huge wheel was clawed the dead landlord, with every bone in his body broken to pieces.

Gerard averted his head and hurried by. Denys lingered, and crowed over his dead foes. "Times are changed, my lads, since we two sat shaking in the cold awaiting you seven to come and cut our throats."

"Fie, Denys! Death squares all reckonings. Prithee pass on without another word, if you prize my respect a groat."

To this earnest remonstrance Denys yielded. He even said thoughtfully "you have been better brought up than I."

About three in the afternoon they reached a little town with the people buzzing in knots. The wolves, starved by the cold, had entered, and eaten two grown-up persons over-night, in the main street: so some were blaming the eaten; "none but fools or knaves are about after nightfall;" others the law for not protecting the town, and others the corporation for not enforcing what laws there were.

"Bah! this is nothing to us," said Denys, and was for resuming their march.

"Ay, but 'tis," remonstrated Gerard.

"What, are we the pair they ate?"

"No, but we may be the next pair."

"Ay, neighbour," said an ancient man, " 'tis the town's fault for not obeying the ducal ordinance, which bids every shopkeeper light a lamp o'er his door at sunset, and burn it till sunrise."

On this Denys asked him somewhat derisively, "What made him fancy rush dips would scare away empty wolves? Why mutton fat is all their joy."

" 'Tis not the fat, vain man, but the light. All ill things hate light; especially wolves and the imps that lurk, I ween, under their fur. Example; Paris city stands in a wood like, and the wolves do howl around it all night: yet of late years wolves come but little in the streets. For why, in that burgh the watchmen do thunder at each door that is dark, and make the weary wight rise and light. 'Tis my son tells me. He is a great voyager, my son Nicholas."

In further explanation he assured them that previously to that ordinance no city had been worse infested with wolves than Paris; a troop had boldly assaulted the town in 1420, and in 1438 they had eaten fourteen persons in a single month between Montmartre and the gate St. Antoine, and that not a winter month even, but September: and as for the dead, which nightly lay in the streets slain in midnight brawls, or assassinated, the wolves had used to devour them, and to grub up the fresh graves in the churchyards and tear out the bodies.

Here a thoughtful citizen suggested that probably the wolves had been bridled of late in Paris, not by candle-lights, but owing to the English having been driven out of the kingdom of France. "For those English be very wolves themselves for fierceness and greediness." What marvel then that under their rule our neighbours of France should be wolf-eaten? This logic was too suited to the time and place, not to be received with acclamation. But the old man stood his ground. "I grant ye those islanders are wolves: but two-legged ones, and little apt to favour their four-footed cousins. One greedy thing loveth it another? I trow not. By the same token, and this too I have from my boy Nicole, Sir Wolf dare not show his nose in London city; though 'tis smaller than Paris, and thick woods hard by the north wall, and therein great store of deer, and wild boars rife as flies at midsummer."

"Sir," said Gerard, "you seem conversant with wild beasts, prithee advise my comrade here and me: we would not waste time on the road, and if we may go forward to the next town with reasonable safety."

"Young man, I trow 'twere an idle risk. It lacks but an hour of dusk, and you must pass nigh a wood, where lurk some thousands of these half-starved vermin, rank cowards single; but in great bands bold as lions. Wherefore I rede you sojourn here the night; and journey on betimes. By the dawn the vermin will be tired out with roaring and rampaging; and mayhap will have filled their lank bellies with flesh of my good neighbours here, the unteachable fools."

Gerard hoped not; and asked could he recommend them to a good inn?

"Humph? there is the 'Tête d'Or.' My granddaughter keeps it. She is a mijaurée, but not so knavish as most hotel-keepers, and her house indifferent clean."

"Hey, for the 'Tête d'Or,'" struck in Denys, decided by his ineradicable foible.

On the way to it, Gerard inquired of his companion what "a mijaurée" was?

Denys laughed at his ignorance. "Not know what a mijaurée is? why all the world knows that. It is neither more nor less than a mijaurée."

As they entered the "Tête d'Or" they met a young lady richly dressed, with the velvet chaperon on her head, which was confined by law to the nobility. They unbonneted and louted low, and she curtsied, but fixed her eye on vacancy the while, which had a curious rather than a genial effect. However nobility was not so unassuming in those days as it is now. So they were little surprised. But the next minute supper was served, and lo! in came this princess and carved the goose.

"Holy St. Bavon," cried Gerard. "'Twas the landlady all the while."

A young woman, cursed with nice white teeth and lovely hands:

for these beauties being misallied to homely features had turned her head. She was a feeble carver, carving not for the sake of others but herself, *i. e.,* to display her hands. When not carving she was eternally either taking a pin out of her head or her body, or else putting a pin into her head or her body. To display her teeth, she laughed indifferently at gay or grave; and from ear to ear. And she "sat at ease" with her mouth ajar.

Now there is an animal in creation of no great general merit; but it has the eye of a hawk for affectation. It is called "a boy." And Gerard was but a boy still in some things; swift to see, and to loathe, affectation. So Denys sat casting sheep's eyes, and Gerard, daggers, at one comedian.

Presently, in the midst of her minauderies, she gave a loud shriek and bounded out of her chair like hare from form, and ran backwards out of the room uttering little screams, and holding her farthingale tight down to her ankles with both hands. And, as she scuttled out of the door, a mouse scuttled back to the wainscot in a state of equal, and perhaps more reasonable, terror. The guests, who had risen in anxiety at the principal yell, now stood irresolute awhile, then sat down laughing. The tender Denys, to whom a woman's cowardice, being a sexual trait, seemed a lovely and pleasant thing, said he would go comfort her and bring her back.

"Nay! nay! nay! for pity's sake let her bide," cried Gerard earnestly. "Oh blessed mouse! sure some saint sent thee to our aid."

Now at his right hand sat a sturdy middle-aged burgher, whose conduct up to date had been cynical. He had never budged, nor even rested his knife, at all this fracas. He now turned on Gerard and inquired haughtily whether he really thought that "grimacière" was afraid of a mouse.

"Ay. She screamed hearty."

"Where is the coquette that cannot scream to the life? These she tavern-keepers do still ape the nobles. Some princess or duchess hath lain here a night, that was honestly afeared of a mouse, having been brought up to it. And this ape hath seen her, and said, 'I will start at a mouse, and make a coil.' She has no more right to start at a mouse, than to wear that fur on her bosom, and that velvet on her monkey's head. I am of the town, young man, and have known the mijaurée all her life, and I mind when she was no more afeard of a mouse than she is of a man." He added that she

The Cloister and the Hearth

was fast emptying the inn with these "singeries." "All the world is so sick of her hands, that her very kinsfolk will not venture themselves anigh them." He concluded with something like a sigh, "The 'Tête d'Or' was a thriving hostelry under my old chum her good father; but she is digging its grave tooth and nail."

"Tooth and nail? good! a right merry conceit and a true," said Gerard. But the right merry conceit was an inadvertence as pure as snow, and the stout burgher went to his grave and never knew what he had done: for just then attention was attracted by Denys returning pompously. He inspected the apartment minutely, and with a high official air: he also looked solemnly under the table; and during the whole inquisition a white hand was placed conspicuously on the edge of the open door, and a tremulous voice inquired behind it whether the horrid thing was quite gone.

"The enemy has retreated, bag and baggage," said Denys: and handed in the trembling fair, who, sitting down, apologized to her guests for her foolish fears, with so much earnestness, grace, and seeming self-contempt, that, but for a sour grin on his neighbour's face, Gerard would have been taken in as all the other strangers were. Dinner ended, the young landlady begged an Augustine friar at her right hand to say grace. He delivered a longish one. The moment he began, she clapped her white hands piously together, and held them up joined for mortals to admire; 'tis an excellent pose for taper white fingers; and cast her eyes upward towards heaven, and felt as thankful to it as a magpie does while cutting off with your thimble.

After supper the two friends went to the street-door and eyed the market-place. The mistress joined them, and pointed out the town hall, the borough jail, St. Catherine's church, &c. This was courteous, to say the least. But the true cause soon revealed itself: the fair hand was poked right under their eyes every time an object was indicated; and Gerard eyed it like a basilisk, and longed for a bunch of nettles. The sun set, and the travellers, few in number, drew round the great roaring fire, and, omitting to go on the spit, were frozen behind though roasted in front. For if the German stoves were oppressively hot, the French salles à manger were bitterly cold, and above all stormy. In Germany men sat bareheaded round the stove, and took off their upper clothes, but in Burgundy they kept on their hats, and put on their warmest furs to sit round the great open chimney-places, at which the external air rushed furiously from door and ill-fitting window. However it seems their mediæval backs were broad enough to bear it: for they made themselves not only comfortable but merry, and broke harmless jests over each other in turn. For instance Denys's new shoes, though not in direct communication, had this day exploded with twin-like sympathy and unanimity. "Where do you buy your shoon, soldier?" asked one.

Denys looked askant at Gerard, and not liking the theme, shook it off. "I gather 'em off the trees by the road-side," said he surlily.

"Then you gathered these too ripe," said the hostess, who was only a fool externally.

"Ay, rotten ripe," observed another, inspecting them.

Gerard said nothing, but pointed the circular satire by panto-mime. He slily put out both his feet, one after another, under Denys's eye, with their German shoes, on which a hundred leagues of travel had produced no effect. They seemed hewn out of a rock.

At this "I'll twist the smooth varlet's neck that sold me mine," shouted Denys, in huge wrath, and confirmed the threat with singular oaths peculiar to the mediæval military. The landlady put her fingers in her ears, thereby exhibiting the hand in a fresh attitude. "Tell me when he has done his orisons, somebody," said she minc-ingly. And after that they fell to telling stories.

Gerard, when his turn came, told the adventure of Denys and Gerard at the inn in Domfront, and so well, that the hearers were rapt into sweet oblivion of the very existence of mijaurée and hands. But this made her very uneasy, and she had recourse to her grand coup. This misdirected genius had for a twelvemonth past practised yawning, and could do it now at any moment so naturally as to set all creation gaping, could all creation have seen her. By this means she got in all her charms. For first she showed her teeth, then, out of good breeding, you know, closed her mouth with three taper fingers. So the moment Gerard's story got too interesting and absorbing, she turned to and made yawns, and "croix sur la bouche."

This was all very fine: but Gerard was an artist, and artists are chilled by gaping auditors. He bore up against the yawns a long time: but finding they came from a bottomless reservoir, lost both heart and temper, and suddenly rising in mid narrative, said, "But

The Cloister and the Hearth

I weary our hostess, and I am tired myself: so good night!" whipped a candle off the dresser, whispered Denys, "I cannot stand her," and marched to bed in a moment.

The mijaurée coloured and bit her lips. She had not intended her by-play for Gerard's eye: and she saw in a moment she had been rude, and silly, and publicly rebuked. She sat with cheek on fire, and a little natural water in her eyes, and looked ten times comelier and more womanly, and interesting than she had done all day. The desertion of the best narrator broke up the party, and the unassuming Denys approached the meditating mijaurée, and invited her in the most flattering terms, to gamble with him. She started from her reverie, looked him down into the earth's centre with chilling dignity, and consented, for she remembered all in a moment what a show of hands gambling admitted.

The soldier and the mijaurée rattled the dice. In which sport she was so taken up with her hands, that she forgot to cheat, and Denys won "écu au soleil" of her. She fumbled slowly with her purse, partly because her sex do not burn to pay debts of honour: partly to admire the play of her little knuckles peeping between their soft white cushions. Denys proposed a compromise. "Three silver franks I win of you, fair hostess. Give me now three kisses of this white hand, and we'll e'en cry quits."

"You are malapert," said the lady with a toss of her head; "besides they are so dirty. See! they are like ink:" and, to convince him, she put them out to him and turned them up and down. They were no dirtier than cream fresh from the cow. And she knew it: she was eternally washing and scenting them.

Denys read the objection like the observant warrior he was, seized them and mumbled them.

Finding him so appreciative of her charm, she said timidly, "Will you do me a kindness, good soldier?"

"A thousand, fair hostess an you will."

"Nay, I ask but one. 'Tis to tell thy comrade I was right sorry to lose his most thrilling story, and I hope he will tell me the rest to-morrow morning. Meantime I shall not sleep for thinking on't. Wilt tell him that—to pleasure me?"

"Ay, I'll tell the young savage. But he is not worthy of your condescension, sweet hostess. He would rather be aside a man than a woman any day."

The Cloister and the Hearth

"So would—ahem. He is right: the young women of the day are not worthy of *him,* 'un tas des mijaurées.' He has a good, honest, and right comely face. Any way I would not guest of mine should think me unmannerly, not for all the world. Wilt keep faith with me and tell him?"

"On this fair hand I swear it: and thus I seal the pledge."

"There; no need to melt the wax, though. Now go to bed. And tell him ere you sleep."

The perverse toad (I thank thee, Marion, for teaching me that word) was inclined to bestow her slight affections upon Gerard. Not that she was inflammable: far less so than many that passed for prudes in the town. But Gerard possessed a triple attraction that has ensnared coquettes in all ages. 1. He was very handsome. 2. He did not admire her the least. 3. He had given her a good slap in the face.

Denys woke Gerard and gave the message. Gerard was not enchanted. "Dost wake a tired man to tell him that? Am I to be pestered with 'mijaurées' by night as well as day?"

"But I tell thee, novice, thou hast conquered her: trust to my experience: her voice sank to melodious whispers: and the cunning jade did in a manner bribe me to carry thee her challenge to Love's lists: for so I read her message."

Denys then, assuming the senior and the man of the world, told Gerard the time was come to show him how a soldier understood friendship and camaraderie. Italy was now out of the question. Fate had provided better; and the blind jade Fortune had smiled on merit for once. The "Head of Gold" had been a prosperous inn, would be again with a man at *its* head. A good general laid far-sighted plans; but was always ready to abandon them, should some brilliant advantage offer; and to reap the full harvest of the unforeseen: 'twas chiefly by this trait great leaders defeated little ones; for these latter could do nothing not cut and dried beforehand.

"Sorry friendship, that would marry me to a mijaurée," interposed Gerard yawning.

"Comrade, be reasonable; 'tis not the friskiest sheep that falls down the cliff. All creatures must have their flings soon, or late; and why not a woman? What more frivolous than a kitten? what graver than a cat?"

The Cloister and the Hearth

"Hast a good eye for nature, Denys," said Gerard, "that I proclaim."

"A better for thine interest, boy. Trust then to me; these little doves they are my study day and night; happy the man whose wife taketh her fling before wedlock; and trippeth up the altar-steps instead of down 'em. Marriage it always changeth them for better or else for worse. Why, Gerard, she is honest when all is done: and he is no man, nor half a man, that cannot mould any honest lass like a bit of warm wax, and she aye aside him at bed and board. I tell thee in one month thou wilt make of this coquette the matron the most sober in the town, and of all its wives the one most docile, and submissive. Why she is half tamed already. Nine in ten meek and mild ones had gently hated thee like poison all their lives, for wounding of their hidden pride. But she for an affront proffers affection. By Joshua his bugle a generous lass, and void of petty malice. When thou wast gone she sat a thinking and spoke not. A sure sign of love in one of her sex: for of all things else they speak ere they think. Also her voice did sink exceedingly low in discoursing of thee, and murmured sweetly; another infallible sign. The bolt hath struck and wrankles in her; oh be joyful! Art silent? I see; 'tis settled. I shall go alone to Remiremont, alone and sad. But, pillage and poleaxes! what care I for that, since my dear comrade will stay here, landlord of the 'Tête d'Or,' and safe from all storms of life? Wilt think of me, Gerard, now and then by thy warm fire, of me camped on some windy heath, or lying in wet trenches or wounded on the field and far from comfort? Nay" (and this he said in a manner truly noble), "not comfortless. For cold, or wet, or bleeding, 'twill still warm my heart to lie on my back and think that I have placed my dear friend, and comrade true, in the 'Tête d'Or,' far from a soldier's ills."

"I let you run on, dear Denys," said Gerard softly, "because at each word you show me the treasure of a good heart. But now bethink thee, my troth is plighted there where my heart it clingeth. You so leal, would you make me disloyal?"

"Perdition seize me, but I forgot that," said Denys.

"No more then, but hie thee to bed, good Denys. Next to Margaret I love thee best on earth, and value thy 'cœur d'or' far more than a dozen of these 'Têtes d'Or.' So prithee call me at the first blush of rosy-fingered morn, and let's away ere the woman with the hands be stirring."

They rose with the dawn, and broke their fast by the kitchen fire. Denys inquired of the girl whether the mistress was about.

"Nay: but she hath risen from her bed: by the same token I am carrying her this to clean her withal;" and she filled a mug with boiling water and took it upstairs.

"Behold," said Gerard, "the very elements must be warmed to suit her skin; what had the saints said, which still chose the coldest pool? Away, ere she come down and catch us."

They paid the score, and left the "Tête d'Or," while its mistress was washing her hands.

CHAPTER XXXVIII

OUTSIDE the town they found the snow fresh trampled by innumerable wolves every foot of the road.

"We did well to take the old man's advice Denys."

"Ay did we. For now I think on't I did hear them last night a-scurrying under our window and howling and whining for man's flesh in yon market-place. But no fat burgher did pity the poor vagabones, and drop out o' window."

Gerard smiled, but with an air of abstraction.

And they plodded on in silence.

"What dost meditate so profoundly?"

"Thy goodness."

Denys was anything but pleased at this answer. Amongst his oddities you may have observed that he could stand a great deal of real impertinence, he was so good-humoured. But would fire up now and then where not even the shadow of a ground for anger existed.

"A civil question merits a civil reply," said he very drily.

"Alas, I meant no other," said Gerard.

"Then why pretend you were thinking of my goodness, when you know I have no goodness under my skin."

"Had another said this, I had answered 'thou liest.' But to thee

I say: 'hast no eye for men's qualities, but only for women's.'
And, once more, I do defy thy unreasonable choler, and say I was
thinking of thy goodness of overnight. Wouldst have wedded me
to the 'Tête d'Or,' or rather to the 'tête de veau dorée,' and left thyself solitary."

"Oh, are ye there, lad?" said Denys recovering his good-humour
in a moment. "Well, but to speak sooth, I meant that not for goodness; but for friendship and true fellowship, no more. And let
me tell you, my young master, my conscience it pricketh me even
now for letting you turn your back thus on fortune and peaceful
days. A truer friend than I had ta'en and somewhat hamstrung
thee. Then hadst thou been fain to lie smarting at the 'Tête d'Or'
a month or so: yon skittish lass had nursed thee tenderly, and all had
been well. Blade I had in hand to do't, but, remembering how thou
hatest pain though it be but a scratch, my craven heart it failed me
at the pinch." And Denys wore a look of humble apology for his
lack of virtuous resolution when the path of duty lay so clear.

Gerard raised his eyebrows with astonishment at this monstrous
but thoroughly characteristic revelation; however this new and delicate point of friendship was never discussed; viz., whether one ought
in all love to cut the tendon Achilles of one's friend. For an incident interposed.

"Here cometh one in our rear a-riding on his neighbour's mule,"
shouted Denys.

Gerard turned round. "And how know ye 'tis not his own, pray?"

"Oh blind! Because he rides it with no discretion."

And in truth the man came galloping like a fury. But what
astonished the friends most was that on reaching them the rustic
rider's eyes opened saucer-like, and he drew the rein so suddenly and
powerfully, that the mule stuck out her fore legs, and went sliding
between the pedestrians like a four-legged table on casters.

"I trow ye are from the 'Tête d'Or.'" They assented. "Which
of ye is the younger?"

"He that was born the later," said Denys winking at his companion.

"Gramercy for the news."

"Come, divine then!"

"And shall. Thy beard is ripe; thy fellow's is green; he shall be the younger; here, youngster." And he held him out a paper packet. "Ye left this at the 'Tête d'Or': and our mistress sends it ye."

"Nay, good fellow, methinks I left nought." And Gerard felt his pouch, etc.

"Would ye make our burgess a liar," said the rustic reproachfully: "and shall I have no pourboire?" (still more reproachfully); "and came ventre à terre."

"Nay, thou shalt have pourboire," and he gave him a small coin.

"A la bonne heure," cried the clown, and his feature beamed with disproportionate joy. "The Virgin go with ye; come up, Jenny!" and back he went "stomach to earth," as his nation is pleased to call it.

Gerard undid the packet: it was about six inches square, and inside it he found another packet, which contained a packet, and so on. At the fourth he hurled the whole thing into the snow. Denys took it out and rebuked his petulance. He excused himself on the ground of hating affectation.

Denys attested "'The great toe of the little daughter of Herodias' there was no affectation here, but only woman's good wit. Doubtless the wraps contained something which out of delicacy, or her sex's lovely cunning, she would not her hind should see her bestow on a young man; thy garter, to wit."

"I wear none."

"Her own then; or a lock of her hair. What is this? A piece of raw silk fresh from the worm. Well of all the love tokens!"

"Now who but thee ever dreamed that she is so naught as send me love tokens? I saw no harm in her—barring her hands."

"Stay, here is something hard lurking in this soft nest. Come forth I say, little nestling! Saints and pikestaves! look at this!"

It was a gold ring, with a great amethyst glowing and sparkling, full coloured, but pure as crystal.

"How lovely!" said Gerard, innocently.

"And here is something writ: read it thou! I read not so glib as some; when I know not the matter beforehand."

Gerard took the paper. "'Tis a posy: and fairly enough writ." He read the lines, blushing like a girl. They were very naïve, and may be thus Englished:—

The Cloister and the Hearth

"Youth, with thee my heart is fledde,
Come back to the 'golden Hedde!'
Wilt not? yet this token keepe
Of her who doëth thy goeing weepe.
Gyf the world prove harsh and cold,
Come back to 'the Hedde of gold.'"

"The little dove!" purred Denys.

"The great owl! To go and risk her good name thus. However, thank Heaven she has played this prank with an honest lad that will ne'er expose her folly. But oh, the perverseness! Could she not bestow her nauseousness on thee?" Denys sighed and shrugged. "On thee that art as ripe for folly as herself?"

Denys confessed that his young friend had harped his very thought. 'Twas passing strange to him that a damsel with eyes in her head should pass by a man, and bestow her affections on a boy. Still he could not but recognize in this the bounty of Nature. Boys were human beings after all, and, but for this occasional caprice of women, their lot would be too terrible; they would be out of the sun altogether, blighted, and never come to anything: since only the fair could make a man out of such unpromising materials as a boy. Gerard interrupted this flattering discourse to beg the warrior-philosopher's acceptance of the lady's ring. He refused it flatly, and insisted on Gerard going back to the "Tête d'Or" at once, ring and all, like a man, and not letting a poor girl hold out her arms to him in vain.

"Her hands you mean."

"Her hand, with the 'Tête d'Or' in it."

Failing in this he was for putting the ring on his friend's finger. Gerard declined. "I wear a ring already."

"What that sorry gimcrack? Why 'tis pewter, or tin at best: and this virgin gold, forbye the jewel."

"Ay, but 'twas Margaret gave me this one: and I value it above rubies. I'll neither part with it nor give it a rival:" and he kissed the base metal, and bade it fear nought.

"I see the owl hath sent her ring to a goose," said Denys, sorrowfully. However he prevailed on Gerard to fasten it inside his bonnet. To this indeed the lad consented very readily. For sovereign qualities were universally ascribed to certain jewels; and the amethyst ranked high among these precious talismans.

When this was disposed of, Gerard earnestly requested his friend to let the matter drop, since speaking of the other sex to him made him pine so for Margaret, and almost unmanned him with the thought that each step was taking him farther from her. "I am no general lover, Denys. There is room in my heart for one sweetheart, and for one friend. I am far from my dear mistress: and my friend, a few leagues more and I must lose him too. Oh let me drink thy friendship pure while I may, and not dilute with any of these stupid females."

"And shalt, honey-pot, and shalt," said Denys, kindly. "But as to my leaving thee at Remiremont, reckon thou not on that! For" (three consecutive oaths) "if I do. Nay, I shall propose to thee to stay forty-eight hours there while I kiss my mother and sisters, and the females generally, and on go you and I together to the sea."

"Denys! Denys!"

"Denys not me! 'Tis settled. Gainsay me not! or I'll go with thee to Rome. Why not? his holiness the Pope hath ever some little merry pleasant war toward, and a Burgundian soldier is still welcome in his ranks."

On this Gerard opened his heart. "Denys, ere I fell in with thee, I used often to halt on the road, unable to go farther: my puny heart so pulled me back: and then, after a short prayer to the saints for aid, would I rise and drag my most unwilling body onward. But since I joined company with thee, great is my courage. I have found the saying of the ancients true, that better is a bright comrade on the weary road than a horse litter; and, dear brother, when I do think of what we have done and suffered together! Savedst my life from the bear, and from yet more savage thieves; and even poor I did make shift to draw thee out of Rhine, and somehow loved thee double from that hour. How many ties tender and strong between us! Had I my will, I'd never, never, never, never, part with my Denys on this side the grave. Well-a-day! God his will be done."

"No, my will shall be done this time," shouted Denys. "Le bon Dieu has bigger fish to fry than you or me. I'll go with thee to Rome. There is my hand on it."

"Think what you say! 'Tis impossible. 'Tis too selfish of me."

"I tell thee, 'tis settled. No power can change me. At Remiremont I borrow ten pieces of my uncle, and on we go: 'tis fixed; irrevocable as fate."

They shook hands over it. Then Gerard said nothing, for his heart was too full: but he ran twice round his companion as he walked, then danced backwards in front of him, and finally took his hand, and so on they went hand-in-hand like sweethearts, till a company of mounted soldiers, about fifty in number, rose to sight on the brow of a hill.

"See the banner of Burgundy," said Denys, joyfully. "I shall look out for a comrade among these."

"How gorgeous is the standard in the sun," said Gerard; "and how brave are the leaders with velvet and feathers, and steel breast-plates like glassy mirrors!"

When they came near enough to distinguish faces, Denys uttered an exclamation: "Why 'tis the Bastard of Burgundy, as I live. Nay, then; there is fighting a foot since he is out; a gallant leader, Gerard, rates his life no higher than a private soldier's, and a soldier's no higher than a tomtit's; and that is the captain for me."

"And see Denys, the very mules with their great brass frontlets and trappings seem proud to carry them; no wonder men itch to be soldiers;" and in the midst of this innocent admiration the troop came up with them.

"Halt," cried a stentorian voice. The troop halted. The Bastard of Burgundy bent his brow gloomily on Denys: "How now, arbalestrier, how comes it thy face is turned southward, when every good hand and heart is hurrying northward?"

Denys replied respectfully that he was going on leave, after some years of service, to see his kindred at Remiremont.

"Good. But this not the time for't, the duchy is disturbed. Ho! bring that dead soldier's mule to the front; and thou mount her and forward with us to Flanders."

"So please your highness," said Denys, firmly, "that may not be. My home is close at hand. I have not seen it these three years and, above all, I have this poor youth in charge; whom I may not, cannot leave, till I see him shipped for Rome."

"Dost bandy words with me?" said the chief, with amazement turning fast to wrath. "Art weary o' thy life? Let go the youth's hand, and into the saddle without more idle words."

Denys made no reply: but he held Gerard's hand the tighter, and looked defiance.

At this the bastard roared, "Jarnac, dismount six of thy archers, and shoot me this whitelivered cur dead where he stands—for an example."

The young Count de Jarnac, second in command, gave the order, and the men dismounted to execute it.

"Strip him naked," said the bastard, in the cold tone of military business, "and put his arms and accoutrements on the spare mule. We'll may be find some clown worthier to wear them."

Denys groaned aloud, "Am I to be shamed as well as slain?"

"Oh, nay! nay! nay!" cried Gerard, awaking from the stupor into which this thunderbolt of tyranny had thrown him. "He shall go with you on the instant. I'd liever part with him for ever than see a hair of his dear head harmed. Oh sir, oh, my lord, give a poor boy but a minute to bid his only friend farewell! he will go with you. I swear he shall go with you."

The stern leader nodded a cold contemptuous assent. "Thou, Jarnac, stay with them, and bring him on alive or dead.—Forward!" And he resumed his march, followed by all the band but the young count and six archers, one of whom held the spare mule.

Denys and Gerard gazed at one another haggardly. Oh! what a look!

And after this mute interchange of anguish, they spoke hurriedly, for the moments were flying by.

"Thou goest to Holland: thou knowest where she bides. Tell her all. She will be kind to thee for my sake."

"Oh, sorry tale that I shall carry her! For God's sake go back to the 'Tête d'Or.' I am mad."

"Hush! Let me think: have I nought to say to thee, Denys? my head! my head!"

"Ah! I have it. Make for the Rhine, Gerard! Strasbourg. 'Tis but a step. And down the current to Rotterdam. Margaret is there: I go thither. I'l tell her thou art coming. We shall all be together."

"My lads, haste ye, or you will get us into trouble," said the count firmly, but not harshly now.

"Oh, sir, one moment! one little moment!" panted Gerard.

"Cursed be the land I was born in; cursed be the race of man; and he that made them what they are," screamed Denys.

"Hush! Denys, hush! blaspheme not! oh, God, forgive him, he wots not what he says. Be patient, Denys,—be patient! though we meet no more on earth, let us meet in a better world, where no blasphemer may enter. To my heart, lost friend; for what are words now?" He held out his arms, and they locked one another in a close embrace. They kissed one another again and again, speechless, and the tears rained down their cheeks. And the Count Jarnac looked on amazed, but the rougher soldiers, to whom comrade was a sacred name, looked on with some pity in their hard faces. Then at a signal from Jarnac, with kind force and words of rude consolation, they almost lifted Denys on to the mule; and putting him in the middle of them, spurred after their leader. And Gerard ran wildly after (for the lane turned), to see the very last of him; and the last glimpse he caught, Denys was rocking to and fro on his mule, and tearing his hair out. But at this sight something rose in Gerard's throat so high, so high, he could run no more nor breathe, but gasped, and leaned against the snow-clad hedge, seizing it, and choking piteously.

The thorns ran into his hand.

After a bitter struggle he got his breath again: and now began to see his own misfortune. Yet not all at once to realize it, so sudden and numbing was the stroke. He staggered on, but scarce feeling or caring whither he was going: and every now and then he stopped, and his arms fell and his head sank on his chest: and he stood motionless: then he said to himself, "Can this thing be? This must be a dream. 'Tis scarce five minutes since we were so happy, walking handed, faring to Rome together, and we admired them and their gay banners and helmets—oh hearts of hell!"

All nature seemed to stare now as lonely as himself. Not a creature in sight. No colour but white. He, the ghost of his former self, wandered alone among the ghosts of trees, and fields, and hedges. Desolate! desolate! desolate! All was desolate.

He knelt and gathered a little snow. "Nay, I dream not; for this *is* snow: cold as the world's heart. It is bloody, too: what may that mean? Fool! 'tis from thy hand. I mind not the wound. Ay, I see: thorns. Welcome! kindly foes: I felt ye not, ye ran not into my heart. Ye are not cruel like men."

He had risen, and was dragging his leaden limbs along, when he heard horses' feet and gay voices behind him. He turned with a joyful but wild hope that the soldiers had relented and were bringing Denys back. But no: it was a gay cavalcade. A gentleman of rank and his favourites in velvet and furs and feathers; and four or five armed retainers in buff jerkins.

They swept gaily by.

Gerard never looked at them after they were gone by: certain gay shadows had come and passed: that was all. He was like one in a dream. But he was rudely wakened: suddenly a voice in front of him cried harshly, "Stand and deliver!" and there were three of the gentleman's servants in front of him. They had ridden back to rob him.

"How, ye false knaves," said he quite calmly: "would ye shame your noble master? He will hang ye to the nearest tree:" and with these words he drew his sword doggedly, and set his back to the hedge.

One of the men instantly levelled his petronel at him.

But another, less sanguinary, interposed. "Be not so hasty! And be not thou so mad! Look yonder!"

Gerard looked, and scarce a hundred yards off the nobleman and his friends had halted, and sat on their horses, looking at the lawless act, too proud to do their own dirty work, but not too proud to reap the fruit, and watch lest their agents should rob them of another man's money.

The milder servant then, a good-natured fellow, showed Gerard resistance was vain; reminded him common thieves often took the life as well as the purse, and assured him it cost a mint to be a gentleman; his master had lost money at play overnight, and was going to visit his leman, and so must take money where he saw it.

"Therefore, good youth, consider that we rob not for ourselves, and deliver us that fat purse at thy girdle without more ado, nor put us to the pain of slitting thy throat and taking it all the same."

"This knave is right," said Gerard calmly, aloud but to himself. "I ought not to fling away my life; Margaret would be so sorry. Take then the poor man's purse to the rich man's pouch; and with it this; tell him, I pray the Holy Trinity each coin in it may burn his hand, and freeze his heart, and blast his soul for ever. Begone and leave me to my sorrow!" He flung them the purse.

They rode away muttering; for his words pricked them a little; a very little: and he staggered on, penniless now as well as friendless, till he came to the edge of a wood. Then, though his heart could hardly feel this second blow, his judgment did; and he began to ask himself what was the use going further? He sat down on the hard road, and ran his nails into his hair and tried to think for the best; a task all the more difficult that a strange drowsiness was stealing over him. Rome he could never reach without money. Denys had said "go to Strasbourg, and down the Rhine home." He would obey Denys. But how get to Strasbourg without money?

Then suddenly seemed to ring in his ears—

> "Gyf the world prove harsh and cold,
> Come back to the hedde of gold."

"And if I do I must go as her servant; I who am Margaret's. I am a-weary, a-weary. I will sleep, and dream all is as it was. Ah me, how happy were we an hour agone, we little knew how happy. There is a house: the owner well to do. What if I told him my wrong, and prayed his aid to retrieve my purse, and so to Rhine? Fool! is he not a man, like the rest? He would scorn me and trample me lower. Denys cursed the race of men. That will I never: but oh, I 'gin to loathe and dread them. Nay, here will I lie till sunset: then darkling creep into this rich man's barn, and take by stealth a draught of milk or a handful o' grain, to keep body and soul together. God, who hath seen the rich rob me, will peradventure forgive me. They say 'tis ill sleeping on the snow. Death steals on such sleepers with muffled feet and honey breath. But what can I? I am a-weary, a-weary. Shall this be the wood where lie the wolves yon old man spoke of? I must e'en trust them: they are not men; and I am so a-weary."

He crawled to the road-side, and stretched out his limbs on the snow, with a deep sigh.

"Ah tear not thine hair so! teareth my heart to see thee.

"Mar—garet. Never see me more. Poor Mar—ga—ret."

And the too tender heart was still.

And the constant lover, and friend of antique mould, lay silent on the snow; in peril from the weather, in peril from wild beasts, in peril from hunger, friendless and penniless, in a strange land, and not half way to Rome.

CHAPTER XXXIX

RUDE travel is enticing to us English. And so are its records; even though the adventurer be no pilgrim of love. And antique friendship has at least the interest of a fossil. Still, as the true centre of this story is in Holland, it is full time to return thither, and to those ordinary personages and incidents, whereof life has been mainly composed in all ages.

Jorian Ketel came to Peter's house to claim Margaret's promise; but Margaret was ill in bed, and Peter, on hearing his errand, affronted him and warned him off the premises, and one or two that stood by were for ducking him; for both father and daughter were favourites, and the whole story was in every mouth, and the Sevenbergens in that state of hot, undiscriminating, irritation which accompanies popular sympathy.

So Jorian Ketel went off in dudgeon, and repented him of his good deed. This sort of penitence is not rare, and has the merit of being sincere. Dierich Brower, who was discovered at "The Three Kings," making a chatterbox drunk in order to worm out of him the whereabouts of Martin Wittenhaagen, was actually taken and flung into a horse-pond, and threatened with worse usage, should he ever show his face in the burgh again; and finally, municipal jealousy being roused, the burgomaster of Sevenbergen sent a formal missive being sincere. Dierich Brower, who was discovered at "The Three to the burgomaster of Tergou, reminding him he had overstepped the law, and requesting him to apply to the authorities of Sevenbergen on any future occasion when he might have a complaint, real or imaginary, against any of its townsfolk.

The wily Ghysbrecht, suppressing his rage at this remonstrance, sent back a civil message to say that the person he had followed to Sevenbergen was a Tergovan, one Gerard, and that he had stolen the town records: that Gerard having escaped into foreign parts, and probably taken the documents with him, the whole matter was at an end.

Thus he made a virtue of necessity. But in reality his calmness was but a veil: baffled at Sevenbergen, he turned his views elsewhere; he set his emissaries to learn from the family at Tergou whither Gerard had fled, and "to his infinite surprise" they did not know.

This added to his uneasiness. It made him fear Gerard was only lurking in the neighborhood: he would make a certain discovery, and would come back and take a terrible revenge. From this time Dierich and others that were about him noticed a change for the worse in Ghysbrecht Van Swieten. He became a moody, irritable man. A dread lay on him. His eyes cast furtive glances, like one who expects a blow, and knows not from what quarter it is to come. Making others wretched had not made him happy. It seldom does.

The little family at Tergou, which, but for his violent interference, might in time have cemented its difference without banishing spem gregis to a distant land, wore still the same outward features, but within was no longer the simple happy family this tale opened with. Little Kate knew the share Cornelis and Sybrandt had in banishing Gerard, and though, for fear of making more mischief still, she never told her mother, yet there were times she shuddered at the bare sight of them, and blushed at their hypocritical regrets. Catherine, with a woman's vigilance, noticed this, and with a woman's subtlety said nothing, but quietly pondered it, and went on watching for more. The black sheep themselves, in their efforts to partake in the general gloom and sorrow, succeeded so far as to impose upon their father and Giles: but the demure satisfaction that lay at their bottom could not escape these feminine eyes—

"That, noting all, seem'd nought to note."

Thus mistrust and suspicion sat at the table, poor substitutes for Gerard's intelligent face, that had brightened the whole circle, unobserved till it was gone. As for the old hosier, his pride had been wounded by his son's disobedience, and so he bore stiffly up, and did his best never to mention Gerard's name; but underneath his Spartan cloak Nature might be seen tugging at his heartstrings. One anxiety he never affected to conceal. "If I but knew where the boy is, and that his life and health are in no danger, small would be my care," would he say; and then a deep sigh would follow. I cannot help thinking that if Gerard had opened the door just then, and walked in, there would have been many tears and embraces for him, and few reproaches, or none.

One thing took the old couple quite by surprise—publicity. Ere Gerard had been gone a week, his adventures were in every mouth;

and, to make matters worse, the popular sympathy declared itself warmly on the side of the lovers, and against Gerard's cruel parents, and that old busy-body the burgomaster, "who must put his nose into a business that nowise concerned him."

"Mother," said Kate, "it is all over the town that Margaret is down with a fever—a burning fever; her father fears her sadly."

"Margaret? what Margaret?" inquired Catherine, with a treacherous assumption of calmness and indifference.

"Oh, mother! whom should I mean? Why Gerard's Margaret."

"Gerard's Margaret," screamed Catherine; "how dare you say such a word to me? And I rede you never mention that hussy's name in this house, that she has laid bare. She is the ruin of my poor boy, the flower of all my flock. She is the cause that he is not a holy priest in the midst of us, but is roaming the world, and I a desolate broken-hearted mother. There, do not cry, my girl, I do ill to speak harsh to you. But, oh, Kate! you know not what passes in a mother's heart. I bear up before you all; it behoves me swallow my fears: but at night I see him in my dreams and still some trouble or other near him: sometimes he is torn by wild beasts; other times he is in the hands of robbers, and their cruel knives uplifted to strike his poor pale face, that one should think would move a stone. Oh! when I remember that, while I sit here in comfort, perhaps my poor boy lies dead in some savage place: and all along of that girl: there, her very name is ratsbane to me. I tremble all over when I hear it."

"I'll not say anything, nor do anything to grieve you worse, mother," said Kate tenderly; but she sighed.

She whose name was so fiercely interdicted in this house, was much spoken of, and even pitied, elsewhere. All Sevenbergen was sorry for her, and the young men and maidens cast many a pitying glance, as they passed, at the little window where the beauty of the village lay "dying for love." In this familiar phrase they underrated her spirit and unselfishness. Gerard was not dead, and she was too loyal herself to doubt his constancy. Her father was dear to her and helpless; and, but for bodily weakness, all her love for Gerard would not have kept her from doing her duties, though she might have gone about them with drooping head and heavy heart. But physical and mental excitement had brought on an attack of fever so violent, that nothing but youth and constitution saved her. The malady left her at last, but in that terrible state of bodily weakness in which the patient feels life a burden.

Then it is that love and friendship by the bedside are mortal angels with comfort in their voices, and healing in their palms.

But this poor girl had to come back to life and vigour how she could. Many days she lay alone, and the heavy hours rolled like leaden waves over her. In her enfeebled state existence seemed a burden, and life a thing gone by. She could not try her best to get well. Gerard was gone. She had not him to get well for. Often she lay for hours quite still, with the tears welling gently out of her eyes.

One day, waking from an uneasy slumber, she found two women in her room. One was a servant, the other by the deep fur on her collar and sleeves was a person of consideration: a narrow band of silvery hair, being spared by her coiffure, showed her to be past the age when women of sense conceal their years. The looks of both were kind and friendly. Margaret tried to raise herself in the bed, but the old lady placed a hand very gently on her.

"Lie still, sweetheart; we come not here to put you about, but to comfort you, God willing. Now cheer up a bit, and tell us, first, who think you we are?"

"Nay, madam, I know you, though I never saw you before: you are the demoiselle Van Eyck, and this is Reicht Heynes. Gerard has oft spoken of you, and of your goodness to him. Madam, he has no friend like you near him now," and at this thought she lay back and the tears welled out of her eyes in a moment.

The good-natured Reicht Heynes began to cry for company; but her mistress scolded her. "Well, you are a pretty one for a sick-room," said she: and she put out a world of innocent art to cheer the patient: and not without some little success. An old woman, that has seen life and all its troubles, is a sovereign blessing by a sorrowful young woman's side. She knows what to say, and what to avoid. She knows how to soothe her and interest her. Ere she had been there a hour, she had Margaret's head lying on her shoulder instead of on the pillow, and Margaret's soft eyes dwelling on her with gentle gratitude.

"Ah! this is hair," said the old lady, running her fingers through it. "Come and look at it, Reicht!"

Reicht came and handled it, and praised it unaffectedly. The poor girl that owned it was not quite out of the reach of flattery; owning doubtless to not being dead.

"In sooth, madam, I did use to think it hideous: but *he* praised it, and ever since then I have been almost vain of it, saints forgive me. You know how foolish those are that love."

"They are greater fools that don't," said the old lady, sharply.

Margaret opened her lovely eyes, and looked at her for her meaning.

This was only the first of many visits. In fact either Margaret Van Eyck or Reicht came nearly every day until their patient was convalescent: and she improved rapidly under their hands. Reicht attributed this principally to certain nourishing dishes she prepared in Peter's kitchen: but Margaret herself thought more of the kind words and eyes that kept telling her she had friends to live for.

Martin Wittenhaagen went straight to Rotterdam, to take the bull by the horns. The bull was a biped, with a crown for horns. It was Philip the Good, duke of this, earl of that, lord of the other. Arrived at Rotterdam, Martin found the court was at Ghent. To Ghent he went, and sought an audience, but was put off and baffled by lacqueys and pages. So he threw himself in his sovereign's way cut hunting, and, contrary to all court precedents, commenced the conversation—by roaring rustily for mercy.

"Why, where is the peril, man?" said the duke, looking all round and laughing.

"Grace for an old soldier hunted down by burghers!"

Now kings differ in character like other folk; but there is one trait they have in common; they are mightily inclined to be affable to men of very low estate. These do not vie with them in anything whatever, so jealousy cannot creep in; and they amuse them by their bluntness and novelty, and refresh the poor things with a touch of nature—a rarity in courts. So Philip the Good reined in his horse and gave Martin almost a *tête-à-tête,* and Martin reminded him of a certain battle-field where he had received an arrow intended for his sovereign. The duke remembered the incident perfectly, and was graciously pleased to take a cheerful view of it. He could afford to, not having been the one hit. Then Martin told his majesty of Gerard's first capture in the church, his imprisonment in the tower, and the manœuvre by which they got him out, and all the details of the hunt; and, whether he told it better than I have, or the duke had not heard so many good stories as you have, certain it is that sovereign got so wrapt up in it, that, when a number of courtiers came galloping up and interrupted Martin, he swore like a costermonger, and threatened, only half in jest, to cut off the next head that should come between him and a good story: and when Martin had done, he cried out:—

"St. Luke! what sport goeth on in this mine earldom, ay! in my own woods, and I see it not. You base fellows have all the luck." And he was indignant at the partiality of Fortune. "Lo you now! this was a man-hunt," said he. "*I* never had the luck to be at a man-hunt."

"My luck was none so great," replied Martin bluntly; "I was on the wrong side of the dogs' noses."

"Ah! so you were: I forgot that." And royalty was more reconciled to its lot. "What would you then?"

"A free pardon, your highness, for myself and Gerard."

"For what?"

"For prison-breaking."

"Go to: the bird will fly from the cage. 'Tis instinct. Besides, coop a young man up for loving a young woman? These burgomasters must be void of common sense. What else?"

"For striking down the burgomaster."

"Oh, the hunted boar will turn to bay. 'Tis his right: and I hold him less than man that grudges it him. What else?"

"For killing of the bloodhounds."

The duke's countenance fell.

"'Twas their life or mine," said Martin eagerly.

"Ay! but I can't have my bloodhounds, my beautiful bloodhounds, sacrificed to——"

"No, no, no! They were not your dogs."

"Whose dogs, then?"

"The ranger's."

"Oh. Well, I am very sorry for him, but, as I was saying, I can't have my old soldiers sacrificed to his bloodhounds. Thou shalt have thy free pardon."

"And poor Gerard."

"And poor Gerard too, for thy sake. And more, tell thou this burgomaster his doings mislike me: this is to set up for a king, not a burgomaster. I'll have no kings in Holland but one. Bid him be more humble: or by St. Jude I'll hang him before his own door, as I hanged the burgomaster of what's the name, some town or other in Flanders it was: no, 'twas somewhere in Brabant—no matter—I hanged him, I remember that much—for oppressing poor folk."

The duke then beckoned his chancellor, a pursy old fellow that rode like a sack, and bade him write out a free pardon for Martin and one Gerard.

This precious document was drawn up in form, and signed next day, and Martin hastened home with it.

Margaret had left her bed some days, and was sitting pale and pensive by the fireside, when he burst in, waving the parchment, and crying, "A free pardon, girl, for Gerard as well as me! Send for him back when you will; all the burgomasters on earth daren't lay a finger on him."

She flushed all over with joy, and her hands trembled with eagerness as she took the parchment and devoured it with her eyes, and kissed it again and again, and flung her arms round Martin's neck, and kissed *him.* When she was calmer, she told him Heaven had raised her up a friend in the dame Van Eyck. "And I would fain consult her on this good news: but I have not strength to walk so far."

"What need to walk? There is my mule."

"Your mule, Martin?"

The old soldier or professional pillager laughed, and confessed he had got so used to her, that he forgot at times Ghysbrecht had a prior claim. To-morrow he would turn her into the burgomaster's yard, but to-night she should carry Margaret to Tergou.

It was nearly dusk; so Margaret ventured, and about seven in the evening she astonished and gladdened her new but ardent friend, by arriving at her house with unwonted roses on her cheeks, and Gerard's pardon in her bosom.

The Cloister and the Hearth

CHAPTER XL

SOME are old in heart at forty, some are young at eighty. Margaret Van Eyck's heart was an evergreen. She loved her young namesake with youthful ardour. Nor was this new sentiment a mere caprice: she was quick at reading character, and saw in Margaret Brandt that which in one of her own sex goes far with an intelligent woman; genuineness. But, besides her own sterling qualities, Margaret had from the first a potent ally in the old artist's bosom.

Human nature.

Strange as it may appear to the unobservant, our hearts warm more readily to those we have benefited than to our benefactors. Some of the Greek philosophers noticed this; but the British Homer has stamped it in immortal lines:—

> "I heard, and thought how side by side
> We two had stemmed the battle's tide
> In many a well-debated field,
> Where Bertram's breast was Philip's shield.
> I thought on Darien's deserts pale,
> Where Death bestrides the evening gale,
> How o'er my friend my cloak I threw,
> And fenceless faced the deadly dew.
> I thought on Quariana's cliff,
> Where, rescued from our foundering skiff,
> Through the white breakers' wrath I bore
> Exhausted Mortram to the shore;
> And when his side an arrow found,
> I sucked the Indian's venom'd wound.
> These thoughts like torrents rushed along
> To sweep away my purpose strong."

Observe! this assassin's hand is stayed by memory, not of benefits received, but benefits conferred.

Now Margaret Van Eyck had been wonderfully kind to Margaret Brandt; had broken through her own habits to go and see her; had nursed her, and soothed her, and petted her, and cured her more than all the medicine in the world. So her heart opened to the recipient of her goodness, and she loved her now far more tenderly than she had ever loved Gerard, though, in truth, it was purely out of regard for Gerard she had visited her in the first instance.

When, therefore, she saw the roses on Margaret's cheek, and read the bit of parchment that had brought them there, she gave up her own views without a murmur.

"Sweetheart," said she, "I did desire he should stay in Italy five or six years, and come back rich, and, above all, an artist. But your happiness is before all, and I see you cannot live without him, so we must have him home as fast as may be."

"Ah, madam! you see my very thoughts." And the young woman hung her head a moment and blushed. "But how to let him know, madam? That passes my skill. He is gone to Italy; but what part, that I know not. Stay! he named the cities he should visit. Florence was one, and Rome. But then—"

Finally, being a sensible girl, she divined that a letter, addressed "My Gerard—Italy," might chance to miscarry, and she looked imploringly at her friend for counsel.

"You are come to the right place, and at the right time," said the old lady. "Here was this Hans Memling with me to-day; he is going to Italy, girl, no later than next week, 'to improve his hand,' he says. Not before 'twas needed, I do assure you."

"But how is he to find my Gerard?"

"Why, he knows your Gerard, child. They have supped here more than once, and were like hand and glove. Now, as his business is the same as Gerard's—"

"What! he is a painter then?"

"He passes for one. He will visit the same places as Gerard, and, soon or late, he must fall in with him. Wherefore, get you a long letter written, and copy out this pardon into it, and I'll answer for the messenger. In six months at farthest Gerard shall get it; and when he shall get it, then will he kiss it, and put it in his bosom, and come flying home. What are you smiling at? And now what makes your cheeks so red? And what you are smothering me for, I cannot think. Yes! happy days are coming to my little pearl."

Meantime, Martin sat in the kitchen, with the black-jack before him and Reicht Heynes spinning beside him: and, wow! but she pumped him that night.

This Hans Memling was an old pupil of Jan Van Eyck and his

sister. He was a painter, notwithstanding Margaret's sneer, and a good soul enough, with one fault. He loved the "nipperkin, canakin, and the brown bowl" more than they deserve. This singular penchant kept him from amassing fortune, and was the cause that he often came to Margaret Van Eyck for a meal, and sometimes for a groat. But this gave her a claim on him, and she knew he would not trifle with any commission she should intrust to him.

The letter was duly written, and left with Margaret Van Eyck; and, the following week, sure enough, Hans Memling returned from Flanders. Margaret Van Eyck gave him the letter, and a piece of gold towards his travelling expenses. He seemed in a hurry to be off.

"All the better," said the old artist; "he will be the sooner in Italy."

But as there are horses who burn and rage to start, and after the first yard or two want the whip, so all this hurry cooled into inaction when Hans got as far as the principal hostelry of Tergou, and saw two of his boon companions sitting in the bay window. He went in for a parting glass with them; but when he offered to pay, they would not hear of it. No; he was going a long journey; they would treat him; everybody must treat him, the landlord and all.

It resulted from this treatment that his tongue got as loose as if the wine had been oil; and he confided to the convivial crew that he was going to show the Italians how to paint: next he sang his exploits in battle, for he had handled a pike; and his amorous successes with females, not present to oppose their version of the incidents. In short, 'plenus rimarum erat: huc illuc diffluebat:' and among the miscellaneous matters that oozed out, he must blab that he was intrusted with a letter to a townsman of theirs, one Gerard, a good fellow: he added "you are all good fellows:" and, to impress his eulogy, slapped Sybrandt on the back so heartily, as to drive the breath out of his body.

Sybrandt got round the table to avoid this muscular approval; but listened to every word, and learned for the first time that Gerard was gone to Italy. However, to make sure, he affected to doubt it.

"My brother Gerard is never in Italy."

"Ye lie, ye cur," roared Hans, taking instantly the irascible turn, and not being clear enough to see that he, who now sat opposite him, was the same he had praised, and hit, when beside him. "If he is ten times your brother, he is in Italy. What call ye this? There, read me that superscription!" and he flung down a letter on the table.

Sybrandt took it up, and examined it gravely; but eventually laid it down, with the remark, that he could not read. However one of the company, by some immense fortuity, could read; and, proud of so rare an accomplishment, took it, and read it out: "To Gerard Eliassoen, of Tergou. These by the hand of the trusty Hans Memling, with all speed."

"'Tis excellently well writ," said the reader, examining every letter.

"Ay!" said Hans bombastically "and small wonder: 'tis writ by a famous hand; by Margaret, sister of Jan Van Eyck. Blessed and honoured be his memory! She is an old friend of mine, is Margaret Van Eyck."

Miscellaneous Hans then diverged into forty topics.

Sybrandt stole out of the company, and went in search of Cornelis.

They put their heads together over the news: Italy was an immense distance off. If they could only keep him there?

"Keep him there? Nothing would keep him long from his Margaret."

"Curse her!" said Sybrandt. "Why didn't she die when she was about it?"

"*She* die? She would outlive the pest to vex us." And Cornelis was wroth at her selfishness in not dying, to oblige.

These two black sheep kept putting their heads together, and tainting each other worse and worse, till at last their corrupt hearts conceived a plan for keeping Gerard in Italy all his life, and so securing his share of their father's substance.

But when they had planned it they were no nearer the execution; for that required talent: so iniquity came to a standstill. But presently, as if Satan had come between the two heads, and whispered into the right ear of one and the left of the other simultaneously, they both burst out

"THE BURGOMASTER!"

They went to Ghysbrecht Van Swieten, and he received them at once: for the man who is under the torture of suspense catches eagerly at knowledge. Certainty is often painful, but seldom, like suspense, intolerable.

The Cloister and the Hearth

"You have news of Gerard?" said he eagerly.

Then they told about the letter and Hans Memling. He listened with restless eye. "Who writ the letter?"

"Margaret Van Eyck," was the reply: for they naturally thought the contents were by the same hand as the superscription.

"Are ye sure?" And he went to a drawer and drew out a paper written by Margaret Van Eyck while treating with the burgh for her house. "Was it writ like this?"

"Yes. 'Tis the same writing," said Sybrandt, boldly.

"Good. And now what would ye of me?" said Ghysbrecht, with beating heart, but a carelessness so well feigned that it staggered them. They fumbled with their bonnets, and stammered and spoke a word or two, then hesitated and beat about the bush, and let out by degrees that they wanted a letter written, to say something that might keep Gerard in Italy: and this letter they proposed to substitute in Hans Memling's wallet for the one he carried. While these fumbled with their bonnets and their iniquity, and vacillated between respect for a burgomaster, and suspicion that this one was as great rogue as themselves, and, somehow or other, on their side against Gerard, pros and cons were coursing one another to and fro in the keen old man's spirit. Vengeance said let Gerard come back and feel the weight of the law. Prudence said keep him a thousand miles off. But then prudence said also, why do dirty work on a doubtful chance? Why put it in the power of these two rogues to tarnish your name? Finally, his strong persuasion that Gerard was in possession of a secret by means of which he could wound him to the quick, coupled with his caution, found words thus: "It is my duty to aid the citizens that cannot write. But for their matter I will not be responsible. Tell me, then, what I shall write."

"Something about this Margaret."

"Ay, ay! that she is false, that she is married to another, I'll go bail."

"Nay, burgomaster, nay! not for all the world!" cried Sybrandt; "Gerard would not believe it, or but half, and then he would come back to see. No; say that she is dead."

"Dead! what at her age? will he credit that?"

"Sooner than the other. Why she *was nearly* dead; so it is not to say a downright lie, after all."

286

"Humph? And you think that will keep him in Italy?"

"We are sure of it, are we not, Cornelis?"

"Ay," said Cornelis, "our Gerard will never leave Itay now he is there. It was always his dream to get there. He would come back for his Margaret, but not for us. What cares he for us? He despises his own family; always did."

"This would be a bitter pill to him," said the old hypocrite. "It will be for his good in the end," replied the young one.

"What avails Famine wedding Thirst?" said Cornelis.

"And the grief you are preparing for him so coolly?" Ghysbrecht spoke sarcastically, but tasted his own vengeance all the time.

"Oh, a lie is not like a blow with a curtal axe. It hacks no flesh, and breaks no bones."

"A curtal axe?" said Sybrandt; "no, nor even like a stroke with a cudgel." And he shot a sly envenomed glance at the burgomaster's broken nose.

Ghysbrecht's face darkened with ire when this adder's tongue struck his wound. But it told, as intended: the old man bristled with hate.

"Well," said he, "tell me what to write for you, and I must write it: but, take notice, you bear the blame if aught turns amiss. Not the hand which writes, but the tongue which dictates, doth the deed."

The brothers assented warmly, sneering within. Ghysbrecht then drew his inkhorn towards him, and laid the specimen of Margaret Van Eyck's writing before him, and made some inquiries as to the size and shape of the letter; when an unlooked-for interruption occured; Jorian Ketel burst hastily into the room, and looked vexed at not finding him alone.

"Thou seest I have matter on hand, good fellow."

"Ay; but this is grave. I bring good news; but 'tis not for every ear."

The burgomaster rose, and drew Jorian aside into the embrasure of his deep window, and then the brothers heard them converse in low but eager tones. It ended by Ghysbrecht sending Jorian out to saddle his mule. He then addressed the black sheep with a sudden coldness that amazed them:

"I prize the peace of households; but this is not a thing to be done in a hurry: we will see about, we will see."

"But, burgomaster, the man will be gone. It will be too late."

"Where is he?"

"At the hostelry, drinking."

"Well, keep him drinking! We will see, we will see." And he sent them off discomfited.

To explain all this we must retrograde a step. This very morning then, Margaret Brandt had met Jorian Ketel near her own door. He passed her with a scowl. This struck her, and she remembered him.

"Stay," said she. "Yes! it is the good man who saved him. Oh! why have you not been near me since? And why have you not come for the parchments? Was it not true about the hundred crowns?"

Jorian gave a snort: but, seeing her face that looked so candid, began to think there might be some mistake. He told her he had come, and how he had been received.

"Alas!" said she, "I knew nought of this. I lay at death's door." She then invited him to follow her, and took him into the garden and showed him the spot where the parchments were buried. "Martin was for taking them up, but I would not let him. *He* put them there: and I said none should move them but you, who had earned them so well of him and me."

"Give me a spade!" cried Jorian, eagerly. "But stay! No; he is a suspicious man. You are sure they are there still?"

"I will openly take the blame if human hand hath touched them."

"Then keep them but two hours more, I prithee, good Margaret," said Jorian, and ran off to the Stadthouse of Tergou a joyful man.

The burgomaster jogged along towards Sevenbergen, with Jorian striding beside him, giving him assurance that in an hour's time the missing parchments would be in his hand.

"Ah, master!" said he, "lucky for us it wasn't a thief that took them."

"Not a thief? not a thief? what call you him, then?"

"Well, saving your presence, I call him a jackdaw. This is jack-daw's work, if ever there was; 'take the thing you are least in need of, and hide it'—that's a jackdaw. I should know," added Jorian, oracularly, "for I was brought up along with a chough. He and I were born the same year, but he cut his teeth long before me, and, wow! but my life was a burden for years all along of him. If you had but a hole in your hose no bigger than a groat, in went his beak like a gimlet; and, for stealing, Gerard all over. What he wanted least, and any poor Christian wanted most, that went first. Mother was a notable woman, so, if she did but look round, away flew her thimble. Father lived by cordwaining, so about sunrise Jack went diligently off with his awl, his wax, and his twine. After that, make your bread how you could! One day I heard my mother tell him to his face he was enough to corrupt half a dozen other children; and he only cocked his eye at her, and next minute away with the nurseling shoe off his very foot. Now this Gerard is tarred with the same stick. The parchments are no more use to him than a thimble or an awl to Jack. He took 'em out of pure mischief and hid them, and you would never have found them but for me."

"I believe you are right," said Ghysbrecht, "and I have vexed myself more than need."

When they came to Peter's gate he felt uneasy.

"I wish it had been anywhere but here."

Jorian reassured him.

"The girl is honest and friendly," said he. "She had nothing to do with taking them, I'll be sworn:" and he led him into the garden. "There, master, if a face is to be believed, here they lie; and, see, the mould *is* loose."

He ran for a spade which was stuck up in the ground at some distance, and soon went to work and uncovered a parchment. Ghysbrecht saw it and thrust him aside and went down on his knees and tore it out of the hole. His hands trembled and his face shone. He threw out parchment after parchment, and Jorian dusted them and cleaned them and shook them. Now, when Ghysbrecht had thrown out a great many, his face began to darken and lengthen, and, when he came to the last, he put his hands to his temples and seemed to be all amazed.

"What mystery lies here?" he gasped. "Are fiends mocking me? Dig deeper! There *must* be another."

Jorian drove the spade in and threw out quantities of hard mould. In vain. And even while he dug, his master's mood had changed.

"Treason! treachery!" he cried. "You knew of this."

289

"Knew what, master, in Heaven's name?"

"Caitiff, you knew there was another one worth all these twice told."

"'Tis false," cried Jorian, made suspicious by the other's suspicion. "'Tis a trick to rob me of my hundred crowns. Oh! I know you, burgomaster." And Jorian was ready to whimper.

A mellow voice fell on them both like oil upon the waves. "No, good man, it is not false, nor yet is it quite true: there was another parchment."

"There, there, there! Where is it?"

"But," continued Margaret calmly, "it was not a town record (so you have gained your hundred crowns, good man): it was but a private deed between the burgomaster here and my grandfather Flor——"

"Hush, hush!"

"——is Brandt."

"Where is it, girl? that is all we want to know."

"Have patience, and I shall tell you. Gerard read the title of it, and he said, "This is as much yours as the burgomaster's," and he put it apart, to read it with me at his leisure."

"It is in the house, then?" said the burgomaster, recovering his calmness.

"No, sir," said Margaret, bravely, "it is not." Then, in a voice that faltered suddenly, "You hunted—my poor Gerard—so hard—and so close—that you gave him—no time—to think of aught—but his life—and his grief.—The parchment was in his bosom, and he hath ta'en it with him."

"Whither, whither?"

"Ask me no more, sir. What right is yours to question me thus? It was for *your* sake, good man, I put force upon my heart, and came out here, and bore to speak at all to this hard old man. For, when I think of the misery he has brought on *him* and me, the sight of him is more than I can bear:" and she gave an involuntary shudder, and went slowly in, with her hand to her head, crying bitterly.

Remorse for the past, and dread of the future—the slow, but, as he now felt, the inevitable future—avarice, and fear, all tugged in one short moment at Ghysbrecht's tough heart. He hung his head, and his arms fell listless by his sides. A coarse chuckle made him start round, and there stood Martin Wittenhaagen leaning on his bow, and sneering from ear to ear. At sight of the man and his grinning face, Ghysbrecht's worst passions awoke.

"Ho! attach him, seize him, traitor and thief!" cried he. "Dog, thou shalt pay for all."

Martin, without a word, calmly thrust the duke's pardon under Ghysbrecht's nose. He looked, and had not a word to say. Martin followed up his advantage.

"The duke and I are soldiers. He won't let you greasy burghers trample on an old comrade. He bade me carry you a message too."

"The duke send a message to me?"

"Ay! I told him of your masterful doings, of your imprisoning Gerard for loving a girl; and says he, 'Tell him this is to be a king, not a burgomaster. I'll have no kings in Holland but one. Bid him be more humble, or I'll hang him at his own door'" (Ghysbrecht trembled. He thought the duke capable of the deed) "'as I hanged the burgomaster of Thingembob.' The duke could not mind which of you he had hung, or in what part; such trifles stick not in a soldier's memory, but he was sure he had hanged one of you for grinding poor folk, 'and I'm the man to hang another,' quoth the good duke."

These repeated insults from so mean a man, coupled with his invulnerability, shielded as he was by the duke, drove the choleric old man into a fit of impotent fury: he shook his fist at the soldier, and tried to threaten him, but could not speak for the rage and mortification that choked him: then he gave a sort of screech, and coiled himself up in eye and form like a rattle-snake about to strike; and spat furiously upon Martin's doublet.

The thick-skinned soldier treated this ebullition with genuine contempt. "Here's a venomous old toad! he knows a kick from this foot would send him to his last home; and he wants me to cheat the gallows. But I have slain too many men in fair fight to lift limb against anything less than a man: and this I count no man; what is it, in Heaven's name? an old goat's-skin bag full o' rotten bones."

"My mule! my mule!" screamed Ghysbrecht.

Jorian helped the old man up trembling in every joint. Once in the saddle, he seemed to gather in a moment unnatural vigour; and the figure that went flying to Tergou was truly weirdlike and terrible: so old and wizened the face; so white and reverend the streaming hair; so baleful the eye; so fierce the fury which shook the bent frame that went spurring like mad; while the quavering voice yelled, "I'll make their hearts ache.—I'll make their hearts ache.—I'll make their hearts ache.—I'll make their hearts ache. All of them. All!—all!—all!"

The black sheep sat disconsolate amidst the convivial crew, and eyed Hans Memling's wallet. For more ease he had taken it off, and flung it on the table. How readily they could have slipped out that letter and put in another. For the first time in their lives they were sorry they had not learned to write, like their brother.

And now Hans began to talk of going, and the brothers agreed in a whisper to abandon their project for the time. They had scarcely resolved this, when Dierich Brower stood suddenly in the doorway, and gave them a wink.

They went out to him. "Come to the burgomaster with all speed," said he.

They found Ghysbrecht seated at a table, pale and agitated. Before him lay Margaret Van Eyck's handwriting. "I have written what you desired," said he. "Now for the superscription. What were the words? did ye see?"

"We cannot read," said Cornelis.

"Then is all this labour lost," cried Ghysbrecht angrily. "Dolts!"

"Nay, but," said Sybrandt, "I heard the words read, and I have not lost them. They were, 'To Gerard Eliassoen, these by the hand of the trusty Hans Memling with all speed.'"

" 'Tis well. Now, how was the letter folded? how big was it?"

"Longer than that one, and not so long as this."

" 'Tis well. Where is he?"

"At the hostelry."

"Come, then, take you this groat, and treat him. Then ask to see the letter, and put this in place of it. Come to me with the other letter."

The brothers assented, took the letter, and went to the hostelry.

They had not been gone a minute, when Dierich Brower issued from the Stadthouse, and followed them. He had his orders not to let them out of his sight till the true letter was in his master's hands. He watched outside the hostelry.

He had not long to wait. They came out almost immediately, with downcast looks. Dierich made up to them.

"Too late!" they cried; "too late! He is gone."

"Gone? How long?"

"Scarce five minutes. Cursed chance!"

"You must go back to the burgomaster at once," said Dierich Brower.

"To what end?"

"No matter; come:" and he hurried them to the Stadthouse.

Ghysbrecht Van Swieten was not the man to accept a defeat. "Well," said he, on hearing the ill news, "suppose he is gone. Is he mounted?"

"No."

"Then what hinders you to come up with him?"

"But what avails coming up with him? there are no hostelries on the road he is gone."

"Fools!" said Ghysbrecht, "is there no way of emptying a man's pockets but liquor and sleight of hand?"

A meaning look, that passed between Ghysbrecht and Dierich, aided the brothers' comprehension. They changed colour, and lost all zeal for the business.

"No! no! we don't hate our brother. We won't get ourselves hanged to spite him," said Sybrandt; "that would be a fool's trick."

"Hanged?" cried Ghysbrecht. "Am I not the burgomaster? How can ye be hanged? I see how 'tis: ye fear to tackle one man, being two: hearts of hare, that ye are! O! why cannot I be young again? I'd do it single-handed."

The old man now threw off all disguise, and showed them his heart was in this deed. He then flattered and besought, and jeered them alternately, but he found no eloquence could move them to an action, however dishonourable, which was attended with danger. At last he opened a drawer, and showed them a pile of silver coins.

"Change but those letters for me," he said, "and each of you shall thrust one hand into this drawer, and take away as many of them as you can hold."

The effect was magical. Their eyes glittered with desire. Their whole bodies seemed to swell, and rise into male energy.

"Swear it, then," said Sybrandt.

"I swear it."

"No; on the crucifix."

Ghysbrecht swore upon the crucifix.

The next minute the brothers were on the road, in pursuit of Hans Memling. They came in sight of him about two leagues from Tergou: but though they knew he had no weapon but his staff, they were too prudent to venture on him in daylight; so they fell back.

But being now three leagues and more from the town, and on a grassy road,—sun down, moon not yet up,—honest Hans suddenly found himself attacked before and behind at once by men with up-lifted knives, who cried in loud though somewhat shaky voices, "Stand and deliver!"

The attack was so sudden, and so well planned, that Hans was dismayed. "Slay me not, good fellows," he cried: "I am but a poor man, and ye shall have my all."

"So be it then. Live! But empty thy wallet."

"There is nought in my wallet, good friends, but one letter."

"That we shall see," said Sybrandt, who was the one in front. "Well: it *is* a letter."

"Take it not from me, I pray you. 'Tis worth nought, and the good dame would fret that writ it."

"There," said Sybrandt, "take back thy letter: and now empty thy pouch. Come! tarry not!"

But by this time Hans had recovered his confusion: and, from a certain flutter in Sybrandt, and hard breathing of Cornelis, aided by an indescribable consciousness, felt sure the pair he had to deal with were no heroes. He pretended to fumble for his money: then suddenly thrust his staff fiercely into Sybrandt's face, and drove him staggering, and lent Cornelis a back-handed slash on the ear that sent him twirling like a weather-cock in March: then whirled his weapon over his head and danced about the road like a figure on springs, shouting "Come on, ye thieving loons! Come on!"

It was a plain invitation: yet they misunderstood it so utterly as to take to their heels, with Hans after them, he shouting "Stop thieves!" and they howling with fear and pain as they ran.

CHAPTER XLI

DENYS, placed in the middle of his companions, lest he should be so mad as attempt escape, was carried off in an agony of grief and remorse. For his sake Gerard had abandoned the German route to Rome; and what was his reward? left all alone in the centre of Burgundy. This was the thought which maddened Denys most, and made him now rave at heaven and earth, now fall into a gloomy silence so savage and sinister that it was deemed prudent to disarm him. They caught up their leader just outside the town, and the whole cavalcade drew up and baited at the "Tête d'Or."

The young landlady, though much occupied with the count, and still more with the Bastard, caught sight of Denys, and asked him somewhat anxiously what had become of his young companion?

Denys, with a burst of grief, told her all, and prayed her to send after Gerard. "Now he is parted from me, he will maybe listen to my rede," said he; "poor wretch he loves not solitude."

The landlady gave a toss of her head. "I trow I have been some-what over-kind already," said she, and turned rather red.

"You will not?"

"Not I."

"Then,"—and he poured a volley of curses and abuse upon her.

She turned her back upon him, and went off whimpering, and saying she was not used to be cursed at; and ordered her hind to saddle two mules.

Denys went north with his troop, mute and drooping over his saddle, and, quite unknown to him, that veracious young lady made an equestrian toilet in only forty minutes, she being really in a hurry, and spurred away with her servant in the opposite direction.

At dark, after a long march, the Bastard and his men reached "the White Hart;" their arrival caused a prodigious bustle, and it was some time before Manon discovered her old friend among so many. When she did, she showed it only by heightened colour. She did not claim the acquaintance. The poor soul was already beginning to scorn

The Cloister and the Hearth

"The base degrees by which she did ascend."

Denys saw, but could not smile. The inn reminded him too much of Gerard.

Ere the night closed the wind changed. She looked into the room and beckoned him with her finger. He rose sulkily, and his guards with him.

"Nay, I would speak a word to thee in private." She drew him to a corner of the room, and there asked him under her breath, would he do her a kindness.

He answered out loud, "No, he would not, he was not in the vein to do kindnesses to man or woman. If he did a kindness it should be to a dog: and not that if he could help it."

"Alas, good archer, I did you one eftsoons, you and your pretty comrade," said Manon, humbly.

"You did, dame, you did; well then, for his sake—what is't to do?"

"Thou knowest my story. I had been unfortunate. Now I am worshipful. But a woman did cast him in my teeth this day. And so 'twill be ever while he hangs there. I would have him ta'en down; well-a-day!"

"With all my heart."

"And none dare I ask but thee. Wilt do't?"

"Not I, even were I not a prisoner."

On this stern refusal the tender Manon sighed, and clasped her palms together despondently. Denys told her she need not fret. There were soldiers of a lower stamp, who would not make two bites of such a cherry. It was a mere matter of money; if she could find two angels, he would find two soldiers to do the dirty work of the "White Hart."

This was not very palatable. However, reflecting that soldiers were birds of passage, drinking here to-night, knocked on the head there to-morrow, she said, softly, "Send them out to me. But prithee, tell them that 'tis for one that is my friend; let them not think 'tis for me. I should sink into th' earth; times are changed."

Denys found warriors glad to win an angel apiece so easily. He sent them out, and instantly dismissing the subject with contempt, sat brooding on his lost friend.

Manon and the warriors soon came to a general understanding.

But what were they to do with the body when taken down? She murmured, "The river is nigh the—the—place."

"Fling him in, eh?"

"Nay, nay; be not so cruel! Could ye not put him—gently—in—with somewhat weighty?"

She must have been thinking on the subject in detail; for she was not one to whom ideas came quickly.

All was speedily agreed, except the time of payment. The mail-clad itched for it, and sought it in advance. Manon demurred to that.

What, did she doubt their word? then let her come along with them, or watch them at a distance.

"Me?" said Manon, with horror. "I would liever die than see it done."

"Which yet you would have done."

"Ay, for sore is my need. Times are changed." She had already forgotten her precept to Denys.

An hour later the disagreeable relic of caterpillar existence ceased to canker the worshipful matron's public life, and the grim eyes of the past to cast malignant glances down into a white hind's clover field.

Total. She made the landlord an average wife, and a prime house-dog, and outlived everybody.

Her troops, when they returned from executing with mediæval naïveté the precept "Off wi' the auld love," received a shock. They found the market-place black with groups; it had been empty an hour ago. Conscience smote them. This came of meddling with the dead. However, the bolder of the two, encouraged by the darkness, stole forward alone, and slily mingled with a group: he soon returned to his companion, saying, in a tone of reproach not strictly reasonable,

"Ye born fool, it is only a miracle."

CHAPTER XLII

LETTERS of fire on the church wall had just inquired, with an appearance of genuine curiosity, why there was no mass for the duke in this time of trouble. The supernatural expostulation had been seen by many, and had gradually faded, leaving the spectators glued there gaping. The upshot was, that the corporation, not choosing to be behind the angelic powers in loyalty to a temporal sovereign, invested freely in masses. By this an old friend of ours, the curé, profited in hard cash; for which he had a very pretty taste. But for this I would not of course have detained you over so trite an occurence as a miracle.

Denys begged for his arms, "Why disgrace him as well as break his heart?"

"Then swear on the cross of thy sword not to leave the Bastard's service until the sedition shall be put down." He yielded to necessity, and delivered three volleys of oaths, and recovered his arms and liberty.

The troops halted at "The Three Fish," and Marion at sight of him cried out, "I'm out of luck; who would have thought to see you again?" then seeing he was sad, and rather hurt than amused at this blunt jest, she asked him what was amiss? He told her. She took a bright view of the case. Gerard was too handsome and well-behaved to come to harm. The women too would always be on his side. Moreover, it was clear that things must either go well or ill with him. In the former case he would strike in with some good company going to Rome; in the latter, he would return home, perhaps be there before his friend; "for you have a trifle of fighting to do in Flanders by all accounts." She then brought him his gold pieces, and steadily refused to accept one, though he urged her again and again. Denys was somewhat convinced by her argument, because she concurred with his own wishes, and was also cheered a little by finding her so honest. It made him think a little better of that world in which his poor little friend was walking alone.

Foot-soldiers in small bodies down to twos and threes were already on the road, making lazily towards Flanders, many of them penniless, but passed from town to town by the bailiffs, with orders for food and lodging on the innkeepers.

Anthony of Burgundy overtook numbers of these, and gathered them under his standard, so that he entered Flanders at the head of six hundred men. On crossing the frontier he was met by his brother Baldwyn, with men, arms, and provisions; he organized his whole force and marched on in battle array through several towns, not only without impediment, but with great acclamations. This loyalty called forth comments not altogether gracious.

"This rebellion of ours is a bite," growled a soldier called Simon, who had elected himself Denys's comrade.

Denys said nothing, but made a little vow to St. Mars to shoot this Anthony of Burgundy dead, should the rebellion, that had cost him Gerard, prove no rebellion.

That afternoon they came in sight of a strongly fortified town; and a whisper went through the little army that this was a disaffected place.

But, when they came in sight, the great gate stood open, and the towers that flanked it on each side were manned with a single sentinel apiece. So the advancing force somewhat broke their array and marched carelessly.

When they were within a furlong, the draw-bridge across the moat rose slowly and creaking till it stood vertical against the fort, and, the very moment it settled into this warlike attitude, down rattled the portcullis at the gate, and the towers and curtains bristled with lances and cross-bows.

A stern hum ran through the Bastard's front rank and spread to the rear.

"Halt!" cried he. The word went down the line, and they halted. "Herald to the gate!" A pursuivant spurred out of the ranks, and, halting twenty yards from the gate, raised his bugle with his herald's flag hanging down round it, and blew a summons. A tall figure in brazen armour appeared over the gate. A few fiery words passed between him and the herald, which were not audible, but their import clear, for the herald blew a single keen and threatening note at the walls, and came galloping back with war in his face. The Bastard moved out of the line to meet him, and their heads had not been together two seconds ere he turned in his saddle and shouted, "Pioneers, to the van!" and in a moment hedges were levelled, and the force took the field and encamped just out of shot from the walls; and away went mounted officers flying south, east, and west, to the friendly towns, for catapults, palisades, mantelets, raw hides, tar barrels, carpenters, provisions, and all the materials for a siege.

The bright perspective mightily cheered one drooping soldier. At the first clang of the portcullis his eyes brightened and his temple flushed; and when the herald came back with battle in his eye he saw it in a moment, and for the first time this many days cried, "Courage, tout le monde, le diable est mort."

If that great warrior heard, how he must have grinned!

CHAPTER XLIII

THE besiegers encamped a furlong from the walls and made roads; kept their pikemen in camp ready for an assault when practicable; and sent forward their sappers, pioneers, catapultiers, and cross-bowmen. These opened a siege by filling the moat, and mining, or breaching the wall, etc. And, as much of their work had to be done under close fire of arrows, quarels, bolts, stones, and little rocks, the above artists "had need of a hundred eyes," and acted in concert with a vigilance, and an amount of individual intelligence, daring and skill, that made a siege very interesting, and even amusing; to lookers on.

The first thing they did was to advance their carpenters behind rolling mantelets, to erect a stockade high and strong on the very edge of the moat. Some lives were lost at this, but not many; for a strong force of cross-bowmen, including Denys, rolled their mantelets up and shot over the workmen's heads at every besieged who showed his nose, and at every loophole, arrow-slit, or other aperture, which commanded the particular spot the carpenters happened to be upon. Covered by their condensd fire, these soon raised a high palisade between them and the ordinary missiles from the pierced masonry.

But the besieged expected this, and ran out at night their hoards, or wooden penthouses on the top of the curtains. The curtains were built with square holes near the top to receive the beams, that supported these structures, the true defence of mediaeval forts, from which the besieged delivered their missiles with far more freedom and variety of range than they could shoot through the oblique but immovable loopholes of the curtain, or even through the sloping crenelets of the higher towers. On this the besiegers brought up mangonels, and set them hurling huge stones at these wood works and battering them to pieces. Contemporaneously they built a triangular wooden tower as high as the curtain, and kept it ready for use, and just out of shot.

This was a terrible sight to the besieged. These wooden towers had taken many a town. They began to mine underneath that part of the moat the tower stood frowning at; and made other preparations to give it a warm reception. The besiegers also mined, but at another part, their object being to get under the square barbican and throw it down. All this time Denys was behind his mantelet with another arbalestrier, protecting the workmen and making some excellent shots. These ended by earning him the esteem of an unseen archer, who every now and then sent a winged compliment quivering into his mantelet. One came and struck within an inch of the narrow slit through which Denys was squinting at the moment. "Peste," cried he, "you shoot well, my friend. Come forth and receive my congratulations! Shall merit such as thine hide its head? Comrade, it is one of those cursed Englishmen, with his half ell shaft. I'll not die till I've had a shot at London wall."

On the besiegers' side was a figure that soon attracted great notice by promenading under fire. It was a tall knight, clad in complete brass, and carrying a light but prodigiously long lance with which he directed the movements of the besieged. And, when any disaster befell the besiegers, this long knight and his tall lance were pretty sure to be concerned in it.

My young reader will say, "Why did not Denys shoot him?"

Denys did shoot him; every day of his life: other arbalestriers shot him; archers shot him. Everybody shot him. He was there to be shot, apparently. But the abomination was, he did not mind being shot. Nay, worse, he got at last so demoralized as not to seem to know when he was shot. He walked his battlements under fire, as some stout skipper paces his deck in a suit of Flushing, calmly oblivious of the April drops that fall on his woolen armour. At last the besiegers got spiteful, and would not waste any more good steel on him; but cursed him and his impervious coat of mail.

He took these missiles like the rest.

The Cloister and the Hearth

Gunpowder has spoiled war. War was always detrimental to the solid interests of mankind. But in old times it was good for something: it painted well, sang divinely, furnished Iliads. But invisible butchery, under a pall of smoke a furlong thick, who is any the better for that? Poet with his note-book may repeat, "Suave etiam belli certamina magna tueri;" but the sentiment is hollow and savours of cuckoo. You can't tueri anything but a horrid row. He didn't say "Suave etiam ingentem caliginem tueri per campos instructam."

They managed better in the middle ages.

This siege was a small affair: but, such as it was, a writer or minstrel could see it; and turn an honest penny by singing it; so far then the sport was reasonable, and served an end.

It was a bright day, clear, but not quite frosty. The efforts of the besieging force were concentrated against a space of about two hundred and fifty yards, containing two curtains, and two towers, one of which was the square barbican, the other had a pointed roof that was built to overlap, resting on a stone machicolade, and by this means a row of dangerous crenelets between the roof and the masonry grinned down at the nearer assailants, and looked not very unlike the grinders of a modern frigate with each port nearly closed. The curtains were overlapped with pent-houses somewhat shattered by the mangonels, trébuchets, and other slinging engines of the besiegers. On the besiegers' edge of the moat was what seemed at first sight a gigantic arsenal, longer than it was broad, peopled by human ants, and full of busy, honest industry, and displaying all the various mechanical science of the age in full operation. Here the lever at work, there the winch and pulley, here the balance, there the capstan. Everywhere heaps of stones, and piles of fascines, mantelets, and rows of fire-barrels. Mantelets rolling, the hammer tapping all day, horses and carts in endless succession rattling up with materials. Only, on looking closer into the hive of industry, you might observe that arrows were constantly flying to and fro, that the cranes did not tenderly deposit their masses of stone, but flung them with an indifference to property, though on scientific principles, and that among the tubs full of arrows, and the tar-barrels and the beams, the fagots, and other utensils, here and there a workman or a soldier lay flatter than is usual in limited naps, and something more or less feathered stuck in them, and blood, and other essentials, oozed out.

The Cloister and the Hearth

At the edge of the moat opposite the wooden tower, a strong penthouse which they called "a cat" might be seen stealing towards the curtain, and gradually filling up the moat with fascines and rubbish, which the workmen flung out at its mouth. It was advanced by two sets of ropes passing round pulleys, and each worked by a windlass at some distance from the cat. The knight burnt the first cat by flinging blazing tar-barrels on it. So the besiegers made the roof of this one very steep, and covered it with raw hides, and the tar-barrels could not harm it. Then the knight made signs with his spear, and a little trébuchet behind the walls began dropping stones just clear of the wall into the moat, and at last they got the range, and a stone went clean through the roof of the cat, and made an ugly hole.

Baldwyn of Burgundy saw this, and losing his temper, ordered the great catapult that was battering the wood-work of the curtain opposite it to be turned and levelled slantwise at this invulnerable knight. Denys and his Englishman went to dinner. These two worthies being eternally on the watch for one another had made a sort of distant acquaintance, and conversed by signs, especially on a topic that in peace or war maintains the same importance. Sometimes Denys would put a piece of bread on the top of his mantelet, and then the archer would hang something of the kind out by a string; or the order of invitation would be reversed. Any way they always managed to dine together.

And now the engineers proceeded to the unusual step of slinging fifty-pound stones at an individual.

This catapult was a scientific, simple, and beautiful engine, and very effective in vertical fire at the short ranges of the period.

Imagine a fir-tree cut down, and set to turn round a horizontal axis on lofty uprights, but not in equilibrio; three-fourths of the tree being on the hither side. At the shorter and thicker end of the tree was fastened a weight of half a ton. This butt end just before the discharge pointed towards the enemy. By means of a powerful winch the long tapering portion of the tree was forced down to the very ground; and fastened by a bolt; and the stone placed in a sling attached to the tree's nose. But this process of course raised the butt end with its huge weight high in the air, and kept it there struggling in vain to come down. The bolt was now drawn; Gravity, an institution which flourished even then, resumed its sway, the short end swung furiously down, the long end went as furiously round up, and at its highest elevation flung the huge stone out of the sling with a tremendous jerk. In this case the huge mass so flung missed the knight, but came down near him on the penthouse, and went through it like paper, making an awful gap in roof and floor. Through the latter fell out two inanimate objects, the stone itself and the mangled body of a besieger it had struck. They fell down the high curtain side, down, down, and struck almost together the sullen waters of the moat, which closed bubbling on them, and kept both the stone and the bone two hundred years, till cannon mocked those oft perturbed waters, and civilization dried them.

"Aha! a good shot," cried Baldwyn of Burgundy.

The tall knight retired. The besiegers hooted him.

He reappeared on the platform of the barbican, his helmet being just visible above the parapet. He seemed very busy, and soon an enormous Turkish catapult made its appearance on the platform, and aided by the elevation at which it was planted, flung a twenty-pound stone two hundred and forty yards in the air; it bounded after that, and knocked some dirt into the Lord Anthony's eye, and made him swear. The next stone struck a horse that was bringing up a sheaf of arrows in a cart, bowled the horse over dead like a rabbit, and spilt the cart. It was then turned at the besiegers' wooden tower, supposed to be out of shot. Sir Turk slung stones cut with sharp edges on purpose, and struck it repeatedly, and broke it in several places. The besiegers turned two of their slinging engines on this monster, and kept constantly slinging smaller stones on to the platform of the barbican, and killed two of the engineers. But the Turk disdained to retort. He flung a forty-pound stone on to the besiegers' great catapult, and hitting it in the neighbourhood of the axis, knocked the whole structure to pieces and sent the engineers skipping and yelling.

In the afternoon, as Simon was running back to his mantelet from a palisade where he had been shooting at the besieged, Denys, peeping through his slit, saw the poor fellow suddenly stare and hold out his arms, then roll on his face, and a feathered arrow protruded from his back. The archer showed himself a moment to enjoy his skill. It was the Englishman. Denys, already prepared, shot his bolt and the murderous archer staggered away wounded. But poor Simon never moved. His wars were over.

The Cloister and the Hearth

"I am unlucky in my comrades," said Denys.

The next morning an unwelcome sight greeted the besieged. The cat was covered with mattresses and raw hides, and fast filling up the moat. The knight stoned it, but in vain; flung burning tar-barrels on it, but in vain. Then with his own hands he let down by a rope a bag of burning sulphur and pitch, and stunk them out. But Baldwyn, armed like a lobster, ran, and bounding on the roof, cut the string, and the work went on. Then the knight sent fresh engineers into the mine, and undermined the place and underpinned it with beams, and covered the beams thickly with grease and tar.

At break of day the moat was filled, and the wooden tower began to move on its wheels towards a part of the curtain on which two catapults were already playing to breach the hoards, and clear the way. There was something awful and magical in its approach without visible agency, for it was driven by internal rollers worked by leverage. On the top was a platform, where stood the first assailing party protected in front by the drawbridge of the turret, which stood vertical till lowered on to the wall; but better protected by full suits of armour. The besieged slung at the tower, and struck it often, but in vain. It was well defended with mattresses and hides, and presently was at the edge of the moat. The knight bade fire the mine underneath it.

Then the Turkish engine flung a stone of half a hundredweight right amongst the knights and carried two away with it off the tower on to the plain. One lay and writhed: the other neither moved nor spake.

And now the besieging catapults flung blazing tar-barrels, and fired the hoards on both sides, and the assailants ran up the ladders behind the tower, and lowered the drawbridge on to the battered curtain, while the catapults in concert flung tar-barrels and fired the adjoining works to dislodge the defenders. The armed men on the platform sprang on the bridge, led by Baldwyn. The invulnerable knight and his men-at-arms met them, and a fearful combat ensued, in which many a figure was seen to fall headlong down off the narrow bridge. But fresh besiegers kept swarming up behind the tower, and the besieged were driven off the bridge.

Another minute, and the town was taken, but so well had the firing of the mine been timed, that just at this instant the underpinners gave way, and the tower suddenly sank away from the walls tearing the drawbridge clear and pouring the soldiers off it against the masonry and on to the dry moat. The besieged uttered a fierce shout and in a moment surrounded Baldwyn and his fellows; but strange to say offered them quarter. While a party disarmed and disposed of these, others fired the turret in fifty places with a sort of hand grenades. At this work who so busy as the tall knight. He put fire-bags on his long spear, and thrust them into the doomed structure late so terrible. To do this he was obliged to stand on a projecting beam of the shattered hoard, holding on by the hand of a pikeman to steady himself. This provoked Denys, he ran out from his mantelet, hoping to escape notice in the confusion, and levelling his cross-bow missed the knight clean, but sent his bolt into the brain of the pikeman, and the tall knight fell heavily from the wall lance and all. Denys gazed wonderstruck: and, in that unlucky moment suddenly he felt his arm hot, then cold, and there was an English arrow skewering it.

This episode was unnoticed in a much greater matter. The knight, his armour glittering in the morning sun, fell headlong, but, turning as he neared the water, struck it with a slap that sounded a mile off.

None ever thought to see him again. But he fell at the edge of the fascines on which the turret stood all cocked on one side, and his spear stuck into them under water, and by a mighty effort he got to the side, but could not get out. Anthony sent a dozen knights with a white flag to take him prisoner. He submitted like a lamb, but said nothing.

He was taken to Anthony's tent.

That worthy laughed at first at the sight of his muddy armour. But presently, frowning, said, "I marvel, sir, that so good a knight as you should know his devoir so ill as turn rebel, and give us all this trouble."

"I am nun—nun—nun—nun—nun—no knight."

"What, then?"

"A hosier."

"A what? Then thy armour shall be stripped off, and thou shalt be tied to a stake in front of the works, and riddled with arrows for a warning to traitors."

"N—n—n—n—no! duda—duda—duda—duda—don't do that."

"Why not?"

"Tuta—tuta—tuta—townsfolk will—h—h—h—hang t'other buba
—buba—buba—buba—bastard."

"What, whom?"

"Your bub—bub—bub—brother Baldwyn."

"What, have yon knaves ta'en him?"

The warlike hosier nodded.

"Hang the fool!" said Anthony peevishly.

The warlike hosier watched his eye, and, doffing his helmet took
out of the lining an intercepted letter from the duke, bidding the
said Anthony come to court immediately, as he was to represent
the court of Burgundy at the court of England: was to go over and
receive the English king's sister and conduct her to her bridegroom
the Earl of Charolois. The mission was one very soothing to Anthony's pride, and also to his love of pleasure. For Edward the
Fourth held the gayest and most luxurious court in Europe. The
sly hosier saw he longed to be off, and said, "We'll gega—gega—
gega—gega—give ye a thousand angels to raise the siege."

"And Baldwyn?"

"I'll gega—gega—gega—gega—go and send him with the money."

It was now dinner-time; and, a flag of truce being hoisted on both
sides, the sham knight and the true one dined together and came
to a friendly understanding.

"But what is your grievance, my good friend?"

"Tuta—tuta—tuta—tuta—too much taxes."

Denys on finding the arrow in his right arm, turned his back,
which was protected by a long shield, and walked sulkily into camp.
He was met by the Comte de Jarnac, who had seen his brilliant shot,
and finding him wounded into the bargain, gave him a handful of
broad pieces.

"Hast got the better of thy grief, arbalestrier, methinks.'

"My grief, yes; but not my love. As soon as ever I have put
down this rebellion, I go to Holland, and there I shall meet with
him."

This event was nearer than Denys thought. He was relieved
from service next day, and, though his wound was no trifle, set out
with a stout heart to rejoin his friend in Holland.

CHAPTER XLIV

A CHANGE came over Margaret Brandt. She went about her household duties like one in a dream. If Peter did but speak a little quickly to her, she started and fixed two terrified eyes on him. She went less often to her friend Margaret Van Eyck, and was ill at her ease when there. Instead of meeting her warm old friend's caresses, she used to receive them passive and trembling, and sometimes almost shrink from them. But the most extraordinary thing was, she never would go outside her own house in daylight. When she went to Tergou it was after dusk, and she returned before daybreak. She would not even go to matins. At last Peter, unobservant as he was, noticed it, and asked her the reason.

"The folk all look at me so."

One day, Margaret Van Eyck asked her what was the matter. A scared look and a flood of tears were all the reply: the old lady expostulated gently. "What, sweetheart, afraid to confide your sorrows to me?"

"I have no sorrows, madam, but of my own making. I am kinder treated than I deserve; especially in this house."

"Then why not come oftener, my dear?"

"I come oftener than I deserve:" and she sighed deeply.

"There, Reicht is bawling for you," said Margaret Van Eyck; "go child!—what on earth can it be?"

Turning possibilities over in her mind, she thought Margaret must be mortified at the contempt with which she was treated by Gerard's family. "I will take them to task for it, at least such of them as are women;" and, the very next day, she put on her hood and cloak, and, followed by Reicht, went to the hosier's house. Catherine received her with much respect, and thanked her with tears for her kindness to Gerard. But when, encouraged by this, her visitor diverged to Margaret Brandt, Catherine's eyes dried, and her lips turned to half the size, and she looked as only obstinate, ignorant women can look. When they put on this cast of features, you might as well attempt to soften or convince a brick wall. Margaret

Van Eyck tried, but all in vain. So then, not being herself used to be thwarted, she got provoked, and at last went out hastily with an abrupt and mutilated curtsy, which Catherine returned with an air rather of defiance than obeisance. Outside the door Margaret Van Eyck found Reicht conversing with a pale girl on crutches. Margaret Van Eyck was pushing by them with heightened colour, and a scornful toss intended for the whole family, when suddenly a little delicate hand glided timidly into hers, and looking round she saw two dove-like eyes, with the water in them, that sought hers gratefully, and at the same time, imploringly. The old lady read this wonderful look, complex as it was, and down went her choler. She stooped and kissed Kate's brow. "I see," said she. "Mind, then, I leave it to you." Returned home, she said,—"I have been to a house to-day, where I have seen a very common thing and a very uncommon thing: I have seen a stupid, obstinate woman, and I have seen an angel in the flesh, with a face—if I had it here I'd take down my brushes once more, and try and paint it."

Little Kate did not belie the good opinion so hastily formed of her. She waited a better opportunity, and told her mother what she had learned from Reicht Heynes, that Margaret had shed her very blood for Gerard in the wood.

"See, mother, how she loves him."

"Who would not love him?"

"Oh, mother, think of it! Poor thing."

"Ay, wench. She has her own trouble, no doubt, as well as we ours. I can't abide the sight of blood, let alone my own."

This was a point gained; but when Kate tried to follow it up she was stopped short.

About a month after this a soldier of the Dalgetty tribe, returning from service in Burgundy, brought a letter one evening to the hosier's house. He was away on business: but the rest of the family sat at supper. The soldier laid the letter on the table by Catherine, and, refusing all guerdon for bringing it, went off to Sevenbergen.

The letter was unfolded and spread out: and curiously enough, though not one of them could read, they could all tell it was Gerard's handwriting.

"And your father must be away," cried Catherine. "Are ye not ashamed of yourselves? not one that can read your brother's letter?"

The Cloister and the Hearth

But although the words were to them what hieroglyphics are to us, there was something in the letter they could read. There is an art can speak without words: unfettered by the penman's limits, it can steal through the eye into the heart and brain, alike of the learned and unlearned: and it can cross a frontier or a sea, yet lose nothing. It is at the mercy of no translator: for it writes an universal language.

When, therefore, they saw this,

which Gerard had drawn with his pencil between the two short paragraphs, of which his letter consisted, they read it, and it went straight to their hearts.

Gerard was bidding them farewell.

As they gazed on that simple sketch, in every turn and line of which they recognized his manner, Gerard seemed present, and bidding them farewell.

The women wept over it till they could see it no longer.

Giles said, "Poor Gerard!" in a lower voice than seemed to belong to him.

Even Cornelis and Sybrandt felt a momentary remorse, and sat silent and gloomy.

But how to get the words read to them. They were loth to show their ignorance and their emotion to a stranger.

"The Dame Van Eyck?" said Kate, timidly.

"And so I will, Kate. She has a good heart. She loves Gerard, too. She will be glad to hear of him. I was short with her when she came here: but I will make my submission, and then she will tell me what my poor child says to me."

The Cloister and the Hearth

She was soon at Maragaret Van Eyck's house. Reicht took her into a room, and said, "Bide a minute; she is at her orisons."

There was a young woman in the room seated pensively by the stove; but she rose and courteously made way for the visitor.

"Thank you, young lady; the winter nights are cold, and your stove is a treat." Catherine then, while warming her hands, inspected her companion furtively from head to foot, both inclusive. The young person wore an ordinary wimple, but her gown was trimmed with fur, which was, in those days, almost a sign of superior rank or wealth. But what most struck Catherine was the candour and modesty of the face. She felt sure of sympathy from so good a countenance, and began to gossip.

"Now, what think you brings me here, young lady? It is a letter: a letter from my poor boy that is far away in some savage part or other. And I take shame to say that none of us can read it. I wonder whether you can read?"

"Yes."

"Can ye, now? It is much to your credit, my dear. I dare say she won't be long; but every minute is an hour to a poor longing mother."

"I will read it to you."

"Bless you, my dear; bless you!"

In her unfeigned eagerness she never noticed the suppressed eagerness, with which the hand was slowly put out to take the letter. She did not see the tremor with which the fingers closed on it.

"Come then, read it to me, prithee. I am wearying for it."

"The first words are, 'To my honoured parents.'"

"Ay! and he always did honour us, poor soul."

"'God and the saints have you in his holy keeping, and bless you by night and by day. Your one harsh deed is forgotten; your years of love remembered.'"

Catherine laid her hand on her bosom, and sank back in her chair with one long sob.

"Then comes this, madam. It doth speak for itself; 'a long farewell.'"

"Ay, go on: bless you, girl; you give me sorry comfort. Still 'tis comfort."

311

" 'To my brothers Cornelis and Sybrandt:—Be content; you will see me no more!' "

"What does that mean? Ah."

" 'To my sister Kate. Little angel of my father's house. Be kind to *her*—' Ah!' "

"That is Margaret Brandt, my dear,—his sweetheart, poor soul. I've not been kind to her, my dear. Forgive me, Gerard!"

" '—for poor Gerard's sake: since grief to her is death—to—me ——' Ah!" And nature, resenting the poor girl's struggle for un-natural composure, suddenly gave way, and she sank from her chair and lay insensible, with the letter in her hand, and her head on Catherine's knees.

CHAPTER XLV

EXPERIENCED women are not frightened when a woman faints, nor do they hastily attribute it to anything but phys-ical causes, which they have often seen produce it. Cather-ine bustled about; laid the girl down with her head on the floor quite flat, opened the window, and unloosed her dress as she lay. Not till she had done all this did she step to the door and say, rather loudly:

"Come here, if you please."

Margaret Van Eyck and Reicht came and found Margaret lying quite flat, and Catherine beating her hands.

"Oh, my poor girl! What have you done to her?"

"Me?" said Catherine, angrily.

"What has happened, then?"

"Nothing, madam; nothing more than is natural in her situa-tion."

Margaret Van Eyck coloured with ire.

"You do well to speak so coolly," said she, "you that are the cause of her situation."

"That I am not," said Catherine, bluntly, "nor any woman born."

"What? was it not you and your husband that kept them apart: and now he is gone to Italy all alone. Situation indeed? You have broken her heart amongst you."

"Why, madam? Who is it then? in Heaven's name? to hear you

312

one would think this was my Gerard's lass. But that can't be. This fur never cost less than five crowns the ell; besides, this young gentlewoman is a wife; or ought to be."

"Of course she ought. And who is the cause she is none? Who came between them at the very altar?"

"God forgive them, whoever it was," said Catherine, gravely: "me it was not, nor my man."

"Well," said the other, a little softened, "now you have seen her perhaps you will not be quite so bitter against her, madam. She is coming to, thank Heaven."

"Me bitter against her?" said Catherine: "no; that is all over. Poor soul! trouble behind her and trouble afore her; and to think of my setting her, of all living women, to read Gerard's letter to me. Ay, and that was what made her go off, I'll be sworn. She is coming to. What, sweetheart? be not afeard, none are here but friends."

They seated her in an easy chair. As the colour was creeping back to her face and lips, Catherine drew Margaret Van Eyck aside.

"Is she staying with you, if you please?"

"No, madam."

"I wouldn't let her go back to Sevenbergen to-night, then."

"That is as she pleases. She still refuses to bide the night."

"Ay, but you are older than she is; you can make her. There, she is beginning to notice." Catherine then put her mouth to Margaret Van Eyck's ear for half a moment; it did not seem time enough to whisper a word, far less a sentence. But on some topics females can flash communication to female like lightning, or thought itself.

The old lady started, and whispered back.

"It's false! it is a calumny! it is monstrous! Look at her face. It is blasphemy to accuse such a face."

"Tut! tut! tut!" said the other, "you might as well say this is not my hand. I ought to know; and I tell ye it is so."

Then much to Margaret Van Eyck's surprise she went up to the girl, and, taking her round the neck, kissed her warmly. "I suffered for Gerard, and you shed your blood for him I do hear: his own words show me I have been to blame, the very words you have read to me. Ay, Gerard, my child, I have held aloof from her.

But I'll make it up to her, once I begin. You are my daughter from this hour."

Another warm embrace sealed this hasty compact, and the woman of impulse was gone.

Margaret lay back in her chair, and a feeble smile stole over her face. Gerard's mother had kissed her and called her daughter; but the next moment she saw her old friend looking at her with a vexed air.

"I wonder you let that woman kiss you."

"His mother!" murmured Margaret, half reproachfully.

"Mother, or no mother, you would not let her touch you if you knew what she whispered in my ear about you."

"About me?" said Margaret, faintly.

"Ay, about you whom she never saw till to-night." The old lady was proceeding, with some hesitation and choice of language, to make Margaret share her indignation, when an unlooked-for interruption closed her lips.

The young woman slid from her chair to her knees, and began to pray piteously to her for pardon. From the words and the manner of her penitence a bystander would have gathered she had inflicted some cruel wrong, some intolerable insult, upon her venerable friend.

CHAPTER XLVI

THE little party at the hosier's house sat at table discussing the recent event, when their mother returned, and, casting a piercing glance all round the little circle, laid the letter flat on the table. She repeated every word of it by memory, following the lines with her finger, to cheat herself and hearers into the notion that she could read the words or nearly. Then, suddenly lifting her head, she cast another keen look on Cornelis and Sybrandt: their eyes fell.

On this the storm that had long been brewing burst on their heads.

Catherine seemed to swell like an angry hen ruffling her feathers, and out of her mouth came a Rhone and Saône of wisdom and twaddle, of great and mean invective, such as no male that ever was born could utter in one current; and not many women.

The following is a fair though a small sample of her words: only they were uttered all in one breath:—

"I have long had my doubts that you blew the flame betwixt Gerard and your father, and set that old rogue, Ghysbrecht, on. And now here are Gerard's own written words to prove it. You have driven your own flesh and blood into a far land, and robbed the mother that bore you of her darling, the pride of her eye, the joy of her heart. But you are all of a piece from end to end. When you were all boys together, my others were a comfort; but you were a curse: mischievous and sly; and took a woman half a day to keep your clothes whole: for why? work wears cloth, but play cuts it. With the beard comes prudence: but none came to you: still the last to go to bed, and the last to leave it; and why? because honesty goes to bed early, and industry rises betimes; where there are two lie-abeds in a house there are a pair of ne'er-do-weels. Often I've sat and looked at your ways, and wondred where ye came from: ye don't take after your father, and ye are no more like me than a wasp is to an ant; sure ye were changed in the cradle, or the cuckoo dropped ye on my floor: for ye have not our hands, nor our hearts: of all my blood none but you ever jeered them that God afflicted; but often when my back was turned I've heard you mock at Giles, because he is not so big as some; and at my lily Kate, because she is not so strong as a Flanders mare. After that rob a church an you will! for you can be no worse in His eyes that made both Kate and Giles, and in mine that suffered for them, poor darlings, as I did for you, you paltry, unfeeling, treasonable curs! No, I will not hush, my daughter; they have filled the cup too full. It takes a deal to turn a mother's heart against the sons she has nursed upon her knees; and many is the time I have winked and wouldn't see too much, and bitten my tongue, lest their father should know them as I do; he would have put them to the door that moment. But now they have filled the cup too full. And where got ye all this money? For this last month you have been rolling in it. You never wrought for it. I wish I may never hear from other mouths how ye got it. It is since that night you were out so late, and *your* head came back so swelled, Cornelis. Sloth and greed are ill mated, my masters. Lovers of money must sweat or steal. Well, if you robbed any poor soul of it, it was some woman, I'll go bail; for a man would drive you with his naked hand. No matter; it is good for one thing. It has shown me how you will guide our gear if ever it comes to be yourn. I have watched you, my lads, this while. You have spent a groat to-day between you. And I spend scarce a groat a week, and keep you all, good *and* bad. No! give up waiting for the shoes that will maybe walk behind your coffin; for this shop and this house shall never be yourn. Gerard is our heir: poor Gerard whom you have banished and done your best to kill; after that never call me mother again! But you have made him tenfold dearer to me. My poor lost boy! I shall soon see him again; shall hold him in my arms, and set him on my knees. Ay, you may stare! You are too crafty, and yet not crafty enow. You cut the stalk away; but you left the seed —the seed that shall outgrow you, and outlive you. Margaret Brandt is quick, and it is Gerard's, and what is Gerard's is mine; and I have prayed the saints it may be a boy: and it will—it must. Kate, when I found it was so, my bowels yearned over her child unborn as if it had been my own. He is our heir. He will outlive us. You will not: for a bad heart in a carcass is like the worm in a nut, soon brings the body to dust. So, Kate, take down Gerard's bib and tucker that are in the drawer you wot of, and one of these days we will carry them to Sevenbergen. We will borrow Peter Buyskens' cart, and go comfort Gerard's wife under her burden. She is his wife. Who is Ghysbrecht Van Swieten? Can he come between a couple and the altar, and sunder those that God and the priest make one? She is my daughter, and I am as proud of her as I am of you, Kate, almost; and as for *you,* keep out of my way awhile: for you are like the black dog in my eyes."

Cornelis and Sybrandt took the hint and slunk out, aching with remorse, and impenitence, and hate. They avoided her eye as much as ever they could: and for many days she never spoke a word good, bad, or indifferent, to either of them. Liberaverat animum suum.

CHAPTER XLVII

CATHERINE was a good housewife who seldom left home for a day, and then one thing or another always went amiss. She was keenly conscious of this, and, watching for a slack tide in things domestic, put off her visit to Sevenbergen from day to day, and one afternoon that it really could have been managed Peter Buyskens' mule was out of the way.

At last, one day Eli asked her before all the family, whether it was true she had thought of visiting Margaret Brandt.

"Ay, my man."

"Then I do forbid you."

"Oh, do you?"

"I do."

"Then there is no more to be said, I suppose," said she, colouring.

"Not a word," replied Eli, sternly.

When she was alone with her daughter she was very severe, not upon Eli, but upon herself.

"Behoved me rather go thither like a cat at a robin. But this was me all over. I am like a silly hen that can lay no egg without cackling, and convening all the house to rob her on't. Next time you and I are after aught the least amiss, let's do't in Heaven's name then and there, and not take time to think about it, far less talk; so then, if they take us to task we can say, alack we knew nought; we thought no ill; now, who'd ever? and so forth. For two pins I'd go thither in all their teeth."

Defiance so wild and picturesque staggered Kate. "Nay, mother; with patience father will come round."

"And so will Michaelmas; but when? and I was so bent on you seeing the girl. Then we could have put our heads together about her. Say what they will, there is no judging body or beast but by the eye. And were I to have fifty more sons I'd ne'er thwart one of them's fancy, till such time as I had clapped my eyes upon her and seen Quicksands: say you, I should have thought of that before condemning Gerard his fancy; but there, life is a school, and the lesson ne'er done; we put down one fault and take up t'other, and so go blundering here, and blundering there, till we blunder into our graves, and there's an end of us."

"Mother," said Kate, timidly.

"Well, what is a-coming now? no good news though, by the look of you. What on earth can make the poor wench so scared?"

"An avowal she hath to make," faltered Kate, faintly.

"Now, there is a noble word for ye," said Catherine, proudly. "Our Gerard taught thee that, I'll go bail. Come then, out with thy vowel."

"Well then, sooth to say, I have seen her."

"Anan?"

"And spoken with her to boot."

"And never told me? After this marvels are dirt."

"Mother, you were so hot against her. I waited till I could tell you without angering you worse."

"Ay," said Catherine, half sadly, half bitterly, "like mother like daughter: cowardice it is our bane. The others I whiles buffet; or how would the house fare? but did you, Kate, ever have harsh word or look from your poor mother, that you——. Nay, I will not have ye cry, girl; ten to one ye had your reason; so rise up, brave heart, and tell me all, better late than ne'er; and first and foremost when ever, and how ever, wond you to Sevenbergen wi' your poor crutches, and I not know?"

"I never was there in my life; and, mammy dear, to say that I ne'er wished to see her that I will not, but I ne'er went, nor sought, to see her."

"There, now," said Catherine, disputatively, "said I not 'twas all unlike my girl to seek her unbeknown to me. Come now, for I'm all agog."

"Then thus 'twas. It came to my ears, no matter how, and prithee, good mother, on my knees ne'er ask me how, that Gerard was a prisoner in the Stadthouse tower."

"Ah!"

"By father's behest as 'twas pretended."

Catherine uttered a sigh that was almost a moan. "Blacker than I thought," she muttered, faintly.

"Giles and I went out at night to bid him be of good cheer. And there at the tower foot was a brave lass, quite strange to me I vow, on the same errand."

"Lookee there now, Kate."

"At first we did properly frighten one another, through the place his bad name, and our poor heads being so full o' divels, and we whitened a bit in moonshine. But next moment, quo' I 'You are Margaret:' 'And you are Kate,' quo' she. Think on't!"

"Did one ever?—'Twas Gerard! He will have been talking backwards and forrards of thee to her, and her to thee."

In return for this, Kate bestowed on Catherine one of the prettiest presents in nature—the composite kiss: *i. e.,* she imprinted on her cheek a single kiss, which said—

1. Quite correct.
2. Good, clever mother, for guessing so right and quick.
3. How sweet for us twain to be of one mind again after never having been otherwise.
4. Etc.

"Now then, speak thy mind, child, Gerard is not here. Alas, what am I saying? would to Heaven he were."

"Well then, mother, she is comely, and wrongs her picture but little."

"Eh, dear; hark to young folk! I am for good acts, not good looks. Loves she my boy as he did ought to be loved?"

"Sevenbergen is farther from the Stadthouse than we are," said Kate, thoughtfully; "yet she was there afore me."

Catherine nodded intelligence.

"Nay, more, she had got him out ere I came. Ay, down from the captives' tower."

Catherine shook her head incredulously. "The highest tower for miles! It is not feasible."

"'Tis sooth though. She and an old man she brought found means and wit to send him up a rope. There 'twas dangling from his prison, and our Giles went up it. When first I saw it hang, I said, 'This is glamour.' But when the frank lass's arms came round me, and her bosom did beat on mine, and her cheeks wet, then said I, ''Tis not glamour: 'tis love.' For she is not like me, but lusty and able; and, dear heart, even I, poor frail creature, do feel sometimes as I could move the world for them I love: I love *you,* mother. And she loves Gerard."

"God bless her for't! God bless her!"

"But."

"But what, lamb?"

"Her love, is it for very certain honest? 'Tis most strange; but that very thing, which hath warmed your heart, hath somewhat cooled mine towards her; poor soul. She is no wife, you know mother when all is done."

"Humph! They have stood at th' altar together."

"Ay, but they went as they came, maid and bachelor."

The Cloister and the Hearth

"The parson, saith he so?"

"Nay, for that I know not."

"Then I'll take no man's word but his in such a tangled skein." After some reflection she added, "Natheless art right, girl; I'll to Sevenbergen alone. A wife I am but not a slave. We are all in the dark here. And she holds the clue. I must question her, and no one by; least of all you. I'll not take my lily to a house wi' a spot, no, not to a palace o' gold and silver."

The more Catherine pondered this conversation, the more she felt drawn towards Margaret, and moreover "she was all agog" with curiosity, a potent passion with us all, and nearly omnipotent with those, who, like Catherine, do not slake it with reading. At last, one fine day, after dinner, she whispered to Kate, "Keep the house from going to pieces, an ye can;" and donned her best kirtle and hood, and her scarlet clocked hose and her new shoes, and trudged briskly off to Sevenbergen, troubling no man's mule.

When she got there she inquired where Margaret Brandt lived. The first person she asked shook his head, and said, "The name is strange to me." She went a little farther and asked a girl of about fifteen who was standing at a door: "Father," said the girl, speaking into the house, "here is another after that magician's daughter." The man came out and told Catherine Peter Brandt's cottage was just outside the town on the east side. "You may see the chimney hence:" and he pointed it out to her. "But you will not find them there, nother father nor daughter; they have left the town this week, bless you."

"Say not so, good man, and me walken all the way from Tergou."

"From Tergou? then you must ha' met the soldier."

"What soldier? ay, I did meet a soldier."

"Well, then, yon soldier was here seeking that selfsame Margaret."

"Ay, and warn't a mad with us because she was gone?" put in the girl. "His long beard and her cheek are no strangers, I warrant."

"Say no more than ye know," said Catherine, sharply. "You are young to take to slandering your elders. Stay! tell me more about this soldier, good man."

"Nay, I know no more than that he came hither seeking Margaret Brandt, and I told him she and her father had made a moonlight flit on't this day sennight, and that some thought the devil had flown

320

away with them, being magicians. 'And,' says he, 'the devil fly away with thee for thy ill news:' that was my thanks. 'But I doubt 'tis a lie,' said he. 'An you think so,' said I, 'go and see.' 'I will,' said he, and burst out wi' a hantle o' gibberish: my wife thinks 'twas curses: and hied him to the cottage. Presently back a comes, and sings t'other tune. 'You were right and I was wrong,' says he, and shoves a silver coin in my hand. Show it the wife, some of ye; then she'll believe me; I have been called a liar once to-day."

"It needs not," said Catherine, inspecting the coin all the same.

"And he seemed quiet and sad-like, didn't he now, wench?"

"That a did," said the young woman warmly; "and, dame, he was just as pretty a man as ever I clapped eyes on. Cheeks like a rose, and shining beard, and eyes in his head like sloes."

"I saw he was well bearded," said Catherine; "but, for the rest, at my age I scan them not as when I was young and foolish. But he seemed right civil: doffed his bonnet to me as I had been a queen, and I did drop him my best reverence, for manners beget manners. But little I wist he had been her light o' love, and most likely the—— Who bakes for this town?"

The man, not being acquainted with her, opened his eyes at this transition, swift and smooth.

"Well, dame, there be two; John Bush and Eric Donaldson, they both bide in this street."

"Then, God be with you, good people" said she, and proceeded: but her sprightly foot came flat on the ground now, and no longer struck it with little jerks and cocking heel. She asked the bakers whether Peter Brandt had gone away in their debt. Bush said they were not customers. Donaldson said "not a stiver: his daughter had come round and paid him the very night they went. Didn't believe they owed a copper in the town." So Catherine got all the information of that kind she wanted with very little trouble.

"Can you tell me what sort this Margaret was?" said she, as she turned to go.

"Well, somewhat too reserved for my taste. I like a chatty customer—when I'm not too busy. But she bore a high character for being a good daughter."

"'Tis no small praise. A well-looking lass I am told?"

"Why, whence come you, wyfe?"

"From Tergou."

"Oh, ay. Well you shall judge: the lads clept her 'the beauty of Sevenbergen;' the lasses did scout it merrily, and terribly pulled her to pieces, and found so many faults no two could agree where the fault lay."

"That is enough," said Catherine. "I see, the bakers are no fools in Sevenbergen, and the young women no shallower than in other burghs."

She bought a manchet of bread, partly out of sympathy and justice (she kept a shop), partly to show her household how much better bread she gave them daily; and returned to Tergou dejected.

Kate met her outside the town with beaming eyes.

"Well, Kate lass; it is a happy thing I went; I am heart-broken. Gerard has been sore abused. The child is none of ourn, nor the mother from this hour."

"Alas, mother, I fathom not your meaning."

"Ask me no more, girl, but never mention her name to me again. That is all."

Kate acquiesced with a humble sigh, and they went home together.

They found a soldier seated tranquilly by their fire. The moment they entered the door, he rose, and saluted them civilly. They stood and looked at him, Kate with some little surprise, but Catherine with a great deal, and with rising indignation.

CHAPTER XLVIII

"WHAT makes you here?" was Catherine's greeting.

"I came to seek after Margaret."

"Well, we know no such person."

"Say not so, dame; sure you know her by name, Margaret Brandt."

"We have heard of her for that matter—to our cost."

"Come, dame, prithee tell me at least where she bides."

"I know not where she bides, and care not."

Denys felt sure this was a deliberate untruth. He bit his lip. "Well, I looked to find myself in an enemy's country at this Tergou; but maybe if ye knew all ye would not be so dour."

"I do know all," replied Catherine bitterly. "This morn I knew nought." Then suddenly setting her arms akimbo she told him with a raised voice and flashing eyes she wondered at his cheek sitting down by that hearth of all hearths in the world.

"May Satan fly away with your hearth to the lake of fire and brimstone," shouted Denys, who could speak Flemish fluently. "Your own servant bade me sit there till you came, else I had ne'er troubled your hearth. My malison on it, and on the churlish roof-tree that greets an unoffending stranger this way," and he strode scowling to the door.

"Oh! oh!" ejaculated Catherine frightened, and also a little con-science-stricken; and the virago sat suddenly down and burst into tears. Her daughter followed suit quietly, but without loss of time.

A shrewd writer, now unhappily lost to us, has somewhere the following dialogue:—

She.] "I feel all a woman's weakness."

He.] "Then you are invincible."

Denys, by anticipation, confirmed that valuable statement; he stood at the door looking ruefully at the havoc his thunderbolt of eloquence had made.

"Nay, wife," said he, "weep not neither for a soldier's hasty word. I mean not all I said. Why your house is your own, and what right in it have I? There now, I'll go."

"What is to do?" said a grave manly voice. It was Eli; he had come in from the shop.

"Here is a ruffian been a-scolding of your womenfolk and making them cry," explained Denys.

"Little Kate, what is't? for ruffians do not use to call themselves ruffians," said Eli the sensible.

Ere she could explain, "Hold your tongue, girl," said Catherine; "Muriel bade him sat down, and I knew not that, and wyted on him; and he was going and leaving his malison on us, root and branch. I was never so becursed in all my days, oh! oh! oh!"

"You were both somewhat to blame; both you and he," said Eli calmly. "However, what the servant says the master should still stand to. We keep not open house, but yet we are not poor enough to grudge a seat at our hearth in a cold day to a wayfarer with an honest face, and as, I think, a wounded man. So, end all malice, and sit ye down!"

"Wounded?" cried mother and daughter in a breath.

"Think you a soldier slings his arm for sport?"

"Nay, 'tis but an arrow," said Denys cheerfully.

"But an arrow?" said Kate with concentrated horror. "Where were our eyes, mother?"

"Nay, in good sooth, a trifle. Which however I will pray mesdames to accept as an excuse for my vivacity. 'Tis these little foolish trifling wounds that fret a man, worthy sir. Why, look ye now, sweeter temper than our Gerard never breathed, yet, when the bear did but strike a piece no bigger than a crown out of his calf, he turned so hot and choleric y'had said he was no son of yours, but got by the good knight Sir John Pepper on his wife dame Mustard; who is this? a dwarf? your servant, master Giles."

"Your servant, soldier," roared the new-comer. Denys started. He had not counted on exchanging greetings with a petard.

Denys's words had surprised his hosts, but hardly more than their deportment now did him. They all three came creeping up to where he sat, and looked down into him with their lips parted, as if he had been some strange phenomenon.

And growing agitation succeeded to amazement.

"Now hush!" said Eli, "let none speak but I. Young man," said he solemnly, "in God's name who are you, that know us though we know you not, and that shake our hearts speaking to us of—the absent—our poor rebellious son: whom Heaven forgive and bless?"

"What, master," said Denys lowering his voice, "hath he not writ to you? hath he not told you of me, Denys of Burgundy?"

"He hath writ, but three lines, and named not Denys of Burgundy, nor any stranger."

"Ay, I mind the long letter was to his sweetheart, this Margaret, and she has decamped, plague take her, and how I am to find her Heaven knows."

"What, she is not your sweetheart, then?"

"Who, dame? an't please you."

"Why, Margaret Brandt."

"How can my comrade's sweetheart be mine? I know her not from Noah's niece; how should I? I never saw her."

"Whist with this idle chat, Kate," said Eli impatiently, "and let the young man answer me. How came you to know Gerard, our son? Prithee now think on a parent's cares, and answer me straight-forward, like a soldier as thou art."

"And shall. I was paid off at Flushing, and started for Bur-gundy. On the German frontier I lay at the same inn with Gerard. I fancied him. I said 'Be my comrade.' He was loth at first: con-sented presently. Many a weary league we trode together. Never were truer comrades: never will be while earth shall last. First I left my route a bit to be with him: then he his to be with me. We talked of Sevenbergen, and Tergou, a thousand times; and of all in this house. We had our troubles on the road: but battling them together made them light. I saved his life from a bear; he mine in the Rhine: for he swims like a duck and I like a hod o' bricks; and one another's lives at an inn in Burgundy, where we two held a room for a good hour against seven cutthroats, and crippled one and slew two; and your son did his devoir like a man, and met the stoutest champion I ever countered, and spitted him like a suck-ing-pig. Else I had not been here. But just, when all was fair, and I was to see him safe aboard ship for Rome, if not to Rome itself, met us that son of a —— the Lord Anthony of Burgundy, and his men, making for Flanders, then in insurrection, tore us by force apart, took me where I got some broad pieces in hand, and a broad ar-row in my shoulder, and left my poor Gerard lonesome. At that sad parting, soldier though I be, these eyes did rain salt scalding tears, and so did his, poor soul. His last word to me was 'Go comfort Margaret!' so here I be. Mine to him was 'Think no more of Rome. Make for Rhine, and down stream home.' Now say, for you know best, did I advise him well or ill?"

"Soldier, take my hand," said Eli. "God bless thee! God bless thee!" and his lip quivered. It was all his reply, but more eloquent than many words.

Catherine did not answer at all, but she darted from the room and bade Muriel bring the best that was in the house, and returned with wood in both arms, and heaped the fire, and took out a snow-white cloth from the press, and was going in a great hurry to lay it for Gerard's friend, when suddenly she sat down and all the power ebbed rapidly out of her body.

"Father!" cried Kate, whose eye was as quick as her affection. Denys started up; but Eli waived him back and flung a little water sharply in his wife's face. This did her instant good. She gasped, "So sudden. My poor boy!" Eli whispered Denys, "Take no notice! she thinks of him night and day." They pretended not to observe her, and she shook it off, and bustled and laid the cloth with her own hands; but, as she smoothed it, her hands trembled and a tear or two stole down her cheeks.

They could not make enough of Denys. They stuffed him, and crammed him: and then gathered round him and kept filling his glass in turn, while by that genial blaze of fire and ruby wine and eager eyes he told all that I have related, and a vast number of minor details which an artist, however minute, omits.

But how different the effect on my readers and on this small circle! To them the interest was already made before the first word came from his lips. It was all about Gerard, and he, who sat there telling it them, was warm from Gerard and an actor with him in all these scenes.

The flesh and blood around that fire quivered for their severed member, hearing its struggles and perils.

I shall ask my readers to recall to memory all they can of Gerard's journey with Denys, and in their mind's eye to see those very matters told by his comrade to an exile's father, all stoic outside, all father within, and to two poor women, an exile's mother and a sister, who were all love and pity and tender anxiety both outside and in. Now would you mind closing this book for a minute and making an effort to realize all this? It will save us so much repetition.

Then you will not be surprised when I tell you that after a while Giles came softly and curled himself up before the fire, and lay gazing at the speaker with a reverence almost canine; and that, when the rough soldier had unconsciously but thoroughly betrayed his better qualities, and above all his rare affection for Gerard, Kate, though timorous as a bird, stole her little hand into the warrior's huge brown palm, where it lay an instant like a teaspoonful of cream spilt on a platter, then nipped the ball of his thumb and served for a Kardiometer. In other words Fate is just even to rival story-tellers, and balances matters. Denys had to pay a tax to his audience which I have not. Whenever Gerard was in too much danger, the female faces became so white, and their poor little throats gurgled so, he was obliged in common humanity to spoil his recital. Suspense is the soul of narrative, and thus dealt Rough-and-Tender of Burgundy with his best suspenses. "Now, dame, take not on till ye hear the end: Ma'amselle, let not your cheek blanch so, courage! it looks ugly: but you shall hear how we wond through. Had he miscarried, and I at hand, would I be alive?"

And I called Kate's little hand a Kardiometer, or heart-measurer, because it graduated emotion, and pinched by scale. At its best it was by no means a high-pressure engine. But all is relative. Denys soon learned the tender gamut; and when to water the suspense, and extract the thrill as far as possible. On one occasion only he cannily indemnified his narrative for this drawback. Falling personally into the Rhine, and sinking, he got pinched, he Denys, to his surprise and satisfaction. "Oho!" thought he, and on the principle of the anatomists, "experimentum in corpore vili," kept himself a quarter of an hour under water; under pressure all the time. And even when Gerard had got hold of him, he was loth to leave the river, so, less conscientious than I was, swam with Gerard to the east bank first, and was about to land, but detected the officers, and their intent, chaffed them a little space, treading water, then turned and swam wearily all across, and at last was obliged to get out, for very shame, or else acknowledge himself a pike; so permitted himself to land, exhausted: and the pressure relaxed.

It was eleven o'clock, an unheard-of hour, but they took no note of time this night; and Denys had still much to tell them, when the door was opened quietly, and in stole Cornelis and Sybrandt looking hang-dog. They had this night been drinking the very last drop of their mysterious funds.

Catherine feared her husband would rebuke them before Denys: but he only looked sadly at them, and motioned them to sit down quietly.

Denys it was who seemed discomposed. He knitted his brows and eyed them thoughtfully and rather gloomily. Then turned to Catherine. "What say you, dame? the rest tomorrow? for I am somewhat weary and it waxes late."

"So be it," said Eli. But when Denys rose to go to his inn, he was instantly stopped by Catherine.

"And think you to lie from this house? Gerard's room has been got ready for you hours agone: the sheets I'll not say much for, see-ing I spun the flax and wove the web."

"Then would I lie in them blindfold," was the gallant reply.

"Ah, dame, our poor Gerard was the one for fine linen. He could hardly forgive the honest Germans their coarse flax, and, when-e'er my traitors of countrymen did amiss, a would excuse them saying, 'Well, well; bonnes toiles sont en Bourgogne:' that means 'there be good lenten cloths in Burgundy.' But indeed he beat all for bywords and cleanliness."

"Oh Eli! Eli! doth not our son come back to us at each word?"

"Ay. Buss me, my poor Kate. You and I know all that passeth in each other's hearts this night. None other can, but God."

CHAPTER XLIX

DENYS took an opportunity next day, and told mother and daughter the rest, excusing himself characteristically for not letting Cornelis and Sybrandt hear of it. "It is not for me to blacken them: they come of a good stock. But Gerard looks on them as no friends of his in this matter; and I'm Gerard's comrade; and it is a rule with us soldiers not to tell the enemy aught; but lies."

Catherine sighed, but made no answer.

The adventures he related cost them a tumult of agitation and grief, and sore they wept at the parting of the friends, which, even now, Denys could not tell without faltering. But at last all merged in the joyful hope and expectation of Gerard's speedy return. In this Denys confidently shared; but reminded them that was no reason why he should neglect his friend's wishes and last words. In fact should Gerard return next week, and no Margaret to be found, what sort of figure should he cut?

Catherine had never felt so kindly towards the truant Margaret as now: and she was fully as anxious to find her, and be kind to her before Gerard's return as Denys was: but she could not agree with him that anything was to be gained by leaving this neighbourhood to search for her. "She must have told somebody whither she was going. It is not as though they were dishonest folk flying the country: they owe not a stiver in Sevenbergen: and dear heart, Denys, you can't hunt all Holland for her."

"Can I not?" said Denys grimly. "That we shall see." He added, after some reflection, that they must divide their forces: she stay here with eyes and ears wide open, and he ransack every town in Holland for her, if need be. "But she will not be many leagues from here. They be three. Three fly not so fast, nor far, as one."

"That is sense," said Catherine. But she insisted on his going first to the demoiselle Van Eyck. "She and our Margaret were bosom friends. She knows where the girl is gone, if she will but tell us." Denys was for going to her that instant, so Catherine, in a turn of the hand, made herself one shade neater, and took him with her.

She was received graciously by the old lady sitting in a richly furnished room; and opened her business. The tapestry dropped out of Margaret Van Eyck's hands. "Gone? Gone from Sevenbergen and not told me: the thankless girl."

This turn greatly surprised the visitors. "What you knew not? when was she here last?"

"Maybe ten days agone. I had ta'en out my brushes, after so many years, to paint her portrait. I did not do it though; for reasons."

Catherine remarked it was "a most strange thing she should go away bag and baggage like this, without with your leave or by your leave, why, or wherefore. Was ever aught so untoward; just when all our hearts are warm to her: and here is Gerard's mate come from the ends o' the earth with comfort for her from Gerard, and can't find her, and Gerard himself expected. What to do I know not. But sure she is not parted like this without a reason. Can ye not give us the clue, my good demoiselle? Prithee now."

"I have it not to give," said the elder lady, rather peevishly.

"Then I can," said Reicht Heynes, showing herself in the doorway, with colour somewhat heightened.

"So you have been hearkening all the time, eh?"

"What are my ears for, mistress?"

"True. Well throw us the light of thy wisdom on this dark matter."

The Cloister and the Hearth

There is no darkness that I see," said Reicht. "And the clue, why an' ye call't a two-plye twine, and the ends on't in this room e'en now, ye'll not be far out. Oh, mistress, I wonder at you sitting there pretending."

"Marry, come up!" and the mistress's cheek was now nearly as red as the servant's. "So 'twas I drove the foolish girl away."

"You did your share, mistress. What sort of greeting gave you her last time she came? Think you she could miss to notice it, and she all friendless? And you said, 'I have altered my mind about painting of you,' says you, a turning up your nose at her."

"I did not turn up my nose. It is not shaped like yours for looking heavenward."

"Oh, all our nosen can follow our heartys bent, for that matter. Poor soul. She did come into the kitchen to me. 'I am not to be painted now,' said she, and the tears in her eyes. She said no more. But I knew well what she did mean. I had seen ye."

"Well," said Margaret Van Eyck, "I do confess so much, and I make you the judge, madam. Know that these young girls can do nothing of their own heads, but are most apt at mimicking aught their sweethearts do. Now your Gerard is reasonably handy at many things, and among the rest at the illuminator's craft. And Margaret she is his pupil, and a patient one: what marvel? having a woman's eye for colour, and eke a lover to ape. 'Tis a trick I despise at heart: for by it the great art of colour, which should be royal, aspiring, and free, becomes a poor slave to the petty crafts of writing and printing, and is fettered, imprisoned, and made little, body and soul, to match the littleness of books, and go to church in a rich fool's pocket. Natheless affection rules us all, and, when the poor wench would bring me her thorn leaves, and lilies, and ivy, and dewberries, and ladybirds, and butterfly grubs, and all the scum of nature—stuck fast in gold-leaf like wasps in a honey-pot, and, withal her diurnal book, showing she had pored an hundred, or an hundred and fifty, or two hundred, hours over each singular page, certes I was wroth that an immortal soul and many hours of labour, and much manual skill, should be flung away on Nature's trash, leaves, insects, grubs, and on barren letters: but, having bowels, I did perforce restrain, and, as it were, dam my better feelings, and looked kindly at the work to see how it might be bettered: and said I, 'Sith Heaven for our sins hath doomed us to spend time, and soul, and colour, on great letters and little beetles, omitting such small fry as saints and heroes, their acts and passions, why not present the scum naturally?' I told her 'the grapes I saw, walking abroad, did hang i' the air, not stick in a wall: and even these insects,' quo' I, 'and Nature her slime in general, pass not their noxious lives wedged miserably in metal prisons like flies in honey-pots and glue-pots, but do crawl or hover at large, infesting air.' 'Ah! my dear friend,' says she, 'I see now whither you drive: but this ground is gold; whereon we may not shade.' 'Who says so?' quoth I. 'All teachers of this craft,' says she: and (to make an end o' me at once, I trow) 'Gerard himself!' 'That for Gerard himself,' quoth I, 'and all the gang; gi'e me a brush!'

"Then chose I, to shade her fruit and reptiles, a colour false in nature, but true relatively to that monstrous ground of glaring gold; and in five minutes out came a bunch of raspberries, stalk and all, and a'most flew in your mouth: likewise a butterfly grub she had so truly presented as might turn the stoutest stomach. My lady she flings her arms round my neck, and says she, 'Oh!' "

"Did she now?"

"The little love!" observed Denys, succeeding at last in wedging in a word.

Margaret Van Eyck stared at him; and then smiled. She went on to tell them how from step to step she had been led on to promise to resume the art she had laid aside with a sigh when her brothers died, and to paint the Madonna once more—with Margaret for model. Incidentally she even revealed how girls are turned into saints. " 'Thy hair is adorable,' said I. 'Why, 'tis red,' quo' she. 'Ay,' quoth I, 'but what a red! how brown! how glossy! most hair is not worth a straw to us painters: thine the artist's very hue. But thy violet eyes, which smack of earth, being now languid for lack of one Gerard, now full of fire in hopes of the same Gerard, these will I lift to heaven in fixed and holy meditation, and thy nose, which doth already somewhat aspire that way (though not so piously as Reicht's), will I debase a trifle, and somewhat enfeeble thy chin.' "

"Enfeeble her chin? Alack! what may that mean? Ye go beyond me, mistress."

" 'Tis a resolute chin. Not a jot too resolute for this wicked world: but, when ye come to a Madonna? No thank you."

"Well I never. A resolute chin."

Denys.] "The darling!"

"And now comes the rub. When you told me she was—the way she is, it gave me a shock: I dropped my brushes. Was I going to turn a girl, that couldn't keep her lover at a distance, into the Virgin Mary, at my time of life? I love the poor ninny still. But I adore our blessed Lady. Say you, 'a painter must not be peevish in such matters.' Well, most painters are men: and men are fine fellows. They can do aught. Their saints and virgins are neither more nor less than their lemans, saving your presence. But know that for this very reason half their craft is lost on me, which find beneath their angels' white wings the very trollops I have seen flaunting it on the streets, bejewelled like Paynim idols, and put on like the queens in a pack o' cards. And I am not a fine fellow, but only a woman, and my painting is but one half craft, and t'other half devotion. So now you may read me. 'Twas foolish, maybe, but I could not help it: yet am I sorry." And the old lady ended despondently a discourse which she had commenced in a mighty defiant tone.

"Well, you know, dame," observed Catherine, "you must think it would go to the poor girl's heart, and she so fond of ye?"

Margaret Van Eyck only sighed.

The Frisian girl, after biting her lips impatiently a little while, turned upon Catherine. "Why, dame, think you 'twas for that alone Margaret and Peter hath left Sevenberg? Nay."

"For what else, then?"

"What else? Why because Gerard's people slight her so cruel. Who would bide among hard-hearted folk that ha' driven her lad t'Italy, and, now he is gone, relent not, but face it out, and ne'er come anigh her that is left?"

"Reicht, I was going."

"Oh, ay, going, and going, and going. Ye should ha' said less or else done more. But with your words you did uplift her heart and let it down wi' your deeds. 'They have never been,' said the poor thing to me, with such a sigh. Ay, here is *one* can feel for her: for I too am far from my friends, and often, when first I came to Holland, I did use to take a hearty cry all to myself. But ten times liever would I be Reicht Heynes with nought but the leagues atween me and all my kith, than be as she is i' the midst of them that ought to warm to her, and yet to fare as lonesome as I."

"Alack, Reicht, I did go but yestreen, and had gone before, but one plaguy thing or t'other did still come and hinder me."

"Mistress, did aught hinder ye to eat your dinner any one of those days? I trow not. And had your heart been as good towards your own flesh and blood, as 'twas towards your flesher's meat, nought had prevailed to keep you from her that sat lonely, a watching the road for you and comfort, wi' your child's child a beating 'neath her bosom."

Here this rude young woman was interrupted by an incident not uncommon in a domestic's bright existence. The Van Eyck had been nettled by the attack on her, but with due tact had gone into ambush. She now sprang out of it. "Since you disrespect my guests, seek another place!"

"With all my heart," said Reicht stoutly.

"Nay, mistress," put in the good-natured Catherine. "True folk will still speak out. Her tongue is a stinger." Here the water came into the speaker's eyes by way of confirmation. "But better she said it than thought it. So now 'twon't rankle in her. And, part with her for me, that shall ye not. Beshrew the wench, she kens she is a good servant, and takes advantage. We poor wretches which keep house must still pay 'em tax for value. I had a good servant once, when I was a young 'oman. Eh dear, how she did grind me down into the dust. In the end, by Heaven's mercy, she married the baker, and I was my own woman again. 'So,' said I, 'no more good servants shall come hither, a hectoring o' me.' I just get a fool and learn her: and whenever she knoweth her right hand from her left, she sauceth me: then out I bundle her neck and crop, and take another dunce in her place. Dear heart, 'tis wearisome, teaching a string of fools by ones; but there—I am mistress:" here she forgot that she was defending Reicht, and turning rather spitefully upon her, added, "and you be mistress here, I trow."

"No more than that stool," said the Van Eyck, loftily. "She is neither mistress nor servant: but Gone. She is dismissed the house, and there's an end of *her*. What did ye not hear me turn the saucy baggage off?"

"Ay, ay. We all heard ye," said Reicht, with vast indifference.

"Then hear me!" said Denys, solemnly.

The Cloister and the Hearth

They all went round like things on wheels, and fastened their eyes on him.

"Ay, let us hear what the man says," urged the hostess. "Men are fine fellows; with their great hoarse voices."

"Mistress Reicht," said Denys, with great dignity and ceremony, indeed so great as to verge on the absurd, "you are turned off. If on a slight acquaintance I might advise, I'd say, since you are a servant no more, be a mistress, a queen."

"Easier said than done," replied Reicht bluntly.

"Not a jot. You see here one who is a man, though but half an arbalestrier, owing to that devilish Englishman's arrow, in whose carcass I have, however, left a like token, which is a comfort. I have twenty gold pieces" (he showed them) "and a stout arm. In another week or so I shall have twain. Marriage is not a habit of mine: but I capitulate to so many virtues. You are beautiful, good hearted, and outspoken, and above all, you take the part of my she-comrade. Be then an arbalestriesse!"

"And what the dickens is that?" inquired Reicht.

"I mean, be the wife, mistress, and queen, of Denys of Burgundy here present!"

A dead silence fell on all.

It did not last long though: and was followed by a burst of unreasonable indignation.

Catherine.] "Well, did you ever?"

Margaret.] "Never in all my born days."

Catherine.] "Before our very faces."

Margaret.] "Of all the absurdity, and insolence of this ridiculous sex——"

Here Denys observed somewhat drily, that the female to whom he had addressed himself was mute; and the others, on whose eloquence there was no immediate demand, were fluent: on this the voices stopped, and the eyes turned pivot-like upon Reicht.

She took a sly glance from under her lashes at her military assailant, and said, "I mean to take a good look at any man ere I leap into his arms."

Denys drew himself up majestically. "Then look your fill, and leap away."

This proposal led to a new and most unexpected result. A long white finger was extended by the Van Eyck in a line with the

334

speaker's eye, and an agitated voice bade him stand, in the name of all the saints. "You are beautiful, so," cried she. "You are inspired—with folly. What matters that? you are inspired. I must take off your head." And in a moment she was at work with her pencil. "Come out, hussy," she screamed to Reicht; "more in front of him, and keep the fool inspired and beautiful. Oh, why had I not this maniac for my good centurion? They went and brought me a brute with a low forehead and a shapeless beard."

Catherine stood and looked with utter amazement at this pantomime, and secretly resolved that her venerable hostess had been a disguised lunatic all this time, and was now busy throwing off the mask. As for Reicht, she was unhappy and cross. She had left her caldron in a precarious state, and made no scruple to say so, and that duties so grave as hers left her no "time to waste a playing the statee and the fool all at one time." Her mistress in reply reminded her that it was possible to be rude and rebellious to one's poor old, affectionate, desolate mistress, without being utterly heartless, and savage; and a trampler on arts.

On this Reicht stopped, and pouted, and looked like a little basilisk at the inspired model who caused her woe. He retorted with unshaken admiration. The situation was at last dissolved by the artist's wrist becoming cramped from disuse; this was not, however, until she had made a rough but noble sketch. "I can work no more at present," said she, sorrowfully.

"Then, mistress, I may go and mind my pot?"

"Ay, ay, go to your pot! And get into it, do; you will find your soul in it: so then you will all be together."

"Well, but Reicht," said Catherine, laughing, "she turned you off."

"Boo, boo, boo!" said Reicht, contemptuously. "When she wants to get rid of me, let her turn herself off and die. I am sure she is old enough for't. But take your time, mistress; if you are in no hurry, no more am I. When that day doth come, 'twill take a man to dry my eyes: and if you should be in the same mind then, soldier, you can say so; and if you are not, why, 'twill be all one to Reicht Heynes."

And the plain speaker went her way. But her words did not fall to the ground. Neither of her female hearers could disguise from herself that this blunt girl, solitary herself, had probably read

The Cloister and the Hearth

Margaret Brandt aright, and that she had gone away from Sevenbergen broken hearted.

Catherine and Denys bade the Van Eyck adieu, and that same
afternoon Denys set out on a wild goose chase. His plan, like all
great things, was simple. He should go to a hundred towns and
villages, and ask in each after an old physician with a fair daughter,
and an old long-bow soldier. He should inquire of the burgomasters about all new-comers, and should go to the fountains and
watch the women and girls as they came with their pitchers for
water.

And away he went, and was months and months on the tramp
and could not find her.

Happily, this chivalrous feat of friendship was in some degree
its own reward.

Those, who sit at home blindfolded by self-conceit, and think
camel or man out of the depths of their inner consciousness, alas!
their ignorance, will tell you that in the intervals of war and danger, peace and tranquil life acquire their true value and satisfy the
heroic mind. But those, who look before they babble or scribble,
will see, and say, that men, who risk their lives habitually, thirst
for exciting pleasures between the acts of danger, and not for innocent tranquillity.

To this Denys was no exception. His whole military life had
been half Sparta, half Capua. And he was too good a soldier, and
too good a libertine, to have ever mixed either habit with the other.
But now for the first time he found himself mixed; at peace and
yet on duty; for he took this latter view of his wild goose chase,
luckily. So all these months he was a demi-Spartan; sober, prudent, vigilant, indomitable; and happy, though constantly disappointed, as might have been expected. He flirted gigantically on
the road; but wasted no time about it. Nor in these his wander-
ings did he tell a single female that "marriage was not one of his
habits, etc."

And so we leave him on the tramp, "Pilgrim of Friendship,"
as his poor comrade was of Love.

CHAPTER L

THE good-hearted Catherine was not happy. Not that she reproached herself very deeply for not having gone quickly enough to Sevenbergen, whither she was not bound to go at all—except on the score of having excited false hopes in Margaret. But she was in dismay when she reflected that Gerard must reach home in another month at farthest, more likely in a week. And how should she tell him she had not even kept an eye upon his betrothed? Then there was the uncertainty as to the girl's fate: and this uncertainty sometimes took a sickening form.

"Oh, Kate," she groaned, "if she should have gone and made herself away."

"Mother, she would never be so wicked."

"Ah, my lass, you know not what hasty fools young lasses be, that have no mothers to keep 'em straight. They will fling themselves into the water for a man that the next man they meet would ha' cured 'em of in a week. I have known 'em to jump in like brass one moment and scream for help in the next. Couldn't know their own minds ye see even such a trifle as yon. And then there's times when their bodies ail like no other living creatures ever I could hear of, and that strings up their feelings so, the patience, that belongs to them at other times beyond all living souls barring an ass, seems all to jump out of 'em at one turn, and into the water they go. Therefore, I say that men are monsters."

"Mother!"

"Monsters, and no less, to go making such heaps o' canals just to tempt the poor women in. They know we shall not cut our throats, hating the sight of blood, and rating our skins a hantle higher nor our lives; and as for hanging, while she is fixing of the nail and a making of the noose she has time t'alter her mind. But a jump into a canal is no more than into bed; and the water it does all the lave, will ye, nill ye. Why, look at me, the mother o' nine, wasn't I agog to make a hole in our canal for the nonce?"

"Nay, mother, I'll never believe it of you."

"Ye may, though. 'Twas in the first year of our keeping house together. Eli hadn't found out my weak stitches then, nor I his;

so we made a rent, pulling contrariwise; had a quarrel. So then I ran crying, to tell some gabbling fool like myself what I had no business to tell out o' doors except to the saints, and there was one of our precious canals in the way; do they take us for teal? Oh, how tempting it did look! Says I to myself, 'Sith he has let me go out of his door quarrelled, he shall see me drowned next, and then he will change his key. He will blubber a good one, and I shall look down from heaven' (I forgot I should be in t'other part), 'and see him take on, and, oh, but that will be sweet!' and I was all a tiptoe and going in, only just then I thought I wouldn't. I had got a new gown a-making, for one thing, and hard upon finished. So I went home instead, and what was Eli's first word? 'Let yon flea stick i' the wall, my lass,' says he. 'Not a word of all I said t' anger thee was sooth, but this: 'I love thee.' These were his very words, I minded 'em, being the first quarrel. So I flung my arms about his neck and sobbed a bit, and thought o' the canal; and he was no colder to me than I to him, being a man and a young one: and so then that was better than lying in the water; and spoiling my wedding kirtle and my fine new shoon, old John Bush made 'em, that was uncle to him keeps the shop now. And what was my grief to hers?"

Little Kate hoped that Margaret loved her father too much to think of leaving him so at his age. "He is father and mother and all to her, you know."

"Nay, Kate, they do forget all these things in a moment o' despair, when the very sky seems black above them. I place more faith in him that is unborn, than on him that is ripe for the grave, to keep her out o' mischief. For certes it do go sore against us to die when there's a little innocent a-pulling at our hearts to let un live, and feeding at our very veins."

"Well, then, keep up a good heart, mother." She added, that very likely all these fears were exaggerated. She ended by solemnly entreating her mother at all events not to persist in naming the sex of Margaret's infant. It was so unlucky, all the gossips told her; "dear heart, as if there were not as many girls born as boys."

This reflection, though not unreasonable, was met with clamour. "Have you the cruelty to threaten me with a girl!!? I want no more girls, while I have you. What use would a lass be to me?

Can I set her on my knee and see my Gerard again as I can a boy?
I tell thee 'tis all settled."

"How may that be?"

"In my mind. And if I am to be disappointed i' the end, t'isn't
for you to disappoint me beforehand, telling me it is not to be a
child, but only a girl."

All these anxieties, and, if I may be permitted, without disrespect to the dead, to add, all this twaddle, that accompanied them,
were shortly suspended by an incident that struck nearer home;
made Tergou furiously jealous of Catherine, and Catherine weep.
And, if my reader is fond of wasting his time, as some novel readers
are, he cannot do it more effectually than by guessing what could
produce results so incongruous.

Marched up to Eli's door a pageant brave to the eye of sense,
and to the vulgar judgment noble, but, to the philosophic, pitiable
more or less.

It looked one animal, a centaur: but on severe analysis proved
two. The human half was sadly bedizened with those two metals,
to clothe his carcass with which and line his pouch, man has now
and then disposed of his soul: still the horse was the vainer brute
of the two; he was far worse beflounced, bebonneted, and bemantled,
than any fair lady regnante crinolinâ. For the man, under the
colour of a warming-pan, retained Nature's outline. But it was
"subaudi equum!" Scarce a pennyweight of honest horseflesh to
be seen. Our crinoline spares the noble parts of woman, and makes
but the baser parts gigantic (why this preference?): but this poor
animal from stem to stern was swamped in finery. His ears were
hid in great sheaths of white linen tipped with silver and blue.
His body swaddled in stiff gorgeous cloths descending to the ground,
except just in front, where they left him room to mince. His tail,
though dear to memory, no doubt, was lost to sight, being tucked in
heaven knows how. Only his eyes shone out like goggles, through
two holes pierced in the wall of haberdashery, and his little front
hoofs peeped in and out like rats.

Yet did this compound, gorgeous and irrational, represent power;
absolute power: it came straight from a tournament at the duke's
court, which being on a progress, lay last night at a neighboring
town—to execute the behests of royalty.

The Cloister and the Hearth

"What ho!" cried the upper half, and on Eli emerging, with his wife behind him, saluted them. "Peace be with you, good people. Rejoice! I am come for your dwarf."

Eli looked amazed, and said nothing. But Catherine screamed over his shoulder, "You have mistook your road, good man; here abides no dwarf."

"Nay, wife, he means our Giles, who is somewhat small of stature: why gainsay what gainsayed may not be?"

"Ay!" cried the pageant, "that is he, and discourseth like the big tabor."

"His breast is sound for that matter," said Catherine, sharply.

"And prompt with his fists though at long odds."

"Else how would the poor thing keep his head in such a world as this?"

"'Tis well said, dame. Art as ready with thy weapon as he; art his mother, likely. So bring him forth and that presently. See, they lead a stunted mule for him. The duke hath need of him; sore need; we are clean out o' dwarven; and tigercats; which may not be, whiles earth them yieldeth. Our last hop o' my thumb tumbled down the well t'other day."

"And think you I'll let my darling go to such an ill-guided house as yon, where the reckless trollops of servants close not the well mouth, but leave it open to trap innocents like wolven?"

The representative of autocracy lost patience at this unwonted opposition, and with stern look and voice bade her bethink her whether it was the better of the two; "to have your abortion at court fed like a bishop and put on like a prince, or to have all your heads stricken off and borne on poles, with the bell-man crying, 'Behold the heads of hardy rebels, which having by good luck a misbegotten son, did traitorously grudge him to the duke, who is the true father of all his folk, little or mickle?'"

"Nay," said Eli, sadly, "miscall us not. We be true folk, and neither rebels nor traitors. But 'tis sudden, and the poor lad is our true flesh and blood, and hath of late given proof of more sense than heretofore."

"Avails not threatening our lives," whimpered Catherine, "we grudge him not to the duke: but in sooth he cannot go: his linen is all in holes. So there is an end."

But the male mind resisted this crusher.

The Cloister and the Hearth

"Think you the duke will not find linen, and cloth of gold to boot? None so brave, none so affected, at court, as our monsters, big or wee."

How long the dispute might have lasted, before the iron arguments of despotism achieved the inevitable victory, I know not; but it was cut short by a party whom neither disputant had deigned to consult.

The bone of contention walked out of the house, and sided with monarchy.

"If my folk are mad, I am not," he roared. "I'll go with you, and on the instant."

At this Catherine set up a piteous cry. She saw another of her brood escaping from under her wing into some unknown element. Giles was not quite insensible to her distress so simple yet so eloquent. He said, "Nay take not on, mother! Why 'tis a godsend. And I am sick of this ever since Gerard left it."

"Ah, cruel Giles! Should ye not rather say she is bereaved of Gerard: the more need of you to stay aside her and comfort her!"

"Oh! I am not going to Rome. Not such a fool I shall never be farther than Rotterdam: and I'll often come and see you; and, if I like not the place, who shall keep me there? Not all the dukes in Christendom."

"Good sense lies in little bulk," said the emissary approvingly. "Therefore, master Giles, buss the old folk, and thank them for misbegetting of thee, and—ho! you—bring hither his mule!"

One of his retinue brought up the dwarf mule. Giles refused it with scorn. And, on being asked the reason, said it was not just. "What would ye throw all into one scale? Put muckle to muckle, and little to wee? Besides I hate and scorn small things. I'll go on the highest horse here, or not at all."

The pursuivant eyed him attentively a moment. He then adopted a courteous manner. "I shall study your will in all things reasonable. (Dismount, Eric, yours is the highest horse.) And if you would halt in the town an hour or so, while you bid them farewell, say but the word, and your pleasure shall be my delight."

Giles reflected.

"Master," said he, "if we wait a month 'twill be still the same: my mother is a good soul, but her body is bigger than her spirit. We

341

shall not part without a tear or two, and the quicker 'tis done the fewer; so, bring yon horse to me."

Catherine threw her apron over her face and sobbed. The high horse was brought, and Giles was for swarming up his tail, like a rope; but one of the servants cried out hastily "forbear, for he kicketh." "I'll kick him," said Giles. "Bring him close beneath this window, and I'll learn you all how to mount a horse which kicketh, and will not be clomb by the tail, the staircase of an horse." And he dashed into the house and almost immediately reappeared at an upper window with a rope in his hand. He fastened an end somehow and holding the other descended as swift and smooth as an oiled thunderbolt in a groove; and lighted astride his high horse as unperceived by that animal as a fly settling on him.

The official lifted his hands to heaven in mawkish admiration. "I have gotten a pearl," thought he; "and wow but this will be a good day's work for me."

"Come, father, come, mother, buss me, and bless me, and off I go."

Eli gave him his blessing, and bade him be honest and true, and a credit to his folk. Catherine could not speak, but clung to him with many sobs and embraces; and even through the mist of tears her eye detected in a moment a little rent in his sleeve he had made getting out of window, and she whipped out her needle and mended it then and there, and her tears fell on his arm the while, unheeded—except by those unfleshly eyes, with which they say the very air is thronged.

And so the dwarf mounted the high horse, and rode away complacent, with the old hand laying the court butter on his back with a trowel. Little recked Perpusillus of two poor silly females that sat by the bereaved hearth, rocking themselves, and weeping, and discussing all his virtues, and how his mind had opened lately, and blind as two beetles to his faults, who rode away from them jocund and bold,

Ingentes animos angusto pectore versans.

Arrived at court he speedily became a great favourite.

One strange propensity of his electrified the palace: but, on account of his small size, and for variety's sake, and as a monster, he was indulged on it. In a word he was let speak the truth.

The Cloister and the Hearth

It is an unpopular thing.
He made it an intolerable one.
Bawled it.

CHAPTER LI

MARGARET BRANDT had always held herself apart from Sevenbergen; and her reserve had passed for pride; this had come to her ears, and she knew many hearts were swelling with jealousy and malevolence. How would they triumph over her when her condition could no longer be concealed! This thought gnawed her night and day. For some time it had made her bury herself in the house, and shun daylight even on those rare occasions when she went abroad.

Not that in her secret heart and conscience she mistook her moral situation, as my unlearned readers have done perhaps. Though not acquainted with the nice distinctions of the contemporary law, she knew that betrothal was a marriage contract, and could no more be legally broken on either side than any other compact written and witnessed: and that marriage with another party than the betrothed had been formally annulled both by Church and State; and that betrothed couples often came together without any further ceremony, and their children were legitimate.

But what weighed down her simple mediæval mind was this: that very contract of betrothal was not forthcoming. Instead of her keeping it, Gerard had got it, and Gerard was far, far away. She hated and despised herself for the miserable oversight, which had placed her at the mercy of false opinion.

For though she had never heard of Horace's famous couplet *Segnius irritant,* &c., she was Horatian by the plain, hard, positive intelligence, which strange to say characterizes the judgment of her sex, when feeling happens not to blind it altogether. She gauged the understanding of the world to a T. Her marriage lines being out of sight, and in Italy, would never prevail to balance her visible pregnancy, and the sight of her child when born. What sort of a tale was this to stop slanderous tongues? "I have got my marriage lines, but I cannot show them you." What woman would believe her? or even pretend to believe her? And, as she was in

343

reality one of the most modest girls in Holland, it was women's good opinion she wanted, not men's.

Even barefaced slander attacks her sex at a great advantage; but here was slander with a face of truth. "The strong-minded woman" had not yet been invented; and Margaret, though by nature and by having been early made mistress of a family, she was resolute in some respects, was weak as water in others, and weakest of all in this. Like all the élite of her sex she was a poor little leaf trembling at each gust of the world's opinion, true or false. Much misery may be contained in few words; I doubt if pages of description from any man's pen could make any human creature, except virtuous women(and these need no such aid) realize the anguish of a virtuous woman foreseeing herself paraded as a frail one. Had she been frail at heart, she might have brazened it out. But she had not that advantage. She was really pure as snow, and saw the pitch coming nearer her and nearer. The poor girl sat listless hours at a time, and moaned with inner anguish. And often, when her father was talking to her and she giving mechanical replies, suddenly her cheek would burn like fire, and the old man would wonder what he had said to discompose her. Nothing. His words were less than air to her. It was the ever present dread sent the colour of shame into her burning cheek, no matter what she seemed to be talking and thinking about. But both shame and fear rose to a climax when she came back that night from Margaret Van Eyck's. Her condition was discovered, and by persons of her own sex. The old artist, secluded like herself, might not betray her: but Catherine, a gossip in the centre of a family, and a thick neighbourhood? One spark of hope remained. Catherine had spoken kindly, even lovingly. The situation admitted no half course. Gerard's mother thus roused must either be her best friend or worst enemy. She waited then in racking anxiety to hear more. No word came. She gave up hope. Catherine was not going to be her friend. Then she would expose her, since she had no strong and kindly feeling to balance the natural love of babbling.

Then it was, the wish to fly from this neighbourhood began to grow and gnaw upon her, till it became a wild and passionate desire. But how persuade her father to this? Old people cling to places. He was very old and infirm to change his abode. There was no course but to make him her confidant; better so than to run away from him: and she felt that would be the alternative. And now between her uncontrollable desire to fly and hide, and her invincible aversion to speak out to a man, even to her father, she vibrated in a suspense full of lively torture. And presently betwixt these two came in one day the fatal thought "end all!" Things foolishly worded are not always foolish; one of poor Catherine's bugbears, these numerous canals, did sorely tempt this poor fluctuating girl. She stood on the bank one afternoon, and eyed the calm deep water. It seemed an image of repose, and she was so harassed. No more trouble. No more fear of shame. If Gerard had not loved her, I doubt she had ended there.

As it was, she kneeled by the waterside, and prayed fervently to God to keep such wicked thoughts from her. "Oh! selfish wretch," said she, "to leave thy father. Oh wicked wretch to kill thy child, and make thy poor Gerard lose all his pain and peril undertaken for thy sight. I will tell father all, ay ere this sun shall set." And she went home with eager haste lest her good resolution should ooze out ere she got there.

Now in matters domestic the learned Peter was simple as a child, and Margaret from the age of sixteen had governed the house gently but absolutely. It was therefore a strange thing in this house, the faltering irresolute way in which its young but despotic mistress addressed that person, who in a domestic sense was less important than Martin Wittenhaagen, or even than the little girl, who came in the morning and for a pittance washed the vessels, &c., and went home at night.

"Father, I would speak to thee."

"Speak on, girl."

"Wilt listen to me? And—and—not—and try to excuse my faults."

"We have all our faults, Margaret, thou no more than the rest of us; but fewer, unless parental feeling blinds me."

"Alas, no, father: I am a poor foolish girl, that would fain do well, but have done ill, most ill, most unwisely: and now must bear the shame. But, father, I love you, with all my faults, and will not you forgive my folly, and still love your motherless girl?"

"That ye may count on," said Peter, cheerfully.

"Oh, well, smile not. For then how can I speak and make you sad?"

"Why, what is the matter?"

"Father, disgrace is coming on this house: it is at the door. And I the culprit. Oh, father, turn your head away. I—I—father, I have let Gerard take away my marriage lines."

"Is that all? 'Twas an oversight."

" 'Twas the deed of a mad woman. But woe is me! that is not the worst."

Peter interrupted her. "The youth is honest, and loves you dear. You are young. What is a year or two to you? Gerard will assuredly come back and keep troth."

"And meantime, know you what is coming?"

"Not I, except that I shall be gone first for one."

"Worse than that. There is worse pain than death. Nay, for pity's sake, turn away your head, father."

"Foolish wench!" muttered Peter, but turned his head.

She trembled violently, and with her cheeks on fire began to falter out, "I did look on Gerard as my husband—we being betrothed—and he was in so sore danger, and I thought I had killed him, and I— Oh, if you were but my mother I might find courage: you would question me. But you say not a word."

"Why, Margaret, what is all this coil about? and why are thy cheeks crimson, speaking to no stranger but to thy old father?"

"Why are my cheeks on fire? Because—because— Father, kill me! send me to heaven! bid Martin shoot me with his arrow! And then the gossips will come and tell you why I blush so this day. And then, when I am dead, I hope you will love your girl again for her mother's sake."

"Give me thy hand, mistress," said Peter, a little sternly.

She put it out to him trembling. He took it gently, and began with some anxiety in his face to feel her pulse.

"Alas, nay!" said she. " 'Tis my soul that burns, not my body with fever. I cannot, will not, bide in Sevenbergen." And she wrung her hands impatiently.

"Be calm now," said the old man, soothingly, "nor torment thyself for nought. Not bide in Sevenbergen? What need to bide a day, as it vexes thee, and puts thee in a fever: for fevered thou art, deny it not."

"What!" cried Margaret, "would you yield to go hence, and—and ask no reason but my longing to be gone?" and, suddenly throwing herself on her knees beside him, in a fervour of supplication she clutched his sleeve, and then his arm, and then his shoulder, while imploring him to quit this place, and not ask her why. "Alas! what needs it? You will soon see it. And I could never say it. I would liever die."

"Foolish child! Who seeks thy girlish secrets? Is it I, whose life hath been spent in searching Nature's? And, for leaving Sevenbergen, what is there to keep me in it, thee unwilling? Is there respect for me here, or gratitude? Am I not yclept quack-salver by those that come not near me, and wizard by those I heal? And give they not the guerdon and the honour they deny me, to the empirics that slaughter them? Besides, what is't to me where we sojourn? Choose thou that, as did thy mother before thee."

Margaret embraced him tenderly, and wept upon his shoulder. She was respited.

Yet as she wept, respited, she almost wished she had had the courage to tell him.

After a while nothing would content him but her taking a medicament he went and brought her. She took it submissively, to please him. It was the least she could do. It was a composing draught, and though administered under an error, and a common one, did her more good than harm: she awoke calmed by a long sleep, and that very day began her preparations.

Next week they went to Rotterdam, bag and baggage, and lodged above a tailor's shop in the Brede-Kirk Straet.

Only one person in Tergou knew whither they were gone.

The Burgomaster.

He locked the information in his own breast.

The use he made of it ere long, my reader will not easily divine: for he did not divine it himself.

But time will show.

CHAPTER LII

AMONG strangers Margaret Brandt was comparatively happy. And soon a new and unexpected cause of content arose. A civic dignitary being ill, and fanciful in propor-tion, went from doctor to doctor; and having arrived at Death's door, sent for Peter. Peter found him bled and purged to nothing.

The Cloister and the Hearth

He flung a battalion of bottles out of the window, and left it open; beat up yolks of eggs in neat Schiedam, and administered it in small doses: followed this up by meat stewed in red wine and water, shredding into both mild febrifugal herbs, that did no harm. Finally, his patient got about again, looking something between a man and a pillow-case, and being a voluble dignitary, spread Peter's fame in every street; and that artist, who had long merited a reputation in vain, made one rapidly by luck. Things looked bright. The old man's pride was cheered at last, and his purse began to fill. He spent much of his gain, however, in sovereign herbs and choice drugs, and would have so invested them all, but Margaret white-mailed a part. The victory came too late. Its happy excitement was fatal.

One evening, in bidding her good-night, his voice seemed rather inarticulate.

The next morning he was found speechless, and only just sensible.

Margaret, who had been for years her father's attentive pupil, saw at once that he had had a paralytic stroke. But not trusting to herself, she ran for a doctor. One of those, who, obstructed by Peter, had not killed the civic dignitary, came, and cheerfully confirmed her views. He was for bleeding the patient. She declined. "He was always against blooding," said she, "especially the old." Peter lived, but was never the same man again. His memory became much affected, and of course he was not to be trusted to prescribe: and several patients had come, and one or two, that were bent on being cured by the new doctor and no other, awaited his convalescence. Misery stared her in the face. She resolved to go for advice and comfort to her cousin William Johnson, from whom she had hitherto kept aloof out of pride and poverty. She found him and his servant sitting in the same room, and neither of them the better for liquor. Mastering all signs of surprise, she gave her greetings, and presently told him she had come to talk on a family matter, and with this glanced quietly at the servant by way of hint. The woman took it, but not as expected.

"Oh, you can speak before me, can she not, my old man?"

At this familiarity Margaret turned very red, and said,—

"I cry your mercy, mistress. I knew not my cousin had fallen

348

into the custom of this town. Well, I must take a fitter opportunity"; and she rose to go.

"I wot not what ye mean by custom o' the town," said the woman, bouncing up. "But this I know: 'tis the part of a faithful servant to keep her master from being preyed on by his beggarly kin."

Margaret retorted: "Ye are too modest, mistress. Ye are no servant. Your speech betrays you. 'Tis not till the ape hath mounted the tree that she shows her tail so plain. Nay, there sits the servant; God help him! And while so it is, fear not thou his kin will ever be so poor in spirit, as come where the likes of you can flout their dole." And casting one look of mute reproach at her cousin for being so little of a man as to sit passive and silent all this time, she turned and went haughtily out; nor would she shed a single tear till she got home and thought of it. And now here were two men to be lodged and fed by one pregnant girl; and another mouth coming into the world.

But this last, though the most helpless of all, was their best friend.

Nature was strong in Margaret Brandt; that same nature which makes the brutes, the birds and the insects, so cunning at providing food and shelter for their progeny yet to come.

Stimulated by nature she sat and brooded, and brooded, and thought, and thought, how to be beforehand with destitution. Ay, though she had still five gold pieces left, she saw starvation coming with inevitable foot.

Her sex, when, deviating from custom, it thinks with male intensity, thinks just as much to the purpose as we do. She rose, bade Martin move Peter to another room, made her own very neat and clean, polished the glass globe, and suspended it from the ceiling, dusted the crocodile and nailed him to the outside wall: and, after duly instructing Martin, set him to play the lounging sentinel about the street door, and tell the crocodile-bitten that a great, and aged, and learned alchymist abode there, who in his moments of recreation would sometimes amuse himself by curing mortal diseases.

Patients soon came, and were received by Margaret, and demanded to see the leech. "That might not be. He was deep in his studies, searching for the grand elixir, and not princes could have speech of him. They must tell her their symptoms, and return in two hours." And, oh! mysterious powers! when they did return, the drug or draught was always ready for them. Sometimes, when it was a worshipful patient, she would carefully scan his face, and feeling both pulse and skin, as well as hearing his story, would go softly with it to Peter's room; and there think and ask herself how her father, whose system she had long quietly observed, would have treated the case. Then she would write an illegible scrawl with a cabalistic letter, and bring it down, reverentially, and show it the patient, and "Could he read that?" Then it would be either "I am no reader," or, with admiration, "Nay mistress, nought can I make on't."

"Ay, but I can. 'Tis sovereign. Look on thyself as cured!" If she had the materials by her, and she was too good an economist not to favour somewhat those medicines she had in her own stock, she would sometimes let the patient see her compound it, often and anxiously consulting the sacred prescription lest great Science should suffer in her hands. And so she would send them away relieved of cash, but with their pockets full of medicine, and minds full of faith, and humbugged to their heart's content. *Populus vult decipi.* And when they were gone, she would take down two little boxes Gerard had made her; and on one of these she had written *To-day,* and on the other *To-morrow,* and put the smaller coins into "To-day," and the larger into "To-morrow," along with such of her gold pieces as had survived the journey from Sevenbergen, and the expenses of housekeeping in a strange place. And so she met current expenses, and laid by for the rainy day she saw coming, and mixed drugs with simples, and vice with virtue. On this last score her conscience pricked her sore, and after each day's comedy, she knelt down and prayed God to forgive her "for the sake of her child." But lo and behold cure after cure was reported to her: so then her conscience began to harden. Martin Wittenhaagen had of late been a dead weight on her hands. Like most men who have endured great hardships, he had stiffened rather suddenly. But, though less supple, he was as strong as ever, and at his own pace could have carried the doctor herself round Rotterdam city. He carried her slops instead.

In this new business he showed the qualities of a soldier: unreasoning obedience, punctuality, accuracy, despatch and drunkenness.

He fell among "good fellows"; the blackguards plied him with Schiedam; he babbled, he bragged.

Doctor Margaret had risen very high in his estimation. All this brandishing of a crocodile for a standard, and setting a dotard in ambush, and getting rid of slops, and taking good money in exchange, struck him not as Science but something far superior, Strategy. And he boasted in his cups and before a mixed company how "me and my General we are a biting of the burghers."

When this revelation had had time to leaven the city, his General, Doctor Margaret, received a call from the constables: they took her, trembling and begging subordinate machines to forgive her, before the burgomaster; and by his side stood real physicians, a terrible row, in long robes and square caps, accusing her of practising unlawfully on the bodies of the duke's lieges. At first she was too frightened to say a word. Novice like, the very name of "Law" paralyzed her. But being questioned closely, but not so harshly as if she had been ugly, she told the truth; she had long been her father's pupil, and had but followed his system, and she had cured many; "and it is not for myself in very deed, sirs, but I have two poor helpless honest men at home upon my hands, and how else can I keep them? Ah, good sirs, let a poor girl make her bread honestly; ye hinder them not to make it idly and shamefully: and oh, sirs, ye are husbands, ye are fathers; ye cannot but see I have reason to work and provide as best I may"; and ere this woman's appeal had left her lips, she would have given the world to recall it, and stood with one hand upon her heart and one before her face, hiding it, but not the tears that trickled underneath it. All which went to the wrong address. Perhaps a female bailiff might have yielded to such arguments, and bade her practise medicine, and break law, till such time as her child should be weaned, and no longer.

"What have we to do with that," said the burgomaster, "save and except that if thou wilt pledge thyself to break the law no more, I will remit the imprisonment, and exact but the fine."

On this Doctor Margaret clasped her hands together, and vowed most pentitently never, never, never, to cure body or beast again; and being dismissed with the constables to pay the fine, she turned at the door, and curtsied, poor soul, and thanked the gentlemen for their forbearance.

The Cloister and the Hearth

And to pay the fine the "to-morrow box" must be opened on the instant; and with excess of caution she had gone and nailed it up, that no slight temptation might prevail to open it. And now she could not draw the nails, and the constables grew impatient, and doubted its contents, and said, "Let us break it for you." But she would not let them. "Ye will break it worse than I shall." And she took a hammer, and struck too faintly, and lost all strength for a minute, and wept hysterically; and at last she broke it, and a little cry broke from her when it broke: and she paid the fine, and it took all her unlawful gains and two gold pieces to boot; and, when the men were gone, she drew the broken pieces of the box, and what little money they had left her, all together on the table, and her arms went round them, and her rich hair escaped and fell down all loose, and she bowed her forehead on the wreck, and sobbed, "My love's box it is broken, and my heart withal"; and so remained. And Martin Wittenhaagen came in, and she could not lift her head, but sighed out to him what had befallen her, ending, "My love his box is broken, and so mine heart is broken."

And Martin was not so sad as wroth. Some traitor had betrayed him. What stony heart had told and brought her to this pass? Whoever it was should feel his arrow's point. The curious attitude in which he must deliver the shaft never occurred to him.

"Idle chat! idle chat!" moaned Margaret, without lifting her brow from the table. "When you have slain all the gossips in this town, can we eat them? Tell me how to keep you all, or prithee hold thy peace, and let the saints get leave to whisper me." Martin held his tongue, and cast uneasy glances at his defeated General.

Towards evening she rose, and washed her face and did up her hair, and doggedly bade Martin take down the crocodile, and put out a basket instead.

"I can get up linen better than they seem to do it in this street," said she, "and you must carry it in the basket."

"That will I for thy sake," said the soldier.

"Good Martin! forgive me that I spake shrewishly to thee."

Even while they were talking came a male for advice. Margaret told it the mayor had interfered and forbidden her to sell drugs. "But," said she, "I will gladly iron and starch your linen for you, and—I will come and fetch it from your house."

"Are ye mad, young woman?" said the male. "I come for a

leech, and ye proffer me a washerwoman;" and it went out in dudgeon.

"There is a stupid creature," said Margaret sadly.

Presently came a female to tell the symptoms of her sick child. Margaret stopped it.

"We are forbidden by the bailiff to sell drugs. But I will gladly wash, iron, and starch your linen for you—and—I will come and fetch it from your house."

"Oh, ay," said the female. "Well, I have some smocks and ruffs foul. Come for them; and when you *are* there, you can look at the boy"; and it told her where it lived, and when its husband would be out; yet it was rather fond of its husband than not.

An introduction is an introduction. And two or three patients, out of all those who came and were denied medicine, made Doctor Margaret their washerwoman.

"Now, Martin, you must help. I'll no more cats than can slay mice "

"Mistress, the stomach is not a wanting for't, but the head-piece, worse luck."

"Oh! I mean not the starching and ironing; that takes a woman and a handy one. But the bare washing; a man can surely contrive that. Why, a mule has wit enough in's head to do't with his hoofs, an ye could drive him into the tub. Come, off doublet, and try."

"I am your man," said the brave old soldier, stripping for the unwonted toil. "I'll risk my arm in soapsuds, an' you will risk your glory."

"My what?"

"Your glory and honour as a—washerwoman."

"Gramercy! if you are man enough to bring me half-washed linen t'iron, I am woman enough to fling't back i' the suds."

And so the brave girl, and the brave soldier, worked with a will, and kept the wolf from the door. More they could not do. Margaret had repaired "the to-morrow box," and, as she leaned over the glue, her tears mixed with it, and she cemented her exiled lover's box with them, at which a smile is allowable, but an intelligent smile tipped with pity, please, and not the empty guffaw of the nineteenth-century-jackass, burlesquing Bibles, and making fun of all things except fun. But when mended it stood unreplenished.

The Cloister and the Hearth

They kept the weekly rent paid, and the pot boiling, but no more.

And now came a concatenation. Recommended from one to another, Margaret washed for the mayor. And bringing home the clean linen one day she heard in the kitchen that his worship's only daughter was stricken with disease, and not like to live. Poor Margaret could not help cross-questioning, and a female servant gave her such of the symptoms as she had observed. But they were too general. However, one gossip would add one fact, and another another. And Margaret pondered them all.

At last one day she met the mayor himself. He recognized her directly. "Why, you are the unlicensed doctor." "I was," said she, "but now I'm your worship's washerwoman." The dignitary coloured, and said that was rather a come down.

"Nay, I bear no malice; for your worship might have been harder. Rather would I do you a good turn. Sir, you have a sick daughter. Let me see her."

The mayor shook his head. "That cannot be. The law I do enforce on others I may not break myself." Margaret opened her eyes.

"Alack, sir, I seek no guerdon now for curing folk; why, I am a washerwoman. I trow one may heal all the world, an if one will but let the world starve one in return." "That is no more than just," said the mayor: he added, "an ye make no trade on't; there is no offence." "Then let me see her."

"What avails it? The learnedst leeches in Rotterdam have all seen her, and bettered her nought. Her ill is inscrutable. One skilled wight saith spleen; another, liver; another, blood; another, stomach; and another, that she is possessed: and, in very truth, she seems to have a demon; shunneth all company; pineth alone; eateth no more victuals than might diet a sparrow. Speaketh seldom, nor hearkens them that speak, and weareth thinner and paler and nearer and nearer the grave, well-a-day." "Sir," said Margaret, "an if you take your velvet doublet to half a dozen of shops in Rotterdam, and speer is this fine or sorry velvet, and worth how much the ell, those six traders will eye it and feel it, and all be in one story to a letter. And why? Because they know their trade. And your leeches are all in different stories. Why? Because they know not their trade. I have heard my father say each is enamoured of some one evil, and seeth it with his bat's eyn in every patient. Had they stayed at home, and ne'er seen your daughter, they had

354

answered all the same, spleen, blood, stomach, lungs, liver, lunacy, or, as they call it, possession. Let me see her. We are of a sex, and that is much." And when he still hesitated, "Saints of Heaven!" cried she, giving way to the irritability of a breeding woman, "is this how men love their own flesh and blood? Her mother had ta'en me in her arms ere this, and carried me to the sick room." And two violet eyes flashed fire.

"Come with me," said the mayor, hastily.

"Mistress, I have brought thee a new doctor."

The person addressed, a pale young girl of eighteen, gave a contemptuous wrench of her shoulder, and turned more decidedly to the fire she was sitting over.

Margaret came softly and sat beside her. "But 'tis one that will not torment you."

"A woman!" exclaimed the young lady, with surprise and some contempt.

"Tell her your symptoms."

"What for? You will be no wiser."

"You will be none the worse."

"Well, I have no stomach for food, and no heart for anything. Now cure me, and go."

"Patience awhile! Your food, is it tasteless like in your mouth?"

"Ay. How knew you that?"

"Nay, I knew it not till you did tell me. I trow you would be better for a little good company."

"I trow not. What is their silly chat to me?"

Here Margaret requested the father to leave them alone: and in his absence put some practical questions. Then she reflected.

"When you wake i' the morning you find yourself quiver, as one may say?"

"Nay. Ay. How knew you that?"

"Shall I dose you, or shall I but tease you a bit with my 'silly chat'?"

"Which you will."

"Then I will tell you a story. 'Tis about two true lovers."

"I hate to hear of lovers," said the girl; "nevertheless canst tell me, 'twill be less nauseous than your physic—maybe."

Margaret then told her a love story. The maiden was a girl

The Cloister and the Hearth

called Ursel, and the youth one Conrad; she an old physician's daughter, he the son of a hosier at Tergou. She told their adventures, their troubles, their sad condition. She told it from the female point of view, and in a sweet and winning and earnest voice, that by degrees soon laid hold of this sullen heart, and held it breathless; and when she broke it off her patient was much disappointed.

"Nay, nay, I must hear the end. I will hear it."

"Ye cannot, for I know it not; none knoweth that but God."

"Ah, your Ursel was a jewel of worth," said the girl earnestly. "Would she were here."

"Instead of her that is here."

"I say not that;" and she blushed a little.

"You do but think it."

"Thought is free. Whether or no, an she were here, I'd give her a buss, poor thing."

"Then give it me, for I am she."

"Nay, nay, that I'll be sworn y' are not."

"Say not so; in very truth I am she. And prithee, sweet mistress, go not from your word, but give me the buss ye promised me, and with a good heart, for oh, my own heart lies heavy: heavy as thine, sweet mistress."

The young gentlewoman rose and put her arms round Margaret's neck and kissed her. "I am woe for you," she sighed. "You are a good soul; you have done me good—a little." (A gulp came in her throat.) "Come again! come often!"

Margaret did come again, and talked with her, and gently, but keenly, watched what topics interested her, and found there was but one. Then she said to the mayor, "I know your daughter's trouble, and 'tis curable."

"What is't? the blood?"

"Nay."

"The stomach?"

"Nay."

"The liver?"

"Nay."

"The foul fiend?"

"Nay."

"What then?"

356

The Cloister and the Hearth

"Love."

"Love? stuff, impossible! She is but a child; she never stirs abroad unguarded. She never hath from a child."

"All the better; then we shall not have far to look for him."

"I trow not. I shall but command her to tell me the catiff's name, that hath by magic arts ensnared her young affections."

"Oh, how foolish be the wise!" said Margaret; "what, would ye go and put her on her guard? Nay, let us work by art first; and if that fails, then 'twill still be time for violence and folly."

Margaret then with some difficulty prevailed on the mayor to take advantage of its being Saturday, and pay all his people their salaries in his daughter's presence and hers.

It was done: some fifteen people entered the room, and received their pay with a kind word from their employer. Then Margaret, who had sat close to the patient all the time, rose and went out. The mayor followed her.

"Sir, how call you yon black haired lad?"

"That is Ulrich, my clerk."

"Well then, 'tis he."

"Now heaven forbid! a lad I took out of the streets."

"Well, but your worship is an understanding man. You took him not up without some merit of his."

"Merit? not a jot. I liked the looks of the brat, that was all."

"Was that no merit? He pleased the father's eye. And now he hath pleased the daughter's. That has oft been seen since Adam."

"How know ye 'tis he?"

"I held her hand, and with my finger did lightly touch her wrist; and, when the others came and went, 'twas as if dogs and cats had fared in and out. But at this Ulrich's coming her pulse did leap, and her eyes shine; and, when he went, she did sink back and sigh; and 'twas to be seen the sun had gone out of the room for her. Nay, burgomaster, look not on me so scared: no witch nor magician I, but a poor girl that hath been docile, and so bettered herself by a great neglected leech's art and learning. I tell ye all this hath been done before, thousands of years ere we were born. Now bide thou there till I come to thee, and prithee, prithee, spoil not good work wi' meddling." She then went back and asked her patient for a lock of her hair.

"Take it," said she, more listlessly than ever.

"Why, 'tis a lass of marble. How long do you count to be like that, mistress?"

"Till I am in my grave, sweet Peggy."

"Who knows? may be in ten minutes you will be altogether as hot."

She ran into the shop, but speedily returned to the mayor and said, "Good news! He fancies her and more than a little. Now how is't to be? Will you marry your child, or bury her, for there is no third way, sith shame and love they do rend her virgin heart to death."

The dignitary decided for the more cheerful rite, but not without a struggle; and, with its marks on his face, he accompanied Margaret to his daughter. But as men are seldom in a hurry to drink their wormwood, he stood silent. So Doctor Margaret said cheerfully, "Mistress, your lock is gone, I have sold it."

"And who was so mad as to buy such a thing?" inquired the young lady, scornfully.

"Oh, a black haired laddie wi' white teeth. They call him Ulrich."

The pale face reddened directly—brow and all.

"Says he, 'Oh, sweet mistress, give it me.' I had told them all whose 'twas. 'Nay,' said I, 'selling is my livelihood, not giving.' So he offered me this, he offered me that, but nought less would I take than his next quarter's wages."

"Cruel," murmured the girl, scarce audibly.

"Why, you are in one tale with your father. Says he to me when I told him, 'Oh, an he loves her hair so well, 'tis odd but he loves the rest of her. Well,' quoth he, ' 'tis an honest lad, and a' shall have her, gien she will but leave her sulks and consent.' So, what say ye, mistress will you be married to Ulrich, or buried i' the kirkyard?"

"Father? father!"

" 'Tis so, girl, speak thy mind."

"I—will—obey—my father—in all things," stammered the poor girl, trying hard to maintain the advantageous position in which Margaret had placed her. But nature, and the joy and surprise, were too strong even for a virgin's bashful cunning. She cast an eloquent look on them both, and sank at her father's knees, and begged his pardon, with many sobs for having doubted his tenderness.

The Cloister and the Hearth

He raised her in his arms, and took her, radiant through her tears with joy, and returning life, and filial love, to his breast; and the pair passed a truly sacred moment, and the dignitary was as happy as he thought to be miserable: so hard is it for mortals to foresee. And they looked round for Margaret, but she had stolen away softly.

The young girl searched the house for her.

"Where is she hid? Where on earth is she?"

Where was she? why in her own house dressing meat for her two old children, and crying bitterly the while at the living picture of happiness she had just created.

"Well-a-day, the odds between her lot and mine; well-a-day!"

Next time she met the dignitary, he hemm'd and hawed, and remarked what a pity it was the law forbade him to pay her who had cured his daughter. "However, when all is done, 'twas not art, 'twas but woman's wit."

"Nought but that, burgomaster," said Margaret, bitterly. "Pay the men of art for not curing her: all the guerdon I seek, that cured her, is this; go not and give your foul linen away from me by way of thanks."

"Why should I?" inquired he.

"Marry, because there be fools about ye will tell ye she that hath wit to cure dark diseases, cannot have wit to take dirt out o' rags; so pledge me your faith."

The dignitary promised pompously, and felt all the patron.

Something must be done to fill "to-morrow's box." She hawked her initial letters and her illuminated vellums all about the town. Printing had by this time dealt caligraphy in black and white a terrible blow in Holland and Germany. But some copies of the printed books were usually illuminated and lettered. The printers offered Margaret prices for work in these two kinds.

"I'll think on't," said she.

She took down her diurnal book, and calculated that the price of an hour's work on those arts would be about one fifth what she got for an hour at the tub and mangle. "I'll starve first," said she; "what, pay a craft and a mystery five times less than a handi-craft!"

The Cloister and the Hearth

Martin, carrying the dry clothes-basket, got treated, and drunk. This time he babbled her whole story. The girls got hold of it and gibed her at the fountain.

All she had gone through was light to her, compared with the pins and bodkins her own sex drove into her heart, whenever she came near the merry crew with her pitcher, and that was every day. Each sex has its form of cruelty; man's is more brutal and terrible; but shallow women, that have neither read nor suffered, have an unmuscular barbarity of their own (where no feeling of sex steps in to overpower it). This defect, intellectual perhaps rather than moral, has been mitigated in our day by books, especially by able works of fiction; for there are two roads to that highest effort of intelligence, Pity; Experience of sorrows, and Imagination, by which alone we realize the grief we never felt. In the fifteenth century girls with pitchers had but one; Experience; and at sixteen years of age or so, that road had scarce been trodden. These girls persisted that Margaret was deserted by her lover. And to be deserted was a crime. [They had not been deserted yet.] Not a word against the Gerard they had created out of their own heads. For his imaginary crime they fell foul of the supposed victim. Sometimes they affronted her to her face. Oftener they talked at her backwards and forwards with a subtle skill, and a perseverence which, "oh, that they had bestowed on the arts," as poor Ague Cheek says.

Now Margaret was brave, and a coward; brave to battle difficulties and ill fortune; brave to shed her own blood for those she loved. Fortitude she had. But she had no true fighting courage. She was a powerful young woman, rather tall, full, and symmetrical; yet had one of those slips of girls slapped her face, the poor fool's hands would have dropped powerless, or gone to her own eyes instead of her adversary's. Nor was she even a match for so many tongues; and, besides, what could she say? She knew nothing of these girls, except that somehow they had found out her sorrows, and hated her; only she thought to herself they must be very happy, or they would not be so hard on her.

So she took their taunts in silence; and all her struggle was not to let them see their power to make her writhe within.

360

Here came in her fortitude; and she received their blows with well-feigned, icy, hauteur. They slapped a statue.

But one day, when her spirits were weak, as happens at times to females in her condition, a dozen assailants followed suit so admirably, that her whole sex seemed to the dispirited one to be against her, and she lost heart, and the tears began to run silently at each fresh stab.

On this their triumph knew no bounds, and they followed her half way home casting barbed speeches.

After that exposure of weakness the statue could be assumed no more. So then she would stand timidly aloof out of tongue-shot, till her young tyrants' pitchers were all filled, and they gone; and then creep up with hers. And one day she waited so long that the fount had ceased to flow. So the next day she was obliged to face the phalanx, or her house go dry. She drew near slowly, but with the less tremor, that she saw a man at the well talking to them. He would distract their attention, and, besides, they would keep their foul tongues quiet if only to blind the male to their real character. This conjecture, though shrewd, was erroneous. They could not all flirt with that one man: so the outsiders indemnified themselves by talking at her the very moment she came up.

"Any news from foreign parts, Jacqueline?"

"None for me, Martha. My lad goes no farther from me than the town wall."

"I can't say as much," says a third.

"But if he goes t' Italy I have got another ready to take the fool's place."

"He'll not go thither, lass. They go not so far till they are sick of us that bide in Holland."

Surprise, and indignation, and the presence of a man, gave Margaret a moment's fighting courage. "Oh, flout me not, and show your ill nature before the very soldier. In Heaven's name, what ill did I ever to ye; what harsh word cast back, for all you have flung on me, a desolate stranger in your cruel town, that ye flout me for my bereavement and my poor lad's most unwilling banishment? Hearts of flesh would surely pity us both, for that ye cast in my teeth these many days, ye brows of brass, ye bosoms of stone."

They stared at this novelty, resistance; and ere they could recover and make mincemeat of her, she put her pitcher quietly down, and threw her coarse apron over her head, and stood there grieving, her short-lived spirit oozing fast. "Hallo!" cried the soldier, "why, what is your ill?" She made no reply. But a little girl, who had long secretly hated the big ones, squeaked out, "They did flout her, they are aye flouting her: she may not come nigh the fountain for fear o' them, and 'tis a black shame."

"Who spoke to her? Not I for one."

"Nor I. I would not bemean myself so far."

The man laughed heartily at this display of dignity. "Come, wife," said he, "never lower thy flag to such light skirmishers as these. Hast a tongue i' thy head as well as they."

"Alack, good soldier, I was not bred to bandy foul terms."

"Well, but hast a better arm than these. Why not take 'em by twos across thy knee, and skelp 'em till they cry Meculpee?"

"Nay, I would not hurt their bodies for all their cruel hearts."

"Then ye must e'en laugh at them, wife. What! a woman grown, and not see why mesdames give tongue? You are a buxom wife; they are a bundle of thread-papers. You are fair and fresh: they have all the Dutch rim under their bright eyes, that comes of dwelling in eternal swamps. There lies your crime. Come, gie me thy pitcher, and, if they flout me, shalt see me scrub 'em all wi' my beard till they squeak holy mother." The pitcher was soon filled, and the soldier put it in Margaret's hand. She murmured "Thank you kindly, brave soldier."

He patted her on the shoulder. "Come, courage, brave wife; the divell is dead!" She let the heavy pitcher fall on his foot directly. He cursed horribly, and hopped in a circle, saying, "No, the Thief's alive and has broken my great toe."

The apron came down, and there was a lovely face all flushed with emotion, and two beaming eyes in front of him, and two hands held out clasped.

"Nay, nay, 'tis nought," said he, good-humouredly, mistaking.

"Denys?"

"Well?—But—Hallo! How know you my name is—"

"Denys of Burgundy!"

"Why, odsbodikins! I know you not, and you know me."

"By Gerard's letter. Cross-bow! beard! handsome! The divell is dead,"

"Sword of Goliah! this must be she. Red hair, violet eyes, lovely face. But I took ye for a married wife, seeing ye—"

"Tell me my name," said she quickly.

"Margaret Brandt."

"Gerard? Where is he? Is he in life? Is he well? Is he come? Why is he not here? Where have ye left him? Oh, tell me! prithee, prithee, prithee, tell me!"

"Ay, ay, but not here. Oh, ye are all curiosity now, mesdames, eh? Lass, I have been three months a-foot travelling all Holland to find ye, and here you are. Oh, be joyful!" and he flung his cap in the air, and seizing both her hands kissed them ardently. "Ah, my pretty she-comrade, I have found thee at last. I knew I should. Shalt be flouted no more. I'll twist your necks at the first word, ye little trollops. And I have got fifteen gold angels left for thee, and our Gerard will soon be here. Shalt wet thy purple eyes no more."

But the fair eyes were wet even now, looking kindly and gratefully at the friend that had dropped among her foes as if from heaven: Gerard's comrade. "Prithee come home with me, good, kind Denys. I cannot speak of him before these." They went off together, followed by a chorus. "She has gotten a man. She has gotten a man at last. Hoo! hoo! hoo!"

Margaret quickened her steps; but Denys took down his crossbow and pretended to shoot them all dead: they fled quadrivious, shrieking.

CHAPTER LIII

THE reader already knows how much these two had to tell one another. It was a sweet yet bitter day for Margaret, since it brought her a true friend, and ill news: for now first she learned that Gerard was all alone in that strange land. She could not think with Denys that he would come home; indeed he would have arrived before this.

Denys was a balm. He called her his she-comrade, and was always cheering her up with his formula and hilarities, and she petted him and made much of him, and feebly hectored it over him as well as over Martin, and would not let him eat a single meal out of her house, and forbade him to use naughty words. "It spoils you, Denys. Good lack, to hear such ugly words come forth so comely a head: forbear, or I shall be angry: so be civil." Whereupon Denys was upon his good behaviour, and ludicrous the struggle between his native politeness and his acquired ruffianism. And as it never rains but it pours, other persons now solicited Margaret's friendship. She had written to Margaret Van Eyck a humble letter telling her she knew she was no longer the favourite she had been, and would keep her distance; but could not forget her benefactress's past kindness. She then told her briefly how many ways she had battled for a living, and, in conclusion, begged earnestly that her residence might not be betrayed, "least of all to his people. I do hate them, they drove him from me. And, even when he was gone, their hearts turned not to me as they would an if they had repented their cruelty to him."

The Van Eyck was perplexed. At last she made a confidante of Reicht. The secret ran through Reicht, as through a cylinder, to Catherine.

"Ay, and is she turned that bitter against us?" said that good woman. "She stole our son from us, and now she hates us for not running into her arms. Natheless it is a blessing she is alive and no farther away than Rotterdam."

The English princess now Countess Charolois, made a stately progress through the northern states of the duchy, accompanied by her step-daughter the young heiress of Burgundy, Marie de Bourgogne. Then the old duke, the most magnificent prince in Europe, put out his splendour. Troops of dazzling knights, and bevies of fair ladies gorgeously attired, attended the two princesses; and minstrels, jongleurs, or storytellers, bards, musicians, actors, tumblers, followed in the train; and there were fencing, dancing, and joy in every town they shone on. Giles, a court favourite, sent a timely mesage to Tergou, inviting all his people to meet the pageant at Rotterdam.

They agreed to take a holiday for once in a way, and setting their married daughter to keep the shop, came to Rotterdam. But to two of them, not the great folk, but little Giles, was the main attraction. They had been in Rotterdam some days, when Denys met Catherine accidentally in the street, and after a warm greeting on both sides, bade her rejoice, for he had found the she-comrade, and crowed; but Catherine cooled him by showing him how much earlier he would have found her by staying quietly at Tergou, than by vagabondizing it all over Holland. "And being found, what the better are we? her heart is set dead against us now."

"Oh let that flea stick, come you with me to her house."

No, she would not go where she was sure of an ill welcome. "Them that come unbidden sit unseated." No, let Denys be mediator, and bring the parties to a good understanding. He undertook the office at once, and with great pomp and confidence. He trotted off to Margaret and said, "She-comrade, I met this day a friend of thine."

"Thou didst look into the Rotter then, and see thyself."

"Nay, 'twas a female, and one that seeks thy regard; 'twas Catherine, Gerard's mother."

"Oh, was it?" said Margaret; "then you may tell her she comes too late. There was a time I longed and longed for her; but she held aloof in my hour of most need, so now we will be as we ha' been."

Denys tried to shake this resolution. He coaxed her, but she was bitter and sullen, and not to be coaxed. Then he scolded her well; then, at that she went into hysterics.

He was frightened at this result of his eloquence, and being off his guard allowed himself to be entrapped into a solemn promise never to recur to the subject. He went back to Catherine crestfallen, and told her. She fired up and told the family how his overtures had been received. Then they fired up; it became a feud and burned fiercer every day. Little Kate alone made some excuses for Margaret.

The very next day another visitor came to Margaret, and found the military enslaved and degraded, Martin up to his elbows in soapsuds, and Denys ironing very clumsily, and Margaret plaiting ruffs, but with a mistress's eye on her raw levies. To these there entered an old man, venerable at first sight, but on nearer view keen and wizened.

"Ah," cried Margaret. Then swiftly turned her back on him and hid her face with invincible repugnance. "Oh, that man! that man!"

"Nay, fear me not," said Ghysbrecht; "I come on a friend's errand. I bring ye a letter from foreign parts."

"Mock me not, old man," and she turned slowly round.

"Nay, see," and he held out an enormous letter. Margaret darted on it, and held it with trembling hands and glistening eyes. It was Gerard's handwriting.

"Oh, thank you, sir, bless you for this. I forgive you all the ill you ever wrought me." And she pressed the letter to her bosom with one hand, and glided swiftly from the room with it.

As she did not come back, Ghysbrecht went away, but not without a scowl at Martin. Margaret was hours alone with her letter.

CHAPTER LIV

WHEN she came down again she was a changed woman. Her eyes were wet, but calm, and all her bitterness and excitement charmed away.

"Denys," said she, softly, "I have got my orders. I am to read my lover's letter to his folk."

"Ye will never do that?"

"Ay will I."

"I see there is something in the letter has softened ye towards them."

"Not a jot, Denys, not a jot. But an I hated them like poison I would not disobey my love. Denys, 'tis so sweet to obey, and sweetest of all to obey one who is far, far away and cannot enforce my duty, but must trust my love for my obedience. Ah, Gerard, my darling, at hand I might have slighted thy commands, misliking thy folk as I have cause to do; but now, didst bid me go into the raging sea and read thy sweet letter to the sharks there I'd go. Therefore, Denys, tell his mother I have got a letter, and if she and hers would hear it, I am their servant, let them say their hour, and I'll seat them as best I can, and welcome them as best I may."

Denys went off to Catherine with this good news. He found the family at dinner, and told them there was a long letter from Gerard. Then in the midst of the joy this caused, he said, "And her heart is softened, and she will read it to you herself; you are to choose your own time."

"What, does she think there are none can read but her?" asked Catherine. "Let her send the letter and we will read it."

"Nay, but mother," objected little Kate; "mayhap she cannot bear to part it from her hand; she loves him dearly."

"What, thinks she we shall steal it?"

Cornelis suggested that she would fain wedge herself into the family by means of this letter.

Denys cast a look of scorn on the speaker. "There spoke a bad heart," said he. "La Camarade hates you all like poison. Oh, mistake me not, dame; I defend her not, but so 'tis; yet maugre her spleen at a word from Gerard she proffers to read you his letter with her own pretty mouth, and hath a voice like honey—sure 'tis a fair proffer."

"'Tis so, mine honest soldier," said the father of the family, "and merits a civil reply, therefore hold your whisht ye that be women, and I shall answer her. Tell her I, his father, setting aside all past grudges, do for this grace thank her, and, would she have double thanks, let her send my son's letter by thy faithful hand, the which will I read to his flesh and blood, and will then to her so surely and faithfully return, as I am Eli a Dierich a William a Luke, free burgher of Tergou, like my forbears, and, like them, a man of my word."

"Ay, and a man who is better than his word," cried Catherine; "the only one I ever did foregather."

"Hold thy peace, wife."

"Art a man of sense, Eli, a dirk, a chose, a chose," * shouted Denys. "The she-comrade will be right glad to obey Gerard and yet not face you all, whom she hates as wormwood, saving your presence. Bless ye, the world hath changed, she is all submission to-day: 'Obedience is honey,' quoth she; and in sooth 'tis a sweet-meat she cannot but savour, eating so little on't, for what with her fair face, and her mellow tongue; and what wi' flying in fits and terrifying us that be soldiers to death, and we thwart her; and what wi' chiding us one while, and petting us like lambs t'other, she hath made two of the crawlingest slaves ever you saw out of two honest swashbucklers. I be the ironing ruffian, t' other washes."

"What next?"

"What next? why whenever the brat is in the world I shall rock cradle, and t' other knave will wash tucker and bib. So, then, I'll

* Anglice, a Thing-em-bob.

go fetch the letter on the instant. Ye will let me bide and hear it read, will ye not?"

"Else our hearts were black as coal," said Catherine.

So Denys went for the letter. He came back crestfallen. "She will not let it out of her hand neither to me nor you, nor any he or she that lives."

"I knew she would not," said Cornelis.

"Whisht! whisht!" said Eli, "and let Denys tell his story."

"'Nay,' said I, 'but be ruled by me.' 'Not I,' quoth she. 'Well but,' quoth I, 'that same honey Obedience ye spake of.' 'You are a fool,' says she; 'obedience to Gerard is sweet, but obedience to any other body, who ever said that was sweet?'"

"At last she seemed to soften a bit, and did give me a written paper for you, mademoiselle. Here 'tis."

"For me?" said little Kate, colouring.

"Give that here!" said Eli, and he scanned the writing, and said almost in a whisper, "These be words from the letter. Hearken!

"'And, sweetheart, an' if these lines should travel safe to thee, make thou trial of my people's hearts withal. Maybe they are somewhat turned toward me, being far away. If 'tis so, they will show it to thee, since now to me they may not. Read, then, this letter! But I do strictly forbid thee to let it from thy hands; and if they still hold aloof from thee, why then say nought, but let them think me dead. Obey me in this; for, if thou dost disrespect my judgment and my will in this thou lovest me not.'"

There was a silence, and Gerard's words copied by Margaret were handed round and inspected.

"Well," said Catherine, "that is another matter. But methinks 'tis for her to come to us, not we to her."

"Alas, mother! what odds does that make?"

"Much," said Eli. "Tell her we are over many to come to her, and bid her hither, the sooner the better."

When Denys was gone, Eli owned it was a bitter pill to him. "When that lass shall cross my threshold, all the mischief and misery she hath made here will seem to come in adoors in one heap. But what could I do, wife? We *must* hear the news of Gerard. I saw that in thine eyes, and felt it in my own heart. And she is backed by our undutiful but still beloved son, and so is she stronger than we, and brings our noses down to the grindstone, the sly, cruel, jade. But never heed. We will hear the letter: and then let her go unblessed, as she came unwelcome."

"Make your mind easy," said Catherine. "She will not come at all." And a tone of regret was visible.

Shortly after Richart, who had been hourly expected, arrived from Amsterdam grave and dignified in his burgher's robe and gold chain, ruff, and furred cap, and was received not with affection only, but respect; for he had risen a step higher than his parents, and such steps were marked in mediæval society almost as visibly as those in their staircases.

Admitted in due course to the family council, he showed plainly, though not discourteously, that his pride was deeply wounded by their having deigned to treat with Margaret Brandt. "I see the temptation," said he. "But which of us hath not at times to wish one way and do another?"

This threw a considerable chill over the old people. So little Kate put in a word. "Vex not thyself, dear Richart. Mother says she will not come."

"All the better, sweetheart. I fear me, if she do, I shall hie me back to Amsterdam."

Here Denys popped his head in at the door, and said "She will be here at three on the great dial."

They all looked at one another in silence.

CHAPTER LV

"NAY, Richart," said Catherine at last, "for Heaven's sake let not this one sorry wench set us all by the ears: hath she not made ill blood enough already?"

"In very deed she hath. Fear me not, good mother. Let her come and read the letter of the poor boy she hath by devilish arts bewitched, and then let her go. Give me your words to show her no countenance beyond decent and constrained civility: less we may not, being in our own house; and I will say no more." On this understanding they awaited the foe. She, for her part, prepared for the interview in a spirit little less hostile.

When Denys brought word they would not come to her, but would receive her, her lip curled, and she bade him observe how in them every feeling, however small, was larger than the love for Gerard.

"Well," said she, "I have not that excuse; so why mimic the pretty burgher's pride, the pride of all unlettered folk? I will go to them for Gerard's sake. Oh, how I loathe them!"

Thus poor good-natured Denys was bringing into one house the materials of an explosion.

Margaret made her toilet in the same spirit that a knight of her day dressed for battle—he to parry blows, and she to parry glances—glances of contempt at her poverty, or of irony at her extravagance. Her kirtle was of English cloth, dark blue, and her farthingale and hose of the same material, but a glossy roan, or claret colour. Not an inch of pretentious fur about her, but plain snowy linen wristbands, and curiously-plaited linen from the bosom of the kirtle up to the commencement of the throat; it did not encircle her throat, but framed it, being square, not round. Her front hair still peeped in two waves much after the fashion which Mary Queen of Scots revived a century later; but instead of the silver net, which would have ill become her present condition, the rest of her head was covered with a very small tight-fitting hood of dark blue cloth, hemmed with silver. Her shoes were red; but the roan petticoat and hose prepared the spectator's mind for the shock, and they set off the arched instep and shapely foot.

Beauty knew its business then as now.

And with all this she kept her enemies waiting, though it was three by the dial.

At last she started, attended by her he-comrade. And when they were half way, she stopped and said thoughtfully, "Denys!"

"Well, she-general?"

"I must go home" (piteously).

"What have ye left somewhat behind?"

"Ay."

"What?"

"My courage. Oh! oh! oh!"

"Nay, nay, be brave, she-general. I shall be with you."

"Ay, but wilt keep close to me when I be there?"

Denys promised, and she resumed her march, but gingerly.

Meantime, they were all assembled, and waiting for her with a strange mixture of feelings.

Mortification, curiosity, panting affection, aversion to her who came to gratify those feelings, yet another curiosity to see what she was like, and what there was in her to bewitch Gerard, and make so much mischief.

At last Denys came alone, and whispered, "The she-comrade is without."

"Fetch her in," said Eli. "Now whist, all of ye. None speak to her but I."

They all turned their eyes to the door in dead silence.

A little muttering was heard outside; Denys's rough organ, and a woman's soft and mellow voice.

Presently that stopped; and then the door opened slowly, and Margaret Brandt, dressed as I have described, and somewhat pale, but calm and lovely, stood on the threshold, looking straight before her.

They all rose but Kate, and remained mute and staring.

"Be seated, mistress," said Eli, gravely, and motioned to a seat that had been set apart for her.

She inclined her head, and crossed the apartment; and in so doing her condition was very visible, not only in her shape, but in her languor.

Cornelis and Sybrandt hated her for it. Richart thought it spoiled her beauty.

It softened the women somewhat.

She took her letter out of her bosom, and kissed it as if she had been alone; then disposed herself to read it with the air of one who knew she was there for that single purpose.

But, as she began, she noticed they had seated her all by herself like a leper. She looked at Denys, and putting her hand down by her side, made him a swift furtive motion to come by her.

He went with an obedient start as if she had cried "March!" and stood at her shoulder like a sentinel; but this zealous manner of doing it revealed to the company that he had been ordered thither; and at that she coloured. And now she began to read her Gerard, their Gerard, to their eager ears, in a mellow, but clear voice, so soft, so earnest, so thrilling, her very soul seemed to cling about each precious sound. It was a voice as of a woman's bosom set speaking by Heaven itself.

"I do nothing doubt, my Margaret, that long ere this shall meet thy beloved eyes, Denys, my most dear friend, will have sought thee out, and told thee the manner of our unlooked-for and most tearful parting. Therefore I will e'en begin at that most doleful day. What befell him after, poor faithful soul, fain, fain would I hear, but may not. But I pray for him day and night next after thee, dearest. Friend more stanch and loving had not David in Jonathan than I in him. Be good to him for poor Gerard's sake."

At these words, which came quite unexpectedly to him, Denys leaned his head on Margaret's high chair, and groaned aloud.

She turned quickly as she sat, and found his hand, and pressed it.

And so the sweetheart and the friend held hands while the sweetheart read.

"I went forward all dizzied, like one in an ill dream; and presently a gentleman came up with his servants, all on horseback, and had like to have rid o'er me. And he drew rein at the brow of the hill, and sent his armed men back to rob me. They robbed me civilly enough; and took my purse and the last copper, and rid gaily away. I wandered stupid on, a friendless pauper."

There was a general sigh, followed by an oath from Denys.

"Presently a strange dimness came o'er me, I lay down to sleep on the snow. 'Twas ill done, and with store of wolves hard by. Had I loved thee as thou dost deserve, I had shown more manhood. But oh, sweet love, the drowsiness that did crawl o'er me desolate, and benumb me, was more than nature. And so I slept; and but that God was better to us, than I to thee or to myself, from that sleep I ne'er had waked; so all do say. I had slept an hour or two, as I supposed, but no more, when a hand did shake me rudely. I awoke to my troubles. And there stood a servant girl in her holiday suit. 'Are ye mad,' quoth she, in seeming choler, 'to sleep in snow, and under wolves' nosen? Art weary o' life, and not long weaned? Come, now,' said she, more kindly, 'get up like a good lad'; so I did rise up. 'Are ye rich, or are ye poor?' But I stared at her as one amazed. 'Why 'tis easy of reply,' quoth she. 'Are ye rich, or are ye poor?' Then I gave a great, loud cry; that she did start back. 'Am I rich, or am I poor? Had ye asked me an hour agone, I had said I am rich. But now I am so poor as sure earth beareth on her bosom none poorer. An hour agone I was rich in a friend, rich in money, rich in hope and spirits of youth; but now the Bastard of Burgundy hath taken my friend and another gentleman my purse; and I can neither go forward to Rome nor back to her I left in Holland. I am poorest of the poor.' 'Alack!'

said the wench. 'Natheless, an ye had been rich ye might ha' lain down again in the snow for any use I had for ye; and then I trow ye had soon fared out o' this world as bare as ye came into 't. But, being poor, you are our man: so come wi' me.' Then I went because she bade me, and because I recked not now whither I went. And she took me to a fine house hard by, and into a noble dining-hall hung with black: and there was set a table with many dishes, and but one plate and one chair. 'Fall to!' said she, in a whisper. 'What, alone?' said I. 'Alone? And which of us, think ye, would eat out of the same dish with ye? Are we robbers o' the dead?' Then she speered where I was born. 'At Tergou,' said I. Says she, 'And, when a gentleman dies in that country, serve they not the dead man's dinner up as usual, till he be in the ground, and set some poor man down to it?' I told her nay. 'She blushed for us then. Here they were better Christians.' So I behoved to sit down. But small was my heart for meat. Then this kind lass sat by me and poured me out wine; and, tasting it, it cut me to the heart Denys was not there to drink with me. He doth so love good wine, and women good, bad, or indifferent. The rich, strong wine curled round my sick heart; and that day first I did seem to glimpse why folk in trouble run to drink so. She made me eat of every dish. ' 'Twas unlucky to pass one. Nought was here but her master's *daily* dinner.' 'He had a good stomach, then,' said I. 'Ay, lad, and a good heart. Leastways, so we all say now he is dead; but, being alive, no word on't e'er heard I.' So I did eat as a bird; nibbling of every dish. And she hearing me sigh, and seeing me like to choke at the food, took pity and bade me be of good cheer. I should sup and lie there that night. And she went to the hind, and he gave me a right good bed; and I told him all, and asked him would the law give me back my purse. 'Law!' quoth he; 'law there was none for the poor in Burgundy. Why, 'twas the cousin of the Lady of the Manor, he that had robbed me. He knew the wild spark. The matter must be judged before the lady; and she was quite young, and far more like to hang me for slandering her cousin, and a gentleman, and a handsome man, than to make him give me back my own. Inside the liberties of a town a poor man might now and then see the face of justice; but out among the grand seigneurs and dames—never.' So I said, 'I'll sit down robbed rather than seek justice and find gallows.' They were all most kind to me next day; and the girl proffered me money from her small wage to help me towards Rhine."

"Oh, then, he is coming home! he is coming home!' shouted Denys, interrupting the reader. She shook her head gently at him, by way of reproof.

"I beg pardon, all the company," said he stiffly.

"'Twas a sore temptation; but, being a servant, my stomach rose against it. 'Nay, nay,' said I. She told me I was wrong. ''Twas pride out o' place; poor folk should help one another; or who on earth would?' I said if I could do aught in return 'twere well; but for a free gift, nay: I was over much beholden already. Should I write a letter for her? 'Nay, he is in the house at present,' said she. 'Should I draw her picture, and so earn my money?' 'What, can ye?' said she. I told her I could try; and her habit would well become a picture. So she was agog to be limned, and give it her lad. And I set her to stand in a good light, and soon made sketches two, whereof I send thee one, coloured at odd hours. The other I did most hastily, and with little conscience daub, for which may Heaven forgive me; but time was short. They, poor things, knew no better, and were most proud and joyous; and, both kissing me after their country fashion, 'twas the hind that was her sweetheart, they did bid me God-speed; and I towards Rhine."

Margaret paused here, and gave Denys the coloured drawing to hand round. It was eagerly examined by the females on account of the costume, which differed in some respects from that of a Dutch domestic: the hair was in a tight linen bag, a yellow half kerchief crossed her head from ear to ear, but threw out a rectangular point that descended the centre of her forehead, and it met in two more points over her bosom. She wore a red kirtle with long sleeves, kilted very high in front, and showing a green farthingale and a great red leather purse hanging down over it; red stockings, yellow leathern shoes, ahead of her age; for they were low-quartered and square-toed, secured by a strap buckling over the instep, which was not uncommon, and was perhaps the rude germ of the diamond buckle to come.

Margaret continued:—

"But, oh! how I missed my Denys at every step! often I sat down on the road and groaned. And in the afternoon it chanced that I did so set me down where two roads met, and with heavy head in hand, and heavy heart, did think of thee, my poor sweetheart, and of my lost friend, and of the little house at Tergou, where they all loved me once; though now it is turned to hate."

Catherine.] "Alas! that he will think so."

Eli.] "Whist! wife!"

"And I did sigh loud, and often. And me sighing so, one came carolling like a bird adown t'other road. 'Ay, chirp and chirp,' cried I, bitterly. 'Thou hast not lost sweetheart, and friend, thy father's hearth, thy mother's smile, and every penny in the world.' And at last he did so carol, and carol, I jumped up in ire to get away from his most jarring mirth. But, ere I fled from it, I looked down the path to see what could make a man so light hearted in this weary world; and lo! the songster was a humpbacked cripple, with a bloody bandage o'er his eye, and both legs gone at the knee.'

"He! he! he! he! he!" went Sybrandt, laughing and cackling.

Margaret's eyes flashed: she began to fold the letter up.

"Nay, lass," said Eli, "heed him not! Thou unmannerly cur, offer't but again and I put thee to the door."

"Why, what was there to gibe at, Sybrandt?" remonstrated Catherine, more mildly. "Is not our Kate afflicted? and is she not the most content of us all, and singeth like a merle at times between her pains? But I am as bad as thou; prithee read on, lass, and stop our gabble wi' somewhat worth the hearkening."

"Then, said I, 'may this thing be?' And I took myself to task. 'Gerard, son of Eli, dost thou well to bemoan thy lot, that hast youth and health; and here comes the wreck of nature on crutches, praising God's goodness with singing like a mavis?'"

Catherine.] "There you see."

Eli.] "Whist, dame, whist!"

"And whenever he saw me, he left carolling and presently hobbled up and chanted, 'Charity, for love of Heaven, sweet master, charity,' with a whine as piteous as wind at keyhole. 'Alack, poor soul,' said I, 'charity is in my heart, but not my purse; I am poor as thou.' Then he believed me none, and to melt me undid his sleeve, and showed a sore wound on his arm, and said he: 'Poor cripple though I be, I am like to lose this eye to boot, look else.' I saw and groaned for him, and to excuse myself let him wot how I have been robbed of my last copper. Thereat he left whining all in a moment, and said, in a big manly voice, 'Then I'll e'en take a rest. Here, youngster, pull thou this strap: nay, fear not!' I pulled, and down·came a stout pair of legs out of his back; and half his hump had melted away, and the wound in his eye no deeper than the bandage."

"Oh!" ejaculated Margaret's hearers, in a body.

"Whereat, seeing me astounded, he laughed in my face, and told me I was not worth gulling, and offered me his protection. 'My face was prophetic,' he said. 'Of what?' said I. 'Marry,' said he, 'that its owner will starve in this thievish land.' Travel teaches e'en the young wisdom. Time was I had turned and fled this impostor as a pestilence; but now I listened patiently to pick up crumbs of counsel. And well I did: for nature and his adventurous life had crammed the poor knave with shrewdness and knowledge of the homelier sort—a child was I beside him. When he had turned me inside out, said he, 'Didst well to leave France and make for Germany; but think not of Holland again. Nay, on to Augsburg and Nürnberg, the Paradise of craftsmen: thence to Venice, an thou wilt. But thou wilt never bide in Italy nor any other land, having once tasted the great German cities. Why there is but one honest country in Europe, and that is Germany; and since thou art honest, and since I am a vagabone, Germany was made for us twain.' I bade him make that good: how might one country fit true men and knaves? 'Why, thou novice,' said he, 'because in an honest land are fewer knaves to bite the honest man, and many honest men for the knave to bite. I was in luck, being honest, to have fallen in with a friendly sharp. Be my pal,' said he. 'I go to Nürnberg, we will reach it with full pouches. I'll learn ye the cul de bois, and the cul de jatte, and how to maund, and chant, and patter, and to raise swellings, and paint sores and ulcers on thy body would take in the divell.' I told him, shivering, I'd liever die than shame myself and my folk so."

Eli.] "Good lad! good lad!"

"Why what shame was it for such as I to turn beggar? Beggary was an ancient and most honourable mystery. What did holy monks, and bishops, and kings, when they would win Heaven's smile? why, wash the feet of beggars, those favourites of the saints. 'The saints were no fools,' he told me. Then he did put out his foot. 'Look at that, that was washed by the greatest king alive, Louis of France, the last holy Thursday that was. And the next day, Friday, clapped in the stocks by the warden of a petty hamlet.' So I told him my foot should walk between such high honour and such low disgrace, on the safe path of honesty, please God. Well then, since I had not spirit to beg, he would indulge my perversity. I should work under him, he be the head, I the fingers. And with that he set himself up like a judge, on a heap of dust by the road's side, and questioned me strictly what I could do. I began to say I was strong and willing. 'Bah!' said he, 'so is an ox. Say, what canst do that Sir Ox cannot?' I could write; I had won a prize for it. 'Canst write as fast as the printers?' quo' he, jeering. 'What else?' I could paint. 'That was better.' I was like to tear my hair to hear him say so, and me going to Rome to write. I could twang the psaltery a bit. 'That was well. Could I tell stories?' Ay, by the score. 'Then,' said he, 'I hire you from this moment.' 'What to do?' said I. 'Nought crooked, Sir Candour,' says he. 'I will feed thee all the way and find thee work; and take half thine earnings, no more.' 'Agreed,' said I, and gave my hand on it. 'Now, servant,' said he, 'we will dine. But ye need not stand behind my chair, for two reasons, first I ha' got no chair, and, next, good fellowship likes me better than state.' And out of his wallet he brought flesh, fowl, and pastry, a good dozen of spices lapped in flax paper, and wine fit for a king. Ne'er feasted I better than out of this beggar's wallet, now my master. When we had well eaten I was for going on. 'But,' said he, 'servants should not drive their masters too hard, especially after feeding, for then the body is for repose, and the mind turns to contemplation;' and he lay on his back gazing calmly at the sky, and presently wondered whether there were any beggars up there. I told him I knew but of one; called Lazarus. 'Could he do the cul de jatte better than I?' said he, and looked quite jealous like. I told him nay; Lazarus was honest, though a beggar, and fed daily of the crumbs fal'n from a rich man's table, and the dogs licked his sores. 'Servant,' quo' he, 'I spy a foul fault in thee. Thou liest without discretion: now the end of lying being to gull, this is no better than fumbling with the divell's tail. I pray Heaven thou mayest prove to paint better than thou cuttest whids, or I am done out of a dinner. No beggar eats crumbs, but only the fat of the land; and dogs lick not a beggar's sores, being made with spearwort, or ratsbane, or biting acids, from all which dogs, and even pigs, abhor. My sores are made after my proper receipt; but no dog would lick e'en them twice. I have made a scurvy bargain: art a cozening knave. I doubt, as well as a nincompoop.' I deigned no reply to this bundle of lies, which did accuse heavenly truth of falsehood for not being in a tale with him. He rose and we took the road; and presently we came to a place where were two little wayside inns, scarce a furlong apart. 'Halt,' said my master. 'Their armories are sore faded—all the better. Go thou in; shun the master; board the wife; and flatter her inn sky high, all but the armories, and offer to colour them dirt cheap.' So I went in and told the wife I was a painter, and would revive her armories cheap; but she sent me away with a rebuff. I to my master. He groaned. 'Ye are all fingers and no tongue,' said he; 'I have made a scurvy bargain. Come and hear me patter and flatter.' Between the two inns was a high hedge. He goes behind it a minute and comes out a decent tradesman. We went on to the other inn, and then I heard him praise it so fulsome as the very wife did blush. 'But,' says he, 'there is one little, little fault; your armories are dull and faded. Say but the word, and for a silver franc my apprentice here, the cunningest e'er I had, shall make them bright as ever.' Whilst she hesitated, the rogue told her he had done it to a little inn hard by, and now the inn's face was like the starry firmament. "D'ye hear that, my man?' cries she, 'The Three Frogs' have been and painted up their armories: shall 'The Four Hedgehogs' be outshone by them?'" So I painted, and my master stood by like a lord, advising me how to do, and winking to me to heed him none, and I got a silver franc. And he took me back to 'The Three Frogs,' and on the way put me on a beard and disguised me, and flattered 'The Three Frogs,' and told them how he had adorned 'The Four Hedgehogs,' and into the net jumped the three poor simple frogs, and I earned another silver franc. Then we went on and he found his crutches, and sent me forward, and showed his 'cicatrices d'emprunt,' as he called them, and all his infirmities, at 'The Four Hedgehogs,' and got both food and money. 'Come, share and share,' quoth he: so I gave him one franc. 'I have made a good bargain,' said he. 'Art a master limner, but takest too much time.' So I let him know that in matters of honest craft things could not be done quick and well. 'Then do them quick,' quoth he. And he told me my name was Bon Bec; and I might call him Cul de Jatte, because that was his lay at our first meeting. And at the next town my master, Cul de Jatte, bought me a psaltery, and sat himself up again by the roadside in state like him that erst judged Marsyas and Apollo, piping for vain glory. So I played a strain. 'Indifferent well, harmonious Bon Bec,' said he, haughtily. 'Now tune thy pipes.' So I did sing a sweet strain the good monks taught me; and singing it reminded poor Bon Bec, Gerard erst, of his young days and home, and brought the water to mine een. But, looking up, my master's visage was as the face of a little boy whipt soundly, or sipping foulest medicine. 'Zounds, stop that belly-ache blether,' quoth he, 'that will ne'er wile a stiver out o' peasants' purses; 'twill but sour the nurses' milk, and gar the kine jump into rivers to be out of earshot on't. What, false knave, did I buy thee a fire new psaltery to be minded o' my latter end withal? Hearken! these be the songs that glad the heart, and fill the minstrel's purse.' And he sung so blasphemous a stave, and eke so obscene, as I drew away from him a space that the lightning might not spoil the new psaltery. However, none came, being winter, and then I said, 'Master, the Lord is débonair. Held I the thunder yon ribaldry had been thy last, thou foul mouthed wretch.'

" 'Why, Bon Bec, what is to do?' quoth he. 'I have made an ill bargain. Oh, perverse heart, that turneth from doctrine.' So I bade him keep his breath to cool his broth, ne'er would I shame my folk with singing ribald songs. 'Then,' says he, sulkily, 'the first fire we light by the way side, clap thou on the music-box! so 'twill make our pot boil for the nonce; but with your

> Good people, let us peak and pine,
> Cut tristful mugs, and miaul and whine
> Thorough our nosen chaunts divine

never, never, never. Ye might as well go through Lorraine crying, Mulleygrubs, Mulleygrubs, who'll buy my Mulleygrubs?' So we fared on, bad friends. But I took a thought, and prayed him hum me one of his naughty ditties again. Then he brightened, and broke forth into ribaldry like a nightingale. Finger in ears stuffed I. 'No words; nought but the bare melody.' For oh, Margaret, note the sly malice of the Evil One! Still to the scurviest matter he weddeth the tunablest ditties."

Catherine.] "That is true as Holy Writ."

The Cloister and the Hearth

Sybrandt.] "How know you that, mother?"

Cornelis.] "He! he! he!"

Eli.] "Whisht, ye uneasy wights, and let me hear the boy. He is wiser than ye; wiser than his years."

" 'What tomfoolery is this?' said he; yet he yielded to me, and soon I garnered three of his melodies; but I would not let Cul de Jatte wot the thing I meditated. 'Show not fools nor bairns unfinished work,' saith the byword. And by this time 'twas night, and a little town at hand, where we went each to his inn; for my master would not yield to put off his rags and other sores till morning; nor I to enter an inn with a tatterdemalion. So we were to meet on the road at peep of day. And, indeed, we still lodged apart, meeting at morn and parting at eve, outside each town we lay at. And waking at midnight and cogitating, good thoughts came down to me, and sudden my heart was enlightened. I called to mind that my Margaret had withstood the taking of the burgomaster's purse. ''Tis theft,' said you; 'disguise it how ye will.' But I must be wiser than my betters: and now that which I had as good as stolen, others had stolen from me. As it came so it was gone. Then I said, 'Heaven is not cruel, but just;' and I vowed a vow, to repay our burgomaster every shilling an I could. And I went forth in the morning sad, but hopeful. I felt lighter for the purse being gone. My master was at the gate becrutched. I told him I'd liever have seen him in another disguise. 'Beggars must not be choosers,' said he. However, soon be bade me untruss him, for he felt sadly. His head swam. I told him, forcefully to deform nature thus could scarce be wholesome. He answered none; but looked scared, and hand on head. By-and-by he gave a groan, and rolled on the ground like a ball, and writhed sore. I was scared, and wist not what to do, but went to lift him; but his trouble rose higher and higher, he gnashed his teeth fearfully, and the foam did fly from his lips; and presently his body bended itself like a bow, and jerked and bounded many times into the air. I exorcised him; it but made him worse. There was water in a ditch hard by, not very clear; but, the poor creature struggling between life and death, I filled my hat withal, and came flying to souse him. Then my lord laughed in my face. 'Come, Bon Bec, by thy white gills, I have not forgotten my trade.' I stood with watery hat in hand, glaring. 'Could this be feigning?' 'What else?' said he. 'Why, a real fit is the sorriest thing; but a

stroke with a feather compared with mine. Art still betters nature.'
'But look, e'en now blood trickleth from your nose,' said I. 'Ay,
ay, pricked my nostrils with a straw.' 'But ye foamed at the lips.'
'Oh, a little soap makes a mickle foam.' And he drew out a morsel
like a bean from his mouth. 'Thank thy stars, Bon Bec,' says he,
'for leading thee to a worthy master. Each day his lesson. To-
morrow we will study the cul de bois and other branches. To-day,
own me prince of demoniacs, and indeed of all good fellows.' Then,
being puffed up, he forgot yesterday's grudge, and discoursed me
freely of beggars; and gave me, who eftsoons thought a beggar was
a beggar, and there an end, the names and qualities of full thirty
sorts of masterful and crafty mendicants in France and Germany,
and England; his three provinces; for so the poor, proud knave
yclept those kingdoms three; wherein his throne it was the stocks
I ween. And outside the next village one had gone to dinner, and
left his wheel-barrow. So says he, 'I'll tie myself in a knot, and
shalt wheel me through; and what with my crippledom and thy
piety, a-wheeling of thy poor old dad, we'll bleed the bumpkins of
a dacha-saltee.' I did refuse. I would work for him; but no hand
would have in begging. 'And wheeling an "asker" in a barrow, is
not that work?' said he; 'then fling yon muckle stone in to boot:
stay, I'll soil it a bit, and swear it is a chip of the holy sepulchre;
and you wheeled us both from Jerusalem.' Said I, 'Wheeling a
pair o' lies, one stony, one fleshly, may be work, and hard work,
but honest work 'tis not. 'Tis fumbling with his tail you wot of.
And,' said I, 'master, next time you go to tempt me to knavery,
speak not to me of my poor old dad.' Said I, 'you have minded me
of my real father's face, the truest man in Holland. He and I are
ill friends now, worse luck. But though I offend him, shame him
I never will.' Dear Margaret, with this knave saying, 'your poor
old dad,' it had gone to my heart like a knife. ' 'Tis well,' said
my master, gloomily; 'I have made a bad bargain.' Presently he
halts, and eyes a tree by the wayside. 'Go spell me what is writ
on yon tree.' So I went, and there was nought but a long square
drawn in outline. I told him so. 'So much for thy monkish lore,'
quoth he. A little farther, and he sent me to read a wall. There
was nought but a circle scratched on the stone with a point of nail
or knife, and in the circle two dots. I said so. Then said he,
'Bon Bec, that square was a warning. Some good Truand left it,

that came through this village faring west; that means "dangerous." The circle with the two dots was writ by another of our brotherhood; and it signifies as how the writer, soit Rollin Trapu, soit Triboulet, soit Catin Cul de Bois, or what not, was *becked* for *asking* here, and lay two months in Starabin.' Then he broke forth, 'Talk of your little snivelling books that go in pouch. Three books have I, France, England, and Germany; and they are writ all over in one tongue, that my brethren of all countries understand; and that is what I call learning. So sith here they whip sores, and imprison infirmities, I to my tiring room.' And he popped behind the hedge, and came back worshipful. We passed through the village, and I sat me down on the stocks, and even as the barber's apprentice whets his razor on a block, so did I flesh my psaltery on this village, fearing great cities. I tuned it, and coursed up and down the wires nimbly with my two wooden strikers; and then chanted loud and clear, as I had heard the minstrels of the country,

'QUI VEUT OUÏR QUI VEUT SAVOIR,'

some trash, I mind not what. And soon the villagers, male and female, thronged about me; thereat I left singing, and recited them to the psaltery a short but right merry tale out of 'the lives of the saints,' which it is my handbook of pleasant figments: and this ended, instantly struck up and whistled one of Cul de Jatte's devil's ditties, and played it on the psaltery to boot. Thou knowest Heaven hath bestowed on me a rare whistle, both for compass and tune. And with me whistling bright and full this sprightly air, and making the wires slow when the tune did gallop, and tripping when the tune did amble, or I did stop and shake on one note like a lark i' the air, they were like to eat me; but looking round, lo! my master had given way to his itch, and there was his hat on the ground, and copper pouring in. I deemed it cruel to whistle the bread out of poverty's pouch; so broke off and away; yet could not get clear so swift, but both men and women did slobber me sore, and smelled all of garlic. 'There, master,' said I, 'I call that cleaving the divell in twain and keeping his white half.' Said he, 'Bon Bec, I have made a good bargain.' Then he bade me stay where I was while he went to the Holy Land. I stayed, and he leaped the churchyard dike, and the sexton was digging a grave, and my master chaffered with him, and came back with a knuckle bone. But, why he clept

The Cloister and the Hearth

a churchyard Holy Land, that I learned not then, but after dinner.
I was colouring the armories of a little inn; and he sat by me most
peaceable, a cutting, and filing, and polishing bones, sedately; so
I speered was not honest work sweet? 'As rain water,' said he,
mocking. 'What was he a making?' 'A pair of bones to play on
with thee; and with the refuse a St. Anthony's thumb and a St.
Martin's little finger, for the devout.' The vagabone! And now,
sweet Margaret, thou seest our manner of life faring Rhineward.
I with the two arts I had least prized or counted on for bread was
welcome everywhere; too poor now to fear robbers, yet able to keep
both master and man on the road. For at night I often made a
portraiture of the innkeeper or his dame, and so went richer from
an inn; the which it is the lot of few. But my master despised
this even way of life. 'I love ups and downs,' said he. And certes
he lacked them not. One day he would gather more than I in
three; another, to hear his tale, it had rained kicks all day in lieu
of 'saltees,' and that is pennies. Yet even then at heart he despised
me for a poor, mechanical soul, and scorned my arts, extolling his
own, the art of feigning.

"Natheless, at odd times was he ill at his ease. Going through
the town of Aix, we came upon a beggar walking, fast by one hand
to a cart-tail, and the hangman a lashing his bare bloody back. He,
stout knave, so whipt, did not a jot relent; but I did wince at every
stroke; and my master hung his head.

"'Soon or late, Bon Bec,' quoth he. 'Soon or late.' I seeing his
haggard face knew what he meaned. And at a town whose name
hath slipped me, but 'twas on a fair river, as we came to the foot of
the bridge, he halted and shuddered. 'Why, what is the coil,' said
I? 'Oh, blind,' said he, 'they are justifying there.' So nought
would serve him but take a boat, and cross the river by water. But
'twas out of the frying-pan, as the word goeth. For the boatmen
had scarce told us the matter, and that it was a man and a woman
for stealing glazed windows out of housen, and that the man was
hanged at daybreak, and the quean to be drowned, when lo; they
did fling her off the bridge, and fell in the water not far from us.
And oh! Margaret, the deadly splash! It ringeth in mine ears
even now. But worse was coming; for, though tied, she came up
and cried 'help help!' and I, forgetting all, and hearing a woman's
voice cry 'help!' was for leaping in to save her, and had surely done

383

it, but the boatmen and Cul de Jatte clung round me, and in a
moment the bourreau's man, that waited in a boat, came and entangled his hooked pole in her long hair, and so thrust her down and
ended her. Oh! if the saints answered so our cries for help! And
poor Cul de Jatte groaned, and I sat sobbing and beat my breast and
cried, 'Of what hath God made men's hearts?' "

The reader stopped, and the tears trickled down her cheeks.
Gerard crying in Lorraine made her cry at Rotterdam. The
leagues were no more to her heart than the breadth of a room.

Eli, softened by many touches in the letter, and by the reader's
womanly graces, said kindly enough, "Take thy time, lass. And
methinks some of ye might find her a creepie to rest her foot, and
she so near her own trouble."

"I'd do more for her than that an I durst," said Catherine.
"Here, Cornelis," and she held out her little wooden stool, and that
worthy, who hated Margaret worse than ever, had to take the
creepie and put it carefully under her foot.

"You are very kind, dame," she faltered. "I will read on; 'tis
all I can do for you in turn."

"Thus seeing my master ashy and sore shaken, I deemed this
horrible tragic act came timeously to warn him, so I strove sore to
turn him from his ill ways, discoursing of sinners and their lethal
end. 'Too late!' said he, 'too late!' and gnashed his teeth. Then
I told him 'too late' was the divell's favourite whisper in repentant
ears. Said I—

> "The Lord is débonair,
> Let sinners nought despair.'

'Too late!' said he, and gnashed his teeth, and writhed his face, as
though vipers were biting his inward parts. But, dear heart, his
was a mind like running water. Ere we cleared the town he was
carolling, and outside the gate hung the other culprit from the
bough of a little tree, and scarce a yard above the ground. And
that stayed my vagabone's music. But, ere we had gone another
furlong, he feigned to have dropped his rosary, and ran back, with
no good intent, as you shall hear. I strolled on very slowly, and
often halting, and presently he came stumping up on one leg, and
that bandaged. I asked him how he could contrive that, for 'twas
masterly done. 'Oh, that was his mystery. Would I know that I

must join the brotherhood.' And presently we did pass a narrow lane, and at the mouth on't espied a written stone, telling beggars by a word like a wee pitchfork to go that way. ''Tis yon farmhouse,' said he: 'bide thou at hand.' And he went to the house, and came back with money, food, and wine. 'This lad did the business,' said he, slapping his one leg proudly. Then he undid the bandage, and with prideful face showed me a hole in his calf you could have put your neef in. Had I been strange to his tricks, here was a leg had drawn my last penny. Presently another farmhouse by the road. He made for it. I stood and asked myself should I run away and leave him, not to be shamed in my own despite by him? But, while I doubted, there was a great noise, and my master well cudgelled by the farmer and his men, and came towards me hobbling and holloaing; for the peasants had layed on heartily. But more trouble was at his heels. Some mischievous wight loosed a dog as big as a jackass colt, and came roaring after him, and downed him momently. I deeming the poor rogue's death certain, and him least fit to die, drew my sword and ran shouting. But, ere I could come near, the muckle dog had torn away his bad leg, and ran growling to his lair with it; and Cul de Jatte slipped his knot, and came running like a lapwing, with his hair on end, and so striking with both crutches before and behind at unreal dogs as 'twas like a windmill crazed. He fled adown the road. I followed leisurely, and found him at dinner. 'Curse the quiens,' said he. And not a word all dinner-time but 'curse the quiens!'

"I said I must know who they were before I would curse them.

" 'Quiens? why that was dogs. And I knew not even that much? He had made a bad bargain.' 'Well, well,' said he; 'to-morrow we shall be in Germany. There the folk are music-bitten, and they molest not beggars, unless they fake to boot, and then they drown us out of hand that moment, curse 'em!' We came to Strasburgh. And I looked down Rhine with longing heart. The stream how swift! It seemed running to clip Sevenbergen to its soft bosom. With but a piece of timber and an oar, I might drift at my ease to thee, sleeping yet gliding still. 'Twas a sore temptation. But the fear of an ill welcome from my folk, and of the neighbours' sneers, and the hope of coming back to thee victorious, not, as now I must, defeated and shamed, and thee with me, it did withhold me; and so, with many sighs, and often turning of the head to look on beloved Rhine, I turned sorrowful face and heavy heart towards Augsburg."

"Alas, dame, alas. Good master Eli, forgive me! But I ne'er can win over this part all at one time. It taketh my breath away. Well-a-day! Why did he not listen to his heart? Had he not gone through peril enow, sorrow enow? Well-a-day! well-a-day!"

The letter dropped from her hand, and she drooped like a wounded lily.

Then there was a clatter on the floor, and it was little Kate going on her crutches, with flushed face, and eyes full of pity, to console her. "Water, mother," she cried. "I am afeard she shall swoon."

"Nay, nay, fear me not," said Margaret, feebly. "I will not be so troublesome. Thy good will it maketh me stouter hearted, sweet mistress Kate. For, if thou carest how I fare, sure Heaven is not against me."

Catherine.] "D'ye hear that, my man?"

Eli.]"Ay, wife, I hear; and mark to boot."

Little Kate went back to her place, and Margaret read on. "The Germans are fonder of armorials than the French. So I found work every day. And, whiles I wrought, my master would leave me, and doff his raiment and don his rags, and other infirmities, and cozen the world, which he did clepe it 'plucking of the goose:' this done, would meet me and demand half my earnings; and with restless piercing eye ask me would I be so base as cheat my poor master by making three parts in lieu of two, till I threatened to lend him a cuff to boot in requital of his suspicion; and thenceforth took his due, with feigned confidence in my good faith, the which his dancing eye belied. Early in Germany we had a quarrel. I had seen him buy a skull of a jailer's wife, and mighty zealous a polishing it. Thought I, 'How can he carry yon memento, and not repent, seeing where ends his way?' Presently I did catch him selling it to a woman for the head of St. Barnabas, with a tale had cozened an Ebrew. So I snatched it out of their hands, and trundled it into the ditch. 'How, thou impious knave,' said I, 'wouldst sell for a saint the skull of some dead thief, thy brother.' He slunk away. But shallow she did crawl after the skull, and with apron reverently dust it for Barnabas, and it Barabbas; and so home with it. Said I, 'non vult anser velli, sed populus vult decipi.' "

Catherine.] "Oh, the goodly Latin!"

The Cloister and the Hearth

Eli.] "What meaneth it?"

Catherine.] "Nay, I know not; but 'tis Latin: is not that enow? He was the flower of the flock."

"Then I to him, 'Take now thy psaltery, and part we here, for art a walking prison, a walking hell.' But lo! my master fell on his knees, and begged me for pity's sake not turn him off. 'What would become of him? He did so love honesty.' 'Thou love honesty?' said I. 'Ay,' said he, 'not to enact it; the saints forbid. But to look on. 'Tis so fair a thing to look on. Alas, good Bon Bec,' said he; 'hadst starved peradventure but for me. Kick not down thy ladder! Call ye that just? Nay, calm thy choler! Have pity on me! I must have a pal: and how could I bear one like myself after one so simple as thou? He might cut my throat for the money that is hid in my belt. 'Tis not much; 'tis not much. With thee I walk at mine ease; with a sharp I dare not go before in a narrow way. Alas! forgive me. Now I know where in thy bonnet lurks the bee, I will ware his sting; I will but pluck the secular goose.' 'So be it,' said I. 'And example was contagious: he should be a true man by then we reached Nurnberg. 'Twas a long way to Nurnberg.' Seeing him so humble, I said, 'Well, doff rags, and make thyself decent; 'twill help me forget what thou art.' And he did so; and we sat down to our nonemete. Presently came by a reverend palmer with hat stuck round with cockle shells from Holy Land, and great rosary of beads like eggs of teal, and sandals for shoes. And he leaned aweary on his long staff, and offered us a shell apiece. My master would none. But I to set him a better example, took one, and for it gave the poor pilgrim two batzen, and had his blessing. And he was scarce gone, when we heard savage cries, and came a sorry sight, one leading a wild woman in a chain, all rags, and howling like a wolf. And when they came nigh us, she fell to tearing her rags to threads. The man sought an alms of us, and told us his hard case. 'Twas his wife, stark raving mad; and he could not work in the fields, and leave her in his house to fire it, nor cure her could he without the Saintys help, and had vowed six pounds of wax to St. Anthony to heal her, and so was fain beg of charitable folk for the money. And now she espied us, and flew at me with her long nails, and I was cold with fear, so devilish showed her face and rolling eyes and nails like birdys talons. But he with the chain checked her sudden, and with his whip did cruelly

387

lash her for it, that I cried 'Forbear! forbear! She knoweth not
what she doth;' and gave him a batz. And being gone, said I,
'Master of those twain I know not which is the more pitiable.' And
he laughed in my face. 'Behold thy justice, Bon Bec,' said he.
'Thou railest on thy poor, good, within-an-ace-of-honest, master, and
bestowest alms on a "vopper."' 'Vopper,' said I; 'what is a vopper?
Why a trull that feigns madness. That was one of us, that sham
maniac, and wow but she did it clumsily. I blushed for her and
thee. Also gavest two batzen for a shell from Holy Land, that
came no farther than Normandy. I have culled them myself on
that coast by scores, and sold them to pilgrims true and pilgrims
false, to gull flats like thee withal.' 'What!' said I; 'that reverend
man?' 'One of us!' cried Cul de Jatte; 'one of us! In France
we call them "Coquillarts," but here "Calmierers." Railest on me
for selling a false relic now and then, and wastest thy earnings on
such as sell nought else. I tell thee, Bon Bec,' said he, 'there is
not one true relic on earth's face. The saints died a thousand
years agone, and their bones mixed with the dust; but the trade in
relics, it is of yesterday; and there are forty thousand tramps in
Europe live by it; selling relics of forty or fifty bodies; oh, threadbare lie! And of the true Cross enow to build Cologne Minster.
Why then may not poor Cul de Jatte turn his penny with the
crowd? Art but a scurvy tyrannical servant to let thy poor master from his share of the swag with your whorson pilgrims, palmers,
and friars, black, grey, and crutched; for all these are of our
brotherhood, and of our art, only masters they, and we but poor ap-
prentices, in guile.' For his tongue was an ell and a half.

"'A truce to thy irreverend sophistries,' said I, 'and say what
company is this a-coming.' 'Bohemians,' cried he. 'Ay, ay, this
shall be the rest of the band.' With that came along so motley a
crew as never your eyes beheld, dear Margaret. Marched at their
head one with a banner on a steel-pointed lance, and girded with a
great long sword, and in velvet doublet and leathern jerkin, the
which stuffs ne'er saw I wedded afore on mortal flesh, and a gay
feather in his lordly cap, and a couple of dead fowls at his back,
the which, an the spark had come by honestly, I am much mistook.
Him followed wives and babes on two lean horses, whose flanks still
rattled like parchment drum, being beaten by kettles and caldrons.
Next an armed man a-riding of a horse, which drew a cart full of

females and children: and in it, sitting backwards, a lusty lazy
knave, lance in hand, with his luxurious feet raised on a holy water-
pail, that lay along, and therein a cat, new kittened, sat glowing
o'er her brood, and sparks for eyes. And the cart-horse cavalier
had on his shoulders a round bundle, and thereon did perch a cock
and crowed with zeal, poor ruffler, proud of his brave feathers as
the rest, and haply with more reason, being his own. And on an
ass another wife and new-born child; and one poor quean a-foot
scarce dragged herself along, so near her time was she, yet held two
little ones by the hand, and helplessly helped them on the road.
And the little folk were just a farce; some rode sticks, with horses'
heads, between their legs, which pranced and caracoled, and soon
wearied the riders so sore, they stood stock still and wept, which
cavaliers were presently taken into cart and cuffed. And one more
grave, lost in a man's hat and feather, walked in Egyptian darkness, handed by a girl; another had the great saucepan on his back,
and a tremendous three-footed clay pot sat on his head and shoulders, swallowing him so as he too went darkling led by his sweetheart three foot high. When they were gone by, and we had both
laughed lustily, said I, 'Natheless, master, my bowels they yearn
for one of that tawdry band, even for the poor wife so near the
down-lying, scarce able to drag herself, yet still, poor soul, helping
the weaker on the way.'"

Catherine.] "Nay, nay, Margaret. Why, wench, pluck up heart.
Certes thou art no Bohemian."

Kate.] "Nay, mother, 'tis not that, I trow, but her father. And,
dear heart, why take notice to put her to the blush?"

Richart.] "So I say."

"And he derided me. 'Why that is a "biltreger,"' said he, 'and
you waste your bowels on a pillow, or so forth.' I told him he
lied. 'Time would show,' said he, 'wait till they camp.' And
rising after meat and meditation, and travelling forward, we found
them camped between two great trees on a common by the wayside;
and they had lighted a great fire, and on it was their caldron; and,
one of the trees slanting o'er the fire, a kid hung down by a chain
from the tree-fork to the fire, and in the fork was wedged an urchin
turning still the chain to keep the meat from burning, and a gay
spark with a feather in his cap cut up a sheep; and another had

spitted a leg of it on a wooden stake; and a woman ended chanticleer's pride with wringing of his neck. And under the other tree four ruffers played at cards and quarrelled, and no word sans oath; and of these lewd gamblers one had cockles in his hat, and was my reverend pilgrim. And a female, young and comely, and dressed like a butterfly, sat and mended a heap of dirty rags. And Cul de Jatte said, 'Yon is the "vopper," ' and I looked incredulous and looked again, and it was so, and at her feet sat he that had so late lashed her; but I ween he had wist where to strike, or woe betide him; and she did now oppress him sore, and made him thread her very needle, the which he did with all humility; so was their comedy turned seamy side without: and Cul de Jatte told me 'twas still so with 'voppers' and their men in camp; they would don their bravery though but for an hour, and, with their tinsel, empire, and the man durst not the least gainsay the 'vopper,' or she would turn him off at these times, as I my master, and take another tyrant more submissive. And my master chuckled over me. Natheless we soon espied a wife set with her back against the tree, and her hair down, and her face white, and by her side a wench held up to her eye a new-born babe, with words of cheer, and the rough fellow, her husband, did bring her hot wine in a cup, and bade her take courage. And, just o'er the place she sat, they had pinned from bough to bough of those neighbouring trees two shawls, and blankets two, together, to keep the drizzle off her. And so had another poor little rogue come into the world: and by her own particular folk tended gipsywise, but of the roasters, and boilers, and voppers, and gamblers, no more noticed, no not for a single moment, than sheep which droppeth her lamb in a field, by travellers upon the way. Then said I, 'What of thy foul suspicions, master? overknavery blinds the eye as well as over-simplicity.' And he laughed and said, 'Triumph, Bon Bec, triumph. The chances were nine in ten against thee.' Then I did pity her, to be in a crowd at such a time; but he rebuked me. 'I should pity rather your queens and royal duchesses, which by law are condemned to groan in a crowd of nobles and courtiers, and do writhe with shame as well as sorrow, being come of decent mothers, whereas these gipsy women have no more shame under their skins than a wolf ruth, or a hare valour. And, Bon Bec,' quoth he, 'I espy in thee a lamentable fault. Wastest thy bowels. Wilt have none left for thy poor good master which doeth thy will by night and day.' Then we came forward; and he talked with the men in some strange Hebrew cant whereof no word knew I; and the poor knaves bade us welcome and denied us nought. With them, and all they had, 'twas lightly come and lightly go; and when we left them my master said to me, 'This is thy first lesson, but to-night we shall lie at Hansburgh. Come with me to the "rotboss" there, and I'll show thee all our folk and their lays, and especially "the lossners," "the dutzers," "the schleppers," "the gickisses," "the schwanfelders," whom in England we call "shivering Jemmies," "the süntvegers," "the schwiegers," "the joners," "the sessel-degers," "the gensscherers," in France "marcandiers or rifodés," "the veranerins," "the stabulers," with a few foreigners like ourselves, such as "pietres," "francmitoux," "polissons," "malingreux," "traters," "rufflers," "whipjalks," "dommerars," "glymmerars," "jarkmen," "patricos," "swadders," "autem morts," "walking morts," '—'Enow,' cried I, stopping him, 'art as gleesome as the Evil one a counting of his imps. I'll jot down in my tablet all these caitiffs and their accursed names, for knowledge is knowledge. But go among them, alive or dead, that will I not with my good will. Moreover,' said I, 'what need? since I have a companion in thee who is all the knaves on earth in one?' and thought to abash him; but his face shone with pride, and hand on breast he did bow low to me. 'If thy wit be scant, good Bon Bec, thy manners are a charm. I have made a good bargain.' So he to the 'rotboss,' and I to a decent inn, and sketched the landlord's daughter by candle-light, and started at morn batzen three the richer, but could not find my master, so loitered slowly on, and presently met him coming west for me, and cursing the quiens. Why so? Because he could blind the culls but not the quiens. At last I prevailed on him to leave cursing and canting, and tell me his adventure. Said he, 'I sat outside the gate of yon monastery, full of sores, which I showed the passers-by. Oh, Bon Bec, beautifuller sores you never saw: and it rained coppers in my hat. Presently the monks came home from some procession, and the convent dogs ran out to meet them, curse the quiens!' 'What, did they fall on thee and bite thee, poor soul?' 'Worse, worse, dear Bon Bec. Had they bitten me I had earned silver. But the great idiots, being, as I think, puppies, or little better, fell on me where I sat, downed me, and fell a licking my sores among them.

As thou, false knave, didst swear the whelps in heaven licked the
sores of Lazybones, a beggar of old.' 'Nay, nay,' said I, 'I said
no such thing. But tell me, since they bit thee not, but sportfully
licked thee, what harm?' 'What harm, noodle, why the sores came
off.' 'How could that be?' 'How could aught else be? and them
just fresh put on. Did I think he was so weak as bite holes in
his flesh with ratsbane? Nay, he was an artist, a painter like his
servant, and had put on sores made of pig's blood, rye meal, and
glue. So when the folk saw my sores go on tongues of puppies,
they laughed, and I saw cord or sack before me. So up I jumped,
and shouted, "a miracle! a miracle! The very dogs of this holy
convent be holy, and have cured me. Good fathers," cried I,
"whose day is this?" "St. Isidore's," said one. "St. Isidore,"
cried I, in a sort of rapture. "Why, St. Isidore is my patron
saint: so that accounts." And the simple folk swallowed my miracle as those accursed quiens my wounds. But the monks took
me inside and shut the gate, and put their heads together; but I
have a quick ear, and one did say "caret miraculo monasterium,"
which is Greek patter I trow, leastways it is no beggar's cant.
Finally they bade the lay-brethren give me a hiding, and take me
out a back way and put me on the road, and threatened me did I
come back to the town to hand me to the magistrate and have me
drowned for a plain impostor. "Profit now by the Church's grace,"
said they, "and mend thy ways." So forward, Bon Bec, for my
life is not sure nigh hand this town.' As he went he worked his
shoulders, 'Wow but the brethren laid on. And what means yon
piece of monk's cant, I wonder?' So I told him the words meant
'the monastery is in want of a miracle,' but the application thereof
was dark to me. 'Dark,' cried he, 'dark as noon. Why it means
they are going to work the miracle, my miracle, and gather all the
grain I sowed. Therefore these blows on their benefactor's shoulders; therefore is he that wrought their scurvy miracle driven
forth with stripes and threats. Oh, cozening knaves!' Said I,
'becomes you to complain of guile.' 'Alas, Bon Bec,' said he, 'I but
outwit the simple; but these monks would pluck Lucifer of his wing
feathers.' And went a league bemoaning himself that he was not
convent-bred like his servant. 'He would put it to more profit;'
and railing on quiens. 'And as for those monks, there was one
Above.' 'Certes,' said I, 'there is one Above. What then?' 'Who

will call those shavelings to compt, one day,' quoth he. 'And all deceitful men,' said I. At one that afternoon I got armories to paint:
so my master took the yellow jaundice and went begging through the
town, and with his oily tongue, and saffron-water face, did fill his hat.
Now in all the towns are certain licensed beggars, and one of these was
an old favourite with the townsfolk: had his station at St. Martin's
porch, the greatest church: a blind man: they called him blind Hans.
He saw my master drawing coppers on the other side of the street,
and knew him by his tricks for an impostor, so sent and warned
the constables, and I met my master in the constables' hands, and
going to his trial in the town hall. I followed and many more;
and he was none abashed, neither by the pomp of justice, nor
memory of his misdeeds, but demanded his accuser like a trumpet.
And blind Hans's boy came forward, but was sifted narrowly by my
master, and stammered, and faltered, and owned he had seen nothing,
but only carried blind Hans's tale to the chief constable. 'This
is but hearsay,' said my master. 'Lo ye now, here standeth Misfortune backbit by Envy. But stand thou forth, blind Envy, and
vent thine own lie.' And blind Hans behoved to stand forth, sore
against his will. Him did my master so press with questions, and
so pinch and torture, asking him again and again, how, being blind,
he could see all that befell, and some that befell not, across a
way; and why, an he could not see, he came there holding up his per-
jured hand, and maligning the misfortunate, that at last he groaned
aloud and would utter no word more. And an alderman said,
'In sooth, Hans, ye are to blame: hast cast more dirt of suspicion
on thyself than on him." But the burgomaster, a wondrous fat
man, and methinks of his fat some had gotten into his head, checked
him and said, 'Nay, Hans we know this many years, and, be he
blind or not, he hath passed for blind so long, 'tis all one. Back
to thy porch, good Hans, and let the strange varlet leave the town
incontinent on pain of whipping.' Then my master winked to me;
but there rose a civic officer in his gown of state and golden chain,
a Dignity with us lightly prized, and even shunned of some, but in
Germany and France much courted, save by condemned malefactors;
to wit the hangman; and says he, 'An't please you, first let us see
why he weareth his hair so thick and low.' And his man went and
lifted Cul de Jatte's hair, and lo the upper gristle of both ears
was gone. 'How is this, knave?' quoth the burgomaster. My

master said, carelessly, he minded not precisely: his had been a
life of misfortunes and losses. 'When a poor soul has lost use
of his leg, noble sirs, these more trivial woes rest lightly in his
memory.' When he found this would not serve his turn, he named
two famous battles, in each of which he had lost half an ear, a
fighting like a true man against traitors and rebels. But the hangman showed them the two cuts were made at one time, and by meas-
urement. ''Tis no bungling soldier's work, my masters,' said he,
''tis ourn.' Then the burgomaster gave judgment: 'The present
charge is not proven against thee; but, an thou beest not guilty now,
thou hast been at other times, witness thine ears. Wherefore I send
thee to prison for one month, and to give a florin towards the new hall
of the guilds now a building, and to be whipt out of the town, and
pay the hangman's fee for the same.' And all the aldermen
approved, and my master was haled to prison with one look of
anguish. It did strike my bosom. I tried to get speech of him,
but the jailer denied me. But lingering near the jail I heard a
whistle, and there was Cul de Jatte at a narrow window twenty
feet from earth. I went under, and he asked me what made I
there? I told him I was loth to go forward and not bid him farewell. He seemed quite amazed; but soon his suspicious soul got
the better. That was not all mine errand. I told him not all: the
psaltery: 'Well, what of that?' 'Twas not mine, but his; I would
pay him the price of it. 'Then throw me a rix dollar,' said he.
I counted out my coins, and they came to a rix dollar and two batzen.
I threw him up his money in three throws, and when he had got it
all he said, softly, 'Bon Bec.' 'Master,' said I. Then the poor
rogue was greatly moved. 'I thought ye had been mocking
me,' said he; 'oh, Bon Bec, Bon Bec, if I had found the world
like thee at starting I had put my wit to better use, and I had not
lain here.' Then he whimpered out, 'I gave not quite a rix dollar
for the jingler;' and threw me back that he had gone to cheat
me of; honest for once, and over late; and so, with many sighs,
bade me Godspeed. Thus did my master, after often baffling men's
justice, fall by their injustice; for his lost ears proved not his guilt
only, but of that guilt the bitter punishment: so the account was
even; yet they for his chastisement did chastise him. Natheless
he was a parlous rogue. Yet he holp to make a man of me.
Thanks to his good wit I went forward richer far with my psaltery

and brush, than with yon as good as stolen purse; for that must have run dry in time, like a big trough, but these a little fountain."

Richart.] "How pregnant his reflections be; and but a curly pated lad when last I saw him. Asking your pardon, mistress. Prithee read on."

"One day I walked alone, and, sooth to say, light hearted, for mine honest Denys sweetened the air on the way; but poor Cul de Jatte poisoned it. The next day, passing a grand house, out came on prancing steeds a gentleman in brave attire and two servants; they overtook me. The gentleman bade me halt. I laughed in my sleeve; for a few batzen were all my store. He bade me doff my doublet and jerkin. Then I chuckled no more. 'Bethink you, my lord,' said I, ' 'tis winter. How may a poor fellow go bare and live?' So he told me I shot mine arrow wide of his thought; and off with his own gay jerkin, richly furred, and doublet to match, and held them forth to me. Then a servant let me know it was a penance. 'His lordship had had the ill luck to slay his cousin in their cups.' Down to my shoes he changed with me; and set me on his horse like a popinjay, and fared by my side in my worn weeds, with my psaltery on his back. And said he, 'Now, good youth, thou art Count Detstein; and I, late count, thy Servant. Play thy part well, and help me save my blood-stained soul! Be haughty and choleric, as any noble; and I will be as humble as I may.' I said I would do my best to play the noble. But what should I call him? He bade me call him nought but Servant. That would mortify him most, he wist. We rode on a long way in silence: for I was meditating this strange chance, that from a beggar's servant had made me master to a count, and also cudgelling my brains how best I might play the master, without being run through the body all at one time like his cousin. For I mistrusted sore my spark's humility; your German nobles being, to my knowledge, proud as Lucifer, and choleric as fire. As for the servants, they did slily grin to one another to see their master so humbled—"

"Ah! what is that?"

A lump, as of lead, had just bounced against the door, and the latch was fumbled with unsuccessfully. Another bounce, and the door swung inwards with Giles arrayed in cloth of gold sticking to it like a wasp. He landed on the floor and was embraced; but, on learning what was going on, trumpeted that he would much liever hear of Gerard than gossip.

Sybrandt pointed to a diminutive chair.

Giles showed his sense of this civility by tearing the said Sybrandt out of a very big one, and there ensconced himself gorgeous and glowing. Sybrandt had to wedge himself into the one, which was too small for the magnificent dwarf's soul, and Margaret resumed. But as this part of the letter was occupied with notices of places, all which my reader probably knows, and, if not, can find handled at large in a dozen well-known books, from Munster to Murray, I skip the topography, and hasten to that part where it occurred to him to throw his letter into a journal. The personal narrative that intervened may be thus condensed.

He spoke but little at first to his new companions, but listened to pick up their characters. Neither his noble Servant nor *his* servants could read or write; and as he often made entries in his tablets, he impressed them with some awe. One of his entries was "Le peu que sont les hommes." For he found the surly innkeepers licked the very ground before him now; nor did a soul suspect the hosier's son in the count's feathers, nor the count in the minstrel's weeds. This seems to have surprised him; for he enlarged on it with the naïveté and pomposity of youth. At one place, being humbly requested to present the inn with his armorial bearings, he consented loftily; but painted them himself, to mine host's wonder, who thought he lowered himself by handling brush. The true count stood grinning by, and held the paint-pot, while the sham count painted a shield with three red herrings rampant under a sort of Maltese cross made with two ell-measures. At first his plebeian servants were insolent. But this coming to the notice of his noble one, he forgot what he was doing penance for, and drew his sword to cut off their ears, heads included. But Gerard interposed and saved them, and rebuked the count severely. And finally they all understood one another, and the superior mind obtained its natural influence. He played the barbarous noble of that day vilely. For his heart would not let him be either tyrannical or cold. Here were three human beings. He tried to make them all happier than he was; held them ravished with stories, and songs, and set Herr Penitent & Co. dancing, with his whistle and psaltery. For his own convenience he made them ride and tie, and thus pushed rapidly through the country, travelling generally fifteen leagues a day.

The Cloister and the Hearth

'THIS first of January I observed a young man of the country to meet a strange maiden, and kissed his hand, and then held it out to her. She took it with a smile, and lo! acquaintance made; and babbled like old friends. Greetings so pretty and delicate I ne'er did see. Yet were they both of the baser sort. So the next lass I saw a coming, I said to my servant lord, 'For further penance bow thy pride; go meet yon base-born girl; kiss thy homicidal hand, and give it her, and hold her in discourse as best ye may.' And my noble Servant said, humbly, 'I shall obey my lord.' And we drew rein and watched while he went forward, kissed his hand and held it out to her. Forthwith she took it smiling, and was most affable with him, and he with her. Presently came up a band of her companions. So this time I bade him doff his bonnet to them, as though they were empresses; and he did so. And lo! the lasses drew up as stiff as hedge-stakes, and moved not nor spake."

Denys.] "Aie! aie! aie! Pardon, the company."

"This surprised me none; for so they did discountenance poor Denys. And that whole day I wore in experimenting these German lasses; and 'twas still the same. An' ye doff bonnet to them they stiffen into statues; distance for distance. But accost them with honest freedom, and with that customary, and, though rustical, most gracious proffer, of the kissed hand, and they withhold neither their hands in turn nor their acquaintance in an honest way. Seeing which I vexed myself that Denys was not with us to prattle with them; he is so fond of women." ("Are you fond of *women*, Denys?") And the reader opened two great violet eyes upon him with gentle surprise.

Denys.] "Ahem! He says so, she-comrade. By Hannibal's helmet 'tis their fault, not mine. They *will* have such soft voices, and white skins, and sunny hair, and dark blue eyes, and—"

Margaret.] (Reading suddenly.) "Which their affability I put to profit thus. I asked them how they made shift to grow roses in yule? For know, dear Margaret, that throughout Germany the baser sort of lasses wear for head-dress nought but a 'crantz,' or wreath of roses, encircling their bare hair, as laurel Cæsar's; and though of the worshipful scorned, yet is braver, I wist, to your eye and mine which painters be, though sorry ones, than the gorgeous, uncouth, mechanical head-gear of the time, and adorns, not hides her hair, that goodly ornament fitted to her head by craft divine. So the good lasses, being questioned close, did let me know, the rosebuds are cut in summer and laid then in great clay pots, thus ordered:—first bay salt, then a row of buds, and over that row bay salt sprinkled; then another row of buds placed crosswise; for they say it is death to the buds to touch one another; and so on, buds and salt in layers. Then each pot is covered and soldered tight, and kept in cool cellar. And on Saturday night the master of the house, or mistress, if master be none, opens a pot, and doles the rose-buds out to every female in the house, high or low, withouten grudge; then solders it up again. And such, as of these buds would full-blown roses make, put them in warm water a little space, or else in the stove, and then with tiny brush and soft, wetted in Rhenish wine, do coax them till they ope their folds. And some perfume them with rose-water. For, alack, their smell it is fled with the summer; and only their fair bodyes lie withouten soul, in tomb of clay, awaiting resurrection.

"And some with the roses and buds mix nutmegs gilded, but not by my good will; for gold, brave in itself, cheek by jowl with roses, is but yellow earth. And it does the eye's heart good to see these fair heads of hair come, blooming with roses, over snowy roads, and by snow capt hedges, setting winter's beauty by the side of summer's glory. For what so fair as winter's lilies, snow yclept, and what so brave as roses? And shouldst have had a picture here, but for their superstition. Leaned a lass in Sunday garb, cross ankled, against her cottage corner, whose low roof was snowclad, and with her crantz did seem a summer flower sprouting from winter's bosom. I drew rein, and out pencil and brush to limn her for thee. But the simpleton, fearing the evil eye, or glamour, claps both hands to her face and flies panic-stricken. But, indeed, they are not more superstitious than the Sevenbergen folk, which take thy father for a magician. Yet softly, sith at this moment I profit by this darkness of their minds; for, at first sitting down to write this diary, I could frame nor thought nor word, so harried and deaved was I with noise of mechanical persons, and hoarse laughter at dull jests of one of these parti-coloured 'fools,' which are so rife in Germany. But, oh, sorry wit, that is driven to the poor resource of pointed ear-caps, and a green and yellow body. True wit, methinks, is of the mind. We met in Burgundy an honest wench, though over free for my palate, a chambermaid, had made havoc of all these zanies, droll by brute force. Oh, Digressor! Well then, I to be rid of roaring rusticalls, and mindless jests, put my finger in a glass and drew on the table a great watery circle; whereat the rusticalls did look askant, like venison at a cat; and in that circle a smaller circle. The rusticalls held their peace; and besides these circles cabalistical, I laid down on the table solemnly yon parchment deed I had out of your house. The rusticalls held their breath. Then did I look as glum as might be, and muttered slowly thus: 'Videamus—quam diu tu fictus morio—vosque veri stulti—audebitis—in hâc aulâ morari, strepitantes ita—et olentes—ut dulcissimæ nequeam miser scribere.' They shook like aspens, and stole away on tiptoe one by one at first, then in a rush and jostling, and left me alone; and most scared of all was the fool: never earned jester fairer his ass's ears. So rubbed I their foible, who first rubbed mine; for of all a traveller's foes I dread those giants twain, Sir Noise, and eke Sir Stench. The saints and martyrs forgive my peevishness. Thus I write to thee in balmy peace, and tell thee trivial things scarce worth ink, also how I love thee, which there was no need to tell, for well thou knowest it. And, oh, dear Margaret, looking on their roses, which grew in summer, but blow in winter, I see the picture of our true affection; born it was in smiles and bliss, but soon adversity beset us sore with many a bitter blast. Yet our love hath lost no leaf, thank God, but blossoms full and fair as ever, proof against frowns, and jibes, and prison, and banishment, as those sweet German flowers a blooming in winter's snow.

"*January 2nd.*—My servant, the count, finding me curious, took me to the stables of the prince that rules this part. In the first court was a horse-bath, adorned with twenty-two pillars, graven with the prince's arms; and also the horse-leech's shop, so furnished as a rich apothecary might envy. The stable is a fair quadrangle, whereof three sides filled with horses of all nations. Before each horse's nose was a glazed window, with a green curtain to be drawn at pleasure, and at his tail a thick wooden pillar with a brazen shield, whence by turning of a pipe he is watered, and serves too for a cupboard to keep his comb and rubbing clothes. Each rack was iron, and each manger shining copper, and each nag covered with a scarlet mantle, and above him his bridle and saddle hung, ready to gallop forth in a minute; and not less than two hundred horses, whereof twelve score of foreign breed. And we returned to our inn full of admiration, and the two varlets said sorrowfully, 'Why were we born with two legs?' And one of the grooms that was civil and had of me trinkgeld, stood now at his cottage-door and asked us in. There we found his wife and children of all ages, from five to eighteen, and had but one room to bide and sleep in, a thing pestiferous and most uncivil. Then I asked my Servant, knew he this prince? Ay, did he, and had often drunk with him in a marble chamber above the stable, where, for table, was a curious and artificial rock, and the drinking vessels hang on its pinnacles, and at the hottest of the engagement a statue of a horseman in bronze came forth bearing a bowl of liquor, and he that sat nearest behoved to drain it. ' 'Tis well,' said I: 'now for thy penance, whisper thou in yon prince's ear, that God hath given him his people freely, and not sought a price for them as for horses. And pray him look inside the huts at his horse-palace door, and bethink himself it is well to house his horses, and stable his folk.' Said he, ' 'Twill give sore offence.' 'But,' said I, 'ye must do it discreetly and choose your time.' So he promised. And riding on we heard plaintive cries. 'Alas,' said I, 'some sore mischance hath befallen some poor soul: what may it be?' And we rode up, and lo! it was a wedding feast, and the guests were plying the business of drinking sad and silent, but ever and anon cried loud and dolefully, 'Seyte frolich! Be merry.'

"*January* 3.—Yesterday between Nurnberg and Augsburg we parted company. I gave my lord, late Servant, back, his brave clothes for mine, but his horse he made me keep, and five gold pieces, and said he was still my debtor, his penance it had been slight along of me, but profitable. But his best word was this: 'I see 'tis more noble to be loved than feared.' And then he did so praise me as I blush to put on paper; yet, poor fool, would fain thou couldst hear his words, but from some other pen than mine. And the servants did heartily grasp my hand, and wish me good luck. And riding apace, yet could I not reach Augsburg till the gates were closed; but it mattered little, for this Augsburg it is an enchanted

The Cloister and the Hearth

city. For a small coin one took me a long way round to a famous postern called der Einlasse. Here stood two guardians, like statues. To them I gave my name and business. They nodded me leave to knock; I knocked; and the iron gate opened with a great noise and hollow rattling of a chain, but no hand seen nor chain; and he, who drew the hidden chain, sits a butt's length from the gate; and I rode in, and the gate closed with a clang after me. I found myself in a great building with a bridge at my feet. This I rode over and presently came to a porter's lodge, where one asked me again my name and business, then rang a bell, and a great portcullis that barred the way began to rise, drawn by a wheel overhead, and no hand seen. Behind the portcullis was a thick oaken door studded with steel. It opened without hand, and I rode into a hall as dark as pitch. Trembling there a while, a door opened and showed me a smaller hall lighted. I rode into it: a tin goblet came down from the ceiling by a little chain: I put two batzen into it, and it went up again. Being gone, another thick door creaked and opened, and I rid through. It closed on me with a tremendous clang, and behold me in Augsburg city. I lay at an inn called 'The Three Moors,' over an hundred years old; and, this morning, according to my way of viewing towns to learn their compass and shape, I mounted the highest tower I could find, and setting my dial at my foot surveyed the beautiful city: whole streets of palaces, and churches tiled with copper burnished like gold; and the house fronts gaily painted and all glazed, and the glass so clean and burnished as 'tis most resplendent and rare; and I, now first seeing a great citie, did crow with delight, and like a cock on his ladder, and at the tower foot was taken into custody for a spy; for whilst I watched the city the watchman had watched me. The burgomaster received me courteously and heard my story; then rebuked he the officers. 'Could ye not question him yourselves, or read in his face? This is to make our city stink in stranger's report.' Then he told me my curiosity was of a commendable sort: and seeing I was a craftsman and inquisitive, bade his clerk take me among the guilds. God bless the city where the very burgomaster is cut of Solomon's cloth!

"*January* 5.—Dear Margaret, it is a noble city, and a kind mother to arts. Here they cut in wood and ivory, that 'tis like spiders' work, and paint on glass, and sing angelical harmonies. Writing of books is quite gone by; here be six printers. Yet was I offered a bountiful wage to write fairly a merchant's accounts, one Fugger, a grand and wealthy trader, and hath store of ships, yet his father was but a poor weaver. But here in commerce, her very garden, men swell like mushrooms. And he bought my horse of me, and abated me not a jot, which way of dealing is not known in Holland. But, oh, Margaret, the workmen of all the guilds are so kind and brotherly to one another, and to me. Here, methinks, I have found the true German mind, loyal, frank, and kindly, somewhat choleric withal, but nought revengeful. Each mechanic wears a sword. The very weavers at the loom sit girded with their weapons, and all Germans on too slight occasion draw them and fight; but no treachery: challenge first, then draw, and with the edge only, mostly the face, not with Sir Point; for if in these combats one thrust at his adversary and hurt him, 'tis called ein schelemstucke, a heinous act; both men and women turn their backs on him, and even the judges punish thrusts bitterly, but pass over cuts. Hence in Germany be good store of scarred faces, three in five at least, and in France scarce more than one in three.

"But in arts mechanical no citizens may compare with these. Fountains in every street that play to heaven, and in the gardens seeming trees, which being approached, one standing afar touches a spring, and every twig shoots water, and souses the guests to their host's much delectation. Big culverins of war they cast with no more ado than our folk horse-shoes, and have done this fourscore years. All stuffs they weave, and linen fine as ours at home, or nearly, which elsewhere in Europe vainly shall you seek. Sir Printing Press—sore foe to poor Gerard, but to other humans beneficial —plieth by night and day, and casteth goodly words like sower afield; while I, poor fool, can but sow them as I saw women in France sow rye, dribbling it in the furrow grain by grain. And of their strange mechanical skill take two examples. For ending of exemplary rogues they have a figure like a woman, seven feet high, and called Jung Frau; but lo a spring is touched, she seizeth the poor wretch with iron arms, and opening herself hales him inside her, and there pierces him through and through with two score lances. Secondly, in all great houses the spit is turned not by a scrubby boy, but by smoke. Ay, mayst well admire, and judge me a lying knave. These cunning Germans do set in the chimney a little windmill, and the smoke struggling to wend past, turns it.

and from the mill a wire runs through the wall and turns the spit on wheels; beholding which I doffed my bonnet to the men of Augsburg, for who but these had ere devised to bind ye so dark and subtle a knave as Sir Smoke, and set him to roast Dame Pullet?

"This day, January 8, with three craftsmen of the town, I painted a pack of cards. They were for a senator in a hurry. I the diamonds. My queen came forth with eyes like spring violets, hair a golden brown, and witching smile. My fellow-craftsmen saw her, and put their arms round my neck and hailed me master. Oh, noble Germans! No jealousy of a brother-workman: no sour looks at a stranger: and would have me spend Sunday with them after matins; and the merchant paid me so richly, as I was ashamed to take the guerdon: and I to my inn, and tried to paint the queen of diamonds for poor Gerard; but no, she would not come like again. Luck will not be bespoke. Oh, happy rich man that hath got her! Fie! fie! Happy Gerard, that shall have herself one day, and keep house with her at Augsburg.

"*January* 8.—With my fellows, and one Veit Stoss, a wood-carver, and one Hafnagel, of the goldsmiths' guild, and their wives and lasses, to Hafnagel's cousin, a senator of this free city, and his stupendious wine-vessel. It is ribbed like a ship, and hath been eighteen months in hand, and finished but now, and holds a hundred and fifty hogsheads, and standeth not, but lieth; yet even so ye get not on his back withouten ladders two, of thirty steps. And we sat about the miraculous mass, and drank Rhenish from it, drawn by a little artificial pump, and the lasses pinned their crantzes to it, and we danced round it, and the senator danced on its back, but with drinking of so many garausses, lost his footing and fell off, glass in hand, and broke an arm and a leg in the midst of us. So scurvily ended our drinking bout for this time.

"*January* 10.—This day started for Venice with a company of merchants, and among them him who had desired me for his scrivener; and so we are now agreed, I to write at night the letters he shall dict, and other matters, he to feed and lodge me on the road. We be many and armed, and soldiers with us to boot, so fear not the thieves which men say lie on the borders of Italy. But an if I find the printing press at Venice I trow I shall not go on to Rome, for man may not vie with iron.

"Imprimit una dies quantum non scribitur anno. And, dearest, something tells me you and I shall end our days at Augsburg, whence going, I shall leave it all I can—my blessing.

"*January* 12.—My master affecteth me much, and now maketh me sit with him in his horse-litter. A grave good man, of all respected, but sad for loss of a dear daughter, and loveth my psaltery: not giddy-paced ditties, but holy harmonies such as Cul de Jatte made wry mouths at. So many men, so many minds. But cooped in horse-litter and at night, writing his letters, my journal halteth.

"*January* 14.—When not attending on my good merchant, I consort with such of our company as are Italians, for 'tis to Italy I wend, and I am ill seen in Italian tongue. A courteous and a subtle people, at meat delicate feeders, and cleanly: love not to put their left hand in the dish. They say Venice is the garden of Lombardy, Lombardy the garden of Italy, Italy of the world.

"*January* 16.—Strong ways and steep, and the mountain girls so girded up, as from their armpits to their waist is but a handful. Of all the garbs I yet have seen the most unlovely.

"*January* 18.—In the midst of life we are in death. Oh! dear Margaret, I thought I had lost thee. Here I lie in pain and dole, and shall write thee that, which read you it in a romance ye should cry 'most improbable!' And so still wondering that I am alive to write it, and thanking for it God and the saints, this is what befell thy Gerard. Yestreen I wearied of being shut up in litter, and of the mule's slow pace, and so went forward; and being, I know not why, strangely full of spirit and hope, as I have heard befall some men when on trouble's brink, seemed to tread on air, and soon outdistanced them all. Presently I came to two roads; and took the larger: I should have taken the smaller. After travelling a good half-hour I found my error and returned, and deeming my company had long passed by, pushed bravely on, but I could not overtake them; and small wonder, as you shall hear. Then I was anxious, and ran, but bare was the road of those I sought, and night came down, and the wild beasts afoot, and I bemoaned my folly, also I was hungered. The moon rose clear and bright exceedingly, and presently, a little way off the road, I saw a tall wind-mill. 'Come,' said I, 'mayhap the miller will take ruth on me.' Near the mill was a haystack, and scattered about were store of little barrels, but lo, they were not flour-barrels but tar-barrels, one or two, and the rest of spirits, Brant vein and Schiedam; I knew them momently, having seen the like in

Holland. I knocked at the mill door, but none answered. I lifted the latch and the door opened inwards. I went in, and gladly, for the night was fine but cold, and a rime on the trees, which were a kind of lofty sycamores. There was a stove, but black; I lighted it with some of the hay and wood, for there was a great pile of wood outside: and, I know not how, I went to sleep. Not long had I slept, I trow, when hearing a noise I awoke, and there were a dozen men around me, with wild faces, and long black hair, and black sparkling eyes."

Catherine.] "Oh, my poor boy! those blackhaired ones do still scare me to look on."

"I made my excuses in such Italian as I knew, and eking out by signs. They grinned. 'I had lost my company.' They grinned. I was an hungered. Still they grinned, and spoke to one another in a tongue I knew not. At last one gave me a piece of bread and a tin mug of wine, as I thought, but it was spirits neat. I made a wry face, and asked for water: then these wild men laughed a horrible laugh. I thought to fly, but, looking towards the door, it was bolted with two enormous bolts of iron, and now first, as I ate my bread, I saw it was all guarded too, and ribbed with iron. My blood curdled within me, and yet I could not tell thee why; but hadst thou seen the faces, wild, stupid, and ruthless. I mumbled my bread, not to let them see I feared them; but oh, it cost me to swallow it and keep it in me. Then it whirled in my brain, was there no way to escape? Said I, 'They will not let me forth by the door; these be smugglers or robbers.' So I feigned drowsiness, and taking out two batzen said, 'Good men, for our Lady's grace let me lie on a bed and sleep, for I am faint with travel.' They nodded and grinned their horrible grin, and bade one light a lanthorn and lead me. He took me up a winding staircase, up, up, and I saw no windows, but the wooden walls were pierced like a barbican tower, and methinks for the same purpose, and through these slits I got glimpses of the sky, and thought, 'Shall I e'er see thee again?' He took me to the very top of the mill, and there was a room with a heap of straw in one corner, and many empty barrels, and by the wall a truckle bed. He pointed to it, and went down stairs heavily, taking the light, for in this room was a great window, and the moon came in bright. I looked out to see, and lo it was so high that even the mill sails at their highest came not up to my window by some feet, but turned

The Cloister and the Hearth

very slow and stately underneath, for wind there was scarce a breath: and the trees seemed silver filagree made by angel craftsmen. My hope of flight was gone.

"But now, those wild faces being out of sight, I smiled at my fears: what an if they were ill men, would it profit them to hurt me? Natheless, for caution against surprise, I would put the bed against the door. I went to move it, but could not. It was free at the head, but at the foot fast clamped with iron to the floor. So I flung my psaltery on the bed, but for myself made a layer of straw at the door, so as none could open on me unawares. And I laid my sword ready to my hand. And said my prayers for thee and me, and turned to sleep.

"Below they drank and made merry. And hearing this gave me confidence. Said I, 'Out of sight, out of mind. Another hour and the good Schiedam will make them forget that I am here.' And so I composed myself to sleep. And for some time could not for the boisterous mirth below. At last I dropped off. How long I slept I knew not; but I woke with a start: the noise had ceased below, and the sudden silence woke me. And scarce was I awake, when sudden the truckle bed was gone with a loud clang all but the feet, and the floor yawned, and I heard my psaltery fall and break to atoms deep, deep below the very floor of the mill. It had fallen into a well. And so had I done, lying where it lay."

Margaret shuddered and put her face in her hands. But speedily resumed.

"I lay stupefied at first. Then horror fell on me and I rose, but stood rooted there, shaking from head to foot. At last I found myself looking down into that fearsome gap, and my very hair did bristle as I peered. And then, I remember, I turned quite calm, and made up my mind to die sword in hand. For I saw no man must know this their bloody secret and live. And I said 'Poor Margaret!' And I took out of my bosom, where they lie ever, our marriage lines, and kissed them again and again. And I pinned them to my shirt again, that they might lie in one grave with me, if die I must. And I thought 'All our love and hopes to end thus!' "

Eli.] "Whist all! Their marriage lines? Give her time! But no word. I can bear no chat. My poor lad!"

During the long pause that ensued Catherine leaned forward and

406

The Cloister and the Hearth

passed something adroitly from her own lap under her daughter's apron who sat next her.

"Presently thinking, all in a whirl, of all that ever passed between us, and taking leave of all those pleasant hours, I called to mind how one day at Sevenbergen thou taughtest me to make a rope of straw. Mindst thou? The moment memory brought that happy day back to me, I cried out very loud: 'Margaret gives me a chance for life even here.' I woke from my lethargy. I seized on the straw and twisted it eagerly, as thou didst teach me, but my fingers trembled and delayed the task. Whiles I wrought I heard a door open below. That was a terrible moment. Even as I twisted my rope I got to the window and looked down at the great arms of the mill coming slowly up, then passing, then turning less slowly down, as it seemed; and I thought 'They go not as when there is wind: yet, slow or fast, what man rid ever on such steed as these, and lived? Yet, said I, 'better trust to them and God, than to ill men.' And I prayed to him whom even the wind obeyeth.

"Dear Margaret, I fastened my rope, and let myself gently down, and fixed my eye on that huge arm of the mill, which then was creeping up to me, and went to spring on to it. But my heart failed me at the pinch. And methought it was near enow. And it passed calm and awful by. I watched for another; they were three. And after a little while one crept up slower than the rest methought. And I with my foot thrust myself in good time somewhat out from the wall, and crying aloud 'Margaret!' did grip with all my soul the wood work of the sail, and that moment was swimming in the air."

Giles.] "WELL DONE! WELL DONE!"

"Motion I felt little; but the stars seemed to go round the sky, and then the grass came up to me nearer and nearer, and when the hoary grass was quite close I was sent rolling along it as if hurled from a catapult, and got up breathless, and every point and tie about me broken. I rose, but fell down again in agony. I had but one leg I could stand on."

Catherine.] "Eh! dear! his leg is broke, my boy's leg is broke."

"And, e'en as I lay groaning, I heard a sound like thunder. It was the assassins running up the stairs. The crazy old mill shook under them. They must have found I had not fallen into their bloody trap, and were running to despatch me. Margaret, I felt no fear, for I had now no hope. I could neither run, nor hide; so wild the place, so bright the moon. I struggled up all agony and revenge, more like some wounded wild beast than your Gerard. Leaning on my sword hilt I hobbled round; and swift as lightning, or vengeance, I heaped a great pile of their hay and wood at the mill door; then drove my dagger into a barrel of their smuggled spirits, and flung it on; then out with my tinder and lighted the pile. 'This will bring true men round my dead body,' said I. 'Aha!' I cried, 'think you I'll die alone, cowards, assass'ns! reckless fiends!' and at each word on went a barrel pierced. But, oh, Margaret! the fire fed by the spirits surprised me: it shot up and singed my very hair, it went roaring up the side of the mill, swift as falls the lightning: and I yelled and laughed in my torture and despair, and pierced more barrels, and the very tar-barrels, and flung them on. The fire roared like a lion for its prey, and voices answered it inside from the top of the mill, and the feet came thundering down, and I stood as near that awful fire as I could with uplifted sword to slay and be slain. The bolt was drawn. A tar-barrel caught fire. The door was opened. What followed? Not the men came out, but the fire rushed in at them like a living death, and the first I thought to fight with was blackened and crumpled on the floor like a leaf. One fearsome yell, and dumb for ever. The feet ran up again, but fewer. I heard them hack with their swords a little way up, at the mill's wooden sides; but they had no time to hew their way out: the fire and reek were at their heels, and the smoke burst out at every loophole, and oozed blue in the moonlight through each crevice. I hobbled back, racked with pain and fury. There were white faces up at my window. They saw me. They cursed me. I cursed them back and shook my naked sword: 'Come down the road I came,' I cried. 'But ye must come one by one, and, as ye come, ye die upon this steel.' Some cursed at that, but others wailed. For I had them all at deadly vantage. And doubtless with my smoke-grimed face and fiendish rage I looked a demon. And now there was a steady roar inside the mill. The flame was going up it as furnace up its chimney. The mill caught fire. Fire glimmered through it. Tongues of flame darted through each loophole and shot sparks and fiery flakes into the night. One of the assassins leaped on to the sail, as I had done. In his hurry he missed his grasp and fell at my feet, and bounded from the hard ground like a ball, and never spoke, nor moved again. And the rest screamed like women, and with their despair came back to me both ruth for them and hope of life for myself. And the fire gnawed through the mill in placen, and shot forth showers of great flat sparks like flakes of fiery snow; and the sails caught fire one after another; and I became a man again and staggered away terror-stricken, leaning on my sword, from the sight of my revenge, and with great bodily pain crawled back to the road. And, dear Margaret, the rimy trees were now all like pyramids of golden filagree, and lace, cobweb fine, in the red firelight. Oh! most beautiful! And a poor wretch got entangled in the burning sails, and whirled round screaming, and lost hold at the wrong time, and hurled like stone from mangonel high into the air; then a dull thump; it was his carcass striking the earth. The next moment there was a loud crash. The mill fell in on its destroyer, and a million great sparks flew up, and the sails fell over the burning wreck, and at that a million more sparks flew up, and the ground was strewn with burning wood and men. I prayed God forgive me, and kneeling with my back to that fiery shambles, I saw lights on the road; a welcome sight. It was a company coming towards me, and scarce two furlongs off. I hobbled towards them. Ere I gone far I heard a swift step behind me. I turned. One had escaped; how escaped, who can divine? His sword shone in the moonlight. I feared him, methought the ghost of all those dead sat on that glittering glaive. I put my other foot to the ground, maugre the anguish, and fled towards the torches, moaning with pain, and shouting for aid. But what could I do? He gained on me. Behooved me turn and fight. Denys had taught me sword play in sport. I wheeled, our swords clashed. His clothes they smelled all singed. I cut swiftly upward with supple hand, and his dangled bleeding at the wrist, and his sword fell; it tinkled on the ground. I raised my sword to hew him should he stoop for't. He stood and cursed me. He drew his dagger with his left; I opposed my point and dared him with my eye to close. A great shout arose behind me from true men's throats. He started. He spat at me in his rage, then gnashed his teeth and fled blaspheming. I turned and saw torches close at hand. Lo, they fell to dancing up and down methought, and the next—moment—all—was—dark. I had ·—ah!"

Catherine.] "Here, help! water! Stand aloof, you that be men!"

Margaret had fainted away.

CHAPTER LVI

WHEN she recovered, her head was on Catherine's arm, and the honest half of the family she had invaded like a foe stood round her uttering rough homely words of encouragement, especially Giles, who roared at her that she was not to take on like that. "Gerard was alive and well, or he could not have writ this letter, the biggest mankind had seen as yet, and," as he thought, "the beautifulest, and most moving, and smallest writ."

"Ay, good Master Giles," sighed Margaret feebly, "he *was* alive. But how know I what hath since befallen him? Oh, why left he Holland to go among strangers fierce as lions? And why did I not drive him from me sooner than part him from his own flesh and blood? Forgive me, you that are his mother!"

And she gently removed Catherine's arm, and made a feeble attempt to slide off the chair on to her knees, which, after a brief struggle with superior force ended in her finding herself on Catherine's bosom. Then Margaret held out the letter to Eli, and said faintly but sweetly, "I will trust it from my hand now. In sooth, I am little fit to read any more—and—and—loth to leave my comfort:" and she wreathed her other arm round Catherine's neck.

"Read thou, Richart," said Eli; "thine eyes be younger than mine."

Richart took the letter. "Well," said he, "such writing saw I never. A writeth with a needle's point; and clear to boot. Why is he not in my counting-house at Amsterdam instead of vagabonding it out yonder?"

"When I came to myself I was seated in the litter, and my good merchant holding of my hand. I babbled I know not what, and then shuddered awhile in silence. He put a horn of wine to my lips."

Catherine.] "Bless him! bless him!"

Eli.] "Whist!"

"And I told him what had befallen. He would see my leg. It

was sprained sore, and swelled at the ankle; and all my points were broken, as I could scarce keep up my hose; and I said, 'Sir, I shall be but a burden to you, I doubt, and can make you no harmony now; my poor psaltery it is broken;' and I did grieve over my broken music, companion of so many weary leagues. But he patted me on the cheek, and bade me not fret; also he did put up my leg on a pillow, and tended me like a kind father.

"*January* 14.—I sit all day in the litter, for we are pushing forward with haste, and at night the good kind merchant sendeth me to bed, and will not let me work. Strange! whene'er I fall in with men like fiends, then the next moment God still sendeth me some good man or woman, lest I should turn away from human kind. Oh, Margaret! how strangely mixed they be, and how old I am by what I was three months agone! And lo! if good Master Fugger hath not been and bought me a psaltery."

Catherine.] "Eli, my man, an yon merchant comes our way let us buy a hundred ells of cloth of him, and not higgle."

Eli.] "That will I, take your oath on't!"

While Richart prepared to read, Kate looked at her mother, and with a faint blush drew out the piece of work from under her apron, and sewed, with head depressed a little more than necessary. On this her mother drew a piece of work out of her pocket, and sewed too, while Richart read. Both the specimens these sweet surreptitious creatures now first exposed to observation were babies' caps, and more than half finished, which told a tale. Horror! they were like little monk's cowls in shape and delicacy.

"*January* 12.—Laid up in the litter, and as good as blind, but, halting to bait, Lombardy plains burst on me. Oh, Margaret! a land flowing with milk and honey; all sloping plains, goodly rivers, jocund meadows, delectable orchards, and blooming gardens; and, though winter, looks warmer than poor beloved Holland at midsummer, and makes the wanderer's face to shine and his heart to leap for joy to see earth so kind and smiling. Here be vines, cedars, olives, and cattle plenty, but three goats to a sheep. The draught oxen wear white linen on their necks, and standing by dark green olive-trees each one is a picture, and the folk, especially women wear delicate strawen hats with flowers and leaves fairly imitated in silk, with silver mixed. This day we crossed a river prettily in a chained ferry-boat. On either bank was a windlass, and a single man by turning of it drew our whole company to his shore, whereat I did admire, being a stranger. Passed over with us some country folk. And, an old woman looking at a young wench, she did hide her face with her hand, and held her crucifix out like knight his sword in tournay, dreading the evil eye.

"*January* 15.—Safe at Venice. A place whose strange and passing beauty is well known to thee by report of our mariners. Dost mind too how Peter would oft fill our ears withal, we handed beneath the table, and he still discoursing of this sea-enthroned and peerless citie, in shape a bow, and its great canal and palaces on piles, and its watery ways plied by scores of gilded boats; and that market-place of nations, orbis, non urbis, forum, St. Mark his place? And his statue with the peerless jewels in his eyes, and the lion at his gate? But I, lying at my window in pain, may see none of these beauties as yet, but only a street, fairly paced, which is dull, and houses with oiled paper and linen, in lieu of glass, which is rude; and the passers-by, their habits and their gestures, wherein they are superfluous. Therefore, not to miss my daily comfort of whispering to thee, I will e'en turn mine eyes inward, and bind my sheaves of wisdom reaped by travel. For I love thee so, that no treasure pleases me not shared with thee; and what treasure so good and enduring as knowledge? This then have I, Sir Footsore, learned, that each nation hath its proper wisdom, and its proper folly; and, methinks, could a great king, or duke, tramp like me, and see with his own eyes, he might pick the flowers, and eschew the weeds of nations, and go home and set his own folk on Wisdom's hill. The Germans in the north were churlish, but frank and honest; in the south, kindly and honest too. Their general blot is drunkenness, the which they carry even to mislike and contempt of sober men. They say commonly, 'Kanstu niecht sauffen und fressen so kanstu kienem hern wol dienen.' In England, the vulgar sort drink as deep, but the worshipful hold excess in this a reproach, and drink a health or two for courtesy, not gluttony, and still sugar the wine. In their cups the Germans use little mirth, or discourse, but ply the business sadly crying, 'Seyte frolich!' The best of their drunken sport is 'Kurlemurlehuff,' a way of drinking with touching deftly of the glass the beard, the table, in due turn, intermixed with whistlings and snappings of the finger so curiously ordered as 'tis a labour of Hercules, but to the beholder right pleasant and mirthful, Their topers, by advice of German leeches, sleep with pebbles in their mouths. For, as of a boiling pot the lid must be set ajar, so with these fleshly wine-pots, to vent the heat of their inward parts: spite of which many die suddenly from drink; but 'tis a matter of religion to slur it, and gloze it, and charge some innocent disease therewith. Yet 'tis more a custom than very nature, for their women come among the tipplers, and do but stand a moment, and, as it were, kiss the wine-cup; and are indeed most temperate in eating and drinking, and, of all women, modest and virtuous, and true spouses and friends to their mates; far before our Holland lasses, that being maids, put the question to the men, and being wived, do lord it over them. Why, there is a wife in Tergou, not far from our door. One came to the house and sought her man. Says she, 'You'll not find him: he asked my leave to go abroad this afternoon, and I did give it him.'"

Catherine.] "''Tis sooth! 'tis sooth! 'Twas Beck Hulse, Jonah's wife. This comes of a woman wedding a boy."

"In the south where wine is, the gentry drink themselves bare; but not in the north: for with beer a noble shall sooner burst his body than melt his lands. They are quarrelsome, but 'tis the liquor, not the mind; for they are none revengeful. And when they have made a bad bargain drunk, they stand to it sober. They keep their windows bright: and judge a man by his clothes. Whatever fruit or grain or herb grows by the roadside, gather and eat. The owner seeing you shall say, 'Art welcome, honest man.' But an ye pluck a wayside grape, your very life is in jeopardy. 'Tis eating of that Heaven gave to be drunken. The French are much fairer spoken, and not nigh so true hearted. Sweet words cost them nought. They call it 'payer en blanche.'"

Denys.] "Les coquins! ha! ha!"

"Natheless, courtesy is in their hearts, ay, in their very blood. They say commonly, 'Give yourself the trouble of sitting down.' And such straws of speech show how blows the wind. Also at a public show, if you would leave your seat, yet not lose it, tie but your napkin round the bench, and no French man or women will sit here; but rather keep the place for you."

Catherine.] "Gramercy! that *is* manners. France for me!"

Denys rose and placed his hand gracefully to his breastplate.

"Natheless, they say things in sport which are not courteous, but shocking. 'Le diable t'emporte!' 'Allez au diable!' and so forth. But I trow they mean not such dreadful wishes: custom belike. Moderate in drinking, and mix water with their wine, and sing and dance over their cups, and are then enchanting company. They are curious not to drink in another man's cup. In war the English gain the better of them in the field; but the French are their masters in attack and defence of cities; witness Orleans, where they beseiged their beseigers, and hashed them sore with their double and treble culverines; and many other sieges in this our century. More than all nations they flatter their women, and despise them. No She may be their sovereign ruler. Also they often hang their female male-factors, instead of drowning them decently, as other nations use. The furniture in their inns is walnut, in Germany only deal. French windows are ill. The lower half is of wood, and opens: the upper half is of glass, but fixed; so that the servant cannot come at it to clean it. The German windows are all glass, and movable and shine far and near like diamonds. In France many mean houses are not glazed at all. Once I saw a Frenchman pass a church without unbonneting. This I ne'er witnessed in Holland, Germany, or Italy. At many inns they show the traveller his sheets to give him assurance they are clean, and warm them at the fire before him; a laudable custom. They receive him kindly and like a guest; they mostly cheat him, and whiles cut his throat. They plead in excuse hard and tyrannous laws. And true it is their law thrusteth its nose into every platter, and its finger into every pie. In France worshipful men wear their hats and their furs in-doors, and go abroad lighter clad. In Germany they don hat and furred cloak to go abroad; but sit bareheaded and light clad round the stove.

"The French intermix not the men and women folk in assemblies, as we Hollanders use. Round their preachers the women sit on their heels in rows, and the men stand behind them. Their harvests are rye, and flax, and wine. Three mules shall you see to one horse, and whole flocks of sheep as black as coal.

"In Germany the snails be red. I lie not. The French buy minstrelsy, but breed jests, and make their own mirth. The Germans foster their set fools, with ear-caps, which move them to laughter by simulating madness; a calamity that asks pity, not laughter. In this particular I deem that lighter nation wiser than the graver German. What sayest thou? Alas! canst not answer me now.

"In Germany the petty laws are wondrous wise and just. Those against criminals, bloody. In France bloodier still; and executed a trifle more cruelly there. Here the wheel is common, and the fiery stake; and under this king they drown men by the score in Paris river, Seine yclept. But the English are as peremptory in hanging and drowning for a light fault; so travellers report. Finally, a true-hearted Frenchman, when ye chance on one, is a man as near perfect as earth affords; and such a man is my Denys, spite of his foul mouth."

Denys.] "My foul mouth! Is that so writ, Master Richart?"

Richart.] "Ay, in sooth; see else."

Denys.] (Inspecting the letter gravely.) "I read not the letter so."

Richart.] "How then?"

Denys.] "Humph! ahem! why just the contrary. He added: "'Tis kittle work perusing of these black scratches men are agreed to take for words. And I trow 'tis still by guess you clerks do go, worthy sir. My foul mouth? This the first time e'er I heard on't. Eh, mesdames?"

But the females did not seize the opportunity he gave them, and burst into a loud and general disclaimer. Margaret blushed and said nothing; the other two bent silently over their work with something very like a sly smile. Denys inspected their countenances long and carefully. And the perusal was so satisfactory, that he turned with a tone of injured, but patient, innocence, and bade Richart read on.

"The Italians are a polished and subtle people. They judge a man, not by his habits, but his speech and gesture. Here Sir Chough may by no means pass for falcon gentle, as did I in Germany, pranked in my noble servant's feathers. Wisest of all nations in their singular temperance of food and drink. Most foolish of all to search strangers coming into their borders, and stay them from bringing much money in. They should rather invite it, and, like other nations, let the traveller from taking of it out. Also here in Venice the dames turn their black hair yellow by the sun and art, to be wiser than Him who made them. Ye enter no Italian town without a bill of health, though now is no plague in Europe. This

peevishness is for extortion's sake. The inn-keepers cringe and
fawn, and cheat, and, in country places, murder you. Yet will
they give you clean sheets by paying therefor. Delicate in eating,
and abhor from putting their hand in the plate; sooner they will
apply a crust or what not. They do even tell of a cardinal at
Rome, which armeth his guest's left hand with a little bifurcal dagger to hold the meat, while his knife cutteth it. But methinks
this, too, is to be wiser than Him, who made the hand so supple
and prehensile."

Eli.] "I am of your mind, my lad."

"They are sore troubled with the itch. And ointment for it, un-
guento per la rogna, is cried at every corner of Venice. From this
my window I saw an urchin sell it to three several dames in silken
trains, and to two velvet knights."

Catherine.] "Italy, my lass, I rede ye wash your body i' the tub
o' Sundays; and then ye can put your hand i' the plate o' Thursday
withouten offence."

"Their bread is lovely white. Their meats they spoil with sprinkling cheese over them; O perversity! Their salt is black; without
a lie. In commerce these Venetians are masters of the earth and
sea; and govern their territories wisely. Only one flaw I find; the
same I once heard a learned friar cast up against Plato his republic:
to wit, that here women are encouraged to venal frailty, and do pay
a tax to the State, which, not content with silk and spice, and other
rich and honest freights, good store, must trade in sin. Twenty
thousand of these Jezabels there be in Venice and Candia, and about,
pampered and honoured for bringing strangers to the city, and
many live in princely palaces of their own. But herein methinks
the politic signors of Venice forget what King David saith, 'Except
the Lord keep the citie, the watchman waketh but in vain.' Also,
in religion, they hang their cloth according to the wind, siding now
with the Pope, now with the Turk; but ay with the god of traders,
mammon hight. Shall flower so cankered bloom to the world's end?
But since I speak of flowers, this none may deny them, that they are
most cunning in making roses and gilliflowers to blow unseasonably.
In summer they nip certain of the budding roses and water them not.
Then in winter they dig round these discouraged plants, and put
in cloves; and so with great art rear sweet-scented roses, and bring
them to market in January. And did first learn this art of a cow.

Buds she grazed in summer, and they sprouted at yule. Women have sat in the doctors' chairs at their colleges. But she that sat in St. Peter's was a German. Italy too, for artful fountains and figures that move by water and enact life. And next for fountains is Augsburg, where they harness the foul knave Smoke to good Sir Spit, and he turneth stout Master Roast. But lest any one place should vaunt, two towns there be in Europe, which, scorning giddy fountains, bring water tame in pipes to every burgher's door, and he filleth his vessels with but turning of a cock. One is London, so watered this many a year by pipes of a league from Paddington, a neighbouring city; and the other is the fair town of Lubeck. Also the fierce English are reported to me wise in that they will not share their land and flocks with wolves; but have fairly driven those marauders into their mountains. But neither in France, nor Germany, nor Italy, is a wayfarer's life safe from the vagabones after sundown. I can hear of no glazed house in all Venice; but only oiled linen and paper; and, behind these barbarian eyelets, a wooden jalosy. Their name for a cowardly assassin is 'a brave man,' and for an harlot, 'a courteous person,' which is as much as to say that a woman's worst vice, and a man's worst vice, are virtues. But I pray God for little Holland that there an assassin may be yclept an assassin, and an harlot an harlot, till domesday; and then gloze foul faults with silken names who can!"

Eli.] (With a sigh.) "He should have been a priest, saving your presence, my poor lass."

"Go to, peevish writer; art tied smarting by the leg, and may not see the beauties of Venice. So thy pen kicketh all around like a wicked mule.

"*January* 16.—Sweetheart, I must be brief and tell thee but a part of that I have seen, for this day my journal ends. To-night it sails for thee, and I, unhappy, not with it, but to-morrow, in another ship, to Rome.

"Dear Margaret, I took a hand-litter, and was carried to St. Mark his church. Outside it, towards the market-place, is a noble gallery, and above it four famous horses, cut in brass by the ancient Romans, and seem all moving, and at the very next step must needs leap down on the beholder. About the church are six hundred pillars of marble, porphyry, and ophites. Inside is a treasure greater than either at St. Denys, or Loretto, or Toledo. Here a jewelled pitcher given the seigniory by a Persian king, also the ducal cap blazing with jewels, and on its crown a diamond and a chrysolite, each as big as an almond; two golden crowns and twelve golden stomachers studded with jewels, from Constantinople; item, a monstrous sapphire; item, a great diamond given by a French king; item, a prodigious carbuncle; item, three unicorns' horns. But what are these compared with the sacred relics?

"Dear Margaret, I stood and saw the brazen chest that holds the body of St. Mark the Evangelist. I saw with these eyes, and handled, his ring and his gospel written with his own hand, and all my travels seemed light: for who am I that I should see such things? Dear Margaret, his sacred body was first brought from Alexandria by merchants in 810, and then not prized as now; for between 829, when this church was builded, and 1094, the very place where it lay was forgotten. Then holy priests fasted and prayed many days seeking for light, and lo the Evangelist's body brake at midnight through the marble and stood before them. They fell to the earth: but in the morning found the crevice the sacred body had burst through, and peering through it saw him lie. Then they took and laid him in his chest beneath the altar, and carefully put back the stone with its miraculous crevice, which crevice I saw, and shall gape for a monument while the world lasts. After that they showed me the Virgin's chair, it is of stone; also her picture, painted by St. Luke, very dark, and the features now scarce visible. This picture, in time of drought, they carry in procession, and brings the rain. I wish I had not seen it. Item, two pieces of marble spotted with John the Baptist's blood; item, a piece of the true cross and of the pillar to which Christ was tied; item, the rock struck by Moses, and wet to this hour; also a stone Christ sat on, preaching at Tyre; but some say it is the one the patriach Jacob laid his head on, and I hold with them, by reason our Lord never preached at Tyre. Going hence they showed me the state nursery for the children of those aphrodisian dames, their favourites. Here in the outer wall was a broad niche, and if they bring them so little as they can squeeze them through it alive, the bairn falls into a net inside, and the state takes charge of it, but if too big, their mothers must even take them home again, with whom abiding 'tis like to be mali corvi mali ovum. Coming out of the church we met them carrying in a corpse, with the feet and face bare. This I then first learned is Venetian custom, and sure no other town will ever rob them of it, nor of this that follows. On a great porphyry slab in the piazza were three ghastly heads rotting and tainting the air, and in their hot summers like to take vengeance with breeding of a plague. These were traitors to the state, and a heavy price—two thousand ducats—being put on each head, their friends had slain them and brought all three to the slab, and so sold blood of others and their own faith. No state buys heads so many nor pays half so high a price for that sorry merchandise. But what I most admired was to see over against the duke's palace a fair gallows in alabaster, reared express to hang him, and no other, for the least treason to the state; and there it stands in his eye whispering him memento mori. I pondered, and owned these signors my masters, who will let no man, not even their sovereign, be above the common weal. Hard by, on a wall, the workmen were just finishing, by order of the seigniory, the stone effigy of a tragical and enormous act enacted last year, yet on the wall looks innocent. Here two gentlefolks whisper together, and there other twain, their swords by their side. Four brethren were they, which did on either side conspire to poison the other two, and so halve their land in lieu of quartering it; and at a mutual banquet these twain drugged the wine, and those twain envenomed a marchpane, to such good purpose, that the same afternoon lay four "brave men" around one table grovelling in mortal agony, and cursing of one another and themselves, and so concluded miserably, and the land, for which they had lost their immortal souls went into another family. And why not? it could not go into a worse.

"But O sovereign wisdom of bywords! how true they put the finger on each nation's, or particular's, fault.

> Quand Italie sera sans poison
> Et France sans trahison
> Et l'Angleterre sans guerre,
> Lors sera le monde sans terre."

Richart explained this to Catherine, then proceeded: "And after this they took me to the quay, and presently I espied among the masts one garlanded with amaranth flowers. 'Take me thither,' said I, and I let my guide know the custom of our Dutch skippers to hoist flowers to the masthead when they are courting a maid.

Oft had I scoffed at this saying. 'So then his wooing is the earth's concern.' But now, so far from the Rotter, that bunch at a mast-head made my heart leap with assurance of a countryman. They carried me, and oh, Margaret! on the stern of that Dutch hoy, was writ in muckle letters,

RICHART ELIASSOEN, AMSTERDAM.

'Put me down,' I said: 'for our Lady's sake put me down.' I sat on the bank and looked, scarce believing my eyes, and looked, and presently fell to crying, till I could see the words no more. Ah me, how they went to my heart, those bare letters in a foreign land. Dear Richart! good kind brother Richart! often I have sat on his knee and rid on his back. Kisses many he has given me, unkind word from him had I never. And there was his name on his own ship, and his face and all his grave, but good and gentle ways, came back to me, and I sobbed vehemently, and cried aloud, 'Why, why is not brother Richart here, and not his name only?' I spake in Dutch, for my heart was too full to hold their foreign tongues, and—"

Eli.] "Well, Richart, go on lad, prithee go on. Is this a place to halt at?"

Richart.] "Father, with my duty to you, it is easy to say go on, but think ye I am not flesh and blood? The poor boy's—simple grief and brotherly love coming—so sudden—on me, they go through my heart and—I cannot go on: sink me if I can even see the words, 'tis writ so fine."

Denys.] "Courage, good Master Richart! Take your time. Here are more eyne wet than yours. Ah, little comrade! would God thou wert here, and I at Venice for thee."

Richart.] "Poor little curly-headed lad, what had he done that we have driven him so far?"

"That is what I would fain know," said Catherine, drily, then fell to weeping and rocking herself, with her apron over her head.

"Kind dame, good friends," said Margaret, trembling, "let me tell you how the letter ends. The skipper hearing our Gerard speak his grief in Dutch, accosted him, and spake comfortably to him; and after a while our Gerard found breath to say he was worthy Master Richart's brother. Thereat was the good skipper all agog to serve him."

The Cloister and the Hearth

Richart.] "So! so! skipper! Master Richart aforesaid will be at thy wedding and bring's purse to boot."

Margaret.] "Sir, he told Gerard of his consort that was to sail that very night for Rotterdam; and dear Gerard had to go home and finish his letter and bring it to the ship. And the rest, it is but his poor dear words of love to me, the which, an't please you, I think shame to hear them read aloud, and ends with the lines I sent to Mistress Kate, and *they* would sound so harsh *now* and ungrateful."

The pleading tone, as much as the words, prevailed, and Richart said he would read no more aloud, but run his eye over it for his own brotherly satisfaction. She blushed and looked uneasy, but made no reply.

"Eli," said Catherine, still sobbing a little, "tell me, for our Lady's sake, how our poor boy is to live at that nasty Rome. He is gone there to write, but here be his own words to prove writing avails nought; a had died o' hunger by the way but for paint-brush and psaltery. Well-a-day!"

"Well," said Eli, "he has got brush and music still. Besides, so many men so many minds. Writing, thof it had no sale in other parts, may be merchandise at Rome."

"Father," said little Kate, "have I your good leave to put in my word 'twixt mother and you?"

"And welcome, little heart."

"Then, seems to me painting and music, close at hand, be stronger than writing, but being distant, nought to compare; for see what glamour written paper hath done here but now. Our Gerard, writing at Venice, hath verily put his hand into this room at Rotterdam, and turned all our hearts. Ay, dear dear Gerard, methinks thy spirit hath rid hither on these thy paper wings; and oh! dear father, why not do as we should do were he here in the body?"

"Kate," said Eli, "fear not; Richart and I will give him glamour for glamour. We will write him a letter, and send it to Rome by a sure hand with money, and bid him home on the instant."

Cornelis and Sybrandt exchanged a gloomy look.

"Ah, good father! And meantime?"

"Well, meantime?"

"Dear father, dear mother, what can we do to pleasure the absent, but be kind to his poor lass; and her own trouble afore her?"

421

The Cloister and the Hearth

" 'Tis well!" said Eli; "but I am older than thou." Then he turned gravely to Margaret: "Wilt answer me a question, my pretty mistress?"

"If I may, sir," faltered Margaret.

"What are these marriage lines Gerard speaks of in the letter?"

"Our marriage lines, sir. His and mine. Know you not we are betrothed?"

"Before witnesses?"

"Ay, sure. My poor father and Martin Wittenhaagen."

"This is the first I ever heard of it. How came they in his hands? They should be in yours."

"Alas, sir, the more is my grief; but I ne'er doubted him: and he said it was a comfort to him to have them in his bosom."

"Y'are a very foolish lass."

"Indeed I was, sir. But trouble teaches the simple."

" 'Tis a good answer. Well, foolish or no, y'are honest. I had shown ye more respect at first, but I thought y'had been his leman, and that is the truth."

"God forbid, sir! Denys, methinks 'tis time for us to go. Give me my letter, sir!"

"Bide ye! bide ye! be not so hot, for a word! Natheless, wife, methinks her red cheek becomes her."

"Better than it did you to give it her, my man."

"Softly, wife, softly. I am not counted an unjust man thof I be somewhat slow."

Here Richart broke in. "Why, mistress, did ye shed your blood for our Gerard?"

"Not I, sir. But maybe I would."

"Nay, nay. But he says you did. Speak sooth, now!"

"Alas! I know not what ye mean. I rede ye believe not all that my poor lad says of me. Love makes him blind."

"Traitress!" cried Denys. "Let not her throw dust in thine eyes, Master Richart. Old Martin tells me—ye need not make signals to me, she-comrade; I am as blind as love. Martin tells me she cut her arm, and let her blood flow, and smeared her heels when Gerard was hunted by the bloodhounds, to turn the scent from her lad."

"Well, and if I did, 'twas my own, and spilled for the good of my own," said Margaret, defiantly. But, Catherine suddenly clasping her, she began to cry at having found a bosom to cry on, of one who would have also shed her blood for Gerard in danger.

Eli rose from his chair. "Wife," said he, solemnly, "you will set another chair at our table for every meal: also another plate and knife. They will be for Margaret and Peter. She will come when she likes, and stay away when she pleases. None may take her place at my left hand. Such as can welcome her are welcome to me. Such as cannot, I force them not to bide with me. The world is wide and free. Within my walls I am master, and my son's betrothed is welcome."

Catherine bustled out to prepare supper. Eli and Richart sat down and concocted a letter to bring Gerard home. Richart promised it should go by sea to Rome that very week. Sybrandt and Cornelis exchanged a gloomy wink, and stole out. Margaret, seeing Giles deep in meditation, for the dwarf's intelligence had taken giant strides, asked him to bring her the letter. "You have heard but half, good Master Giles," said she. "Shall I read you the rest?"

"I shall be much beholden to you," shouted the courtier.

She gave him her stool: curiosity bowed his pride to sit on it: and Margaret murmured the first part of the letter into his ear very low, not to disturb Eli and Richart. And, to do this, she leaned forward and put her lovely face cheek by jowl with Giles's hideous one: a strange contrast, and worth a painter's while to try and represent. And in this attitude Catherine found her, and all the mother warmed towards her, and she exchanged an eloquent glance with little Kate.

The latter smiled, and sewed, with drooping lashes.

"Get him home on the instant," roared Giles. "I'll make a man of him. I can do aught with the duke."

"Hear the boy!" said Catherine, half comically, half proudly.

"We hear him," said Richart: "a mostly makes himself heard when a do speak."

Sybrandt.] "Which will get to him first?"
Cornelis.] (Gloomily.) "Who can tell?"

CHAPTER LVII

ABOUT two months before this scene in Eli's home, the natives of a little maritime place between Naples and Rome might be seen flocking to the sea beach, with eyes cast seaward at a ship, that laboured against a stiff gale blowing dead on the shore.

At times she seemed likely to weather the danger, and then the spectators congratulated her aloud: at others the wind and sea drove her visibly nearer, and the lookers-on were not without a secret satisfaction they would not have owned even to themselves.

> Non quia vexari quemquam est jucunda voluptas
> Sed quibus ipse malis careas quia cernere suave est.

And the poor ship, though not scientifically built for sailing, was admirably constructed for going ashore, with her extravagant poop that caught the wind, and her lines like a cocked hat reversed. To those on the beach that battered labouring frame of wood seemed alive, and struggling against death with a panting heart. But could they have been transferred to her deck they would have seen she had not one beating heart but many, and not one nature but a score were coming out clear in that fearful hour.

The mariners stumbled wildly about the deck, handling the ropes as each thought fit, and cursing and praying alternately.

The passengers were huddled together round the mast, some sitting, some kneeling, some lying prostrate, and grasping the bulwarks as the vessel rolled and pitched in the mighty waves. One comely young man, whose ashy cheek, but compressed lips, showed how hard terror was battling in him with self-respect, stood a little apart, holding tight by a shroud, and wincing at each sea. It was the ill-fated Gerard. Meantime prayers and vows rose from the trembling throng amidships, and, to hear them, it seemed there were almost as many gods about as men and women. The sailors, indeed, relied on a single goddess. They varied her titles only, calling on her as "Queen of Heaven," "Star of the Sea," "Mistress of the World," "Haven of Safety." But among the landsmen Polytheism raged. Even those who by some strange chance hit on the same divinity did not hit on the same edition of that divinity. An English merchant vowed a heap of gold to our lady of Walsingham. But a Genoese merchant vowed a silver collar of four pounds to our lady of Loretto; and a Tuscan noble promised ten pounds of wax lights to our lady of Ravenna; and with a similar rage for diversity they pledged themselves, not on the true Cross, but on the true Cross in this, that, or the other, modern city.

Suddenly a more powerful gust than usual catching the sail at a disadvantage, the rotten shrouds gave way, and the sail was torn out with a loud crack and went down the wind smaller and smaller, blacker and blacker, and fluttered into the sea, half a mile off, like a sheet of paper; and, ere the helmsman could put the ship's head before the wind, a wave caught her on the quarter and drenched the poor wretches to the bone, and gave them a foretaste of chill death. Then one vowed aloud to turn Carthusian monk, if St. Thomas would save him. Another would go a pilgrim to Compostella, bareheaded, barefooted, with nothing but a coat of mail on his naked skin, if St. James would save him. Others invoked Thomas, Dominic, Denys, and, above all, Catherine of Sienna.

Two petty Neapolitan traders stood shivering.

One shouted at the top of his voice, "I vow to St. Christopher at Paris a waxen image of his own weight, if I win safe to land."

On this the other nudged him, and said, "Brother, brother, take heed what you vow. Why, if you sell all you have in the world by public auction, 'twill not buy his weight in wax."

"Hold your tongue, you fool," said the vociferator. Then in a whisper,

"Think ye I am in earnest? Let me but win safe to land, I'll not give him a rush dip."

Others lay flat and prayed to the sea. "O most merciful sea! O sea most generous! O bountiful sea! O beautiful sea! be gentle, be kind, preserve us in this hour of peril."

And others wailed and moaned in mere animal terror each time the ill-fated ship rolled or pitched more terribly than usual; and she was now a mere plaything in the arms of the tremendous waves.

A Roman woman of the humbler class sat with her child at her half-bared breast, silent amid that wailing throng: her cheek ashy pale; her eye calm; and her lips moved at times in silent prayer, but she neither wept, nor lamented, nor bargained with the gods.

Whenever the ship seemed really gone under their feet, and bearded men squeaked, she kissed her child; but that was all. And so she sat patient, and suckled him in death's jaws; for why should he lose any joy she could give him; moribundo? Ay, there I do believe, sat Antiquity among those mediævals. Sixteen hundred years had not tainted the old Roman blood in her veins; and the instinct of a race she had perhaps scarce heard of taught her to die with decent dignity.

A gigantic friar stood on the poop with feet apart, like the Colossus of Rhodes, not so much defying, as ignoring, the peril that surrounded him. He recited verses from the canticles with a loud, unwavering voice; and invited the passengers to confess to him. Some did so on their knees, and he heard them, and laid his hands on them, and absolved them as if he had been in a snug sacristy, instead of a perishing ship. Gerard got nearer and nearer to him, by the instinct that takes the wavering to the side of the impregnable. And, in truth, the courage of heroes facing fleshly odds might have paled by the side of that gigantic friar, and his still more gigantic composure. Thus, even here, two were found who maintained the dignity of our race: a woman, tender, yet heroic, and a monk steeled by religion against mortal fears.

And now, the sail being gone, the sailors cut down the useless mast a foot above the board, and it fell with its remaining hamper over the ship's side. This seemed to relieve her a little.

But now the hull, no longer impelled by canvas, could not keep ahead of the sea. It struck her again and again on the poop, and the tremendous blows seemed given by a rocky mountain, not by a liquid.

The captain left the helm and came amidships pale as death. "Lighten her," he cried. "Fling all overboard, or we shall founder ere we strike, and lose the one little chance we have of life." While the sailors were executing this order, the captain, pale himself, and surrounded by pale faces that demanded to know their fate, was talking as unlike an English skipper in like peril as can well be imagined. "Friends," said he, "last night, when all was fair, too fair, alas! there came a globe of fire close to the ship. When a pair of them come it is good luck, and nought can drown her that voyage. We mariners call these fiery globes Castor and Pollux. But if

Castor come without Pollux, or Pollux without Castor, she is doomed. Therefore, like good Christians, prepare to die."

These words were received with a loud wail.

To a trembling inquiry how long they had to prepare, the captain replied, "She may, or may not, last half an hour; over that, impossible; she leaks like a sieve; bustle, men, lighten her."

The poor passengers seized on everything that was on deck and flung it overboard. Presently they laid hold of a heavy sack; an old man was lying on it, sea sick. They lugged it from under him. It rattled. Two of them drew it to the side; up started the owner, and, with an unearthly shriek, pounced on it. "Holy Moses! what would you do? 'Tis my all; 'tis the whole fruits of my journey; silver candlesticks, silver plates, brooches, hanaps—"

"Let go, thou hoary villain," cried the others, "shall all our lives be lost for thy ill-gotten gear?" "Fling him in with it," cried one; "'tis this Ebrew we Christian men are drowned for." Numbers soon wrenched it from him and heaved it over the side. It splashed into the waves. Then its owner uttered one cry of anguish, and stood glaring, his white hair streaming in the wind, and was going to leap after it, and would, had it floated. But it sank, and was gone for ever; and he staggered to and fro, tearing his hair, and cursed them and the ship, and the sea, and all the powers of heaven and hell alike.

And now the captain cried out: "See, there is a church in sight. Steer for that church, mate, and you, friends, pray to the saint, who'er he be."

So they steered for the church and prayed to the unknown god it was named after. A tremendous sea pooped them, broke the rudder, and jammed it immovable, and flooded the deck.

Then wild with superstitious terror some of them came round Gerard. "Here is the cause of all," they cried. "He has never invoked a single saint. He is a heathen; here is a pagan aboard."

"Alas, good friends, say not so," said Gerard, his teeth chattering with cold and fear. "Rather call these heathens, that lie a praying to the sea. Friends, I do honour the saints,—but I dare not pray to them now,—there is no time—(oh!) what avail me Dominic, and Thomas and Catherine? Nearer God's throne than these St. Peter sitteth; and, if I pray to him, it's odd, but I shall be drowned

ere he has time to plead my cause with God. Oh! oh! oh! I must
need go straight to him that made the sea, and the saints, and me.
Our father, which art in heaven, save these poor souls and me that
cry for the bare life! Oh sweet Jesus, pitiful Jesus, that didst
walk Genezaret when Peter sank, and wept for Lazarus dead when
the apostles' eyes were dry, oh save poor Gerard—for dear Margaret's sake!"

At this moment the sailors were seen preparing to desert the
sinking ship in the little boat, which even at that epoch every ship
carried; then there was a rush of egotists; and thirty souls crowded
into it. Remained behind three who were bewildered, and two
who were paralyzed, with terror. The paralyzed sat like heaps
of wet rags, the bewildered ones ran to and fro, and saw the thirty
egotists put off, but made no attempt to join them: only kept run-
ing to and fro, and wringing their hands. Besides these there was
one on his knees praying over the wooden statue of the Virgin
Mary, as large as life, which the sailors had reverently detached
from the mast. It washed about the deck, as the water came slush-
ing in from the sea, and pouring out at the scuppers; and this
poor soul kept following it on his knees, with his hands clasped
at it, and the water playing with it. And there was the Jew,
palsied, but not by fear. He was no longer capable of so petty
a passion. He sat cross-legged, bemoaning his bag, and, whenever
the spray lashed him, shook his fist at where it came from, and
cursed the Nazarenes, and their gods, and their devils, and their
ships, and their waters, to all eternity.

And the gigantic Dominican, having shriven the whole ship,
stood calmly communing with his own spirit. And the Roman
woman sat pale and patient, only drawing her child closer to her
bosom as death came nearer.

Gerard saw this and it awakened his manhood. "See! see!" he
said, "they have ta'en the boat and left the poor woman and her
child to perish."

His heart soon set his wit working.

"Wife, I'll save thee yet, please God." And he ran to find a
cask or a plank to float her. There was none.

Then his eye fell on the wooden image of the Virgin. He caught
it up in his arms, and, heedless of a wail that issued from its worshipper, like a child robbed of its toy, ran aft with it. "Come,

wife," he cried. "I'll lash thee and the child to this. 'Tis sore worm eaten; but 'twill serve."

She turned her great dark eye on him and said a single word: "Thyself?"

But with wonderful magnanimity and tenderness.

"I am a man, and have no child to take care of."

"Ah!" said she, and his words seemed to animate her face with a desire to live. He lashed the image to her side. Then with the hope of life she lost something of her heroic calm; not much: her body trembled a little, but not her eye.

The ship was now so low in the water that by using an oar as a lever he could slide her into the waves.

"Come," said he, "while yet there is time."

She turned her great Roman eyes, wet now, upon him. "Poor youth!—God forgive me!—My child!" And he launched her on the surge, and with his oar kept her from being battered against the ship.

A heavy hand fell on him; a deep sonorous voice sounded in his ear: "'Tis well. Now come with me."

It was the gigantic friar.

Gerard turned, and the friar took two strides, and laid hold of the broken mast. Gerard did the same, obeying him instinctively. Between them, after a prodigious effort, they hoisted up the remainder of the mast, and carried it off. "Fling it in," said the friar, "and follow it." They flung it in; but one of the bewildered passengers had run after them, and jumped first and got on one end. Gerard seized the other, the friar the middle.

It was a terrible situation. The mast rose and plunged with each wave like a kicking horse, and the spray flogged their faces mercilessly, and blinded them; to help knock them off.

Presently was heard a long grating noise ahead. The ship had struck: and soon after, she being stationary now, they were hurled against her with tremendous force. Their companion's head struck against the upper part of the broken rudder with a horrible crack, and was smashed like a cocoa-nut by a sledge-hammer. He sunk directly, leaving no trace but a red stain on the water, and a white clot on the jagged rudder, and a death cry ringing in their ears, as they drifted clear under the lee of the black hull. The friar uttered a short Latin prayer for the safety of his soul, and took his place composedly. They rolled along ὑπεκ Θανατοιο; one moment they saw nothing, and seemed down in a mere basin of watery hills: the next they caught glimpses of the shore speckled bright with people, who kept throwing up their arms with wild Italian gestures to encourage them, and the black boat driving bottom upwards, and between it and them the woman rising and falling like themselves. She had come across a paddle, and was holding her child tight with her left arm, and paddling gallantly with her right.

When they had tumbled along thus a long time, suddenly the friar said quietly: "I touched the ground."

"Impossible, father," said Gerard, "we are more than a hundred yards from shore. Prithee, prithee, leave not our faithful mast."

"My son," said the friar, "you speak prudently. But know that I have business of holy Church on hand, and may not waste time floating when I can walk, in her service. There, I felt it with my toes again; see the benefit of wearing sandals, and not shoon. Again: and sandy. Thy stature is less than mine: keep to the mast! I walk." He left the mast accordingly, and extending his powerful arms, rushed through the water. Gerard soon followed him. At each overpowering wave the monk stood like a tower, and, closing his mouth, threw his head back to encounter it, and was entirely lost under it awhile: then emerged and ploughed lustily on. At last they came close to the shore; but the suction outward baffled all their attempts to land. Then the natives sent stout fishermen into the sea, holding by long spears in a triple chain: and so dragged them ashore.

The friar shook himself, bestowed a short paternal benediction on the natives, and went on to Rome, with eyes bent on earth, according to his rule, and without pausing. He did not even cast a glance back upon that sea, which had so nearly engulfed him, but had no power to harm him, without his master's leave.

While he stalks on alone to Rome without looking back, I who am not in the service of holy Church, stop a moment to say that the reader and I were within six inches of this giant once before: but we escaped him that time. Now, I fear, we are in for him. Gerard grasped every hand upon the beach. They brought him to an enormous fire and with a delicacy he would hardly have encountered in the north, left him to dry himself alone: on this he took out of his bosom a parchment, and a paper, and dried them carefully. When this was done to his mind, and not till then, he consented to put on a fisherman's dress and leave his own by the fire, and went down to the beach. What he saw may be briefly related.

The captain stuck by the ship, not so much from gallantry, as from a conviction that it was idle to resist Castor or Pollux, whichever it was that had come for him in a ball of fire.

Nevertheless the sea broke up the ship and swept the poop, captain and all, clear of the rest, and took him safe ashore. Gerard had a principal hand in pulling him out of the water. The disconsolate Hebrew landed on another fragment, and on touching earth offered a reward for his bag, which excited little sympathy, but some amusement. Two more were saved on pieces of the wreck. The thirty egotists came ashore, but one at a time, and dead; one breathed still. Him the natives, with excellent intentions, took to a hot fire. So then he too retired from this shifting scene.

As Gerard stood by the sea, watching, with horror and curiosity mixed, his late companions washed ashore, a hand was laid lightly on his shoulder. He turned. It was the Roman matron, burning with womanly gratitude. She took his hand gently, and raising it slowly to her lips, kissed it; but so nobly, she seemed to be conferring an honour on one deserving hand. Then, with face all beaming and moist eyes, she held her child up and made him kiss his preserver.

Gerard kissed the child: more than once. He was fond of children. But he said nothing. He was much moved; for she did not speak at all, except with her eyes, and glowing cheeks, and noble antique gesture, so large and stately. Perhaps she was right. Gratitude is not a thing of words. It was an ancient Roman matron thanking a modern from her heart of hearts.

Next day, towards afternoon, Gerard—twice as old as last year, thrice as learned in human ways, a boy no more, but a man who had shed blood in self-defense, and grazed the grave by land and sea— reached the eternal city; *post tot naufragia tutus.*

CHAPTER LVIII

GERARD took a modest lodging on the west bank of the Tiber, and every day went forth in search of work, taking a specimen round to every shop he could hear of that executed such commissions.

They received him coldly. "We make our letter somewhat thinner than this," said one. "How dark your ink is," said another. But the main cry was, "What avails this? Scant is the Latin writ here now. Can ye not write Greek?"

"Ay, but not nigh so well as Latin."

"Then you shall never make your bread at Rome."

Gerard borrowed a beautiful Greek manuscript at a high price, and went home with a sad hole in his purse, but none in his courage.

In a fortnight he had made vast progress with the Greek character; so then, to lose no time, he used to work at it till noon, and hunt customers the rest of the day.

When he carried round a better Greek specimen than any they possessed, the traders informed him that Greek and Latin were alike unsalable; the city was thronged with works from all Europe. He should have come last year.

Gerard bought a psaltery.

His landlady, pleased with his looks and manners, used often to speak a kind word in passing. One day she made him dine with her, and somewhat to his surprise asked him what had dashed his spirits. He told her. She gave him her reading of the matter. "Those sly traders," she would be bound, "had writers in their pay for whose work they received a noble price and paid a sorry one. So no wonder they blow cold on you. Methinks you write too well. How know I that? say you. Marry—marry, because you lock not your door, like the churl Pietro, and women will be curious. Ay, ay, you write too well for *them*."

Gerard asked an explanation.

"Why," said she, "your good work might put out the eyes of that they are selling."

Gerard sighed. "Alas! dame, you read folk on the ill side, and you so kind and frank yourself."

The Cloister and the Hearth

"My dear little heart, these Romans are a subtle race. Me! I am a Siennese, thanks to the Virgin."

"My mistake was leaving Augsburg," said Gerard.

"Augsburg?" said she, haughtily; "is that a place to even to Rome? I never heard of it for my part."

She then assured him that he should make his fortune in spite of the booksellers. "Seeing thee a stranger, they lie to thee without sense or discretion. Why all the world knows that our great folk are bitten with the writing spider this many years, and pour out their money like water, and turn good land and houses into writ sheepskins to keep in a chest or a cupboard. God help them, and send them safe through this fury, as he hath through a heap of others; and in sooth hath been somewhat less cutting and stabbing among rival factions, and vindictive eating of their opposites' livers, minced and fried, since Scribbling came in. Why *I* can tell you two. There is his eminence Cardinal Bassarion, and his holiness the Pope himself. There be a pair could keep a score such as thee a writing night and day. But I'll speak to Teresa; she hears the gossip of the court."

The next day she told him she had seen Teresa, and had heard of five more signors who were bitten with the writing spider. Gerard took down their names, and bought parchment, and busied himself for some days in preparing specimens. He left one, with his name and address, at each of these signors' doors, and hopefully awaited the result.

There was none.

Day after day passed and left him heartsick.

And strange to say this was just the time when Margaret was fighting so hard against odds to feed her male dependents at Rotterdam, and arrested for curing without a licence instead of killing with one.

Gerard saw ruin staring him in the face.

He spent the afternoons picking up canzonets and mastering them. He laid in playing cards to colour, and struck off a meal per day.

This last stroke of genius got him into fresh trouble.

In these "camere locande" the landlady dressed all the meals, though the lodgers bought the provisions. So Gerard's hostess speedily detected him, and asked him if he was not ashamed of himself: by which brusque opening, having made him blush and look

433

scared, she pacified herself all in a moment, and appealed to his good sense whether Adversity was a thing to be overcome on an empty stomach.

"Patienza, my lad! times will mend, meantime I will feed you for the love of heaven" (Italian for "gratis").

"Nay, hostess," said Gerard, "my purse is not yet quite void, and it would add to my trouble an if true folk should lose their due by me."

"Why you are as mad as your neighbour Pietro, with his one bad picture."

"Why, how know you 'tis a bad picture?"

"Because nobody will buy it. There is one that hath no gift. He will have to don casque and glaive, and carry his panel for a shield."

erard pricked up his ears at this: so she told him more. Pietro had come from Florence with money in his purse, and an unfinished picture; had taken her one unfurnished room, opposite Gerard's, and furnished it neatly. When his picture was finished, he received visitors and had offers for it: these, though in her opinion liberal ones, he had refused so disdainfully as to make enemies of his customers. Since then he had often taken it out with him to try and sell, but had always brought it back; and, the last month, she had seen one movable after another go out of his room, and now he wore but one suit, and lay at night on a great chest. She had found this out only by peeping through the keyhole, for he locked the door most vigilantly whenever he went out. "Is he afraid we shall steal his chest, or his picture that no soul in all Rome is weak enough to buy?"

"Nay, sweet hostess, see you not 'tis his poverty he would screen from view?"

"And the more fool he! Are all our hearts as ill as his? A might give us a trial first any way."

"How you speak of him. Why his case is mine; and your countryman to boot."

"Oh, we Siennese love strangers. His case yours? nay 'tis just the contrary. You are the comeliest youth ever lodged in this house; hair like gold; he is a dark sour-visaged loon. Besides you know how to take a woman on her better side; but not he. Natheless I wish he would not starve to death in my house, to get me a bad name. Any way, one starveling is enough in any house. You are far from home, and it is for me, which am the mistress here, to number your meals—for me and the Dutch wife, your mother, that is far away: we two women shall settle that matter. Mind thou thine own business, being a man, and leave cooking and the like to us, that are in the world for little else that I see but to roast fowls, and suckle men at starting, and sweep their grown-up cobwebs."

"Dear kind dame, in sooth you do often put me in mind of my mother that is far away."

"All the better; I'll put you more in mind of her before I have done with you." And the honest soul beamed with pleasure.

Gerard not being an egotist, nor blinded by female partialities, saw his own grief in poor proud Pietro; and the more he thought of it, the more he resolved to share his humble means with that unlucky artist; Pietro's sympathy would repay him. He tried to waylay him: but without success.

One day he heard a groaning in the room. He knocked at the door, but received no answer. He knocked again. A surly voice bade him enter.

He obeyed somewhat timidly, and entered a garret furnished with a chair, a picture, face to wall, an iron basin, an easel, and a long chest, on which was coiled a haggard young man with a wonderfully bright eye. Anything more like a coiled cobra ripe for striking the first comer was never seen.

"Good Signor Pietro," said Gerard, "forgive me that, weary of my own solitude, I intrude on yours; but I am your nighest neighbour in this house, and methinks your brother in fortune. I am an artist too."

"You are a painter? Welcome, signor. Sit down on my bed."

And Pietro jumped off and waved him into the vacant throne with a magnificent demonstration of courtesy.

Gerard bowed, and smiled; but hesitated a little. "I may not call myself a painter. I am a writer, a caligraph. I copy Greek and Latin manuscripts, when I can get them to copy."

"And you call that an artist?"

"Without offense to your superior merit, Signor Pietro."

"No offence, stranger, none. Only, me seemeth an artist is one who thinks and paints his thought. Now a caligraph but draws in black and white the thoughts of another."

The Cloister and the Hearth

"'Tis well distinguished, signor. But then, a writer can write the thoughts of the great ancients, and matters of pure reason, such as no man may paint: ay, and the thoughts of God, which angels could not paint. But let that pass. I am a painter as well; but a sorry one."

"The better thy luck. They will buy thy work in Rome."

"But seeking to commend myself to one of thy eminence, I thought it well rather to call myself a capable writer than a scurvy painter."

At this moment a step was heard on the stair.

"Ah! 'tis the good dame," cried Gerard. "What ho! hostess, I am here in conversation with Signor Pietro. I dare say he will let me have my humble dinner here."

The Italian bowed gravely.

The landlady brought in Gerard's dinner smoking and savory. She put the dish down on the bed with a face divested of all expression, and went.

Gerard fell to. But ere he had eaten many mouthfuls he stopped, and said: "I am an ill-mannered churl, Signor Pietro. I ne'er eat to my mind, when I eat alone. For our Lady's sake put a spoon into this ragout with me; 'tis not unsavoury, I promise you."

Pietro fixed his glittering eye on him.

"What, good youth, thou a stranger, and offerest me thy dinner?"

"Why, see, there is more than one can eat."

"Well, I accept," said Pietro: and took the dish with some appearance of calmness, and flung the contents out of window.

Then he turned trembling with mortification and ire, and said: "Let that teach thee to offer alms to an artist thou knowest not, master writer."

Gerard's face flushed with anger, and it cost him a bitter struggle not to box this high-souled creature's ears. And then to go and destroy good food! His mother's milk curdled in his veins with horror at such impiety. Finally, pity at Pietro's petulance and egotism, and a touch of respect for poverty-struck pride, prevailed.

However he said coldly, "Likely what thou hast done might pass in a novel of thy countryman, Signor Boccaccio; but 'twas not honest."

"Make that good!" said the painter sullenly.

The Cloister and the Hearth

"I offered thee half my dinner; no more. But thou hast ta'en it all. Hadst a right to throw away thy share, but not mine. Pride is well, but justice is better."

Pietro stared, then reflected.

"'Tis well. I took thee for a fool, so transparent was thine artifice. Forgive me! And prithee leave me! Thou seest how 'tis with me. The world hath soured me. I hate mankind. I was not always so. Once more excuse that my discourtesy, and fare thee well!"

Gerard sighed and made for the door.

But suddenly a thought struck him. "Signor Pietro," said he, "we Dutchmen are hard bargainers. We are the lads 'een eij scheeren,' that is 'to shave an egg.' Therefore, I, for my lost dinner, do claim to feast mine eyes on your picture, whose face is toward the wall."

"Nay, nay," said the painter hastily, "ask me not that; I have already misconducted myself enough towards thee. I would not shed thy blood."

"Saints forbid! My blood?"

"Stranger," said Pietro sullenly, "irritated by repeated insults to my picture, which is my child, my heart, I did in a moment of rage make a solemn vow to drive my dagger into the next one that should flout it, and the labour and love that I have given to it."

"What, are all to be slain that will not praise this picture?" and he looked at its back with curiosity.

"Nay, nay: if you would but look at it, and hold your parrot tongues. But you will be talking. So I have turned it to the wall for ever. Would I were dead, and buried in it for my coffin!"

Gerard reflected.

"I accept the conditions. Show me the picture! I can but hold my peace."

Pietro went and turned its face, and put it in the best light the room afforded, and coiled himself again on his chest, with his eye, and stiletto, glittering.

The picture represented the Virgin and Christ, flying through the air in a sort of cloud of shadowy cherubic faces; underneath was a landscape, forty or fifty miles in extent, and a purple sky above.

Gerard stood and looked at it in silence. Then he stepped close, and looked. Then he retired as far off as he could, and looked; but said not a word.

When he had been at this game half an hour, Pietro cried out querulously and somewhat inconsistently: "Well, have you not a word to say about it?"

Gerard started. "I cry your mercy; I forgot there were three of us here. Ay, I have much to say." And he drew his sword.

"Alas! alas!" cried Pietro, jumping in terror from his lair. "What wouldst thou?"

"Marry, defend myself against thy bodkin, signor; and at due odds, being, as aforesaid, a Dutchman. Therefore, hold aloof, while I deliver judgment, or I will pin thee to the wall like a cockchafer."

"Oh! is that all," said Pietro greatly relieved. "I feared you were going to stab my poor picture with your sword, stabbed already by so many foul tongues."

Gerard "pursued criticism under difficulties." Put himself in a position of defence, with his sword's point covering Pietro, and one eye glancing aside at the picture. "First, signor, I would have you know that, in the mixing of certain colours, and in the preparation of your oil, you Italians are far behind us Flemings. But let that flea stick. For as small as I am, I can show you certain secrets of the Van Eycks, that you will put to marvellous profit in your next picture. Meantime I see in this one the great qualities of your nation. Verily, ye are *solis filii*. If we have colour, you have imagination. Mother of heaven! an he hath not flung his immortal soul upon the panel. One thing I go by is this; it makes other pictures I once admired seem drossy, earth-born things. The drapery here is somewhat short and stiff. Why not let it float freely, the figures being in air and motion?"

"I will! I will!" cried Pietro eagerly. "I will do anything for those who will but see what I *have* done."

"Humph! This landscape it enlightens me. Henceforth I scorn those little huddled landscapes that did erst content me. Here is Nature's very face: a spacious plain, each distance marked, and every tree, house, figure, field and river smaller and less plain, by exquisite gradation, till vision itself melts into distance. O beautiful! And the cunning rogue hath hung his celestial figure in air out of the way of his little world below. Here, floating saints beneath heaven's purple canopy. There, far down, earth and her busy hives. And they let you take this painted poetry, this blooming hymn, through the streets of Rome and bring it home unsold. But I tell thee in Ghent or Bruges, or even in Rotterdam, they would tear it out of thy hands. But 'tis a common saying that a stranger's eye sees clearest. Courage, Pietro Vanucci! I reverence thee, and, though myself a scurvy painter, do forgive thee for being a great one. Forgive thee? I thank God for thee and such rare men as thou art; and bow the knee to thee in just homage. Thy picture is immortal, and thou, that hast but a chest to sit on, art a king in thy most royal art. Viva, il maëstro! Viva!"

At this unexpected burst the painter, with all the abandon of his nation, flung himself on Gerard's neck. "They said it was a maniac's dream," he sobbed.

"Maniacs themselves! no, idiots!" shouted Gerard.

"Generous stranger! I will hate men no more since the world hath such as thee. I was a viper to fling thy poor dinner away; a wretch, a monster."

"Well, monster, wilt be gentle now, and sup with me?"

"Ah! that I will. Whither goest thou?"

"To order supper on the instant. We will have the picture for third man."

"I will invite it whiles thou art gone. My poor picture, child of my heart."

"Ah! master; 'twill look on many a supper after the worms have eaten you and me."

"I hope so," said Pietro.

CHAPTER LIX

ABOUT a week after this the two friends sat working together, but not in the same spirit. Pietro dashed fitfully at his, and did wonders in a few minutes, and then did nothing, except abuse it; then presently resumed it in a fury, to lay it down with a groan. Through all which kept calmly working, calmly smiling, the canny Dutchman.

To be plain, Gerard, who never had a friend he did not master, had put his Onagra in harness. The friends were painting playing cards to boil the pot.

When done, the indignant master took up his picture to make his daily tour in search of a customer.

Gerard begged him to take the cards as well, and try and sell them. He looked all the rattlesnake, but eventually embraced Gerard in the Italian fashion, and took them, after first drying the last finished ones in the sun, which was now powerful in that happy clime.

Gerard, left alone, executed a Greek letter or two, and then mended a little rent in his hose. His landlady found him thus employed, and inquired ironically whether there were no women in the house.

"When you have done that," said she, "come and talk to Teresa, my friend I spoke to thee of, that hath a husband not good for much, which brags his acquaintance with the great."

Gerard went down, and who should Teresa be but the Roman matron.

"Ah, madama," said he, "is it you? The good dame told me not that. And the little fair-haired boy, is he well? is he none the worse for his voyage in that strange boat?"

"He is well," said the matron.

"Why, what are you two talking about?" said the landlady, staring at them both in turn; "and why tremble you so, Teresa mia?"

"He saved my child's life," said Teresa, making an effort to compose herself.

"What, my lodger? and he never told me a word of that. Art not ashamed to look me in the face?"

"Alas! speak not harshly to him," said the matron. She then turned to her friend and poured out a glowing description of Gerard's conduct, during which Gerard stood blushing like a girl, and scarce recognizing his own performance, gratitude painted it so fair.

"And to think thou shouldst ask me to serve thy lodger, of whom I knew nought but that he had thy good word, O Fiammina: and that was enough for me. Dear youth, in serving thee I serve myself."

Then ensued an eager description, by the two women, of what had been done, and what should be done, to penetrate the thick wall of fees, commissions, and chicanery, which stood between the patrons of art and an unknown artist in the Eternal city.

Teresa smiled sadly at Gerard's simplicity in leaving specimens of his skill at the doors of the great.

"What!" said she, "without promising the servants a share—without even feeing them, to let the signors see thy merchandize! As well have flung it into Tiber."

"Well-a-day!" sighed Gerard. "Then how is an artist to find a patron? for artists are poor, not rich."

"By going to some city nobler and not so greedy as this," said Teresa. "La corte Romana non vuol' pecora senza lana."

She fell into thought, and said she would come again to-morrow. The landlady felicitated Gerard. "Teresa has got something in her head," said she.

Teresa was scarce gone when Pietro returned with his picture, looking black as thunder. Gerard exchanged a glance with the landlady, and followed him up stairs to console him.

"What, have they let thee bring home thy masterpiece?"

"As heretofore."

"More fools they, then."

"That is not the worst."

"Why, what is the matter?"

"They have bought the cards," yelled Pietro, and hammered the air furiously right and left.

"All the better," said Gerard cheerfully.

"They flew at me for them. They were enraptured with them. They tried to conceal their longing for them, but could not. I saw, I feigned, I pillaged; curse the boobies."

And he flung down a dozen small silver coins on the floor and jumped on them, and danced on them with basilisk eyes, and then kicked them assiduously, and sent them spinning and flying, and running all abroad. Down went Gerard on his knees and followed the maltreated innocents directly, and transferred them tenderly to his purse.

"Shouldst rather smile at their ignorance, and put it to profit," said he.

"And so I will," said Pietro, with concentrated indignation. "The brutes! We will paint a pack a day; we will set the whole city gambling and ruining itself, while we live like princes on its vices and stupidity. There was one of the queens, though, I had fain have kept back. 'Twas you limned her, brother. She had lovely red-brown hair and sapphire eyes, and above all, soul."

"Pietro," said Gerard, softly, "I painted that one from my heart."

The quick-witted Italian nodded, and his eyes twinkled.

"You love her so well, yet leave her."

"Pietro, it is because I love her so dear that I have wandered all this dreary road."

This interesting colloquy was interrupted by the landlady crying from below, "Come down, you are wanted." He went down, and there was Teresa again.

"Come with me, Ser Gerard."

CHAPTER LX

GERARD walked silently beside Teresa, wondering in his own mind, after the manner of artists, what she was going to do with him; instead of asking her. So at last she told him of her own accord. A friend had informed her of a working goldsmith's wife who wanted a writer. "Her shop is hard by; you will not have far to go."

Accordingly they soon arrived at the goldsmith's wife.

"Madama," said Teresa, "Leonora tells me you want a writer: I have brought you a beautiful one, he saved my child at sea. Prithee look on him with favour."

The goldsmith's wife complied in one sense. She fixed her eyes on Gerard's comely face, and could hardly take them off again. But her reply was unsatisfactory. "Nay, I have no use for a writer. Ah! I mind now, it is my gossip, Clælia, the sausage-maker, wants one; she told me, and I told Leonora."

Teresa made a courteous speech and withdrew.

Clælia lived at some distance, and when they reached her house she was out. Teresa said calmly, "I will await her return," and sat so still, and dignified, and statuesque, that Gerard was beginning furtively to draw her, when Clælia returned.

"Madama, I hear from the goldsmith's wife, the excellent Olympia, that you need a writer" (here she took Gerard by the hand and led him forward); "I have brought you a beautiful one,

The Cloister and the Hearth

he saved my child from the cruel waves. For our Lady's sake look with favour on him."

"My good dame, my fair Ser," said Clælia, "I have no use for a writer; but now you remind me, it was my friend Appia Claudia asked me for one but the other day. She is a tailor, lives in the Via Lepida."

Teresa retired calmly.

"Madama," said Gerard, "this is likely to be a tedious business for you."

Teresa opened her eyes.

"What was ever done without a little patience?" She added mildly, "We will knock at every door at Rome but you shall have justice."

"But madama, I think we are dogged. I noticed a man that follows us, sometimes afar, sometimes close."

"I have seen it," said Teresa, coldly: but her cheek coloured faintly. "It is my poor Lodovico."

She stopped and turned, and beckoned with her finger.

A figure approached them somewhat unwillingly.

When he came up, she gazed him full in the face, and he looked sheepish.

"Lodovico mio," said she, "know this young Ser, of whom I have so often spoken to thee. Know him and love him, for he it was who saved thy wife and child."

At these last words Lodovico, who had been bowing and grinning artificially, suddenly changed to an expression of heartfelt gratitude, and embraced Gerard warmly.

Yet somehow there was something in the man's original manner, and his having followed his wife by stealth, that made Gerard uncomfortable under this caress. However he said, "We shall have your company, Ser Lodovico?"

"No, signor," replied Lodovico, "I go not on that side Tiber."

"Addio, then," said Teresa, significantly.

"When shall you return home, Teresa mia?"

"When I have done mine errand, Lodovico."

They pursued their way in silence. Teresa now wore a sad and almost gloomy air.

To be brief, Appia Claudia was merciful, and did not send them

443

over Tiber again, but only a hundred yards down the street to
Lucretia, who kept the glove shop; she it was wanted a writer: but
what for Appia Claudia could not conceive. Lucretia was a merry
little dame, who received them heartily enough, and told them she
wanted no writer, kept all her accounts in her head. "It was
for my confessor, Father Colonna; he is mad after them."

"I have heard of his excellency," said Teresa.

"Who has not?"

"But, good dame, he is a friar; he has made vow of poverty.
I cannot let the young man write and not be paid. He saved my
child at sea."

"Did he now?" And Lucretia cast an approving look on Gerard.
"Well, make your mind easy; a Colonna never wants for money.
The good father has only to say the word, and the princes of his
race will pour a thousand crowns into his lap. And such a confessor,
dame! the best in Rome. His head is leagues and leagues away
all the while; he never heeds what you are saying. Why I think no
more of confessing my sins to him than of telling them to that wall.
Once, to try him, I confessed, along with the rest, as how I had
killed my lodger's little girl and baked her in a pie. Well, when
my voice left off confessing, he started out of his dream, and says he,
a mustering up a gloom, 'My erring sister, say three paternosters
and three ave Marias kneeling, and eat no butter nor eggs next
Wednesday, and pax vobiscum!' and off a went with his hands
behind him, looking as if there was no such thing as me in the
world."

Teresa waited patiently, then calmly brought this discursive lady
back to the point: "Would she be so kind as go with this good
youth to the friar and speak for him?"

"Alack! how can I leave my shop? And what need? His door
is aye open to writers, and painters, and scholars, and all such cattle.
Why, one day he would not receive the Duke d'Urbino, because a
learned Greek was closeted with him, and the friar's head and his
so close together over a dusty parchment just come in from Greece,
as you could put one cowl over the pair. His wench Onesta told
me. She mostly looks in here for a chat when she goes an errand."

"This is the man for thee, my friend," said Teresa.

"All you have to do," continued Lucretia, "is to go to his lodgings
(my boy shall show them you), and tell Onesta you come from

me, and you are a writer, and she will take you up to him. If you put a piece of silver in the wench's hand, 'twill do you no harm: that stands to reason."

"I have silver," said Teresa, warmly.

"But stay," said Lucretia, "mind one thing. What the young man saieth he can do, that he must be able to do, or let him shun the good friar like poison. He is a very wild beast against all bunglers. Why, 'twas but t'other day, one brought him an ill-carved crucifix. Says he: 'Is this how you present "Salvator Mundi?" who died for you in mortal agony; and you go and grudge him careful work. This slovenly gimcrack, a crucifix? But that it *is* a crucifix of some sort, and I am a holy man, I'd dust your jacket with your crucifix,' says he. Onesta heard every word through the keyhole; so mind."

"Have no fears, madama," said Teresa, loftily. "I will answer for his ability; he saved my child."

Gerard was not subtle enough to appreciate this conclusion: and was so far from sharing Teresa's confidence that he begged a respite. He would rather not go to the friar to-day: would not to-morrow do as well?

"Here is a coward for ye," said Lucretia.

"No, he is not a coward," said Teresa, firing up. "He is modest."

"I am afraid of this high-born, fastidious friar," said Gerard. "Consider, he has seen the handywork of all the writers in Italy, dear dame Teresa; if you would but let me prepare a better piece of work than yet I have done, and then to-morrow I will face him with it."

"I consent," said Teresa.

They walked home together.

Not far from his own lodging was a shop that sold vellum. There was a beautiful white skin in the window. Gerard looked at it wistfully; but he knew he could not pay for it; so he went on rather hastily. However, he soon made up his mind where to get vellum: and, parting with Teresa at his own door, ran hastily up stairs, and took the bond he had brought all the way from Sevenbergen, and laid it with a sigh on the table. He then prepared with his chemicals to erase the old writing; but, as this was his last chance of reading it, he now overcame his deadly repugnance to bad writing, and proceeded to decipher the deed in spite of its detestable contractions. It appeared by this deed that Ghysbrecht Van Swieten was to ad-

vance some money to Floris Brandt on a piece of land, and was to
repay himself out of the rent.

On this Gerard felt it would be imprudent and improper to destroy the deed. On the contrary he vowed to decipher every word,
at his leisure. He went down stairs, determined to buy a small
piece of vellum with his half of the card money.

At the bottom of the stairs he found the landlady and Teresa
talking. At sight of him the former cried: "Here he is. You are
caught, donna mia. See what she has bought you!" And whipped
out from under her apron the very skin of vellum Gerard had
longed for.

"Why, dame! why, donna Teresa!" And he was speechless, with
pleasure and astonishment.

"Dear donna Teresa, there is not a skin in all Rome like it. How
ever came you to hit on this one? 'Tis glamour."

"Alas, dear boy, did not thine eye rest on it with desire? and didst
thou not sigh in turning away from it? And was it for Teresa to
let thee want the thing after that?"

"What sagacity! what goodness, madama! Oh, dame, I never
thought I should possess this. What did you pay for it?"

"I forget. Addio, Fiammina. Addio, Ser Gerard. Be happy,
be prosperous, as you are good." And the Roman matron glided
away, while Gerard was hesitating, and thinking how to offer to pay
so stately a creature for her purchase.

The next day in the afternoon he went to Lucretia, and her boy
took him to Fra Colonna's lodgings. He announced his business
and feed Onesta, and she took him up to the friar. Gerard entered
with a beating heart. The room, a large one, was strewed and
heaped with objects of art, antiquity, and learning, lying about in
rich profusion, and confusion. Manuscripts, pictures, carvings in
wood and ivory, musical instruments; and in this glorious chaos sat
the friar, poring intently over an Arabian manuscript.

He looked up a little peevishly at the interruption. Onesta whispered in his ear.

"Very well," said he. "Let him be seated. Stay; young man,
show me how you write!" And he threw Gerard a piece of paper,
and pointed to an inkhorn.

"So please you, reverend father," said Gerard, "my hand, it

trembleth too much at this moment; but last night I wrote a vellum page of Greek, and the Latin version by its side, to show the various character."

"Show it me!"

Gerard brought the work to him in fear and trembling; then stood, heart-sick, awaiting his verdict.

When it came it staggered him. For the verdict was, a Dominican falling on his neck.

CHAPTER LXI

HAPPY the man who has two chain-cables; Merit, and Women.

Oh that I, like Gerard, had a "chaine des dames" to pull up by.

I would be prose laureat, or professor of the spasmodic, or something, in no time. En attendant, I will sketch the Fra Colonna.

The true revivers of ancient learning and philosophy, were two writers of fiction—Petrarch, and Boccaccio.

Their labours were not crowned with great, public, and immediate success; but they sowed the good seed; and it never perished, but quickened in the soil, awaiting sunshine.

From their day Italy was never without a native scholar or two, versed in Greek; and each learned Greek who landed there was received fraternally. The fourteenth century, ere its close, saw the birth of Poggio, Valla, and the elder Guarino: and early in the fifteenth Florence under Cosmo de Medici was a nest of Platonists. These, headed by Gemistus Pletho, a born Greek, began about A. D. 1440, to write down Aristotle. For few minds are big enough to be just to great A without being unjust to capital B.

Theodore Gaza defended that great man with moderation; George of Trebizond with acerbity, and retorted on Plato. Then Cardinal Bessarion, another born Greek, resisted the said George, and his idol, in a tract "Adversus calumniatorem Platonis."

Pugnacity, whether wise or not, is a form of vitality. Born without controversial bile in so zealous an epoch, Francesco Colonna, a young nobleman of Florence, lived for the arts. At twenty he turned Dominican friar. His object was quiet study. He retired

The Cloister and the Hearth

from idle company, and faction fights, the humming and the stinging of the human hive, to St. Dominic and the Nine Muses.

An eager student of languages, pictures, statues, chronology, coins, and monumental inscriptions. These last loosened his faith in popular histories.

He travelled many years in the East, and returned laden with spoils: master of several choice MSS., and versed in Greek and Latin, Hebrew and Syriac. He found his country had not stood still. Other lettered princes besides Cosmo had sprung up. Alfonso King of Naples, Nicolas d'Este, Lionel d'Este, &c. Above all, his old friend Thomas of Sarzana had been made pope, and had lent a mighty impulse to letters; had accumulated 5,000 MSS. in the library of the Vatican, and had set Poggio to translate Diodorus Siculus and Xenophon's Cyropædia, Laurentius Valla to translate Herodotus and Thucydides, Theodore Gaza, Theophrastus; George of Trebizond, Eusebius, and certain treatises of Plato, etc. etc.

The monk found Plato and Aristotle under armistice, but Poggio and Valla at loggerheads over verbs and nouns, and on fire with odium philologicum. All this was heaven; and he settled down in his native land, his life a rosy dream. None so happy as the versatile, provided they have not their bread to make by it. And Fra Colonna was Versatility. He knew seven or eight languages, and a little mathematics; could write a bit, paint a bit, model a bit, sing a bit, strum a bit; and could relish superior excellence in all these branches. For this last trait he deserved to be as happy as he was. For, gauge the intellects of your acquaintances, and you will find but few whose minds are neither deaf, nor blind, nor dead to some great art or science,

"And wisdom at one entrance quite shut out."

And such of them as are conceited as well as stupid, shall even parade, instead of blushing for, the holes in their intellects.

A zealot in art, the friar was a sceptic in religion.

In every age there are a few men, who hold the opinions of another age; past or future. Being a lump of simplicity, his scepticism was as naïf as his enthusiasm. He affected to look on the religious ceremonies of his day as his models, the heathen philosophers, regarded the worship of gods and departed heroes: mummeries good for the populace. But here his mind drew unconsciously a droll distinction. Whatever Christian ceremony his learning taught him was of purely pagan origin, that he respected, out of respect for antiquity; though had he, with his turn of mind, been a pagan and its cotemporary, he would have scorned it from his philosophic heights.

Fra Colonna was charmed with his new artist, and, having the run of half the palaces in Rome, sounded his praises so, that he was soon called upon to resign him. He told Gerard what great princes wanted him. "But I am so happy with you, father," objected Gerard. "Fiddlestick about being happy with me," said Fra Colonna, "you must not be happy; you must be a man of the world; the grand lesson I impress on the young is be a man of the world. Now these Montesini can pay you three times as much as I can, and they shall too—by Jupiter."

And the friar clapped a terrific price on Gerard's pen. It was acceded to without a murmur. Much higher prices were going for *copying,* than *authorship* ever obtained for centuries under the printing press.

Gerard had three hundred crowns for Aristotle's treatise on rhetoric.

The great are mighty sweet upon all their pets, while the fancy lasts: and in the rage for Greek MSS. the handsome writer soon became a pet, and nobles of both sexes caressed him like a lap dog. It would have turned a vain fellow's head; but the canny Dutchman saw the steel hand beneath the velvet glove, and did not presume. Nevertheless it was a proud day for him, when he found himself seated with Fra Colonna at the table of his present employer, Cardinal Bessarion. They were about a mile from the top of that table; but, never mind, there they were; and Gerard had the advantage of seeing roast pheasants dished up with all their feathers as if they had just flown out of a coppice instead of off the spit: also chickens cooked in bottles, and tender as peaches. But the grand novelty was the napkins, surpassingly fine, and folded into cocked hats, and birds' wings, and fans, etc., instead of lying flat. This electrified Gerard: though my readers have seen the dazzling phenomenon without tumbling backwards chair and all.

After dinner the tables were split in pieces, and carried away, and lo under each was another table spread with sweetmeats. The signoras, and signorinas, fell upon them and gormandized; but the signors eyed them with reasonable suspicion.

"But, dear father," objected Gerard, "I see not the bifurcal daggers, with which men say his excellency armeth the left hand of a man."

"Nay, 'tis the Cardinal Orsini which hath invented yon peevish instrument for his guests to fumble their meat withal. One, being in haste, did skewer his tongue to his palate with it I hear; O tempora, O mores! The ancients, reclining godlike at their feasts, how have they spurned such pedantries."

As soon as the ladies had disported themselves among the sugar-plums, the tables were suddenly removed, and the guests sat in a row against the wall. Then came in, ducking and scraping, two ecclesiastics with lutes, and kneeled at the cardinal's feet and there sang the service of the day: then retired with a deep obeisance: in answer to which the cardinal fingered his skull cap as our late Iron Duke his hat: the company dispersed, and Gerard had dined with a cardinal, and one that had thrice just missed being pope.

But greater honour was in store.

One day the cardinal sent for him, and after praising the beauty of his work took him in his coach to the Vatican: and up a private stair to a luxurious little room, with a great oriel window. Here were inkstands, sloping frames for writing on, and all the instruments of art. The cardinal whispered a courtier, and presently the Pope's private secretary appeared with a glorious grimy old MS. of Plutarch's Lives. And soon Gerard was seated alone copying it, awestruck, yet half delighted at the thought that his holiness would handle his work and read it.

The papal inkstands were all glorious externally; but within the ink was vile. But Gerard carried ever good ink, home-made, in a dirty little inkhorn: he prayed on his knees for a firm and skilful hand, and set to work.

One side of his room was nearly occupied by a massive curtain divided in the centre: but its ample folds overlapped. After a while, Gerard felt drawn to peep through that curtain. He resisted the impulse. It returned. It overpowered him. He left Plutarch; stole across the matted floor; took the folds of the curtain, and gently gathered them up with his fingers, and putting his nose through the chink ran it against a cold steel halbert. Two soldiers armed cap-à-pie, were holding their glittering weapons crossed in a triangle. Gerard drew swiftly back: but in that instant he heard the soft murmur of voices and saw a group of persons cringing before some hidden figure.

He never repeated his attempt to pry through the guarded curtain; but often eyed it. Every hour or so an ecclesiastic peeped in, eyed him, chilled him, and exit. All this was gloomy and mechanical. But the next day a gentleman, richly armed, bounced in, and glared at him. "What is toward here?" said he.

Gerard told him he was writing out Plutarch, with the help of the saints. The spark said he did not know the signor in question. Gerard explained the circumstances of time and space, that had deprived the Signor Plutarch of the advantage of the spark's conversation.

"Oh! one of those old dead Greeks they keep such a coil about."

"Ay, signor, one of them, who, being dead, yet live."

"I understand you not, young man," said the noble, with all the dignity of ignorance. "What did the old fellow write? Love stories?" and his eyes sparkled: "merry tales like Boccaccio."

"Nay lives of heroes, and sages."

"Soldiers, and popes?"

"Soldiers, and princes."

"Wilt read me of them some day?"

"And willingly, signor. But what would they say who employ me, were I to break off work?"

"Oh never heed that; know you not who I am? I am Jacques Bonaventura, nephew to his holiness the Pope, and captain of his guards. And I came here to look after my fellows. I trow they have turned them out of their room for you." Signor Bonaventura then hurried away. This lively companion however having acquired a habit of running into that little room, and finding Gerard good company, often looked in on him, and chatted ephemeralities while Gerard wrote the immortal lives.

One day he came a changed, and moody man, and threw himself into a chair, crying "Ah, traitress! traitress!" Gerard inquired what was his ill? "Traitress! traitress!" was the reply. Whereupon Gerard wrote Plutarch. Then says Bonaventura "I am melancholy; and for our Lady's sake read me a story out of Ser

Plutarcho, to sooth my bile: in all that Greek is there nought about lovers betrayed?"

Gerard read him the life of Alexander. He got excited, marched about the room, and embracing the reader, vowed to shun "soft delights," that bed of nettles, and follow glory.

Who so happy now as Gerard? His art was honoured, and fabulous prices paid for it; in a year or two he should return by sea to Holland, with good store of money, and set up with his beloved Margaret in Bruges, or Antwerp, or dear Augsburg, and end their days in peace, and love, and healthy, happy labour. His heart never strayed an instant from her.

In his prosperity he did not forget poor Pietro. He took the Fra Colonna to see his picture. The friar inspected it severely and closely, fell on the artist's neck, and carried the picture to one of the Colonnas, who gave a noble price for it.

Pietro descended to the first floor; and lived like a gentleman.

But Gerard remained in his garret. To increase his expenses would have been to postpone his return to Margaret. Luxury had no charms for the single-hearted one, when opposed to love.

Jacques Bonaventura made him acquainted with other gay young fellows. They loved him, and sought to entice him into vice, and other expenses. But he begged humbly to be excused. So he escaped that temptation. But a greater was behind.

CHAPTER LXII

FRA COLONNA had the run of the Pope's library, and sometimes left off work at the same hour and walked the city with Gerard; on which occasions the happy artist saw all things en beau, and was wrapped up in the grandeur of Rome and its churches, palaces, and ruins.

The friar granted the ruins, but threw cold water on the rest.

"This place Rome? It is but the tomb of mighty Rome." He showed Gerard that twenty or thirty feet of the old triumphal arches were underground, and that the modern streets ran over ancient palaces; and over the tops of columns; and coupling this with the comparatively narrow limits of the modern city, and the gigantic vestiges of antiquity that peeped above ground here and there, he uttered a somewhat remarkable simile. "I tell thee this village they call Rome is but as one of those swallows' nests ye shall see built on the eaves of a decayed abbey."

"Old Rome must indeed have been fair then," said Gerard.

"Judge for yourself, my son; you see the great sewer, the work of the Romans in their very childhood, and shall outlast Vesuvius. You see the fragments of the Temple of Peace. How would you look could you see also the Capitol with its five-and-twenty temples? Do but note this Monte Savello: what is it, an it please you, but the ruins of the ancient theatre of Marcellus? and as for Testacio, one of the highest hills in modern Rome, it is but an ancient dust heap; the women of old Rome flung their broken pots and pans there, and lo; a mountain.

'Ex pede Herculem; ex ungue leonem.'"

Gerard listened respectfully, but when the holy friar proceeded by analogy to imply that the moral superiority of the heathen Romans was proportionably grand, he resisted stoutly. "Has then the world lost by Christ his coming?" said he; but blushed, for he felt himself reproaching his benefactor.

"Saints forbid!" said the friar. "'Twere heresy to say so." And, having made this direct concession, he proceeded gradually to evade it by subtle circumlocution, and reached the forbidden door by the spiral back staircase. In the midst of all which they came to a church with a knot of persons in the porch. A demon was being exorcised within. Now Fra Colonna had a way of uttering a curious sort of little moan, when things Zeno or Epicurus would not have swallowed were presented to him as facts. This moan conveyed to such, as had often heard it, not only strong dissent, but pity for human credulity, ignorance, and error, especially of course when it blinded men to the merits of Pagandom.

The friar moaned, and said, "Then come away."

"Nay, father, prithee! prithee! I ne'er saw a divell cast out."

The friar accompanied Gerard into the church, but had a good shrug first. There they found the demoniac forced down on his knees before the altar with a scarf tied round his neck, by which the officiating priest held him like a dog in a chain.

Not many persons were present, for fame had put forth that the last demon cast out in that church went no farther than into one of the company: "as a cony ferreted out of one burrow runs to the next."

When Gerard and the friar came up the priest seemed to think there were now spectators enough; and began.

He faced the demoniac, breviary in hand, and first set himself to learn the individual's name with whom he had to deal.

"Come out, Ashtaroth. Oho! it is not you then. Come out, Belial. Come out, Tatzi. Come out, Eza. No: he trembles not. Come out, Azymoth. Come out, Feriander. Come out, Foletho. Come out, Astyma. Come out, Nebul. Aha! what, have I found ye? 'tis thou, thou reptile; at thine old tricks. Let us pray!—

"Oh Lord, we pray thee to drive the foul fiend Nebul out of this thy creature: out of his hair, and his eyes, out of his nose, out of his mouth, out of his ears, out of his gums, out of his teeth, out of his shoulders, out of his arms, legs, loins, stomach, bowels, thighs, knees, calves, feet, ankles, fingernails, toe-nails, and soul. Amen."

The priest then rose from his knees, and turning to the company said, with quiet geniality, "Gentles, we have here as obstinate a divell as you may see in a summer day." Then, facing the patient, he spoke to him with great rigour, sometimes addressing the man, and sometimes the fiend, and they answered him in turn through the same mouth, now saying that they hated those holy names the priest kept uttering, and now complaining they did feel so bad in their inside.

It was the priest who first confounded the victim and the culprit in idea, by pitching into the former, cuffing him soundly, kicking him, and spitting repeatedly in his face. Then he took a candle and lighted it, and turned it down, and burned it till it burned his fingers; when he dropped it double quick. Then took the custodial; and showed the patient the Corpus Domini within. Then burned another candle as before, but more cautiously: then spoke civilly to the demoniac in his human character, dismissed him, and received the compliments of the company.

"Good father," said Gerard, "how you have their names by heart. Our northern priests have no such exquisite knowledge of the hellish squadrons."

"Ay, young man, here we know all their names, and eke their ways, the reptiles. This Nebul is a bitter hard one to hunt out."

He then told the company in the most affable way several of his experiences; concluding with his feat of yesterday, when he drove a great hulking fiend out of a woman by her mouth, leaving behind him certain nails, and pins, and a tuft of his own hair, and cried out in a voice of anguish, ' 'Tis not thou that conquers me. See that stone on the window sill. Know that the angel Gabriel coming down to earth once lighted on that stone: 'tis that has done my business.' "

The friar moaned. "And you believed him?"

"Certes! who, but an infidel had discredited a revelation so precise?"

"What, believe the father of lies? That is pushing credulity beyond the age."

"Oh, a liar does not always lie."

"Ay doth he whenever he tells an improbable story to begin, and shows you a holy relic; arms you against the satanic host. Fiends (if any) be not so simple. Shouldst have answered him out of antiquity—

Timeo Danaos et dona ferentes.

Some blackguard chopped his wife's head off on that stone, young man; you take my word for it." And the friar hurried Gerard away.

"Alack, father, I fear you abashed the good priest."

"Ay, by Pollux," said the friar, with a chuckle; "I blistered him with a single touch of 'Socratic interrogation.' What modern can parry the weapons of antiquity?"

One afternoon, when Gerard had finished his day's work, a fine lacquey came and demanded his attendance at the palace Cesarini. He went and was ushered into a noble apartment; there was a girl seated in it, working on a tapestry. She rose and left the room, and said she would let her mistress know.

A good hour did Gerard cool his heels in that great room, and at last he began to fret. "These nobles think nothing of a poor fellow's time." However, just as he was making up his mind to slip out, and go about his business, the door opened, and a superb beauty entered the room followed by two maids. It was the young princess of the house of Cesarini. She came in talking rather loudly and haughtily to her dependents, but at sight of Gerard lowered her voice to a very feminine tone, and said, "Are you the writer, messer?"

"I am, signora."

"'Tis well." She then seated herself; Gerard and her maids remained standing.

"What is your name, good youth?"

"Gerard, signora."

"Gerard? body of Bacchus! is that the name of a human creature?"

"It is a Dutch name, signora. I was born at Tergou, in Holland."

"A harsh name, girls, for so well-favoured a youth; what say you?"

The maids assented warmly.

"What did I send for him for?" inquired the lady, with lofty languor. "Ah, I remember. Be seated, Ser Gerardo, and write me a letter to Ercole Orsini, my lover; at least he says so."

Gerard seated himself, took out paper and ink, and looked up to the princess for instructions.

She, seated on a much higher chair, almost a throne, looked down at him with eyes equally inquiring.

"Well, Gerardo."

"I am ready, your excellence."

"Write, then."

"I but await the words."

"And who, think you, is to provide *them?*"

"Who but your grace, whose letter it is to be."

"Gramercy! what, you writers, find you not the words? What avails your art without the words? I doubt you are an impostor, Gerardo."

"Nay, signora, I am none. I might make shift to put your highness's speech into grammar, as well as writing. But I cannot interpret your silence. Therefore speak what is in your heart, and I will empaper it before your eyes."

"But there is nothing in my heart. And sometimes I think I have got no heart."

"What is in your mind, then?"

"But there is nothing in my mind; nor my head neither."

"Then why write at all?"

"Why, indeed? That is the first word of sense either you or

The Cloister and the Hearth

I have spoken, Gerardo. Pestilence seize him! why writeth he not first? then I could say nay to this, and ay to that, withouten head-ache. Also is it a lady's part to say the first word?"

"No, signora: the last."

"It is well spoken, Gerardo. Ha! ha! Shalt have a gold piece for thy wit. Give me my purse!" And she paid him for the article on the nail à la moyen âge. Money never yet chilled zeal. Gerard, after getting a gold piece so cheap, felt bound to pull her out of her difficulty; if the wit of man might achieve it. "Signorina," said he, "these things are only hard because folk attempt too much, are artificial and labour phrases. Do but figure to yourself the signor you love—"

"I love him not."

"Well, then, the signor you love not—seated at this table, and dict to me just what you would say to him."

"Well if he sat there I should say, 'Go away.'"

Gerard, who was flourishing his pen by way of preparation, laid it down with a groan.

"And when he was gone," said Floretta, "your highness would say, 'Come back.'"

"Like enough, wench. Now silence, all, and let me think. He pestered me to write, and I promised; so mine honour is engaged. What lie shall I tell the Gerardo to tell the fool?" and she turned her head away from them and fell into deep thought, with her noble chin resting on her white hand, half clenched.

She was so lovely and statuesque, and looked so inspired with thoughts celestial, as she sat thus, impregnating herself with mendacity, that Gerard forgot all, except art, and proceeded eagerly to transfer that exquisite profile to paper.

He had very nearly finished when the fair statue turned brusquely round and looked at him.

"Nay, signora," said he, a little peevishly, "for Heaven's sake change not your posture; 'twas perfect. See, you are nearly finished."

All eyes were instantly on the work, and all tongues active. "How like! and done in a minute: nay, methinks her highness's chin is not quite so—"

"Oh, a touch will make that right."

"What a pity 'tis not coloured. I'm all for colours. Hang black

457

and white! And her highness hath such a lovely skin. Take away
her skin, and half her beauty is lost."

"Peace. Can you colour, Ser Gerardo?"

"Ay, signorina. I am a poor hand at oils; there shines my friend
Pietro: but in this small way I can tint you to the life, if you have
time to waste on such vanity."

"Call you this vanity? And for time, it hangs on me like lead.
Send for your colours now,—quick,—this moment,—for love of
all the saints."

"Nay, signorina, I must prepare them. I could come at the same
time to-morrow."

"So be it. And you, Floretta, see that he be admitted at all
hours. Alack! leave my head! leave my head!"

"Forgive me, signora; I thought to prepare it at home to receive
the colours. But I will leave it. And now let us despatch the letter."

"What letter?"

"To the Signor Orsini."

"And shall I waste my *time* on such *vanity* as writing letters—
and to that empty creature, to whom I am as indifferent as the moon?
Nay, not indifferent, for I have just discovered my real sentiments.
I hate him and despise him. Girls, I here forbid you once for all
to mention that signor's name to me again; else I'll whip you till
the blood comes. You know how I can lay on when I'm roused."

"We do. We do."

"Then provoke me not to it;" and her eye flashed daggers, and
she turned to Gerard all instantaneous honey. "Addio, il Gerar-do."
And Gerard bowed himself out of this velvet tiger's den.

He came next day and coloured her; and next he was set to
make a portrait of her on a large scale; and then a full-length figure; and he was obliged to set apart two hours in the afternoon for
drawing and painting this princess, whose beauty and vanity were
prodigious, and candidates for a portrait of her numerous. Here
the thriving Gerard found a new and fruitful source of income.

Margaret seemed nearer and nearer.

It was Holy Thursday. No work this day. Fra Colonna and
Gerard sat in a window and saw the religious processions. Their
number and pious ardour thrilled Gerard with the devotion that

now seemed to animate the whole people, lately bent on earthly joys.

Presently the Pope came pacing majestically at the head of his cardinals, in a red hat, white cloak, a capuchin of red velvet, and riding a lovely white Neapolitan barb, caparisoned with red velvet fringed and tasselled with gold; a hundred horsemen, armed cap-à-pie, rode behind him with their lances erected, the butt-end resting on the man's thigh. The cardinals went uncovered, all but one, de Medicis, who rode close to the Pope and conversed with him as with an equal. At every fifteen steps the Pope stopped a single moment, and gave the people his blessing, then on again.

Gerard and the friar now came down, and threading some by-streets reached the portico of one of the seven churches. It was hung with black, and soon the Pope and cardinals, who had entered the church by another door, issued forth, and stood with torches on the steps, separated by barriers from the people; then a canon read a Latin Bull, excommunicating several persons by name, especially such princes as were keeping the Church out of any of her temporal possessions.

At this awful ceremony Gerard trembled, and so did the people. But two of the cardinals spoiled the effect by laughing unreservedly the whole time.

When this was ended, the black cloth was removed, and revealed a gay panoply; and the Pope blessed the people, and ended by throwing his torch among them; so did two cardinals. Instantly there was a scramble for the torches: they were fought for, and torn in pieces by the candidates, so devoutly that small fragments were gained at the price of black eyes, bloody noses, and burnt fingers; in which hurtling his holiness and suite withdrew in peace.

And now there was a cry, and the crowd rushed to a square where was a large, open stage: several priests were upon it praying. They rose, and with great ceremony donned red gloves. Then one of their number kneeled, and with signs of the lowest reverence drew forth from a shrine a square frame, like that of a mirror, and inside was as it were the impression of a face.

It was the Verum icon, or true impression of our Saviour's face, taken at the very moment of his most mortal agony for us. Received as it was without a grain of doubt, imagine how it moved every Christian heart.

The Cloister and the Hearth

The people threw themselves on their faces when the priest raised it on high; and cries of pity were in every mouth, and tears in almost every eye. After a while the people rose, and then the priests went round the platform, showing it for a single moment to the nearest; and at each sight loud cries of pity and devotion burst forth.

Soon after this the friends fell in with a procession of *Flagellants* flogging their bare shoulders till the blood ran streaming down; but without a sign of pain in their faces, and many of them laughing and jesting as they lashed. The bystanders out of pity offered them wine; they took it, but few drank it, they generally used it to free the tails of the cat, which were hard with clotted blood, and make the next stroke more effective. Most of them were boys, and a young woman took pity on one fair urchin. "Alas! dear child," said she, "why wound thy white skin so?" "Basta," said he, laughing, "'tis for your sins I do it, not for mine."

"Hear you that?" said the friar. "Show me the whip that can whip the vanity out of man's heart! The young monkey; how knoweth he that stranger is a sinner more than he?"

"Father," said Gerard, "surely this is not to our Lord's mind. He was so pitiful."

"Our Lord?" said the friar, crossing himself. "What has he to do with this? This was a custom in Rome six hundred years before he was born. The boys used to go through the streets at the Lupercalia, flogging themselves. And the married women used to shove in, and try and get a blow from the monkeys' scourges; for these blows conferred fruitfulness—in those days. A foolish trick this flagellation; but interesting to the bystander; reminds him of the grand old heathen. We are so prone to forget all we owe them."

Next they got into one of the seven churches, and saw the Pope give the mass. The ceremony was imposing, but again spoiled by the inconsistent conduct of the cardinals, and other prelates, who sat about the altar with their hats on, chattering all through the mass like a flock of geese.

The eucharist in both kinds was tasted by an official before the Pope would venture on it: and this surprised Gerard beyond measure. "Who is that base man? and what doth he there?"

"Oh, that is 'The Preguste,' and he tastes the eucharist by way

The Cloister and the Hearth

of precaution. This is the country for poison; and none fall oftener by it than the poor Popes."

"Alas! so I have heard; but after the miraculous change of the bread and wine to Christ his body and blood, poison cannot remain; gone is the bread with all its properties and accidents; gone is the wine."

"So says faith; but experience tells another tale. Scores have died in Italy poisoned in the host."

"And I tell you, father, that were both bread and wine charged with direst poison before his holiness had consecrated them, yet after consecration I would take them both withouten fear."

"So would I, but for the fine arts."

"What mean you?"

"Marry, that I would be as ready to leave the world as thou, were it not for those arts, which beautify existence here below, and make it dear to men of sense and education. No: so long as the Nine Muses strew my path with roses of learning and art, me may Apollo inspire with wisdom and caution, that knowing the wiles of my countrymen, I may eat poison neither at God's altar nor at a friend's table, since, wherever I eat it or drink it, it will assuredly cut short my mortal thread; and I am writing a book—heart and soul in it—'The Dream of Polifilo,' the man of many arts. So name not poison to me till that is finished and copied."

And now the great bells of St. John Lateran's were rung with a clash at short intervals, and the people hurried thither to see the heads of St. Peter and St. Paul.

Gerard and the friar got a good place in the church, and there was a great curtain, and, after long and breathless expectation of the people, this curtain was drawn by jerks, and at a height of about thirty feet were two human heads with bearded faces that seemed alive. They were shown no longer than the time to say an Ave Maria, and then the curtain drawn. But they were shown in this fashion three times. St. Peter's complexion was pale, his face oval, his beard gray and forked; his head crowned with a papal mitre. St. Paul was dark skinned, with a thick, square beard; his face also and head were more square and massive, and full of resolution.

Gerard was awe-struck. The friar approved after his fashion.

"This exhibition of the 'imagines,' or waxen effigies of heroes and

461

demigods, is a venerable custom, and inciteth the vulgar to virtue by great and visible examples."

"Waxen images? What, are they not the apostles themselves, embalmed, or the like?"

The friar moaned.

"They did not exist in the year 800. The great old Roman families always produced at their funerals a series of these 'imagines,' thereby tying past and present history together, and showing the populace the features of far-famed worthies. I can conceive nothing more thrilling or instructive. But then the effigies were portraits made during life or at the hour of death. These of St. Paul and St. Peter are moulded out of pure fancy."

"Ah! say not so, father."

"But the worst is, this humour of showing them up on a shelf, and half in the dark, and by snatches, and with the poor mountebank trick of a drawn curtain.

Quodcunque ostendis mihi sic incredulus odi.

Enough; the men of this day are not the men of old. Let us have done with these new-fangled mummeries, and go among the Pope's books; there we shall find the wisdom we shall vainly hunt in the streets of modern Rome."

And, this idea having once taken root, the good friar plunged and tore through the crowd, and looked neither to the right hand nor to the left, till he had escaped the glories of the holy week, which had brought fifty thousand strangers to Rome; and had got nice and quiet among the dead in the library of the Vatican.

Presently, going into Gerard's room, he found a hot dispute afoot, between him and Jacques Bonaventura. That spark had come in, all steel from head to toe; doffed helmet, puffed, and railed most scornfully on a ridiculous ceremony, at which he and his soldiers had been compelled to attend the Pope; to wit the blessing of the beasts of burden.

Gerard said it was not ridiculous; nothing a Pope did could be ridiculous.

The argument grew warm, and the friar stood grimly neuter, waiting like the stork that ate the frog and the mouse at the close of their combat, to grind them both between the jaws of antiquity: when lo, the curtain was gently drawn, and there stood a venerable old man in a purple skull cap, with a beard like white floss silk, looking at them with a kind though feeble smile.

"Happy youth," said he, "that can heat itself over such matters."

They all fell on their knees. It was the Pope.

"Nay, rise, my children," said he, almost peevishly. "I came not into this corner to be in state. How goes Plutarch?"

Gerard brought his work, and kneeling on one knee presented it to his holiness, who had seated himself, the others standing.

His holiness inspected it with interest. " 'Tis excellently writ," said he.

Gerard's heart beat with delight.

"Ah! this Plutarch, he had a wondrous art, Francesco. How each character standeth out alive on his page: how full of nature each, yet how unlike his fellow!"

Jacques Bonaventura.] "Give me the signor Boccaccio."

His Holiness.] "An excellent narrator, Capitano, and writeth exquisite Italian. But in spirit a thought too monotonous. Monks and nuns were never all unchaste: one or two such stories were right pleasant and diverting; but five score paint his time falsely, and sadden the heart of such as love mankind. Moreover he hath no skill at characters. Now this Greek is supreme in that great art: he carveth them with pen: and turning his page, see into how real and great a world we enter of war, and policy, and business, and love in its own place: for with him, as in the great world, men are not all running after a wench. With this great open field compare me not the narrow garden of Boccaccio, and his little mill-round of dishonest pleasures."

"Your holiness, they say, hath not disdained to write a novel."

"My holiness hath done more foolish things than one, whereof it repents too late. When I wrote novels I little thought to be head of the Church."

"I search in vain for a copy of it to add to my poor library."

"It is well. Then the strict orders I gave four years ago to destroy every copy in Italy, have been well discharged. However, for your comfort, on my being made Pope, some fool turned it into French: so that you may read it, at the price of exile."

"Reduced to this strait we throw ourselves on your holiness's generosity. Vouchsafe to give us your infallible judgment on it!"

"Gently, gently, good Francesco. A Pope's novels are not matters of faith. I can but give you my sincere impression. Well then the work in question had, as far as I remember, all the vices of Boccaccio, without his choice Italian."

Fra Colonna.] "Your holiness is known for slighting Æneas Silvius as other men never slighted him. I did him injustice to make you his judge. Perhaps your holiness will decide more justly between these two boys—about blessing the beasts."

The Pope demurred. In speaking of Plutarch he had brightened up for a moment, and his eye had even flashed; but his general manner was as unlike what youthful females expect in a Pope as you can conceive. I can only describe it in French. Le gentilhomme blazé. A high bred, and highly cultivated gentleman, who had done, and said, and seen, and known everything, and whose body was nearly worn out. But double languor seem to seize him at the father's proposal.

"My poor Francesco," said he "bethink thee that I have had a life of controversy, and am sick on't, sick as death. Plutarch drew me Jo this calm retreat; not divinity."

"Nay, but, your holiness, for moderating of strife between two hot young bloods.

‘Μακαριοι οἱ ειρηνοποιοι.’ ”

"And know you nature so ill, as to think either of these high-mettled youths will reck what a poor old Pope saith?"

"Oh! your holiness," broke in Gerard, blushing and gasping, "sure, here is one who will treasure your words all his life as words from Heaven."

"In that case," said the Pope, "I am fairly caught. As Francesco here would say—

‘ουκ εστιν ὅστις εστ' ανηρ ελευθερος.’

I came to taste that eloquent heathen, dear to me e'en as to thee, thou paynim monk; and I must talk divinity, or something next door to it. But the youth hath a good, and a winning face, and writeth Greek like an angel. Well then, my children, to comprehend the ways of the Church, we should still rise a little above the earth, since the Church is between heaven and earth, and interprets betwixt them.

"The question is then, not how vulgar men feel, but how the common Creator of man and beast doth feel, towards the lower animals. This, if we are too proud to search for it in the lessons of the

Church, the next best thing is to go to the most ancient history of men and animals."

Colonna.] "Herodotus."

"Nay, nay; in this matter Herodotus is but a mushroom. Finely were we sped for ancient history, if we depended on your Greeks, who did but write on the last leaf of that great book, Antiquity."

The friar groaned. Here was a Pope uttering heresy against his demigods.

"'Tis the Vulgate I speak of. A history that handles matters three thousand years before him pedants call 'the Father of History.'"

Colonna.] "Oh! the Vulgate? I cry your holiness mercy. How you frightened me. I quite forgot the Vulgate."

"Forgot it? art sure thou ever readst it, Francesco mio?"

"Not quite, your holiness. 'Tis a pleasure I long promised myself, the first vacant moment. Hitherto these grand old heathen have left me small time for recreation."

His Holiness.] "First then you will find in Genesis that God, having created the animals, drew a holy pleasure, undefinable by us, from contemplating of their beauty. Was it wonderful? See their myriad forms; their lovely hair, and eyes, their grace, and of some the power and majesty; the colour of others, brighter than roses, or rubies. And when, for man's sin, not their own, they were destroyed, yet were two of each kind spared.

"And when the ark and its trembling inmates tumbled solitary on the world of water, then, saith the word, 'God remembered Noah, *and the cattle that were with him in the ark.*'

"Thereafter God did write his rainbow in the sky as a bond that earth should be flooded no more; and between whom the bond? between God and man, nay: between God and man, *and every living creature of all flesh;* or my memory fails me with age. In Exodus God commanded that the cattle should share the sweet blessing of the one day's rest. Moreover he forbade to muzzle the ox that trod out the corn. 'Nay let the poor overwrought soul snatch a mouthful as he goes his toilsome round: the bulk of the grain shall still be for man.' Ye will object perchance that St. Paul, commenting this, saith rudely, 'Doth God care for oxen?' Verily, had I been Peter, instead of the humblest of his successors, I had answered him. 'Drop thy theatrical poets, Paul, and read the scriptures: then shalt thou know whether God careth only for men and sparrows, or for all his creatures. O Paul,' had I made bold to say, 'think not to learn God by looking into Paul's heart, nor any heart of man, but study that which he hath revealed concerning himself.'

"Thrice he forbade the Jews to boil the kid in his mother's milk; not that this is cruelty, but want of thought and gentle sentiments, and so paves the way for downright cruelty. A prophet riding on an ass did meet an angel. Which of these two, Paulo judice, had seen the heavenly spirit? marry, the prophet. But it was not so. The man, his vision cloyed with sin, saw nought. The poor despised creature saw all. Nor is this recorded as miraculous. Poor proud things, we overrate ourselves. The angel had slain the prophet and spared the ass, but for that creature's clearer vision of essences divine. He said so, methinks. But in sooth I read it many years agone. Why did God spare repentant Nineveh? Because in that city were sixty thousand children, *besides much cattle.*

"Profane history and vulgar experience add their mite of witness. The cruel to animals end in cruelty to man; and strange and violent deaths, marked with retribution's bloody finger, have in all ages fallen from heaven on such as wantonly harm innocent beasts. This I myself have seen. All this duly weighed, and seeing that, despite this Francesco's friends, the Stoics, who in their vanity say the creatures all subsist for man's comfort, there be snakes and scorpions which kill 'Dominum terræ' with a nip, musquitoes which eat him piecemeal, and tigers and sharks, which crack him like an almond, we do well to be grateful to these true, faithful, patient four-footed friends, which, in lieu of powdering us, put forth their strength to relieve our toils, and do feed us like mothers from their gentle dugs.

"Methinks then the Church is never more divine than in this benediction of our four-footed friends, which has revolted yon great theological authority, the captain of the Pope's guards; since here she inculcates humility and gratitude, and rises towards the level of the mind divine, and interprets God to man, God the creator, parent, and friend, of man and beast.

"But all this, young Gentles you will please to receive, not as delivered by the Pope ex cathedrâ, but uttered carelessly, in a free hour, by an aged clergyman. On that score you will perhaps do well to entertain it with some little consideration. For old age must surely bring a man somewhat, in return for his digestion (his "dura puerorum ilia," eh, Francesco), which it carries away."

Such was the purport of the Pope's discourse; but the manner high-bred, languid, kindly, and free from all tone of dictation. He seemed to be gently probing the matter in concert with his hearers, not playing Sir Oracle. At the bottom of all which was doubtless a slight touch of humbug, but the humbug that embellishes life; and all sense of it was lost in the subtle Italian grace of the thing.

"I seem to hear the oracle of Delphi," said Fra Colonna, enthusiastically.

"I call that good sense," shouted Jacques Bonaventura.

"Oh, captain, good sense!" said Gerard, with a deep and tender reproach.

The Pope smiled on Gerard. "Cavil not at words; that was an unheard-of concession from a rival theologian."

He then asked for all Gerard's work, and took it away in his hand. But, before going, he gently pulled Fra Colonna's ear, and asked him whether he remembered when they were school-fellows together, and robbed the Virgin by the roadside of the money dropped into her box. "You took a flat stick and applied birdlime to the top, and drew the money out through the chink, you rogue," said his holiness, severely.

"To every signor his own honour," replied Fra Colonna. "It was your holiness's good wit invented the manœuvre. I was but the humble instrument."

"It is well. Doubtless you know 'twas sacrilege."

"Of the first water: but I did it in such good company, it troubles me not."

"Humph! I have not even that poor consolation. What did we spend it in, dost mind?"

"Can your holiness ask? Why, sugar-plums."

"What, all on't?"

"Every doit."

"These are delightful reminiscences, my Francesco. Alas! I am getting old. I shall not be here long. And I am sorry for it, for thy sake. They will go and burn thee when I am gone. Art far more a heretic than Huss, whom I saw burned with these eyes; and oh, he died like a martyr."

"Ay, your holiness: but I believe in the Pope; and Huss did not."

"Fox! They will not burn thee; wood is too dear. Adieu, old playmate; adieu, young gentlemen; an old man's blessing be on you."

That afternoon the Pope's secretary brought Gerard a little bag: in it were several gold pieces.

He added them to his store.

Margaret seemed nearer and nearer.

For some time past, too, it appeared as if the fairies had watched over him. Baskets of choice provisions and fruits were brought to his door by porters, who knew not who had employed them, or affected ignorance; and one day came a jewel in a letter, but no words.

At this point the suspicions of his landlady broke out. "This is none of thy patrons, silly boy; this is some lady that hath fallen in love with thy sweet face. Marry, I blame her not."

CHAPTER LXIII

THE Princess Clælia ordered a full-length portrait of herself. Gerard advised her to employ his friend Pietro Vanucci.

But she declined. "'Twill be time to put a slight on the Gerardo, when his work discontents me." Then Gerard, who knew he was an excellent draughtsman, but not so good a colourist, begged her to stand to him as a Roman statue. He showed her how closely he could mimic marble on paper. She consented at first; but demurred when this enthusiast explained to her that she must wear the tunic, toga, and sandals of the ancients.

"Why, I had as lieve be presented in my smock," said she, with mediæval frankness.

"Alack! signorina," said Gerard, "you have surely never noted the ancient habit; so free, so ample, so simple, yet so noble; and most becoming your highness, to whom Heaven hath given the Roman features, and eke a shapely arm and hand, hid in modern guise."

"What, can you flatter, like the rest, Gerardo? Well, give me time to think on't. Come o' Saturday, and then I will say ay or nay."

The Cloister and the Hearth

The respite thus gained was passed in making the tunic and toga, &c., and trying them on in her chamber, to see whether they suited her style of beauty well enough to compensate their being a thousand years out of date.

Gerard, hurrying along to this interview, was suddenly arrested, and rooted to earth at a shop window.

His quick eye had discerned in that window a copy of Lactantius, lying open. "That is fairly writ, any way," thought he.

He eyed it a moment more with all his eyes.

It was not written at all. It was printed.

Gerard groaned. "I am sped; mine enemy is at the door. The press is in Rome."

He went into the shop, and, affecting nonchalance, inquired how long the printing-press had been in Rome. The man said he believed there was no such thing in the city. "Oh, the Lactantius; that was printed on the top of the Apennines."

"What, did the printing-press fall down there out o' the moon?"

"Nay, messer," said the trader, laughing, "it shot up there out of Germany. See the title-page!"

Gerard took the Lactantius eagerly, and saw the following:—

Operâ et impensis Sweynheim et Pannartz
Alumnorum Joannis Fust.
Impressum Subiacis. A.D. 1465.

"Will ye buy, messer? See how fair and even be the letters. Few are left can write like that; and scarce a quarter of the price."

"I would fain have it," said Gerard, sadly; "but my heart will not let me. Know that I am a caligraph, and these disciples of Fust run after me round the world a-taking the bread out of my mouth. But I wish them no ill. Heaven forbid!" And he hurried from the shop.

"Dear Margaret," said he to himself, "we must lose no time; we must make our hay while shines the sun. One month more and an avalanche of printer's type shall roll down on Rome from those Apennines, and lay us waste that writers be."

And he almost ran to the princess Clælia.

He was ushered into an apartment new to him. It was not very large, but most luxurious; a fountain played in the centre, and the floor was covered with the skins of panthers, dressed with the hair, so that no footfall could be heard. The room was an antechamber to the princess's boudoir, for on one side there was no door, but an ample curtain of gorgeous tapestry.

Here Gerard was left alone till he became quite uneasy, and doubted whether the maid had not shown him to the wrong place.

These doubts were agreeably dissipated.

A light step came swiftly behind the curtain; it parted in the middle, and there stood a figure the heathens might have worshipped. It was not quite Venus, nor quite Minerva; but between the two; nobler than Venus, more womanly than Jupiter's daughter. Toga, tunic, sandals; nothing was modern. And as for beauty, that is of all times.

Gerard started up, and all the artist in him flushed with pleasure. "Oh!" he cried, innocently, and gazed in rapture.

This added the last charm to his model: a light blush tinted her cheeks, and her eyes brightened, and her mouth smiled with delicious complacency at this genuine tribute to her charms.

When they had looked at one another so some time, and she saw Gerard's eloquence was confined to ejaculating and gazing, she spoke. "Well, Gerardo, thou seest I have made myself an antique monster for thee."

"A monster? I doubt Fra Colonna would fall down and adore your highness, seeing you so habited."

"Nay, I care not to be adored by an old man. I would liever be loved by a young one: of my own choosing."

Gerard took out his pencils, arranged his canvas, which he had covered with stout paper, and set to work; and so absorbed was he that he had no mercy on his model. At last, after near an hour in one posture, "Gerardo," said she, faintly, "I can stand so no more, even for thee."

"Sit down and rest awhile, signora."

"I thank thee," said she; and sinking into a chair turned pale and sighed.

Gerard was alarmed, and saw also he had been inconsiderate. He took water from the fountain and was about to throw it in her face; but she put up a white hand deprecatingly: "Nay, hold it to my brow with thine hand; prithee, do not fling it at me!"

Gerard timidly and hesitating applied his wet hand to her brow.

"Ah!" she sighed, "that is reviving. Again."

The Cloister and the Hearth

He applied it again. She thanked him, and asked him to ring a little hand-bell on the table. He did so, and a maid came, and was sent to Floretta with orders to bring a large fan.

Floretta speedily came with the fan.

She no sooner came near the princess, than that lady's high-bred nostrils suddenly expanded like a blood horse's. "Wretch!" said she; and rising up with a sudden return to vigour, seized Floretta with her left hand, twisted it in her hair, and with the right hand boxed her ears severely three times.

Floretta screamed and blubbered; but obtained no mercy.

The antique toga left quite disengaged a bare arm, that now seemed as powerful as it was beautiful: it rose and fell like the piston of a modern steam-engine, and heavy slaps resounded one after another on Floretta's shoulders; the last one drove her sobbing and screaming through the curtain, and there she was heard crying bitterly for some time after.

"Saints of heaven!" cried Gerard, "what is amiss? what hath she done?"

"She knows right well. 'Tis not the first time. The nasty toad! I'll learn her to come to me stinking of the musk-cat."

"Alas! signora, 'twas a small fault, methinks."

"A small fault? Nay, 'twas a foul fault." She added with an amazing sudden descent to humility and sweetness, "Are you wroth with me for beating her, Gerar-do?"

"Signora, it ill becomes me to school you; but methinks such as Heaven appoints to govern others should govern themselves."

"That is true, Gerardo. How wise you are, to be so young." She then called the other maid, and gave her a little purse. "Take that to Floretta, and tell her 'the Gerardo' hath interceded for her; and so I must needs forgive her. There, Gerardo."

Gerard coloured all over at the compliment; but not knowing how to turn a phrase equal to the occasion, asked her if he should resume her picture.

"Not yet; beating that hussy hath somewhat breathed me. I'll sit awhile, and you shall talk to me. I know you can talk, an it pleases you, as rarely as you draw."

"That were easily done."

"Do it then, Gerardo."

Gerard was taken aback.

"But, signora, I know not what to say. This is sudden."

"Say your real mind. Say you wish you were anywhere but here."

"Nay, signora, that would not be sooth. I wish one thing though."

"Ay, and what is that?" said she, gently.

"I wish I could have drawn you as you were beating that poor lass. You were awful, yet lovely. Oh, what a subject for a Pythoness!"

"Alas! he thinks but of his art. And why keep such a coil about my beauty, Gerardo? You are far fairer than I am. You are more like Apollo than I to Venus. Also, you have lovely hair, and lovely eyes—but you know not what to do with them."

"Ay, do I. To draw you, signora."

"Ah, yes; you can see my features with them; but you cannot see what any Roman gallant had seen long ago in your place. Yet sure you must have noted how welcome you are to me, Gerardo?"

"I can see your highness is always passing kind to me; a poor stranger like me."

"No, I am not, Gerardo. I have often been cold to you; rude sometimes; and you are so simple you see not the cause. Alas! I feared for my own heart. I feared to be your slave. I who have hitherto made slaves. Ah! Gerardo, I am unhappy. Ever since you came here I have lived upon your visits. The day you are to come I am bright. The other days I am listless, and wish them fled. You are not like the Roman gallants. You make me hate them. You are ten times braver to my eye; and you are wise and scholarly, and never flatter and lie. I scorn a man that lies. Gerar-do; teach me thy magic; teach me to make thee as happy by my side as I am still by thine."

As she poured out these strange words, the princess's mellow voice sunk almost to a whisper, and trembled with half-suppressed passion, and her white hand stole timidly yet earnestly down Gerard's arm, till it rested like a soft bird upon his wrist, and as ready to fly away at a word.

Destitute of vanity and experience, wrapped up in his Margaret and his art, Gerard had not seen this revelation coming, though it had come by regular and visible gradations.

He blushed all over. His innocent admiration of the regal beauty that besieged him, did not for a moment displace the absent Margaret's image. Yet it was regal beauty, and wooing with a grace and tenderness he had never even figured in imagination. How to check her without wounding her?

He blushed and trembled.

The siren saw, and encouraged him. "Poor Gerardo," she murmured, "fear not; none shall ever harm thee under my wing. Wilt not speak to me, Gerar-do mio?"

"Signora!" muttered Gerard, deprecatingly.

At this moment his eye, lowered in his confusion, fell on the shapely white arm and delicate hand that curled round his elbow like a tender vine, and it flashed across him how he had just seen that lovely limb employed on Floretta.

He trembled and blushed.

"Alas!" said the princess, "I scare him. Am I then so very terrible? Is it my Roman robe? I'll doff it, and habit me as when thou first camest to me. Mindest thou? 'Twas to write a letter to yon barren knight Ecole d'Orsini. Shall I tell thee? 'twas the sight of thee, and thy pretty ways, and thy wise words, made me hate him on the instant. I liked the fool well enough before; or wist I liked him. Tell me now how many times hast thou been here since then. Ah! thou knowest not; lovest me not, I doubt, as I love thee. Eighteen times, Gerardo. And each time dearer to me. The day thou comest not 'tis night not day, to Clælia. Alas! I speak for both. Cruel boy, am I not worth a word? Hast every day a princess at thy feet? Nay, prithee, prithee, speak to me, Gerar-do."

"Signora," faltered Gerard, "what can I say, that were not better left unsaid? Oh evil day that ever I came here."

"Ah! say not so. 'Twas the brightest day ever shone on me; or indeed on thee. I'll make thee confess so much ere long, ungrateful one."

"Your highness," began Gerard, in a low, pleading voice.

"Call me Clælia, Gerar-do."

"Signora, I am too young and too little wise to know how I ought to speak to you, so as not to seem blind nor yet ungrateful. But this I know, I were both naught and ungrateful, and the worst foe e'er you had, did I take advantage of this mad fancy. Sure some ill spirit hath had leave to afflict you withal. For 'tis all unnatural that a princess adorned with every grace should abase her affections on a churl."

The princess withdrew her hand slowly from Gerard's wrist.

Yet as it passed lightly over his arm it seemed to linger a moment at parting.

"You fear the daggers of my kinsmen," said she, half sadly, half contemptuously.

"No more than I fear the bodkins of your women," said Gerard, haughtily. "But I fear God and the saints, and my own conscience."

"The truth, Gerardo, the truth! Hypocrisy sits awkwardly on thee. Princesses, while they are young, are not despised for love of God, but of some other woman. Tell me whom thou lovest: and if she is worthy thee I will forgive thee."

"No she in Italy, upon my soul."

"Ah! there is one somewhere, then. Where? where?"

"In Holland, my native country."

"Ah! Marie de Bourgoyne is fair, they say. Yet she is but a child."

"Princess, she I love is not noble. She is as I am. Nor is she so fair as thou. Yet is she fair; and linked to my heart for ever by her virtues, and by all the dangers and griefs we have borne together, and for one another. Forgive me; but I would not wrong my Margaret for all the highest dames in Italy."

The slighted beauty started to her feet, and stood opposite him, as beautiful, but far more terrible than when she slapped Floretta, for then her cheeks were red, but now they were pale, and her eyes full of concentrated fury.

"This to my face, unmannered wretch," she cried. "Was I born to be insulted, as well as scorned, by such as thou? Beware! We nobles brook no rivals. Bethink thee whether is better, the love of a Cesarini, or her hate: for after all I have said and done to thee, it must be love or hate between us and to the death. Choose now!"

He looked up at her with wonder and awe, as she stood towering over him in her Roman toga, offering this strange alternative.

He seemed to have affronted a goddess of antiquity; he a poor puny mortal.

He sighed deeply, but spoke not.

The Cloister and the Hearth

Perhaps something in his deep and patient sigh touched a tender chord in that ungoverned creature; or perhaps the time had come for one passion to ebb and another to flow. The princess sank languidly into a seat, and the tears began to steal rapidly down her cheeks.

"Alas! alas!" said Gerard. "Weep not, sweet lady; your tears they do accuse me, and I am like to weep for company. My kind patron; be yourself! you will live to see how much better a friend I was to you than I seemed."

"I see it now, Gerardo," said the princess. "Friend is the word: the only word can ever pass between us twain. I was mad. Any other man had ta'en advantage of my folly. You must teach me to be your friend and nothing more."

Gerard hailed this proposition with joy; and told her out of Cicero how godlike a thing was friendship, and how much better and rarer and more lasting than love: to prove to her he was capable of it, he even told her about Denys and himself.

She listened with her eyes half shut, watching his words to fathom his character, and learn his weak point.

At last, she addressed him calmly thus: "Leave me now, Gerardo; and come as usual to-morrow. You will find your lesson well bestowed." She held out her hand to him: he kissed it; and went away pondering deeply this strange interview, and wondering whether he had done prudently or not.

The next day he was received with marked distance, and the princess stood before him literally like a statue, and after a very short sitting, excused herself and dismissed him. Gerard felt the chilling difference: but said to himself, "She is wise." So she was in her way.

The next day, he found the princess waiting for him surrounded by young nobles flattering her to the skies. She and they treated him like a dog that could do one little trick they could not. The cavaliers in particular criticised his work with a mass of ignorance and insolence combined that made his cheeks burn.

The princess watched his face demurely with half-closed eyes, at each sting the insects gave him: and, when they had fled, had her doors closed against every one of them for their pains.

The next day Gerard found her alone: cold, and silent. After standing to him so some time, she said, "You treated my company with less respect than became you."

"Did I, signora?"

"Did you? you fired up at the comments they did you the honour to make on your work."

"Nay, I said nought," observed Gerard.

"Oh, high looks speak as plain as high words. Your cheeks were red as blood."

"I was nettled a moment at seeing so much ignorance and ill-nature together."

"Now it is me, their hostess, you affront."

"Forgive me, signora, and acquit me of design. It would ill become me to affront the kindest patron and friend I have in Rome—but one."

"How humble we are all of a sudden. In sooth, Ser Gerardo, you are a capital feigner. You can insult or truckle at will."

"Truckle? to whom?"

"To me, for one; to one, whom you affronted for a base-born girl like yourself: but whose patronage you claim all the same."

Gerard rose, and put his hand to his heart. "These are biting words, signora. Have I really deserved them?"

"Oh, what are words to an adventurer like you? cold steel is all you fear."

"I am no swashbuckler, yet I have met steel with steel: and methinks I had rather face your kinsmen's swords than your cruel tongue, lady. Why do you use me so?"

"Gerar-do, for no good reason, but because I am wayward, and shrewish, and curst, and because everybody admires me but you."

"I admire you too, signora. Your friends may flatter you more; but believe me they have not the eye to see half your charms. Their babble yesterday showed me that. None admire you more truly, or wish you better, than the poor artist, who might not be your lover, but hoped to be your friend: but no, I see that may not be between one so high as you, and one so low as I."

"Ay! but it shall, Gerardo," said the princess, eagerly. "I will not be so curst. Tell me now where abides thy Margaret; and I will give thee a present for her; and on that you and I will be friends."

"She is the daughter of a physician called Peter, and

they bide at Sevenbergen; ah me shall I e'er see it again?"

"'Tis well. Now go." And she dismissed him somewhat abruptly.

Poor Gerard. He began to wade in deep waters when he encountered this Italian princess; *callida et calida solis filia.* He resolved to go no more when once he had finished her likeness. Indeed he now regretted having undertaken so long and laborious a task.

This resolution was shaken for a moment by his next reception, which was all gentleness and kindness.

After standing to him some time in her toga, she said she was fatigued, and wanted his assistance in another way: would he teach her to draw a little? He sat down beside her, and taught her to make easy lines. He found her wonderfully apt. He said so.

"I had a teacher before thee, Gerar-do. Ay, and one as handsome as thyself." She then went to a drawer, and brought out several heads drawn with a complete ignorance of the art, but with great patience and natural talent. They were all heads of Gerard, and full of spirit: and really not unlike. One was his very image.

"There," said she. "Now thou seest who was my teacher."

"Not I, signora."

"What, know you not who teaches us women to do all things? 'Tis love, Gerar-do. Love made me draw because thou drawest, Gerar-do. Love prints thine image in my bosom. My fingers touch the pen, and love supplies the want of art, and lo! thy beloved features lie upon the paper."

Gerard opened his eyes with astonishment at this return to an interdicted topic. "Oh, signora, you promised me to be friends and nothing more."

She laughed in his face. "How simple you are; who believes a woman promising nonsense, impossibilities? Friendship, foolish boy, who ever built that temple on red ashes? Nay, Gerardo," she added gloomily, "between thee and me it must be love or hate."

"Which you will, signora," said Gerard, firmly. "But for me I will neither love nor hate you; but with your permission I will leave you." And he rose abruptly.

She rose too pale as death, and said, "Ere thou leavest me so, know thy fate; outside that door are armed men who wait to slay thee at a word from me."

The Cloister and the Hearth

"But you will not speak that word, signora."

"That word I will speak. Nay, more, I shall noise it abroad it was for proffering brutal love to me thou wert slain; and I will send a special messenger to Sevenbergen: a cunning messenger, well taught his lesson. Thy Margaret shall know thee dead, and think thee faithless; now, go to thy grave; a dog's. For a man thou art not."

Gerard turned pale, and stood dumbstricken. "God have mercy on us both."

"Nay, have thou mercy on her, and on thyself. She will never know in Holland what thou dost in Rome; unless I be driven to tell her my tale. Come, yield thee, Gerar-do mio: what will it cost thee to say thou lovest me? I ask thee but to feign it handsomely. Thou art young: die not for the poor pleasure of denying a lady what—the shadow of a heart. Who will shed a tear for thee? I tell thee men will laugh, not weep, over thy tombstone— ah!" She ended in a little scream, for Gerard threw himself in a moment at her feet, and poured out in one torrent of eloquence the story of his love and Margaret's. How he had been imprisoned, hunted with bloodhounds for her, driven to exile for her; how she had shed her blood for him, and now pined at home. How he had walked through Europe, environed by perils, torn by savage brutes, attacked by furious men, with sword and axe and trap, robbed, shipwrecked for her.

The princess trembled, and tried to get away from him: but he held her robe, he clung to her, he made her hear his pitiful story and Margaret's; he caught her hand, and clasped it between both his, and his tears fell fast on her hand, as he implored her to think on all the woes of the true lovers she would part; and what but remorse, swift and lasting, could come of so deep a love betrayed, and so false a love feigned, with mutual hatred lurking at the bottom.

In such moments none ever resisted Gerard.

The princess, after in vain trying to get away from him, for she felt his power over her, began to waver, and sigh, and her bosom to rise and fall tumultuously, and her fiery eyes to fill.

"You conquer me," she sobbed. "You, or my better angel. Leave Rome!"

"I will, I will."

"If you breath a word of my folly, it will be your last."

"Think not so poorly of me. You are my benefactress once more. Is it for me to slander you?"

"Go! I will send you the means. I know myself; if you cross my path again, I shall kill you. Addio; my heart is broken."

She touched her bell. "Floretta," she said, in a choked voice, "take him safe out of the house through my chamber and by the side poster."

He turned at the door; she was leaning with one hand on a chair, crying, with averted head. Then he thought only of her kindness, and ran back and kissed her robe. She never moved.

Once clear of the house he darted home, thanking Heaven for his escape, soul and body.

"Landlady," said he, "there is one would pick a quarrel with me. What is to be done?"

"Strike him first, and at vantage! Get behind him; and then draw."

"Alas, I lack your Italian courage. To be serious, 'tis a noble."

"Oh, holy saints, that is another matter. Change thy lodging awhile, and keep snug; and alter the fashion of thy habits."

She then took him to her own niece, who let lodgings at some little distance, and installed him there.

He had little to do now, and no princess to draw, so he set himself resolutely to read that deed of Floris Brandt, from which he had hitherto been driven by the abominably bad writing. He mastered it, and saw at once that the loan on this land must have been paid over and over again by the rents, and that Ghysbrecht was keeping Peter Brandt out of his own.

"Fool! not to have read this before," he cried. He hired a horse and rode down to the nearest port. A vessel was to sail for Amsterdam in four days.

He took a passage; and paid a small sum to secure it.

"The land is too full of cut-throats for me," said he; "and 'tis lovely fair weather for the sea. Our Dutch skippers are not shipwrecked like these bungling Italians."

When he returned home there sat his old landlady with her eyes sparkling.

"You are in luck, my young master," said she. "All the fish run to your net this day methinks. See what a lacquey hath brought to our house! This bill and this bag."

Gerard broke the seals, and found it full of silver crowns. The letter contained a mere slip of paper with this line, cut out of some MS.—"La lingua non ha osso, ma fa rompere il dosso."

"Fear me not!" said Gerard, aloud. "I'll keep mine between my teeth."

"What is that?"

"Oh, nothing. Am I not happy, dame? I am going back to my sweetheart with money in one pocket, and land in the other." And he fell to dancing around her.

"Well," said she, "I trow nothing could make you happier."

"Nothing, except to be there."

"Well, that is a pity, for I thought to make you a little happier with a letter from Holland."

"A letter? for me? where? how? who brought it? Oh, dame!"

"A stranger; a painter, with a reddish face and an outlandish name; Anselmin, I trow."

"Hans Memling? a friend of mine. God bless him!"

"Ay, that is it; Anselmin. He could scarce speak a word, but a had the wit to name thee: and a puts the letter down, and a nods and smiles, and I nods and smiles, and gives him a pint o'wine, and it went down him like a spoonful."

"That is Hans, honest Hans. Oh, dame, I am in luck to-day: but I deserve it. For, I care not if I tell you, I have just over-come a great temptation for dear Margaret's sake."

"Who is she?"

"Nay, I'd have my tongue cut out sooner than betray her, but oh it *was* a temptation. Gratitude pushing me wrong, Beauty almost divine pulling me wrong: curses, reproaches, and, hardest of all to resist, gentle tears from eyes used to command. Sure some saint helped me; Anthony belike. But my reward is come."

"Ay, is it, lad; and no farther off than my pocket. Come out, Gerard's reward," and she brought a letter out of her capacious pocket.

Gerard threw his arm around her neck and hugged her. "My best friend," said he, "my second mother, I'll read it to you."

"Ay, do, do."

"Alas! it is not from Margaret. This is not her hand." And he turned it about.

"Alack; but may be her bill is within. The lasses are aye for gliding in their bills under cover of another hand."

"True. Whose hand is this? sure I have seen it. I trow 'tis my dear friend the demoiselle VanEyck. Oh, then Margaret's bill *will* be inside." He tore it open. "Nay, 'tis all in one writing. 'Gerard, my well beloved son,' (she never called me that before that I mind) 'this letter brings thee heavy news from one would liever send thee joyful tidings. Know that Margaret Brandt died in these arms on Thursday sennight last.' (What does the doting old woman mean by that?) 'The last word on her lips was "Gerard:" she said "Tell him I prayed for him at my last hour: and bid him pray for me." She died very comfortable, and I saw her laid in the earth, for her father was useless, as you shall know. So no more at present from her that is with sorrowing heart thy loving friend and servant, 'MARGARET VANEYCK.'

"Ay, that is her signature sure enough. Now what d'ye think of that, dame?" cried Gerard, with a grating laugh. "There is a pretty letter to send to a poor fellow so far from home. But it is Reicht Heynes I blame for humouring the old woman and letting her do it; as for the old woman herself, she dotes, she has lost her head, she is fourscore. Oh, my heart, I'm choking. For all that she ought to be locked up, or her hands tied. Say this had come to a fool; say I was idiot enough to believe this; know ye what I should do? run to the top of the highest church tower in Rome and fling myself off it, cursing Heaven. Woman! woman! what are you doing?" And he seized her rudely by the shoulder. "What are ye weeping for?" he cried in a voice all unlike his own, and loud and hoarse as a raven. "Would ye scald me to death with your tears? She believes it. She believes it. Ah! ah! ah! ah! ah! ah!— Then there is no God."

The poor woman sighed and rocked herself. "And must I be the one to bring it thee all smiling and smirking? I could kill myself for't. Death spares none," she sobbed. "Death spares none."

Gerard staggered against the window sill. "But He is master of death," he groaned. "Or they have taught me a lie. I begin to fear there is no God, and the saints are but dead bones, and hell is master of the world. My pretty Margaret; my sweet, my loving Margaret. The best daughter, the truest lover! the pride of Holland! the darling of the world! It is a lie. Where is this caitiff Hans? I'll hunt him round the town. I'll cram his murdering falsehood down his throat."

And he seized his hat and ran furiously about the streets for hours.

Towards sunset he came back white as a ghost. He had not found Memling: but his poor mind had had time to realize the woman's simple words, that Death spares none.

He crept into the house bent, and feeble as an old man, and refused all food. Nor would he speak, but sat, white, with great staring eyes, muttering at intervals "there is no God."

Alarmed both on his account and on her own (for he looked a desperate maniac), his landlady ran for her aunt.

The good dame came, and the two women, braver together, sat one on each side of him, and tried to soothe him with kind and consoling voices. But he heeded them no more than the chairs they sat on. Then the younger held a crucifix out before him, to aid her. "Maria, mother of heaven, comfort him," they sighed. But he sat glaring, deaf to all external sounds.

Presently, without any warning, he jumped up, struck the crucifix rudely out of his way with a curse and made a headlong dash at the door. The poor women shrieked. But, ere he reached the door, something seemed to them to draw him up straight by his hair, and twirl him round like a top. He whirled twice around with arms extended; then fell like a dead log upon the floor, with blood trickling from his nostrils and ears.

CHAPTER LXIV

GERARD returned to consciousness and to despair.

On the second day he was raving with fever on the brain. On a table hard by lay his rich auburn hair, long as a woman's.

The deadlier symptoms succeeded one another rapidly.

On the fifth day his leech retired and gave him up.

The Cloister and the Hearth

On the sunset of that same day he fell into a deep sleep.

Some said he would wake only to die.

But an old gossip, whose opinion carried weight (she had been a professional nurse), declared that his youth might save him yet could he sleep twelve hours.

On this his old landlady cleared the room and watched him alone. She vowed a wax candle to the Virgin for every hour he should sleep.

He slept twelve hours.

The good soul rejoiced, and thanked the Virgin on her knees.

He slept twenty-four hours.

His kind nurse began to doubt. At the thirtieth hour she sent for the woman of art. "Thirty hours! shall we wake him?"

The other inspected him closely for some time.

"His breath is even, his hand moist. I know there be learned leeches would wake him, to look at his tongue, and be none the wiser; but we that be women should have the sense to let bon Nature alone. When did sleep ever harm the racked brain or the torn heart?"

When he had been forty-eight hours asleep, it got wind, and they had much ado to keep the curious out. But they admitted only Fra Colonna and his friend the gigantic Fra Jerome.

These two relieved the women, and sat silent; the former eyeing his young friend with tears in his eyes, the latter with beads in his hand looked as calmly on him, as he had on the sea when Gerard and he encountered it hand to hand.

At last, I think it was about the sixtieth hour of this strange sleep, the landlady touched Fra Colonna with her elbow. He looked. Gerard had opened his eyes as gently as if he had been but dozing.

He stared.

He drew himself up a little in bed.

He put his hand to his head, and found his hair was gone.

He noticed his friend Colonna, and smiled with pleasure. But in the middle of smiling his face stopped, and was convulsed in a moment with anguish unspeakable, and he uttered a loud cry, and turned his face to the wall.

His good landlady wept at this. She had known what it is to awake bereaved.

Fra Jerome recited canticles, and prayers from his breviary.

Gerard rolled himself in the bed-clothes.

The Cloister and the Hearth

Fra Colonna went to him, and, whimpering, reminded him that all was not lost. The divine muses were immortal. He must transfer his affection to them; they would never betray him nor fail him like creatures of clay. The good, simple father then hurried away; for he was overcome by his emotion.

Fra Jerome remained behind. "Young man," said he, "the Muses exist but in the brains of pagans and visionaries. The Church alone gives repose to the heart on earth, and happiness to the soul hereafter. Hath earth deceived thee, hath passion broken thy heart after tearing it, the Church opens her arms: consecrate thy gifts to her! The Church is peace of mind."

He spoke these words solemnly at the door, and was gone as soon as they were uttered.

"The Church!" cried Gerard, rising furiously and shaking his fist after the friar. "Malediction on the Church! But for the Church I should not lie broken here, and she lie cold, cold, cold, in Holland. O my Margaret! O my darling! my darling! And I must run from thee the few months thou hadst to live. Cruel! cruel! The monsters, they let her die. Death comes not without some signs. These the blind, selfish wretches saw not, or recked not; but I had seen them, I that love her. Oh, had I been there, I had saved her, I had saved her. Idiot! idiot! to leave her for a moment."

He wept bitterly a long time.

Then, suddenly bursting into rage again, he cried vehemently, "The Church! for whose sake I was driven from her; my malison be on the Church! and the hypocrites that name it to my broken heart. Accursed be the world! Ghysbrecht lives; Margaret dies. Thieves, murderers, harlots, live for ever. Only angels die. Curse life! Curse death! and whosoever made them what they are!"

The friar did not hear these mad and wicked words; but only the yell of rage with which they were flung after him.

It was as well. For, if he had heard them, he would have had his late shipmate burned in the forum with as little hesitation as he would have roasted a kid.

His old landlady, who had accompanied Fra Colonna down the stair, heard the raised voice, and returned in some anxiety.

She found Gerard putting on his clothes, and crying.

She remonstrated.

"What avails my lying here?" said he gloomily. "Can I find here that which I seek?"

"Saints preserve us! Is he distraught again? What seek ye?"

"Oblivion."

"Oblivion, my little heart? Oh, but y' are young to talk so."

"Young or old, what else have I to live for?"

He put on his best clothes.

The good dame remonstrated. "My pretty Gerard, know that it is Tuesday, not Sunday."

"Oh, Tuesday is it? I thought it had been Saturday."

"Nay, thou has slept long. Thou never wearest thy brave clothes on working days. Consider."

"What I did, when she lived, I did. Now I shall do whatever erst I did not. The past is the past. There lies my hair, and with it my way of life. I have served one Master as well as I could. You see my reward. Now I'll serve another, and give him a fair trial too."

"Alas!" sighed the woman, turning pale, "what mean these dark words? and what new master is this whose service thou wouldst try?"

"SATAN."

And with this horrible declaration on his lips the miserable creature walked out with his cap and feather set jauntily on one side, and feeble limbs, and a sinister face pale as ashes, and all drawn down as if by age.

CHAPTER LXV

A DARK cloud fell on a noble mind.

His pure and unrivalled love for Margaret had been his polar star. It was quenched, and he drifted on the gloomy sea of no hope.

Nor was he a prey to despair alone, but to exasperation at all his self-denial, fortitude, perils, virtue, wasted and worse than wasted; for it kept burning and stinging him, that, had he stayed lazily, selfishly, at home, he should have saved his Margaret's life.

These two poisons, raging together in his young blood, maddened and demoralized him. He rushed fiercely into pleasure. And in those days, even more than now, pleasure was vice.

Wine, women, gambling, whatever could procure him an hour's excitement and a moment's oblivion. He plunged into these things, as men tired of life have rushed among the enemy's bullets.

The large sums he had put by for Margaret gave him ample means for debauchery, and he was soon the leader of those loose companions he had hitherto kept at a distance.

His heart deteriorated along with his morals.

He sulked with his old landlady for thrusting gentle advice and warning on him; and finally removed to another part of the town, to be clear of remonstrance, and reminiscences. When he had carried this game on some time, his hand became less steady, and he could no longer write to satisfy himself. Moreover his patience declined as the habits of pleasure grew on him. So he gave up that art, and took likenesses in colours.

But this he neglected whenever the idle rakes, his companions, came for him.

And so he dived in foul waters, seeking that sorry oyster-shell, Oblivion.

It is not my business to paint at full length the scenes of coarse vice, in which this unhappy young man now played a part. But it *is* my business to impress the broad truth, that he was a rake, a debauchee, and a drunkard, and one of the wildest, loosest, and wickedest young men in Rome.

They are no lovers of truth, nor of mankind, who conceal or slur the wickedness of the good, and so by their want of candour rob despondent sinners of hope.

Enough, the man was not born to do things by halves. And he was not vicious by halves.

His humble female friends often gossiped about him. His old landlady told Teresa he was going to the bad, and prayed her to try and find out where he was.

Teresa told her husband Lodovico his sad story, and bade him look about and see if he could discover the young man's present abode. "Shouldst remember his face, Lodovico mio?"

"Teresa a man in my way of life never forgets a face, least of all a benefactor's. But thou knowest I seldom go abroad by daylight."

Teresa sighed. "And how long is it to be so, Lodovico?"

"Till some cavalier passes his sword through me. They will not let a poor fellow like me take to any honest trade."

Pietro Vanucci was one of those who bear prosperity worse than adversity.

Having been ignominiously ejected for late hours by their old landlady, and meeting Gerard in the street, he greeted him warmly and soon after took up his quarters in the same house.

He brought with him a lad called Andrea, who ground his colours, and was his pupil, and also his model, being a youth of rare beauty, and as sharp as a needle.

Pietro had not quite forgotten old times, and professed a warm friendship for Gerard.

Gerard, in whom all warmth of sentiment seemed extinct, submitted coldly to the other's friendship.

And a fine acquaintance it was. This Pietro was not only a libertine, but half a misanthrope, and an open infidel.

And so they ran in couples, with mighty little in common. O rare phenomenon!

One day, when Gerard had undermined his health, and taken the bloom off his beauty, and run through most of his money, Vanucci got up a gay party to mount the Tiber in a boat drawn by buffaloes. Lorenzo de' Medici had imported these creatures into Florence about three years before. But they were new in Rome, and nothing would content this beggar on horseback, Vanucci, but being drawn by the brutes up the Tiber.

Each libertine was to bring a lady; and she must be handsome, or he be fined. But the one, that should contribute the loveliest, was to be crowned with laurel, and voted a public benefactor. Such was their reading of "Vir bonus est quis?" They got a splendid galley, and twelve buffaloes. And all the libertines and their female accomplices assembled by degrees at the place of embarkation. But no Gerard.

They waited for him some time, at first patiently, then impatiently.

Vanucci excused him. "I heard him say he had forgotten to provide himself with a fardingale. Comrades, the good lad is hunting for a beauty fit to take rank among these peerless dames. Consider the difficulty, ladies, and be patient!"

At last Gerard was seen at some distance with a female in his hand.

"She is long enough," said one of her sex; criticizing her from afar.

"Gemini! what step she takes," said another; "Oh! it is wise to hurry into good company," was Pietro's excuse.

But when the pair came up, satire was choked.

Gerard's companion was a peerless beauty; she extinguished the boat-load, as stars the rising sun. Tall, but not too tall; and straight as a dart, yet supple as a young panther. Her face a perfect oval, her forehead white, her cheeks a rich olive with the eloquent blood mantling below; and her glorious eyes fringed with long thick silken eyelashes, that seemed made to sweep up sensitive hearts by the half-dozen. Saucy red lips, and teeth of the whitest ivory.

The women were visibly depressed by this wretched sight; the men in ecstasies; they received her with loud shouts and waving of caps, and one enthusiast even went down on his knees upon the boat's gunwale, and hailed her of origin divine. But his chère amie pulling his hair for it—and the goddess giving him a little kick—cotemporaneously, he lay supine: and the peerless creature frisked over his body without deigning him a look, and took her seat at the prow. Pietro Vanucci sat in a sort of collapse, glaring at her, and gaping with his mouth open like a dying cod-fish.

The drover spoke to the buffaloes, the ropes tightened, and they moved up stream.

"What think ye of this new beef, mesdames?"

"We ne'er saw monsters so vilely ill-favoured; with their nasty horns that make one afeard, and their foul nostrils cast up into the air. Holes be they; not nostrils."

"Signorina, the beeves are a present from Florence the beautiful. Would ye look a gift beef i' the nose?"

"They are so dull," objected a lively lady. "I went up Tiber twice as fast last time with but five mules and an ass."

"Nay, that is soon mended," cried a gallant, and jumping ashore he drew his sword, and despite the remonstrances of the drivers, went down the dozen buffaloes goading them.

The Cloister and the Hearth

They snorted and whisked their tails and went no faster, at which the boat-load laughed loud and long; finally he goaded a patriarch bull, who turned instantly on the sword, sent his long horns clean through the spark, and with a furious jerk of his prodigious neck sent him flying over his head into the air. He described a bold parabola and fell sitting, and unconsciously waving his glittering blade, into the yellow Tiber. The laughing ladies screamed and wrung their hands, all but Gerard's fair. She uttered something very like an oath, and seizing the helm steered the boat out, and the gallant came up sputtering, gripped the gunwale, and was drawn in dripping.

He glared round him confusedly. "I understand not that," said he a little peevishly; puzzled, and therefore it would seem, discontented. At which, finding he was by some strange accident not slain, his doublet being perforated, instead of his body, they began to laugh again louder than ever.

"What are ye cackling at?" remonstrated the spark. "I desire to know how 'tis that one moment a gentleman is out yonder a pricking of African beef, and the next moment—"

Gerard's lady.] "Disporting in his native stream."

"Tell him not, a soul of ye," cried Vanucci. "Let him find out 's own riddle."

"Confound ye all. I might puzzle my brains till doomsday, I should ne'er find it out. Also, where is my sword?"

Gerard's lady.] "Ask Tiber! Your best way, signor, will be to do it over again: and, in a word, keep pricking of Afric's beef, till your mind receives light. So shall you comprehend the matter by degrees as lawyers mount heaven, and buffaloes Tiber."

Here a chevalier remarked that the last speaker transcended the sons of Adam as much in wit as she did the daughters of Eve in beauty.

At which, and indeed at all their compliments, the conduct of Pietro Vanucci was peculiar. That signor had left off staring, and gaping bewildered: and now sat coiled up snakelike, on a bench, his mouth muffled, and two bright eyes fixed on the lady, and twinkling and scintillating most comically.

He did not appear to interest or amuse her in return. Her glorious eyes and eyelashes swept him calmly at times, but scarce distinguished him from the benches and things.

The Cloister and the Hearth

Presently the unanimity of the party suffered a momentary check. Mortified by the attention the cavaliers paid to Gerard's companion, the ladies began to pick her to pieces sotto voce, and audibly. The lovely girl then showed that, if rich in beauty, she was poor in feminine tact. Instead of revenging herself like a true woman through the men, she permitted herself to overhear, and openly retaliate on her detractors.

"There is not one of you that wears Nature's colours," said she. "Look here," and she pointed rudely in one's face. "This is the beauty that is to be bought in every shop. Here is cerussa, here is stibium, and here purpurissum. Oh I know the articles: bless you, I use them every day—but not on my face, no thank you."

Here Vanucci's eyes twinkled themselves nearly out of sight. "Why your lips are coloured, and the very veins in your forehead: not a charm but would come off with a wet towel. And look at your great coarse black hair like a horse's tail, drugged and stained to look like tow. And then your bodies are as false as your heads and your cheeks, and your hearts I trow. Look at your padded bosoms, and your wooden heeled chopines to raise your little stunted limbs up and deceive the world. Skinny dwarfs ye are, cushioned and stiltified into great fat giants. Aha, mesdames, well is it said of you, grande —di legni: grosse—di straci: rosse—di bettito: bianche—di calcina."

This drew out a rejoinder. "Avaunt, vulgar toad, telling the men everything. Your coarse, ruddy cheeks are your own, and your little handful of African hair. But who is padded more? Why you are shaped like a fireshovel."

"Ye lie, malapert."

"Oh the well educated young person! Where didst pick her up, Ser Gerard?"

"Hold thy peace, Marcia," said Gerard, awakened by the raised trebles from a gloomy reverie. "Be not so insolent! The grave shall close over thy beauty as it hath over fairer than thee."

"They began," said Marcia petulantly.

"Then be thou the first to leave off."

"At thy request, my friend." She then whispered Gerard, "It was only to make you laugh: you are distraught, you are sad. Judge whether I care for the quips of these little fools, or the admiration of these big fools. Dear Signor Gerard, would I were what they

490

take me for? You should not be so sad." Gerard sighed deeply; and shook his head. But, touched by the earnest young tones, caressed the jet black locks, much as one strokes the head of an affectionate dog.

At this moment a galley drifting slowly down stream got entangled for an instant in their ropes: for, the river turning suddenly, they had shot out into the stream: and this galley came between them and the bank. In it a lady of great beauty was seated under a canopy with gallants and dependents standing behind her.

Gerard looked up at the interruption. It was the princess Clælia. He coloured and withdrew his hand from Marcia's head.

Marcia was all admiration. "Aha! ladies," said she, "here is a rival an' ye will. Those cheeks were coloured by Nature—like mine."

"Peace, child! peace!" said Gerard. "Make not too free with the great."

"Why, she heard me not. Oh, Ser Gerard, what a lovely creature!"

Two of the females had been for some time past putting their heads together and casting glances at Marcia.

One of them now addressed her.

"Signorina, do you love almonds?"

The speaker had a lapful of them.

"Yes, I love them; when I can get them," said Marcia, pettishly, and eyeing the fruit with ill-concealed desire; "but yours is not the hand to give me any, I trow."

"You are much mistook," said the other. "Here, catch!"

And suddenly threw a double handful into Marcia's lap.

Marcia brought her knees together by an irresistible instinct.

"Aha! you are caught, my lad," cried she of the nuts. "'Tis a man; or a boy. A woman still parteth her knees to catch the nuts the surer in her apron; but a man closeth his for fear they shall fall between his hose. Confess now, didst never wear fardingale ere today."

"Give me another handful, sweetheart, and I'll tell thee."

"There! I said he was too handsome for a woman."

"Ser Gerard, they have found me out," observed the Epicæne, calmly cracking an almond.

The Cloister and the Hearth

The libertines vowed it was impossible, and all glared at the goddess like a battery. But Vanucci struck in, and reminded the gaping gazers of a recent controversy, in which they had, with an unanimity not often found among dunces, laughed Gerard and him to scorn, for saying that men were as beautiful as women in a true artist's eye.

"Where are ye now? This is my boy Andrea. And you have all been down on your knees to him. Ha! ha! But oh, my little ladies, when he lectured you and flung your stibium, your cerussa, and your purpurissum back in your faces, 'tis then I was like to burst; a grinds my colours. Ha! ha! he! he! he! ho!"

"The little impostor! Duck him!"

"What for, signors?" cried Andrea, in dismay, and lost his rich carnation.

But the females collected round him, and vowed nobody should harm a hair of his head.

"The dear child! How well his pretty little saucy ways become him."

"Oh, what eyes! and teeth!"

"And what eyebrows and hair!"

"And what lashes!"

"And what a nose!"

"The sweetest little ear in the world!"

"And what health! Touch but his cheek with a pin the blood should squirt."

"Who would be so cruel?"

"He is a rosebud washed in dew."

And they revenged themselves for their beaux' admiration of her by lavishing all their tenderness on him.

But one there was who was still among these butterflies but no longer of them.

The sight of the Princess Clælia had torn open his wound.

Scarce three months ago he had declined the love of that peerless creature; a love illicit and insane; but at least refined. How much lower had he fallen now.

How happy he must have been, when the blandishments of Clælia, that might have melted an anchorite, could not tempt him from the path of loyalty!

The Cloister and the Hearth

Now what was he? He had blushed at her seeing him in such company. Yet it was his daily company.

He hung over the boat in moody silence.

And from that hour another phase of his misery began; and grew upon him.

Some wretched fools try to drown care in drink.

The fumes of intoxication vanish; the inevitable care remains, and must be faced at last—with an aching head, a disordered stomach, and spirits artificially depressed.

Gerard's conduct had been of a piece with these maniacs'. To survive his terrible blow he needed all his forces; his virtue, his health, his habits of labour, and the calm sleep that is labour's satellite; above all, his piety.

Yet all these balms to wounded hearts he flung away, and trusted to moral intoxication.

Its brief fumes fled; the bereaved heart lay still heavy as lead within his bosom; but now the dark vulture Remorse sat upon it rending it.

Broken health; means wasted; innocence fled; Margaret parted from him by another gulf wider than the grave!

The hot fit of despair passed away.

The cold fit of despair came on.

Then this miserable young man spurned his gay companions, and all the world.

He wandered alone. He drank wine alone to stupefy himself; and paralyze a moment the dark foes to man that preyed upon his soul. He wandered alone amidst the temples of old Rome, and lay stony-eyed, woe-begone, among their ruins, worse wrecked than they.

Last of all came the climax, to which solitude, that gloomy yet fascinating foe of minds diseased, pushes the hopeless.

He wandered alone at night by dark streams, and eyed them, and eyed them, with decreasing repugnance. There glided peace; perhaps annihilation.

What else was left him?

These dark spells have been broken by kind words, by loving and cheerful voices.

The humblest friend the afflicted one possesses may speak, or

look, or smile, a sunbeam between him and that worst madness
Gerard now brooded.

Where was Teresa?   Where his hearty, kind, old landlady?

They would see with their homely but swift intelligence; they
would see and save.

No: they knew not where he was, or whither he was gliding.

And is there no mortal eye upon the poor wretch, and the dark
road he is going?

Yes: one eye there is upon him; watching his every movement;
following him abroad; tracking him home.

And that eye is the eye of an enemy.

An enemy to the death.

CHAPTER LXVI

IN an apartment richly furnished, the floor covered with striped
and spotted skins of animals, a lady sat with her arms extended
before her, and her hands half clenched. The agitation of her
face corresponded with this attitude: she was pale and red by turns;
and her foot restless.

Presently the curtain was drawn by a domestic.

The lady's brow flushed.

The maid said, in an awe-struck whisper, "Altezza, the man is
here."

The lady bade her admit him, and snatched up a little black mask
and put it on; and in a moment her colour was gone, and the contrast between her black mask and her marble cheeks was strange and
fearful.

A man entered bowing and scraping. It was such a figure as
crowds seem made of; short hair, roundish head, plain, but decent
clothes; features neither comely nor forbidding. Nothing to remark in him but a singularly restless eye.

After a profusion of bows he stood opposite the lady, and awaited
her pleasure.

"They have told you for what you are wanted."

"Yes, signora."

"Did those who spoke to you agree as to what you are to receive?"

"Yes, signora. 'Tis the full price; and purchases the greater vendetta: unless of your benevolence you choose to content yourself with the lesser."

"I understand you not," said the lady.

"Ah; this is the signora's first. The lesser vendetta, lady, is the death of the body only. We watch our man come out of a church; or take him in an innocent hour; and so deal with him. In the greater vendetta we watch him, and catch him hot from some unrepented sin, and so slay his soul as well as his body. But this vendetta is not so run upon now as it was a few years ago."

"Man, silence me his tongue, and let his treasonable heart beat no more. But his soul I have no feud with."

"So be it, signora. He who spoke to me knew not the man, nor his name, nor his abode. From whom shall I learn these?"

"From myself."

At this the man, with the first symptoms of anxiety he had shown, entreated her to be cautious, and particular in this part of the business.

"Fear me not," said she. "Listen. It is a young man, tall of stature, and auburn hair, and dark-blue eyes, and an honest face, would deceive a saint. He lives in the Via Claudia, at the corner house; the glover's. In that house there lodge but three males: he; and a painter short of stature and dark visaged, and a young, slim boy. He that hath betrayed me is a stranger, fair; and taller than thou art."

The bravo listened with all his ears. "It is enough," said he. "Stay, signora, haunteth he any secret place where I may deal with him?"

"My spy doth report me he hath of late frequented the banks of Tiber after dusk; doubtless to meet his light o' love, who calls me her rival; even there slay him! and let my rival come and find him; the smooth, heartless, insolent traitor."

"Be calm, signora. He will betray no more ladies."

"I know not that. He weareth a sword, and can use it. He is young and resolute."

"Neither will avail him."

"Are ye so sure of your hand? What are your weapons?"

The bravo showed her a steel gauntlet. "We strike with such force we needs must guard our hand. This is our mallet." He then undid his doublet, and gave her a glimpse of a coat of mail beneath, and finally laid his glittering stiletto on the table with a flourish.

The lady shuddered at first, but presently took it up in her white hand and tried its point against her finger.

"Beware, madam," said the bravo.

"What, is it poisoned?"

"Saints forbid! We steal no lives. We take them with steel point, not drugs. But 'tis newly ground, and I feared for the signora's white skin."

"His skin is as white as mine," said she, with a sudden gleam of pity. It lasted but a moment. "But his heart is black as soot. Say, do I not well to remove a traitor that slanders me?"

"The signora will settle that with her confessor. I am but a tool in noble hands; like my stiletto."

The princess appeared not to hear the speaker. "Oh, how I could have loved him; to the death; as now I hate him. Fool! he will learn to trifle with princes; to spurn them and fawn on them and prefer the scum of the town to them, and make them a by-word." She looked up; "why loiter'st thou here? haste thee, revenge me."

"It is customary to pay half the price beforehand, signora."

"Ah I forgot; thy revenge is bought. Here is more than half," and she pushed a bag across the table to him. "When the blow is struck, come for the rest."

"You will soon see me again, signora."

And he retired bowing and scraping.

The princess, burning with jealousy, mortified pride, and dread of exposure (for till she knew Gerard no public stain had fallen on her), sat where he left her, masked, with her arms straight out before her, and the nails of her clenched hand nipping the table.

So sat the fabled sphynx: so sits a tigress.

Yet there crept a chill upon her now that the assassin was gone. And moody misgivings heaved within her, precursors of vain remorse. Gerard and Margaret were before their age. *This* was your true mediæval. Proud, amorous, vindictive, generous, foolish, cunning, impulsive, unprincipled: and ignorant as dirt.

Power is the curse of such a creature.

Forced to do her own crimes, the weakness of her nerves would have balanced the violence of her passions, and her bark been worse than her bite. But power gives a feeble, furious, woman, male instruments. And the effect is as terrible as the combination is unnatural.

In this instance it whetted an assassin's dagger for a poor forlorn wretch just meditating suicide.

CHAPTER LXVII

IT happened, two days after the scene I have endeavoured to describe, that Gerard, wandering through one of the meanest streets of Rome, was overtaken by a thunderstorm, and entered a low hostelry. He called for wine, and, the rain continuing, soon drank himself into a half-stupid condition, and dozed with his head on his hands and his hands upon the table.

In course of time the room began to fill and the noise of the rude guests to wake him.

Then it was he became conscious of two figures near him conversing in a low voice.

One was a pardoner. The other by his dress, clean but modest, might have passed for a decent tradesman: but the way he had slouched his hat over his brows so as to hide all his face except his beard, showed he was one of those who shun the eye of honest men, and of the law. The pair were driving a bargain in the sin market. And by an arrangement not uncommon at that date, the crime to be forgiven was yet to be committed—under the celestial contract.

He of the slouched hat was complaining of the price pardons had reached. "If they go up any higher we poor fellows shall be shut out of heaven altogether."

The pardoner denied the charge flatly. "Indulgences were never cheaper to good husbandmen."

The other inquired "Who were they?"

"Why such as sin by the market, like reasonable creatures. But if your will be so perverse as go and pick out a crime the Pope hath set his face against, blame yourself, not me?"

Then, to prove that crime of one sort or another was within the means of all, but the very scum of society, he read out the scale from a written parchment.

It was a curious list: but not one that could be printed in this book. And to mutilate it would be to misrepresent it. It is to be found in any great library. Suffice it to say, that murder of a layman was much cheaper than many crimes my lay readers would deem light by comparison.

This told; and by a little trifling concession on each side, the bargain was closed, the money handed over, and the aspirant to heaven's favour forgiven beforehand for removing 1 layman. The price for disposing of a clerk bore no proportion.

The word assassination was never once uttered by either merchant.

All this buzzed in Gerard's ear. But he never lifted his head from the table; only listened stupidly.

However, when the parties rose and separated, he half raised his head and eyed with a scowl the retiring figure of the purchaser.

"If Margaret was alive," muttered he, "I'd take thee by the throat and throttle thee, thou cowardly stabber. But she is dead; dead; dead. Die all the world; 'tis nought to me: so that I die among the first."

When he got home there was a man in a slouched hat walking briskly to and fro on the opposite side of the way.

"Why there is that cur again," thought Gerard.

But in his state of mind, the circumstance made no impression whatever on him.

CHAPTER LXVIII

TWO nights after this Pietro Vanucci and Andrea sat waiting supper for Gerard.

The former grew peevish. It was past nine o'clock. At last he sent Andrea to Gerard's room on the desperate chance of his having come in unobserved. Andrea shrugged his shoulders and went.

He returned without Gerard, but with a slip of paper. Andrea could not read, as scholars in his day and charity boys in ours understand the art; but he had a quick eye, and had learned how the words Pietro Vanucci looked on paper.

"That is for you, I trow," said he, proud of his intelligence.

Pietro snatched it, and read it to Andrea, with his satirical comments.

" 'Dear Pietro, dear Andrea, life is too great a burden.'

"So 'tis, my lad; but that is no reason for being abroad at supper-time. Supper is not a burden.

" 'Wear my habits!'

"Said the poplar to the juniper bush.

" 'And thou, Andrea, mine amethyst ring; and me in both your hearts, a month or two.'

"Why, Andrea?

" 'For my body, ere this ye read, it will lie in Tiber. Trouble not to look for it. 'Tis not worth the pains. Oh unhappy day that it was born; oh happy night that rids me of it.

" 'Adieu! adieu!

" 'The broken-hearted Gerard."

"Here is a sorry jest of the peevish rogue," said Pietro. But his pale cheek and chattering teeth belied his words. Andrea filled the house with his cries.

"Oh, miserable day! O, calamity of calamities! Gerard, my friend, my sweet patron! Help! help! He is killing himself! Oh, good people, help me save him!" And after alarming all the house he ran into the street, bareheaded, imploring all good Christians to help him save his friend.

A number of persons soon collected.

But poor Andrea could not animate their sluggishness. Go down to the river? No. It was not their business. What part of the river? It was a wild goose chase.

It was not lucky to go down to the river after sunset. Too many ghosts walked those banks all night.

A lacquey, however, who had been standing some time opposite the house, said he would go with Andrea; and this turned three or four of the younger ones.

The little band took the way to the river.

The lacquey questioned Andrea.

Andrea, sobbing, told him about the letter, and Gerard's moody ways of late.

That lacquey was a spy of the Princess Clælia.

Their Italian tongues went fast till they neared the Tiber.

But the moment they felt the air from the river, and the smell of the stream in the calm spring night, they were dead silent.

The Cloister and the Hearth

The moon shone calm and clear in a cloudless sky. Their feet sounded loud and ominous. Their tongues were hushed.

Presently hurrying round a corner they met a man. He stopped irresolute at sight of them.

The man was bareheaded, and his dripping hair glistened in the moonlight: and at the next step they saw his clothes were drenched with water.

"Here he is," cried one of the young men, unacquainted with Gerard's face and figure.

The stranger turned instantly and fled.

They ran after him might and main, Andrea leading, and the princess's lacquey next.

Andrea gained on him: but in a moment he twisted up a narrow alley. Andrea shot by, unable to check himself; and the pursuers soon found themselves in a labyrinth in which it was vain to pursue a quick-footed fugitive who knew every inch of it, and could now only be followed by the ear.

They returned to their companions, and found them standing on the spot where the man had stood, and utterly confounded. For Pietro had assured them that the fugitive had neither the features nor the stature of Gerard.

"Are ye verily sure?" said they. "He had been in the river. Why, in the saints' names, fled he at our approach?"

Then said Vanucci, "Friends, methinks this has nought to do with him we seek. What shall we do, Andrea?"

Here the lacquey put in his word. "Let us track him to the water's side, to make sure. See, he hath come dripping all the way."

This advice was approved, and with very little difficulty they tracked the man's course.

But soon they encountered a new enigma.

They had gone scarcely fifty yards ere the drops turned away from the river, and took them to the gate of a large gloomy building. It was a monastery.

They stood irresolute before it, and gazed at the dark pile. It seemed to them to hide some horrible mystery.

But presently Andrea gave a shout. "Here be the drops again," cried he. "And this road leadeth to the river."

They resumed the chase; and soon it became clear the drops were now leading them home. The track became wetter and wetter, and took them to the Tiber's edge. And there on the bank a bucketful appeared to have been discharged from the stream.

At first they shouted, and thought they had made a discovery; but reflection showed them it amounted to nothing. Certainly a man had been in the water, and had got out of it in safety: but that man was not Gerard. One said he knew a fisherman hard by that had nets and drags. They found the fisher and paid him liberally to sink nets in the river below the place, and to drag it above and below; and promised him gold should he find the body. Then they ran vainly up and down the river, which flowed so calm and voiceless, holding this and a thousand more strange secrets. Suddenly Andrea, with a cry of hope, ran back to the house.

He returned in less than half an hour.

"No," he groaned, and wrung his hands.

"What is the hour?" asked the lacquey.

"Four hours past midnight."

"My pretty lad," said the lacquey, solemnly, "say a mass for thy friend's soul: for he is not among living men."

The morning broke. Worn out with fatigue, Andrea and Pietro went home, heart sick.

The days rolled on, mute as the Tiber as to Gerard's fate.

CHAPTER LXIX

IT would indeed have been strange if with such barren data as they possessed, those men could have read the handwriting on the river's bank.

For there on that spot an event had just occurred, which, take it altogether, was perhaps without a parallel in the history of mankind, and may remain so to the end of time.

But it shall be told in a very few words, partly by me, partly by an actor in the scene.

Gerard, then, after writing his brief adieu to Pietro and Andrea, had stolen down to the river at nightfall.

He had taken his measures with a dogged resolution not uncommon in those who are bent on self-destruction. He filled his pockets with all the silver and copper he possessed, that he might sink the surer; and, so provided, hurried to a part of the stream that he had seen was little frequented.

There are some, especially women, who look about to make sure there is somebody at hand.

But this resolute wretch looked about him to make sure there was nobody.

And, to his annoyance, he observed a single figure leaning against the corner of an alley. So he affected to stroll carelessly away; but returned to the spot.

Lo! the same figure emerged from a side street and loitered about.

"Can he be watching me? Can he know what I am here for?" thought Gerard. "Impossible."

He went briskly off, walked along a street or two, made a detour, and came back.

The man had vanished. But, lo! on Gerard looking all round, to make sure, there he was a few yards behind, apparently fastening his shoe.

Gerard saw he was watched, and at this moment observed in the moonlight a steel gauntlet in his sentinel's hand.

Then he knew it was an assassin.

Strange to say, it never occurred to him that his was the life aimed at. To be sure he was not aware he had an enemy in the world.

He turned and walked up to the bravo. "My good friend," said he, eagerly, "sell me thine arm! a single stroke! See, here is all I have:" and he forced his money into the bravo's hands. "Oh, prithee! prithee! do one good deed, and rid me of my hateful life!" and even while speaking he undid his doublet, and bared his bosom.

The man stared in his face.

"Why do ye hesitate?" shrieked Gerard. "Have ye no bowels? Is it so much pains to lift your arm and fall it? Is it because I am poor, and can't give ye gold? Useless wretch, canst only strike a man behind; not look one in the face. There, then, do but turn thy head and hold thy tongue!"

And with a snarl of contempt he ran from him, and flung himself into the water.

"Margaret!"

At the heavy plunge of his body in the stream the bravo seemed to recover from a stupor. He ran to the bank, and with a strange cry the assassin plunged in after the self-destroyer.

What followed will be related by the assassin.

CHAPTER LXX

A WOMAN has her own troubles, as a man has his.

And we male writers seldom do more than indicate the griefs of the other sex. The intelligence of the female reader must come to our aid, and fill up our cold outlines. So have I indicated, rather than described, what Margaret Brandt went through up to that eventful day, when she entered Eli's house an enemy, read her sweetheart's letter, and remained a friend.

And now a woman's greatest trial drew near, and Gerard far away.

She availed herself but little of Eli's sudden favour: for this reserve she had always a plausible reason ready; and never hinted at the true one, which was this; there were two men in that house at sight of whom she shuddered with instinctive antipathy and dread. She had read wickedness and hatred in their faces, and mysterious signals of secret intelligence. She preferred to receive Catherine and her daughter at home. The former went to see her every day, and was wrapped up in the expected event.

Catherine was one of those females whose office is to multiply, and rear the multiplied: who, when at last they consent to leave off pelting one out of every room in the house with babies, hover about the fair scourges that are still in full swing, and do so cluck, they seem to multiply by proxy. It was in this spirit she entreated Eli to let her stay at Rotterdam while he went back to Tergou.

"The poor lass hath not a soul about her, that knows anything about anything. What avail a pair o' soldiers? Why that sort o' cattle should be putten out o' doors the first, at such an a time."

Need I say that this was a great comfort to Margaret.

Poor soul, she was full of anxiety as the time drew near.

She should die; and Gerard away.

But things balance themselves. Her poverty, and her father's helplessness, which had cost her such a struggle, stood her in good stead now.

Adversity's iron hand had forced her to battle the lassitude that overpowers the rich of her sex, and to be for ever on her feet, working. She kept this up to the last by Catherine's advice.

And so it was, that one fine evening just at sunset, she lay weak as water, but safe; with a little face by her side, and the heaven of maternity opening on her.

"Why dost weep, sweetheart? All of a sudden?"

"He is not here to see it."

"Ah, well, lass, he will be here ere 'tis weaned. Meantime, God hath been as good to thee as to e'er a woman born: and do but bethink thee it might have been a girl; didn't my very own Kate threaten me with one: and here we have got the bonniest boy in Holland, and a rare heavy one, the saints be praised for't."

"Ay, mother, I am but a sorry, ungrateful wretch to weep. If only Gerard were here to see it. 'Tis strange; I bore him well enow to be away from me in my sorrow; but, oh, it doth seem so hard he should not share my joy. Prithee, prithee, come to me, Gerard! dear, dear, Gerard!" And she stretched out her feeble arms.

Catherine bustled about, but avoided Margaret's eyes; for she could not restrain her own tears at hearing her own absent child thus earnestly addressed.

Presently, turning round, she found Margaret looking at her with a singular expression. "Heard you nought?"

"No, my lamb. What?"

"I did cry on Gerard, but now."

"Ay, ay, sure I heard that."

"Well, he answered me."

"Tush, girl: say not that."

"Mother, as sure as I lie here, with his boy by my side, his voice came back to me, 'Margaret!' So. Yet methought 'twas not his *happy* voice. But that might be the distance. All voices go off sad like at a distance. Why art not happy, sweetheart? and I so happy this night? Mother, I seem never to have felt a pain or known a care." And her sweet eyes turned and gloated on the little face in silence.

That very night Gerard flung himself into the Tiber. And, that very hour she heard him speak her name, he cried aloud in death's jaws and despair's.

"Margaret!"

Account for it those who can. I cannot.

CHAPTER LXXI

IN the guest chamber of a Dominican convent lay a single stranger, exhausted by successive and violent fits of nausea, which had at last subsided, leaving him almost as weak as Margaret lay that night in Holland.

A huge wood fire burned on the hearth, and beside it hung the patient's clothes.

A gigantic friar sat by his bedside reading pious collects aloud from his breviary.

The patient at times eyed him, and seemed to listen: at others closed his eyes and moaned.

The monk kneeled down with his face touching the ground and prayed for him: then rose and bade him farewell. "Day breaks," said he, "I must prepare for matins."

"Good Father Jerome, before you go, how came I hither?"

"By the hand of heaven. You flung away God's gift. He bestowed it on you again. Think on it! Hast tried the world, and found its gall. Now try the church! The church is peace. Pax vobiscum."

He was gone. Gerard lay back, meditating and wondering, till weak and wearied he fell into a doze.

When he awoke again he found a new nurse seated beside him. It was a layman, with an eye as small and restless as Friar Jerome's was calm and majestic.

The man inquired earnestly how he felt.

"Very, very weak. Where have I seen you before, Messer?"

"None the worse for my gauntlet?" inquired the other with considerable anxiety; "I was fain to strike you withal, or both you and I should be at the bottom of Tiber."

Gerard stared at him. "What, 'twas you saved me? How?"

"Well, signor, I was by the banks of Tiber on—on—an errand, no matter what. You came to me and begged hard for a dagger stroke. But ere I could oblige you, ay, even as you spoke to me, I knew you for the signor that saved my wife and child upon the sea."

"It *is* Teresa's husband. And an assassin? ! ! ?"

"At your service. Well, Ser Gerard, the next thing was, you flung yourself into Tiber, and bade me hold aloof."

"I remember that."

"Had it been any but you, believe me I had obeyed you, and not wagged a finger. Men are my foes. They may all hang on one rope, or drown in one river for me. But when thou, sinking in Tiber, didst cry 'Margaret!'"

"Ah!"

"My heart it cried 'Teresa!' How could I go home and look her in the face, did I let thee die, and by the very death thou savedst her from? So in I went; and luckily for us both I swim like a duck. You, seeing me near, and being bent on destruction, tried to grip me, and so end us both. But I swam round thee, and (receive my excuses) so buffeted thee on the nape of the neck with my steel glove; that thou lost sense, and I with much ado, the stream being strong, did draw thy body to land, but insensible and full of water. Then I took thee on my back and made for my own home. 'Teresa will nurse him, and be pleased with me,' thought I. But, hard by this monastery, a holy friar, the biggest e'er I saw, met us and asked the matter. So I told him. He looked hard at thee. 'I know the face,' quoth he. ''Tis one Gerard, a fair youth from Holland.' 'The same,' quo' I. Then said his reverence, 'He hath friends among our brethren. Leave him with us! Charity, it is our office.'

"Also he told me they of the convent had better means to tend thee than I had. And that was true enow. So I just bargained to be let in to see thee once a day, and here thou art."

And the miscreant cast a strange look of affection and interest upon Gerard.

Gerard did not respond to it. He felt as if a snake were in the room. He closed his eyes.

"Ah thou wouldst sleep," said the miscreant eagerly. "I go."

And he retired on tiptoe with a promise to come every day.

Gerard lay with his eyes closed: not asleep, but deeply pondering.

Saved from death by an assassin!

Was not this the finger of Heaven?

Of that Heaven he had insulted, cursed, and defied.

He shuddered at his blasphemies. He tried to pray.

He found he could utter prayers. But he could not pray.

"I am doomed eternally," he cried, "doomed, doomed."

The organ of the convent church burst on his ear in rich and solemn harmony.

Then rose the voices of the choir chanting a full service.

Among them was one that seemed to hover above the others, and tower towards heaven; a sweet boy's voice, full, pure, angelic.

He closed his eyes and listened. The days of his own boyhood flowed back upon him in those sweet, pious harmonies. No earthly dross there, no foul, fierce, passions, rending and corrupting the soul.

Peace; peace; sweet, balmy, peace.

"Ay," he sighed, "the Church is peace of mind. Till I left her bosom I ne'er knew sorrow, nor sin."

And the poor torn, worn, creature, wept.

And, even as he wept, there beamed on him the sweet and reverend face of one he had never thought to see again. It was the face of Father Anselm.

The good father had only reached the convent the night before last. Gerard recognized him in a moment, and cried to him, "Oh Father Anselm, you cured my wounded body in Juliers; now cure my hurt soul in Rome! Alas, you cannot."

Anselm sat down by the bedside, and, putting a gentle hand on his head, first calmed him with a soothing word or two.

He then (for he had learned how Gerard came there) spoke to him kindly but solemnly, and made him feel his crime, and urged him to repentance, and gratitude to that Divine Power which had thwarted his will to save his soul.

"Come, my son," said he, "first purge thy bosom of its load."

"Ah, father," said Gerard, "in Juliers I could; then I was innocent; but now, impious monster that I am, I dare not confess to you."

"Why not, my son? Thinkest thou I have not sinned against Heaven in my time, and deeply? oh how deeply! Come, poor laden soul, pour forth thy grief, pour forth thy faults, hold back nought! Lie not oppressed and crushed by hidden sins."

And soon Gerard was at Father Anselm's knees confessing his every sin with sighs and groans of penitence.

"Thy sins are great," said Anselm. "Thy temptation also was great, terribly great. I must consult our good prior."

The Cloister and the Hearth

The good Anselm kissed his brow, and left him to consult the superior as to his penance.

And, lo! Gerard could pray now.

And he prayed with all his heart.

The phase, through which this remarkable mind now passed, may be summed in a word—Penitence.

He turned with terror and aversion from the world, and begged passionately to remain in the convent. To him, convent nurtured, it was like a bird returning wounded, wearied, to its gentle nest.

He passed his noviciate in prayer, and mortification, and pious reading, and meditation.

The Princess Clælia's spy went home and told her that Gerard was certainly dead, the manner of his death unknown at present.

She seemed literally stunned.

When, after a long time, she found breath to speak at all, it was to bemoan her lot, cursed with such ready tools. "So soon," she sighed; "see how swift these monsters are to do ill deeds. They come to us in our hot blood, and first tempt us with their venal daggers, then enact the mortal deeds we ne'er had thought on but for them."

Ere many hours had passed, her pity for Gerard and hatred of his murderer had risen to fever heat; which with this fool was blood heat.

"Poor soul! I cannot call thee back to life. But he shall never live that traitorously slew thee."

And she put armed men in ambush, and kept them on guard all day, ready, when Ludovico should come for his money, to fall on him in a certain antechamber and hack him to pieces.

"Strike at his head," said she, "for he weareth a privy coat of mail; and if he goes hence alive your own heads shall answer it."

And so she sat weeping her victim, and pulling the strings of machines to shed the blood of a second for having been her machine to kill the first.

The Cloister and the Hearth

ONE of the novice Gerard's self-imposed penances was to receive Ludovico kindly, feeling secretly as to a slimy serpent.

Never was self-denial better bestowed: and, like most rational penances, it soon became no penance at all. At first the pride and complacency, with which the assassin gazed on the one life he had saved, was perhaps as ludicrous as pathetic; but it is a great thing to open a good door in a heart. One good thing follows another through the aperture. Finding it so sweet to save life, the miscreant went on to be averse to taking it; and from that to remorse; and from remorse to something very like penitence. And here Teresa co-operated by threatening, not for the first time, to leave him unless he would consent to lead an honest life. The good fathers of the convent lent their aid, and Ludovico and Teresa were sent by sea to Leghorn, where Teresa had friends, and the assassin settled down and became a porter.

He found it miserably dull work at first: and said so.

But methinks this dull life of plodding labour was better for him, than the brief excitement of being hewn in pieces by the Princess Clælia's myrmidons. His exile saved the unconscious penitent from that fate; and the princess, balked of her revenge, took to brooding, and fell into a profound melancholy; dismissed her confessor, and took a new one with a great reputation for piety, to whom she confided what she called her griefs. The new confessor was no other than Fra Jerome. She could not have fallen into better hands.

He heard her grimly out. Then took her and shook the delusions out of her as roughly as if she had been a kitchen-maid. For, to do this hard monk justice, on the path of duty he feared the anger of princes as little as he did the sea. He showed her in a few words, all thunder and lightning, that she was the criminal of criminals.

"Thou art the devil, that with thy money hath tempted one man to slay his fellow, and then, blinded with self-love, instead of blaming and punishing thyself, art thirsting for more blood of guilty men, but not so guilty as thou."

The Cloister and the Hearth

At first she resisted, and told him she was not used to be taken to task by her confessors. But he overpowered her, and so threatened her with the Church's curse here and hereafter, and so tore the scales off her eyes, and thundered at her, and crushed her, that she sank down and grovelled with remorse and terror at the feet of the gigantic Boanerges.

"Oh, holy father, have pity on a poor weak woman, and help me save my guilty soul. I was benighted for want of ghostly counsel like thine, good father. I waken as from a dream."

"Doff thy jewels," said Fra Jerome, sternly.

"I will. I will."

"Doff thy silk and velvet: and, in humbler garb than wears thy meanest servant, wend thou instant to Loretto."

"I will," said the princess, faintly.

"No shoes: but a bare sandal."

"No, father."

"Wash the feet of pilgrims both going and coming; and to such of them as be holy friars tell thy sin, and abide their admonition."

"Oh, holy father, let me wear my mask."

"Humph!"

"Oh, mercy! Bethink thee! My features are known through Italy."

"Ay. Beauty is a curse to most of ye. Well, thou mayst mask thine eyes; no more."

On this concession she seized his hand, and was about to kiss it; but he snatched it rudely from her.

"What would ye do? That hand handled the eucharist but an hour agone: is it fit for such as thou to touch it?"

"Ah, no. But oh, go not without giving your penitent daughter your blessing."

"Time enow to ask it when you come back from Loretto."

Thus that marvellous occurrence by Tiber's banks left its mark on all the actors, as prodigies are said to do. The assassin, softened by saving the life he was paid to take, turned from the stiletto to the porter's knot. The princess went barefoot to Loretto, weeping her crime and washing the feet of base born men.

And Gerard, carried from the Tiber into that convent a suicide, now passed for a young saint within its walls.

510

Loving but experienced eyes were on him.

Upon a shorter probation than usual he was admitted to priests' orders.

And soon after took the monastic vows, and became a friar of St. Dominic.

Dying to the world, the monk parted with the very name by which he had lived in it, and so broke the last link of association with earthly feelings.

Here Gerard ended, and Brother Clement began.

CHAPTER LXXIII

"AS is the race of leaves so is that of man." And a great man budded unnoticed in a tailor's house at Rotterdam this year, and a large man dropped to earth with great éclat.

Philip Duke of Burgundy, Earl of Holland, etc., etc., lay sick at Bruges. Now paupers got sick and got well as Nature pleased: but woe betided the rich in an age when, for one Mr. Malady killed, three fell by Dr. Remedy.

The duke's complaint, nameless then, is now diphtheria. It is, and was, a very weakening malady, and the duke was old; so altogether Dr. Remedy bled him.

The duke turned very cold: wonderful!

Then Dr. Remedy had recourse to the arcana of science.

"Ho! This is grave. Flay me an ape incontinent, and clap him to the duke's breast!"

Officers of state ran septemvious, seeking an ape to counteract the bloodthirsty tomfoolery of the human species.

Perdition! The duke was out of apes. There were buffaloes, lizards, Turks, leopards; any unreasonable beast but the right one.

"Why, there used to be an ape about," said one. "If I stand here I saw him."

So there used; but the mastiff had mangled the sprightly creature for stealing his supper: and so fulfilled the human precept, "Soyez de votre siècle!"

In this emergency the seneschal cast his despairing eyes around; and not in vain. A hopeful light shot into them.

"Here is *this*," said he, sotto voce. "Surely *this* will serve; 'tis altogether apelike, doublet and hose apart."

"Nay," said the chancellor, peevishly, "the Princess Marie would hang us. She doteth on *this*."

Now *this* was our friend Giles, strutting, all unconscious, in cloth of gold.

Then Dr. Remedy grew impatient, and bade flay a dog.

"A dog is next best to an ape; only it must be a dog all of one colour."

So they flayed a liver-coloured dog, and clapped it, yet palpitating, to their sovereign's breast: and he died.

Philip the Good, thus scientifically disposed of, left thirty-one children: of whom one, somehow or another, was legitimate; and reigned in his stead.

The good duke provided for nineteen out of the other thirty; the rest shifted for themselves.

According to the Flemish chronicle the deceased prince was descended from the kings of Troy through Thierry of Aquitaine, and Chilperic, Pharamond, &c., the old kings of Franconia.

But this in reality was no distinction. Not a prince of his day have I been able to discover who did not come down from Troy. "Priam" was mediæval for "Adam."

The good duke's body was carried into Burgundy, and laid in a noble mausoleum of black marble at Dijon.

Holland rang with his death; and little dreamed that anything as famous was born in her territory that year. That judgment has been long reversed. Men gaze at the tailor's house, where the great birth of the fifteenth century took place. In what house the good duke died "no one knows and no one cares," as the song says.

And why?

Dukes Philip the Good come and go, and leave mankind not a halfpenny wiser, nor better, nor other, than they found it. But when, once in three hundred years, such a child is born to the world as Margaret's son, lo! a human torch lighted by fire from heaven; and "FIAT LUX" thunders from pole to pole.

CHAPTER LXXIV

The Cloister

THE Dominicans, or preaching friars, once the most powerful order in Europe, were now on the wane; their rivals and bitter enemies, the Franciscans, were overpowering them throughout Europe; even in England, a rich and religious country, where, under the name of the Black Friars, they had once been paramount.

Therefore the sagacious men, who watched and directed the interests of the order, were never so anxious to incorporate able and zealous sons, and send them forth to win back the world.

The zeal and accomplishments of Clement, especially his rare mastery of language (for he spoke Latin, Italian, French, high and low Dutch) soon transpired, and he was destined to travel and preach in England, corresponding with the Roman centre.

But Jerome, who had the superior's ear, obstructed this design.

"Clement," said he, "has the milk of the world still in his veins, its feelings, its weaknesses; let not his new-born zeal and his humility tempt us to forego our ancient wisdom. Try him first, and temper him, lest one day we find ourselves leaning on a reed for a staff."

"It is well advised," said the prior. "Take him in hand thyself."

Then Jerome, following the ancient wisdom, took Clement and tried him.

One day he brought him to a field where the young men amused themselves at the games of the day; he knew this to be a haunt of Clement's late friends.

And sure enough ere long Pietro Vanucci and Andrea passed by them, and cast a careless glance on the two friars. They did not recognize their dead friend in a shaven monk.

Clement gave a very little start, and then lowered his eyes and said a pater noster.

"Would ye not speak with them, brother?" said Jerome, trying him.

513

"No, brother: yet was it good for me to see them. They remind me of the sins I can never repent enough."

"It is well," said Jerome, and he made a cold report in Clement's favour.

Then Jerome took Clement to many death-beds. And then into noisome dungeons; places where the darkness was appalling, and the stench loathsome, pestilential; and men looking like wild beasts lay coiled in rags and filth and despair. It tried his body hard; but the soul collected all its powers to comfort such poor wretches there as were not past comfort. And Clement shone in that trial. Jerome reported that Clement's spirit was willing, but his flesh was weak.

"Good!" said Anselm; "his flesh is weak, but his spirit is willing."

But there was a greater trial in store.

I will describe it as it was seen by others.

One morning a principal street in Rome was crowded, and even the avenues blocked up with heads. It was an execution. No common crime had been done, and on no vulgar victim.

The governor of Rome had been found in his bed at daybreak, *slaughtered*. His hand, raised probably in self-defence, lay by his side severed at the wrist; his throat was cut, and his temples bruised with some blunt instrument. The murder had been traced to his servant, and was to be expiated in kind this very morning.

Italian executions were not cruel in general. But this murder was thought to call for exact and bloody retribution.

The criminal was brought to the house of the murdered man, and fastened for half an hour to its wall. After this foretaste of legal vengeance his left hand was struck off, like his victim's. A new killed fowl was cut open and fastened round the bleeding stump; with what view I really don't know; but, by the look of it, some mare's nest of the poor dear doctors; and the murderer, thus mutilated and bandaged, was hurried to the scaffold; and there a young friar was most earnest and affectionate in praying with him, and for him, and holding the crucifix close to his eyes.

Presently the executioner pulled the friar roughly on one side, and in a moment felled the culprit with a heavy mallet, and falling on him, cut his throat from ear to ear.

There was a cry of horror from the crowd.

The young friar swooned away.

A gigantic monk strode forward, and carried him off like a child.

Brother Clement went back to the convent sadly discouraged. He confessed to the prior, with tears of regret.

"Courage, son Clement," said the prior. "A Dominican is not made in a day. Thou shalt have another trial. And I forbid thee to go to it fasting." Clement bowed his head in token of obedience. He had not long to wait. A robber was brought to the scaffold; a monster of villainy and cruelty, who had killed men in pure wantonness, after robbing them. Clement passed his last night in prison with him, accompanied him to the scaffold, and then prayed with him and for him so earnestly that the hardened ruffian shed tears and embraced him. Clement embraced him too, though his flesh quivered with repugnance; and held the crucifix earnestly before his eyes. The man was garotted, and Clement lost sight of the crowd, and prayed loud and earnestly while that dark spirit was passing from earth. He was no sooner dead than the hangman raised his hatchet and quartered the body on the spot. And, oh, mysterious heart of man! the people, who had seen the living body robbed of life with indifference, almost with satisfaction, uttered a piteous cry at each stroke of the axe upon his corpse that could feel nought. Clement too shuddered then, but stood firm, like one of those rocks that vibrate but cannot be thrown down. But suddenly Jerome's voice sounded in his ear.

"Brother Clement, get thee on that cart and preach to the people. Nay, quickly! strike with all thy force on all this iron, while yet 'tis hot, and souls are to be saved."

Clement's colour came and went; and he breathed hard. But he obeyed, and with ill-assured step mounted the cart, and preached his first sermon to the first crowd he had ever faced. Oh, that sea of heads! His throat seemed parched, his heart thumped, his voice trembled.

By-and-by the greatness of the occasion, the sight of the eager upturned faces, and his own heart full of zeal, fired the pale monk. He told them this robber's history, warm from his own lips in the prison, and showed his hearers by that example the gradations of folly and crime, and warned them solemnly not to put foot on the first round of that fatal ladder. And as alternately he thundered against the shedders of blood, and moved the crowd to charity and pity, his tremors left him, and he felt all strung up like a lute, and gifted with an unsuspected force; he was master of that listening crowd, could feel their very pulse, could play sacred melodies on them as on his psaltery. Sobs and groans attested his power over the mob already excited by the tragedy before them. Jerome stared like one who goes to light a stick; and fires a rocket. After a while Clement caught his look of astonishment, and seeing no approbation in it, broke suddenly off, and joined him.

"It was my first endeavour," said he, apologetically. "Your behest came on me like a thunderbolt. Was I?— Did I?— Oh, correct me and aid me with your experience, brother Jerome."

"Humph!" said Jerome, doubtfully. He added, rather sullenly after long reflection, "Give the glory to God, brother Clement; my opinion is thou art an orator born."

He reported the same at headquarters, half reluctantly. For he was an honest friar though a disagreeable one.

One Julio Antonelli was accused of sacrilege; three witnesses swore they saw him come out of the church whence the candlesticks were stolen, and at the very time. Other witnesses proved an alibi for him as positively. Neither testimony could be shaken. In this doubt Antonelli was permitted the trial by water, hot or cold. By the hot trial he must put his bare arm into boiling water, fourteen inches deep, and take out a pebble; by the cold trial his body must be let down into eight feet of water. The clergy, who thought him innocent, recommended the hot water trial, which, to those whom they favoured, was not so terrible as it sounded. But the poor wretch had not the nerve, and chose the cold ordeal. And this gave Jerome another opportunity of steeling Clement. Antonelli took the sacrament, and then was stripped naked on the banks of the Tiber, and tied hand and foot, to prevent those struggles by which a man, throwing his arms out of the water, sinks his body.

He was then let down gently into the stream, and floated a moment, with just his hair above water. A simultaneous roar from the crowd on each bank proclaimed him guilty. But the next moment the ropes, which happened to be new, got wet, and he settled down. Another roar proclaimed his innocence. They left him at the bottom of the river the appointed time, rather more than half a minute, then drew him up, gurgling, and gasping, and screaming for mercy;

and, after the appointed prayers, dismissed him, cleared of the charge.

During the experiment Clement prayed earnestly on the bank. When it was over he thanked God in a loud but slightly quavering voice.

By-and-by he asked Jerome whether the man ought not to be compensated.

"For what?"

"For the pain, the dread, the suffocation. Poor soul, he liveth, but hath tasted all the bitterness of death. Yet he had done no ill."

"He is rewarded enough in that he is cleared of his fault."

"But, being innocent of that fault, yet hath he drunk Death's cup, though not to the dregs; and his accusers, less innocent than he, do suffer nought."

Jerome replied, somewhat sternly:

"It is not in this world men are really punished, brother Clement. Unhappy they who sin yet suffer not. And happy they who suffer such ills as earth hath power to inflict; 'tis counted to them above, ay, and a hundredfold."

Clement bowed his head submissively.

"May thy good words not fall to the ground, but take root in my heart, brother Jerome."

But the severest trial Clement underwent at Jerome's hands was unpremeditated. It came about thus. Jerome, in an indulgent moment, went with him to Fra Colonna, and there "The Dream of Polifilo" lay on the table just copied fairly. The poor author, in the pride of his heart, pointed out a master-stroke in it.

"For ages," said he, "fools have been lavishing poetic praise and amorous compliment on mortal women, mere creatures of earth, smacking palpably of their origin; Sirens at the windows, where our Roman women in particular have by lifelong study learned the wily art to show their one good feature, though but an ear or an eyelash, at a jalosy, and hide all the rest; Magpies at the door, Capre n' i giardini, Angeli in Strada, Sante in chiesa, Diavoli in casa. Then come I and ransack the minstrels' lines for amorous turns, not forgetting those which Petrarch wasted on that French jilt Laura, the slyest of them all; and I lay you the whole bundle of spice at the feet of the only females worthy amorous incense; to wit, the Nine Muses."

"By which goodly stratagem," said Jerome, who had been turning the pages all this time, "you, a friar of St. Dominic, have produced an obscene book." And he dashed Polifilo on the table.

"Obscene? thou discourteous monk!" And the author ran round the table, snatched Polifilo away, locked him up, and, trembling with mortification, said, "My Gerard, pshaw! brother What's-his-name, had not found Polifilo obscene. Puris omnia pura."

"Such as read your Polifilo—Heaven grant they may be few!—will find him what I find him."

Poor Colonna gulped down this bitter pill as he might; and had he not been in his own lodgings, and a high born gentleman as well as a scholar, there might have been a vulgar quarrel. As it was, he made a great effort, and turned the conversation to a beautiful chrysolite the Cardinal Colonna had lent him; and, while Clement handled it, enlarged on its moral virtues: for he went the whole length of his age as a worshipper of jewels. But Jerome did not, and expostulated with him for believing that one dead stone could confer valour on its wearer, another chastity, another safety from poison, another temperance.

"The experience of ages proves they do," said Colonna. "As to the last virtue you have named, there sits a living proof. This Gerard—I beg your pardon, brother Thingemy—comes from the north, where men drink like fishes; yet was he ever most abstemious. And why? Carried an amethyst, the clearest and fullest coloured e'er I saw on any but noble finger. Where, in Heaven's name, is thine amethyst? Show it this unbeliever!"

"And 'twas that amethyst made the boy temperate?" asked Jerome, ironically.

"Certainly. Why, what is the derivation and meaning of amethyst? a negative, and μεθύω to tipple. Go to, names are but the signs of things. A stone is not called αμεθυστος for two thousand years out of mere sport, and abuse of language."

He then went through the prime jewels, illustrating their moral properties, especially of the ruby, the sapphire, the emerald, and the opal, by anecdotes out of grave historians.

"These be old wives' fables," said Jerome, contemptuously. "Was ever such credulity as thine?"

Now credulity is a reproach sceptics have often the ill-luck to incur: but it mortifies them none the less for that.

The believer in stones writhed under it, and dropped the subject. Then Jerome, mistaking his silence, exhorted him to go a step farther, and give up from this day his vain pagan lore, and study the lives of the saints. "Blot out these heathen superstitions from thy mind, brother, as Christianity hath blotted them from the earth."

And in this strain he proceeded, repeating, incautiously, some current but loose theological statements. Then the smarting Polifilo revenged himself. He flew out, and hurled a mountain of crude, miscellaneous lore upon Jerome, of which partly for want of time, partly for lack of learning, I can reproduce but a few fragments.

"The heathen blotted out? Why they hold four-fifths of the world. And what have we Christians invented without their aid? painting? sculpture? these are heathen arts, and we but pigmies at them. What modern mind can conceive and grave so god-like forms as did the chief Athenian sculptors, and the Libyan Licas, and Dinocrates of Macedon, and Scopas, Timotheus, Leochares, and Briaxis; Chares, Lysippus, and the immortal three of Rhodes, that wrought Laocoon from a single block? What prince hath the genius to turn mountains into statues, as was done at Bagistan, and projected at Athos? what town the soul to plant a colossus of brass in the sea, for the tallest ships to sail in and out between his legs? Is it architecture we have invented? Why here too we are but children. Can we match for pure design the Parthenon, with its clusters of double and single Doric columns? (I do adore the Doric when the scale is large), and, for grandeur and finish, the theatres of Greece and Rome, or the prodigious temples of Egypt, up to whose portals men walked awe-struck through avenues a mile long of sphinxes, each as big as a Venetian palace. And all these prodigies of porphyry cut and polished like crystal, not rough hewn as in our puny structures. Even now their polished columns and pilasters lie o'erthrown and broken, o'ergrown with acanthus and myrtle, but sparkling still, and flouting the slovenly art of modern workmen. Is it sewers, aqueducts, viaducts?

"Why we have lost the art of making a road—lost it with the world's greatest models under our very eye. Is it sepulchres of the dead? Why no Christian nation has ever erected a tomb, the sight of which does not set a scholar laughing. Do but think of the Mausoleum, and the Pyramids, and the monstrous sepulchres of the Indus and Ganges, which outside are mountains, and within are mines of precious stones. Ah, you have not seen the East, Jerome, or you could not decry the heathen."

Jerome observed that these were mere material things. True greatness was in the soul.

"Well then," replied Colonna, "in the world of mind, what have we discovered? Is it geometry? Is it logic? Nay, we are all pupils of Euclid and Aristotle. Is it written characters, an invention almost divine? We no more invented it than Cadmus did. Is it poetry? Homer hath never been approached by us, nor hath Virgil, nor Horace. Is it tragedy or comedy? Why poets, actors, theatres, all fell to dust at our touch. Have we succeeded in reviving them? Would you compare our little miserable mysteries and moralities, all frigid personification and dog Latin, with the glories of a Greek play (on the decoration of which a hundred thousand crowns had been spent) performed inside a marble miracle, the audience a seated city, and the poet a Sophocles?

"What then have we invented? Is it monotheism? Why the learned and philosophical among the Greeks and Romans held it; even their more enlightened poets were monotheists in their sleeves.

$$\text{Zευς εστιν ϝρανος, Zευς τε γῆ Zευς τοι παντα,}$$

saith the Greek, and Lucan echoes him:

'Jupiter est quod cunque vides quo cunque moveris.'

"Their vulgar were polytheists; and what are ours? We have not invented 'invocation of the saints.' Our sancti answer to their Dæmones and Divi, and the heathen used to pray their Divi or deified mortals to intercede with the higher divinity; but the ruder minds among them, incapable of nice distinctions, worshipped those lesser gods they should have but invoked. And so do the mob of Christians in our day, following the heathen vulgar by unbroken tradition. For in holy writ is no polytheism of any sort or kind.

"We have not invented so much as a form, or variety, of polytheism. The pagan vulgar worshipped all sorts of deified mortals, and each had his favourite, to whom he prayed ten times for once to the Omnipotent. Our vulgar worship canonized mortals, and each has his favourite, to whom he prays ten times for once to God. Call you that invention? Invention is confined to the East. Among the ancient vulgar only the mariners were monotheists; they worshipped Venus; called her 'Stella maris,' and 'Regina cælorum.' Among our vulgar only the mariners are monotheists; they worship the Virgin Mary, and call her 'the Star of the Sea,' and 'the Queen of Heaven.' Call you theirs a new religion? An old doublet with a new button. Our vulgar make images, and adore them, which is absurd; for adoration is the homage due from a creature to its creator; now here man is the creator; so the statues ought to worship him, and would, if they had brains enough to justify a rat in worshipping *them*. But even this abuse, though childish enough to be modern, is ancient. The pagan vulgar in these parts made their images, then knelt before them, adorned them with flowers, offered incense to them, lighted tapers before them, carried them in procession, and made pilgrimages to them just to the smallest tittle as we their imitators do."

Jerome here broke in impatiently, and reminded him that the images the most revered in Christendom were made by no mortal hand, but had dropt from heaven.

"Ay," cried Colonna, "such are the tutelary images of most great Italian towns. I have examined nineteen of them, and made draughts of them. If they came from the sky, our worst sculptors are our angels. But my mind is easy on that score. Ungainly statue, or villanous daub fell never yet from heaven to smuggle the bread out of capable workmen's mouths. All this is Pagan, and arose thus. The Trojans had oriental imaginations, and feigned that their Palladium, a wooden statue three cubits long, fell down from heaven. The Greeks took this fib home among the spoils of Troy, and soon it rained statues on all the Grecian cities, and their Latin apes. And one of these Palladia gave St. Paul trouble at Ephesus; 'twas a statue of Diana that fell down from Jupiter: credat qui credere possit."

"What would you cast your profane doubts on that picture of our blessed Lady, which scarce a century agone hung lustrous in the air over this very city, and was taken down by the Pope and bestowed in St. Peter's Church?"

"I have no profane doubts on the matter, Jerome. This is the story of Numa's shield, revived by theologians with an itch for fiction, but no talent that way; not being orientals. The 'ancile,' or sacred shield of Numa hung lustrous in the air over this very city, till that pious prince took it down and hung it in the temple of

Jupiter. Be just, swallow both stories or neither. The 'Bocca della Verita' passes for a statue of the Virgin, and convicted a woman of perjury the other day; it is in reality an image of the goddess Rhea, and the modern figment is one of its ancient traditions; swallow both or neither.

'Qui Bavium non odit amet tua carmina, Mavi.'

"But indeed we owe all our Palladiuncula, and all our speaking, nodding, winking, sweating, bleeding statues to these poor abused heathens: the Athenian statues all sweated before the battle of Chæronea, so did the Roman statues during Tully's consulship, viz., the statue of Victory at Capua, of Mars at Rome, and of Apollo outside the gates. The Palladium itself was brought to Italy by Æneas, and after keeping quiet three centuries, made an observation in Vesta's Temple: a trivial one, I fear, since it hath not survived; Juno's statue at Veii assented with a nod to go to Rome. Anthony's statue on Mount Alban bled from every vein in its marble, before the fight of Actium. Others cured diseases: as that of Pelichus, derided by Lucian; for the wiser among the heathen believed in sweating marble, weeping wood, and bleeding brass—as I do. Of all our marks and dents made in stone by soft substances, this saint's knee, and that saint's finger, and t'other's head, the original is heathen. Thus the foot-prints of Hercules were shown on a rock in Scythia. Castor and Pollux fighting on white horses for Rome against the Latians, left the prints of their hoofs on a rock at Regillum. A temple was built to them on the spot, and the marks were to be seen in Tully's day. You may see near Venice a great stone cut nearly in half by St. George's sword. This he ne'er had done but for the old Roman who cut the whetstone in two with his razor.

'Qui Bavium non odit amet tua carmina, Mavi.'

"Kissing of images, and the Pope's toe, is Eastern Paganism. The Egyptians had it of the Assyrians, the Greeks of the Egyptians, the Romans of the Greeks, and we of the Romans, whose Pontifex Maximus had his toe kissed under the Empire. The Druids kissed their High Priest's toe a thousand years B. C. The Mussulmans, who like you, profess to abhor Heathenism, kiss the stone of the Caaba: a Pagan practice.

"The Priests of Baal kissed their idols so.

The Cloister and the Hearth

"Tully tells us of a fair image of Hercules at Agrigentum, whose chin was worn by kissing. The lower parts of the statue we call Peter are Jupiter. The toe is sore worn, but not all by Christian mouths. The heathen vulgar laid their lips there first, for many a year, and ours have but followed them, as monkeys their masters. And that is why, down with the poor heathen! Pereant qui ante nos nostra fecerint.

"Our infant baptism is Persian, with the font, and the signing of the child's brow. Our throwing three handfuls of earth on the coffin, and saying dust to dust, is Egyptian.

"Our incense is Oriental, Roman, Pagan; and the early Fathers of the Church regarded it with superstitious horror, and died for refusing to handle it. Our holy water is Pagan, and all its uses. See, here is a Pagan aspersorium. Could you tell it from one of ours? It stood in the same part of their temples, and was used in ordinary worship as ours, and in extraordinary purifications. They called it Aqua lustralis. Their vulgar, like ours, thought drops of it falling on the body would wash out sin; and their men of sense, like ours, smiled or sighed at such credulity. What saith Ovid of this folly, which hath outlived him?

'Ah nimium faciles, qui tristia crimina cœdis
Flumineâ tolli posse putetis aquâ.'

Thou seest the heathen were not *all* fools. No more are we. Not *all*."

Fra Colonna uttered all this with such volubility, that his hearers could not edge in a word of remonstrance; and not being interrupted in praising his favourites, he recovered his good humour, without any diminution of his volubility.

"We celebrate the miraculous Conception of the Virgin on the 2nd of February. The old Romans celebrated the miraculous Conception of Juno on the 2nd of February. Our feast of All Saints is on the 2nd of November. The Festum Dei Mortis was on the 2nd of November. Our Candlemas is also an old Roman feast: neither the date nor the ceremony altered one tittle. The patrician ladies carried candles about the city that night as our signoras do now. At the gate of San Croce our courtezans keep a feast on the 20th August. Ask them why! The little noodles cannot tell you. On that very spot stood the Temple of Venus. Her building

is gone; but her rite remains. Did we discover Purgatory?
On the contrary, all we really know about it is from two treatises
of Plato, the Gorgias and the Phædo, and the sixth book of Virgil's
Æneid."

"I take it from a holier source: St. Gregory": said Jerome,
sternly.

"Like enough," replied Colonna, drily. "But St. Gregory was
not so nice; he took it from Virgil. Some souls, saith Gregory,
are purged by fire, others by water, others by air.

"Says Virgil:—

> 'Aliæ panduntur inanes,
> Suspensæ ad ventos, aliis sub gurgite vasto
> Infectum eluitur scelus, aut exuritur igni.'

But peradventure, you think Pope Gregory I. lived before Virgil,
and Virgil versified him.

"But the doctrine is Eastern, and as much older than Plato as
Plato than Gregory. Our prayers for the dead came from Asia
with Æneas. Ovid tells, that when he prayed for the soul of An-
chises, the custom was strange in Italy.

> 'Hunc morem Ænæas, pietatis idoneus auctor
> Attulit in terras, juste Latine, tuas.'

The 'Biblicæ Sortes,' which I have seen consulted on the altar,
are a parody on the 'Sortes Virgilianæ.' Our numerous altars
in one church are heathen: the Jews, who are monotheists, have but
one altar in a church. But the Pagans had many, being polytheists.
In the temple of Paphian Venus were a hundred of them. 'Centum que Sabæo thure calent aræ.' Our altars and our hundred
lights around St. Peter's tomb are Pagan. 'Centum aras posuit
vigilemque sacraverat ignem.' We invent nothing, not even nu-
merically. Our very Devil is the god Pan: horns and hoofs and all;
but blackened. For we cannot draw; we can but daub the figures of
Antiquity with a little sorry paint or soot. Our Moses hath stolen
the horns of Ammon; our Wolfgang the hook of Saturn; and Janus
bore the keys of heaven before St. Peter. All our really old Italian
bronzes of the Virgin and Child are Venuses and Cupids. So is
the wooden statue, that stands hard by this house, of Pope Joan
and the child she is said to have brought forth there in the middle
of a procession. Idiots! are new-born children thirteen years old?

And that boy is not a day younger. Cupid! Cupid! Cupid! And since you accuse me of credulity, know that to my mind that Papess is full as mythological, born of froth, and every way unreal, as the goddess who passes for her in the next street, or as the saints you call St. Baccho and St. Quirina: or St. Oracte, which is a dunce-like corruption of Mount Soracte, or St. Amphibolus, an English saint, which is a dunce-like corruption of the cloak worn by their St. Alban, or as the Spanish saint, St. Viar, which words on his tombstone, written thus: 'S. Viar,' prove him no saint, but a good old nameless heathen, and 'præfectus Viarum,' or overseer of roads (would he were back to earth, and paganizing of our Christian roads!), or as our St. Veronica of Benasco, which Veronica is a dunce-like corruption of the 'Vera icon,' which this saint brought into the church. I wish it may not be as unreal as the donor, or as the eleven thousand virgins of Cologne, who were but a couple."

Clement interrupted him to inquire what he meant. "I have spoken with those who have seen their bones."

"What of eleven thousand virgins all collected in one place and at one time? Do but bethink thee, Clement. Not one of the great Eastern cities of antiquity could collect eleven thousand Pagan virgins at one time, far less a puny Western city. Eleven thousand *Christian virgins* in a little, wee Paynim city!

'Quod cunque ostendis mihi sic incredulus odi.'

The simple sooth is this. The martyrs were two: the Breton princess herself, falsely called British, and her maid Onesimilla, which is a Greek name, Onesima, diminished. This some fool did mispronounce undecim mille, eleven thousand: loose tongue found credulous ears, and so one fool made many; eleven thousand of *them,* an you will. And you charge me with credulity, Jerome? and bid me read the lives of the saints. Well, I have read them: and many a dear old Pagan acquaintance I found there. The best fictions in the book are Oriental, and are known to have been current in Persia and Arabia eight hundred years and more before the dates the Church assigns to them as facts. As for the true Western figments, they lack the Oriental plausibility. Think you I am credulous enough to believe that St. Ida joined a decapitated head to its body? that Cuthbert's carcass directed his bearers where to go, and where to stop; that a city was eaten up of rats to punish one Hatto for comparing the poor to mice; that angels have a little horn in their foreheads, and that this was seen and recorded at the time by St. Veronica of Benasco, who never existed, and hath left us this information and a miraculous handkercher? For my part, I think the holiest woman the world ere saw must have an existence ere she can have a handkercher, or an eye to take unicorns for angels. Think you I believe that a brace of lions turned sextons and helped Anthony bury Paul of Thebes? that Patrick, a Scotch saint, stuck a goat's beard on all the descendants of one that offended him? that certain thieves, having stolen the convent ram, and denying it, St. Pol de Leon bade the ram bear witness, and straight the mutton bleated in the thief's belly? Would you have me give up the skilful figments of antiquity for such old wives' fables as these? The ancients lied about animals, too: but then they lied logically; we unreasonably. Do but compare Ephis and his lion, or, better still, Androcles and his lion, with Anthony and his two lions. Both the pagan lions do what lions never did; but at least they act in character. A lion with a bone in his throat, or a thorn in his foot, could not do better than be civil to a man. But Anthony's lions are asses in a lion's skin. What leonine motive could they have in turning sextons? A lion's business is to make corpses, not inter them." He added with a sigh, "Our lies are as inferior to the lies of the ancients as our statues, and for the same reason; we do not study nature as they did. We are imitatores, servum pecus. Believe you 'the lives of the saints;' that Paul the Theban was the first hermit, and Anthony the first Cænobite? Why, Pythagoras was an Eremite, and under ground for seven years: and his daughter was an abbess. Monks and hermits were in the East long before Moses, and neither old Greece nor Rome was ever without them. As for St. Francis and his snowballs, he did but mimic Diogenes, who, naked, embraced statues on which snow had fallen. The folly without the poetry. Ape of an ape—for Diogenes was but a mimic therein of the Brahmins and Indian gymnosophists. Natheless, the children of this Francis bid fair to pelt us out of the church with their snowballs. Tell me now, Clement, what habit is lovelier than the vestments of our priests? Well, we owe them all to Numa Pompilius, except the girdle and the stole, which are judaical. As for the amice and the albe, they retain the very names they bore in Numa's day. The 'pelt' worn by the canons comes from primeval Paganism. 'Tis a relic of those rude times when the sacrificing priest wore the skins of the beasts with the fur outward. Strip off thy black gown, Jerome, thy girdle and cowl, for they come to us all three from the Pagan ladies. Let thy hair grow like Absalom's, Jerome! for the tonsure is as Pagan as the Muses."

"Take care what thou sayest," said Jerome, sternly. "We know the very year in which the church did first ordain it."

"But not invent it, Jerome. The Brahmins wore it a few thousand years ere that. From them it came through the Assyrians to the priests of Isis in Egypt, and afterwards of Serapis at Athens. The late Pope (the saints be good to him) once told me the tonsure was forbidden by God to the Levites in the Pentateuch. If so, this was because of the Egyptian priests wearing it. I trust to his holiness. I am no biblical scholar. The Latin of thy namesake Jerome is a barrier I cannot overleap. 'Dixit ad me Dominus Deus. Dixi ad Dominum Deum.' No, thank you, holy Jerome; I can stand a good deal, but I cannot stand thy Latin. Nay; give me the New Testament! 'Tis not the Greek of Xenophon; but 'tis Greek. And there be heathen sayings in it too. For St. Paul was not so spiteful against them as thou. When the heathen said a good thing that suited his matter, by Jupiter he just took it, and mixed it to all eternity with the inspired text."

"Come forth, Clement, come forth!" said Jerome, rising; "and thou, profane monk, know that but for the powerful house that upholds thee, thy accursed heresy should go no farther, for I would have thee burned at the stake." And he strode out white with indignation.

Colonna's reception of this threat did credit to him as an enthusiast. He ran and hallowed joyfully after Jerome. "And *that* is Pagan. Burning of men's bodies for the opinions of their souls is a purely Pagan custom—as Pagan as incense, holy water, a hundred altars in one church, the tonsure, the cardinal's, or flamen's hat, the word Pope, the——"

Here Jerome slammed the door.

But ere they could get clear of the house a jalosy was flung open, and the Paynim monk came out head and shoulders, and overhung the street, shouting—

"'Affecti suppliciis Christiani, genus hominum
Novæ superstitionis ac maleficæ.'"

And having delivered this parting blow, he felt a great triumphant joy, and strode exultant to and fro; and not attending with his usual care to the fair way (for his room could only be threaded by little paths wriggling among the antiquities), tripped over the beak of an Egyptian stork, and rolled upon a regiment of Armenian gods, which he found tough in argument though small in stature.

"You will go no more to that heretical monk," said Jerome to Clement.

Clement sighed. "Shall we leave him and not try to correct him? Make allowance for heat of discourse! He was nettled. His words are worse than his acts. Oh! 'tis a pure and charitable soul."

"So are all arch-heretics. Satan does not tempt them like other men. Rather he makes them more moral, to give their teaching weight. Fra Colonna cannot be corrected; his family is all-powerful in Rome. Pray we the saints he blasphemes to enlighten him. 'Twill not be the first time they have returned good for evil. Meantime thou art forbidden to consort with him. From this day go alone through the city! Confess and absolve sinners! exorcise demons! comfort the sick! terrify the impenitent! preach wherever men are gathered and occasion serves! and hold no converse with the Fra Colonna!"

Clement bowed his head.

Then the prior, at Jerome's request, had the young friar watched. And one day the spy returned with the news that brother Clement had passed by the Fra Colonna's lodging, and had stopped a little while in the street and then gone on, but with his hand to his eyes, and slowly.

This report Jerome took to the prior. The prior asked his opinion, and also Anselm's, who was then taking leave of him on his return to Juliers.

Jerome.] "Humph! He obeyed, but with regret, ay, with childish repining."

Anselm.] "He shed a natural tear at turning his back on a friend and a benefactor. But he obeyed."

Now Anselm was one of your gentle irresistibles. He had at times a mild ascendant even over Jerome.

"Worthy brother Anselm," said Jerome, "Clement is weak to the **very** bone. He will disappoint thee. He will do nothing *great,* either for the Church or for our holy order. Yet he is an orator, and hath drunken of the spirit of St. Dominic. Fly him, then, with a string."

That same day it was announced to Clement that he was to go to England immediately with brother Jerome.

Clement folded his hands on his breast, and bowed his head in calm submission.

CHAPTER LXXV

The Hearth

A CATHERINE is not an unmixed good in a strange house. The governing power is strong in her. She has scarce crossed the threshold ere the utensils seem to brighten; the hearth to sweep itself; the windows to let in more light; and the soul of an enormous cricket to animate the dwelling-place. But this cricket is a Busy Body. And that is a tremendous character. It has no discrimination. It sets everything to rights, and everybody. Now many things are the better for being set to rights. But everything is not. Everything is the one thing that won't stand being set to rights; except in that calm and cool retreat, the grave.

Catherine altered the position of every chair and table in Margaret's house; and perhaps for the better.

But she must go farther and upset the live furniture.

When Margaret's time was close at hand, Catherine treacherously invited the aid of Denys and Martin: and, on the poor simple-minded fellows asking her earnestly what service they could be, she told them they might make themselves comparatively useful by going for a little walk. So far so good. But she intimated further that should the promenade extend into the middle of next week all the better. This was not ingratiating.

The subsequent conduct of the strong under the yoke of the weak might have propitiated a she-bear with three cubs, one sickly. They generally slipped out of the house at daybreak: and stole in like thieves at night: and if by any chance they were at home, they went about like cats on a wall tipped with broken glass, and wearing awe-struck visages, and a general air of subjugation and depression.

But all would not do. Their very presence was ill timed: and jarred upon Catherine's nerves.

Did instinct whisper, a pair of depopulators had no business in a house with multipliers twain?

The breastplate is no armour against a female tongue: and Catherine ran infinite pins and needles of speech into them. In a word, when Margaret came down stairs, she found the kitchen swept of heroes.

Martin, old and stiff, had retreated no farther than the street, and with the honours of war: for he had carried off his baggage, a stool: and sat on it in the air.

Margaret saw he was out in the sun: but was not aware he was a fixture in that luminary. She asked for Denys. "Good, kind Denys; he will be right pleased to see me about again."

Catherine, wiping a bowl with now superfluous vigour, told her Denys was gone to his friends in Burgundy. "And high time. Hasn't been anigh them this three years, by all accounts."

"What, gone without bidding me farewell?" said Margaret, opening two tender eyes like full-blown violets.

Catherine reddened. For this new view of the matter set her conscience pricking her.

But she gave a little toss, and said, "Oh, you were asleep at the time: and I would not have you wakened."

"Poor Denys," said Margaret: and the dew gathered visibly on the open violets.

Catherine saw out of the corner of her eye, and without taking a bit of open notice, slipped off and lavished hospitality and tenderness on the surviving depopulator.

It was sudden; and Martin old and stiff in more ways than one.

"No, thank you, dame. I have got used to out o' doors. And I love not changing and changing. I meddle wi' nobody here: and nobody meddles wi' me."

"Oh, you nasty, cross, old wretch!" screamed Catherine, passing in a moment from treacle to sharpest vinegar. And she flounced back into the house.

On calm reflection she had a little cry. Then she half reconciled herself to her conduct by vowing to be so kind Margaret should never miss her plagues of soldiers. But, feeling still a little uneasy, she dispersed all regrets by a process at once simple and sovereign.

She took and washed the child.

From head to foot she washed him in tepid water: and heroes, and their wrongs, became as dust in an ocean—of soap and water.

While this celestial ceremony proceeded, Margaret could not keep quiet. She hovered round the fortunate performer. She must have an apparent hand in it, if not a real. She put her finger into the water—to pave the way for her boy, I suppose; for she could not have deceived herself so far as to think Catherine would allow her to settle the temperature. During the ablution she kneeled down opposite the little Gerard, and prattled to him with amazing fluency; taking care, however, not to articulate like grown-up people; for, how could a cherub understand *their* ridiculous pronunciation?

"I wish you could wash out THAT," said she, fixing her eyes on the little boy's hand.

"What?"

"What, have you not noticed? on his little finger."

Granny looked, and there was a little brown mole.

"Eh! but this is wonderful!" she cried. "Nature, my lass, y' are strong; and meddlesome to boot. Hast noticed such a mark on some one else. Tell the truth, girl!"

"What, on *him?* Nay, mother, not I."

"Well then he has; and on the very spot. And you never noticed that much. But, dear heart, I forgot; you han't known him from child to man as I have. I have had him hundreds o' times on my knees, the same as this, and washed him from top to toe in lu-warm water." And she swelled with conscious superiority; and Margaret looked meekly up to her as a woman beyond competition.

Catherine looked down from her dizzy height, and moralized. She differed from other busy-bodies in this, that she now and then reflected: not deeply; or of course I should take care not to print it.

"It is strange," said she, "how things come round and about. Life is but a whirligig. Leastways, we poor women, *our* lives are cut upon one pattern. Wasn't I for washing out my Gerard's mole in his young days? 'Oh, fie! her's a foul blot,' quo' I; and scrubbed away at it I did till I made the poor wight cry; so then

I thought 'twas time to give over. And now says you to me, 'Mother,' says you, 'do try and wash yon out o' my Gerard's finger,' says you. Think on't!"

"Wash it out?" cried Margaret; "I wouldn't for all the world. Why it is the sweetest bit in his little darling body. I'll kiss it morn and night till he, that owned it first, comes back to us three. Oh, bless you, my jewel of gold and silver, for being marked like your own daddy to comfort me."

And she kissed little Gerard's little mole; but she could not stop there; she presently had him sprawling on her lap, and kissed his back all over again and again, and seemed to worry him as wolf a lamb; Catherine looking on and smiling. She had seen a good many of these savage onslaughts in her day.

And this little sketch indicates the tenor of Margaret's life for several months. One or two small things occurred to her during that time, which must be told; but I reserve them, since one string will serve for many glass beads. But, while her boy's father was passing through those fearful tempests of the soul ending in the dead monastic calm, her life might fairly be summed in one great blissful word—

Maternity.

You, who know what lies in that word, enlarge my little sketch, and see the young mother nursing and washing, and dressing and undressing, and crowing and gambolling with her first-born; then swifter than lightning dart your eye into Italy, and see the cold cloister; and the monks passing like ghosts, eyes down, hands meekly crossed over bosoms dead to earthly feelings.

One of these cowled ghosts is he, whose return, full of love and youth, and joy, that radiant young mother awaits.

In the valley of Grindelwald the traveller has on one side the perpendicular Alps, all rock, ice, and everlasting snow, towering above the clouds, and piercing to the sky; on his other hand little every-day slopes, but green as emeralds, and studded with cows, and pretty cots, and life; whereas those lofty neighbours stand leafless, lifeless, inhuman, sublime. Elsewhere sweet commonplaces of nature are apt to pass unnoticed; but, fronting the grim Alps, they soothe, and even gently strike, the mind by contrast with their tremendous opposites. Such, in their way, are the two halves of this story, rightfully looked at; on the Italian side rugged adventure, strong passion, blasphemy, vice, penitence, pure ice, holy snow, soaring direct at heaven. On the Dutch side, all on a humble scale and womanish, but ever green. And as a pathway parts the ice towers of Grindelwald, aspiring to the sky, from its little sunny braes, so here is but a page between "the Cloister and the Hearth."

CHAPTER LXXVI

The Cloister

THE new pope favoured the Dominican order. The convent received a message from the Vatican, requiring a capable friar to teach at the university of Basle. Now Clement was the very monk for this: well versed in languages, and in his worldly days had attended the lectures of Guarini the younger. His visit to England was therefore postponed, though not resigned; and meantime he was sent to Basle: but not being wanted there for three months, he was to preach on the road.

He passed out of the northern gate with his eyes lowered, and the whole man wrapped in pious contemplation.

Oh, if we could paint a mind and its story, what a walking fresco was this bare-footed friar!

Hopeful, happy love, bereavement, despair, impiety, vice, suicide, remorse, religious despondency, penitence, death to the world, resignation.

And all in twelve short months.

And now the traveller was on foot again. But all was changed: no perilous adventures now. The very thieves and robbers bowed to the ground before him, and, instead of robbing him, forced stolen money on him, and begged his prayers.

This journey therefore furnished few picturesque incidents. I have, however, some readers to think of, who care little for melodrama, and expect a quiet peep at what passes inside a man. To such students things undramatic are often vocal, denoting the progress of a mind.

The first Sunday of Clement's journey was marked by this. He prayed for the soul of Margaret. He had never done so before.

Not that her eternal welfare was not dearer to him than anything on earth. It was his humility. The terrible impieties that burst from him on the news of her death horrified my well-disposed readers; but not as on reflection they horrified him who had uttered them. For a long time during his novitiate he was oppressed with religious despair. He thought he must have committed that sin against the Holy Spirit which dooms the soul for ever. By degrees that dark cloud cleared away, Anselmo juvante: but deep self-abasement remained. He felt his own salvation insecure, and moreover thought it would be mocking Heaven, should he, the deeply stained, pray for a soul so innocent, comparatively, as Margaret's. So he used to coax good Anselm and another kindly monk to pray for her. They did not refuse, nor do it by halves. In general the good old monks (and there were good, bad, and indifferent, in every convent) had a pure and tender affection for their younger brethren, which, in truth, was not of this world.

Clement then, having preached on Sunday morning in a small Italian town, and being mightily carried onward, was greatly encouraged; and that day a balmy sense of God's forgiveness and love descended on him. And he prayed for the welfare of Margaret's soul. And from that hour this became his daily habit, and the one purified tie, that by memory connected his heart with earth.

For his family were to him as if they had never been.

The Church would not share with earth. Nor could even the Church cure the great love without annihilating the smaller ones.

During most of this journey Clement rarely felt any spring of life within him, but when he was in the pulpit. The other exceptions were, when he happened to relieve some fellow-creature.

A young man was tarantula bitten, or perhaps, like many more, fancied it. Fancy or reality, he had been for two days without sleep, and in most extraordinary convulsions, leaping, twisting, and beating the walls. The village musicians had only excited him worse with their music. Exhaustion and death followed the disease, when it gained such a head. Clement passed by and learned what was the matter. He sent for a psaltery, and tried the patient with soothing melodies; but, if the other tunes maddened him, Clement's seem to crush him. He groaned and moaned under them, and grovelled on the floor. At last the friar observed that at intervals his lips kept going. He applied his ear, and found the patient was whispering a tune; and a very singular one, that had no existence. He learned this tune, and played it. The patient's face brightened amazingly. He marched about the room on the light fantastic toe enjoying it; and when Clement's fingers ached nearly off with playing it, he had the satisfaction of seeing the young man sink complacently to sleep to this lullaby, the strange creation of his own mind; for it seems he was no musician, and never composed a tune before or after. This sleep saved his life. And Clement, after teaching the tune to another, in case it should be wanted again, went forward with his heart a little warmer. On another occasion he found a mob haling a decently-dressed man along, who struggled and vociferated, but in a strange language. This person had walked into their town erect and sprightly, waving a mulberry branch over his head. Thereupon the natives first gazed stupidly, not believing their eyes, then pounced on him and dragged him before the podesta.

Clement went with them: but on the way drew quietly near the prisoner and spoke to him in Italian; no answer. In French; German; Dutch; no assets. Then the man tried Clement in tolerable Latin, but with a sharpish accent. He said he was an Englishman, and, oppressed with the heat of Italy, had taken a bough off the nearest tree, to save his head. "In my country anybody is welcome to what grows on the highway. Confound the fools; I am ready to pay for it. But here is all Italy up in arms about a twig and a handful of leaves."

The pig-headed podesta would have sent the dogged islander to prison: but Clement mediated, and with some difficulty made the prisoner comprehend that silkworms, and by consequence mulberry leaves, were sacred, being under the wing of the Sovereign, and his source of income; and urged on the podesta that ignorance of his mulberry laws was natural in a distant country, where the very tree perhaps was unknown. The opinionative islander turned the still vibrating scale by pulling out a long purse and repeating his original theory, that the whole question was mercantile. "Quid damni?" said he. "Dic; et cito solvam." The podesta snuffed the gold: fined him a ducat for the duke; about the value of the whole tree: and pouched the coin.

The Cloister and the Hearth

The Englishman shook off his ire the moment he was liberated, and laughed heartily at the whole thing: but was very grateful to Clement.

"You are too good for this hole of a country, father," said he. "Come to England! That is the only place in the world. I was an uneasy fool to leave it, and wander among mulberries and their idiots. I am a Kentish squire, and educated at Cambridge University. My name it is Rolfe, my place Betshanger. The man and the house are both at your service. Come over and stay till domesday. We sit down forty to dinner every day at Betshanger. One more or one less at the board will not be seen. You shall end your days with me and my heirs if you will. Come now! What an Englishman says he means." And he gave him a great hearty grip of the hand to confirm it.

"I will visit thee some day, my son," said Clement: "but not to weary thy hospitality."

The Englishman then begged Clement to shrive him. "I know not what will become of my soul," said he. "I live like a heathen since I left England."

Clement consented gladly, and soon the islander was on his knees to him by the road-side, confessing the last month's sins.

Finding him so pious a son of the Church, Clement let him know he was really coming to England. He then asked him whether it was true that country was overrun with Lollards and Wickliffites.

The other coloured up a little. "There be black sheep in every land," said he. Then after some reflection he said, gravely, "Holy father, hear the truth about these heretics. None are better disposed towards holy Church than we English. But we are ourselves, and by ourselves. Wo love our own ways, and, above all, our own tongue. The Norman could conquer our billhooks, but not our tongues; and hard they tried it for many a long year by law and proclamation. Our good foreign priests utter God to plain English folk in Latin, or in some French or Italian lingo, like the bleating of a sheep. Then come the fox Wickliff and his crew, and read him out of his own book in plain English, that all men's hearts warm to. Who can withstand this? God forgive me, I believe the English would turn deaf ears to St. Peter himself, spoke he not to them in the tongue their mothers sowed in their ears and their hearts along with mothers' kisses." He added hastily, "I say not this for myself; I am Cambridge bred; and good words come not amiss to me in Latin; but for the people in general. Clavis ad corda Anglorum est lingua materna."

"My son," said Clement, "blessed be the hour I met thee; for thy words are sober and wise. But, alas! how shall I learn your English tongue? No book have I."

"I would give you my book of hours, father. 'Tis in English and Latin, cheek by jowl. But, then, what would become of my poor soul, wanting my 'hours' in a strange land? Stay, you are a holy man, and I am an honest one; let us make a bargain; you to pray for me every day for two months, and I to give you my book of hours. Here it is. What say you to that?" And his eyes sparkled, and he was all on fire with mercantility.

Clement smiled gently at this trait: and quietly detached a MS. from his girdle, and showed him that it was in Latin and Italian.

"See, my son," said he, "Heaven hath forseen our several needs, and given us the means to satisfy them: let us change books; and, my dear son, I will give thee my poor prayers and welcome, not sell them thee. I love not religious bargains."

The islander was delighted. "So shall I learn the Italian tongue without risk to my eternal weal. Near is my purse, but nearer is my soul."

He forced money on Clement. In vain the friar told him it was contrary to his vow to carry more of that than was barely necessary.

"Lay it out for the good of the Church and of my soul," said the islander. "I ask you not to keep it, but take it you must and shall." And he grasped Clement's hand warmly again: and Clement kissed him on the brow, and blessed him, and they went each his way.

About a mile from where they parted, Clement found two tired wayfarers lying in the deep shade of a great chestnut-tree, one of a thick grove the road skirted. Near the men was a little cart, and in it a printing-press, rude and clumsy as a vine-press. A jaded mule was harnessed to the cart.

And so Clement stood face to face with his old enemy.

And as he eyed it, and the honest, blue-eyed faces of the wearied craftsmen, he looked back as on a dream at the bitterness he had once felt towards this machine. He looked kindly down on them, and said, softly,

"Sweynheim!"

The men started to their feet.

"Pannartz!"

They scuttled into the wood, and were seen no more.

Clement was amazed, and stood puzzling himself.

Presently a face peeped from behind a tree.

Clement addressed it. "What fear ye?"

A quavering voice replied, "Say, rather, by what magic you, a stranger, can call us by our names! I never clapt eyes on you till now."

"O superstition! I know ye, as all good workmen are known—by your works. Come hither and I will tell ye."

They advanced gingerly from different sides; each regulating his advance by the other's.

"My children," said Clement, "I saw a Lactantius in Rome, printed by Sweynheim and Pannartz, disciples of Fust."

"D'ye hear that, Pannartz? our work has gotten to Rome already."

"By your blue eyes and flaxen hair I wist ye were Germans: and the printing-press spoke for itself. Who then should ye be but Fust's disciples, Pannartz and Sweynheim?"

The honest Germans were now astonished that they had suspected magic in so simple a matter.

"The good father hath his wits about him, that is all," said Pannartz.

"Ay," said Sweynheim, "and with those wits would he could tell us how to get this tired beast to the next town."

"Yea," said Sweynheim, "and where to find money to pay for his meat and ours when we get there."

"I will try," said Clement. "Free the mule of the cart, and of all harness but the bare halter."

This was done, and the animal immediately lay down and rolled on his back in the dust like a kitten. Whilst he was thus employed, Clement assured them he would rise up a new mule. "His Creator hath taught him this art to refresh himself, which the nobler horse knoweth not. Now, with regard to money, know that a worthy Englishman hath intrusted me with a certain sum to bestow in charity. To whom can I better give a stranger's money than to strangers? Take it, then, and be kind to some Englishman or other stranger in his need; and may all nations learn to love one another one day."

The Cloister and the Hearth

The tears stood in the honest workmen's eyes. They took the money with heartfelt thanks.

"It is your nation we are bound to thank and bless, good Father, if we but knew it."

"My nation is the Church."

Clement was then for bidding them farewell, but the honest fellows implored him to wait a little; they had no silver nor gold, but they had something they could give their benefactor. They took the press out of the cart, and, while Clement fed the mule, they bustled about, now on the white hot road, now in the deep cool shade, now half in and half out, and presently printed a quarto sheet of eight pages, which was already set up. They had not type enough to print two sheets at a time. When, after the slower preliminaries, the printed sheet was pulled all in a moment, Clement was amazed in turn.

"What are all these words really fast upon the paper?" said he. "Is it verily certain they will not go as swiftly as they came? And *you* took *me* for a magician! 'Tis 'Augustine de civitate Dei.' My sons, you carry here the very wings of knowledge. Oh, never abuse this great craft! Print no ill books! They would fly abroad countless as locusts, and lay waste men's souls."

The workmen said they would sooner put their hands under the screw than so abuse their goodly craft.

And so they parted.

There is nothing but meeting and parting in this world.

At a town in Tuscany the holy friar had a sudden and strange rencontre with the past. He fell in with one of those motley assemblages of patricians and plebeians, piety and profligacy, "a company of pilgrims"; a subject too well painted by others for me to go and daub.

They were in an immense barn belonging to the inn. Clement, dusty and wearied, and no lover of idle gossip, sat in a corner studying the Englishman's hours, and making them out as much by his own Dutch as by the Latin version.

Presently a servant brought a bucket half full of water, and put it down at his feet. A female servant followed with two towels. And then a woman came forward, and, crossing herself, kneeled down without a word at the bucket-side, removed her sleeves entirely, and motioned to him to put his feet into the water. It was some lady of rank doing penance. She wore a mask scarce an inch broad, but effectual. Moreover, she handled the friar's feet more delicately than those do who are born to such offices.

These penances were not uncommon; and Clement, though he had little faith in this form of contrition, received the services of the incognita as a matter of course. But presently she sighed deeply, and, with her heartfelt sigh and her head bent low over her menial office, she seemed so bowed with penitence, that he pitied her and said, calmly but gently, "Can I aught for your soul's weal, my daughter?"

She shook her head with a faint sob. "Nought, holy father, nought: only to hear the sin of her who is most unworthy to touch thy holy feet. 'Tis part of my penance to tell sinless men how vile I aim."

"Speak, my daughter."

"Father," said the lady, bending lower and lower, "these hands of mine look white, but they are stained with blood,—the blood of the man I loved. Alas! you withdraw your foot. Ah me! What shall I do? All holy things shrink from me."

"Culpa mea! culpa mea!" said Clement eagerly. "My daughter, it was an unworthy movement of earthly weakness, for which I shall do penance. Judge not the Church by her feebler servants. Not her foot, but her bosom, is offered to thee, repenting truly. Take courage, then, and purge thy conscience of his load."

On this the lady, in a trembling whisper, and hurriedly, and cringing a little, as if she feared the Church would strike her bodily for what she had done, made this confession.

"He was a stranger, and base-born, but beautiful as Spring, and wise beyond his years. I loved him. I had not the prudence to conceal my love. Nobles courted me. I ne'er thought one of humble birth could reject me. I showed him my heart; oh, shame of my sex! He drew back; yet he admired me: but innocently. He loved another: and he was constant. I resorted to a woman's wiles. They availed not. I borrowed the wickedness of men, and threatened his life, and to tell his true lover he died false to her. Ah! you shrink; your foot trembles. Am I not a monster? Then he wept and prayed to me for mercy; then my good angel helped me; I bade him leave Rome. Gerard, Gerard, why did you not obey me?

I thought he was gone. But two months after this I met him. Never shall I forget it. I was descending the Tiber in my galley, when he came up it with a gay company, and at his side a woman beautiful as an angel, but bold and bad. That woman claimed me aloud for her rival. Traitor and hypocrite, he had exposed me to her, and to all the loose tongues in Rome. In terror and revenge I hired—a bravo. When he was gone on his bloody errand, I wavered too late. The dagger I had hired struck. He never came back to his lodgings. He was dead. Alas! perhaps he was not so much to blame: none have ever cast his name in my teeth. His poor body is not found: or I should kiss its wounds; and slay myself upon it. All around his very name seems silent as the grave, to which this murderous hand has sent him." (Clement's eyes were drawn by her movement. He recognized her shapely arm, and soft white hand.) "And oh! he was so young to die. A poor thoughtless boy, that had fallen a victim to that bad woman's arts, and she had made him tell her everything. Monster of cruelty, what penance can avail me? Oh, holy father, what shall I do?"

Clement's lips moved in prayer, but he was silent. He could not see his duty clear.

Then she took his feet and began to dry them. She rested his foot upon her soft arm, and pressed it with the towel so gently she seemed incapable of hurting a fly. Yet her lips had just told another story, and a true one.

While Clement was still praying for wisdom, a tear fell upon his foot. It decided him. "My daughter," said he, "I myself have been a great sinner."

"You, father?"

"I; quite as great a sinner as thou; though not in the same way. The devil has gins and snares, as well as traps. But penitence softened my impious heart, and then gratitude remoulded it. Therefore, seeing you penitent, I hope you can be grateful to Him, who has been more merciful to you than you have to your fellow-creature. Daughter, the Church sends you comfort."

"Comfort to me? ah! never! unless it can raise my victim from the dead."

"Take this crucifix in thy hand, fix thine eyes on it, and listen to me," was all the reply.

"Yes, father; but let me thoroughly dry your feet first: 'tis ill sitting in wet feet: and you are the holiest man of all whose feet I have washed. I know it by your voice."

"Woman, I am not. As for my feet, they can wait their turn. Obey thou me!"

"Yes, father," said the lady, humbly. But with a woman's evasive pertinacity she wreathed one towel swiftly round the foot she was drying, and placed his other foot on the dry napkin; then obeyed his command.

And, as she bowed over the crucifix, the low, solemn, tones of the friar fell upon her ear, and his words soon made her whole body quiver with various emotions, in quick succession.

"My daughter, he you murdered—in intent—was one Gerard, a Hollander. He loved a creature, as man should love none but their Redeemer and his Church. Heaven chastised him. A letter came to Rome. She was dead."

"Poor Gerard! Poor Margaret!" moaned the penitent.

Clement's voice faltered at this a moment. But soon, by a strong effort, he recovered all his calmness.

"His feeble nature yielded, body and soul, to the blow. He was stricken down with fever. He revived only to rebel against Heaven. He said 'There is no God.'"

"Poor, poor, Gerard!"

"Poor Gerard? thou feeble, foolish woman! Nay, wicked, impious Gerard. He plunged into vice, and soiled his eternal jewel: those you met him with were his daily companions: but know, rash creature, that the seeming woman you took to be his leman was but a boy, dressed in woman's habits to flout the others, a fair boy called Andrea. What that Andrea said to thee I know not; but be sure neither he, *nor any layman,* knows thy folly. This Gerard, rebel against Heaven, was no traitor to thee, unworthy."

The lady moaned like one in bodily agony, and the crucifix began to tremble in her trembling hands.

"Courage!" said Clement. "Comfort is at hand.

"From crime he fell into despair, and, bent on destroying his soul, he stood one night by Tiber, resolved on suicide. He saw one watching him. It was a bravo."

"Holy saints!"

"He begged the bravo to despatch him; he offered him all his money, to slay him body and soul. The bravo would not. Then this desperate sinner, not softened even by that refusal, flung himself into Tiber."

"Ah!"

"And the assassin saved his life. Thou hadst chosen for the task Lodovico, husband of Teresa, whom this Gerard had saved at sea, her and her infant child."

"He lives! he lives! he lives! I am faint."

The friar took the crucifix from her hands, fearing it might fall. A shower of tears relieved her. The friar gave her time; then continued, calmly. "Ay, he lives; thanks to thee and thy wickedness, guided to his eternal good by an almighty and all-merciful hand. Thou art his greatest earthly benefactor."

"Where is he? where? where?"

"What is that to thee?"

"Only to see him alive. To beg him on my knees forgive me. I swear to you I will never presume again to— How could I? He knows all. Oh, shame! Father, *does* he know?"

"All."

"Then never will I meet his eye; I should sink into the earth. But I would repair my crime. I would watch his life unseen. He shall rise in the world, whence I so nearly thrust him, poor soul; the Cæsare, my family, are all-powerful in Rome; and I am near their head."

"My daughter," said Clement, coldly, "he you call Gerard needs nothing man can do for him. Saved by a miracle from double death, he has left the world, and taken refuge from sin and folly in the bosom of the Church."

"A priest?"

"A priest, and a friar."

"A friar? Then you are not his confessor? Yet you know all. That gentle voice!"

She raised her head slowly, and peered at him through her mask.

The next moment she uttered a faint shriek, and lay with her brow upon his bare feet.

The Cloister and the Hearth

CHAPTER LXXVII

CLEMENT sighed. He began to doubt whether he had taken the wisest course with a creature so passionate.

But young as he was, he had already learned many lessons of ecclesiastical wisdom. For one thing he had been taught to pause: *i. e.,* in certain difficulties, neither to do nor say anything, until the matter should clear itself a little.

He therefore held his peace and prayed for wisdom.

All he did was gently to withdraw his foot.

But his penitent flung her arms round it with a piteous cry, and held convulsively, and wept over it.

And now the agony of shame, as well as penitence, she was in, showed itself by the bright red that crept over her very throat, as she lay quivering at his feet.

"My daughter," said Clement gently, "take courage. Torment thyself no more about this Gerard, who is not. As for me, I am brother Clement, whom Heaven hath sent to thee this day to comfort thee, and help thee save thy soul. Thou hast made me thy confessor. I claim, then, thine obedience."

"Oh, yes," sobbed the penitent.

"Leave this pilgrimage, and instant return to Rome. Penitence abroad is little worth. There where we live lie the temptations we must defeat, or perish; not fly in search of others more showy, but less lethal. Easy to wash the feet of strangers, masked ourselves. Hard to be merely meek and charitable with those about us."

"I'll never, never, lay finger on her again."

"Nay, I speak not of servants only, but of dependents, kinsmen, friends. This be thy penance; the last thing at night, and the first thing after matins, call to mind thy sin, and God his goodness; and so be humble, and gentle to the faults of those around thee. The world it courts the rich; but seek thou the poor: not beggars; these for the most are neither honest nor truly poor. But rather find out those who blush to seek thee, yet need thee sore. Giving to them shalt lend to Heaven. Marry a good son of the Church."

"Me? I will never marry."

"Thou wilt marry within the year. I do entreat and command

544

thee to marry one that feareth God. For thou art very clay. Mated ill thou shalt be nought. But wedding a worthy husband thou mayest, Dei gratiâ, live a pious princess; ay, and die a saint."

"I?"

"Thou."

He then desired her to rise and go about the good work he had set her.

She rose to her knees, and, removing her mask, cast an eloquent look upon him, then lowered her eyes meekly.

"I will obey you as I would an angel. How happy I am, yet unhappy; for oh my heart tells me I shall never look on you again. I will not go till I have dried your feet."

"It needs not. I have excused thee this bootless penance."

" 'Tis no penance to me. Ah! you do not forgive me, if you will not let me dry your poor feet."

"So be it then," said Clement, resignedly; and thought to himself "Levius quid fœminâ."

But these weak creatures, that gravitate towards the small, as heavenly bodies towards the great, have yet their own flashes of angelic intelligence.

When the princess had dried the friar's feet, she looked at him with tears in her beautiful eyes, and murmured with singular tenderness and goodness—

"I will have masses said for her soul. May I?" she added timidly.

This brought a faint blush into the monk's cheek, and moistened his cold blue eye. It came so suddenly from one he was just rating so low.

"It is a gracious thought," he said. "Do as thou wilt: often such acts fall back on the doer like blessed dew. I am thy confessor; not hers; thine is the soul I must now do my all to save, or woe be to my own. My daughter, my dear daughter, I see good and ill angels fighting for thy soul this day, ay, this moment; oh, fight thou on thine own side. Doth thou remember all I bade thee?"

"Remember!" said the princess. "Sweet saint, each syllable of thine is graved in my heart."

"But one word more then. Pray much to Christ, and little to his saints."

"I will."

"And that is the best word I have light to say to thee. So part we on it. Thou to the place becomes thee best, thy father's house: I to my holy mother's work."

"Adieu," faltered the princess. "Adieu thou that I have loved too well, hated too ill, known and revered too late; forgiving angel adieu—for ever."

The monk caught her words, though but faltered in a sigh.

"FOR EVER?" he cried aloud with sudden ardour. "Christians live 'FOR EVER,' and love 'FOR EVER,' but they never part 'FOR EVER.' They part, as part the earth and sun, to meet more brightly in a little while. You and I part here for life. And what is our life? One line in the great story of the Church, whose son and daughter we are; one handful in the sand of time, one drop in the ocean of 'FOR EVER.' Adieu—for the little moment called 'a life!' We part in trouble, we shall meet in peace: we part creatures of clay, we shall meet immortal spirits: we part in a world of sin and sorrow, we shall meet where all is purity and love divine; where no ill passions are, but Christ is, and his saints around him clad in white. There, in the turning of an hour-glass, in the breaking of a bubble, in the passing of a cloud, she, and thou, and I, shall meet again; and sit at the feet of angels and archangels, apostles and saints, and beam like them with joy unspeakable, in the light of the shadow of God upon his throne, FOR EVER—AND EVER—AND EVER."

And so they parted. The monk erect, his eyes turned heavenwards and glowing with the sacred fire of zeal; the princess slowly retiring and turning more than once to cast a lingering glance of awe and tender regret on that inspired figure.

She went home subdued, and purified. Clement, in due course, reached Basle, and entered on his duties, teaching in the University, and preaching in the town and neighbourhood. He led a life that can be comprised in two words; deep study, and mortification. My reader has already a peep into his soul. At Basle he advanced in holy zeal and knowledge.

The brethren of his order began to see in him a descendant of the saints and martyrs.

CHAPTER LXXVIII

The Hearth

WHEN little Gerard was nearly three months old, a messenger came hot from Tergou for Catherine.

"Now just you go back," said she, "and tell them I can't come and I won't: they have got Kate." So he departed, and Catherine continued her sentence; "there, child, I *must* go: they are all at sixes and sevens: this is the third time of asking; and to-morrow my man would come himself and take me home by the ear, with a flea in't." She then recapitulated her experiences of infants, and instructed Margaret what to do in each coming emergency, and pressed money upon her. Margaret declined it with thanks. Catherine insisted, and turned angry. Margaret made excuses all so reasonable that Catherine rejected them with calm contempt: to her mind they lacked femininity. "Come, out with your heart," said she; "and you and me parting; and mayhap shall never see one another's face again."

"Oh! mother, say not so."

"Alack, girl, I have seen it so often; 'twill come into my mind now at each parting. When I was your age, I never had such a thought. Nay, we were all to live for ever then: so out wi' it."

"Well then, mother—I would rather not have told you—your Cornelis must say to me, 'So you are come to share with us, eh, mistress?' those were his words. I told him I would be very sorry."

"Beshrew his ill tongue! What signifies it? He will never know."

"Most likely he would sooner or later. But, whether or no, I will take no grudge bounty from any family; unless I saw my child starving, and then Heaven only knows what I might do. Nay, mother, give me but thy love—I do prize that above silver, and they grudge me not that, by all I can find—for not a stiver of money will I take out of your house."

"You are a foolish lass. Why, were it me, I'd take it just to spite him."

"No, you would not. You and I are apples off one tree."

The Cloister and the Hearth

Catherine yielded with a good grace; and, when the actual parting came, embraces and tears burst forth on both sides.

When she was gone the child cried a good deal; and all attempts to pacify him failing, Margaret suspected a pin, and, searching between his clothes and his skin, found a gold angel incommoding his backbone.

"There now, Gerard," said she to the babe; "I *thought* granny gave in rather *sudden.*"

She took the coin and wrapped it in a piece of linen, and laid it at the bottom of her box, bidding the infant observe she could be at times as resolute as granny herself.

Catherine told Eli of Margaret's foolish pride, and how she had baffled it. Eli said Margaret was right, and she was wrong. Catherine tossed her head. Eli pondered.

Margaret was not without domestic anxieties. She had still two men to feed, and could not work so hard as she had done. She had enough to do to keep the house, and the child, and cook for them all. But she had a little money laid by, and she used to tell her child his father would be home to help them before it was spent. And with these bright hopes, and that treasury of bliss, her boy, she spent some happy months.

Time wore on: and no Gerard came; and, stranger still, no news of him.

Then her mind was disquieted, and, contrary to her nature, which was practical, she was often lost in sad reverie; and sighed in silence. And, while her heart was troubled, her money was melting. And so it was, that one day she found the cupboard empty, and looked in her dependents' faces; and, at the sight of them, her bosom was all pity; and she appealed to the baby whether she could let grandfather and poor old Martin want a meal; and went and took out Catherine's angel. As she unfolded the linen a tear of gentle mortification fell on it. She sent Martin out to change it. While he was gone a Frenchman came with one of the dealers in illuminated work, who had offered her so poor a price. He told her he was employed by his sovereign to collect masterpieces for her book of hours. Then she showed him the two best things she had; and he was charmed with one of them, viz., the flowers and raspberries and creeping things, which Margaret Van Eyck had shaded. He offered her an unheard-of price. "Nay, flout not my need, good stranger," said she: "three mouths there be in this house, and none to fill them but me."

Curious arithmetic! Left out No. 1.

"I flout thee not, fair mistress. My princess charged me strictly, 'Seek the best craftsmen; but I will no hard bargains; make them content with me, and me with them.'"

The next minute Margaret was on her knees kissing little Gerard in the cradle, and showering four gold pieces on him again and again, and relating the whole occurrence to him in very broken Dutch.

"And oh what a good princess: wasn't she? We will pray for her, won't we, my lambkin; when we are old enough?"

Martin came in furious. "They will not change it. I trow they think I stole it."

"I am beholden to thee," said Margaret, hastily, and almost snatched it from Martin, and wrapped it up again, and restored it to its hiding-place.

Ere these unexpected funds were spent, she got to her ironing and starching again. In the midst of which Martin sickened; and died after an illness of nine days.

Nearly all of her money went to bury him decently.

He was gone; and there was an empty chair by her fireside. For he had preferred the hearth to the sun as soon as the Busybody was gone.

Margaret would not allow anybody to sit in this chair now. Yet whenever she let her eye dwell too long on it, vacant, it was sure to cost her a tear.

And now there was nobody to carry her linen home. To do it herself she must leave little Gerard in charge of a neighbour. But she dared not trust such a treasure to mortal; and besides she could not bear him out of her sight for hours and hours. So she set inquiries on foot for a boy to carry her basket on Saturday and Monday.

A plump, fresh-coloured youth, called Luke Peterson, who looked fifteen, but was eighteen, came in, and blushing, and twiddling his bonnet, asked her if a man would not serve her turn as well as a boy.

Before he spoke she was saying to herself, "This boy will just do."

But she took the cue, and said, "Nay; but a man will maybe seek more than I can well pay."

"Not I," said Luke, warmly. "Why, Mistress Margaret, I am your neighbour, and I do very well at the coopering. I can carry your basket for you before or after my day's work, and welcome. You have no need to pay *me* anything. 'Tisn't as if we were strangers, ye know."

"Why, Master Luke, I know your face, for that matter; but I cannot call to mind that ever a word passed between us."

"Oh yes, you did, Mistress Margaret. What have you forgotten? One day you were trying to carry your baby and eke your pitcher full o' water: and, quo' I, 'Give me the baby to carry.' 'Nay,' says you, 'I'll give you the pitcher, and keep the bairn myself:' and I carried the pitcher home, and you took it from me at this door, and you said to me, 'I am muckle obliged to you, young man,' with such a sweet voice; not like the folk in this street speak to a body."

"I do mind now, Master Luke; and methinks it was the least I could say."

"Well, Mistress Margaret, if you will say as much every time I carry your basket, I care not how often I bear it, nor how far."

"Nay, nay," said Margaret, colouring faintly. "I would not put upon good nature. You are young, Master Luke, and kindly. Say I give you your supper on Saturday night, when you bring the linen home, and your dawn-mete o' Monday; would that make us anyways even?"

"As you please; only say not I sought a couple o' diets, I, for such a trifle as yon."

With chubby-faced Luke's timely assistance, and the health and strength which Heaven gave this poor young woman, to balance her many ills, the house went pretty smoothly awhile. But the heart became more and more troubled by Gerard's long and now most mysterious silence.

And then that mental torture, Suspense, began to tear her heavy heart with his hot pinchers, till she cried often and vehemently, "Oh, that I could know the worst."

While she was in this state, one day she heard a heavy step mount the stair. She started and trembled. "That is no step that I know. Ill tidings!"

The door opened, and an unexpected visitor, Eli, came in, looking grave and kind.

Margaret eyed him in silence, and with increasing agitation.

"Girl," said he, "the skipper is come back."

"One word," gasped Margaret, "is he alive?"

"Surely, I hope so. No one has seen him dead."

"Then they must have seen him alive."

"No girl; neither dead nor alive hath he been seen this many months in Rome. My daughter Kate thinks he is gone to some other city. She bade me tell you her thought."

"Ay, like enough," said Margaret, gloomily; "like enough. My poor babe!"

The old man in a faintest voice asked her for a morsel to eat: he had come fasting.

The poor thing pitied him with the surface of her agitated mind, and cooked a meal for him, trembling, and scarce knowing what she was about.

Ere he went he laid his hand upon her head, and said, "Be he alive, or be he dead, I look on thee as my daughter. Can I do nought for thee this day? bethink thee now."

"Ay, old man. Pray for him; and for me!"

Eli sighed, and went sadly and heavily down the stairs.

She listened half stupidly to his retiring footsteps till they ceased. Then she sank moaning down by the cradle, and drew little Gerard tight to her bosom. "Oh, my poor fatherless boy; my fatherless boy!"

CHAPTER LXXIX

NOT long after this, as the little family at Tergou sat at dinner, Luke Peterson burst in on them, covered with dust. "Good people, Mistress Catherine is wanted instantly at Rotterdam."

"My name is Catherine, young man. Kate, it will be Margaret."

"Ay dame, she said to me, 'Good Luke, hie thee to Tergou, and ask for Eli the hosier, and pray his wife Catherine to come to me, for God his love.' I didn't wait for daylight."

"Holy saints! He has come home, Kate. Nay, she would sure have said so. What on earth can it be?" And she heaped conjecture on conjecture.

"Mayhap the young man can tell us," hazarded Kate, timidly.

"That I can," said Luke. "Why, her babe is a-dying. And she was so wrapped up in it!"

Catherine started up: "What is his trouble?"

"Nay, I know not. But it has been peaking and pining worse and worse this while."

A furtive glance of satisfaction passed between Cornelis and Sybrandt. Luckily for them Catherine did not see it. Her face was turned towards her husband. "Now, Eli," cried she, furiously, "if you say a word against it, you and I shall quarrel, after all these years."

"Who gainsays thee, foolish woman? Quarrel with your own shadow; while I go borrow Peter's mule for ye."

"Bless thee, my good man! Bless thee! Didst never yet fail me at a pinch. Now eat your dinners who can, while I go and make ready."

She took Luke back with her in the cart, and, on the way, questioned and cross-questioned him, severely, and seductively, by turns, till she had turned his mind inside out, what there was of it.

Margaret met her at the door, pale and agitated, and threw her arms round her neck, and looked imploringly in her face.

"Come, he is alive, thank God," said Catherine, after scanning her eagerly.

She looked at the failing child, and then at the poor hollow-eyed mother, alternately. "Lucky you sent for me," said she. "The child is poisoned."

"Poisoned! by whom?"

"By you. You have been fretting."

"Nay, indeed, mother. How can I help fretting?"

"Don't tell me, Margaret. A nursing mother has no business to fret. She must turn her mind away from her grief to the comfort that lies in her lap. Know you not that the child pines if the mother vexes herself? This comes of your reading and writing.

Those idle crafts befit a man; but they keep all useful knowledge out of a woman. The child must be weaned."

"Oh, you cruel woman," cried Margaret, vehemently; "I am sorry I sent for you. Would you rob me of the only bit of comfort I have in the world? A-nursing my Gerard, I forget I am the most unhappy creature beneath the sun."

"That you do not," was the retort, "or he would not be the way he is."

"Mother!" said Margaret, imploringly.

"'Tis hard," replied Catherine, relenting. "But bethink thee; would it not be harder to look down and see his lovely wee face a-looking up at you out of a little coffin?"

"O, Jesu!"

"And how could you face your other troubles with your heart aye full, and your lap empty?"

"Oh, mother, I consent to anything. Only save my boy."

"That is a good lass. Trust to me! I do stand by, and see clearer than thou."

Unfortunately there was another consent to be gained; the babe's: and he was more refractory than his mother.

"There," said Margaret, trying to affect regret at his misbehaviour; "he loves me too well."

But Catherine was a match for them both. As she came along she had observed a healthy young woman, sitting outside her own door, with an infant hard by. She went and told her the case; and would she nurse the pining child for the nonce, till she had matters ready to wean him?

The young woman consented with a smile, and popped her child into the cradle and came into Margaret's house. She dropped a curtsy, and Catherine put the child into her hands. She examined, and pitied it, and purred over it, and proceeded to nurse it, just as if it had been her own.

Margaret, who had been paralyzed at her assurance, cast a rueful look at Catherine, and burst out crying.

The visitor looked up. "What is to do? Wife, ye told me not the mother was unwilling."

"She is not: she is only a fool. Never heed her: and you, Margaret, I am ashamed of you."

"You are a cruel, hard-hearted woman," sobbed Margaret.

"Them as take in hand to guide the weak, need be hardish. And you will excuse me; but you are not my flesh and blood: and your boy is."

After giving this blunt speech time to sink, she added, "Come now, she is robbing her own to save yours, and you can think of nothing better than bursting out a-blubbering in the woman's face. Out fie, for shame?"

"Nay, wife," said the nurse. "Thank Heaven, I have enough for my own and for hers to boot. And prithee wyte not on her! Maybe the troubles o' life ha' soured her own milk."

"And her heart into the bargain," said the remorseless Catherine.

Margaret looked her full in the face; and down went her eyes.

"I know I ought to be very grateful to you," sobbed Margaret to the nurse: then turned her head and leaned away over the chair, not to witness the intolerable sight of another nursing her Gerard, and Gerard drawing no distinction between this new mother, and her the banished one.

The nurse replied, "You are very welcome, my poor woman. And so are you, Mistress Catherine, which are my townswoman, and know it not."

"What, are ye from Tergou? all the better. But I cannot call your face to mind."

"Oh, you know not me: my husband and me, we are very humble folk by you. But true Eli and his wife are known of all the town; and respected. So I am at your call, dame; and at yours, wife; and yours, my pretty poppet; night or day."

"There's a woman of the right old sort," said Catherine, as the door closed upon her.

"I HATE her. I HATE her. I HATE her," said Margaret, with wonderful fervour.

Catherine only laughed at this outburst.

"That is right," said she, "better say it, as set sly and think it. It is very natural after all. Come, here is your bundle o' comfort. Take and hate that; if ye can:" and she put the child in her lap.

"No, no;" said Margaret, turning her head half away from him: she could not for her life turn the other half. "He is not my child now; he is hers. I know not why she left him here, for my part. It was very good of her not to take him to her house, cradle and all; oh! oh! oh! oh! oh! oh! oh! oh!"

"Ah! well, one comfort, *he* is not dead. This gives me light; some other woman has got him away from me; like father, like son; oh! oh! oh! oh! oh!"

Catherine was sorry for her, and let her cry in peace. And after that, when she wanted Joan's aid, she used to take Gerard out, to give him a little fresh air. Margaret never objected; nor expressed the least incredulity; but on their return was always in tears.

This connivance was short lived. She was now altogether as eager to wean little Gerard. It was done; and he recovered health and vigour: and another trouble fell upon him directly: teething. But here Catherine's experience was invaluable: and now, in the midst of her grief and anxiety about the father, Margaret had moments of bliss, watching the son's tiny teeth come through. "Teeth, mother? I call them not teeth, but pearls of pearls." And each pearl that peeped and sparkled on his red gums, was to her the greatest feat Nature had ever achieved.

Her companion partook the illusion. And, had we told them a field of standing corn was equally admirable, Margaret would have changed to a reproachful gazelle, and Catherine turned us out of doors; so each pearl's arrival was announced with a shriek of triumph by whichever of them was the fortunate discoverer.

Catherine gossiped with Joan and learned that she was the wife of Jorian Ketel of Tergou, who had been servant to Ghysbrecht Van Swieten, but fallen out of favour, and come back to Rotterdam, his native place. His friends had got him the place of sexton to the parish, and what with that and carpentering, he did pretty well.

Catherine told Joan in return whose child it was she had nursed, and all about Margaret and Gerard, and the deep anxiety his silence had plunged them in. "Ay," said Joan, "the world is full of trouble." One day she said to Catherine, "It's my belief my man knows more about your Gerard than anybody in these parts: but he has got to be closer than ever of late. Drop in some day just afore sunset, and set him talking. And, for our Lady's sake, say not I set you on. The only hiding he ever gave me was for babbling his business: and I do not want another. Gramercy! I married a man for the comfort of the thing: not to be hided."

Catherine dropped in. Jorian was ready enough to tell her how he had befriended her son and perhaps saved his life. But this was no news to Catherine: and the moment she began to cross-question him as to whether he could guess why her lost boy neither came, nor wrote, he cast a grim look at his wife, who received it with a calm air of stolid candour and innocent unconsciousness; and his answers became short and sullen. "What should he know more than another?" and so on. He added, after a pause, "Think you the burgomaster takes such as me into his secrets?"

"Oh, then the burgomaster knows something?" said Catherine, sharply.

"Likely. Who else should?"

"I'll ask him."

"I would."

"And tell him you say he knows."

"That is right, dame. Go make him mine enemy. That is what a poor fellow always gets if he says a word to you women." And Jorian from that moment shrunk in and became impenetrable as a hedgehog, and almost as prickly.

His conduct caused both the poor women agonies of mind; alarm, and irritated curiosity. Ghysbrecht was for some cause Gerard's mortal enemy; had stopped his marriage, imprisoned him, hunted him. And here was his late servant, who when off his guard had hinted that this enemy had the clue to Gerard's silence. After sifting Jorian's every word and look, all remained dark and mysterious. Then Catherine told Margaret to go herself to him. "You are young; you are fair. You will, maybe, get more out of him than I could."

The conjecture was a reasonable one.

Margaret went with her child in her arms and tapped timidly at Jorian's door just before sunset. "Come in," said a sturdy voice. She entered, and there sat Jorian by the fireside. At sight of her he rose, snorted, and burst out of the house. "Is that for me, wife?" inquired Margaret, turning very red.

"You must excuse him," replied Joan, rather coldly; "he lays it to your door that he is a poor man instead of a rich one. It is something about a piece of parchment. There was one missing, and he got nought from the burgomaster all along of that one."

"Alas! Gerard took it!"

"Likely. But my man says you should not have let him: you were pledged to him to keep them all safe. And, sooth to say, I blame not my Jorian for being wroth. 'Tis hard for a poor man to be so near

556

fortune and lose it by those he has befriended. However, I tell *him* another story. Says I, 'Folk that are out o' trouble, like you and me, didn't ought to be too hard on folk that are in trouble: and she has plenty.' Going already? What is all your hurry, mistress?"

"Oh, it is not for me to drive the good man out of his own house."

"Well, let me kiss the bairn afore ye go. He is not in fault any way, poor innocent."

Upon this cruel rebuff Margaret came to a resolution, which she did not confide even to Catherine.

After six weeks' stay that good woman returned home.

On the child's birthday, which occurred soon after, Margaret did no work: but put on her Sunday clothes, and took her boy in her arms and went to the church and prayed there long and fervently for Gerard's safe return.

That same day and hour Father Clement celebrated a mass and prayed for Margaret's departed soul in the minster church at Basle.

CHAPTER LXXX

SOME blackguard or other, I think it was Sybrandt, said, "A lie is not like a blow with a curtal axe."

True: for we can predict in some degree the consequences of a stroke with any material weapon. But a lie has no bounds at all. The nature of the thing is to ramify beyond human calculation.

Often in the every-day world a lie has cost a life, or laid waste two or three.

And so, in this story, what tremendous consequences of that one heartless falsehood!

Yet the tillers reaped little from it.

The brothers, who invented it merely to have one claimant the less for their father's property, saw little Gerard take their brother's place in their mother's heart. Nay, more, one day Eli openly proclaimed that, Gerard being lost, and probably dead, he had provided by will for little Gerard, and also for Margaret, his poor son's widow.

At this the look that passed between the black sheep was a caution to traitors. Cornelis had it on his lips to say Gerard was most likely alive. But he saw his mother looking at him, and checked himself in time.

The Cloister and the Hearth

Ghysbrecht Van Swieten, the other partner in that lie, was now a failing man. He saw the period fast approaching when all his wealth would drop from his body, and his misdeeds cling to his soul.

Too intelligent to deceive himself entirely, he had never been free from gusts of remorse. In taking Gerard's letter to Margaret he had compounded. "I cannot give up land and money," said his giant Avarice. "I will cause her no unnecessary pain," said his dwarf Conscience.

So, after first tampering with the seal, and finding there was not a syllable about the deed, he took it to her with his own hand; and made a merit of it to himself: a set-off; and on a scale not uncommon where the self-accuser is the judge.

The birth of Margaret's child surprised and shocked him, and put his treacherous act in a new light. Should his letter take effect he should cause the dishonour of her, who was the daughter of one friend, the granddaughter of another, and whose land he was keeping from her too.

These thoughts preying on him at that period of life, when the strength of body decays, and the memory of old friends revives, filled him with gloomy horrors. Yet he was afraid to confess. For the curé was an honest man, and would have made him disgorge. And with him Avarice was an ingrained habit, Penitence only a sentiment.

Matters were thus when, one day, returning from the town-hall to his own house, he found a woman waiting for him in the vestibule, with a child in her arms. She was veiled, and so, concluding she had something to be ashamed of, he addressed her magisterially. On this she let down her veil and looked him full in the face.

It was Margaret Brandt.

Her sudden appearance and manner startled him, and he could not conceal his confusion.

"Where is my Gerard?" cried she, her bosom heaving. "Is he alive?"

"For aught I know," stammered Ghysbrecht. "I hope so, for your sake. Prithee come into this room. The servants!"

"Not a step," said Margaret, and she took him by the shoulder, and held him with all the energy of an excited woman. "You know the secret of that which is breaking my heart. Why does not my Gerard

558

come, nor send a line this many months? Answer me, or all the town is like to hear me; let alone thy servants. My misery is too great to be sported with."

In vain he persisted he knew nothing about Gerard. She told him those who had sent her to him told her another tale. "You do know why he neither comes nor sends," said she, firmly.

At this Ghysbrecht turned paler and paler; but he summoned all his dignity, and said, "Would you believe those two knaves against a man of worship?"

"What two knaves?" said she, keenly.

He stammered, "Said ye not——? There, I am a poor old broken man, whose memory is shaken. And you come here, and confuse me so. I know not what I say."

"Ay, sir, your memory *is* shaken, or sure you would not be my enemy. My father saved you from the plague, when none other would come anigh you; and was ever your friend. My grandfather Floris helped you in your early poverty, and loved you, man and boy. Three generations of us you have seen; and here is the fourth of us; this is your old friend Peter's grandchild, and your old friend Floris his great-grandchild. Look down on his innocent face, and think of theirs!"

"Woman, you torture me," sighed Ghysbrecht, and sank upon a bench. But she saw her advantage, and kneeled before him, and put the boy on his knees. "This fatherless babe is poor Margaret Brandt's, that never did you ill, and comes of a race that loved you. Nay, look at his face. 'Twill melt thee more than any word of mine, Saints of heaven, what can a poor desolate girl and her babe have done to wipe out all memory of thine own young days, when thou wert guiltless as he is, that now looks up in thy face and implores thee to give him back his father?"

And with her arms under the child she held him up higher and higher, smiling under the old man's eyes.

He cast a wild look of anguish on the child, and another on the kneeling mother, and started up shrieking, "Avaunt, ye pair of adders."

The stung soul gave the old limbs a momentary vigour, and he walked rapidly, wringing his hands and clutching at his white hair. "Forget those days? I forget all else. Oh, woman, woman, sleeping or waking I see but the faces of the dead, I hear but the voices of the dead, and I shall soon be among the dead. There, there, what is done is done. I am in hell. I am in hell."

And unnatural force ended in prostration.

He staggered, and but for Margaret would have fallen. With her one disengaged arm she supported him as well as she could, and cried for help.

A couple of servants came running, and carried him away in a state bordering on syncope. The last Margaret saw of him was his old furrowed face, white and helpless as his hair that hung down over the servant's elbow.

"Heaven forgive me," she said. "I doubt I have killed the poor old man."

Then this attempt to penetrate the torturing mystery left it as dark, or darker than before. For when she came to ponder every word, her suspicion was confirmed that Ghysbrecht did know something about Gerard. "And who were the two knaves he thought had done a good deed, and told me? Oh, my Gerard, my poor deserted babe, you and I are wading in deep waters."

The visit to Tergou took more money than she could well afford: and a customer ran away in her debt. She was once more compelled to unfold Catherine's angel. But, strange to say, as she came down stairs with it in her hand she found some loose silver on the table, with a written line—

For Gerard His Wife

She fell with a cry of surprise on the writing: and soon it rose into a cry of joy.

"He is alive. He sends me this by some friendly hand."

She kissed the writing again and again, and put it in her bosom.

Time rolled on: and no news of Gerard.

And about every two months a small sum in silver found its way into the house. Sometimes it lay on the table. Once it was flung in through the bedroom window in a purse. Once it was at the bottom of Luke's basket. He had stopped at the public-house to talk to a friend. The giver or his agent was never detected. Catherine disowned it. Margaret Van Eyck swore she had no hand in it. So did Eli. And Margaret, whenever it came, used to say to little Gerard, "Oh, my poor deserted child, you and I are wading in deep waters."

She applied at least half this modest, but useful supply, to dressing the little Gerard beyond his station in life. "If it does come from Gerard, he shall see his boy neat." All the mothers in the street began to sneer, especially such as had brats out at elbows.

The months rolled on, and dead sickness of heart succeeded to these keener torments. She returned to her first thought: "Gerard must be dead. She should never see her boy's father again, nor her marriage lines." This last grief, which had been somewhat allayed by Eli and Catherine recognizing her bethrothal, now revived in full force; others would not look so favourably on her story. And often she moaned over her boy's illegitimacy. "Is it not enough for us to be bereaved? Must we be dishonoured too? Oh, that we had ne'er been born."

A change took place in Peter Brandt. His mind, clouded for nearly two years, seemed now to be clearing; he had intervals of intelligence; and then he and Margaret used to talk of Gerard till he wandered again. But one day, returning after an absence of some hours, Margaret found him conversing with Catherine, in a way he had never done since his paralytic stroke. "Eh, girl, why must you be out?" said she. "But indeed I have told him all; and we have been a-crying together over thy troubles."

Margaret stood silent, looking joyfully from one to the other.

Peter smiled on her, and said, "Come, let me bless thee."

She kneeled at his feet, and he blessed her most eloquently. He told her she had been all her life the lovingest, truest, and most obedient daughter Heaven ever sent to a poor old widowed man. "May thy son be to thee what thou hast been to me!"

After this he dozed. Then the females whispered together: and Catherine said—"All our talk e'en now was of Gerard. It lies heavy on his mind. His poor head must often have listened to us when it seemed quite dark. Margaret, he is a very understanding man; he thought of many things: 'He may be in prison,' says he, 'or forced to go fighting for some king, or sent to Constantinople to copy books there, or gone into the Church after all.' He had a bent that way."

"Ah, mother," whispered Margaret, in reply, "he doth but deceive himself as we do."

Ere she could finish the sentence, a strange interruption occurred. A loud voice cried out, "I SEE HIM. I SEE HIM."

And the old man with dilating eyes seemed to be looking right through the wall of the house.

"IN A BOAT; on a GREAT RIVER; COMING THIS WAY. Sore disfigured; but I knew him. Gone! gone! all dark."

And he sank back, and asked feebly where was Margaret.

"Dear father, I am by thy side. Oh, mother! mother, what is this?"

"I cannot see thee, and but a moment agone I saw all round the world. Ay, ay. Well, I am ready. Is this thy hand? Bless thee, my child, bless thee! Weep not! The tree is ripe."

The old physician read the signs aright. These calm words were his last. The next moment he drooped his head, and gently, placidly, drifted away from earth, like an infant sinking to rest. The torch had flashed up, before going out.

CHAPTER LXXXI

SHE who had wept for poor old Martin was not likely to bear this blow so stoically as the death of the old is apt to be borne. In vain Catherine tried to console her with commonplaces; in vain told her it was a happy release for him; and that, as he himself had said, the tree was ripe. But her worst failure was, when she urged that there were now but two mouths to feed: and one care the less.

"Such cares are all the joys I have," said Margaret. "They fill my desolate heart, which now seems void as well as waste. Oh, empty chair, my bosom it aches to see thee. Poor old man, how could I love him by halves, I that did use to sit and look at him and think 'But for me thou wouldst die of hunger.' He, so wise, so learned erst, was got to be helpless as my own sweet babe, and I loved him as if he had been my child instead of my father. Oh, empty chair! Oh, empty heart! Well-a-day! well-a-day!"

And the pious tears would not be denied.

Then Catherine held her peace: and hung her head. And one day she made this confession, "I speak to thee out o' my head, and not out o' my bosom; thou dost well to be deaf to me. Were I in thy place I should mourn the old man all one as thou dost."

Then Margaret embraced her, and this bit of true sympathy did her a little good. The commonplaces did none.

Then Catherine's bowels yearned over her, and she said, "My poor girl, you were not born to live alone. I have got to look on you as my own daughter. Waste not thine youth upon my son Gerard. Either he is dead or he is a traitor. It cuts my heart to say it; but who can help seeing it? Thy father is gone: and I cannot always be aside thee. And here is an honest lad that loves thee well this many a day. I'd take him and Comfort together. Heaven hath sent us these creatures to torment us and comfort us and all; we are just nothing in the world without 'em." Then seeing Margaret look utterly perplexed, she went on to say, "Why sure you are not so blind as not to see it?"

"What? Who?"

"Who but this Luke Peterson."

"What, our Luke? The boy that carries my basket?"

"Nay, he is over nineteen, and a fine, healthy lad: and I have made inquiries for you; and they all do say he is a capable workman and never touches a drop; and that is much in a Rotterdam lad, which they are mostly half man, half sponge."

Margaret smiled for the first time this many days. "Luke loves dried puddings dearly," said she: "and I made them to his mind. 'Tis them he comes a-courting here." Then she suddenly turned red. "But if I thought he came after your son's wife that is, or ought to be, I'd soon put him to the door."

"Nay, nay; for Heaven's sake let me not make mischief. Poor lad! Why, girl, Fancy will not be bridled. Bless you, I wormed it out of him near a twelvemonth agone."

"Oh, mother, and you *let* him!?"

"Well, I thought of you. I said to myself, 'If he is fool enough to be her slave for nothing, all the better for her. A lone woman is lost without a man about her to fetch and carry her little matters.' But now my mind is changed, and I think the best use you can put him to is to marry him."

"So then his own mother is against him, and would wed me to the first comer. Ah, Gerard, thou hast but me; I will not believe thee dead till I see thy tomb, nor false till I see thee with another lover in thine hand. Foolish boy, I shall ne'er be civil to him again."

The Cloister and the Hearth

Afflicted with the busybody's protection, Luke Peterson met a cold reception in the house where he had hitherto found a gentle and kind one. And by-and-by, finding himself very little spoken to at all, and then sharply and irritably, the great, soft, fellow fell to whimpering, and asked Margaret plump if he had done anything to offend her.

"Nothing. I am to blame. I am curst. If you will take my counsel you will keep out of my way awhile."

"It is all along of me, Luke," said the busybody.

"You, Mistress Catherine. Why what have I done for you to set her against me?"

"Nay, I meant all for the best. I told her I saw you were looking towards her through a wedding-ring. But she won't hear of it."

"There was no need to tell her that, wife, she knows I am courting her this twelvemonth."

"Not I," said Margaret, "or I should never have opened the street door to you."

"Why, I come here every Saturday night. And that is how the lads in Rotterdam do court. If we sup with a lass o' Saturdays, that's wooing."

"Oh, that is Rotterdam, is it? Then next time you come let it be Thursday, or Friday. For my part I thought you came after my puddings, boy."

"I like your puddings well enough. You make them better than mother does. But I like you still better than the puddings," said Luke, tenderly.

"Then you have seen the last of them. How dare you talk so to another man's wife, and him far away?" She ended gently, but very firmly, "You need not trouble yourself to come here any more, Luke; I can carry my basket myself."

"Oh, very well," said Luke, and after sitting silent and stupid for a little while, he rose, and said sadly to Catherine, "Dame, I dare say I have got the sack;" and went out.

But the next Saturday Catherine found him seated on the door-step blubbering. He told her he had got used to come there, and every other place seemed strange. She went in and told Margaret and Margaret sighed and said, "Poor Luke, he might come in for her, if he could know his place, and treat her like a married wife." On this being communicated to Luke, he hesitated. "Pshaw!" said Catherine, "promises are pie-crusts. Promise her all the world, sooner than sit outside like a fool, when a word will carry you inside. Now you humour her in everything, and then, if poor Gerard come not home and claim her, you will be sure to have her—in time. A lone woman is aye to be tired out, thou foolish boy."

CHAPTER LXXXII

The Cloister

BROTHER CLEMENT had taught and preached in Basle more than a twelvemonth, when one day Jerome stood before him, dusty, with a triumphant glance in his eye.

"Give the glory to God, brother Clement; thou canst now wend to England with me."

"I am ready, brother Jerome: and, expecting thee these many months, have in the intervals of teaching and devotion studied the English tongue somewhat closely."

"'Twas well thought of," said Jerome. He then told him he had but delayed till he could obtain extraordinary powers from the Pope to collect money for the Church's use in England, and to hear confession in all the secular monasteries. "So now gird up thy loins and let us go forth and deal a good blow for the Church, and against the Franciscans."

The two friars went preaching down the Rhine, for England. In the larger places they both preached. At the smaller they often divided, and took different sides of the river, and met again at some appointed spot. Both were able orators, but in different styles.

Jerome's was noble and impressive, but a little contracted in religious topics, and a trifle monotonous in delivery compared with Clement's, though in truth not so compared with most preachers.

Clement's was full of variety, and often remarkably colloquial. In its general flow tender and gently winning, it curled round the reason and the heart. But it always rose with the rising thought; and so at times Clement soared as far above Jerome as his level speaking was below him. Indeed, in these noble heats he was all that we have read of inspired prophet or heathen orator: Vehemens ut procella, excitatus ut torrens, incensus ut fulmen, tonabat, fulgurabat, et rapidis eloquentiæ fluctibus cuncta proruebat et porturbabat.

I would give liberal specimens, but for five objections: it is difficult; time is short; I have done it elsewhere; an able imitator has since done it better; and similarity, a virtue in peas, is a vice in books.

But (not to evade the matter entirely) Clement used secretly to try and learn the recent events and the besetting sin of each town he was to preach in.

But Jerome the unbending scorned to go out of his way for any people's vices. At one great town some leagues from the Rhine, they mounted the same pulpit in turn. Jerome preached against vanity in dress, a favourite theme of his. He was eloquent and satirical, and the people listened with complacency. It was a vice that they were little given to.

Clement preached against drunkenness. It was a besetting sin, and sacred from preaching in these parts: for the clergy themselves were infected with it, and popular prejudice protected it. Clement dealt it merciless blows out of Holy Writ and worldly experience. A crime itself, it was the nursing-mother of most crimes, especially theft and murder. He reminded them of a parricide that had lately been committed in their town by an honest man in liquor, and also how a band of drunkards had roasted one of their own comrades alive at a neighbouring village. "Your last prince," said he, "is reported to have died of apoplexy, but well you know he died of drink: and of your aldermen one perished miserably last month dead drunk, suffocated in a puddle. Your children's backs go bare that you may fill your bellies with that which makes you the worst of beasts, silly as calves, yet fierce as boars; and drive your families to need, and your souls to hell. I tell ye your town, ay, and your very nation would sink to the bottom of mankind did your women drink as you do. And how long will they be temperate, and, contrary to nature, resist the example of their husbands and fathers? Vice ne'er yet stood still. Ye must amend yourselves or see them come down to your mark. Already in Bohemia they drink along with the men. How shows a drunken woman? Would you love to see your wives drunken, your mothers drunken?" At this there was a shout of horror, for mediæval audiences had not learned to sit mumchance at a moving sermon. "Ah, that comes home to you," cried the friar. "What? madmen! think you it doth not more shock the all pure God to see a man, his noblest work, turned to a drunken beast, than it can shock you creatures of sin and unreason to see a woman turned into a thing no better nor worse than yourselves?"

The Cloister and the Hearth

He ended with two pictures; a drunkard's house and family, and a sober man's; both so true and dramatic in all their details that the wives fell to "ohing" and "ahing," and "Eh, but that is a true word."

This discourse caused quite an uproar. The hearers formed knots: the men were indignant; so the women flattered them, and took their part openly against the preacher. A married man had a right to a drop: he needed it, working for all the family. And for their part they did not care to change their men for milksops.

The double faces! That very evening a band of men caught near a hundred of them round brother Clement, filling his wallet with the best, and offering him the very roses off their heads, and kissing his frock, and blessing him "for taking in hand to mend their sots."

Jerome thought this sermon too earthly.

"Drunkenness is not heresy, Clement, that a whole sermon should be preached against it."

As they went on he found to his surprise that Clement's sermons sank into his hearers deeper than his own; made them listen, think, cry, and sometimes even amend their ways. "He hath the art of sinking to their peg," thought Jerome. "Yet he can soar high enough at times."

Upon the whole, it puzzled Jerome, who had a secret sense of superiority to his tenderer brother. And, after about two hundred miles of it, it got to displease him as well as puzzle him. But he tried to check this sentiment as petty and unworthy. "Souls differ like locks," said he, "and preachers must differ like keys, or the fewer should the Church open for God to pass in. And, certes, this novice hath the key to these northern souls, being himself a northern man."

And so they came slowly down the Rhine, sometimes drifting a few miles on the stream: but in general walking by the banks preaching, and teaching, and confessing sinners in the towns and villages; and they reached the town of Dusseldorf.

There was the little quay where Gerard and Denys had taken boat up the Rhine. The friars landed on it. There were the streets, there was "The Silver Lion." Nothing had changed but he, who walked through it barefoot, with his heart calm and cold, his hands across his breast, and his eyes bent meekly on the ground, a true son of Dominic and holy Church.

CHAPTER LXXXIII

The Hearth

"ELI," said Catherine, "answer me one question like a man, and I'll ask no more to-day. What is wormwood?"

Eli looked a little helpless at this sudden demand upon his faculties; but soon recovered enough to say it was something that tasted main bitter.

"That is a fair answer, my man, but not the one I look for."

"Then answer it yourself."

"And shall. Wormwood is—to have two in the house a-doing nought, but waiting for thy shoes and mine." Eli groaned. The shaft struck home.

"Methinks waiting for their best friend's coffin, that and nothing to do, are enow to make them worse than Nature meant. Why not let them up somewhere, to give 'em a chance?"

Eli said he was willing, but afraid they would drink and gamble their very shelves away.

"Nay," said Catherine. "Dost take me for a simpleton? Of course I mean to watch them at starting, and drive them wi' a loose rein, as the saying is."

"Where did you think of? Not here; to divide our own custom."

"Not likely. I say Rotterdam, against the world. Then I could start them."

Oh, self-deception! The true motive of all this was to get near little Gerard.

After many discussions, and eager promises of amendment on these terms from Cornelis and Sybrandt, Catherine went to Rotterdam shop-hunting, and took Kate with her; for a change. They soon found one, and in a good street: but it was sadly out of order. However they got it cheaper for that, and instantly set about brushing it up, fitting proper shelves for the business, and making the dwelling house habitable.

Luke Peterson was always asking Margaret what he could do for her. The answer used to be in a sad tone, "Nothing, Luke, nothing."

"What you that are so clever, can you think of nothing for me to do for you?"

"Nothing, Luke, nothing."

But at last she varied the reply thus: "If you could make something to help my sweet sister Kate about."

The slave of love consented joyfully, and soon made Kate a little cart, and cushioned it, and yoked himself into it, and at eventide drew her out of the town, and along the pleasant boulevard, with Margaret and Catherine walking beside. It looked a happier party than it was.

Kate, for one, enjoyed it keenly; for little Gerard was put in her lap, and she doted on him: and it was like a cherub carried by a little angel, or a rosebud lying in the cup of a lily.

So the vulgar jeered: and asked Luke how a thistle tasted, and if his mistress could not afford one with four legs, etc.

Luke did not mind these jeers; but Kate minded them for him.

"Thou hast made the cart for me, good Luke," said she. " 'Twas much. I did ill to let thee draw me too; we can afford to pay some poor soul for that. I love my rides, and to carry little Gerard; but I'd liever ride no more than thou be mocked for't."

"Much I care for their tongues," said Luke, "if I did care I'd knock their heads together. I shall draw you till my mistress says give over."

"Luke, if you obey Kate, you will oblige me."

"Then I will obey Kate."

An honourable exception to popular humour was Jorian Ketel's wife. "That is strength well laid out, to draw the weak. And her prayers will be your guerdon: she is not long for this world: she smileth in pain." These were the words of Joan.

Singleminded Luke answered that he did not want the poor lass's prayers; he did it to please his mistress, Margaret.

After that Luke often pressed Margaret to give him something to do—without success.

But one day, as if tired with his importuning, she turned on him, and said with a look and accent, I should in vain try to convey—

"Find me my boy's father!"

CHAPTER LXXXIV

"MISTRESS, they all say he is dead."

"Not so. They feed me still with hopes."

"Ay, to your face, but behind your back they all **say** he is dead."

At this revelation Margaret's tears began to flow.

Luke whimpered for company. He had the body of a man, but the heart of a girl.

"Prithee, weep not so, sweet mistress," said he. "I'd bring him back to life, an' I could, rather than see thee weep so sore."

Maragret said she thought she was weeping because they were so double-tongued with her.

She recovered herself, and laying her hand on his shoulder, said solemnly, "Luke, he is not dead. Dying men are known to have a strange sight. And listen, Luke! My poor father, when he was a-dying, and I, simple fool, was so happy, thinking he was going to get well altogether, he said to mother and me—he was sitting in that very chair where you are now, and mother was as might be here, and I was yonder making a sleeve—said he, 'I see him! I see him!' Just so. Not like a failing man at all, but all o' fire. 'Sore disfigured—on a great river—coming this way.'

"Ah, Luke, if you were a woman, and had the feeling for me you think you have, you would pity me, and find him for me. Take a thought! The father of my child!"

"Alack, I would, if I knew how," said Luke. "But how can I?"

"Nay, of course you cannot. I am mad to think it. But, oh, if any one really cared for me, they *would;* that is all I know."

Luke reflected in silence for some time.

"The old folk all say dying men can see more than living wights. Let me think: for my mind cannot gallop like thine. On a great river? Well, the Maas is a great river." He pondered on.

"Coming this way? Then if it 'twas the Maas, he would have been here by this time, so 'tis not the Maas. The Rhine is a great river, greater than the Maas; and very long. I think it will be the Rhine."

The Cloister and the Hearth

"And so do I, Luke; for Denys bade him come down the Rhine.
But even if it is, he may turn off before he comes anigh his birthplace. He does not pine for me as I for him; that is clear. Luke,
do you not think he has deserted me?" She wanted him to contradict her; but he said "It looks very like it; what a fool he
must be!"

"What do we know?" objected Margaret, imploringly.

"Let me think again," said Luke. "I cannot gallop."

The result of this meditation was this. He knew a station about
sixty miles up the Rhine, where all the public boats put in; and
he would go to that station, and try and cut the truant off. To be
sure he did not even know him by sight; but as each boat came in
he would mingle with the passengers, and ask if one Gerard was
there. "And, mistress, if you were to give me a bit of a letter
to him; for, with us being strangers, mayhap a won't believe a word
I say."

"Good, kind, thoughtful Luke, I will (how I have undervalued
thee!). But give me till supper-time to get it writ." At supper
she put a letter into his hand with a blush: it was a long letter
tied round with silk after the fashion of the day, and sealed over
the knot.

Luke weighed it in his hand, with a shade of discontent, and said
to her very gravely, "Say your father was not dreaming, and say
I have the luck to fall in with this man, and say he should turn
out a better bit of stuff than I think him, and come home to you
then and there—what is to become o' me?"

Margaret coloured to her very brow. "Oh, Luke, Heaven will
reward thee. And I shall fall on my knees and bless thee; and I
shall love thee all my days, sweet Luke; as a mother does her son.
I am so old by thee: trouble ages the heart. Thou shalt not go:
'tis not fair of me; Love maketh us to be all self."

"Humph!" said Luke. "And if," resumed he, in the same grave
way, "yon scapegrace shall read thy letter, and hear me tell him
how thou pinest for him, and yet, being a traitor, or a mere idiot,
will not turn to thee—what shall become of me then? Must I die
a bachelor, and thou fare lonely to thy grave, neither maid, wife,
nor widow?"

Margaret panted with fear and emotion at this terrible piece of
good sense, and the plain question that followed it. But at last

she faltered out, "If, which our Lady be merciful to me, and forbid— Oh!"

"Well, mistress?"

"If he should read my letter, and hear thy words—and, sweet Luke, be just and tell him what a lovely babe he hath, fatherless, fatherless. Oh Luke, can he be so cruel?"

"I trow not: but if?"

"Then he will give thee up my marriage lines, and I shall be an honest woman; and a wretched one; and my boy will not be a bastard: and, of course, then we *could* both go into any honest man's house that would be troubled with us: and even for thy goodness this day, I will—I will—ne'er be so ungrateful as go past thy door to another man's."

"Ay, but will you come in at mine? Answer me that!"

"Oh, ask me not! Some day, perhaps, when my wounds leave bleeding. Alas, I'll try. If I don't fling myself and my child into the Maas. Do not go, Luke! do not think of going! 'Tis all madness from first to last."

But Luke was as slow to forego an idea as to form one.

His reply showed how fast love was making a man of him. "Well," said he, "madness is something any way; and I am tired of doing nothing for thee: and I am no great talker. To-morrow, at peep of day, I start. But, hold, I have no money. My mother, she takes care of all mine; and I ne'er see it again."

Then Margaret took out Catherine's gold angel, which had escaped so often, and gave it to Luke; and he set out on his mad errand.

It did not however seem so mad to him as to us. It was a superstitious age: and Luke acted on the dying man's dream, or vision, or illusion, or whatever it was, much as we should act on respectable information.

But Catherine was downright angry when she heard of it. To send the poor lad on such a wild-goose chase! "But you are like a many more girls; and mark my words: by the time you have worn that Luke fairly out, and made him as sick of you as a dog, you will turn as fond on him as a cow on a calf, and 'Too late' will be the cry."

The Cloister and the Hearth

The Cloister

The two friars reached Holland from the south just twelve hours after Luke started up the Rhine.

Thus, wild-goose chase or not, the parties were nearing each other, and rapidly too. For Jerome, unable to preach in low Dutch, now began to push on towards the coast, anxious to get to England as soon as possible.

And, having the stream with them, the friars would in point of fact have missed Luke by passing him in full stream below his station, but for the incident which I am about to relate.

About twenty miles above the station Luke was making for, Clement landed to preach in a large village; and towards the end of his sermon he noticed a grey nun weeping.

He spoke to her kindly, and asked her what was her grief. "Nay," said she, " 'tis not for myself flow these tears; 'tis for my lost friend. Thy words reminded me of what she was, and what she is, poor wretch. But you are a Dominican, and I am a Franciscan nun."

"It matters little, my sister, if we are both Christians and if I can aid thee in aught."

The nun looked in his face, and said, "These are strange words, but methinks they are good; and thy lips are oh most eloquent. I will tell thee our grief."

She then let him know that a young nun, the darling of the convent, and her bosom friend, had been lured away from her vows, and, after various gradations of sin, was actually living in a small inn as chambermaid, in reality as a decoy, and was known to be selling her favours to the wealthier customers. She added, "Anywhere else we might by kindly violence force her away from perdition. But this innkeeper was the servant of the fierce baron on the height there, and hath his ear still, and he would burn our convent to the ground, were we to take her by force."

"Moreover, souls will not be saved by brute force," said Clement.

While they were talking Jerome came up, and Clement persuaded him to lie at the convent that night. But when in the morning Clement told him he had had a long talk with the abbess, and that she was very sad, and he had promised her to try and win back her nun, Jerome objected, and said, "It was not their business, and was a waste of time." Clement, however, was no longer a mere pupil. He stood firm, and at last they agreed that Jerome should go forward, and secure their passage in the next ship for England, and Clement be allowed time to make his well-meant but idle experiment.

About ten o'clock that day, a figure in a horseman's cloak, and great boots to match, and a large flapping felt hat, stood like a statue near the auberge, where was the apostate nun, Mary. The friar thus disguised was at that moment truly wretched. These ardent natures undertake wonders; but are dashed when they come hand to hand with the sickening difficulties. But then, as their hearts are steel, though their nerves are anything but iron, they turn not back, but panting and dispirited, struggle on to the last.

Clement hesitated long at the door, prayed for help and wisdom, and at last entered the inn and sat down faint at heart, and with his body in a cold perspiration.

But outside he was another man. He called lustily for a cup of wine: it was brought him by the landlord. He paid for it with money the convent had supplied him: and made a show of drinking it.

"Landlord," said he, "I hear there is a fair chambermaid in thine house."

"Ay, stranger, the buxomest in Holland. But she gives not her company to all comers; only to good customers."

Friar Clement dangled a massive gold chain in the landlord's sight. He laughed, and shouted, "Here, Janet, here is a lover for thee would bind thee in chains of gold: and a tall lad into the bargain I promise thee."

"Then I am in double luck," said a female voice: "send him hither."

Clement rose, shuddered, and passed into the room, where Janet was seated playing with a piece of work, and laying it down every minute, to sing a mutilated fragment of a song. For, in her mode of life, she had not the patience to carry anything out.

After a few words of greeting, the disguised visitor asked her if they could not be more private somewhere.

"Why not?" said she. And she rose and smiled, and went tripping before him. He followed, groaning inwardly, and sore perplexed.

The Cloister and the Hearth

"There," said she. "Have no fear! Nobody ever comes here, but such as pay for the privilege."

Clement looked round the room, and prayed silently for wisdom. Then he went softly, and closed the window-shutters carefully.

"What on earth is that for?" said Janet in some uneasiness.

"Sweetheart," whispered the visitor, with a mysterious air, "it is that God may not see us."

"Madman," said Janet, "think you a wooden shutter can keep out his eye?"

"Nay, I know not. Perchance he has too much on hand to notice *us*. But I would not the saints and angels should see us. Would you?"

"My poor soul, hope not to escape their sight! The only way is not to think of them; for if you do, it poisons your cup. For two pins I'd run and leave thee. Art pleasant company in sooth."

"After all, girl, so that men see us not, what signify God and the saints seeing us? Feel this chain! 'Tis virgin gold. I shall cut two of these heavy links off for thee."

"Ah! now thy discourse is to the point." And she handled the chain greedily. "Why, 'tis as massy as the chain round the Virgin's neck at the conv—" She did not finish the word.

"Whisht! whisht! whisht! 'Tis *it*. And thou shalt have thy share. But betray me not."

"Monster!" cried Janet, drawing back from him with repugnance, "what rob the blessed Virgin of her chain, and give it to an—"

"You are none," cried Clement, exultingly, "or you had not recked for that.—Mary!"

"Ah! ah! ah!"

"Thy patron saint, whose chain this is, sends me to greet thee."

She ran screaming to the window and began to undo the shutters.

Her fingers trembled, and Clement had time to debarass himself of his boots, and his hat, before the light streamed in upon him. He then let his cloak quietly fall, and stood before her, a Dominican friar, calm and majestic as a statue, and held his crucifix towering over her with a loving, sad, and solemn look, that somehow relieved her of the physical part of fear, but crushed her with religious terror and remorse. She crouched and cowered against the wall.

"Mary," said he, gently; "one word! Are you happy?"

"As happy as I shall be in hell."

"And they are not happy at the convent; they weep for you."

"For me?"

"Day and night; above all the Sister Ursula."

"Poor Ursula!" And the strayed nun began to weep herself at the thought of her friend.

"The angels weep still more. Wilt not dry all their tears in earth and heaven, and save thyself?"

"Ah! would I could: but it is too late."

"Satan avaunt," cried the monk, sternly. " 'Tis thy favourite temptation; and thou, Mary, listen not to the enemy of man, belying God, and whispering despair. I who come to save thee have been a far greater sinner than thou. Come, Mary, sin, thou seest, is not so sweet e'en in this world, as holiness; and eternity is at the door."

"How can they ever receive me again?"

" 'Tis their worthiness thou doubtest now. But in truth they pine for thee. 'Twas in pity of their tears that I, a Dominican, undertook this task; and broke the rule of my order by entering an inn; and broke it again by donning these lay vestments. But all is well done, and quit for a light penance, if thou will let us rescue thy soul from this den of wolves and bring thee back to thy vows."

The nun gazed at him with tears in her eyes. "And thou a Dominican hast done this for a daughter of St. Francis! Why the Franciscans and Dominicans hate one another."

"Ay, my daughter; but Francis and Dominic love one another."

The recreant nun seemed struck and affected by this answer.

Clement now reminded her how shocked she had been that the Virgin should be robbed of her chain. "But see now," said he, "the convent and the Virgin too think ten times more of their poor nun than of golden chains; for they freely trusted their chain to me a stranger, that peradventure the sight of it might touch their lost Mary and remind her of their love." Finally he showed her with such terrible simplicity the end of her present course, and on the other hand so revived her dormant memories and better feelings, that she kneeled sobbing at his feet, and owned she had never known happiness nor peace since she betrayed her vows; and said she would go back if he would go with her; but alone she dared not, could not: even if she reached the gate she could never enter. How could she face the abbess and the sisters? He told her he would go with her as joyfully as the shepherd bears a strayed lamb to the fold.

But when he urged her to go at once, up sprung a crop of those prodigiously petty difficulties that entangle her sex, like silken nets, liker iron cobwebs.

He quietly swept them aside.

"But how can I walk beside thee in this habit?"

"I have brought the gown and cowl of thy holy order. Hide thy bravery with them. And leave thy shoes as I leave these" (pointing to his horseman's boots).

She collected her jewels and ornaments.

"What are these for?" inquired Clement.

"To present to the convent, father."

"Their source is too impure."

"But," objected the penitent, "it would be a sin to leave them here. They can be sold to feed the poor."

"Mary, fix thine eye on this crucifix, and trample those devilish baubles beneath thy feet."

She hesitated; but soon threw them down and trampled on them.

"Now open the window and fling them out on that dung-hill. 'Tis well done. So pass the wages of sin from thy hands, its glittering yoke from thy neck, its pollution from thy soul. Away, daughter of St. Francis, we tarry in this vile place too long." She followed him.

But they were not clear yet.

At first the landlord was so astounded at seeing a black friar and a grey nun pass through his kitchen from the inside, that he gaped, and muttered "Why, what mummery is this?" But he soon comprehended the matter, and whipped in between the fugitives and the door. "What ho! Reuben! Carl! Gavin! here is a false friar spiriting away our Janet."

The men came running in with threatening looks. The friar rushed at them crucifix in hand. "Forbear," he cried, in a stentorian voice. "She is a holy nun returning to her vows. The hand that touches her cowl, or her robe, to stay her, it shall wither, his body shall lie unburied, cursed by Rome, and his soul shall roast in eternal fire." They shrank back as if a flame had met them. "And thou—miserable panderer!—"

He did not end the sentence in words, but seized the man by the neck, and, strong as a lion in his moments of hot excitement, whirled him furiously from the door and sent him all across the room, pitching headforemost on to the stone floor; then tore the door open and carried the screaming nun out into the road. "Hush! poor trembler," he gasped; "they dare not molest thee on the high road. Away!"

The landlord lay terrified, half stunned, and bleeding: and Mary, though she often looked back apprehensively, saw no more of him.

On the road he bade her observe his impetuosity.

"Hitherto," said he, "we have spoken of thy faults: now for mine. My choler is ungovernable; furious. It is by the grace of God I am not a murderer. I repent the next moment; but a moment too late is all too late. Mary, had the churls laid finger on thee, I should have scattered their brains with my crucifix. Oh, I know myself, go to; and tremble at myself. There lurketh a wild beast beneath this black gown of mine."

"Alas, father," said Mary, "were you other than you are I had been lost. To take me from that place needed a man wary as a fox; yet bold as a lion."

Clement reflected. "Thus much is certain: God chooseth well his fleshly instruments: and with imperfect hearts doeth his perfect work. Glory be to God!"

When they were near the convent Mary suddenly stopped, and seized the friar's arm, and began to cry. He looked at her kindly, and told her she had nothing to fear. It would be the happiest day she had ever spent. He then made her sit down and compose herself till he should return. He entered the convent, and desired to see the abbess.

"My sister, give the glory to God: Mary is at the gate."

The astonishment and delight of the abbess were unbounded. She yielded at once to Clement's earnest request that the road of penitence might be smoothed at first to this unstable wanderer, and, after some opposition, she entered heartily into his views as to her actual reception. To give time for their little preparations Clement went slowly back, and seating himself by Mary soothed her: and heard her confession.

"The abbess has granted me that you shall propose your own penance."

"It shall be none the lighter," said she.

"I trow not," said he: "but that is future: to-day is given to joy alone."

He then led her round the building to the abbess's postern. As they went they heard musical instruments and singing.

"'Tis a feast-day," said Mary: "and I come to mar it."

"Hardly," said Clement, smiling; "seeing that you are the queen of the fête."

"I, father? what mean you?"

"What, Mary, have you never heard that there is more joy in heaven over one sinner that repenteth, than over ninety-nine just persons which need no repentance? Now this convent is not heaven; nor the nuns angels; yet are there among them some angelic spirits; and these sing and exult at thy return. And here methinks comes one of them; for I see her hand trembles at the keyhole."

The postern was flung open, and in a moment sister Ursula clung sobbing and kissing round her friend's neck. The abbess followed more sedately, but little less moved.

Clement bade them farewell. They entreated him to stay: but he told them with much regret he could not. He had already tried his good brother Jerome's patience, and must hasten to the river: and perhaps sail for England to-morrow.

So Mary returned to the fold, and Clement strode briskly on towards the Rhine, and England.

This was the man for whom Margaret's boy lay in wait with her letter.

The Hearth

And that letter was one of those simple, touching appeals only her sex can write to those who have used them cruelly, and they love them. She began by telling him of the birth of the little boy, and the comfort he had been to her in all the distress of mind his long and strange silence had caused her. She described the little Gerard minutely, not forgetting the mole on his little finger. "Know you any one that hath the like on his? If you only saw him you could not choose but be proud of him; all the mothers in the street do envy me: but I the wives; for thou comest not to us. My own Gerard, some say thou art dead. But if thou wert dead how could I be alive? Others say that thou, whom I love so truly, art false. But this will I believe from no lips but thine. My father loved thee well; and as he lay a-dying he thought he saw thee on a great river, with thy face turned towards thy Margaret, but sore disfigured. Is't so, perchance? Have cruel men scarred thy sweet face? or hast thou lost one of thy precious limbs? Why then thou hast the more need of me, and I shall love thee not worse, alas! thinkest thou a woman's love is light as a man's? but better, than I did when I shed those few drops from my arm, not worth the tears thou didst shed for them; mindest thou? 'tis not so very long agone, dear Gerard."

The letter continued in this strain, and concluded without a word of reproach or doubt as to his faith and affection. Not that she was free from most distressing doubts: but they were not certainties; and to show them might turn the scale, and frighten him away from her with fear of being scolded. And of this letter she made soft Luke the bearer.

So she was not an angel after all.

Luke mingled with the passengers of two boats, and could hear nothing of Gerard Eliassoen. Nor did this surprise him. He was more surprised when, at the third attempt, a black friar said to him, somewhat severely, "And what would you with him you call Gerard Eliassoen?"

"Why, father, if he is alive I have got a letter for him."

"Humph!" said Jerome. "I am sorry for it. However, the flesh is weak. Well, my son, he you seek will be here by the next boat, or the next boat after. And if he chooses to answer to that name— After all, I am not the keeper of his conscience."

"Good father, one plain word, for Heaven's sake. This Gerard Eliassoen of Tergou—is he alive?"

"Humph! Why, certes, he that went by that name is alive."

"Well, then, that is settled," said Luke, drily. But the next moment he found it necessary to run out of sight and blubber.

"Oh, why did the Lord make any women?" said he to himself.

"I was content with the world till I fell in love. Here his little finger is more to her than my whole body, and he is not dead. And here I have got to give him this." He looked at the letter and dashed it on the ground. But he picked it up again with a spiteful snatch, and went to the landlord, with tears in his eyes, and begged for work. The landlord declined, said he had his own people.

"Oh, I seek not your money," said Luke. "I only want some work to keep me from breaking my heart about another man's lass."

"Good lad! good lad!" exploded the landlord; and found him lots of barrels to mend—on these terms. And he coopered with fury in the interval of the boats coming down the Rhine.

CHAPTER LXXXV

The Hearth

WRITING an earnest letter seldom leaves the mind in *statu quo*. Margaret, in hers, vented her energy and her faith in her dying father's vision, or illusion; and, when this was done, and Luke gone, she wondered at her credulity, and her conscience pricked her about Luke; and Catherine came and scolded her, and she paid the price of false hopes, and elevation of spirits, by falling into deeper despondency. She was found in this state by a stanch friend she had lately made; Joan Ketel. This good woman came in radiant with an idea.

"Margaret, I know the cure for thine ill: the hermit of Gouda, a wondrous holy man. Why, he can tell what is coming, when he is in the mood."

"Ay, I have heard of him," said Margaret hopelessly. Joan with some difficulty persuaded her to walk out as far as Gouda, and consult the hermit. They took some butter, and eggs, in a basket, and went to his cave.

What had made the pair such fast friends? Jorian some six weeks ago fell ill of a bowel disease; it began with raging pain; and when this went off, leaving him weak, an awkward symptom succeeded; nothing, either liquid or solid, would stay in his stomach a minute. The doctor said: "He must die if this goes on many hours; therefore, boil thou now a chicken with a golden angel in the

581

water, and let him sup that!" Alas! Gilt chicken broth shared the fate of the humbler viands, its predecessors. Then the curé steeped the thumb of St. Sergius in beef broth. Same result. Then Joan ran weeping to Margaret to borrow some linen to make his shroud. "Let me see him," said Margaret. She came in and felt his pulse. "Ah!" said she, "I doubt they have not gone to the root. Open the window! Art stifling him; now change all his linen."

"Alack, woman, what for? Why foul more linen for a dying man?" objected the mediæval wife.

"Do as thou art bid," said Margaret dully, and left the room.

Joan somehow found herself doing as she was bid. Margaret returned with her apron full of a flowering herb. She made a decoction, and took it to the bedside; and before giving it to the patient, took a spoonful herself, and smacked her lips hypocritically. "That is fair," said he with a feeble attempt at humour. "Why, 'tis sweet, and now 'tis bitter." She engaged him in conversation as soon as he had taken it. This bitter-sweet stayed by him. Seeing which she built on it as cards are built: mixed a very little schiedam in the third spoonful, and a little beaten yolk of egg in the seventh. And so with the patience of her sex she coaxed his body out of Death's grasp; and finally, Nature, being patted on the back, instead of kicked under the bed, set Jorian Ketel on his legs again. But the doctress made them both swear never to tell a soul her guilty deed. "They would put me in prison, away from my child."

The simple that saved Jorian was called sweet feverfew. She gathered it in his own garden. Her eagle eye had seen it growing out of the window.

Margaret and Joan, then, reached the hermit's cave, and placed their present on the little platform. Margaret then applied her mouth to the aperture, made for that purpose, and said: "Holy hermit, we bring thee butter and eggs of the best: and I a poor deserted girl, wife, yet no wife, and mother of the sweetest babe, come to pray thee tell me whether he is quick or dead, true to his vows or false."

A faint voice issued from the cave: "Trouble me not with the things of earth, but send me a holy friar. I am dying."

"Alas!" cried Margaret. "Is it e'en so, poor soul? Then let us in to help thee."

"Saints forbid! Thine is a woman's voice. Send me a holy friar!"

They went back as they came. Joan could not help saying, "Are women imps o' darkness then, that they must not come anigh a dying bed?"

But Margaret was too deeply dejected to say anything. Joan applied rough consolation. But she was not listened to till she said: "And Jorian will speak out ere long; he is just on the boil. He is very grateful to thee, believe it."

"Seeing is believing," replied Margaret with quiet bitterness.

"Not but what he thinks you might have saved him with something more out o' the common than yon. 'A man of my inches to be cured wi' feverfew,' says he. 'Why, if there is a sorry herb,' says he. 'Why, I was thinking o' pulling all mine up,' says he. I up and told him remedies were none the better for being far-fetched; you and feverfew cured him, when the grand medicines came up faster than they went down. So says I, 'You may go down on your four bones to feverfew.' But indeed, he is grateful at bottom; you are all his thought and all his chat. But he sees Gerard's folk coming around ye, and good friends, and he said only last night—"

"Well?"

"He made me vow not to tell ye."

"Prithee, tell me."

"Well, he said: 'An' if I tell what little I know, it won't bring him back, and it will set them all by the ears. I wish I had more head-piece,' said he, 'I am sore perplexed. But least said is soonest mended.' Yon is his favourite word; he comes back to't from a mile off."

Margaret shook her head. "Ay, we are wading in deep waters, my poor babe and me."

It was Saturday night: and no Luke.

"Poor Luke!" said Margaret. "It was very good of him to go on such an errand."

"He is one out of a hundred," replied Catherine warmly.

"Mother, do you think he would be kind to little Gerard?"

"I am sure he would. So do you be kinder to *him* when he comes back! Will ye now?"

"Ay."

The Cloister

Brother Clement, directed by the nuns, avoided a bend in the river, and, striding lustily forward, reached a station some miles nearer the coast than that where Luke lay in wait for Gerard Eliassoen. And the next morning he started early, and was in Rotterdam at noon. He made at once for the port, not to keep Jerome waiting.

He observed several monks of his order on the quay; he went to them: but Jerome was not amongst them. He asked one of them whether Jerome had arrived? "Surely, brother," was the reply.

"Prithee, where is he?"

"Where? Why, there!" said the monk, pointing to a ship in full sail. And Clement now noticed that all the monks were looking seaward.

"What, gone without me! Oh Jerome! Jerome!" cried he in a voice of anguish. Several of the friars turned round and stared.

"You must be brother Clement," said one of them at length; and on this they kissed him and greeted him with brotherly warmth, and gave him a letter Jerome had charged them with for him. It was a hasty scrawl. The writer told him coldly a ship was about to sail for England, and he was loth to lose time. He (Clement) might follow if he pleased, but he would do much better to stay behind, and preach to his own country folk. "Give the glory to God, brother; you have a wonderful power over Dutch hearts: but you are no match for those haughty islanders: you are too tender.

"Know thou that on the way I met one, who asked me for thee under the name thou didst bear in the world. Be on thy guard! Let not the world catch thee again by any silken net. And remember, Solitude, Fasting, and Prayer are the sword, spear, and shield of the soul. Farewell."

Clement was deeply shocked and mortified at this contemptuous desertion, and this cold-blooded missive.

He promised the good monks to sleep at the convent, and to

preach wherever the prior should appoint (for Jerome had raised
him to the skies as a preacher), and then withdrew abruptly, for
he was cut to the quick, and wanted to be alone. He asked himself, was there some incurable fault in him, repulsive to so true
a son of Dominic? Or was Jerome himself devoid of that Christian Love which St. Paul had placed above Faith itself? Shipwrecked with him, and saved on the same fragment of the wreck;
his pupil, his penitent, his son in the Church, and now for four
hundred miles his fellow-traveller in Christ; and to be shaken off
like dirt, the first opportunity, with harsh and cold disdain. "Why,
worldly hearts are no colder nor less trusty than this," said he.
"The only one that ever really loved me lies in a grave hard by.
Fly me, fly to England, man born without a heart; I will go
and pray over a grave at Sevenbergen."

Three hours later he passed Peter's cottage. A troop of noisy
children were playing about the door, and the house had been repaired, and a new outhouse added. He turned his head hastily
away, not to disturb a picture his memory treasured; and went to
the churchyard.

He sought among the tombstones for Margaret's. He could
not find it. He could not believe they had begrudged her a tombstone, so searched the churchyard all over again.

"Oh, poverty! stern poverty! Poor soul, thou wert like me; no
one was left that loved thee, when Gerard was gone."

He went into the church, and after kissing the steps, prayed long
and earnestly for the soul of her whose resting-place he could not
find.

Coming out of the church he saw a very old man looking over
the little churchyard gate. He went towards him, and asked him
did he live in the place.

"Four score and twelve years, man and boy. And I come here
every day of late, holy father, to take a peep. This is where I
look to bide ere long."

"My son, can you tell me where Margaret lies?"

"Margaret? There's a many Margarets here."

"Margaret Brandt. She was daughter to a learned physician."

"As if I didn't know that," said the old man, pettishly. "But
she doesn't lie here. Bless you, they left this a longful while ago.
Gone in a moment, and the house empty. What, is she dead?

Margaret a Peter dead? Now only think on't. Like enow; like enow. They great towns do terribly disagree wi' country folk."

"What great towns, my son?"

"Well 'twas Rotterdam they went to from here, so I heard tell; or was it Amsterdam? Nay, I trow 'twas Rotterdam. And gone there to die!"

Clement sighed.

" 'Twas not in her face now, that I saw. And I can mostly tell. Alack, there was a blooming young flower to be cut off so soon, and an old weed like me left standing still. Well, well, she was a May rose yon; dear heart, what a winsome smile she had, and—"

"God bless thee, my son," said Clement; "farewell!" and he hurried away.

He reached the convent at sunset, and watched and prayed in the chapel for Jerome, and Margaret, till it was long past midnight, and his soul had recovered its cold calm.

CHAPTER LXXXVI

The Hearth

THE next day, Sunday, after mass, was a bustling day at Catherine's house in the Hoog Straet. The shop was now quite ready, and Cornelis and Sybrandt were to open it next day; their names were above the door; also their sign, a white lamb sucking a gilt sheep. Eli had come, and brought them some more goods from his store to give them a good start. The hearts of the parents glowed at what they were doing, and the pair themselves walked in the garden together, and agreed they were sick of their old life, and it was more pleasant to make money than waste it; they vowed to stick to business like wax. Their mother's quick and ever watchful ear overheard this resolution through an open window and she told Eli. The family supper was to include Margaret and her boy, and be a kind of inaugural feast, at which good trade advice was to flow from the elders, and good wine to be drunk to the success of the converts to Commerce from Agriculture in its unremunerative form,—wild oats. So Margaret had come over to help her mother-in-law, and also to shake off her own deep languor; and both their faces were as red as the fire. Presently in came Joan with a salad from Jorian's garden.

"He cut it for you, Margaret; you are all his chat; I shall be jealous. I told him you were to feast to-day. But oh, lass, what a sermon in the new kerk! Preaching? I never heard it till this day."

"Would I had been there then," said Margaret; "for I am dried up for want of dew from heaven."

"Why, he preacheth again this afternoon. But mayhap you are wanted here."

"Not she," said Catherine. "Come, away ye go, if y' are minded."

"Indeed," said Margaret, "methinks I should not be such a damper at table if I could come to't warm from a good sermon."

"Then you must be brisk," observed Joan. "See the folk are wending that way, and as I live, there goes the holy friar. Oh bless us and save us, Margaret; the hermit! We forgot." And this active woman bounded out of the house, and ran across the road, and stopped the friar. She returned as quickly. "There, I was bent on seeing him nigh hand."

"What said he to thee?"

"Says he, 'My daughter, I will go to him ere sunset, God willing.' The sweetest voice. But, oh, my mistresses, what thin cheeks for a young man, and great eyes, not far from your colour, Margaret."

"I have a great mind to go hear him," said Margaret. "But my cap is not very clean, and they will all be there in their snow-white mutches."

"There, take my handkerchief out of the basket," said Catherine; "you cannot have the child, I want him for my poor Kate. It is one of her ill days."

Margaret replied by taking the boy upstairs. She found Kate in bed.

"How art thou, sweetheart? Nay, I need not ask. Thou art in sore pain; thou smilest so. See, I have brought thee one thou lovest."

"Two, by my way of counting," said Kate, with an angelic smile. She had a spasm at that moment would have made some of us roar like bulls.

"What, in your lap?" said Margaret, answering a gesture of

the suffering girl. "Nay, he is too heavy, and thou in such pain."
"I love him too dear to feel his weight," was the reply.

Margaret took this opportunity, and made her toilet. "I am for the kerk," said she, "to hear a beautiful preacher." Kate sighed. "And a minute ago, Kate, I was all agog to go: that is the way with me this month past; up and down, up and down, like the waves of the Zuyder Zee. I'd as lieve stay aside thee; say the word!"

"Nay," said Kate, "prithee go; and bring me back every word. Well-a-day that I cannot go myself." And the tears stood in the patient's eyes. This decided Margaret, and she kissed Kate, looked under her lashes at the boy, and heaved a little sigh.

"I trow I must not," said she. "I never could kiss him a little; and my father was dead against waking a child by day or night. When 'tis thy pleasure to wake, speak thy aunt Kate the two new words thou hast gotten." And she went out, looking lovingly over her shoulder, and shut the door inaudibly.

"Joan, you will lend me a hand, and peel these?" said Catherine.

"That I will dame." And the cooking proceeded with silent vigour.

"Now, Joan, them which help me cook and serve the meat, they help me eat it; that's a rule."

"There's worse laws in Holland than that. Your will is my pleasure, mistress; for my Luke hath got his supper i' the air. He is digging to-day, by good luck." (Margaret came down.)

"Eh, woman, yon is an ugly trade. There, she has just washed her face and gi'en her hair a turn, and now who is like her? Rotterdam, that for you!" and Catherine snapped her fingers at the capital. "Give us a buss, hussy! Now mind, Eli won't wait supper for the duke. Wherefore, loiter not after your kerk is over."

Joan and she both followed her to the door, and stood at it watching her a good way down the street. For among homely housewives going out o' doors is half an incident. Catherine commented on the launch; "there, Joan, it is almost to me as if I had just started my own daughter for kerk, and stood a looking after; the which I've done it manys and manys the times. Joan, lass, she won't hear a word against our Gerard; and, be he alive, he has used her cruel; that is why my bowels yearn for the poor wench. I'm older and wiser than she; and so I'll wed her to yon simple Luke, and there an end. What's one grandchild?"

CHAPTER LXXXVII

The Cloister and The Hearth

THE sermon had begun when Margaret entered the great church of St. Laurens. It was a huge edifice, far from completed. Churches were not built in a year. The side aisles were roofed, but not the mid aisle nor the chancel; the pillars and arches were pretty perfect, and some of them whitewashed. But only one window in the whole church was glazed; the rest were at present great jagged openings in the outer walls.

But to-day all these uncouth imperfections made the church beautiful. It was a glorious summer afternoon, and the sunshine came broken into marvellous forms through those irregular openings, and played bewitching pranks upon so many broken surfaces.

It streamed through the gaping walls, and clove the dark cool side aisles with rivers of glory, and dazzled and glowed on the white pillars beyond.

And nearly the whole central aisle was chequered with light and shade in broken outlines; the shades seeming cooler and more soothing than ever shade was, and the light like patches of amber diamond, animated with heavenly fire. And above, from west to east the blue sky vaulted the lofty aisle, and seemed quite close.

The sunny caps of the women made a sea of white contrasting exquisitely with that vivid vault of blue.

For the mid aisle huge as it was, was crammed, yet quite still. The words and the mellow, gentle, earnest voice of the preacher held them mute.

Margaret stood spell-bound at the beauty, the devotion, "the great calm." She got behind a pillar in the north aisle; and there, though she could hardly catch a word, a sweet devotional languor crept over her at the loveliness of the place and the preacher's musical voice: and balmy oil seemed to trickle over the waves in her heart and smooth them. So she leaned against the pillar with eyes half closed, and all seemed soft and dreamy. She felt it good to be there.

Presently she saw a lady leave an excellent place opposite, to get out of the sun, which was indeed pouring on her head from the window. Margaret went round softly but swiftly; and was fortunate enough to get the place. She was now beside a pillar of the south aisle, and not above fifty feet from the preacher. She was at his side, a little behind him, but could hear every word.

Her attention however was soon distracted by the shadow of a man's head and shoulders bobbing up and down so drolly she had some ado to keep from smiling.

Yet it was nothing essentially droll.

It was the sexton digging.

She found that out in a moment by looking behind her, through the window, to whence the shadow came.

Now as she was looking at Jorian Ketel digging, suddenly a tone of the preacher's voice fell upon her ear and her mind so distinctly, it seemed literally to strike her, and make her vibrate inside and out.

Her hand went to her bosom, so strange and sudden was the thrill. Then she turned round and looked at the preacher. His back was turned and nothing visible but his tonsure. She sighed. That tonsure being all she saw, contradicted the tone effectually.

Yet she now leaned a little forward with downcast eyes, hoping for that accent again. It did not come. But the whole voice grew strangely upon her. It rose and fell as the preacher warmed: and it seemed to waken faint echoes of a thousand happy memories. She would not look to dispel the melancholy pleasure this voice gave her.

Presently, in the middle of an eloquent period, the preacher stopped.

She almost sighed; a soothing music had ended. Could the sermon be ended already? No: she looked around; the people did not move.

A good many faces seemed now to turn her way. She looked behind her sharply. There was nothing there.

Startled countenances near her now eyed the preacher. She followed their looks; and there, in the pulpit, was a face of a staring corpse. The friar's eyes, naturally large, and made larger by the thinness of his cheeks, were dilated to supernatural size, and glaring, her way, out of a bloodless face.

She cringed and turned fearfully round; for she thought there *must* be some terrible thing near her. No: there was nothing; she was the outside figure of the listening crowd.

At this moment the church fell into commotion. Figures got up all over the building, and craned forward; agitated faces by hundreds gazed from the friar to Margaret, and from Margaret to the friar. The turning to and fro of so many caps made a loud rustle. Then came shrieks of nervous women, and buzzing of men: and Margaret, seeing so many eyes levelled at her, shrank terrified behind the pillar, with one scared, hurried glance at the preacher.

Momentary as that glance was, it caught in that stricken face an expression that made her shiver.

She turned faint and sat down on a heap of chips the workmen had left, and buried her face in her hands. The sermon went on again. She heard the sound of it; but not the sense. She tried to think, but her mind was in a whirl. Thought would fix itself in no shape but this: that on that prodigy-stricken face she had seen a look stamped. And the recollection of that look now made her quiver from head to foot.

For that look was "RECOGNITION."

The sermon, after wavering some time, ended in a strain of exalted, nay, feverish eloquence, that went far to make the crowd forget the preacher's strange pause and ghastly glare.

Margaret mingled hastily with the crowd, and went out of the church with them.

They went their ways home. But she turned at the door, and went into the churchyard; to Peter's grave. Poor as she was, she had given him a slab and a headstone. She sat down on the slab, and kissed it. Then threw her apron over her head that no one might distinguish her by her hair.

"Father," she said, "thou hast often heard me say I am wading in deep waters; but now I begin to think God only knows the bottom of them. I'll follow that friar round the world, but I'll see him at arm's length. And he shall tell me why he looked towards me like a dead man wakened: and not a soul behind me. Oh father; you often praised me here: speak a word for me *there*. For I am wading in deep waters."

Her father's tomb commanded a side view of the church door.

And on that tomb she sat, with her face covered, waylaying the holy preacher.

CHAPTER LXXXVIII

The Cloister and The Hearth

THE cool church, chequered with sunbeams and crowned with heavenly purple, soothed and charmed father Clement, as it did Margaret; and more, it carried his mind direct to the Creator of all good and pure delights. Then his eye fell on the great aisle crammed with his country-folk; a thousand snowy caps, filigreed with gold. Many a hundred leagues he had travelled; but seen nothing like them, except snow. In the morning he had thundered: but this sweet afternoon seemed out of tune with threats. His bowels yearned over that multitude; and he must tell them of God's love: poor souls, they heard almost as little of it from the pulpit then a days as the heathen used. He told them the glad tidings of salvation. The people hung upon his gentle, earnest tongue.

He was not one of those preachers who keep gyrating in the pulpit like the weathercock on the steeple. He moved the hearts of others more than his own body. But on the other hand he did not entirely neglect those who were in bad places. And presently, warm with this theme, that none of all that multitude might miss the joyful tidings of Christ's love, he turned him towards the south aisle.

And there, in a stream of sunshine from the window, was the radiant face of Margaret Brandt. He gazed at it without emotion. It just benumbed him soul and body.

But soon the words died in his throat, and he trembled as he glared at it.

There, with her auburn hair bathed in sunbeams, and glittering like the gloriola of a saint, and her face glowing doubly, with its own beauty, and the sunshine it was set in—stood his dead love.

She was leaning very lightly against a white column. She was listening with tender, downcast lashes.

He had seen her listen so to him a hundred times.

There was no change in *her*. This was the blooming Margaret he had left: only a shade riper and more lovely.

He stared at her with monstrous eyes and bloodless cheeks.

The peopie died out of his sight. He heard, as in a dream, a rustling and rising all over the church; but could not take his prodigy-stricken eyes off that face, all life, and bloom, and beauty, and that wondrous auburn hair glistening gloriously in the sun.

He gazed, thinking she must vanish.

She remained.

All in a moment she was looking at him, full.

Her own violet eyes!!

At this he was beside himself, and his lips parted to shriek out her name, when she turned her head swiftly, and soon after vanished, but not without one more glance, which, though rapid as lightning, encountered his, and left her crouching and quivering with her mind in a whirl, and him panting and gripping the pulpit convulsively. For this glance of hers, though not recognition, was the startled inquiring, nameless, indescribable look, that precedes recognition. He made a mighty effort, and muttered something nobody could understand: then feebly resumed his discourse; and stammered and babbled on a while, till by degrees forcing himself, now she was out of sight, to look on it as a vision from the other world, he rose into a state of unnatural excitement, and concluded in a style of eloquence that electrified the simple; for it bordered on rhapsody.

The sermon ended, he sat down on the pulpit stool, terribly shaken. But presently an idea very characteristic of the time took possession of him. He had sought her grave at Sevenbergen in vain. She had now been permitted to appear to him, and show him that she was buried *here*; probably hard by that very pillar, where her spirit had showed itself to him.

This idea once adopted soon settled on his mind with all the certainty of a fact. And he felt he had only to speak to the sexton, (whom to his great disgust he had seen working during the sermon) to learn the spot, where she was laid.

The church was now quite empty. He came down from the pulpit and stepped through an aperture in the south wall onto the grass, and went up to the sexton. He knew him in a moment. But Jorian never suspected the poor lad, whose life he had saved, in this holy friar. The loss of his shapely beard had wonderfully altered the outline of his face. This had changed him even more than his tonsure, his short hair sprinkled with premature grey, and his cheeks thinned and paled by fasts and vigils.

The Cloister and the Hearth

"My son," said friar Clement, softly, "if you keep any memory of those whom you lay in the earth, prithee tell me is any Christian buried inside the church, near one of the pillars."

"Nay, father," said Jorian, "here in the churchyard lie buried all that buried be. Why?"

"No matter. Prithee tell me then where lieth Margaret Brandt."

"Margaret Brandt?" And Jorian stared stupidly at the speaker.

"She died about three years ago, and was buried here."

"Oh, that is another matter," said Jorian; "that was before my time; the vicar could tell you, likely; if so be she was a gentlewoman, or at least rich enough to pay him his fee."

"Alas, my son, she was poor (and paid a heavy penalty for it); but born of decent folk. Her father, Peter, was a learned physician; she came hither from Sevenbergen—to die."

When Clement had uttered these words his head sunk upon his breast, and he seemed to have no power nor wish to question Jorian more. I doubt even if he knew where he was. He was lost in the past.

Jorian put down his spade, and standing upright in the grave, set his arms akimbo, and said sulkily, "Are you making a fool of me, holy sir, or has some wag been making a fool of you?"

And having relieved his mind thus, he proceeded to dig again, with a certain vigour that showed his somewhat irritable temper was ruffled.

Clement gazed at him with a puzzled but gently reproachful eye; for the tone was rude, and the words unintelligible.

Good natured, though crusty, Jorian had not thrown up three spadesful ere he became ashamed of it himself. "Why what a base churl am I to speak thus to thee, holy father; and thou standing there, looking at me like a lamb. Aha! I have it; 'tis Peter Brandt's grave, you would fain see, not Margaret's. He does lie here; hard by the west door. There; I'll show you." And he laid down his spade, and put on his doublet and jerkin to go with the friar.

He did not know there was anybody sitting on Peter's tomb. Still less that she was watching for this holy friar.

---

* Pietro Vanucci, and Andrea, did not recognize him without his beard. The fact is, that the beard, which has never known a razor, grows in a very picturesque and characteristic form, and becomes a feature in the face; so that its removal may in some cases be an effectual disguise.

CHAPTER LXXXIX

WHILE Jorian was putting on his doublet and jerkin to go to Peter's tomb, his tongue was not idle. "They used to call him a magician out Sevenbergen way. And they do say he gave 'em a touch of his trade at parting; told 'em he saw Margaret's lad a coming down Rhine in brave clothes and store o' money, but his face scarred by foreign glaive, and not altogether so many arms and legs as a went away wi'. But, dear heart, nought came on't. Margaret is still wearying for her lad; and Peter, he lies as quiet as his neighbours, not but what she hath put a stone slab over him, to keep him where he is: as you shall see."

He put both hands on the edge of the grave, and was about to raise himself out of it, but the friar laid a trembling hand on his shoulder, and said in a strange whisper—

"How long since died Peter Brandt?"

"About two months. Why?"

"And his daughter buried him, say you?"

"Nay, I buried him, but she paid the fee and reared the stone. Why?"

"Then—but he had but one daughter; Margaret?"

"No more; leastways, that he owned to."

"Then you think Margaret is—is alive?"

"Think? Why I should be dead else. Riddle me that."

"Alas, how can I? You love her!"

"No more than reason, being a married man and father of four more sturdy knaves like myself. Nay, the answer is, she saved my life scarce six weeks agone. Now had she been dead she couldn't ha' kept me alive. Bless your heart I couldn't keep a thing on my stomach; nor doctors couldn't make me. My Joan says ' 'Tis time to buy thee a shroud.' 'I dare say, so 'tis,' says I; 'but try and borrow one first.' In comes my lady, this Margaret, which she died three years ago, by your way on't, opens the windows, makes 'em shift me where I lay, and cures me in the twinkling of a bed post; but wi' what? there pinches the shoe; with the scurviest herb, and out of my own garden, too; with sweet feverfew. A herb, quotha, 'tis a weed; leastways it was a weed till it cured me; but now whene'er I pass my bunch I doff bonnet, and, says I, 'My service t'ye.' Why, how now, father, you look wondrous pale, and now you are red; and now you are white? Why, what is the matter? What in Heaven's name is the matter?"

"The surprise—the joy—the wonder—the fear," gasped Clement.

"Why what is it to thee? Art thou of kin to Margaret Brandt?"

"Nay; but I knew one that loved her well, so well her death nigh killed him, body and soul. And yet thou sayest she lives. And I believe thee."

Jorian stared, and after a considerable silence, said very gravely, "Father, you have asked me many questions, and I have answered them truly; now for our Lady's sake answer me but two. Did you in very sooth know one who loved this poor lass? Where?"

Clement was on the point of revealing himself, but he remembered Jerome's letter, and shrank from being called by the name he had borne in the world.

"I knew him in Italy," said he.

"If you knew him you can tell me his name," said Jorian, cautiously.

"His name was Gerard Eliassoen."

"Oh, but this is strange. Stay, what made thee say Margaret Brandt was dead?"

"I was with Gerard when a letter came from Margaret Van Eyck. The letter told him she he loved was dead and buried. Let me sit down, for my strength fails me. Foul play! Foul play!"

"Father," said Jorian, "I thank Heaven for sending thee to me. Ay, sit ye down; ye do look like a ghost; ye fast overmuch to be strong. My mind misgives me; methinks I hold the clue to this riddle, and, if I do, there be two knaves in this town whose heads I would fain batter to pieces as I do this mould"; and he clenched his teeth and raised his long spade above his head, and brought it furiously down upon the heap several times. "Foul play? You never said a truer word i' your life; and, if you know where Gerard is now, lose no time, but show him the trap they have laid for him. Mine is but a dull head, but whiles the slow hound puzzles out the scent—go to. And I do think you and I ha' got hold of two ends o' one stick, and a main foul one."

Jorian then, after some of those useless preliminaries men of his class always deal in, came to the point of his story. He had been employed by the burgomaster of Tergou to repair the floor of an upper room in his house, and, when it was almost done, coming suddenly to fetch away his tools, curiosity had been excited by some loud words below, and he had lain down on his stomach, and heard the burgomaster talking about a letter, which Cornelis and Sybrandt were minded to convey into the place of one that a certain Hans Memling was taking to Gerard: "and it seems their will was good, but their stomach was small; so to give them courage the old man showed them a drawer full of silver, and if they did the trick they should each put a hand in, and have all the silver they could hold in't. Well, father," continued Jorian, "I thought not much on't at the time, except for the bargain itself, *that* kept me awake mostly all night. Think on't! Next morning at peep of day who should I see but my masters Cornelis and Sybrandt come out of their house each with a black eye. 'Oho,' says I, 'what yon Hans hath put his mark on ye; well now I hope that is all you have got for your pains.' Didn't they make for the burgomaster's house? I to my hiding-place."

At this part of Jorian's revelation the monk's nostril dilated, and his restless eye showed the suspense he was in.

"Well, father," continued Jorian, "the burgomaster brought them into that same room. He had a letter in his hand; but I am no scholar; however, I have got as many eyes in my head as the Pope hath, and I saw the drawer opened, and those two knaves put in each a hand and draw it out full. And, saints in glory, how they tried to hold more, and more, and more o' yon stuff! And Sybrandt, he had daubed his hand in something sticky, I think 'twas glue, and he made shift to carry one or two pieces away a sticking to the back of his hand, he! he! he! 'Tis a sin to laugh. So you see luck was on the wrong side as usual; they had done the trick; but how they did it, that, methinks, will never be known till doomsday. Go to, they left their immortal jewels in yon drawer. Well, they got a handful of silver for them; the devil had the worst o' yon bargain. There, father, that is off my mind; often I longed to tell it some one, but I durst not to the women; or Margaret would not have had a friend left in the world; for those two black-hearted villains are the favourites. 'Tis always so. Have not the old folk just taken a brave new shop for them in this very town, in the Hoog Straet? There may you see their sign, a gilt sheep and a lambkin; a brace of wolves sucking their dam would be nigher the mark. And there the whole family feast this day; oh, 'tis a fine world. What, not a word, holy father; you sit there like stone, and have not even a curse to bestow on them, the stony-hearted miscreants. What, was it not enough the poor lad was all alone in a strange land; must his own flesh and blood go and lie away the one blessing his enemies had left him? And then think of her pining and pining all these years, and sitting at the window looking adown the street for Gerard! and so constant, so tender, and true: my wife says she is sure no woman ever loved a man truer, than she loves the lad those villains have parted from her: and the day never passes but she weeps salt tears for him. And, when I think, that, but for those two greedy lying knaves, yon winsome lad, whose life I saved, might be by her side this day the happiest he in Holland; and the sweet lass, that saved my life, might be sitting with her cheek upon her sweetheart's shoulder, the happiest she in Holland in place of the saddest; oh, I thirst for their blood, the nasty, sneaking, lying, cogging, cowardly, heartless, bowelless—how now?!''

The monk started wildly up, livid with fury and despair, and rushed headlong from the place with both hands clenched and raised on high. So terrible was this inarticulate burst of fury, that Jorian's puny ire died out at sight of it, and he stood looking dismayed after the human tempest he had launched.

While thus absorbed he felt his arm grasped by a small, tremulous, hand.

It was Margaret Brandt.

He started: her coming there just then seemed so strange.

She had waited long on Peter's tombstone, but the friar did not come. So she went into the church to see if he was there still. She could not find him.

Presently, going up the south aisle, the gigantic shadow of a friar came rapidly along the floor and part of a pillar, and seemed to pass through her. She was near screaming: but in a moment remembered Jorian's shadow had come in so from the churchyard: and tried to clamber out the nearest way. She did so, but with some difficulty; and by that time Clement was just disappearing down the street: yet, so expressive at times is the body as well as the face, she could see he was greatly agitated. Jorian and she looked at one another, and at the wild figure of the distant friar.

"Well?" said she to Jorian, trembling.

"Well," said he, "you startled me. How come you here of all people?"

"Is this a time for idle chat? What said he to you? He has been speaking to you; deny it not."

"Girl, as I stand here, he asked me, where-about you were buried in this churchyard."

"Ah?"

"I told him, nowhere, thank Heaven: you were alive and saving other folk from the churchyard."

"Well?"

"Well, the long and the short is, he knew thy Gerard in Italy: and a letter came, saying you were dead; and it broke thy poor lad's heart. Let me see; who was the letter written by? Oh, by the demoiselle Van Eyck. That was *his* way of it. But I up and told him nay; 'twas neither demoiselle nor dame that penned yon lie, but Ghysbrecht Van Swieten, and those foul knaves, Cornelis and Sybrandt; these changed the true letter for one of their own; I told him as how I saw the whole villainy done, through a chink; and now, if I have not been and told you!"

"Oh, cruel! cruel! But he lives. The fear of fears is gone. Thank God!"

"Ay, lass; and as for thine enemies, I have given them a dig. For yon friar is friendly to Gerard, and he is gone to Eli's house, methinks. For I told him where to find Gerard's enemies and thine, and wow but he will give them their lesson. If ever a man was mad with rage, it's yon. He turned black and white, and parted like a stone from a sling. Girl, there was thunder in his eye and silence on his lips. Made me cold a did."

"Oh, Jorian, what have you done?" cried Margaret. "Quick! quick! help me thither, for the power is gone all out of my body. You know him not as I do. Oh, if you had seen the blow he gave Ghysbrecht; and heard the frightful crash! Come, save him from worse mischief. The water is deep enow; but not bloody yet; come!"

Her accents were so full of agony that Jorian sprang out of the grave and came with her, huddling on his jerkin as he went.

But, as they hurried along, he asked her what on earth she meant? "I talk of this friar, and you answer me of Gerard."

The Cloister and the Hearth

"Man, see you not, *this* is Gerard!"

"This, Gerard? what mean ye?"

"I mean, yon friar is my boy's father. I have waited for him long, Jorian. Well, he is come to me at last. And thank God for it. Oh, my poor child! Quicker, Jorian, quicker!"

"Why, thou art mad as he. Stay! By St. Bavon, yon *was* Gerard's face; 'twas nought like it; yet somehow,—'twas it. Come on! come on! let me see the end of this."

"The end? How many of us will live to see that?"

They hurried along in breathless silence, till they reached Hoog Straet.

Then Jorian tried to reassure her. "You are making your own trouble," said he; "who says he has gone thither? more likely to the convent to weep and pray, poor soul. Oh, cursed, cursed villains!"

"Did you tell him where those villains bide?"

"Ay, that I did."

"Then quicker, oh Jorian, quicker. I see the house. Thank God and all the saints, I shall be in time to calm him. I know what I'll say to him; Heaven forgive me! Poor Catherine; 'tis of her I think: she has been a mother to me."

The shop was a corner house, with two doors: one in the main street, for customers, and a house-door round the corner.

Margaret and Jorian were now within twenty yards of the shop, when they heard a roar inside, like as of some wild animal, and the friar burst out, white and raging, and went tearing down the street.

Margaret screamed, and sank fainting on Jorian's arm.

Jorian shouted after him, "Stay, Madman, know thy friends."

But he was deaf, and went headlong, shaking his clenched fists high, high, in the air.

"Help me in, good Jorian," moaned Margaret, turning suddenly calm. "Let me know the worst; and die."

He supported her trembling limbs into the house.

It seemed unnaturally still; not a sound.

Jorian's own heart beat fast.

A door was before him, unlatched. He pushed it softly with his left hand, and Margaret and he stood on the threshold.

What they saw there you shall soon know.

CHAPTER XC

IT was supper-time. Eli's family were collected round the board; Margaret only was missing. To Catherine's surprise Eli said he would wait a bit for her.

"Why, I told her you would not wait for the duke."

"She is not the duke: she is a poor, good lass, that hath waited not minutes, but years, for a graceless son of mine. You can put the meat on the board all the same; then we can fall to, without further loss o' time, when she does come."

The smoking dishes smelt so savoury that Eli gave way. "She will come if we begin," said he; "they always do. Come, sit ye down, Mistress Joan; y' are not here for a slave, I trow, but a guest. There, I hear a quick step—off covers, and fall to."

The covers were withdrawn, and the knives brandished. Then burst into the room, not the expected Margaret, but a Dominican friar, livid with rage.

He was at the table in a moment, in front of Cornelis and Sybrandt, threw his tall body over the narrow table, and, with two hands hovering above their shrinking heads, like eagles over a quarry, he cursed them by name, soul and body, in this world and the next. It was an age eloquent in curses: and this curse was so full, so minute, so blighting, blasting, withering, and tremendous, that I am afraid to put all the words on paper. "Cursed be the lips," he shrieked, "which spoke the lie that Margaret was dead; may they rot before the grave, and kiss the white-hot iron in hell thereafter; doubly cursed be the hands that changed those letters, and be they struck off by the hangman's knife, and handle hell-fire for ever; thrice accursed be the cruel hearts that did conceive that damned lie, to part true love for ever; may they sicken and wither on earth joyless, loveless, hopeless; and wither to dust before their time; and burn in eternal fire." He cursed the meat at their mouths, and every atom of their bodies, from their hair to the soles of their feet. Then turning from the cowering, shuddering pair, who had almost hid themselves beneath the table, he tore a letter out of his bosom, and flung it down before his father.

"Read that, thou hard old man, that didst imprison thy son, read,

and see what monsters thou hast brought into the world. The
memory of my wrongs, and hers, dwell with you all for ever! I
will meet you again at the judgment day; on earth ye will never see
me more."

And in a moment, as he had come, so he was gone, leaving them
stiff, and cold, and white as statues, round the smoking board.

And this was the sight that greeted Margaret's eyes and Jorian's
—pale figures of men and women petrified around the untasted food,
as Eastern poets feigned.

Margaret glanced her eye round, and gasped out, "Oh, joy! all
here; no blood hath been shed. Oh, you cruel, cruel men! I
thank God he hath not slain you."

At sight of her Catherine gave an eloquent scream; then turned
her head away. But Eli, who had just cast his eye over the false
letter, and begun to understand it all, seeing the other victim come
in at that very moment with *her* wrongs reflected in her sweet,
pale face, started to his feet in a transport of rage, and shouted,
"Stand clear, and let me get at the traitors. I'll hang for them."
And in a moment he whipped out his short sword, and fell upon
them.

"Fly!" screamed Margaret. "Fly!"

They slipped howling under the table, and crawled out the other
side.

But, ere they could get to the door, the furious old man ran
round and intercepted them. Catherine only screamed and wrung
her hands; your notables are generally useless at such a time; and
blood would certainly have flowed, but Margaret and Jorian seized
the fiery old man's arms, and held them with all their might, whilst
the pair got clear of the house; then they let him go; and he went
vainly raging after them out into the street.

They were a furlong off, running like hares.

He hacked down the board on which their names were written,
and brought it in doors, and flung it into the chimney-place.

Catherine was sitting rocking herself with her apron over her
head. Joan had run to her husband. Margaret had her arms
round Catherine's neck; and, pale and panting, was yet making
efforts to comfort her.

But it was not to be done. "O my poor children!" she cried.

The Cloister and the Hearth

"O miserable mother! 'Tis a mercy Kate was ill upstairs. There, I have lived to thank God for that!" she cried, with a fresh burst of sobs. "It would have killed her. He had better have stayed in Italy, as come home to curse his own flesh and blood, and set us all by the ears."

"Oh, hold your chat, woman," cried Eli, angrily; "you are still on the side of the ill-doer. You are cheap served; your weakness made the rogues what they are; I was for correcting them in their youth: for sore ills, sharp remedies; but you still sided with their faults, and undermined me, and baffled wise severity. And you, Margaret, leave comforting her that ought rather to comfort you; for what is her hurt to yours? But she never had a grain of justice under her skin; and never will. So come thou to me; that am thy father from this hour."

This was a command; so she kissed Catherine, and went tottering to him, and he put her on a chair beside him, and she laid her feeble head on his honest breast: but not a tear: it was too deep for that.

"Poor lamb," said he. After awhile—"Come, good folks," said true Eli, in a broken voice, to Jorian and Joan, "we are in a little trouble, as you see; but that is no reason you should starve. For our Lady's sake, fall to; and add not to my grief the reputation of a churl. What the dickens!" added he, with a sudden ghastly attempt at stout-heartedness, "the more knaves I have the luck to get shut of, the more my need of true men and women, to help me clear the dish, and cheer mine eye with honest faces about me where else were gaps. Fall to, I do entreat ye."

Catherine, sobbing, backed his request. Poor, simple, antique, hospitable souls! Jorian, whose appetite, especially since his illness, was very keen, was for acting on this hospitable invitation; but Joan whispered a word in his ear, and he instantly drew back. "Nay, I'll touch no meat that holy Church hath cursed."

"In sooth, I forgot," said Eli, apologetically. "My son, who was reared at my table, hath cursed my victuals. That seems strange. Well, what God wills, man must bow to."

The supper was flung out into the yard.

Jorian took his wife home, and heavy sadness reigned in Eli's house that night.

Meantime, where was Clement?

Lying at full length upon the floor of the convent church, with his lips upon the lowest step of the altar, in an indescribable state of terror, misery, penitence, and self-abasement: through all which struggled gleams of joy that Margaret was alive.

Night fell and found him lying there weeping, and praying: and morning would have found him there too; but he suddenly remembered that, absorbed in his own wrongs and Margaret's, he had committed another sin besides intemperate rage. He had neglected a dying man.

He rose instantly, groaning at his accumulated wickedness, and set out to repair the omission. The weather had changed; it was raining hard, and, when he got clear of the town, he heard the wolves baying; they were on foot. But Clement was himself again, or nearly; he thought little of danger or discomfort, having a shameful omission of religious duty to repair: he went stoutly forward through rain and darkness.

And, as he went, he often beat his breast, and cried, "Mea Culpa! Mea Culpa!"

CHAPTER XCI

WHAT that sensitive mind, and tender conscience, and loving heart, and religious soul, went through even in a few hours, under a situation so sudden and tremendous, is perhaps beyond the power of words to paint.

Fancy yourself the man; then put yourself in his place!

Were I to write a volume on it, we should have to come to that at last.

I shall relate his next two overt acts. They indicate his state of mind after the first fierce tempest of the soul had subsided.

After spending the night with the dying hermit in giving and receiving holy consolations, he set out not for Rotterdam, but for Tergou. He went there to confront his fatal enemy the burgomaster, and, by means of that parchment, whose history by-the-by was itself a romance, to make him disgorge; and give Margaret her own.

Heated and dusty, he stopped at the fountain, and there began to eat his black bread and drink of the water. But in the middle of his frugal meal a female servant came running, and begged him to come and shrive her dying master. He returned the bread to his wallet, and followed her without a word.

She took him—to the Stadthouse.

He drew back with a little shudder when he saw her go in.

But he almost instantly recovered himself, and followed her into the house, and up the stairs. And there in bed, propped up by pillows, lay his deadly enemy, looking already like a corpse.

Clement eyed him a moment from the door, and thought of all —the tower, the wood, the letter. Then he said in a low voice, "Pax vobiscum!" He trembled a little while he said it.

The sick man welcomed him as eagerly as his weak state permitted. "Thank Heaven, thou art come in time to absolve me from my sins, father, and pray for my soul, thou and thy brethren."

"My son," said Clement, "before absolution cometh confession. In which act there must be no reservation, as thou valuest thy soul's weal. Bethink thee, therefore, wherein thou hast most offended God and the Church, while I offer up a prayer for wisdom to direct thee."

Clement then kneeled and prayed; and, when he rose from his knees, he said to Ghysbrecht, with apparent calmness, "My son, confess thy sins."

"Ah, father," said the sick man, "they are many and great."

"Great then be thy penitence, my son; so shalt thou find God's mercy great."

Ghysbrecht put his hands together, and began to confess with every appearance of contrition.

He owned he had eaten meat in mid-Lent. He had often absented himself from mass on the Lord's day, and saints' day: and had trifled with other religious observances, which he enumerated with scrupulous fidelity.

When he had done, the friar said, quietly, " 'Tis well, my son. These be faults. Now to thy crimes. Thou hadst done better to begin with them."

"Why, father, what crimes lie to my account if these be none?"

"Am I confessing to thee, or thou to me?" said Clement, somewhat severely.

"Forgive me, father! Why, surely, I to you. But I know not what you call crimes."

"The seven deadly sins, art thou clear of them?"

"Heaven forfend I should be guilty of them. I know them not by name."

"Many do them all that cannot name them. Begin with that one which leads to lying, theft, and murder."

"I am quit of that one any way. How call you it?"

"AVARICE, my son."

"Avarice? Oh, as to that, I have been a saving man all my day; but I have kept a good table, and not altogether forgotten the poor. But, alas, I am a great sinner. Mayhap the next will catch me. What is the next?"

"We have not yet done with this one. Bethink thee, the Church is not to be trifled with."

"Alas! am I in a condition to trifle with her now? Avarice? Avarice?"

He looked puzzled and innocent.

"Hast thou ever robbed the fatherless?" inquired the friar.

"Me? robbed the fatherless?" gasped Ghysbrecht; "not that I mind."

"Once more, my son, I am forced to tell thee thou art trifling with the Church. Miserable man! another evasion, and I leave thee, and fiends will straightway gather round thy bed, and tear thee down to the bottomless pit."

"Oh, leave me not! leave me not!" shrieked the terrified old man. "The Church knows all. I *must* have robbed the fatherless. I will confess. Who shall I begin with? My memory for names is shaken."

The defence was skilful, but in this case failed.

"Hast thou forgotten Floris Brandt?" said Clement stonily.

The sick man reared himself in bed in a pitiable state of terror.

"How knew you that?" said he.

"The Church knows many things," said Clement, coldly, "and by many ways that are dark to thee. Miserable impenitent, you called her to your side hoping to deceive her. You said 'I will not confess to the curé, but to some friar who knows not my misdeeds. So will I cheat the Church on my death-bed, and die as I have lived.' But God, kinder to thee than thou art to thyself, sent to thee one whom thou couldst not deceive. He has tried thee; he was patient with thee, and warned thee not to trifle with holy Church; but all is in vain; thou canst not confess; for thou art impenitent as a stone. Die, then, as thou hast lived. Methinks I see the fiends crowding round the bed for their prey. They wait but for me to go. And I go."

He turned his back; but Ghysbrecht, in extremity of terror, caught him by the frock. "Oh, holy man, mercy! stay. I will confess all, all. I robbed my friend Floris. Alas, would it had ended there; for he lost little by me; but I kept the land from Peter his son, and from Margaret, Peter's daughter. Yet I was always going to give it back; but I couldn't, I couldn't."

"Avarice, my son, avarice. Happy for thee 'tis not too late."

"No. I will leave it her by will. She will not have long to wait for it now: not above a month or two at farthest."

"For which month's possession thou wouldst damn thy soul for ever. Thou fool!"

The sick man groaned, and prayed the friar to be reasonable. The friar firmly, but gently and persuasively, persisted, and with infinite patience detached the dying man's gripe from another's property. There were times when his patience was tried, and he was on the point of thrusting his hand into his bosom and producing the deed, which he had brought for that purpose; but after yesterday's outbreak he was on his guard against choler; and, to conclude, he conquered his impatience; he conquered a personal repugnance to the man, so strong as to make his own flesh creep all the time he was struggling with this miser for his soul: and at last, without a word about the deed, he won him to make full and prompt restitution.

How the restitution was made will be briefly related elsewhere: also certain curious effects produced upon Ghysbrecht by it; and when and on what terms Ghysbrecht and Clement parted.

I promise to relate two acts of the latter, indicative of his mind. This is one. The other is told in two words.

As soon as he was quite sure Margaret had her own, and was a rich woman—

HE DISAPPEARED.

IT was the day after that terrible scene: the little house in the Hoog Straet was like a grave, and none more listless and dejected than Catherine, so busy and sprightly by nature. After dinner, her eyes red with weeping, she went to the convent to try and soften Gerard, and lay the first stone at least of a reconcilation. It was some time before she could make the porter understand whom she was seeking. Eventually she learned he had left late last night and was not expected back. She went sighing with the news to Margaret. She found her sitting idle, like one with whom life had lost its savour; she had her boy clasped so tight in her arms, as if he was all she had left, and she feared some one would take him too. Catherine begged her to come to the Hoog Straet.

"What for?" sighed Margaret. "You cannot but say to yourselves, 'she is the cause of all.'"

"Nay, nay," said Catherine, "we are not so ill-hearted, and Eli is so fond on you; you will, may be, soften him."

"Oh, if you think I can do any good, I'll come," said Margaret, with a weary sigh.

They found Eli and a carpenter putting up another name in place of Cornelis's and Sybrandt's and what should that name be but Margaret Brandt's.

With all her affection for Margaret this went through poor Catherine like a knife. "The bane of one is another's meat," said she.

"Can he make me spend the money unjustly?" replied Margaret, coldly.

"You are a good soul," said Catherine. "Ay, so best, sith he is the strongest."

The next day Giles dropped in, and Catherine told the story all in favour of the black sheep, and invited his pity for them, anathematized by their brother, and turned on the wide world by their father. But Giles's prejudices ran the other way; he heard her out, and told her bluntly the knaves had got off cheap; they deserved to be hanged at Margaret's door into the bargain, and, dismissing them with contempt, crowed with delight at the return of his favourite. "I'll show him," said he, "what 'tis to have a brother at court with a heart to serve a friend, and a head to point the way."

The Cloister and the Hearth

"Bless thee, Giles," murmured Margaret, softly.

"Thou wast ever his stanch friend, dear Giles," said little Kate; "but alack I know not what thou canst do for him now."

Giles had left them, and all was sad and silent again, when a well-dressed man opened the door softly and asked was Margaret Brandt here.

"D'ye hear, lass? You are wanted," said Catherine, briskly. In her the Gossip was indestructible.

"Well, mother," said Margaret, listlessly, "and here I am."

A shuffling of feet was heard at the door, and a colourless, feeble, old man was assisted into the room. It was Ghysbrecht Van Swieten. At sight of him Catherine shrieked and threw her apron over her head and Margaret shuddered violently and turned her head swiftly away not to see him.

A feeble voice issued from the strange visitor's lips, "Good people, a dying man hath come to ask your forgiveness."

"Come to look on your work, you mean," said Catherine, taking down her apron and bursting out sobbing. "There, there, she is fainting; look to her, Eli, quick."

"Nay," said Margaret, in a feeble voice, "the sight of him gave me a turn, that is all. Prithee let him say his say; and go; for he is the murtherer of me and mine."

"Alas," said Ghysbrecht, "I am too feeble to say it standing, and no one biddeth me sit down."

Eli, who had followed him into the house, interfered here, and said half sullenly, half apologetically, "Well, burgomaster, 'tis not our wont to leave a visitor standing whiles we sit. But, man, man, you have wrought us too much ill." And the honest fellow's voice began to shake with anger he fought hard to contain, because it was his own house.

Then Ghysbrecht found an advocate in one who seldom spoke in vain in that family.

It was little Kate. "Father, mother," said she, "my duty to you, but this is not well. Death squares all accounts. And see you not death in his face? I shall not live long, good friends: and his time is shorter than mine."

Eli made haste and set a chair for their dying enemy with his own hands. Ghysbrecht's attendants put him into it. "Go fetch the boxes," said he. They brought in two boxes, and then retired,

609

leaving their master alone in the family he had so cruelly injured.

Every eye was now bent on him, except Margaret's. He undid the boxes, with unsteady fingers, and brought out of one the title-deeds of a property at Tergou. "This land and these houses belonged to Floris Brandt, and do belong to thee of right, his grand-daughter. These I did usurp for a debt long since defrayed with interest. These I now restore their rightful owner with penitent tears. In this other box are three hundred and forty golden angels, being the rent and fines I have received from that land more than Floris Brandt's debt to me. I have kept compt, still meaning to be just one day; but Avarice withheld me. Pray, good people, against temptation! I was not born dishonest: yet you see."

"Well, to be sure," cried Catherine. "And you the burgomaster! Hast whipt good store of thieves in thy day. However," said she, on second thoughts, " 'tis better late than never. What, Margaret? art deaf? The good man hath brought thee back thine own. Art a rich woman. Alack, what a mountain o' gold!"

"Bid him keep land and gold, and give me back my Gerard, that he stole from me with his treason;" said Margaret, with her head still averted.

"Alas!" said Ghysbrecht; "would I could. What I can I have done. Is it nought? It cost me a sore struggle; and I rose from my last bed to do it myself, lest some mischance should come between her and her rights."

"Old man," said Margaret, "since thou, whose idol is pelf, hast done this, God and his saints will, as I hope, forgive thee. As for me, I am neither saint nor angel, but only a poor woman, whose heart thou hast broken. Speak to him, Kate; for I am like the dead."

Kate meditated a little while; and then her soft silvery voice fell like a soothing melody upon the air. "My poor sister hath a sorrow that riches cannot heal. Give her time, Ghysbrecht; 'tis not in nature she should forgive thee all. Her boy is fatherless; and she is neither maid, wife, nor widow; and the blow fell but two days syne, that laid her heart a bleeding."

A single heavy sob from Margaret was the comment to these words.

"Therefore, give her time! And, ere thou diest, she will forgive thee all, ay, even to pleasure me, that haply shall not be long behind thee, Ghysbrecht. Meantime, we, whose wounds be sore, but not so deep as hers, do pardon thee, a penitent and a dying man; and I, for one, will pray for thee from this hour; go in peace!"

Their little oracle had spoken; it was enough. Eli even invited him to break a manchet and drink a stoup of wine to give him heart for his journey.

But Ghysbrecht declined, and said what he had done was a cordial to him. "Man seeth but a little way before him, neighbour. This land I clung so to it was a bed of nettles to me all the time. 'Tis gone; and I feel happier and livelier like for the loss on't."

He called his men and they lifted him into the litter.

When he was gone Catherine gloated over the money. She had never seen so much together, and was almost angry with Margaret, for "sitting out there like an image." And she dilated on the advantages of money.

And she teased Margaret till at last she prevailed on her to come and look at it.

"Better let her be, mother," said Kate. "How can she relish gold, with a heart in her bosom liker lead?" But Catherine persisted.

The result was, Margaret looked down at all her wealth, with wondering eyes. Then suddenly wrung her hands and cried with piercing anguish, "TOO LATE! TOO LATE!"

And shook off her leaden despondency, only to go into strong hysterics over the wealth that came too late to be shared with him she loved.

A little of this gold, a portion of this land, a year or two ago, when it was as much her own as now; and Gerard would have never left her side for Italy or any other place.

Too late! Too late!

CHAPTER XCIII

NOT many days after this came the news that Margaret Van Eyck was dead and buried. By a will she had made a year before, she left all her property, after her funeral expenses and certain presents to Reicht Heynes, to her dear daughter Margaret Brandt, requesting her to keep Reicht as long as unmarried. By this will Margaret inherited a furnished house, and pictures and sketches that in the present day would be a fortune: among the pictures was one she valued more than a gallery of others. It represented "a Betrothal." The solemnity of the ceremony was marked in the grave face of the man, and the demure complacency of the woman. She was painted almost entirely by Margaret Van Eyck, but the rest of the picture by Jan. The accessories were exquisitely finished, and remain a marvel of skill to this day. Margaret Brandt sent word to Reicht to stay in the house till such time as she could find the heart to put foot in it, and miss the face and voice that used to meet her there: and to take special care of the picture "in the little cubboard": meaning the diptych.

The next thing was, Luke Peterson came home, and heard that Gerard was a monk.

He was like to go mad with joy. He came to Margaret and said,

"Never heed, mistress. If he cannot marry you I can."

"You?" said Margaret. "Why, I have seen him."

"But he is a friar."

"He was my husband, and my boy's father long ere he was a friar. And I have seen him. I've *seen* him."

Luke was thoroughly puzzled. "I'll tell you what," said he; "I have got a cousin a lawyer. I'll go and ask him whether you are married or single."

"Nay, I shall ask my own heart, not a lawyer. So that is your regard for me; to go making me the town talk, oh, fie!"

"That is done already without a word from me."

"But not by such as seek my respect. And if you do it, never come nigh me again."

"Ay," said Luke, with a sigh, "you are like a dove to all the rest; but you are a hard-hearted tyrant to me."

" 'Tis your own fault, dear Luke, for wooing me. That is what lets me from being as kind to you as I desire. Luke, my bonny lad, listen to me. I am rich now; I can make my friends happy, though not myself. Look round the street, look round the parish. There is many a quean in it, fairer than I twice told, and not spoiled with weeping. Look high; and take your choice. Speak you to the lass herself, and I'll speak to the mother; they shall not say thee nay; take my word for't."

The Cloister and the Hearth

"I see what ye mean," said Luke, turning very red. "But if I can't have your liking, I will none o' your money. I was your servant when you were poor as I; and poorer. No: if you would liever be a friar's leman than an honest man's wife, you are not the woman I took you for; so part we withouten malice: seek you your comfort on yon road, where never a she did find it yet, and, for me, I'll live and die a bachelor. Good even, mistress."

"Farewell, dear Luke: and God forgive you for saying *that* to me."

For some days Margaret dreaded, almost as much as she desired, the coming interview with Gerard. She said to herself, "I wonder not he keeps away a while; for so should I." However he would hear he was a father: and the desire to see their boy would overcome everything; "And," said the poor girl to herself, "if so be that meeting does not kill me, I feel I shall be better after it than I am now."

But when day after day went by, and he was not heard of, a freezing suspicion began to crawl and creep towards her mind. What if his absence was intentional? What if he had gone to some cold-blooded monks his fellows, and they had told him never to see her more? The convent had ere this shown itself as merciless to true lovers as the grave itself.

At this thought the very life seemed to die out of her.

And now for the first time deep indignation mingled at times with her grief and apprehension. "Can he have ever loved me? To run from me and his boy without a word! Why this poor Luke thinks more of me than he does."

While her mind was in this state, Giles came roaring, "I've hit the clout; OUR GERARD IS VICAR OF GOUDA."

A very brief sketch of the dwarf's court life will suffice to prepare the reader for his own account of this feat. Some months before he went to court his intelligence had budded. He himself dated the change from a certain 8th of June, when, swinging by one hand along with the week's washing on a tight rope in the drying ground, something went crack inside his head; and lo! intellectual powers unchained. At court his shrewdness and bluntness of speech, coupled with his gigantic voice and his small stature, made him a Power: without the last item I fear they would have conducted him to that unpopular gymnasium, the gallows. The young Duchess of Burgundy, and Marie the heiress apparent, both petted him, as great ladies have petted dwarfs in all ages; and the court poet melted butter by the six-foot rule, and poured enough of it down his back to stew Goliah in. He even amplified, versified, and enfeebled, certain rough and ready sentences dictated by Giles.

The centipedal prolixity that resulted went to Eli by letter, thus entitled,

> "The high and puissant Princess Marie
> of Bourgogne her lytel jantilman hys
> complaynt of yᵉ Coort, and
> praise of a rusticall lyfe, versificated, and empapyred
> by me the lytel jantilman's right lovynge
> and obsequious servitor, etc.

But the dwarf reached his climax by a happy mixture of mind and muscle; thus:

The day before a grand court joust he challenged the duke's giant to a trial of strength. This challenge made the gravest grin, and aroused expectation.

Giles had a lofty pole planted ready, and at the appointed hour went up it like a squirrel, and by strength of arm made a right angle with his body, and so remained: then slid down so quickly, that the high and puissant princess squeaked, and hid her face in her hands, not to see the demise of her pocket-Hercules.

The giant effected only about ten feet, then looked ruefully up and ruefully down, and descended, bathed in perspiration, to argue the matter.

"It was not the dwarf's greater strength, but his smaller body."

The spectators received this excuse with loud derision. There was the fact. The dwarf was great at mounting a pole: the giant only great at excuses. In short Giles had gauged their intellects: with his own body no doubt.

"Come," said he, "an' ye go to that, I'll wrestle ye, my lad, if so be you will let me blindfold your eyne."

The giant, smarting under defeat, and thinking he could surely recover it by this means, readily consented.

"Madam," said Giles, "see you yon blind Samson? At a signal from me he shall make me a low obeisance, and unbonnet to me."

614

"How may that be, being blinded?" inquired a maid of honour. "That is my affair."

"I wager on Giles for one," said the princess.

When several wagers were laid pro and con, Giles hit the giant in the bread-basket. He went double (the obeisance), and his bonnet fell off.

The company yelled with delight at this delicate stroke of wit, and Giles took to his heels. The giant followed as soon as he could recover his breath and tear off his bandage. But it was too late; Giles had prepared a little door in the wall, through which he could pass, but not a giant, and had coloured it so artfully it looked like wall; this door he tore open, and went headlong through, leaving no vestige but this posy, written very large upon the reverse of his trick door:

> Long limbs, big body, wanting wit,
> By wee and wise is bet and bit.

After this Giles became a Force.

He shall now speak for himself.

Finding Margaret unable to believe the good news, and sceptical as to the affairs of holy Church being administered by dwarfs, he narrated as follows:

"When the princess sent for me to her bedroom as of custom, to keep her out of languor, I came not mirthful nor full of country dicts, as is my wont, but dull as lead.

" 'Why what aileth thee?' quo' she. 'Art sick?' 'At heart,' quo' I. 'Alas, he is in love,' quo' she. Whereat five brazen hussies, which they call them maids of honour, did giggle loud. 'Not so mad as that,' said I, 'seeing what I see at court of women folk.'

" 'There, ladies,' quo' the princess, 'best let him a be. 'Tis a liberal mannikin, and still giveth more than he taketh of saucy words.'

" 'In all sadness,' quo' she, 'what is the matter?'

"I told her I was meditating, and what perplexed me was, that other folk could now and then keep their word, but princes never.

" 'Heyday,' says she, 'thy shafts fly high this morn.' I told her, 'Ay, for they hit the Truth.'

"She said I was as keen as keen; but it became not me to put riddles to her, nor her to answer them. 'Stand aloof a bit, mesdames,' said she, 'and thou speak without fear'; for she saw I was in sad earnest.

"I began to quake a bit; for mind ye, she can doff freedom and don dignity quicker than she can slip out of her dressing-gown into kirtle of state. But I made my voice so soft as honey; (wherefore smilest?) and I said, 'Madam, one evening, a matter of five years agone, as ye sat with your mother, the Countess of Charolois, who is now in heaven, worse luck, you wi' your lute, and she wi' her tapestry, or the like; do ye mind there came in to ye a fair youth—with a letter from a painter body, one Margaret Van Eyck?'

"She said she thought she did. 'Was it not a tall youth, exceedingly comely?'

"'Ay, madam,' said I; 'he was my brother.'

"'Your brother?' said she, and did eye me like all over. (What dost smile at?)

"So I told her all that passed between her and Gerard, and how she was for giving him a bishopric; but the good countess said, 'Gently, Marie! He is too young;' and with that they did both promise him a living; 'Yet,' said I, 'he hath been a priest a long while, and no living. Hence my bile.'

"'Alas!' said she, ''tis not by my good will. For all this thou hast said is sooth; and more, I do remember, my dear mother said to me, "See thou to it if I be not here."' So then she cried out 'Ay, dear mother, no word of thine shall ever fall to the ground.'

"I seeing her so ripe, said quickly, 'Madam, the Vicar of Gouda died last week.' (For when ye seek favours of the great, behoves ye know the very thing ye aim at.)

"'Then thy brother is vicar of Gouda,' quo' she, 'so sure as I am heiress of Burgundy and the Netherlands. Nay, thank me not, good Giles,' quo' she; 'but my good mother. And I do thank thee for giving of me somewhat to do for her memory.' And doesn't she fall a weeping for her mother? and doesn't that set me off a snivelling for my good brother that I love so dear, and to think that a poor little elf like me could yet speak in the ear of princes, and make my beautiful brother vicar of Gouda; eh, lass, it is a bonny place, and a bonny manse, and hawthorn in every bush at spring-tide, and dog-roses and eglantine in every summer hedge. I know what the poor fool affects, leave that to me."

The dwarf began his narrative strutting to and fro before Margaret; but he ended it in her arms. For she could not contain herself, but caught him, and embraced him warmly. "Oh, Giles," she said, blushing, and kissing him, "I cannot keep my hands off thee, thy body it is so little, and thy heart so great. Thou art his true friend. Bless thee! bless thee! bless thee! Now we shall see him again. We have not set eyes on him since that terrible day."

"Gramercy, but that is strange," said Giles. "Maybe he is ashamed of having cursed those two vagabones, being our own flesh and blood, worse luck."

"Think you that is why he hides?" said Margaret, eagerly.

"Ay, if he is hiding at all. However, I'll cry him by bellman."

"Nay, that might much offend him."

"What care I? Is Gouda to go vicarless, and the manse in nettles?"

And, to Margaret's secret satisfaction, Giles had the new vicar cried in Rotterdam, and the neighbouring towns. He easily persuaded Margaret that, in a day or two, Gerard would be sure to hear, and come to his benefice. She went to look at his manse, and thought how comfortable it might be made for him, and how dearly she should love to do it.

But the days rolled on, and Gerard came neither to Rotterdam nor Gouda. Giles was mortified, Margaret indignant, and very wretched. She said to herself, "Thinking me dead, he comes home, and now, because I am alive, he goes back to Italy; for that is where he has gone."

Joan advised her to consult the hermit of Gouda.

"Why sure he is dead by this time."

"Yon one, belike. But the cave is never long void; Gouda ne'er wants a hermit."

But Margaret declined to go again to Gouda on such an errand. "What can he know, shut up in a cave? less than I, belike. Gerard hath gone back t' Italy. He hates me for not being dead."

Presently a Tergovian came in with a word from Catherine that

The Cloister and the Hearth

Ghysbrecht Van Swieten had seen Gerard later than any one else. On this Margaret determined to go and see the house and goods that had been left her, and take Reicht Heynes home to Rotterdam. And, as may be supposed, her steps took her first to Ghysbrecht's house. She found him in his garden, seated in a chair with wheels. He greeted her with a feeble voice, but cordially; and when she asked him whether it was true he had seen Gerard since the fifth of August, he replied, "Gerard, no more, but Friar Clement. Ay, I saw him; and blessed be the day he entered my house."

He then related in his own words his interview with Clement. He told her moreover that the friar had afterwards acknowledged he came to Tergou with the missing deed in his bosom on purpose to make him disgorge her land; but that finding him disposed towards penitence, he had gone to work the other way.

"Was not this a saint; who came to right thee; but must needs save his enemy's soul in the doing it?"

To her question, whether he had recognized him, he said, "I ne'er suspected such a thing. 'Twas only when he had been three days with me that he revealed himself. Listen while I speak my shame and his praise.

"I said to him 'The land is gone home, and my stomach feels lighter; but there is another fault that clingeth to me still;' then told I him of the letter I had writ at request of his brethren, I whose place it was to check them. Said I, 'Yon letter was writ to part true lovers, and, the devil aiding, it hath done the foul work. Land and houses I can give back; but yon mischief is done for ever.' 'Nay,' quoth he, 'not for ever; but for life. Repent it then while thou livest.' 'I shall,' said I, 'but how can God forgive it? I would not,' said I, 'were I He.'

" 'Yet will He certainly forgive it,' quoth he; 'for He is ten times more forgiving than I am; and I forgive thee.' I stared at him; and then he said softly, but quavering like, 'Ghysbrecht, look at me closer. I am Gerard the son of Eli.' And I looked, and looked, and at last, lo! it was Gerard. Verily I had fallen at his feet with shame and contrition; but he would not suffer me. 'That became not mine years and his, for a particular fault. I say not I forgive thee without a struggle,' said he, 'not being a saint. But these three days, thou hast spent in penitence, I have worn under thy roof in prayer: and I do forgive thee.' Those were his very words."

Margaret's tears began to flow; for it was in a broken and contrite voice the old man told her this unexpected trait in her Gerard. He continued, "And even with that he bade me farewell.

" 'My work here is done now,' said he. I had not the heart to stay him; for, let him forgive me ever so, the sight of me must be wormwood to him. He left me in peace, and may a dying man's blessing wait on him, go where he will. Oh, girl, when I think of his wrongs, and thine, and how he hath avenged himself by saving this stained soul of mine, my heart is broken with remorse, and these old eyes shed tears by night and day."

"Ghysbrecht," said Margaret, weeping, "since he hath forgiven thee, I forgive thee too: what is done, is done; and thou hast let me know this day that which I had walked the world to hear. But oh, burgomaster, thou art an understanding man, now help a poor woman, which hath forgiven thee her misery."

She then told him all that had befallen; "And," said she, "they will not keep the living for him for ever. He bids fair to lose that, as well as break all our hearts."

"Call my servant," cried the burgomaster, with sudden vigour.

He sent him for a table and writing materials, and dictated letters to the burgomasters in all the principal towns in Holland, and one to a Prussian authority, his friend. His clerk, and Margaret, wrote them, and he signed them. "There," said he, "the matter shall be despatched throughout Holland by trusty couriers; and as far as Basle in Switzerland; and fear not, but we will soon have the vicar of Gouda to his village."

She went home animated with fresh hopes, and accusing herself of ingratitude to Gerard. "I value my wealth now," said she.

She also made a resolution never to blame his conduct, till she should hear from his own lips his reasons.

Not long after her return from Tergou, a fresh disaster befell. Catherine, I must premise, had secret interviews with the black sheep, the very day after they were expelled; and Cornelis followed her to Tergou, and lived there on secret contribution; but Sybrandt chose to remain in Rotterdam. Ere Catherine left, she asked Margaret to lend her two gold angels; "For," said she, "all mine are spent." Margaret was delighted to lend them or give them; but the words were scarce out of her mouth, ere she caught a look of regret and distress on Kate's face; and she saw directly whither

her money was going. She gave Catherine the money, and went and shut herself up with her boy. Now this money was to last Sybrandt till his mother could make some good excuse for visiting Rotterdam again; and then she would bring the idle dog some of her own industrious scrapings.

But Sybrandt, having gold in his pocket, thought it inexhaustible; and, being now under no shadow of restraint, led the life of a complete sot; until one afternoon, in a drunken frolic, he climbed on the roof of the stable at the inn he was carousing in, and proceeded to walk along it, a feat he had performed many times when sober. But now his unsteady brain made his legs unsteady, and he rolled down the roof and fell with a loud thwack on to a horizontal paling, where he hung a moment in a semicircle: then toppled over and lay silent on the ground, amidst roars of laughter from his boon companions.

When they came to pick him up he could not stand; but fell down giggling at each attempt.

On this they went staggering and roaring down the street with him, and carried him at great risk of another fall, to the shop in the Hoog Straet. For he had babbled his own shame all over the place.

As soon as he saw Margaret he hiccupped out, "Here is the doctor that cures all hurts; a bonny lass." He also bade her observe he bore her no malice, for he was paying her a visit, sore against his will. "Wherefore, prithee send away these drunkards; and let you and me have t'other glass, to drown all unkindness."

All this time Margaret was pale and red by turns at sight of her enemy and at his insolence. But one of the men whispered what had happened, and a streaky something in Sybrandt's face arrested her attention.

"And he cannot stand up, say you?"

"A couldn't just now. Try, comrade! Be a man now!"

"I am a better man than thou," roared Sybrandt. "I'll stand up and fight ye all for a crown."

He started to his feet, and instantly rolled into his attendant's arms with a piteous groan. He then began to curse his boon companions, and declare they had stolen away his legs. "He could feel nothing below the waist."

"Alas, poor wretch," said Margaret. She turned very gravely to the men, and said, "Leave him here. And if you have brought him to this, go on your knees; for you have spoiled him for life. He will never walk again: his back is broken."

The drunken man caught these words, and the foolish look of intoxication fled, and a glare of anguish took its place. "The curse," he groaned; "the curse!'"

Margaret and Reicht Heynes carried him carefully, and laid him on the softest bed.

"I must do as *he* would do," whispered Margaret. "He was kind to Ghysbrecht."

Her opinion was verified. Sybrandt's spine was fatally injured; and he lay groaning, and helpless, fed and tended by her he had so deeply injured.

The news was sent to Tergou; and Catherine came over.

It was a terrible blow to her. Moreover she accused herself as the cause. "Oh, false wife, oh, weak mother," she cried. "I am rightly punished for my treason to my poor Eli."

She sat for hours at a time by his bedside rocking herself in silence; and was never quite herself again; and the first grey hairs began to come in her poor head from that hour.

As for Sybrandt, all his cry was now for Gerard. He used to whine to Margaret like a suffering hound, "Oh, sweet Margaret, oh, bonny Margaret, for our Lady's sake find Gerard, and bid him take his curse off me. Thou art gentle, thou art good; thou wilt entreat for me, and he will refuse thee nought." Catherine shared his belief that Gerard could cure him, and joined her entreaties to his. Margaret hardly needed this. The burgomaster and his agents having failed, she employed her own, and spent money like water. And among these agents poor Luke enrolled himself. She met him one day looking very thin, and spoke to him compassionately. On this he began to blubber, and say he was more miserable than ever; he would like to be good friends again upon almost any terms.

"Dear heart," said Margaret, sorrowfully, "why can you not say to yourself, now I am her little brother, and she is my old, married sister, worn down with care? Say so, and I will indulge thee, and pet thee, and make thee happier than a prince."

"Well, I will," said Luke savagely, "sooner than keep away from you altogether. But above all give me something to do. Perchance I may have better luck this time."

The Cloister and the Hearth

"Get me my marrige lines," said Margaret, turning sad and gloomy in a moment.

"That is as much as to say, get me *him!* for where they are he is."

"Not so. He may refuse to come nigh me; but certes he will not deny a poor woman, who loved him once, her lines of betrothal. How can she go without them into any honest man's house?"

"I'll get them you if they are in Holland," said Luke.

"They are as like to be in Rome," replied Margaret.

"Let us begin with Holland," observed Luke, prudently.

The slave of love was furnished with money by his soft tyrant, and wandered hither and thither, coopering, and carpentering, and looking for Gerard. "I can't be worse if I find the vagabone," said he, "and I may be a handle better."

The months rolled on, and Sybrandt improved in spirit, but not in body, he was Margaret's pensioner for life; and a long-expected sorrow fell upon poor Catherine, and left her still more bowed down; and she lost her fine hearty bustling way, and never went about the house singing now; and her nerves were shaken, and she lived in dread of some terrible misfortune falling on Cornelis. The curse was laid on him as well as Sybrandt.

She prayed Eli, if she had been a faithful partner all these years, to take Cornelis into his house again; and let her live awhile at Rotterdam.

"I have good daughters here," said she; "but Margaret is so tender, and thoughtful, and the little Gerard, he is my joy; he grows liker his father every day, and his prattle cheers my heavy heart; and I do love children."

And Eli, sturdy but kindly, consented sorrowfully.

And the people of Gouda petitioned the duke for a vicar, a real vicar. "Ours cometh never nigh us," said they, "this six months past: our children they die unchristened, and our folk unburied, except by some chance comer." Giles's influence baffled this just complaint once; but a second petition was prepared, and he gave Margaret little hope that the present position could be maintained a single day.

So then Margaret went sorrowfully to the pretty manse to see it for the last time, ere it should pass forever into a stranger's hands.

"I think he would have been happy here," she said, and turned heartsick away.

On their return, Reicht Heynes proposed to her to go and consult the hermit.

"What," said Margaret, "Joan has been at you. She is the one for hermits. I'll go, if 'tis but to show thee they know no more than we do." And they went to the cave.

It was an excavation partly natural, partly artificial, in a bank of rock overgrown by brambles. There was a rough stone door on hinges, and a little window high up, and two apertures, through one of which the people announced their gifts to the hermit, and put questions of all sorts to him; and, when he chose to answer, his voice came dissonant and monstrous out at another small aperture.

On the face of the rock this line was cut—

Felix qui in Domino nirus ab orbe fugit.

Margaret observed to her companion that this was new since she was here last.

"Ay," said Reicht, "like enough," and looked up at it with awe. Writing even on paper she thought no trifle: but on rock!

She whispered, " 'Tis a far holier hermit than the last; he used to come in the town now and then; but this one ne'er shows his face to mortal man."

"And that is holiness?"

"Ay, sure."

"Then what a saint a dormouse must be!"

"Out, fie, mistress. Would ye even a beast to a man?"

"Come Reicht," said Margaret, "my poor father taught me overmuch. So I will e'en sit here; and look at the manse once more. Go thou forward and question thy solitary; and tell me whether ye get nought or nonsense out of him; for 'twill be one."

As Reicht drew near the cave, a number of birds flew out of it. She gave a little scream, and pointed to the cave to show Margaret they had come thence. On this Margaret felt sure there was no human being in the cave, and gave the matter no further attention. She fell into a deep reverie while looking at the little manse.

She was startled from it by Reicht's hand upon her shoulder, and a faint voice, saying, "Let us go home."

"You got no answer at all, Reicht," said Margaret, calmly.

"No, Margaret," said Reicht, despondently. And they returned home.

Perhaps after all Margaret had nourished some faint secret hope in her heart, though her reason had rejected it; for she certainly went home more dejectedly.

Just as they entered Rotterdam, Reicht said, "Stay! Oh, Margaret, I am ill at deceit; but 'tis death to utter ill news to thee; I love thee so dear."

"Speak out, sweetheart," said Margaret. "I have gone through so much, I am almost past feeling any fresh trouble."

"Margaret, the hermit did speak to me."

"What, a hermit there? among all those birds."

"Ay; and doth not that show him a holy man?"

"I' God's name, what said he to thee, Reicht?"

"Alas! Margaret, I told him thy story, and I prayed him for our Lady's sake, tell me where thy Gerard is. And I waited long for an answer, and presently a voice came like a trumpet. 'Pray for the soul of Gerard, the son of Eli!'"

"Ah!"

"Oh, woe is me that I have this to tell thee, sweet Margaret! bethink thee thou hast thy boy to live for yet."

"Let me get home," said Margaret, faintly.

Passing down the Brede Kirk Straet they saw Joan at the door.

Reicht said to her, "Eh, woman, she has been to your hermit, and heard no good news."

"Come in," said Joan, eager for a gossip.

Margaret would not go in. But she sat down disconsolate on the lowest step but one of the little external staircase that led into Joan's house; and let the other two gossip their fill at the top of it.

"Oh," said Joan, "what yon hermit says is sure to be sooth. He is that holy, I am told, that the very birds consort with him."

"What does that prove?" said Margaret, deprecatingly. "I have seen my Gerard tame the birds in winter till they would eat from his hand."

A look of pity at this parallel passed between the other two. But they were both too fond of her to say what they thought. Joan proceeded to relate all the marvellous tales she had heard of this hermit's sanctity. How he never came out but at night, and prayed among the wolves, and they never molested him: and how he bade the people not bring him so much food to pamper his body, but to bring him candles."

"The candles are to burn before his saint," whispered Reicht, solemnly.

"Ay, lass; and to read his holy books wi'. A neighbour o' mine saw his hand come out, and the birds sat thereon and pecked crumbs. She went for to kiss it; but the holy man whippit it away in a trice. They can't abide a woman to touch 'em, or even look at 'em, saints can't."

"What like was his hand, wife? Did you ask her?"

"What is my tongue for, else? Why, dear heart, all one as ourn; by the same token a had a thumb and four fingers."

"Look ye there now."

"But a deal whiter nor yourn and mine."

"Ay, ay."

"And main skinny."

"Alas."

"What could ye expect? Why a live upon air, and prayer: and candles."

"Ah, well," continued Joan, "poor thing, I whiles think 'tis best for her to know the worst. And now she hath gotten a voice from heaven, or almost as good: and behoves her pray for his soul. One thing she is not so poor now as she was; and never fell riches to a better hand; and she is only come into her own for that matter: so she can pay the priest to say masses for him, and that is a great comfort."

In the midst of their gossip Margaret, in whose ears it was all buzzing, though she seemed lost in thought, got softly up; and crept away with her eyes on the ground, and her brows bent.

"She hath forgotten I am with her," said Reicht Heynes, ruefully.

She had her gossip out with Joan, and then went home.

She found Margaret seated cutting out a pelisse of grey cloth, and a cape to match. Little Gerard was standing at her side, inside her left arm, eyeing the work, and making it more difficult by wriggling about, and fingering the arm with which she held the cloth steady; to all which she submitted with imperturbable patience and complacency. Fancy a male workman so entangled, impeded, worried!

"Ot's that, mammy?"

"A pelisse, my pet."

"Ot's a p'lisse?"

"A great frock. And this is the cape to't."

"Ot's it for?"

"To keep his body from the cold; and the cape is for his shoulders, or to go over his head like the country folk. 'Tis for a hermit."

"Ot's a 'ermit?"

"A holy man that lives in a cave all by himself."

"In de dark?"

"Ay, whiles."

"Oh."

In the morning Reicht was sent to the hermit with the pelisse, and a pound of thick candles.

As she was going out of the door, Margaret said to her, "Said you whose son Gerard was?"

"Nay, not I."

"Think, girl! How could he call him Gerard, son of Eli, if you had not told him?"

Reicht persisted she had never mentioned him but as plain Gerard. But Margaret told her flatly she did not believe her; at which Reicht was affronted, and went out with a little toss of the head. However she determined to question the hermit again, and did not doubt he would be more liberal in his communication, when he saw his nice new pelisse and the candles.

She had not been gone long when Giles came in with ill news. The living of Gouda would be kept vacant no longer.

Margaret was greatly distressed at this. "Oh, Giles," said she. "ask for another month. They will give thee another month, maybe."

He returned in an hour to tell her he could not get a month. "They have given me a week," said he. "And what is a week?"

"Drowning bodies catch at strawen," was her reply. "A week? a little week?"

Reicht came back from her errand out of spirits. Her oracle had declined all further communications. So at least its obstinate silence might fairly be interpreted.

The next day Margaret put Reicht in charge of the shop, and

disappeared all day. So the next day; and so the next. Nor would she tell any one where she had been. Perhaps she was ashamed. The fact is she spent all those days on one little spot of ground. When they thought her dreaming she was applying to every word that fell from Joan and Reicht the whole powers of a far acuter mind than either of them possessed.

She went to work on a scale that never occurred to either of them. She was determined to see the hermit, and question him face to face, not through a wall. She found that by making a circuit she could get above the cave and look down without being seen by the solitary. But when she came to do it she found an impenetrable mass of brambles. After tearing her clothes and her hands and feet, so that she was soon covered with blood, the resolute, patient girl took out her scissors and steadily snipped and cut till she made a narrow path through the enemy. But so slow was the work that she had to leave it half done. The next day she had her scissors fresh ground, and brought a sharp knife as well; and gently, silently cut her way through to the roof of the cave. There she made an ambush of some of the cut brambles, so that the passers-by might not see her, and couched with watchful eye till the hermit should come out. She heard him move underneath her. But he never left his cell. She began to think it was true that he only came out at night. The next day she came early, and brought a jerkin she was making for little Gerard, and there she sat all day working and watching with dogged patience.

At four o'clock the birds began to feed; and a great many of the smaller kinds came fluttering round the cave, and one or two went in. But most of them taking a preliminary seat on the bushes suddenly discovered Margaret, and went off with an agitated flirt of their little wings. And although they sailed about in the air they would not enter the cave. Presently, to encourage them, the hermit all unconscious of the cause of their tremors put out a thin white hand with a few crumbs in it. Margaret laid down her work softly, and gliding her body forward like a snake, looked down at it from above: it was but a few feet from her. It was as the woman described it, a thin, white hand.

Presently the other hand came out with a piece of bread, and the two hands together broke it and scattered the crumbs.

But that other hand had hardly been out two seconds ere the

violet eyes, that were watching above, dilated; and the gentle bosom heaved and the whole frame quivered like a leaf in the wind.

What her swift eye had seen I leave the reader to guess. She suppressed the scream that rose to her lips; but the effort cost her dear. Soon the left hand of the hermit began to swim indistinctly before her gloating eyes: and with a deep sigh her head drooped, and she lay like a broken lily.

She was in a deep swoon, to which perhaps her long fast to-day, and the agitation and sleeplessness of many preceding days contributed.

And there lay beauty, intelligence, and constancy; pale and silent. And little that hermit guessed who was so near him. The little birds hopped on her now; and one nearly entangled his little feet in her rich auburn hair.

She came back to her troubles. The sun was set. She was very cold. She cried a little; but I think it was partly from the remains of physical weakness. And then she went home, praying God and the saints to enlighten her and teach her what to do for the best.

When she got home she was pale and hysterical, and would say nothing in answer to all their questions but her favourite word, "We are wading in deep waters."

The night seemed to have done wonders for her.

She came to Catherine who was sitting sighing by the fireside, and kissed and said, "Mother, what would you like best in the world?"

"Eh, dear," replied Catherine, despondently. "I know nought that would make me smile now; I have parted from too many that were dear to me. Gerard lost again as soon as found. Kate in heaven; and Sybrandt down for life."

"Poor mother! Mother dear, Gouda manse is to be furnished, and cleaned, and made ready all in a hurry. See here be ten gold angels. Make them go far, good mother; for I have ta'en over many already from my boy for a set of useless loons that were aye going to find him for me."

Catherine and Reicht stared at her a moment in silence; and then out burst a flood of questions, to none of which would she give a reply. "Nay," said she, "I have lain on my bed, and thought, and thought, and thought, whiles you were all sleeping; and methinks

I have got a clue to all. I love you, dear mother; but I'll trust no woman's tongue. If I fail this time, I'll have none to blame but Margaret Brandt."

A resolute woman is a very resolute thing. And there was a deep dogged determination in Margaret's voice and brow, that at once convinced Catherine it would be idle to put any more questions at that time. She and Reicht lost themselves in conjectures; and Catherine whispered Reicht, "Bide quiet; then 'twill leak out;" a shrewd piece of advice founded on general observation.

Within an hour Catherine was on the road to Gouda in a cart with two stout girls to help her, and quite a siege artillery of mops, and pails, and brushes. She came back with heightened colour and something of the old sparkle in her eye, and kissed Margaret with a silent warmth that spoke volumes; and at five in the morning was off again to Gouda.

That night as Reicht was in her first sleep a hand gently pressed her shoulder, and she awoke, and was going to scream.

"Whisht," said Margaret, and put her finger to her lips.

She then whispered. "Rise softly, don thy habits, and come with me!"

When she came down, Margaret begged her to loose Dragon and bring him along. Now Dragon was a great mastiff, who had guarded Margaret Van Eyck and Reicht, two lone women, for some years, and was devotedly attached to the latter.

Margaret and Reicht went out with Dragon walking majestically behind them. They came back long after midnight and retired to rest.

Catherine never knew.

Margaret read her friends: she saw the sturdy faithful Frisian could hold her tongue; and Catherine could not. Yet I am not sure she would have trusted even Reicht, had her nerve equalled her spirit: but with all her daring and resolution, she was a tender, timid woman, a little afraid of the dark, very afraid of being alone in it, and desperately afraid of wolves. Now Dragon could kill a wolf in a brace of shakes; but then Dragon would not go with her, but only with Reicht. So altogether she made one confidante.

The next night they made another moonlight reconnaissance; and, as I think, with some result. For not the next night (it rained that night and extinguished their courage), but the next after, they took with them a companion; the last in the world Reicht Heynes would have thought of; yet she gave her warm approval as soon as she was told he was to go with them.

Imagine how these stealthy assailants trembled and panted, when the moment of action came: imagine, if you can, the tumult in Margaret's breast, the thrilling hopes, chasing and chased by, sickening fears; the strange, and perhaps unparalleled mixture of tender familiarity and distant awe, with which a lovely, and high spirited, but tender adoring woman, wife in the eye of the Law, and no wife in the eye of the Church, trembling, blushing, paling, glowing, shivering, stole at night, noiseless as the dew, upon the hermit of Gouda.

And the stars above seemed never so bright and calm.

CHAPTER XCIV

YES, the hermit of Gouda was the vicar of Gouda, and knew it not, so absolute was his seclusion.

My reader is aware that the moment the phrenzy of his passion passed, he was seized with remorse for having been betrayed into it. But perhaps only those who have risen as high in religious spirit as he had, and suddenly fallen, can realize the terror at himself that took possession of him. He felt like one whom self-confidence had betrayed to the very edge of a precipice. "Ah, good Jerome," he cried, "how much better you knew me than I knew myself! How bitter yet wholesome was your admonition!"

Accustomed to search his own heart, he saw at once that the true cause of his fury was Margaret. "I love her better than God," said he, despairingly, "better than the Church. From such a love what can spring to me, or to her?" He shuddered at the thought. "Let the strong battle temptation; 'tis for the weak to flee. And who is weaker than I have shown myself? What is my penitence, my religion? A pack of cards built by degrees into a fair-seeming structure: and lo! one breath of earthly love, and it lies in the dust. I must begin again: and on a surer foundation." He resolved to leave Holland at once, and spend years of his life in some distant convent before returning to it. By that time the temptations of earthly passion would be doubly baffled; an older, and a better, monk, he should be more master of his earthly affections, and Margaret, seeing herself abandoned, would marry, and love another.

The very anguish this last thought cost him showed the self-searcher and self-denier, that he was on the path of religious duty.

But in leaving her for his immortal good and hers, he was not to neglect her temporal weal. Indeed, the sweet thought he could make her comfortable for life, and rich in this world's goods, which she was not bound to despise, sustained him in the bitter struggle it cost him to turn his back on her without one kind word or look. "Oh, what will she think of me?" he groaned. "Shall I not seem to her of all creatures the most heartless, inhuman? but so best: ay, better she should hate me, miserable that I am. Heaven is merciful, and giveth my broken heart this comfort; I can make that villain restore her own, and she shall never lose another true lover by poverty. Another? Ah me! ah me! God and the saints to mine aid!"

How he fared on this errand has been related. But first, as you may perhaps remember, he went at night to shrive the hermit of Gouda. He found him dying, and never left him till he had closed his eyes and buried him beneath the floor of the little oratory attached to his cell. It was the peaceful end of a stormy life. The hermit had been a soldier, and even now carried a steel corselet next his skin, saying he was now Christ's soldier as he had been Satan's. When Clement had shriven him and prayed by him, he, in his turn, sought counsel of one who was dying in so pious a frame. The hermit advised him to be his successor in this peaceful retreat. "His had been a hard fight against the world, the flesh, and the devil, and he had never thoroughly baffled them till he retired into the citadel of Solitude."

These words and the hermit's pious and peaceful death, which speedily followed, and set as it were the seal of immortal truth on them, made a deep impression upon Clement. Nor in his case had they any prejudice to combat; the solitary recluse was still profoundly revered in the Church, whether immured as an anchorite, or anchoress, in some cave or cell belonging to a monastery, or hidden in the more savage but laxer seclusion of the independent hermitage. And Clement knew more about the hermits of the Church than most divines at his time of life; he had read much thereon at the monastery near Tergou; had devoured their lives with wonder and delight in the manuscripts of the Vatican, and conversed earnestly about them with the mendicant friars of several nations. Before Printing these friars were the great circulators of those local annals and biographies which accumulated in the convents of every land. Then, his teacher, Jerome, had been three years an anchorite on the heights of Camaldoli, where for more than four centuries the Thebaid had been revived; and Jerome, cold and curt on most religious themes, was warm with enthusiasm on this one. He had pored over the annals of St. John Baptist's abbey, round about which the hermits' caves were scattered, and told him the names of many a noble, and many a famous warrior, who had ended his days there a hermit, and of many a bishop and archbishop who had passed from the see to the hermitage, or from the hermitage to the see. Among the former the archbishop of Ravenna; among the latter Pope Victor the Ninth. He told him too, with grim delight, of their multifarious austerities, and how each hermit set himself to find where he was weakest, and attacked himself without mercy or remission till there, even there, he was strongest. And how seven times in the twenty-four hours, in thunder, rain, or snow, by daylight, twilight, moonlight or torchlight, the solitaries flocked from distant points, over rugged precipitous ways, to worship in the convent church; at matins, at prime, tierce, sexte, nones, vespers, and complin. He even, under eager questioning, described to him the persons of famous anchorites he had sung the Psalter and prayed with there; the only intercourse their vows allowed, except with special permission. Moncata, Duke of Moncata and Cardova, and Hidalgo of Spain, who in the flower of his youth had retired thither from the pomps, vanities, and pleasures of the world; Father John Baptist of Novara, who had led armies to battle, but was now a private soldier of Christ; Cornelius, Samuel, and Sylvanus. This last, when the great Duchess de' Medici obtained the Pope's leave, hitherto refused, to visit Camaldoli, went down and met her at the first wooden cross, and there, surrounded as she was with courtiers and flatterers, remonstrated with her and persuaded her, and warned her, not to profane that holy mountain, where no woman for so many centuries had placed her foot; and she, awed by the place and the man, retreated with all her captains, soldiers, courtiers, and pages, from that one hoary hermit. At Basle Clement found fresh materials, especially with respect to German and English anchorites; and he had even prepared a "Catena Eremitarum" from the year of our Lord 250, when Paul of Thebes commenced his ninety years of solitude, down to the year 1470. He called them *Angelorum amici et animalium, i. e.,*

FRIENDS OF ANGELS AND ANIMALS.

Thus, though in those days he never thought to be a recluse, the road was paved, so to speak: and when the dying hermit of Gouda blessed the citadel of Solitude, where he had fought the good fight and won it, and invited him to take up the breastplate of faith, that now fell off his own shrunken body, Clement said within himself: "Heaven itself led my foot hither to this end." It struck him too, as no small coincidence, that his patron, St. Bavon, was a hermit, and an austere one, a cuirassier* of the solitary cell.

As soon as he was reconciled to Ghysbrecht Van Swieten, he went eagerly to his new abode, praying Heaven it might not have been already occupied in these three days. The fear was not vain; these famous dens never wanted a human tenant long. He found the rude stone door ajar; then he made sure he was too late; he opened the door and went softly in. No; the cell was vacant, and there were the hermit's great ivory crucifix, his pens, ink, seeds, and memento mori, a skull; his cilice of hair, and another of bristles; his well-worn sheepskin pelisse and hood, his hammer, chisel, and psaltery, &c. Men and women had passed that way, but none had ventured to intrude, far less to steal. Faith and simplicity had guarded that keyless door more securely than the houses of the laity were defended by their gates like a modern jail, and thick iron bars at every window, and the gentry by moat, bastion, chevaux de frise, and portcullis.

As soon as Clement was fairly in the cell there was a loud flap, and a flutter, and down came a great brown owl from a corner, and whirled out of the window, driving the air cold on Clement's face. He started and shuddered.

Was this seeming owl something diabolical? trying to deter him from his soul's good? On second thoughts, might it not be some

* "Loricatus," vide Ducange, in voce

good spirit the hermit had employed to keep the cell for him, perhaps the hermit himself? Finally he concluded that it was just an owl; and that he would try and make friends with it.

He kneeled down and inaugurated his new life with prayer.

Clement had not only an earthly passion to quell, the power of which made him tremble for his eternal weal, but he had a penance to do for having given way to ire, his besetting sin, and cursed his own brothers.

He looked round this roomy cell furnished with so many comforts, and compared it with the pictures in his mind of the hideous place, eremus in eremo, a desert in a desert, where holy Jerome, hermit, and the Plutarch of hermits had wrestled with sickness, temptation, and despair, four mortal years; and with the inaccessible and thorny niche, a hole in a precipice, where the boy hermit Benedict buried himself and lived three years on the pittance the good monk Romanus could spare him from his scanty commons; and subdivided that mouthful with his friend, a raven; and the hollow tree of his patron St. Bavon, and the earthly purgatory at Fribourg, where lived a nameless saint in a horrid cavern, his eyes chilled with perpetual gloom, and his ears stunned with an eternal waterfall; and the pillar on which St. Simeon Stylita existed forty-five years, and the destina, or stone box, of St. Dunstan, where like Hilarion in his bulrush hive, sepulchro potius quam domu, he could scarce sit, stand or lie; and the living tombs, sealed with lead, of Thais, and Christina, and other recluses; and the damp dungeon of St. Alred. These and scores more of the dismal dens in which true hermits had worn out their wasted bodies on the rock, and the rock under their sleeping bodies, and their praying knees, all came into his mind, and he said to himself, "This sweet retreat is for safety of the soul; but what for penance? Jesu aid me against faults to come; and for the fault I rue, face of man I will not see for a twelvemonth and a day." He had famous precedents in his eye even for this last and unusual severity. In fact the original hermit of this very cell was clearly under the same vow. Hence the two apertures through which he was spoken to, and replied.

Adopting, in other respects, the uniform rule of hermits and anchorites, he divided his day into the seven offices, ignoring the petty accidents of light and dark, creations both of Him to whom he prayed so unceasingly.   He learned the psalter by heart, and in all the intervals of devotion, not occupied by broken slumbers, he worked hard with his hands.   No article of the hermit's rule was more strict or more ancient than this.   And here his self-imposed penance embarrassed him, for what work could he do, without being seen, that should benefit his neighbours? for the hermit was to labour *for himself* in those cases only where his subsistence depended on it. Now Clement's modest needs were amply supplied by the villagers.

On moonlight nights he would steal out like a thief, and dig some poor man's garden on the outskirts of the village.   He made baskets and dropped them slily at humble doors.

And since he could do nothing for the bodies of those who passed by his cell in daytime, he went out in the dead of the night with his hammer and his chisel, and carved moral and religious sentences all down the road upon the sandstone rocks.   "Who knows?" said he, "often a chance shaft striketh home.   Oh, sore heart, comfort thou the poor and bereaved with holy words of solace in their native tongue; for *he* said well, ''tis clavis ad corda plebis.'"   Also he remembered the learned Colonna had told him of the written mountains in the east where kings had inscribed their victories. "What," said Clement, "are they so wise, those Eastern monarchs, to engrave their warlike glory upon the rock, making a blood bubble endure so long as earth; and shall I leave the rocks about me silent on the King of Glory, at whose word they were, and at whose breath they shall be dust?   Nay, but these stones shall speak to weary way-farers of eternal peace, and of the Lamb, whose frail, and afflicted, yet happy servant worketh them among."

Now at this time the inspired words that have consoled the poor and the afflicted for so many ages, were not yet printed in Dutch, so that these sentences of gold from the holy Evangelists came like fresh oracles from heaven, or like the dew on parched flowers; and the poor hermit's written rocks softened a heart or two, and sent the heavy laden singing on their way.*

These holy oracles that seemed to spring up around him like magic; his prudent answers through his window to such as sought ghostly

* It requires now-a-days a strong effort of the imagination to realize the effect on poor people who had never seen them before, of such sentences as this: "Blessed are the poor," &c.

counsel; and above all, his invisibility, soon gained him a prodigious reputation. This was not diminished by the medical advice they now and then extorted from him, sore against his will, by tears and entreaties; for if the patients got well, they gave the holy hermit the credit, and if not, they laid all the blame on the devil. I think he killed nobody, for his remedies were "womanish and weak." Sage, and wormwood, sion, hyssop, borage, spikenard, dog's-tongue, our Lady's mantle, feverfew, and Faith, and all in small quantities except the last.

Then his abstinence, sure sign of a saint. The eggs and milk they brought him at first he refused with horror. Know ye not the hermit's rule is bread, or herbs, and water? Eggs, they are birds in disguise; for when the bird dieth then the egg rotteth. As for milk, it is little better than white blood. And when they brought him too much bread he refused it. Then they used to press it on him. "Nay, holy father; give the overplus to the poor."

"You who go among the poor can do that better. Is bread a thing to fling haphazard from an hermit's window?" And to those who persisted after this: "To live on charity, yet play Sir Bountiful, is to lie with the right hand. Giving another's to the poor, I should beguile them of their thanks, and cheat thee the true giver. Thus do thieves, whose boast it is they bleed the rich into the lap of the poor. Occasio avaritiæ nomen pauperum."

When nothing else would convince the good souls, this piece of Latin always brought them round. So would a line of Virgil's Æneid.

This great reputation of sanctity was all external. Inside the cell was a man who held the hermit of Gouda as cheap as dirt.

"Ah!" said he, "I cannot deceive myself; I cannot deceive God's animals. See the little birds, how coy they be! I feed and feed them and long for their friendship, yet will they never come within, nor take my hand, by lighting on't. For why? No Paul, no Benedict, no Hugh of Lincoln, no Columbia, no Guthlac bides in this cell. Hunted doe flieth not hither, for here is no Fructuosus, nor Aventine, nor Albert of Suabia: nor e'en a pretty squirrel cometh from the wood hard by for the acorns I have hoarded; for here abideth no Columban. The very owl that was here hath fled. They are not to be deceived; I have a Pope's word for that; Heaven rest his soul."

The Cloister and the Hearth

Clement had one advantage over her, whose image in his heart he was bent on destroying.

He had suffered and survived the pang of bereavement; and the mind cannot quite repeat such anguish. Then he had built up a habit of looking on her as dead. After that strange scene in the church and churchyard of St. Laurens, that habit might be compared to a structure riven by a thunderbolt. It was shattered, but stones enough stood to found a similar habit on; to look on her as dead *to him.*

And, by severe subdivision of his time and thoughts, by unceasing prayers, and manual labour, he did, in about three months, succeed in benumbing the earthly half of his heart.

But, lo! within a day or two of this first symptom of mental peace returning slowly, there descended upon his mind a horrible despondency.

Words cannot utter it; for words never yet painted a likeness of despair. Voices seemed to whisper in his ear, "Kill thyself, kill! kill! kill!"

And he longed to obey the voices; for life was intolerable. He wrestled with his dark enemy with prayers and tears; he prayed God but to vary his temptation. "Oh let mine enemy have power to scourge me with red-hot whips, to tear me leagues and leagues over rugged places by the hair of my head, as he has served many a holy hermit, that yet baffled him at last; to fly on me like a raging lion; to gnaw me with a serpent's fangs: any pain, any terror, but this horrible gloom of the soul that shuts me from all light of Thee and of the saints."

And now a freezing thought crossed him. What if the triumphs of the powers of darkness over Christian souls in desert places, had been suppressed; and only their defeats recorded, or at least in full: for dark hints were scattered about antiquity that now first began to grin at him with terrible meaning.

"THEY WANDERED IN THE DESERT AND PERISHED BY SERPENTS," said an ancient father, of hermits that went into solitude, "and were seen no more." And another at a more recent epoch, wrote: "Vertunter ad melancoliam;" "they turn to gloomy madness." These two statements were they not one? for the ancient fathers never spoke with regret of the death of the body. No,

637

the hermits so lost were perished souls, and the serpents were diabolical * thoughts, the natural brood of solitude.

St. Jerome went into the desert with three companions; one fled in the first year; two died: how? The single one that lasted, was a gigantic soul with an iron body.

The cotemporary who related this made no comment; expressed no wonder. What then if here was a glimpse of the true proportion in every age, and many souls had always been lost in solitude for one gigantic mind and iron body that survived this terrible ordeal.

The darkened recluse now cast his despairing eyes over antiquity to see what weapons the Christian arsenal contained, that might befriend him. The greatest of all was prayer. Alas! it was a part of his malady to be unable to pray with true fervour. The very system of mechanical supplication he had for months carried out so severely by rule had rather checked than fostered his power of originating true prayer.

He prayed louder than ever, but the heart hung back cold and gloomy, and let the words go up alone.

"Poor wingless prayers," he cried; "you will not get half way to heaven."

A fiend of this complexion had been driven out of King Saul by music.

Clement took up the hermit's psaltery, and with much trouble mended the strings and tuned it.

No, he could not play it. His soul was so out of tune. The sounds jarred on it, and made him almost mad.

"Ah, wretched me!" he cried. "Saul had a saint to play to him. He was not alone with the spirits of darkness; but here is no sweet bard of Israel to play to me; I, lonely, with crushed heart, on which a black fiend sitteth mountain high, must make the music to uplift that heart to heaven; it may not be." And he grovelled on the earth weeping and tearing his hair.

VERTEBATUR AD MELANCHOLIAM.

---

* The primitive writer was so interpreted by others besides Clement; and, in particular by Peter of Blois, a divine of the twelfth century, whose comment is noteworthy, as he himself was a forty-year hermit.

The Cloister and the Hearth

CHAPTER XCV

ONE day as he lay there sighing, and groaning, prayerless, tuneless, hopeless, a thought flashed into his mind. What he had done for the poor and the wayfarer, he would do for himself. He would fill his den of despair with the name of God and the magic words of holy writ, and the pious, prayerful, consolations of the Church.

Then, like Christian at Apollyon's feet, he reached his hand suddenly out and caught, not his sword, for he had none, but peaceful labour's humbler weapon, his chisel, and worked with it as if his soul depended on his arm.

They say that Michael Angelo in the next generation used to carve statues, not like our timid sculptors, by modelling the work in clay, and then setting a mechanic to chisel it; but would seize the block, conceive the image, and, at once, with mallet and steel make the marble chips fly like mad about him, and the mass sprout into form. Even so Clement drew no lines to guide his hand. He went to his memory for the gracious words, and then dashed at his work and eagerly graved them in the soft stone, between working and fighting.

He begged his visitors for candle ends, and rancid oil.

"Anything is good enough for *me*," he said, "if 'twill but burn." So at night the cave glowed afar off like a blacksmith's forge, through the window and the gaping chinks of the rude stone door, and the rustics beholding crossed themselves and suspected deviltries, and, within, the holy talismans one after another came upon the walls, and the sparks and the chips flew day and night, night and day, as the soldier of Solitude and of the Church plied, with sighs and groans, his bloodless weapon, between working and fighting.

Kyrie Eleeison
Christe Eleeison

Τον Σαταναν συντριψον ύπο τους ποδας ήμων.

Sursum corda [2]

Deus refugium nostrum et virtus [3]

[1] Beat down Satan under our feet.
[2] Up, Hearts!
[3] Oh God our refuge and strength.

639

The Cloister and the Hearth

Agnus Dei, qui tollis peccata mundi, miserere mihi.[1]

Sancta Trinitas unus Deus, miserere nobis.[2]

Ab infestationibus Daemonum, a ventura ira, a damnatione perpetua.[3]

Libera nos Domine

Deus, qui miro ordine Angelorum ministeria, etc. (the whole collect).[4]

Quem quaerimus adjutorem nisi te Domine, qui pro peccatis nostris juste irascaris?[5]

Sancte Deus, Sancte fortis, Sancte et misericors Salvator, amarae morti ne tradas nos.

And underneath the great crucifix, which was fastened to the wall, he graved this from Augustine:—

O anima Christiana, respice vulnera patientis, sanguinem morientis, pretium redemptionis.—Haec quanta sint cogitate, et in statera mentis vestrae appendite, ut totus vobis figatur in corde, qui pro vobis totus firus est in cruce. Nam, si passio Christi ad memoriam revocetur, nihil est tam durum quod non aequo animo toleretur.

Which may be thus rendered:—

O Christian soul, look on the wounds of the suffering One, the blood of the dying One, the price paid for our redemption! These things, oh think how great they be, and weigh them in the balance of thy mind: that He may be wholly nailed to thy heart, who for thee was all nailed unto the cross. For do but call to mind the sufferings of Christ, and there is nought on earth too hard to endure with composure.

Soothed a little, a very little, by the sweet and pious words he was raising all round him, and weighed down with watching and working night and day, Clement one morning sank prostrate with fatigue; and a deep sleep overpowered him for many hours.

---

[1] Oh! Lamb of God, that takest away the Sins of the world, have mercy upon me!

[2] Oh! Holy Trinity, one God, have mercy upon us.

[3] From the assaults of demons—from the wrath to come—from everlasting damnation—

Deliver us, O Lord!

[4] See the English collect, St. Michael and all Angels.

[5] Of whom may we seek succour, but of thee, Oh Lord, who for our sins art justly displeased (and that torrent of prayer, the following verse).

The Cloister and the Hearth

Awaking quietly, he heard a little cheep; he opened his eyes, and, lo! upon his breviary which was on a lone stool near his feet, ruffling all his feathers with a single pull, and smoothing them as suddenly, and cocking his bill this way and that with a vast display of cunning purely imaginary, perched a robin redbreast.

Clement held his breath.

He half closed his eyes lest they should frighten the airy guest.

Down came robin on the floor.

When there he went through his pantomime of astuteness; and then, pim, pim, pim, with three stiff little hops, like a ball of worsted on vertical wires, he was on the hermit's bare foot. On this eminence he swelled, and contracted again, with ebb and flow of feathers; but Clement lost this, for he quite closed his eyes and scarce drew his breath in fear of frightening and losing his visitor. He was content to feel the minute claw on his foot. He could but just feel it, and that by help of knowing it was there.

Presently a little flirt with two little wings, and the feathered busy-body was on the breviary again.

Then Clement determined to try and feed this pretty little fidget without frightening it away. But it was very difficult. He had a piece of bread within reach, but how get at it? I think he was five minutes creeping his hand up to that bread, and when there he must not move his arm.

He slily got a crumb between a finger and thumb and shot it as boys do marbles, keeping the hand quite still.

Cockrobin saw it fall near him, and did sagacity, but moved not.

When another followed, and then another: he popped down and caught up one of the crumbs, but not quite understanding this mystery fled with it, for more security, to an eminence; to wit the hermit's knee.

And so the game proceeded till a much larger fragment than usual rolled along.

Here was a prize. Cockrobin pounced on it, bore it aloft and fled so swiftly into the world with it, the cave resounded with the buffeted air.

"Now, bless thee, sweet bird," sighed the stricken solitary; "thy wings are music, and thou a feathered ray camedst to light my darkened soul."

And from that to his orisons; and then to his tools with a little bit of courage; and this was his day's work:—

> *Veni Creator Spiritus*
> *Mentes tuorum visita*
> *Imple superna gratia*
> *Quae tu creasti pectora*
>
> *Accende lumen sensibus*
> *Mentes tuorum visita*
> *Infirma nostri corporis*
> *Virtute firmans perpetim.*

And so the days rolled on; and the weather got colder and Clement's heart got warmer; and despondency was rolling away; and by-and-by, somehow or another, it was gone. He had outlived it.

It had come like a cloud, and it went like one.

And presently all was reversed; his cell seemed illuminated with joy. His work pleased him; his prayers were full of unction; his psalms of praise. Hosts of little birds followed their crimson leader, and flying from snow, and a parish full of Cains, made friends one after another with Abel; fast friends. And one keen frosty night as he sang the praises of God to his tuneful psaltery, and his hollow cave rang forth the holy psalmody upon the night, as if that cave itself was Tubal's sounding shell, or David's harp, he heard a clear whine, not unmelodious; it became louder and less in tune. He peeped through the chinks of his rude door, and there sat a great red wolf moaning melodiously with his nose high in the air.

Clement was rejoiced. "My sins are going," he cried, "and the creatures of God are owning me, one after another." And in a burst of enthusiasm he struck up the laud:

"Praise Him all ye creatures of His!

"Let everything that hath breath praise the Lord."

And all the time he sang the wolf bayed at intervals.

But above all he seemed now to be drawing nearer to that celestial intercourse, which was the sign, and the bliss of the true hermit; for he had dreams about the saints and angels, so vivid, they were more like visions. He saw bright figures clad in woven snow. They bent on him eyes lovelier than those of the antelopes he had seen at Rome.

and fanned him with broad wings hued like the rainbow, and their
gentle voices bade him speed upon his course.

He had not long enjoyed this felicity, when his dreams began to
take another and a strange complexion. He wandered with Fra Colonna over the relics of antique nations, and the friar was lame and
had a staff, and this staff he waved over the mighty ruins, and were
they Egyptian, Greek, or Roman, straightway the temples and palaces
whose wrecks they were, rose again like an exhalation, and were
thronged with the famous dead. Songsters that might have eclipsed
both Apollo and his rival, poured forth their lays; women, godlike
in form, and draped like Minerva, swam round the marble courts in
voluptuous but easy and graceful dances. Here sculptors carved away
amidst admiring pupils, and forms of supernatural beauty grew out
of Parian marble in a quarter of an hour; and grave philosophers
conversed on high and subtle matters, with youth listening reverently;
it was a long time ago. And still beneath all this wonderful pan-
orama a sort of suspicion or expectation lurked in the dreamer's
mind. "This is a prologue, a flourish, there is something behind;
something that means me no good, something mysterious, awful."

And one night that the wizard Colonna had transcended himself,
he pointed with his stick, and there was a swallowing up of many
great ancient cities, and the pair stood on a vast sandy plain with a
huge crimson sun sinking to rest. There were great palm-trees; and
there were bulrush hives, scarce a man's height, dotted all about to
the sandy horizon, and the crimson sun.

"These are the anchorites of the Theban desert," said Colonna,
calmly; "followers not of Christ and his apostles, and the great
fathers, but of the Greek pupils of the Egyptian pupils of the Brach-
mans and Gymnosophists."

And Clement thought that he burned to go and embrace the holy
men and tell them his troubles, and seek their advice. But he was
tied by the feet somehow, and could not move, and the crimson sun
sank; and it got dusk, and the hives scarce visible. And Colonna's
figure became shadowy and shapeless, but his eyes glowed ten times
brighter: and this thing all eyes spoke and said: "Nay, let them
be, a pack of fools! see how dismal it all is." Then with a sudden
sprightliness, "But I hear one of them has a manuscript of Petronius,
on papyrus; I go to buy it, farewell for ever, for ever, for ever."

And it was pitch dark, and a light came at Clement's back like a gentle stroke; a glorious roseate light. It warmed as well as brightened. It loosened his feet from the ground; he turned round, and there, her face irradiated with sunshine, and her hair glittering like the gloriola of a saint, was Margaret Brandt.

She blushed and smiled and cast a look of ineffable tenderness on him. "Gerard," she murmured, "be whose thou wilt by day, but at night be mine!"

Even as she spoke, the agitation of seeing her so suddenly awakened him, and he found himself lying trembling from head to foot.

That radiant figure, and mellow voice, seemed to have struck his nightly keynote.

Awake he could pray, and praise, and worship God; he was master of his thoughts. But, if he closed his eyes in sleep, Margaret, or Satan in her shape, beset him, a seeming angel of light. He might dream of a thousand different things, wide as the poles asunder, ere he woke the imperial figure was sure to come and extinguish all the rest in a moment stellas exortus uti ætherius sol: for she came glowing with two beauties never before united, an angel's radiance and a woman's blushes.

Angels cannot blush. So he knew it was a fiend.

He was alarmed, but not so much surprised as at the demon's last artifice. From Anthony to Nicholas of the Rock scarce a hermit that had not been thus beset; sometimes with gay voluptuous visions, sometimes with lovely phantoms, warm, tangible, and womanly without, demons within, nor always baffled even by the saints. Witness that "angel form with a devil's heart," that came hanging its lovely head, like a bruised flower, to St. Macarius, with a feigned tale; and wept, and wept, and wept, and beguiled him first of his tears and then of half his virtue.

But with the examples of Satanic power and craft had come down copious records of the hermits' triumphs and the weapons by which they had conquered.

Domandum est corpus; the body must be tamed; this had been their watchword for twelve hundred years. It was a tremendous war-cry; for they called the earthly affections, as well as appetites, body; and crushed the whole heart through the suffering and mortified flesh.

Clement then said to himself that the great enemy of man had retired but to spring with more effect, and had allowed him a few

The Cloister and the Hearth

days of true purity and joy only to put him off his guard against the soft blandishments he was pouring over the soul, that had survived the buffeting of his black wings. He applied himself to tame the body; he shortened his sleep, lengthened his prayers, and increased his severe temperance to abstinence. Hitherto, following the ordinary rule, he had eaten only at sunset. Now he ate but once in forty-eight hours, drinking a litle water every day.

On this the visions became more distinct.

Then he flew to a famous antidote; to "the grand febrifuge" of anchorites—cold water.

He found the deepest part of the stream that ran by his cell; it rose not far off at a holy well; and, clearing the bottom of the large stones, made a hole where he could stand in water to the chin, and, fortified by so many examples, he sprang from his rude bed upon the next diabolical assault, and entered the icy water.

It made him gasp and almost shriek with the cold. It froze his marrow. "I shall die," he cried, "I shall die: but better this, than fire eternal."

And the next day he was so stiff in all his joints he could not move, and he seemed one great ache. And even in sleep he felt that his very bones were like so many raging teeth, till the phantom he dreaded came and gave one pitying smile, and all the pain was gone.

Then, feeling that to go into the icy water again, enfeebled by fasts, as he was, might perhaps carry the guilt of suicide, he scourged himself till the blood ran, and so lay down smarting.

And when exhaustion began to blunt the smart down to a throb, that moment the present was away, and the past came smiling back. He sat with Margaret at the duke's feast, the minstrels played divinely, and the purple fountains gushed. Youth and love reigned in each heart, and perfumed the very air.

Then the scene shifted and they stood at the altar together man and wife. And no interruption this time, and they wandered hand in hand, and told each other their horrible dreams. As for him "he had dreamed she was dead, and he was a monk; and really the dream had been so vivid and so full of particulars that only his eyesight could even now convince him it was only a dream, and they were really one."

And this new keynote once struck, every tune ran upon it. Awake he was Clement the hermit, risen from unearthly visions of the night, as dangerous as they were sweet; asleep he was Gerard Eliassoen, the happy husband of the loveliest and best, and truest girl in Holland: all the happier that he had been for some time the sport of hideous dreams, in which he had lost her.

His constant fasts, coupled with other austerities, and the deep mental anxiety of a man fighting with a supernatural foe, had now reduced him nearly to a skeleton; but still on those aching bones hung flesh unsubdued, quivering with an earthly passion; so however, he thought; "or why had ill spirits such power over him?" His opinion was confirmed, when one day he detected himself sinking to sleep actually with a feeling of complacency, because now Margaret would come and he should feel no more pain, and the unreal would be real, and the real unreal, for an hour.

On this he rose hastily with a cry of dismay, and stripping to the skin climbed up to the brambles above his cave, and flung himself on them, and rolled on them writhing with the pain: then he came into his den a mass of gore, and lay moaning for hours; till, out of sheer exhaustion, he fell into a deep and dreamless sleep.

He awoke to bodily pain, and mental exultation; he had broken the fatal spell. Yes, it was broken; another and another day passed, and her image molested him no more. But he caught himself sighing at his victory.

The birds got tamer and tamer, they perched upon his hand. Two of them let him gild their little claws. Eating but once in two days he had more to give them.

His tranquillity was not to last long.

A woman's voice came in from the outside, told him his own story in a very few words, and asked him to tell her where Gerard was to be found.

He was so astounded he could only say, with an instinct of self-defence, "Pray for the soul of Gerard, the son of Eli!" meaning that he was dead to the world. And he sat wondering.

When the woman was gone, he determined, after an inward battle, to risk being seen, and he peeped after her to see who it could be: but he took so many precautions, and she ran so quickly back to her friend that the road was clear.

"Satan!" said he, directly.

And that night back came his visions of earthly love and happiness so vividly, he could count every auburn hair in Margaret's head, and see the pupils of her eyes.

Then he began to despair, and said, "I must leave this country; here I am bound fast in memory's chain:" and began to dread his cell. He said "A breath from hell hath infected it, and robbed even these holy words of their virtue." And unconsciously imitating St. Jerome, a victim of earthly hallucinations, as overpowering, and coarser, he took his warmest covering out into the wood hard by, and there flung down under a tree that torn and wrinkled leather bag of bones, which a little ago might have served a sculptor for Apollo.

Whether the fever of his imagination intermitted, as a master mind of our day has shown that all things intermit,* or that this really broke some subtle link, I know not, but his sleep was dreamless.

He awoke nearly frozen, but warm with joy within.

"I shall yet be a true hermit, Dei gratiâ," said he.

The next day some good soul left on his little platform a new lambs-wool pelisse and cape, warm, soft, and ample.

He had a moment's misgiving on account of its delicious softness and warmth; but that passed. It was the right skin, † and a mark that Heaven approved his present course.

It restored warmth to his bones after he came in from his short rest.

And now, at one moment he saw victory before him if he could but live to it; at another, he said to himself, " 'Tis but another lull; be on thy guard, Clement."

And this thought agitated his nerves and kept him in continual awe.

He was like a soldier within the enemy's lines.

One night, a beautiful clear frosty night, he came back to his cell, after a short rest. The stars were wonderful. Heaven seemed a thousand times larger as well as brighter than earth, and to look with a thousand eyes instead of one.

"Oh, wonderful," he cried, "that there should be men who do crimes by night; and others scarce less mad, who live for this little world, and not for that great and glorious one, which nightly. to all eyes not blinded by custom, reveals its glowing glories. Thank God I am a hermit."

* Dr. Dickson, author of *Fallacies of the Faculty*, etc.

† It is related of a mediæval hermit, that being offered a garment made of cats' skins, he rejected it, saying, "I have heard of a lamb of God, but I never heard of a cat of God."

And in this mood he came to his cell door.

He paused at it; it was closed.

"Why, methought I left it open," said he. "The wind. There is not a breath of wind. What means this?"

He stood with his hand upon the rugged door. He looked through one of the great chinks, for it was much smaller in places than the aperture it pretended to close, and saw his little oil wick burning just where he had left it.

"How is it with me," he sighed, "when I start and tremble at nothing? Either I did shut it, or the fiend hath shut it after me to disturb my happy soul. Retro Sathanas!"

And he entered his cave rapidly, and began with somewhat nervous expedition to light one of his largest tapers. While he was lighting it, there was a soft sigh in the cave.

He started and dropped the candle just as it was lighting, and it went out.

He stooped for it hurriedly and lighted it, listening intently. When it was lighted he shaded it with his hand from behind, and threw the faint light all round the cell.

In the farthest corner the outline of the wall seemed broken.

He took a step towards the place with his heart beating.

The candle at the same time getting brighter, he saw it was the figure of a woman.

Another step with his knees knocking together.

IT WAS MARGARET BRANDT.

CHAPTER XCVI

HER attitude was one to excite pity rather than terror, in eyes not blinded by a preconceived notion. Her bosom was fluttering like a bird, and the red and white coming and going in her cheeks, and she had her hand against the wall by the instinct of timid things, she trembled so; and the marvellous mixed gaze of love, and pious awe, and pity, and tender memories, those purple eyes cast on the emaciated and glaring hermit, was an event in nature.

"Aha!" he cried. "Thou art come at last in flesh and blood; come to me as thou camest to holy Anthony. But I am ware of thee; I thought thy wiles were not exhausted. I am armed." With this he snatched up his small crucifix and held it out at her, astonished, and the candle in the other hand, both crucifix and candle shaking violently, "Exorcizo te."

"Ah, no!" cried she, piteously; and put out two pretty deprecating palms. "Alas! work me no ill! It is Margaret."

"Liar!" shouted the hermit. "Margaret was fair, but not so supernatural fair as thou. Thou didst shrink at that sacred name, thou subtle hypocrite. In Nomine Dei exorcizo vos."

"Ah, Jesu!" gasped Margaret, in extremity of terror, "curse me not! I will go home. I thought I might come. For very manhood be-Latin me not! Oh Gerard, is it thus you and I meet after all; after all?"

And she cowered almost to her knees, and sobbed with superstitious fear, and wounded affection.

Impregnated as he was with Satanophobia, he might perhaps have doubted still whether this distressed creature, all woman, and nature, was not all art, and fiend. But her spontaneous appeal to that sacred name dissolved his chimera; and let him see with his eyes, and hear with his ears.

He uttered a cry of self-reproach, and tried to raise her; but what with fasts, what with the over-powering emotion of a long solitude so broken, he could not. "What," he gasped shaking over her, "and is it thou? And have I met thee with hard words? Alas!" And they were both choked with emotion, and could not speak for a while.

"I heed it not much," said Margaret, bravely, struggling with her tears; "you took me for another: for a devil; oh! oh! oh! oh! oh!"

"Forgive me, sweet soul!" And as soon as he could speak more than a word at a time, he said, "I have been much beset by the evil one since I came here."

Margaret looked round with a shudder. "Like enow. Then oh take my hand, and let me lead thee from this foul place."

He gazed at her with astonishment.

"What, desert my cell; and go into the world again? Is it for that thou hast come to me?" said he, sadly and reproachfully.

"Ay, Gerard. I am come to take thee to thy pretty vicarage: art vicar of Gouda, thanks to Heaven and thy good brother Giles: and mother and I have made it so neat for thee, Gerard. 'Tis well enow in winter I promise thee. But bide a bit till the hawthorn bloom, and anon thy walls put on their kirtle of brave roses, and sweet woodbine. Have we forgotten thee, and the foolish things thou lovest? And, dear Gerard, thy mother is waiting; and 'tis late for her to be out of her bed: prithee; prithee; come! And the moment we are out of this foul hole I'll show thee a treasure thou hast gotten, and knowest nought on't, or sure hadst never fled from us so. Alas! what is to do? What have I ignorantly said; to be regarded thus?"

For he had drawn himself all up into a heap, and was looking at her with a strange gaze of fear and suspicion blended.

"Unhappy girl," said he, solemnly, yet deeply agitated, "would you have me risk my soul and yours for a miserable vicarage and the flowers that grow on it? But this is not thy doing: the bowelless fiend sends thee, poor simple girl, to me with this bait. But oh, cunning fiend, I will unmask thee even to this thine instrument, and she shall see thee, and abhor thee as I do. Margaret, my lost love, why am I here? Because I love thee."

"Oh! no, Gerard, you love me not, or you would not have hidden from me; there was no need."

"Let there be no deceit between us twain: that have loved so true; and after this night, shall meet no more on earth."

"Now God forbid!" said she.

"I love thee, and thou hast not forgotten me, or thou hadst married ere this, and hadst not been the one to find me, buried here from sight of man. I am a priest, a monk: what but folly or sin can come of you and me living neighbours, and feeding a passion innocent once, but now (so Heaven wills it) impious and unholy? No, though my heart break I must be firm. 'Tis I that am the man, 'tis I that am the priest. You and I must meet no more, till I am schooled by solitude, and thou art wedded to another."

"I consent to my doom but not to thine. I would ten times liever die; yet I will marry, ay, wed misery itself sooner than let thee lie in this foul dismal place, with yon sweet manse a waiting for thee." Clement groaned; at each word she spoke out stood clearer and clearer, two things—his duty, and the agony it must cost.

"My beloved," said he, with a strange mixture of tenderness and dogged resolution, "I bless thee for giving me one more sight of thy sweet face, and may God forgive thee, and bless thee, for destroying in a minute the holy peace it hath taken six months of solitude to build. No matter. A year of penance will, Dei gratiâ, restore me to my calm. My poor Margaret, I seem cruel: yet I am kind: 'tis best we part; ay, this moment."

"Part, Gerard? Never: we have seen what comes of parting. Part? Why you have not heard half my story; no nor the tithe. 'Tis not for thy mere comfort I take thee to Gouda manse. Hear me!"

"I may not. Thy very voice is a temptation with its music, memory's delight."

"But I say you shall hear me, Gerard, for forth this place I go not unheard."

"Then must we part by other means," said Clement, sadly.

"Alack! what other means? Wouldst put me to thine own door, being the stronger?"

"Nay, Margaret, well thou knowest I would suffer many deaths rather than put force on thee; thy sweet body is dearer to me than my own: but a million times dearer to me are our immortal souls, both thine and mine. I have withstood this direst temptation of all long enow. Now I must fly it: farewell! farewell!"

He made to the door, and had actually opened it and got half out, when she darted after and caught him by the arm.

"Nay, then another must speak for me. I thought to reward thee for yielding to me: but unkind that thou art, I need his help I find; turn then this way one moment."

"Nay, nay."

"But I say ay! And then turn thy back on us an thou canst." She somewhat relaxed her grasp, thinking he would never deny her so small a favour. But at this he saw his opportunity and seized it.

"Fly, Clement, fly!" he almost shrieked, and, his religious enthusiasm giving him for a moment his old strength, he burst wildly away from her, and after a few steps bounded over the little stream and ran beside it, but finding he was not followed, stopped and looked back.

She was lying on her face, with her hands spread out.

Yes, without meaning it, he had thrown her down and hurt her. When he saw that, he groaned and turned back a step; but suddenly, by another impulse, flung himself into the icy water instead.

"There, kill my body!" he cried, "but save my soul!"

Whilst he stood there, up to his throat in liquid ice, so to speak, Margaret uttered one long, piteous moan, and rose to her knees.

He saw her as plain almost as in midday. Saw her face pale and her eyes glistening; and then in the still night he heard these words: "Oh, God! thou that knowest all, thou seest how I am used. Forgive me then! For I will not live another day." With this she suddenly started to her feet, and flew like some wild creature, wounded to death, close by his miserable hiding-place, shrieking:

"CRUEL!—CRUEL!—CRUEL!—CRUEL!"

What manifold anguish may burst from a human heart in a single syllable. There were wounded love, and wounded pride, and despair, and coming madness, all in that piteous cry. Clement heard, and it froze his heart with terror and remorse, worse than the icy water chilled the marrow of his bones.

He felt he had driven her from him for ever, and in the midst of his dismal triumph, the greatest he had won, there came an almost incontrollable impulse to curse the Church, to curse religion itself, for exacting such savage cruelty from mortal man. At last he crawled half dead out of the water, and staggered to his den. "I am safe here," he groaned; "she will never come near me again; unmanly, ungrateful wretch that I am." And he flung his emaciated, frozen body down on the floor, not without a secret hope that it might never rise thence alive.

But presently he saw by the hour-glass that it was past midnight. On this he rose slowly and took off his wet things, and moaning all the time at the pain he had caused her he loved, put on the old hermit's cilice of bristles, and over that his breastplate. He had never worn either of these before, doubting himself worthy to don the arms of that tried soldier. But now he must give himself every aid: the bristles might distract his earthly remorse by bodily pain, and there might be holy virtue in the breastplate.

Then he kneeled down and prayed God humbly to release him that very night from the burden of the flesh. Then he lighted all his candles and recited his psalter doggedly: each word seemed to come like a lump of lead from a leaden heart, and to fall leaden to the ground: and in this mechanical office every now and then he moaned with all his soul. In the midst of which he suddenly observed a little bundle in the corner he had not seen before in the feebler light, and at one end of it something like gold spun into silk.

He went to see what it could be; and he had no sooner viewed it closer than he threw up his hands with rapture, "It is a seraph," he whispered, "a lovely seraph. Heaven hath witnessed my bitter trial, and approves my cruelty; and this flower of the skies is sent to cheer me, fainting under my burden."

He fell on his knees, and gazed with ectasy on its golden hair, and its tender skin and cheeks like a peach.

"Let me feast my sad eyes on thee ere thou leavest me for thine ever-blessed abode, and my cell darkens again at thy parting, as it did at hers."

With all this the hermit disturbed the lovely visitor. He opened wide two eyes, the colour of heaven; and seeing a strange figure kneeling over him, he cried piteously: "MUM—MA! MUM—MA!" And the tears began to run down his little cheeks.

Perhaps, after all, Clement, who for more than six months had not looked on the human face divine, estimated childish beauty more justly than we can; and in truth, this fair northern child, with its long golden hair, was far more angelic than any of our imagined angels. But now the spell was broken.

Yet not unhappily. Clement, it may be remembered, was fond of children, and true monastic life fosters this sentiment. The innocent distress on the cherubic face, the tears that ran so smoothly from those transparent violets, his eyes, and his pretty, dismal cry for his only friend, his mother, went through the hermit's heart. He employed all his gentleness and all his art to sooth him, and, as the little soul was wonderfuly intelligent for his age, presently succeeded so far that he ceased to cry out, and wonder took the place of fear, while in silence, broken only in little gulps, he scanned, with great tearful eyes, this strange figure that looked so wild, but spoke so kindly, and wore armour, yet did not kill little boys, but coaxed them. Clement was equally perplexed to know how this little human flower came to lie sparkling and blooming in his gloomy cave. But he remembered he had left the door wide open, and he was driven to conclude that, owing to this negligence, some unfortunate creature of high or low degree had seized this opportunity to get rid of her child for ever.* At this his bowels yearned so over the poor deserted cherub that the tears of pure tenderness stood in his eyes, and still, beneath the crime of the mother, he saw the divine goodness, which had so directed her heartlessness as to comfort his servant's breaking heart.

"Now bless thee, bless thee, bless thee, sweet innocent, I would not change thee for e'en a cherub in heaven."

"At's pooty," replied the infant, ignoring contemptuously, after the manner of infants, all remarks that did not interest him.

"What is pretty here, my love, beside thee?"

"Ookum-gars," † said the boy, pointing to the hermit's breast-plate.

"Quot liberi, tot sententiunculæ!" Hector's child screamed at his father's glittering casque and nodding crest: and here was a mediæval babe charmed with a polished cuirass, and his griefs assuaged.

"There are prettier things here than that," said Clement, "there are little birds; lovest thou birds?"

"Nay. Ay. En um ittle, ery ittle? Not ike torks. Hate torks; um bigger an baby."

He then confided, in very broken language, that the storks, with their great flapping wings, scared him, and were a great trouble and worry to him, darkening his existence more or less.

"Ay, but my birds are very little, and good, and oh, so pretty!"

"Den I ikes 'm," said the child, authoritatively. "I ont my mammy."

"Alas, sweet dove! I doubt I shall have to fill her place as best I may. Hast thou no daddy as well as mammy, sweet one?"

Now not only was this conversation from first to last, the relative ages, situations, and all circumstances of the parties considered, as strange a one as ever took place between two mortal creatures, but at or within a second or two of the hermit's last question, to turn the strange into the marvellous, came an unseen witness, to whom every word that passed carried ten times the force it did to either of the speakers.

Since, therefore, it is with her eyes you must now see, and hear with her ears, I go back a step for her.

---

* More than one hermit had received a present of this kind.

† Query? "looking-glass."

The Cloister and the Hearth

Margaret, when she ran past Gerard, was almost mad. She was in that state of mind in which affectionate mothers have been known to kill their children, sometimes along with themselves, sometimes alone, which last is certainly maniacal. She ran to Reicht Heynes pale and trembling, and clasped her round the neck. "Oh, Reicht! oh, Reicht!" and could say no more. Reicht kissed her and began to whimper; and, would you believe it, the great mastiff uttered one long whine: even his glimmer of sense taught him grief was afoot.

"Oh, Reicht!" moaned the despised beauty, as soon as she could utter a word for choking, "see how he has served me;" and she showed her hands that were bleeding with falling on the stony ground. "He threw me down, he was so eager to fly from me. He took me for a devil; he said I came to tempt him. Am I the woman to tempt a man? you know me, Reicht."

"Nay, in sooth, sweet Mistress Margaret, the last i' the world."

"And he would not look at my child. I'll fling myself and him into the Rotter this night."

"Oh fie, fie! eh, my sweet woman, speak not so. Is any man that breathes worth your child's life?"

"My child! where is he? Why, Reicht, I have left him behind. Oh shame! is it possible I can love him to that degree as to forget my child? Ah! I am rightly served for it."

And she sat down, and faithful Reicht beside her, and they sobbed in one another's arms.

After a while Margaret left off sobbing and said, doggedly, "Let us go home."

"Ay, but the bairn?"

"Oh! he is well where he is. My heart is turned against my very child. *He* cares nought for him; wouldn't see him, nor hear speak of him; and I took him there so proud, and made his hair so nice I did, and put his new frock and cowl on him. Nay, turn about: it's his child as well as mine; let him keep it awhile: mayhap that will learn him to think more of its mother and his own."

"High words off an empty stomach," said Reicht.

"Time will show. Come thou home."

They departed, and Time did show quicker than he levels abbeys, for at the second step Margaret stopped, and could neither go one way nor the other, but stood stock still.

"Reicht," said she, piteously, "what else have I on earth? I cannot."

"Who ever said you could? Think you I paid attention? Words are woman's breath. Come back for him without more ado; 'tis time we were in our beds, much more he."

Reicht led the way, and Margaret followed readily enough in that direction; but as they drew near the cell she stopped again.

"Reicht, go you and ask him will he give me back my boy; for I could not bear the sight of him."

"Alas! mistress, this do seem a sorry ending after all that hath been betwixt you twain. Bethink thee now, doth thine heart whisper no excuse for him? dost verily hate him for whom thou hast waited so long? Oh weary world!"

"Hate him, Reicht? I would not harm a hair of his head for all that is in nature; but look on him I cannot; I have taken a horror of him. Oh! when I think of all I have suffered for him, and what I came here this night to do for him, and brought my own darling to kiss him and call him father. Ah; Luke, my poor chap, my wound showeth me thine. I have thought too little of thy pangs, whose true affection I despised: and now my own is despised Reicht, if the poor lad was here now, he would have a good chance."

"Well, he is not far off," said Reicht Heynes, but somehow she did not say it with alacrity.

"Speak not to me of any man," said Margaret, bitterly, "I hate them all."

"For the sake of one?"

"Flout me not, but prithee go forward and get me what *is* my own, my sole joy in the world. Thou knowest I am on thorns till I have him to my bosom again."

Reicht went forward; Margaret sat by the roadside and covered her face with her apron, and rocked herself after the manner of her country, for her soul was full of bitterness and grief. So severe, indeed, was the internal conflict, that she did not hear Reicht running back to her, and started violently when the young woman laid a hand upon her shoulder.

"Mistress Margaret!" said Reicht, quietly, "take a fool's advice that loves ye. Go softly to yon cave wi' all the ears and eyes your mother ever gave you."

"Why?—what,—Reicht?" stammered Margaret.

"I thought the cave was afire, 'twas so light inside; and there were voices."

"Voices?"

"Ay, not one, but twain, and all unlike—a man's and a little child's, talking as pleasant as you and me. I am no great hand at a keyhole for my part, 'tis paltry work; but if so be voices were talking in yon cave, and them that owned those voices were so near to me as those are to thee, I'd go on all fours like a fox, and I'd crawl on my belly like a serpent, ere I'd lose one word that passes *atwixt those twain.*"

"Whisht, Reicht! Bless thee! Bide thou here. Buss me! Pray for me!"

And almost ere the agitated words had left her lips Margaret was flying towards the hermitage as noiselessly as a lapwing. Arrived near it, she crouched, and there was something truly serpentine in the gliding, flexible, noiseless movements by which she reached the very door, and there she found a chink and listened. And often it cost her a struggle not to burst in upon them, but warned by defeat, she was cautious and resolute to let well alone. And after a while slowly and noiselessly she reared her head, like a snake its crest, to where she saw the broadest chink of all, and looked with all her eyes and soul, as well as listened.

The little boy then being asked whether he had no daddy, at first shook his head, and would say nothing; but being pressed, he suddenly seemed to remember something, and said he, "Dad—da ill man; run away and leave poor mum—ma."

She who heard this winced. It was as new to her as to Clement. Some interfering foolish woman had gone and said this to the boy, and now out it came in Gerard's very face. His answer surprised her; he burst out, "The villain! the monster! he must be born without bowels to desert thee, sweet one. Ah! he little knows the joy he hath turned his back on. Well, my little dove, I must be father and mother to thee, since the one runs away, and t'other abandons thee to my care. Now to-morrow I shall ask the good people, that bring me my food, to fetch some nice eggs and milk for thee as well; for bread is good enough for poor old good-for-nothing me, but not for thee. And I shall teach thee to read."

"I can yead, I can yead."

"Ay verily, so young? all the better; we will read good books together, and I shall show thee the way to heaven. Heaven is a beautiful place, a thousand times fairer and better than earth, and there be little cherubs like thyself, in white, glad to welcome thee and love thee. Wouldst like to go to heaven one day?"

"Ay, along wi'—my—mammy."

"What, not without her then?"

"Nay. I ont my mammy. Where is my mammy?"

(Oh! what it cost poor Margaret not to burst in and clasp him to her heart!)

"Well, fret not, sweetheart, mayhap she will come when thou art asleep. Wilt thou be good now and sleep?"

"I not eepy. Ikes to talk."

"Well, talk we then; tell me thy pretty name."

"Baby." And he opened his eyes with amazement at this great hulking creature's ignorance.

"Hast none other?"

"Nay."

"What shall I do to pleasure thee, baby? Shall I tell thee a story?"

"I ikes tories," said the boy, clapping his hands.

"Or sing thee a song?"

"I ikes tongs," and he became excited.

"Choose then, a song or a story."

"Ting I a tong. Nay, tell I a tory. Nay, ting I a tong. Nay—." And the corners of his little mouth turned down and he had half a mind to weep because he could not have both, and could not tell which to forego. Suddenly his little face cleared, "Ting I a tory," said he.

"Sing thee a story, baby? Well, after all, why not? And wilt thou sit o' my knee and hear it?"

"Yea."

"Then I must 'een doff this breastplate. 'Tis too hard for thy soft cheek. So. And now I must doff this bristly cilice; they would prick thy tender skin, perhaps make it bleed, as they have me, I see. So. And now I put on my best pelisse, in honour of thy worshipful visit. See how soft and warm it is; bless the good soul that sent it; and now I sit me down; so. And I take thee on my left knee, and put my arm under thy little head: so. And then the psaltery, and play a little tune; so, not too loud."

"I ikes dat."

"I am right glad on't. Now list the story."

He chanted a child's story in a sort of recitative, singing a little moral refrain now and then. The boy listened with rapture.

"I ikes oo," said he. "Ot is oo? is oo a man?"

"Ay, little heart, and a great sinner to boot."

"I ikes great tingers. Ting one other tory."

Story No. 2 was chanted.

"I ubbs oo," cried the child, impetuously. "Ot caft * is oo?"

"I am a hermit, love."

"I ubbs vermins. Ting other one."

But during this final performance, Nature suddenly held out her leaden sceptre over the youthful eyelids. "I is not eepy," whined he very faintly, and succumbed.

Clement laid down his psaltery softly and began to rock his new treasure in his arms, and to crone over him a little lullaby well known in Tergou, with which his own mother had often set him off.

And the child sank into a profound sleep upon his arm. And he stopped croning, and gazed on him with infinite tenderness, yet sadness; for, at that moment he could not help thinking what might have been but for a piece of paper with a lie in it.

He sighed deeply.

The next moment the moonlight burst into his cell, and with it, and in it, and almost as swift as it, Margaret Brandt was down at his knee with a timorous hand upon his shoulder.

"GERARD, YOU DO NOT REJECT US. YOU CANNOT."

CHAPTER XCVII

THE startled hermit glared from his nursling to Margaret, and from her to him, in amazement, equalled only by his agitation at her so unexpected return. The child lay asleep on his left arm, and she was at his right knee; no longer the pale, scared, panting girl he had overpowered so easily an hour or two ago, but an imperial beauty, with blushing cheeks and sparkling eyes, and lips sweetly parted in triumph, and her whole

* Craft. He means trade or profession.

face radiant with a look he could not quite read; for he had never yet seen it on her; maternal pride.

He stared and stared from the child to her, in throbbing amazement.

"Us?" he gasped at last. And still his wonder-stricken eyes turned to and fro.

Margaret was surprised in her turn. It was an age of impressions not facts. "What!" she cried, "doth not a father know his own child? and a man of God, too? Fie, Gerard, to pretend! nay, thou art too wise, too good, not to have—why I watched thee: and e'en now look at you twain! 'Tis thine own flesh and blood thou holdest to thine heart."

Clement trembled. "What words are these," he stammered, "this angel mine?"

"Whose else? since he is mine."

Clement turned on the sleeping child, with a look beyond the power of the pen to describe, and trembled all over, as his eyes seemed to absorb the little love.

Margaret's eyes followed his. "He is not a bit like me," said she, proudly; "but oh at whiles he is thy very image in little; and see this golden hair. Thine was the very colour at his age; ask mother else. And see this mole on his little finger; now look at thine own; there! 'Twas thy mother let me weet thou wast marked so before him; and oh, Gerard, 'twas this our child found thee for me; for by that little mark on thy finger I knew thee for his father, when I watched above thy window and saw thee feed the birds; here she seized the child's hand and kissed it eagerly, and got half of it into her mouth, heaven knows how. "Ah! bless thee, thou didst find thy poor daddy for her, and now thou hast made us friends again after our little quarrel; the first, the last. Wast very cruel to me but now, my poor Gerard, and I forgive thee; for loving of thy child."

"Ah! ah! ah! ah! ah!" sobbed Clement, choking.

And lowered by fasts, and unnerved by solitude, the once strong man was hysterical, and nearly fainting.

Margaret was alarmed, but, having experience, her pity was greater than her fear. "Nay, take not on so," she murmured soothingly, and put a gentle hand upon his brow. "Be brave! So, so.

Dear heart, thou art not the first man, that hath gone abroad, and come back richer by a lovely little self, than he went forth. Being a man of God take courage, and say He sends thee this to comfort thee for what thou hast lost in me; and that is not so very much, my lamb; for sure the better part of love shall ne'er cool here to thee, though it may in thine, and ought, being a priest, and parson of Gouda."

"I? priest of Gouda? Never!" murmured Clement, in a faint voice, "I am a friar of St. Dominic: yet speak on sweet music, tell me all that has happened thee, before we are parted again."

Now some would on this have exclaimed against parting at all, and raised the true question in dispute. But such women as Margaret do not repeat their mistakes. It is very hard to defeat them *twice,* where their hearts are set on a thing.

She assented, and turned her back on Gouda manse as a thing not to be recurred to; and she told him her tale, dwelling above all on the kindness to her of his parents; and, while she related her troubles, his hand stole to hers, and often she felt him wince and tremble with ire, and often press her hand, sympathizing with her in every vein.

"Oh, piteous tale of a true heart battling alone against such bitter odds," said he.

"It all seems small, when I see thee here again, and nursing my boy. We have had a warning, Gerard. True friends like you and me are rare, and they are mad to part, ere death divideth them."

"And that is true," said Clement, off his guard.

And then she would have him tell her what he had suffered for her, and he begged her to excuse him, and she consented; but by questions quietly revoked her consent and elicited it all; and many a sigh she heaved for him, and more than once she hid her face in her hands with terror at his perils, though past.

And to console him for all he had gone through, she kneeled down and put her arms under the little boy, and lifted him gently up. "Kiss him softly," she whispered. "Again, again! kiss thy fill if thou canst; he is sound. 'Tis all I can do to comfort thee till thou art out of this foul den and in thy sweet manse yonder."

Clement shook his head.

"Well," said she, "let that pass. Know that I have been sore affronted for want of my lines."

"Who hath dared affront thee?"

"No matter, those that will do it again if thou hast lost them, which the saints forbid."

"I lose them? nay, there they lie, close to thy hand."

"Where, where, oh where?"

Clement hung his head. "Look in the Vulgate. Heaven forgive me: I thought thou wert dead, and a saint in heaven."

She looked, and on the blank leaves of the poor soul's Vulgate she found her marriage lines.

"Thank God!" she cried, "thank God! Oh, bless thee, Gerard, bless thee! Why what is here, Gerard?"

On the other leaves were pinned every scrap of paper she had ever sent him, and their two names she had once written together in sport, and the lock of her hair she had given him, and half a silver coin she had broken with him, and a straw she had sucked her soup with the first day he ever saw her.

When Margaret saw these proofs of love and signs of a gentle heart bereaved, even her exultation at getting back her marriage lines was overpowered by gushing tenderness. She almost staggered, and her hand went to her bosom, and she leaned her brow against the stone cell and wept so silently that he did not see she was weeping; indeed she would not let him, for she felt that to befriend him now she must be the stronger; and emotion weakens.

"Gerard," said she, "I know you are wise and good. You must have a reason for what you are doing, let it seem ever so unreasonable. Talk we like old friends. Why are you buried alive?"

"Margaret, to escape temptation. My impious ire against those two had its root in the heart; that heart then I must deaden, and, Dei gratiâ, I shall. Shall I, a servant of Christ and of the Church, court temptation? Shall I pray daily to be led out on't, and walk into it with open eyes?"

"That is good sense any way," said Margaret, with a consummate affection of candour.

"'Tis unanswerable," said Clement, with a sigh.

"We shall see. Tell me, have you escaped temptation here? Why I ask is, when _I_ am alone, my thoughts are far more wild and foolish than in company. Nay, speak sooth; come!"

"I must needs own I have been worse tempted here with evil imaginations than in the world."

The Cloister and the Hearth

"There now."

"Ay, but so were Anthony, and Jerome, Macarius, and Hilarion, Benedict, Bernard, and all the saints. 'Twill wear off."

"How do you know?"

"I feel sure it will."

"Guessing against knowledge. Here 'tis men folk are sillier than us that be but women. Wise in their own conceits, they will not let themselves see; their stomachs are too high to be taught by their eyes. A woman, if she went into a hole in a bank to escape temptation, and there found it, would just lift her farthingale and out on't, and not e'en know how wise she was, till she watched a man in like plight."

"Nay, I grant humility and a teachable spirit are the roads to wisdom; but, when all is said, here I wrestle but with imagination. At Gouda she I love as no priest or monk must love any but the angels, she will tempt a weak soul, unwilling, yet not loth, to be tempted."

"Aye that is another matter; _I_ should tempt thee then? to what, i' God's name?"

"Who knows? The flesh is weak."

"Speak for yourself, my lad. Why you are thinking of some other Margaret, not Margaret à Peter. Was ever my mind turned to folly and frailty? Stay, is it because you were my husband once, as these lines avouch? Think you the road to folly is beaten for you more than for another? Oh! how shallow are the wise, and how little able are you to read me, who can read you so well from top to toe. Come, learn thy A B C. Were a stranger to proffer me unchaste love, I should shrink a bit, no doubt, and feel sore, but I should defend myself without making a coil; for men, I know, are so, the best of them sometimes. But if you, that have been my husband, and are my child's father, were to offer to humble me so in mine own eyes, and thine, and his, either I should spit in thy face, Gerard, or, as I am not a downright vulgar woman, I should snatch the first weapon at hand and strike thee dead."

And Margaret's eyes flashed fire, and her nostrils expanded, that it was glorious to see; and no one that did see her could doubt her sincerity.

"I had not the sense to see that," said Gerard, quietly. And he pondered.

Margaret eyed him in silence, and soon recovered her composure. "Let not you and I dispute," said she, gently; "speak we of other things. Ask me of thy folk."

"My father?"

"Well, and warms to thee and me. Poor soul, a drew glaive on those twain that day, but Jorian Ketel and I we mastered him, and he drove them forth his house for ever."

"That may not be; he must take them back."

"That he will never do for us. You know the man; he is dour as iron: yet would he do it for one word from one that will not speak it."

"Who?"

"The vicar of Gouda. The old man will be at the manse to-morrow, I hear."

"How you come back to that."

"Forgive me: I am but a woman. It is us for nagging; shouldst keep me from it wi' questioning of me."

"My sister Kate?"

"Alas!"

"What hath ill befallen e'en that sweet lily? Out and alas!"

"Be calm, sweetheart, no harm hath her befallen. Oh, nay, nay, far fro' that." Then Margaret forced herself to be composed, and in a low sweet, gentle voice she murmured to him thus: "My poor Gerard, Kate hath left her trouble behind her. For the manner on't, 'twas like the rest. Ah; such as she saw never thirty, nor ever shall while earth shall last. She smiled in pain too. A well, then, thus 'twas; she was took wi' a languor and a loss of all her pains."

"A loss of her pains? I understand you not."

"Ay, you are not experienced; indeed, e'en thy mother almost blinded herself, and said, ''tis maybe a change for the better.' But Joan Ketel, which is an understanding woman, she looked at her and said, 'Down sun, down wind!' And the gossips sided and said, 'Be brave, you that are her mother, for she is half way to the saints.' And thy mother wept sore, but Kate would not let her; and one very ancient woman, she said to thy mother, 'She will die as easy as she lived hard.' And she lay painless best part of three days, a sipping of heaven aforehand. And, my dear, when she was just parting, she asked for 'Gerard's little boy,' and I brought him and set him on the bed, and the little thing behaved as peaceably as he does now. But by this time she was past speaking: but she pointed to a drawer, and her mother knew what to look for: it was two gold angels thou hadst given her years ago. Poor soul! she had kept them till thou shouldst come home. And she nodded towards the little boy, and looked anxious: but we understood her, and put the pieces in his two hands, and, when his little fingers closed on them, she smiled content. And so she gave her little earthly treasures to her favourite's child—for you *were* her favourite—and her immortal jewel to God, and passed so sweetly we none of us knew justly when she left us. Well-a-day, well-a-day!"

Gerard wept.

"She hath not left her like on earth," he sobbed. "Oh how the affections of earth curl softly round my heart! I cannot help it: God made them after all. Speak on, sweet Margaret; at thy voice the past rolls its tides back upon me; the loves and the hopes of youth come fair and gliding into my dark cell, and darker bosom, on waves of memory and music."

"Gerard, I am loth to grieve you, but Kate cried a little when she first took ill, at you not being there to close her eyes."

Gerard sighed.

"You were within a league, but hid your face from her."

He groaned.

"There, forgive me for nagging; I am but a woman: you would not have been so cruel to your own flesh and blood knowingly, would you?"

"Oh, no."

"Well then, know that thy brother Sybrandt lies in my charge with a broken back, fruit of thy curse."

"Mea culpa! mea culpa!"

"He is very penitent; be yourself and forgive him this night!"

"I have forgiven him long ago."

"Think you he can believe that from any mouth but yours? Come! he is but about two butts' length hence."

"So near? Why where?"

"At Gouda manse. I took him there yestreen. For I know you, the curse was scarce cold on your lips when you repented it"

(Gerard nodded assent), "and I said to myself, Gerard will thank me for taking Sybrandt to die under his roof; he will not beat his breast and cry mea culpa, yet grudge three footsteps to quiet a withered brother on his last bed. He may have a bee in his bonnet, but he is not a hypocrite, a thing all pious words and uncharitable deeds."

Gerard literally staggered where he sat at this tremendous thrust.

"Forgive me for nagging," said she. "Thy mother too is waiting for thee. Is it well done to keep her on thorns so long? She will not sleep this night. Bethink thee, Gerard, she is all to thee that I am to this sweet child. Ah, I think so much more of mothers since I had my little Gerard. She suffered for thee, and nursed thee, and tended thee from boy to man. Priest, monk, hermit, call thyself what thou wilt, to her thou art but one thing; her child."

"Where is she?" murmured Gerard, in a quavering voice.

"At Gouda manse, wearing the night in prayer and care."

Then Margaret saw the time was come for that appeal to his reason she had purposely reserved till persuasion should have paved the way for conviction. So the smith first softens the iron by fire; and then brings down the sledge hammer.

She showed him, but in her own good straightforward Dutch, that his present life was only a higher kind of selfishness; spiritual egotism. Whereas a priest had no more right to care only for his own soul than only for his own body. That was not *his* path to heaven. "But," said she, "whoever yet lost his soul by saving the souls of others? the Almighty loves him who thinks of others, and when He shall see thee caring for the souls of the folk the duke hath put into thine hand, He will care ten times more for thy soul than He does now."

Gerard was struck by this remark. "Art shrewd in dispute," said he.

"Far from it," was the reply, "only my eyes are not bandaged with conceit.* So long as Satan walks the whole earth, tempting men, and so long as the sons of Belial do never lock themselves in caves, but run like ants, to and fro, corrupting others, the good man that skulks apart, plays the devil's game, or at least gives him the odds: thou a soldier of Christ? ask thy comrade Denys,

* I think she means prejudice.

who is but a soldier of the duke, ask him if ever he skulked in a hole and shunned the battle because forsooth in battle is danger as well as glory and duty. For thy sole excuse is fear; thou makest no secret on't. Go to; no duke nor king hath such cowardly soldiers as Christ hath. What was that you said in the church at Rotterdam about the man in the parable, that buried his talent in the earth and so offended the giver? Thy wonderful gift for preaching, is it not a talent, and a gift from thy creator?"

"Certes; such as it is."

"And hast thou laid it out? or buried it? To whom hast thou preached these seven months? to bats and owls? Hast buried it in one hole with thyself and thy once good wits.

"The Dominicans are the friars Preachers. 'Tis for preaching they were founded; so thou art false to Dominic as well as to his master.

"Do you remember, Gerard, when we were young together, which now are old before our time, as we walked handed in the fields, did you but see a sheep cast, ay three fields off, you would leave your sweetheart (by her good will), and run and lift the sheep for charity? Well then, at Gouda is not one sheep in evil plight, but a whole flock; some cast, some strayed, some sick, some tainted, some a being devoured, and all for the want of a shepherd. Where is their shepherd? lurking in a den like a wolf; a den in his own parish, out fie! out fie!

"I scented thee out, in part, by thy kindness to the little birds. Take note, you Gerard Eliassoen must love something, 'tis in your blood; you were born to't. Shunning man you do but seek earthly affection a peg lower than man."

Gerard interrupted her. "The birds are God's creatures, his innocent creatures, and I do well to love them, being God's creatures."

"What, are they creatures of the same God that we are, that he is who lies upon thy knee?"

"You know they are."

"Then what pretence for shunning us and being kind to them? Sith man is one of the animals, why pick him out to shun? Is't because he is of animals the paragon? What, you court the young of birds, and abandon your own young? Birds need but bodily food, and, having wings, deserve scant pity if they cannot fly and find it. But that sweet dove upon thy knee, he needeth not carnal only, but spiritual food. He is thine as well as mine: and I have done my share. He will soon be too much for me, and I look to Gouda's parson to teach him true piety and useful lore. Is he not of more value than many sparrows?"

Gerard started and stammered an affirmation. For she waited for his reply.

"You wonder," continued she, "to hear me quote holy writ so glib. I have pored over it this four years, and why? Not because God wrote it, but because I saw it often in thy hands ere thou didst leave me. Heaven forgive me; I am but a woman. What thinkest thou of this sentence? 'Let your work so shine before men that they may see your good works and glorify your Father which is in heaven!' What is a saint in a sink better than 'a light under a bushel'?

"Therefore, since the sheep committed to thy charge bleat for thee and cry: 'Oh desert us no longer, but come to Gouda manse;' since I, who know thee ten times better than thou knowest thyself, do pledge my soul it is for thy soul's weal to go to Gouda manse,—since duty to thy child, too long abandoned, call thee to Gouda Manse,—since thy sovereign, whom holy writ again bids thee honour, sends thee to Gouda manse,—since the Pope, whom the Church teaches thee to revere, hath absolved thee of thy monkish vows, and orders thee to Gouda manse—"

"Ah?"

"Since thy grey-haired mother watches for thee in dole and care, and turneth oft the hour-glass and sigheth sore that thou comest so slow to her at Gouda manse,—since thy brother, withered by thy curse, awaits thy forgiveness and thy prayers for his soul, now lingering in his body, at Gouda manse,—take thou up in thine arms the sweet bird wi' crest of gold that nestles to thy bosom, and give me thy hand; thy sweetheart erst and wife, and now thy friend, the truest friend to thee this night that ere man had; and come with me to Gouda manse!"

"IT IS THE VOICE OF AN ANGEL!" cried Clement loudly.

"Then hearken it, and come forth to Gouda manse!"

The battle was won.

Margaret lingered behind, cast her eye rapidly round the furniture, and selected the Vulgate and the psaltery. The rest she sighed at, and let it lie. The breastplate and the cilice of bristles she took and dashed with feeble ferocity on the floor. Then, seeing Gerard watch her with surprise from the outside, she coloured and said: "I am but a woman: 'little' will still be 'spiteful.'"

"Why encumber thyself with those? They are safe."

"Oh, she had a reason."

And with this they took the road to Gouda parsonage. The moon and stars were so bright, it seemed almost as light as day.

Suddenly Gerard stopped. "My poor little birds!"

"What of them?"

"They will miss their food. I feed them every day."

"The child hath a piece of bread in his cowl. Take that and feed them now, against the morn."

"I will. Nay, I will not. He is as innocent, and nearer to me and to thee."

Margaret drew a long breath. "'Tis well. Hadst taken it, I might have hated thee; I am but a woman."

When they had gone about a quarter of a mile, Gerard sighed. "Margaret," said he, "I must e'en rest; he is too heavy for me."

"Then give him me, and take thou these. Alas! alas! I mind when thou wouldst have run with the child on one shoulder, and the mother on t'other."

And Margaret carried the boy.

"I trow," said Gerard, looking down, "overmuch fasting is not good for a man."

"A many die of it each year, winter time," replied Margaret.

Gerard pondered these simple words, and eyed her askant, carrying the child with perfect ease. When they had gone nearly a mile, he said, with considerable surprise: "You thought it was but two butts' length."

"Not I."

"Why, you said so."

"That is another matter." She then turned on him the face of a Madonna. "I lied," said she, sweetly. "And to save your soul and body, I'd maybe tell a worse lie than that, at need. I am but a woman. Ah, well, it is but two butts' length from here at any rate."

"Without a lie?"

"Humph? Three, without a lie."

And sure enough, in a few minutes they came up to the manse.

The Cloister and the Hearth

A candle was burning in the vicar's parlour. "She is waking still," whispered Margaret.

"Beautiful! beautiful!" said Clement, and stopped to look at it.

"What, in Heaven's name?"

"That little candle, seen through the window at night. Look an it be not like some fair star of size prodigious: it delighteth the eyes and warmeth the heart of those outside."

"Come, and I'll show thee something better," said Margaret, and led him on tiptoe to the window.

They looked in, and there was Catherine kneeling on the hassock, with her "hours" before her.

"Folk can pray out of a cave," whispered Margaret. "Ay and hit heaven with their prayers. For 'tis for a sight of thee she prayeth; and thou art here. Now, Gerard, be prepared; she is not the woman you knew her; her children's troubles have greatly broken the brisk, light-hearted soul. And I see she has been weeping e'en now; she will have given thee up, being so late."

"Let me get to her," said Clement hastily, trembling all over.

"That door! I will bide here."

"When Gerard was gone to the door, Margaret, fearing the sudden surprise, gave one sharp tap at the window, and cried, "Mother!" in a loud, expressive voice that Catherine read at once. She clasped her hands together and had half risen from her kneeling posture, when the door burst open and Clement flung himself wildly on his knees at her knees, with his arms out to embrace her. She uttered a cry such as only a mother could. "Ah! my darling, my darling!" And clung sobbing round his neck. And true it was, she saw neither a hermit, a priest, nor a monk, but just her child, lost, and despaired of, and in her arms. And after a little while Margaret came in, with wet eyes and cheeks, and a holy calm of affection settled by degrees on these sore troubled ones. And they sat all three together, hand in hand, murmuring sweet and loving converse; and he who sat in the middle, drank right and left their true affection and their humble but genuine wisdom, and was forced to eat a good nourishing meal, and at daybreak was packed off to a snowy bed, and by-and-by awoke, as from a hideous dream, friar and hermit no more, Clement no more, but Gerard Eliassoen, parson of Gouda.

CHAPTER XCVIII

MARGARET went back to Rotterdam long ere Gerard awoke, and actually left her boy behind her. She sent the faithful, sturdy Reicht off to Gouda directly with a vicar's grey frock and large felt hat, and with minute instructions how to govern her new master.

Then she went to Jorian Ketel; for she said to herself, "he is the closest I ever met, so he is the man for me," and in concert with him she did two mortal sly things; yet not, in my opinion, virulent, though she thought they were; but if I am asked what were these deeds without a name, the answer is, that as she, who was "but a woman," kept them secret till her dying day, I, who am a man,— Verbum non amplius addam.

She kept away from Gouda parsonage.

Things that pass little noticed in the heat of argument, sometimes rankle afterwards; and, when she came to go over all that had passed, she was offended at Gerard's thinking she could ever forget the priest in the sometime lover. "For what did he take me?" said she. And this raised a great shyness which really she would not otherwise have felt, being downright innocent. And pride sided with modesty, and whispered "Go no more to Gouda parsonage."

She left little Gerard there to complete the conquest her maternal heart ascribed to him, not to her own eloquence and sagacity; and to anchor his father for ever to humanity.

But this generous stroke of policy cost her heart dear. She had never yet been parted from her boy an hour; and she felt sadly strange as well as desolate without him. After the first day it became intolerable; and what does the poor soul do, but creep at dark up to Gouda parsonage, and lurk about the premises like a thief till she saw Reicht Heynes in the kitchen alone. Then she tapped softly at the window and said, "Reicht, for pity's sake bring him out to me unbeknown." With Margaret the person who occupied her thoughts at the time ceased to have a name, and sank to a pronoun.

Reicht soon found an excuse for taking little Gerard out, and there was a scene of mutual rapture; followed by mutual tears when mother and boy parted again.

The Cloister and the Hearth

And it was arranged that Reicht should take him half way to Rotterdam every day, at a set hour, and Margaret meet them. And at these meetings, after the raptures, and after mother and child had gambolled together like a young cat and her first kitten, the boy would sometimes amuse himself alone at their feet, and the two women generally seized this opportunity to talk very seriously about Luke Peterson. This began thus:

"Reicht," said Margaret, "I as good as promised him to marry Luke Peterson. 'Say you the word,' quoth I, 'and I'll wed him.'"

"Poor Luke!"

"Prithee, why poor Luke?"

"To be bandied about so, atwixt yea and nay."

"Why, Reicht, you have not ever been so simple as to cast an eye of affection on the boy, that you take his part?"

"Me?" said Reicht, with a toss of the head.

"Oh, I ask your pardon. Well, then, you can do me a good turn."

"Whist! whisper! that little darling is listening to every word, and eyes like saucers."

On this both their heads would have gone under one cap.

Two women plotting against one boy? Oh you great cowardly serpents!

But when these stolen meetings had gone on about five days Margaret began to feel the injustice of it, and to be irritated as well as unhappy.

And she was crying about it, when a cart came to her door, and in it, clean as a new penny, his beard close shaved, his bands white as snow, and a little colour in his pale face, sat the vicar of Gouda in the grey frock and large felt hat she had sent him.

She ran upstairs directly and washed away all traces of her tears and put on a cap, which, being just taken out of the drawer, was cleaner, theoretically, than the one she had on; and came down to him.

He seized both her hands and kissed them, and a tear fell upon them. She turned her head away at that to hide her own which started.

"My sweet Margaret," he cried, "why is this? Why hold you

672

aloof from your own good deed? we have been waiting and waiting for you every day, and no Margaret."

"You said things."

"What! when I was a hermit; and a donkey."

"Ay! no matter, you said things. And you had no reason."

"Forget all I said there. Who hearkens the ravings of a maniac? for I see now that in a few months more I should have been a gibbering idiot: Yet no mortal could have persuaded me away but you. Oh what an outlay of wit and goodness was yours! But it is not here I can thank and bless you as I ought; no, it is in the home you have given me, among the sheep whose shepherd you have made me; already I love them dearly; there it is I must thank 'the truest friend ever man had.' So now I say to you as erst you said to me, come to Gouda manse."

"Humph! we will see about that."

"Why, Margaret, think you I had ever kept the dear child so long, but that I made sure you would be back to him from day to day? Oh he curls round my very heart strings, but what is my title to him compared to thine? Confess now, thou hast had hard thoughts of me for this."

"Nay, nay, not I. Ah! thou art thyself again; wast ever thoughtful of others. I have half a mind to go to Gouda manse, for your saying that."

"Come then, with half thy mind, 'tis worth the whole of other folk's."

"Well, I dare say I will; but there is no such mighty hurry," said she coolly (she was literally burning to go). "Tell me first how you agree with your folk."

"Why, already my poor have taken root in my heart."

"I thought as much."

"And there are such good creatures among them; simple, and rough, and superstitious, but wonderfully good."

"Oh! leave you alone for seeing a grain of good among a bushel of ill."

"Whisht; whisht! And, Margaret, two of them have been ill friends for four years, and came to the manse each to get on my blind side. But, give the glory to God, I got on their bright side, and made them friends and laugh at themselves for their folly."

"But are you in very deed their vicar? answer me that."

"Certes: have I not been to the bishop and taken the oath, and rung the church bell, and touched the altar, the missal, and the holy cup, before the churchwardens? And they have handed me the parish seal; see here it is. Nay 'tis a real vicar inviting a true friend to Gouda manse."

"Then my mind is at ease. Tell me oceans more."

"Well, sweet one, nearest to me of all my parish is a poor cripple that my guardian angel and his (her name thou knowest even by this turning of thy head away) hath placed beneath my roof. Sybrandt and I are that we never were till now, brothers. 'Twould gladden thee, yet sadden thee to hear how we kissed and forgave one another. He is full of thy praises, and wholly in a pious mind; he says he is happier since his trouble than e'er he was in the days of his strength. Oh! out of my house he ne'er shall go to any place but heaven."

"Tell me somewhat that happened thyself, poor soul! All this is good, but yet no tidings to me. Do I not know thee of old?"

"Well, let me see. At first I was much dazzled by the sunlight, and could not go abroad (owl!); but that is past; and good Reicht Heynes—humph!"

"What of her?"

"This to thine ear only, for she is a diamond. Her voice goes through me like a knife, and all voices seem loud but thine, which is so mellow sweet. Stay, now I'll fit ye with tidings: I spake yesterday with an old man that conceits he is ill-tempered, and sweats to pass for such with others, but oh! so threadbare, and the best good heart beneath."

"Why 'tis a parish of angels," said Margaret, ironically.

"Then why dost thou keep out on't?" retorted Gerard. "Well he was telling me there was no parish in Holland where the devil hath such power as at Gouda; and among his instances, says he, 'We had a hermit, the holiest in Holland; but, being Gouda, the devil came for him this week, and took him, bag and baggage: not a ha'porth of him left but a goodish piece of his skin, just for all the world like a hedgehog's, and a piece o' old iron furbished up."

Margaret smiled.

"Aye, but," continued Gerard, "the strange thing is, the cave has verily fallen in; and, had I been so perverse as resist thee, it had assuredly buried me dead there where I had buried myself alive. Therefore in this I see the finger of Providence, condemning my late, approving my present, way of life. What sayest thou?"

"Nay, can I pierce the like mysteries? I am but a woman."

"Somewhat more, methinks. This very tale proves thee my guardian angel, and all else avouches it: so come to Gouda manse."

"Well, go you on, I'll follow."

"Nay, in the cart with me."

"Not so."

"Why?"

"Can I tell why and wherefore, being a woman? All I know is I seem—to feel—to wish—to come alone."

"So be it then. I leave thee the cart, being, as thou sayest, a woman, and I'll go a-foot being a man again, with the joyful tidings of thy coming."

When Margaret reached the manse the first thing she saw was the two Gerards together, the son performing his capriccios on the plot, and the father slouching on a chair, in his great hat, with pencil and paper, trying very patiently to sketch him.

After a warm welcome he showed her his attempts. "But in vain I strive to fix him," said he, "for he is incarnate quicksilver. Yet do but note his changes, infinite, but none ungracious: all is supple and easy; and how he melteth from one posture to another." He added presently, "Woe to illuminators! looking on thee, sir baby, I see what awkward, lopsided, ungainly toads I and my fellows painted missals with, and called them cherubs and seraphs." Finally he threw the paper away in despair, and Margaret conveyed it secretly into her bosom.

At night when they sat round the peat fire he bade them observe how beautiful the brass candlesticks and other glittering metals were in the glow from the hearth. Catherine's eyes sparkled at this observation. "And oh the sheets I lie in here," said he, "often my conscience pricketh me and saith, 'Who art thou to lie in lint like web of snow?' Dives was ne'er so flaxed as I. And to think that there are folk in the world that have all the beautiful things which I have here, yet not content. Let them pass six months in a hermit's cell, seeing no face of man; then will they find how lovely and pleasant this wicked world is; and eke that men and women are God's fairest creatures. Margaret was always fair: but never to my eye so bright as now." Margaret shook her head incredulously. Gerard continued: "My mother was ever good and kind, but I noted not her exceeding comeliness till now."

"Nor I neither," said Catherine: "a score years ago I might pass in a crowd, but not now."

Gerard declared to her that each age had its beauty: "See this mild grey eye," said he, "that hath looked motherly love upon so many of us, all that love hath left its shadow, and that shadow is a beauty which defieth Time. See this delicate lip, these pure white teeth. See this 'well-shaped brow, where comeliness just passeth into reverence. Art beautiful in my eyes, mother dear."

"And that is enough for me, my darling. 'Tis time you were in bed, child. Ye have to preach the morn."

And Reicht Heynes and Catherine interchanged a look, which said, "We two have an amiable maniac to superintend; calls everything beautiful."

The next day was Sunday; and they heard him preach in his own church. It was crammed with persons, who came curious, but remained devout. Never was his wonderful gift displayed more powerfully: he was himself deeply moved by the first sight of all his people, and his bowels yearned over this flock he had so long neglected. In a single sermon, which lasted two hours and seemed to last but twenty minutes, he declared the whole scripture: he terrified the impenitent and thoughtless, confirmed the wavering, consoled the bereaved and the afflicted, uplifted the hearts of the poor, and, when he ended, left the multitude standing, rapt, and unwilling to believe the divine music of his voice and soul had ceased.

Need I say that two poor women in a corner sat entranced, with streaming eyes.

"Wherever gat he it all?" whispered Catherine with her apron to her eyes. "By our Lady not from me."

As soon as they were by themselves Margaret threw her arms round Catherine's neck and kissed her.

"Mother, mother, I am not quite a happy woman, but oh I am a proud one."

And she vowed on her knees never by word or deed to let her love come between this young saint and heaven.

Reader, did you ever stand by the sea-shore after a storm, when the wind happens to have gone down suddenly? The waves cannot cease with their cause; indeed, they seem at first to the ear to lash the sounding shore more fiercely than while the wind blew. Still we are conscious that inevitable calm has begun, and is now but rocking them to sleep. So it was with those true and tempest-tossed lovers from that eventful night, when they went hand in hand beneath the stars from Gouda hermitage to Gouda manse.

At times a loud wave would every now and then come roaring; but it was only memory's echo of the tempest that had swept their lives: the storm itself was over; and the boiling waters began from that moment to go down, down, down, gently, but inevitably.

This image is to supply the place of interminable details, that would be tedious and tame. What best merits attention at present, is the general situation, and the strange complication of feeling that arose from it. History itself, though a far more daring storyteller than romance, presents few things so strange * as the footing on which Gerard and Margaret now lived for many years. United by present affection, past familiarity, and a marriage irregular, but legal; separated by holy Church and by their own consciences which sided unreservedly with holy Church: separated by the Church, but united by a living pledge of affection, lawful in every sense at its date.

And living but a few miles from one another, and she calling his mother "mother." For some years she always took her boy to Gouda on Sunday, returning home at dark. Go when she would, it was always fête at Gouda manse, and she was received like a little queen. Catherine, in these days, was nearly always with her, and Eli very often. Tergou had so little to tempt them, compared with Rotterdam; and at last they left it altogether, and set up in the capital.

And thus the years glided: so barren now of striking incidents, so void of great hopes, and free from great fears, and so like one

* Let me not be understood to apply this to the bare outline of the relation. Many bishops and priests, and not a few popes had wives and children as laymen; and entering orders were parted from the wives and not from the children. But in the case before the reader are the additional features of a strong surviving attachment on both sides, and of neighbourhood, besides that here the man had been led into holy orders by a false statement of the woman's death. On a summary of all the essential features, the situation was, to the best of my belief, unique.

another, that without the help of dates I could scarcely indicate the progress of time.

However, early next year, 1471, the Duchess of Burgundy with the open dissent, but secret connivance of the duke, raised forces to enable her dethroned brother, Edward the Fourth of England, to invade that kingdom; our old friend Denys thus enlisted, and passing through Rotterdam to the ships, heard on his way that Gerard was a priest, and Margaret alone. On this he told Margaret that marriage was not a habit of his, but that as his comrade had put it out of his own power to keep troth, he felt bound to offer to keep it for him; "for a comrade's honour is dear to us as our own," said he.

She stared, then smiled, "I choose rather to be still thy she-comrade," said she; "closer acquainted we might not agree so well." And in her character of she-comrade she equipped him with a new sword of Antwerp make, and a double handful of silver. "I give thee no gold," said she; "for 'tis thrown away as quick as silver, and harder to win back. Heaven send thee safe out of all thy perils; there be famous fair women yonder to beguile thee with their faces, as well as men to hash thee with their axes."

He was hurried on board at La Vere, and never saw Gerard at that time.

In 1473, Sybrandt began to fail. His pitiable existence had been sweetened by his brother's inventive tenderness, and his own contented spirit, which, his antecedents considered, was truly remarkable. As for Gerard, the day never passed that he did not devote two hours to him; reading or singing to him, praying with him, and drawing him about in a soft carriage Margaret and he had made between them. When the poor soul found his end near, he begged Margaret might be sent for; she came at once, and almost with his last breath he sought once more that forgiveness she had long ago accorded. She remained by him till the last; and he died blessing and blessed, in the arms of the two true lovers he had parted for life. Tantum religio scit suadere boni.

1474 there was a wedding in Margaret's house. Luke Peterson and Reicht Heynes.

This may seem less strange if I give the purport of the dialogue interrupted some time back.

Margaret went on to say; "Then in that case you can easily

make him fancy you, and for my sake you must, for my conscience it pricketh me and I must needs fit him with a wife, the best I know." Margaret then instructed Reicht to be always kind and good humoured to Luke; and she would be a model of peevishness to him. "But be not thou so simple as run me down," said she. "Leave that to me. Make thou excuses for me; I will make myself black enow."

Reicht received these instructions like an order to sweep a room, and obeyed them punctually.

When they had subjected poor Luke to this double artillery for a couple of years, he got to look upon Margaret as his fog and wind, and Reicht as his sunshine: and his affections transferred themselves, he scarce knew how or when.

On the wedding day Reicht embraced Margaret and thanked her almost with tears. "He was always my fancy," said she, "from the first hour I clapped eyes on him."

"Heyday, you never told me that. What, Reicht, are you as sly as the rest?"

"Nay, nay," said Reicht eagerly; "but I never thought you would really part with him to me. In my country the mistress looks to be served before the maid."

Margaret settled them in her shop, and gave them half the profits.

1476 and 7, were years of great trouble to Gerard, whose conscience compelled him to oppose the Pope. His Holiness, siding with the Grey Friars in their determination to swamp every palpable distinction between the Virgin Mary and her Son, bribed the Christian world into his crotchet by proffering pardon of all sins to such as would add to the Ave Mary, this clause: "and blessed be thy Mother Anna, from whom, without blot of original sin, proceeded thy virgin flesh."

Gerard, in common with many of the northern clergy, held this sentence to be flat heresy; he not only refused to utter it in his church, but warned his parishioners against using it in private; and he refused to celebrate the new feast the Pope invented at the same time, viz., "the feast of the miraculous conception of the Virgin."

But this drew upon him the bitter enmity of the Franciscans, and they were strong enough to put him into more than one serious difficulty, and inflict many a little mortification on him.

In emergencies he consulted Margaret, and she always did one of two things, either she said, "I do not see my way"; and refused to

guess; or else she gave him advice that proved wonderfully sagacious. He had genius; but she had marvellous tact.

And where affection came in and annihilated the woman's judgment, he stepped in his turn to her aid. Thus, though she knew
she was spoiling little Gerard, and Catherine was ruining him for
life, she would not part with him, but kept him at home, and his
abilities uncultivated. And there was a shrewd boy of nine years,
instead of learning to work and obey, playing about and learning
selfishness from their infinite unselfishness, and tyrannizing with a
rod of iron over two women, both of them sagacious and spirited, but
reduced by their fondness for him to the exact level of idiots.

Gerard saw this with pain, and interfered with mild but firm
remonstrance; and after a considerable struggle prevailed, and got
little Gerard sent to the best school in Europe, kept by one Haaghe
at Deventer: this was in 1477. Many tears were shed, but the great
progress the boy made at that famous school reconciled Margaret in
some degree, and the fidelity of Reicht Heynes, now her partner in
business, enabled her to spend weeks at a time hovering over her boy
at Deventer.

And so the years glided; and these two persons subjected to as
strong and constant temptation as can well be conceived, were
each other's guardian angels; and not each other's tempters.

To be sure the well greased morality of the next century, which
taught that solemn vows to God are sacred in proportion as they are
reasonable, had at that time entered no single mind; and the alternative to these two minds was self-denial, or sacrilege.

It was a strange thing to hear them talk with unrestrained tenderness to one another of their boy; and an icy barrier between themselves all the time.

Eight years had now passed thus, and Gerard, fairly compared
with men in general, was happy.

But Margaret was not.

The habitual expression of her face was a sweet pensiveness; but
sometimes she was irritable and a little petulant. She even snapped
Gerard now and then. And, when she went to see him, if a monk
was with him, she would turn her back and go home.

She hated the monks for having parted Gerard and her, and she
inoculated her boy with a contempt for them which lasted him till
his dying day.

The Cloister and the Hearth

Gerard bore with her like an angel. He knew her heart of gold, and hoped this ill gust would blow over.

He himself being now the right man in the right place this many years, loving his parishioners, and beloved by them, and occupied from morn till night in good works, recovered the natural cheerfulness of his disposition. To tell the truth, a part of his jocoseness was a blind: he was the greatest peacemaker, except Mr. Harmony in the play, that ever was born. He reconciled more enemies in ten years than his predecessors had done in three hundred; and one of his manœuvres in the peace-making art was to make the quarrellers laugh at the cause of quarrel. So did he undermine the demon of discord. But, independently of that, he really loved a harmless joke. He was a wonderful tamer of animals, squirrels, hares, fawns, &c. So half in jest, a parishoner who had a mule supposed to be possessed with a devil, gave it him, and said, "Tame this vagabone, parson, if ye can." Well, in about six months, Heaven knows how, he not only tamed Jack, but won his affections to such a degree, that Jack would come running to his whistle like a dog. One day, having taken shelter from a shower on the stone settle outside a certain public-house, he heard a toper inside, a stranger, boasting he could take more at a draught than any man in Gouda. He instantly marched in, and said, "What, lads, do none of ye take him up for the honour of Gouda? Shall it be said that there came hither one from another parish a greater sot than any of us? Nay, then, I your parson do take him up. Go to; I'll find thee a parishioner shall drink more at a draught than thou."

A bet was made: Gerard whistled; in clattered Jack—for he was taught to come into a room with the utmost composure—and put his nose into his backer's hand.

"A pair of buckets!" shouted Gerard, "and let us see which of these two sons of asses can drink most at a draught."

On another occasion two farmers had a dispute whose hay was the best. Failing to convince each other, they said, "We'll ask parson;" for by this time he was their referee in every mortal thing.

"How lucky you thought of me!" said Gerard. "Why, I have got one staying with me who is the best judge of hay in Holland. Bring me a double handful apiece."

So when they came, he had them into the parlour, and put each bundle on a chair. Then he whistled, and in walked Jack.

"Lord a mercy!" said one of the farmers.

"Jack," said the parson, in the tone of conversation, "just tell us which is the best hay of these two."

Jack sniffed them both, and made his choice directly; proving his sincerity by eating every morsel. The farmers slapped their thighs, and scratched their heads. "To think of we not thinking o' that." And they each sent Jack a truss.

So Gerard got to be called the merry parson of Gouda. But Margaret, who like most loving women had no more sense of humour than a turtledove, took this very ill. "What!" said she to herself, "is there nothing sore at the bottom of his heart that he can go about playing the zany?" She could understand pious resignation and content, but not mirth, in true lovers parted. And whilst her woman's nature was perturbed by this gust (and women seem more subject to gusts than men) came that terrible animal, a busybody, to work upon her. Catherine saw she was not happy, and said to her, "Your boy is gone from you. I would not live alone all my days if I were you."

"*He* is more alone than I," sighed Margaret.

"Oh, a man is a man: but a woman is a woman. You must not think all of him and none of yourself. Near is your kirtle, but nearer is your smock. Besides, he is a priest, and can do no better. But you are not a priest. He has got his parish, and his heart is in that. Bethink thee! Time flies; overstay not thy market. Wouldst not like to have three or four more little darlings about thy knee now they have robbed thee of poor little Gerard, and sent him to yon nasty school?" And so she worked upon a mind already irritated.

Margaret had many suitors ready to marry her at a word or even a look, and among them two merchants of the better class, Van Schelt and Oostwagen. "Take one of those two," said Catherine.

"Well, I will ask Gerard if I may," said Margaret one day with a flood of tears; "for I cannot go on the way I am."

"Why, you would never be so simple as ask *him*?"

"Think you I would be so wicked as marry without his leave?"

Accordingly she actually went to Gouda, and after hanging her head, and blushing, and crying, and saying she was miserable, told him his mother wished her to marry one of those two; and if he approved of her marrying at all, would he use his wisdom, and tell her which he thought would be the kindest to the little Gerard of those two; for herself she did not care what became of her.

Gerard felt as if she had put a soft hand into his body, and torn his heart out with it. But the priest with a mighty effort mastered the man. In a voice scarcely audible he declined this responsibility. "I am not a saint or a prophet," said he; "I might advise thee ill. I shall read the marriage service for thee," faltered he; "it is my right. No other would pray for thee as I should. But thou must choose for thyself: and oh! let me see thee happy. This four months past thou hast not been happy."

"A discontented mind is never happy," said Margaret.

She left him, and he fell on his knees, and prayed for help from above.

Margaret went home pale and agitated. "Mother," said she, "never mention it to me again, or we shall quarrel."

"He forbade you? Well, more shame for him, that is all."

"He forbid me? He did not condescend so far. He was as noble as I was paltry. He would not choose for me for fear of choosing me an ill husband. But he would read the service for my groom and me: that was his right. Oh, mother, what a heartless creature I was!"

"Well, I thought not he had that much sense."

"Ah, you go by the poor soul's words: but I rate words as air when the face speaketh to mine eye. I saw the priest and the true lover a fighting in his dear face, and his cheek pale with the strife, and oh! his poor lip trembled as he said the stout-hearted words— Oh! oh! oh! oh! oh! oh! oh!" And Margaret burst into a violent passion of tears.

Catherine groaned. "There, give it up without more ado," said she. "You two are chained together for life; and, if God is merciful, that won't be for long; for what are you? neither maid, wife, nor widow."

"Give it up?" said Margaret: "that was done long ago. All I think of now is comforting him; for now I have been and made him unhappy too, wretch and monster that I am."

So the next day they both went to Gouda. And Gerard, who had been praying for resignation all this time, received her with peculiar tenderness as a treasure he was to lose; for she was agitated and eager to let him see without words that she would never marry, and she fawned on him like a little dog to be forgiven. And as she was going away she murmured, "Forgive! and forget! I am but a woman."

He misunderstood her, and said, "All I bargain for is, let me see thee content; for pity's sake, let me not see thee unhappy as I have this while."

"My darling, you never shall again," said Margaret, with streaming eyes, and kissed his hand.

He misunderstood this too at first; but when month after month passed, and he heard no more of her marriage, and she came to Gouda comparatively cheerful, and was even civil to Father Ambrose, a mild benevolent monk from the Dominican convent hard by—then he understood her; and one day he invited her to walk alone with him in the sacred paddock: and before I relate what passed between them, I must give its history. When Gerard had been four or five days at the manse looking out of window, he uttered an exclamation of joy. "Mother, Margaret, here is one of my birds: another, another; four, six, nine. A miracle! a miracle!"

"Why, how can you tell your birds from their fellows?" said Catherine.

"I know every feather in their wings. And see: there is the little darling whose beak I gilt, bless it!"

And presently his rapture took a serious turn, and he saw Heaven's approbation in this conduct of the birds as he did in the fall of the cave. This wonderfully kept alive his friendship for animals: and he enclosed a paddock, and drove all the sons of Cain from it with threats of excommunication. "On this little spot of earth we'll have no murder," said he. He tamed leverets and partridges, and little birds, and hares, and roe-deer. He found a squirrel with a broken leg; he set it with infinite difficulty and patience: and during the cure showed it repositories of acorns, nuts, chestnuts, &c. And this squirrel got well and went off, but visited him in hard weather, and brought a mate, and next year little squirrels were found to have imbibed their parents' sentiments: and of all these animals each generation was tamer than the last. This set the good parson thinking, and gave him the true clue to the great successes of mediæval hermits in taming wild animals.

He kept the key of this paddock, and never let any man but him self enter it: nor would he even let little Gerard go there without him or Margaret. "Children are all little Cains," said he.

In this oasis then he spoke to Margaret, and said, "Dear Margaret, I have thought more than ever of thee of late, and have asked myself why I am content, and thou unhappy."

"Because thou art better, wiser, holier, than I; that is all," said Margaret, promptly.

"Our lives tell another tale," said Gerard, thoughtfully. "I know thy goodness and thy wisdom too well to reason thus perversely. Also I know that I love thee as dear as thou, I think, lovest me. Yet am I happier than thou. Why is this so?"

"Dear Gerard, I am as happy as a woman can hope to be this side the grave."

"Not so happy as I. Now for the reason. First then I am a priest, and this, the one great trial and disappointment God giveth me along with so many joys, why I share it with a multitude. For alas! I am not the only priest by thousands that must never hope for entire earthly happiness. Here then thy lot is harder than mine."

"But Gerard, I have my child to love. Thou canst not fill thy heart with him as his mother can. So you may set this against yon."

"And I have ta'en him from thee; it was cruel; but he would have broken thy heart one day if I had not. Well then, sweet one, I come to where the shoe pincheth, methinks. I have my parish, and it keeps my heart in a glow from morn till night. There is scarce an emotion that my folk stir not up in me many times a day. Often their sorrows make me weep, sometimes their perversity kindles a little wrath, and their absurdity makes me laugh, and sometimes their flashes of unexpected goodness do set me all of a glow: and I could hug 'em. Meantime thou, poor soul, sittest with heart—"

"Of lead, Gerard, of very lead."

"See now, how unkind thy lot compared with mine. Now how if thou couldst be persuaded to warm thyself at the fire that warmeth me."

"Ah, if I could?"

"Hast but to will it. Come among my folk. Take in thine hand the alms I set aside, and give it with kind words; hear their sorrows: they shall show you life is full of troubles, and, as thou sayest truly, no man or woman without their thorn this side the grave. In-doors

I have a map of Gouda parish. Not to o'erburden thee at first, I will put twenty housen under thee with their folk. What sayest thou? but for thy wisdom I had died a dirty maniac, and ne'er seen Gouda manse, nor pious peace. Wilt profit in turn by what little wisdom _I_ have to soften her lot to whom I do owe all?"

Margaret assented warmly: and a happy thing it was for the little district assigned to her: it was as if an angel had descended on them. Her fingers were never tired of knitting, or cutting for them, her heart of sympathizing with them. And that heart expanded and waved its drooping wings; and the glow of good and gentle deeds began to spread over it: and she was rewarded in another way, by being brought into more contact with Gerard, and also with his spirit. All this time malicious tongues had not been idle. "If there is nought between them more than meets the eye, why doth she not marry?" &c. And I am sorry to say our old friend, Joan Ketel, was one of these coarse sceptics. And now, one winter evening she got on a hot scent. She saw Margaret and Gerard talking earnestly together on the Boulevard. She whipped behind a tree. "Now I'll hear something," said she: and so she did. It was winter; there had been one of those tremendous floods followed by a sharp frost, and Gerard in despair as to where he should lodge forty or fifty houseless folk out of the piercing cold. And now it was, "Oh dear, dear Margaret, what shall I do? The manse is full of them, and a sharp frost coming on this night."

Margaret reflected, and Joan listened.

"You must lodge them in the church," said Margaret, quietly.

"In the church? Profanation."

"No: charity profanes nothing; not even a church: soils nought, not even a church. To-day is but Tuesday. Go save their lives; for a bitter night is coming. Take thy stove into the church: and there house them. We will dispose of them here and there ere the Lord's day."

"And I could not think of that: bless thee, sweet Margaret; thy mind is stronger than mine, and readier."

"Nay, nay, a woman looks but a little way; therefore she sees clear. I'll come over myself to-morrow."

And on this they parted with mutual blessings.

Joan glided home remorseful.

And after that she used to check all surmises to their discredit.

The Cloister and the Hearth

"Beware," she would say, "lest some angel should blister thy tongue. Gerard and Margaret paramours? I tell ye they are two saints which meet in secret to plot charity to the poor."

In the summer of 1481 Gerard determined to provide against similar disasters recurring to his poor. Accordingly he made a great hole in his income, and bled his friends (zealous parsons always do that) to build a large Xenodochium to receive the victims of flood or fire. Giles, and all his friends were kind, but all was not enough; when lo! the Dominican monks of Gouda, to whom his parlour and heart had been open for years, came out nobly and put down a handsome sum to aid the charitable vicar.

"The dear good souls," said Margaret, "who would have thought it!"

"Any one who knows them," said Gerard. "Who more charitable than monks?"

"Go to! They do but give the laity back a pig of their own sow."

"And what more do I? What more doth the duke?"

Then the ambitious vicar must build almshouses for decayed true men in their old age, close to the manse, that he might keep, and feed them, as well as lodge them. And, his money being gone, he asked Margaret for a few thousand bricks, and just took off his coat and turned builder: and as he had a good head, and the strength of a Hercules, with the zeal of an artist, up rose a couple of almshouses parson built.

And at this work Margaret would sometimes bring him his dinner, and add a good bottle of Rhenish. And once, seeing him run up a plank with a wheelbarrow full of bricks, which really most bricklayers would have gone staggering under, she said, "Times are changed since I had to carry little Gerard for thee."

"Ay, dear one, thanks to thee."

When the first home was finished, the question was who they should put into it; and being fastidious over it like a new toy, there was much hesitation. But an old friend arrived in time to settle this question.

As Gerard was passing a public-house in Rotterdam one day, he heard a well-known voice. He looked up, and there was Denys of Burgundy; but sadly changed: his beard stained with grey, and his clothes worn and ragged; he had a cuirass still, and gauntlets, but a staff instead of an arbalest. To the company he appeared to be bragging and boasting; but in reality he was giving a true relation of Edward the Fourth's invasion of an armed kingdom with 2000 men, and his march through the country with armies capable of swallowing him, looking on, his battles at Tewkesbury and Barnet, and reoccupation of his capital and kingdom in three months after landing at the Humber with a mixed handful of Dutch, English, and Burgundians.

In this, the greatest feat of arms the century had seen, Denys had shone; and whilst sneering at the warlike pretensions of Charles the Bold, a duke with an itch, but no talent, for fighting, and proclaiming the English king the first captain of the age, did not forget to exalt himself.

Gerard listened with eyes glittering affection and fun. "And now," said Denys, "after all these feats, patted on the back by the gallant young Prince of Gloucester, and smiled on by the great captain himself, here I am lamed for life; by what? by the kick of a horse, and this night I know not where I shall lay my tired bones. I had a comrade once in these parts, that would not have let me lie far from him. But he turned priest and deserted his sweetheart; so 'tis not likely he would remember his comrade. And ten years play sad havoc with our hearts, and limbs, and all." Poor Denys sighed; and Gerard's bowels yearned over him.

"What words are these?" he said, with a great gulp in his throat. "Who grudges a brave soldier supper and bed? Come home with me!"

"Much obliged; but I am no lover of priests."

"Nor I of soldiers; but what is supper and bed between two true men?"

"Not much to you; but something to me. I will come."

"In one hour," said Gerard, and went in high spirits to Margaret, and told her the treat in store, and she must come and share it. She must drive his mother in his little carriage up to the manse with all speed, and make ready an excellent supper.

Then he himself borrowed a cart, and drove Denys up rather slowly, to give the women time.

On the road Denys found out this priest was a kind soul; so told him his trouble, and confessed his heart was pretty near broken. "The great use our stout hearts, and arms, and lives, till we are worn out, and then fling us away like broken tools." He sighed deeply, and it cost Gerard a great struggle, not to hug him then and there, and tell him. But he wanted to do it all like a story book. Who has not had this fancy once in his life? Why Joseph had it; all the better for us.

They landed at the little house. It was as clean as a penny; the hearth blazing, and supper set.

Denys brightened up. "Is this your house, reverend sir?"

"Well, 'tis my work, and with these hands; but 'tis your house."

"Ah, no such luck," said Denys, with a sigh.

"But I say ay," shouted Gerard. "And what is more. I—" (gulp) "say—" (gulp) "Courage, camarade, le diable est mort!"

Denys started, and almost staggered. "Why what?" he stammered, "w—wh—who art thou that bringest me back the merry words and merry days of my youth?" and he was greatly agitated.

"My poor Denys, I am one whose face is changed, but nought else: to my heart, dear trusty comrade, to my heart." And he opened his arms, with the tears in his eyes. But Denys came close to him, and peered in his face, and devoured every feature; and when he was sure it was really Gerard, he uttered a cry so vehement it brought the women running from the house, and fell upon Gerard's neck, and kissed him again and again, and sank on his knees, and laughed and sobbed with joy so terribly that Gerard mourned his folly in doing dramas. But the women with their gentle soothing ways soon composed the brave fellow; and he sat smiling, and holding Margaret's hand and Gerard's. And they all supped together, and went to their beds with hearts warm as a toast, and the broken soldier was at peace, and in his own house, and under his comrade's wing.

His natural gaiety returned, and he resumed his consigne after eight years' disuse, and hobbled about the place enlivening it, but offended the parish mortally by calling the adored vicar comrade, and nothing but comrade.

When they made a fuss about this to Gerard, he just looked in their faces and said, "What does it matter? Break him of swearing, and you shall have my thanks."

This year Margaret went to a lawyer to make her will, for without this she was told her boy might have trouble some day to get his own, not being born in lawful wedlock. The lawyer, however, in conversation, expressed a different opinion.

"This is the babble of churchmen," said he. "Yours is a perfect marriage, though an irregular one."

He then informed her that throughout Europe, excepting only the southern part of Britain, there were three irregular marriages, the highest of which was hers, viz., a betrothal before witnesses.

"This," said he, "if not followed by matrimonial intercourse, is a marriage complete in form, but incomplete in substance. A person so betrothed can forbid any other banns to all eternity. It has, however, been set aside where a party so betrothed contrived to get married regularly and children were born thereafter. But such a decision was for the sake of the offspring, and of doubtful justice. However, in your case, the birth of your child closes that door, and your marriage is complete both in form and substance. Your course, therefore, is to sue for your conjugal rights: it will be the prettiest case of the century. The law is on our side, the Church all on theirs. If you come to that, the old Batavian law, which *compelled* the clergy to marry, hath fallen into disuse, but was never formally repealed."

Margaret was quite puzzled. "What are you driving at, sir? Who am I to go to law with?"

"Who is the defendant? Why, the vicar of Gouda."

"Alas, poor soul! And for what shall I law him?"

"Why, to make him take you into his house, and share bed and board with you, to be sure."

Margaret turned red as fire. "Gramercy for your rede," said she. "What, is yon a woman's part? Constrain a man to be hers by force? That is men's way of wooing, not ours. Say I were so ill a woman as ye think me, I should set myself to beguile him, not to law him;" and she departed, crimson with shame and indignation.

"There is an impracticable fool for you," said the man of art.

Margaret had her will drawn elsewhere, and made her boy safe from poverty, marriage or no marriage.

These are the principal incidents, that in ten whole years befell two peaceful lives, which in a much shorter period had been so thronged with adventures and emotions.

Their general tenor was now peace, piety, the mild content that lasts, not the fierce bliss ever on tiptoe to depart, and, above all, Christian charity.

On this sacred ground these two true lovers met with an uniformity and a kindness of sentiment, which went far to sooth the wound in their own hearts. To pity the same bereaved; to hunt in couples all the ills in Gouda, and contrive and scheme together to remedy all that were remediable; to use the rare insight into troubled hearts, which their own troubles had given them, and use it to make others happier than themselves, this was their daily practice. And in this blessed cause their passion for one another cooled a little, but their affection increased. From the time Margaret entered heart and soul into Gerard's pious charities that affection purged itself of all mortal dross. And, as it had now long outlived scandal and misapprehension, one would have thought that so bright an example of pure self-denying affection was to remain long before the world, to show men how nearly religious faith, even when not quite reasonable, and religious charity, which is always reasonable, could raise two true lovers' hearts to the loving hearts of the angels of heaven. But the great Disposer of events ordered otherwise.

Little Gerard rejoiced both his parents' hearts by the extraordinary progress he made at Alexander Haaghe's famous school at Deventer.

The last time Margaret returned from visiting him she came to Gerard flushed with pride. "Oh, Gerard, he will be a great man one day, thanks to thy wisdom in taking him from us silly women. A great scholar, one Zinthius, came to see the school and judge the scholars, and didn't our Gerard stand up, and not a line in Horace or Terence could Zinthius cite, but the boy would follow him with the rest. 'Why, 'tis a prodigy,' says that great scholar, and there was his poor mother stood by and heard it. And he took our Gerard in his arms and kissed him, and what think you he said?"

"Nay, I know not."

" 'Holland will hear of thee one day: and not Holland only, but all the world.' Why, what a sad brow!"

"Sweet one, I am as glad as thou; yet am I uneasy to hear the child is wise before his time. I love him dear: but he is thine idol; and Heaven doth often break our idols."

"Make thy mind easy," said Margaret. "Heaven will never rob me of my child. What I was to suffer in this world I have suffered. For if any ill happened to my child or thee I should not live a week. The Lord he knows this, and he will leave me my boy."

A month had elapsed after this; but Margaret's words were yet ringing in his ears, when, going his daily round of visits to his poor, he was told quite incidentally and as mere gossip that the plague was at Deventer, carried thither by two sailors from Hamburgh.

His heart turned cold within him. News did not gallop in those days. The fatal disease must have been there a long time before the tidings would reach Gouda. He sent a line by a messenger to Margaret, telling her that he was gone to fetch little Gerard to stay at the manse a little while; and would she see a bed prepared; for he should be back next day. And so he hoped she would not hear a word of the danger till it was all happily over. He borrowed a good horse, and scarce drew rein till he reached Deventer, quite late in the afternoon. He went at once to the school. The boy had been taken away.

As he left the school he caught sight of Margaret's face at the window of a neighbouring house she always lodged at when she came to Deventer.

He ran hastily in to scold her and pack both her and the boy out of the place.

To his surprise the servant told him with some hesitation that Margaret had been there, but was gone.

"Gone, woman?" said Gerard, indignantly. "Art not ashamed to say so? Why, I saw her but now at the window."

"Oh, if you saw her——"

A sweet voice above said, "Stay him not, let him enter." It was Margaret.

Gerard ran up the stairs to her, and went to take her hand.

She drew back hastily.

He looked astounded.

"I am displeased," said she, coldly. "What makes you here? Know you not the plague is in the town?"

"Ay, dear Margaret: and came straightway to take our boy away."

"What, had he no mother?"

"How you speak to me! I hoped you knew not."

"What, think you I leave my boy unwatched? I pay a trusty woman that notes every change in his cheek when I am not here, and lets me know. I am his mother."

"Where is he?"

"In Rotterdam, I hope, ere this."

"Thank Heaven! And why are you not there?"

"I am not fit for the journey: never heed me; go you home on the instant: I'll follow. For shame of you to come here risking your precious life."

"It is not so precious as thine," said Gerard. "But let that pass; we will go home together, and on the instant."

"Nay, I have some matters to do in the town. Go thou at once; and I will follow forthwith."

"Leave thee alone in a plague-stricken town? To whom speak you, dear Margaret?"

"Nay, then, we shall quarrel, Gerard."

"Methinks I see Margaret and Gerard quarreling! Why, it takes two to quarrel, and we are but one."

With this Gerard smiled on her sweetly. But there was no kind responsive glance. She looked cold, gloomy, and troubled. He sighed, and sat patiently down opposite her with his face all puzzled and saddened. He said nothing: for he felt sure she would explain her capricious conduct, or it would explain itself.

Presently she rose hastily, and tried to reach her bedroom: but on the way she staggered and put out her hand. He ran to her with a cry of alarm. She swooned in his arms. He laid her gently on the ground, and beat her cold hands, and ran to her bedroom, and fetched water, and sprinkled her pale face. His own was scarce less pale; for in a basin he had seen water stained with blood: it alarmed him, he knew not why. She was a long time ere she revived, and when she did she found Gerard holding her hand, and bending over her with a look of infinite concern and tenderness. She seemed at first as if she responded to it, but the next moment her eye dilated, and she cried, "Ah, wretch, leave my hand; how dare you touch me?"

"Heaven help her!" said Gerard. "She is not herself."

"You will not leave me, then, Gerard?" said she, faintly. "Alas! why do I ask? Would I leave thee if thou wert—— At least, touch me not, and then I will let thee abide, and see the last of poor Margaret. She ne'er spoke harsh to thee before, sweetheart; and she never will again."

"Alas! what mean these dark words, these wild and troubled looks?" said Gerard, clasping his hands.

"My poor Gerard," said Margaret, "forgive me that I spoke so to thee. I am but a woman, and would have spared thee a sight will make thee weep." She burst into tears. "Ah, me!" she cried, weeping, "that I cannot keep grief from thee: there is a great sorrow before my darling, and this time I shall not be able to come and dry his eyes."

"Let it come, Margaret, so it touch not thee," said Gerard, trembling.

"Dearest," said Margaret, solemnly, "call now religion to thine aid and mine. I must have died before thee one day, or else outlived thee and so died of grief."

"Died? thou die? I will never let thee die. Where is thy pain? What is thy trouble?"

"The plague," said she, calmly. Gerard uttered a cry of horror, and started to his feet: she read his thought. "Useless," said she, quietly. "My nose hath bled; none ever yet survived to whom that came along with the plague. Bring no fools hither to babble over the body they cannot save. I am but a woman; I love not to be stared at; let none see me die but thee."

And even with this a convulsion seized her, and she remained sensible but speechless a long time.

And now for the first time Gerard began to realize the frightful truth, and he ran wildly to and fro, and cried to Heaven for help as drowning men cry to their fellow-creatures. She raised herself on her arm and set herself to quiet him.

She told him she had known the torture of hopes and fears, and was resolved to spare him that agony. "I let my mind dwell too much on the danger," said she, "and so opened my brain to it; through which door when this subtle venom enters it makes short work. I shall not be spotted or loathsome, my poor darling; God is good and spares thee that; but in twelve hours I shall be a dead woman. Ah, look not so, but be a man: be a priest! Waste not one precious minute over my body; it is doomed; but comfort my parting soul."

Gerard sick and cold at heart kneeled down, and prayed for help from Heaven to do his duty.

When he rose from his knees his face was pale and old, but deadly calm and patient. He went softly and brought her bed into the room, and laid her gently down and supported her head with pillows. Then he prayed by her side the prayers for the dying, and she said Amen to each prayer. Then for some hours she wandered, but when the fell disease had quite made sure of its prey, her mind cleared; and she begged Gerard to shrive her; "For oh my conscience it is laden," said she, sadly.

"Confess thy sins to me, my daughter; let there be no reserve."

"My father," said she, sadly, "I have one great sin on my breast this many years. E'en now that death is at my heart I can scarce own it. But the Lord is débonair: if thou wilt pray to him, perchance he may forgive me."

"Confess it first, my daughter."

"I—alas!"

"Confess it!"

"I deceived thee. This many years I have deceived thee."

Here tears interrupted her speech.

"Courage, my daughter, courage," said Gerard, kindly, overpowering the lover in the priest.

She hid her face in her hands, and with many sighs told him it was she who had broken down the hermit's cave with the help of Jorian Ketel. "I, shallow, did it but to hinder thy return thither; but when thou sawest therein the finger of God, I played the traitress, and said, 'While he thinks so he will ne'er leave Gouda manse;' and I held my tongue. Oh false heart."

"Courage, my daughter; thou dost exaggerate a trivial fault."

"Ah, but 'tis not all. The birds."

"Well?"

"They followed thee not to Gouda by miracle but by my treason. I said, he will ne'er be quite happy without his birds that visited him in his cell; and I was jealous of them, and cried, and said, these foul little things, they are my child's rivals. And I bought loaves of bread, and Jorian and me we put crumbs at the cave door, and thence went sprinkling them all the way to the manse, and there a heap. And my wiles succeeded, and they came, and thou wast glad, and I was pleased to see thee glad; and when thou sawest in my guile the finger of Heaven, wicked, deceitful I did hold my tongue. But *die* deceiving thee? ah, no, I could not. Forgive me if thou canst; I was but a woman; I knew no better at the time. 'Twas writ in my bosom with a very sunbeam, ' 'Tis good for him to bide at Gouda manse.' "

"Forgive thee, sweet innocent!" sobbed Gerard, "what have I to forgive? Thou hadst a foolish froward child to guide to his own weal, and didst all this for the best. I thank thee and bless thee. But as thy confessor, all deceit is ill in Heaven's pure eye. Therefore thou hast done well to confess and report it; and even on thy confession and penitence the Church through me absolves thee. Pass to thy graver faults."

"My graver faults? Alas! alas! Why, what have I done to compare? I am not an ill woman, not a very ill one. If He can forgive me deceiving thee, He can well forgive me all the rest ever I did."

Being gently pressed, she said she was to blame not to have done more good in the world. "I had just begun to do a little," she said; "and now I must go. But I repine not, since 'tis Heaven's will. Only I am so afeard thou wilt miss me." And at this she could not restrain her tears, though she tried hard.

Gerard struggled with his as well as he could; and knowing her life of piety, purity, and charity, and seeing that she could not in her present state realize any sin but her having deceived *him,* gave her full absolution. Then he put the crucifix in her hand, and, while he consecrated the oil, bade her fix her mind neither on her merits nor her demerits, but on Him who died for her on the tree.

She obeyed him, with a look of confiding love and submission.

And he touched her eye with the consecrated oil, and prayed aloud beside her.

Soon after she dozed.

He watched beside her, more dead than alive himself.

When the day broke she awoke, and seemed to acquire some energy. She begged him to look in her box for her marriage lines, and for a picture, and bring them both to her. He did so. She then entreated him by all they had suffered for each other, to ease her mind by making a solemn vow to execute her dying requests.

He vowed to obey them to the letter.

"Then, Gerard, let no creature come here to lay me out. I could not bear to be stared at; my very corpse would blush. Also I would not be made a monster of for the worms to sneer at as well as feed on. Also my very clothes are tainted, and shall to earth with me. I am a physician's daughter: and ill becomes me kill folk, being dead, which did so little good to men in the days of health; wherefore lap me in lead, the way I am; and bury me deep\ yet not so deep but what one day thou mayest find the way, and lay thy bones by mine.

"Whiles I lived I went to Gouda but once or twice a week. It cost me not to go each day. Let me gain this by dying, to be always at dear Gouda—in the green kirkyard.

"Also they do say the spirit hovers where the body lies: I would have my spirit hover near thee, and the kirkyard is not far from the manse. I am so afeard some ill will happen thee, Margaret being gone.

"And see, with mine own hands I place my marriage lines in my bosom. Let no living hand move them, on pain of thy curse and mine. Then, when the angel comes for me at the last day, he shall say, this is an honest woman, she hath her marriage lines (for you know I am your lawful wife though holy Church hath come between us), and he will set me where the honest women be. I will not sit among ill women, no, not in heaven; for their mind is not my mind, nor their soul my soul. I have stood, unbeknown, at my window, and heard their talk."

For some time she was unable to say any more, but made signs to him that she had not done.

At last she recovered her breath, and bade him look at the picture.

It was the portrait he had made of her when they were young together, and little thought to part so soon. He held it in his hands and looked at it, but could scarce see it. He had left it in fragments, but now it was whole.

"They cut it to pieces, Gerard. But see, Love mocked at their knives.

"I implore thee with my dying breath, let this picture hang ever in thine eye.

"I have heard that such as die of the plague, unspotted, yet after death spots have been known to come out; and, oh, I could not bear thy last memory of me to be so. Therefore, as soon as the breath is out of my body, cover my face with this handkerchief, and look at me no more till we meet again, 'twill not be so very long. O promise."

"I promise," said Gerard, sobbing.

"But look on this picture instead. Forgive me; I am but a woman. I could not bear my face to lie a foul thing in thy memory.

Nay, I must have thee still think me as fair as I was true. Hast called me an angel once or twice; but be just! did I not still tell thee I was no angel, but only a poor simple woman, that whiles saw clearer than thou because she looked but a little way, and that loves thee dearly, and never loved but thee, and now with her dying breath prays thee indulge her in this, thou that art a man."

"I will. I will. Each word, each wish is sacred."

"Bless thee! Bless thee! So then the eyes that now can scarce see thee, they are so troubled by the pest, and the lips that shall not touch thee to taint thee, will still be before thee, as they were when we were young and thou didst love me."

"When I did love thee, Margaret! Oh, never loved I thee as now."

"Hast not told me so of late."

"Alas! hath love no voice but words? I was a priest; I had charge of thy soul; the sweet offices of a pure love were lawful; words of love imprudent at the least. But now the good fight is won, ah me! Oh my love, if thou hast lived doubting of thy Gerard's heart, die not so: for never was woman loved so tenderly as thou this ten years past."

"Calm thyself, dear one," said the dying woman, with a heavenly smile. "I know it: only being but a woman, I could not die happy till I had heard thee say so. Ah, I have pined ten years for those sweet words. Hast said them; and this is the happiest hour of my life. I had to die to get them; well, I grudge not the price."

From this moment a gentle complacency rested on her fading features. But she did not speak.

Then Gerard, who had loved her soul so many years, feared lest she should expire with a mind too fixed on earthly affection. "Oh my daughter," he cried, "my dear daughter, if indeed thou lovest me as I love thee, give me not the pain of seeing thee die with thy pious soul fixed on mortal things.

"Dearest lamb of all my fold, for whose soul I must answer, oh think not now of mortal love, but of His who died for thee on the tree. Oh let thy last look be heavenwards, thy last word a word of prayer."

She turned a look of gratitude and obedience on him. "What saint?" she murmured: meaning, doubtless, "what saint should she invoke as an intercessor."

"He to whom the saints themselves do pray."

She turned on him one more sweet look of love and submission, and put her pretty hands together in prayer like a child.

"Jesu!"

This blessed word was her last. She lay with her eyes heavenwards, and her hands put together.

Gerard prayed fervently for her passing spirit. And when he had prayed a long time with his head averted, not to see her last breath, all seemed unnaturally still. He turned his head fearfully. It was so.

She was gone.

Nothing left him now, but the earthly shell of as constant, pure, and loving a spirit, as ever adorned the earth.

CHAPTER XCIX

A PRIEST is never more thoroughly a priest than in the chamber of death. Gerard did the last offices of the Church for the departed, just as he should have done them for his smallest parishioner. He did this mechanically, then sat down stupefied by the sudden and tremendous blow; and not yet realizing the pangs of bereavement. Then in a transport of religious enthusiasm he kneeled and thanked Heaven for her Christian end.

And then all his thought was to take her away from strangers, and lay her in his own churchyard. That very evening a covered cart with one horse started for Gouda, and in it was a coffin, and a broken-hearted man lying with his arms and chin resting on it.

The mourner's short-lived energy had exhausted itself in the necessary preparations, and now he lay crushed, clinging to the cold lead that held her.

The man, of whom the cart was hired, walked by the horse's head, and did not speak to him, and when he baited the horse spoke but in a whisper, respecting that mute agony. But, when he stopped for the night, he and the landlord made a well-meaning attempt to get the mourner away to take some rest and food. But Gerard repulsed them, and, when they persisted, almost snarled at them, like a faithful dog, and clung to the cold lead all night. So then they drew a cloak over him, and left him in peace

And at noon the sorrowful cart came up to the manse, and there were full a score of parishioners collected with one little paltry trouble or another. They had missed the parson already. And when they saw what it was, and saw their healer so stricken down, they raised a loud wail of grief, and it roused him from his lethargy of woe, and he saw where he was, and their faces, and tried to speak to them. "Oh my children! my children!" he cried; but choked with anguish could say no more.

Yet the next day, spite of all remonstrances, he buried her himself, and read the service with a voice that only trembled now and then. Many tears fell upon her grave. And when the service ended he stayed there standing like a statue, and the people left the churchyard out of respect.

He stood like one in a dream, till the sexton, who was, as most men are, a fool, began to fill in the grave without giving him due warning.

But at the sound of earth falling on her, Gerard uttered a piercing scream.

The sexton forbore.

Gerard staggered and put his hand to his breast. The sexton supported him, and called for help.

Jorian Ketel, who lingered near, mourning his benefactress, ran into the churchyard, and the two supported Gerard into the manse.

"Ah, Jorian! good Jorian!" said he, "something snapped within me; I felt it, and I heard it: here Jorian, here:" and he put his hand to his breast.

CHAPTER C

A FORTNIGHT after this a pale, bowed figure entered the Dominican convent in the suburbs of Gouda, and sought speech with brother Ambrose, who governed the convent as deputy, the prior having lately died, and his successor, though appointed, not having arrived.

The sick man was Gerard, come to end life as he began it. He entered as a novice, on probation; but the truth was, he was a failing man, and knew it, and came there to die in peace, near kind and gentle Ambrose his friend, and the other monks to whom his house and heart had always been open.

His manse was more than he could bear; it was too full of reminiscences of her.

Ambrose, who knew his value, and his sorrow, was not without a kindly hope of curing him, and restoring him to his parish. With this view he put him in a comfortable cell over the gateway, and forbade him to fast or practise any austerities.

But in a few days the new prior arrived, and proved a very Tartar. At first he was absorbed in curing abuses, and tightening the general discipline; but one day hearing the vicar of Gouda had entered the convent as a novice, he said, " 'Tis well; let him first give up his vicarage then, or go: I'll no fat parsons in my house." The prior then sent for Gerard, and he went to him; and the moment they saw one another they both started.

"Clement!"

"Jerome!"

CHAPTER CI

JEROME was as morose as ever in his general character; but he had somewhat softened towards Gerard. All the time he was in England he had missed him more than he thought possible, and since then had often wondered what had become of him. What he heard in Gouda raised his feeble brother in his good opinion: above all that he had withstood the Pope and the Minorites on "the infernal heresy of the immaculate conception," as he called it. But when one of his young monks told him with tears in his eyes the cause of Gerard's illness, all his contempt revived. "Dying for a woman?"

He determined to avert this scandal: he visited Clement twice a day in his cell, and tried all his old influence and all his eloquence to induce him to shake off this unspiritual despondency, and not rob the Church of his piety and his eloquence at so critical a period.

Gerard heard him, approved his reasoning, admired his strength, confessed his own weakness, and continued visibly to wear away to the land of the leal. One day Jerome told him he had heard his story, and heard it with pride. "But now," said he, "you spoil it all, Clement: for this is the triumph of earthly passion. Better have yielded to it, and repented, than resist it while she lived, and succumb under it now body and soul."

"Dear Jerome," said Clement, so sweetly as to rob his remonstrance of the tone of remonstrance, "here, I think, you do me some injustice. Passion there is none: but a deep affection, for which I will not blush here, since I shall not blush for it in Heaven. Bethink thee, Jerome; the poor dog that dies of grief on his master's grave, is he guilty of passion? Neither am I. Passion had saved my life, and lost my soul. She was my good angel: she sustained me in my duty and charity; her face encouraged me in the pulpit: her lips soothed me under ingratitude. She intertwined herself with all that was good in my life: and after leaning on her so long, I could not go on alone. And, dear Jerome, believe me I am no rebel against Heaven. It is God's will to release me. When they threw the earth upon her poor coffin, something snapped within my bosom here that mended may not be. I heard it and I felt it. And from that time, Jerome, no food that I put in my mouth had any savour. With my eyes bandaged now I could not tell thee which was bread, and which was flesh, by eating of it."

"Holy saints!"

"And again, from that same hour my deep dejection left me, and I smiled again. I often smile—why? I read it thus: He in whose hands are the issues of life and death gave me that minute the great summons; 'twas some cord of life snapped in me. He is very pitiful. I should have lived unhappy; but He said 'No; enough is done, enough is suffered; poor, feeble, loving servant, thy shortcomings are forgiven, thy sorrows touch thine end; come thou to thy rest!' I come, Lord, I come."

Jerome groaned. "The Church had ever her holy but feeble servants," he said. "Now would I give ten years of my life to save thine. But I see it may not be. Die in peace."

And so it was that in a few days more Gerard lay a dying in a frame of mind so holy and happy, that more than one aged saint was there to garner his dying words. In the evening he had seen Giles, and begged him not to let poor Jack starve: and to see that little Gerard's trustees did their duty, and to kiss his parents for him, and to send Denys to his friends in Burgundy: "Poor thing, he will feel so strange here without his comrade." And after that he had an interview with Jerome alone. What passed between them was never distinctly known; but it must have been something remarkable; for Jerome went from the door with his hands crossed on his breast, his high head lowered, and sighing as he went.

The two monks, that watched with him till matins, related that all through the night he broke out from time to time in pious exclamations, and praises, and thanksgivings: only once they said he wandered, and thought he saw her walking in green meadows with other spirits clad in white, and beckoning him; and they all smiled and beckoned him. And both these monks said (but it might have been fancy) that just before dawn there came three light taps against the wall, one after another, very slow; and the dying man heard them, and said "I come, love, I come."

This much is certain, that Gerard did utter these words, and prepare for his departure, having uttered them. He sent for all the monks who at that hour were keeping vigil. They came, and hovered like gentle spirits round him with holy words. Some prayed in silence for him with their faces touching the ground, others tenderly supported his head. But when one of them said something about his life of self-denial and charity, he stopped him, and addressing them all said, "My dear brethren, take note that he, who here dies so happy, holds not these newfangled doctrines of man's merit. Oh, what a miserable hour were this to me an if I did! Nay, but I hold with the Apostles, and their pupils in the Church, the ancient fathers, that 'we are justified, not by our own wisdom, or piety, or the works we have done in holiness of heart, but by faith.' " *

Then there was a silence, and the monks looked at one another significantly.

"Please you sweep the floor," said the dying Christian in a voice to which all its clearness and force seemed supernaturally restored.

They instantly obeyed, not without a sentiment of awe and curiosity.

"Make me a great cross with wood ashes."

* He was citing from Clement of Rome—
'Ὅυ δι ἑαντων δικαιουμεθα ουδε δια της ἡμετερας σοφιας, ἠ ευσεβειας, ἠ εργων ὡν κατειργασαμεθα εν ὁσιοτητι καρδιας, αλλα δια της πιστεως.'——*Epist. ad Corinth.*, i. 32.

They strewed the ashes in form of a great cross upon the floor. "Now lay me down on it: for so will I die."

And they took him gently from his bed, and laid him on the cross of wood ashes.

"Shall we spread out thine arms, dear brother?"

"Now God forbid! Am I worthy of that?"

He lay silent, but with his eyes raised in ecstasy.

Presently he spoke half to them, half to himself. "Oh," he said with a subdued but concentrated rapture, "I feel it buoyant. It lifts me floating in the sky whence my merits had sunk me like lead."

Day broke; and displayed his face cast upward in silent rapture, and his hands together; like Margaret's.

And just about the hour she died he spoke his last word in this world.

"Jesu!"

And even with that word—he fell asleep.

They laid him out for his last resting-place.

Under his linen they found a horse-hair shirt. "Ah!" cried the young monks, "behold a saint!"

Under the hair cloth they found a long thick tress of auburn hair.

They started, and were horrified; and a babel of voices arose, some condemning, some excusing.

In the midst of which Jerome came in, and, hearing the dispute, turned to an ardent young monk called Basil, who was crying scandal the loudest. "Basil," said he, "is she alive or dead that owned this hair?"

"How may I know, father?"

"Then for aught you know it may be the relic of a saint?"

"Certes it may be," said Basil sceptically.

"You have then broken our rule, which saith 'Put ill construction on no act done by a brother which can be construed innocently.' Who are you to judge such a man as this was? go to your cell, and stir not out for a week by way of penance."

He then carried off the lock of hair.

The Cloister and the Hearth

And when the coffin was to be closed, he cleared the cell: and put the tress upon the dead man's bosom. "There, Clement," said he to the dead face. And set himself a penance for doing it; and nailed the coffin up himself.

The next day Gerard was buried in Gouda churchyard. The monks followed him in procession from the convent. Jerome, who was evidently carrying out the wishes of the deceased, read the service. The grave was a deep one, and at the bottom of it was a lead coffin. Poor Gerard's, light as a feather (so wasted was he), was lowered, and placed by the side of it.

After the service Jerome said a few words to the crowd of parishioners that had come to take the last look at their best friend. When he spoke of the virtues of the departed, loud wailing and weeping burst forth, and tears fell upon the coffin like rain.

The monks went home. Jerome collected them in the refectory and spoke to them thus: "We have this day laid a saint in the earth. The convent will keep his trentals, but will feast, not fast; for our good brother is freed from the burden of the flesh; his labours are over, and he has entered into his joyful rest. I alone shall fast, and do penance: for to my shame I say it, I was unjust to him, and knew not his worth, till it was too late. And you, young monks, be not curious to inquire whether a lock he bore on his bosom was a token of pure affection, or the relic of a saint; but remember the heart he wore beneath: most of all, fix your eyes upon his life and conversation; and follow them an ye may: for he was a holy man."

Thus after life's fitful fever these true lovers were at peace. The grave, kinder to them than the Church, united them for ever: and now a man of another age and nation, touched with their fate, has laboured to build their tombstone, and rescue them from long and unmerited oblivion.

He asks for them your sympathy, but not your pity.

No, put this story to a wholesome use.

Fiction must often give false views of life and death. Here as it happens, curbed by history, she gives you true ones. Let the barrier, that kept these true lovers apart, prepare you for this, that here on earth there will nearly always be some obstacle or other to your perfect happiness; to their early death apply your Reason and your Faith, by way of exercise and preparation. For if you

705

cannot bear to be told that these died young, who, had they lived a hundred years, would still be dead, how shall you bear to see the gentle, the loving, and the true, glide from your own bosom to the grave, and fly from your house to heaven?

Yet this is in store for you. In every age the Master of life and death, who is kinder as well as wiser than we are, has transplanted to heaven, young, earth's sweetest flowers.

I ask your sympathy then for their rare constancy, and pure affection, and then cruel separation by a vile heresy * in the bosom of the Church; but not your pity for their early, but happy end.

Beati sunt qui in Domino moriuntur.

CHAPTER CII

IN compliance with a custom I despise, but have not the spirit to resist, I linger on the stage to pick up the smaller fragments of humanity I have scattered about: *i. e.* some of them, for the wayside characters have no claim on me; they have served their turn if they have persuaded the reader that Gerard travelled from Holland to Rome through human beings, and not through a population of dolls.

Eli and Catherine lived to a great age: lived so long that both Gerard and Margaret grew to be dim memories. Giles also was longævous; he went to the court of Bavaria, and was alive there at ninety, but had somehow turned into bones and leather, trumpet toned.

Cornelis, free from all rivals, and forgiven long ago by his mother, who clung to him more and more now all her brood was scattered, waited, and waited, and waited, for his parents' decease. But Catherine's shrewd word came true: ere she and her mate wore out, this worthy rusted away. At sixty-five he lay dying of old age in his mother's arms, a hale woman of eighty-six. He had lain unconscious a while; but came to himself *in articulo mortis,* and seeing her near him, told her how he would transform the shop and premises as soon as they should be his. "Yes, my darling," said the poor old woman, soothingly; and in another minute he was clay:

* Celibacy of the Clergy, an invention truly fiendish.

The Cloister and the Hearth

and that clay was followed to the grave by all the feet whose shoes he had waited for.

Denys, broken-hearted at his comrade's death, was glad to return to Burgundy, and there a small pension the court allowed him kept him until unexpectedly he inherited a considerable sum from a relation. He was known in his native place for many years as a crusty old soldier, who could tell good stories of war, when he chose; and a bitter railer against women.

Jerome, disgusted with northern laxity, retired to Italy, and, having high connections, became at seventy a mitred abbot. He put on the screw of discipline: his monks revered and hated him. He ruled with iron rod ten years. And one night he died, alone; for he had not found the way to a single heart. The Vulgate was on his pillow, and the crucifix in his hand, and on his lips something more like a smile, than was ever seen there while he lived; so that, methinks, at that awful hour he was not quite alone. Requiescat in pace. The Master he served has many servants, and they have many minds, and now and then a faithful one will be a surly one, as it is in these our mortal mansions.

The yellow-haired laddie, Gerard Gerardson, belongs not to Fiction but to History. She has recorded his birth in other terms than mine. Over the tailor's house in the Brede Kirk Straet she has inscribed:—

"Hæc est parva domus natus quâ magnus Erasmus";

and she has written half a dozen lives of him. But there is something left for her yet to do. She has no more comprehended magnum Erasmum, than any other pigmy comprehends a giant, or partisan a judge.

First scholar and divine of his epoch, he was also the heaven-born dramatist of his century. Some of the best scenes in this new book are from his mediæval pen, and illumine the pages where they come; for the words of a genius, so high as his are not born to die: their immediate work upon mankind fulfilled, they may seem to lie torpid; but, at each fresh shower of intelligence Time pours upon their students, they prove their immortal race: they revive, they spring from the dust of great libraries; they bud, they flower, they fruit, they seed, from generation to generation, and from age to age.

On *THE CLOISTER AND THE HEARTH*

On *THE CLOISTER AND THE HEARTH*

When Charles Reade was writing *The Cloister and the Hearth* a century ago, he must have been conscious of the fact that historical fiction, of which his novel is a notable exemplar, had lost much of its early popularity. Following the death of Sir Walter Scott in 1832 there had been a flurry of interest in this form, as Harrison Ainsworth, G. P. R. James, and Bulwer-Lytton, among others, attempted to occupy the place of Scott and to re-establish the popularity of the genre which he had developed. But nothing is more tedious than a bad historical novel, and the post-Scott romancers were often egregiously, even ingeniously, bad. A gifted writer, however, will always rise above the level of mediocrity to which a form seems committed, and thus in 1852 Thackeray proved by the brilliance of *Henry Esmond* that the historical novel was a viable form whose potential was limited only by the skill of individual novelists. *The Cloister and the Hearth* is in the tradition of the best work of its class.

What *is* a historical novel? The question is not as absurd as it may sound, for the usual definition is as ambiguous as the form itself, which covers a wide variety of fictional types. The historical novel comprehends not only the romanticism of Scott with his pageantry of the past, but the realism of John W. DeForest, transcribing Civil War scenes verbatim from his journal, and the romantic realism of Margaret Mitchell, selecting scenes for dra-

711

matic effect but emphasizing the way in which history impinges on the lives of people who are individually unimportant. No doubt most readers, however, think of the historical novel in terms of the modern costume romance, that anomaly which has provoked the irreverent remark that a historical novel is a book with a wench on the jacket but no jacket on the wench.

The writer of historical fiction may take one of two possible approaches to his material. As Bulwer-Lytton put it in a preface to the third edition of his *Harold* (1855):

There are two ways of employing the materials of History in the service of Romance: the one consists in lending to ideal personages, and to an imaginary fable, the additional interest to be derived from historical groupings: the other, in extracting the main interest of romantic narrative from History itself. Those who adopt the former mode are at liberty to exclude all that does not contribute to theatrical effect or picturesque composition; their fidelity to the period they select is towards the manners and costume, not towards the precise order of events, the moral causes from which the events proceeded, and the physical agencies by which they were influenced and controlled. . . . [Scott] had employed History to aid Romance; I contented myself with the humbler task to employ Romance in the aid of History,—to extract from authentic but neglected chronicles, and the unfrequented storehouse of Archeology, the incidents and details that enliven the dry narrative of facts to which the general historian is confined. . . .

Of these two methods the first has proved the more popular. Readers have consistently preferred the historical background for romance to history which is seen through what may be the distortions of fiction. This is why we prefer Scott to Bulwer, and why *The Cloister and the Hearth* is alive and *Harold* is dead. Bulwer was a much more accurate scholar than either Scott or Reade, though, as we shall see, Reade did not neglect his homework for *The Cloister and the Hearth;* but it is clear that the vitality and endurance of a historical novel bear little or no relation to the author's scholarship.

The historical novel at its best, nevertheless, may serve a very useful function in education. Carlyle said that through Scott "the bygone ages of the world were actually fitted with *living men,* not by protocols, state papers, controversies, and abstractions of men." That is, the historical novel can animate history, can show that history is, in some degree at least, the biography of great men. In the nineteenth century the practitioner of this new form, recognizing both the human values and the dramatic values of history, anticipated modern biography, particularly as it has developed since Strachey. It is said that Scott's mother disliked fiction because, she contended, it is just a pack of lies. Her son's work is anchored, however, in a reasonable facsimile of fact, and she could scarcely object because he saw how to do that which is always open to the novelist; that is, to vitalize and clothe with flesh the bare bones of history. Though Charles Reade had no cavalier disdain for fact, it is his distinction that, like Scott, he emphasized the dramatic elements of his material.

What *was* Reade's material? It should be of some interest for us to see to what extent he followed established fact and to what extent he improvised romance. In the 1850's he was collecting material for a book to have been called *Heroes and Martyrs,* glorifying obscure people whose exploits of unassuming virtue had gone unrecognized. This was by way of answer to Carlyle, whose theory of the hero as the determinant of history Reade strongly rejected. At this time he came across the dramatic story of the parents of Erasmus. Since he had reason to oppose the concept of enforced celibacy, as we have already seen, the subject proved doubly attractive.

On the opening page of his novel Reade tells us that he has used as his source "a musty chronicle, written in tolerable Latin." For half a century this material remained unknown. Then in 1910 Andrew Lang, preparing a new edition of *A Good Fight,* an early version of *The Cloister and the Hearth,* discovered Erasmus' *Compendium vitae* (1524), a brief biographical sketch written as part of a letter to a friend. The section from which Reade drew is brief enough to reproduce.

713

He was born in Rotterdam on the eve of Simon and Jude. He computes about 57 years ago. His mother was called Margaret, daughter of a certain doctor named Peter. She came from Septimontium, in the common tongue Zevenberge; he saw two of her brothers at Dordrecht, almost nonagenarians. His father was named Gerard. He secretly had an affair with the said Margaret, hoping for marriage. And there are those who say they were betrothed. Both the parents and brothers of Gerard were incensed at this happening. His father was Elias, his mother Catharine; each of them attained extreme old age, Catharine wellnigh her ninety-fifth year. There were ten brothers but no sister; all born of the same father and mother; all married. Gerard was the youngest, except one. It seemed best to them all that from so great a number one should be consecrated to God. You know old people's moods. The brothers, too, were unwilling that the property should be diminished and liked to have someone with whom they might live. Gerard, seeing he was shut off, in every way, from matrimony by general agreement, did what desperate men are wont to do; he secretly took flight and, while on his journey, sent to his parents and brothers a letter with a hand clasping a hand and one sentence added, "Farewell; I shall never see you again."

In the mean time, his intended wife was left with child. The boy was brought up in his grandmother's home. Gerard betook himself to Rome. There by writing he did a fair business, for the printer's art had not yet arrived. Moreover, he was deft with his hands. And he lived as youths do. Soon he applied his mind to honest studies. He became well versed in Greek and Latin. In jurisprudence, too, he gained more than common skill. For Rome was then most rich in learned men. He heard Guarinus lecture. He copied all authors with his hand. His parents, when they learned he was in Rome, wrote him that the girl whom he had sought to marry was dead. Believing this, he became a priest for grief and turned his whole mind to religion. Returning home, he discovered the trick. Nevertheless she would never marry afterward, nor did he ever lay hand on her.

He had the boy well educated, however, and put him to study his letters when he was barely four. . . . He reached the third class; then a pestilence raging violently there, carried off his mother, leaving the boy now in his thirteenth year. When the disease grew daily more terrible, all the household in which he had been living having been stricken, he returned to his home. Gerard, upon receiving the sad news, began to languish and shortly afterward died. Both parents died not much after their fortieth year.

Erasmus, then, provided Reade with the basic plot outline. The interstices were filled in with material drawn from a mass of miscellaneous reading, recorded in the novelist's famous notebooks and on huge cards. A few months after Reade's death Annie Fields published in the *Century* a letter in which Reade had enumerated the books he had read in preparation for the novel. There are seventy-nine titles in the list. They include not only the standard works on Erasmus but multi-volumed studies in the fine arts, ecclesiastical history, politics, social history, biography, geography, travel, letters, literary history, etc. Six are in Latin, and at least nine (and possibly thirteen) could have been read only in French. Professor Turner, the closest student of Reade's sources, examined 206 volumes in an attempt to duplicate the reading which went into *The Cloister and the Hearth.* It is not contended that Reade mastered all these works or that he did not perhaps receive some help from his scholarly Oxford colleagues. The point is that this mid-Victorian romancer, who wore his learning lightly, took with some seriousness his obligation to the spirit of historical accuracy in the background as well as the forefront of his novel.

But *The Cloister and the Hearth* does not live because it bears a relationship to history. It takes its interest, as do other romances, from an effective blending of vigorous narrative and touching sentiment. Indeed, it might be argued that the history is entirely incidental to a series of picaresque episodes. Such is certainly true of the first half of the book, in which *The Cloister and the Hearth* is simply a romance of hair-raising adventures. Not until chapter lxxiii are we given a hint that there may be more here than a work of fancy, and the name of Erasmus does not appear until the last page.

On The Cloister and the Hearth

The Cloister and the Hearth, therefore, is sustained by plot. However badly the term "sensation novel" needs definition and however inadequately it represents the quality of Reade's best work, it does emphasize the importance which he attached to plot. Reade was devoted to the tradition of French melodrama, and his imagination was essentially dramatic. He visualized a novel in terms of effective "scenes," each one of which was to be wrung dry of its measure of excitement and emotion. The task of the novelist, therefore, was simply to string together a succession of incidents that would provide variety.

This is certainly the purpose of the first half of *The Cloister and the Hearth,* and few readers will deny that it is skillfully accomplished. Gerard's escape from the Stadthouse in the eerie moonlight, with Giles shinnying, monkey-like, up the rope to the top of the tower; Dierich Brower's search for Gerard through Margaret's house, an incident full of high suspense; the breathless pursuit through the forest, with bloodshed and ultimate hairbreadth escape on Ghysbrecht's mule—these are not moments when the reader will yawn and begin to think of going to bed. Even less so are the colorful scenes and episodes after Gerard meets Denys: the harrowing encounter with the bear; the horror of the loaded gibbet; the escape by water; the bloody violence of the fight with the "Abbot"—overdone, perhaps, but spine-tingling; the fortuitous escape from the assassins at the mill, etched in fire against the black night; and finally shipwreck in a tumultuous storm. Few possibilities of the blood-and-thunder romance, medieval-style, have been overlooked, and the play upon the reader's nerves is both relentless and effective.

Most nineteenth-century novels were published serially in magazines or in monthly parts. In either case the writer was obliged to take special pains to maintain reader interest from one installment to another. The obvious way to do so was to end each part upon a point of high interest, particularly on a point of unresolved action. Known familiarly as the "cliff-hanger" technique, this stratagem accorded perfectly with Reade's developed concept of the novel. In its final form *The Cloister and the Hearth* was one of the few Reade novels *not* published serially; the first half, however, under the title of *A Good Fight,* did appear in this manner. Both in this text and elsewhere Reade's artful management of climaxes and curtains reflects his considerable experience in the theater.

Wilkie Collins, in the preface to his novel *Basil* (1852), had stated his understanding of the relation between fiction and drama: "Believing that the Novel and the Play are twin-sisters in the family of Fiction; that the one is a drama narrated, as the other is a drama acted; and that all the strong and deep emotions which the Play-writer is privileged to excite, the Novel-writer is privileged to excite also, I have not thought it either politic or necessary, while adhering to realities, to adhere to everyday realities only." There can be no doubt that Reade was in complete agreement. His novels often suggest a division into acts and scenes, with the action rising to a point of tension, followed by a chapter beginning quietly and proceeding to another climax. Always there is adroitly balanced suspense, an essential of the melodramatic mode. Denys' account of his experiences with Gerard wins Reade's approval because Denys knows how "to water the suspense, and extract the thrill as far as possible." And Reade, who has the chatty Victorian novelist's habit of talking with his readers, adds, "Suspense is the soul of narrative." Collins is supposed to have coined the formula for the sensation novelist: "Make 'em laugh, make 'em weep, make 'em wait." It is certain that for both these writers suspense is of primary importance.

In the preface to *Hard Cash* Reade describes *The Cloister and the Hearth* as "a matter-of-fact romance." By this phrase, which he used many times to describe his novels, he emphasizes what was for him the central responsibility of the novelist—to effect "the union of fact and imagination." In his *Trade Malice* he defines fiction as "the art of weaving fact with invention." *The*

Cloister and the Hearth is a notable exemplar of this technique. The romance of Gerard's more implausible adventures is supported by passages transcribed almost verbatim from Erasmus' *Colloquies,* as Reade candidly acknowledges in the novel's final paragraph. Thus, egregious romance is balanced by solid realism, and the reader does not feel imposed upon. Some Victorian readers, in fact, took exception to Reade's insistence on realism, criticizing, for example, his inclusion of the less pleasant details of life in the dirty and overcrowded German inn, not realizing that the whole description is taken from Erasmus.

Today the criticism must be that the realism does not go far enough. We know, and Reade knew, that speech and manners in the age he was describing were often coarse and vulgar, yet he was forced to bowdlerize at every turn. This form of abject submission to the power of Mrs. Grundy is often called "the Victorian compromise." If Reade had not capitulated, however, his book would not have been published. So he contented himself with reminding us that Denys, as a professional soldier, used rather different language than that attributed to him: "I sacrifice perfect truth of portraiture to decency by thinning those expletives with which [his] talk was garnished . . ." Similarly, the uninhibited Marion "shall not be photographed by me but feebly indicated; . . . she . . . said things without winking which no decent man of our day would say even among men."

The Victorian poet-critic A. C. Swinburne wrote of *The Cloister and the Hearth* that "a story better conceived, better constructed, or better related, it would be difficult to find anywhere." This judgment on the architectonics will find little support today. Reade's warmest admirers will acknowledge that his talent for plotting is to be found more in the handling of single incidents than in structuring and unifying complex material. The evening at "Les Trois Poissons," for example, with its gay good spirits and crackling dialogue, is superbly managed, and we are quite ready to agree with Gerard's judgment of Marion, "Now that is a character." [1] Such a scene is reminiscent of below-stairs high-jinks in the best eighteenth-century comedies. But the integration of this material on a large scale is not always skillfully accomplished. *The Cloister and the Hearth* is built around two narratives—the Dutch story and the Italian story—and there are innumerable picaresque episodes. Tying these stories together proved extremely difficult. Reade must resort to such awkward devices as Gerard's "letter" to Margaret, which runs to sixty-odd pages. The events come, as Reade admits, in clusters, and are separated by often tedious passages, especially in the Italian chapters, in which he unloads upon us the results of his wide reading. There is an unconscionable use of coincidence (e.g., most of the appearances of Father Jerome) and sudden, unconvincing reversals of fortune (e.g., the impressment of Denys, immediately followed by the armed robbery of Gerard). Finally, there are the inset narratives of "Manon's Deposition" and "The Curé's Tale." Reade had already put himself on record in *The Autobiography of a Thief* (1858) as aware that "a story within a story is a frightful flaw in art," but here he falls victim again to a structural malady that plagued the English novel even as late as Stevenson. *The Cloister and the Hearth* is rescued, however, from the chaos into which some of Reade's other novels fell by the relatively simple nature of its two-pronged plot and, especially, by the author's mastery of narrative pace. We are rushed happily from one dramatic scene to another without the leisure to examine closely any single action. That it does not often occur to us to do so is the measure of Reade's success in this phase of his craft.

It would be illusory to expect to find in the dramatic novel patient, detailed, penetrating characterization. While Reade was

[1] You will note how often Reade sets up dialogue with stage directions, naming the speakers. It is clear that he saw his material in dramatic terms.

working on *The Cloister and the Hearth,* George Eliot published *Adam Bede* and *The Mill on the Floss.*[2] As a matter of principle both writers chose to follow the lives of obscure people, but their approach is vastly different. George Eliot, the dedicated realist, was moving towards the psychological novel. Reade, to whom we must apply the term romanticist, though its connotations do not quite apply to him in all respects, was content if his characters were colorful rather than complex, vivid rather than deep. He resolutely declines the attempt to make Kate more than the sweet invalid, Sybrandt and Cornelis more than the scheming brothers, Ghysbrecht more than the crafty miser, brokenly repentant at the end.

The same criticism cannot be leveled at the portraits of Gerard and Margaret without important reservations. It is true that there is little imaginative stretch in Reade's concept of Margaret Brandt, but her pride and a streak of stubbornness do differentiate her in some measure from a long line of fictional suffering heroines. Gerard, while subject to excesses of temperament and emotion that help produce the "situations" of which Reade was so fond, is given more than surface treatment. Though we see him from the outside rather than the inside, though we are *told* what and how he feels rather than allowed to infer it from subtleties of speech and action, we nevertheless follow him with interest and participate with him in the more moving of his experiences.

I think most readers will salute with enthusiasm the skill with which Reade builds sympathy for his star-crossed lovers. The tension is developed and maintained artfully as the novel nears its close, and in the final chapters Reade comes close to being an indisputably great novelist. It would be a very stonyhearted reader, certainly, who could put down this book without having

[2] It is interesting to remember that George Eliot's next novel, published the year after *The Cloister and the Hearth* was *Romola,* her own medieval Italian story.

been deeply moved by its climax. In *A Good Fight,* brought to a hasty close on demand of the editor of the journal in which it was appearing, Reade "revised the catastrophe; made Gerard and his sweetheart happy," as he lamented. Such a denouement is absurd, not to say grotesque, in a novel which logically could be only tragic. *The Cloister and the Hearth* ends with dignity and power, the emotion deriving honestly from the situation and the characters acting out their predestined parts under firm authorial control. It was with pardonable pride that Reade said of the last fifteen pages, "I think they will live."

The power of the final scene has its origin in the emotional context, to be sure, but one should not overlook Reade's triumph here as a stylist. His normal vein, one must admit, was not poetic. Emily Brontë's high imagination and Meredith's delicate fancy were quite beyond him. His careless habits of writing often resulted in absurdity. We are told of Margaret finding the feverfew, that "her eagle eye had seen it growing out of the window." At times he could be insufferably pompous: the old man was "redolent of wealth" and his purse was "plethoric." Some of the worst passages of this kind seem to be an abortive attempt to be funny: when the mule put her foot in a rabbit-hole, "the soil was strewn with dramatis personae"; when Denys threatened the taunting girls of Rotterdam, "they fled quadrivious." Similarly, the attempt to give a medieval flavor to the language by the use of an obsolete vocabulary is not always successful. Critics have objected, with cause, to Reade's use of capitals, exclamation marks, one-page chapters and the like to produce effects that should emerge from the text itself without adventitious aids. And, finally, the use not only of tags of foreign languages but of long passages goes beyond the legitimate purposes of either creating a continental atmosphere for his traveling characters or of suggesting a cosmopolitan culture.

Reade's surest talent as a writer (and it is a very sound one) derives from his experience in the theater. He had a clever hand for dialogue, as the scenes involving Denys and Marion attest, and he had a highly polished skill in the use of puns, witticisms, and other ingenious word-play. He could neatly turn an amusing phrase: Cornelis and Sybrandt were devoted to "agriculture in its unremunerative form—wild oats." On occasion he, like other practiced writers, could say things memorably: Signor Bonaventura "chatted ephemeralities while Gerard wrote the immortal lives"; at "Les Trois Poissons" the peevish old fellow "kept mumchance during the raillery, but crept out into the sunshine of commonplaces." But for the most part Reade's style is functional rather than brilliant. The appropriate descriptive adjectives are not *lambent, shimmering,* and *coruscating,* but, at Reade's best, *clean, bare* and *artless.* Charles Reade may sometimes be a prosy writer, but there are moments when his simplicity makes him a very effective one.

No reader of wide experience in the recognized masterpieces of fiction would call *The Cloister and the Hearth* one of the greatest English novels. It has too many flaws of loose structure and too little insight into the origin of the deeper human emotions. Reade was not a Flaubert or a Dostoevsky or a Henry James, and it would be uncritical to claim too much for him. But he was a man of intelligence with a superb narrative gift. His finest novel has moments of sustained excitement, and his grasp of character is firm enough to maintain if not total credence at least the willing suspension of disbelief. In the final pages he asks our sympathy for the "rare constancy and pure affection" of Gerard and Margaret. It is not likely that this will be denied, for theirs is a touching story of love's exaltation and of love's despair. English fiction is richer for Charles Reade's moving tribute to their memory.

BRADFORD A. BOOTH

University of California, Los Angeles
September, 1960

BIBLIOGRAPHICAL NOTE

BIBLIOGRAPHICAL MATERIAL

Elwin, Malcolm, *Charles Reade: a Biography*, London, 1930. Contains material on Reade's minor writing for periodicals as well as lists of performances of his plays.

Sadleir, Michael, *Excursions in Victorian Bibliography*, London, 1922.

BIOGRAPHY

Elwin, Malcolm, *Charles Reade: a Biography*, London, 1930. There are two earlier studies, largely adulatory and uncritical, but Elwin is the best source.

CRITICAL STUDIES

Books

Phillips, W. C., *Dickens, Reade and Collins: Sensation Novelists*, New York, 1919.

Turner, Albert M., *The Making of The Cloister and the Hearth*, Chicago, 1938.

Articles

Besant, Sir Walter, Introduction to *The Cloister and the Hearth*, London, 1894.

Booth, Bradford A., "Trollope, Reade, and *Shilly-Shally*," *Nineteenth-Century Fiction*, I (March, 1947), 45–57; II (June, 1947), 43–51.

Burns, Wayne, "Pre-Raphaelitism in Reade's Early Fiction," *Publications of the Modern Language Association*, LX (1945), 1149–1164.

Burns, Wayne, *"The Cloister and the Hearth:* a Classic Reconsidered," *Nineteenth-Century Fiction,* II (1947), 71–82.

Burns, Wayne, "The Sheffield Flood: a Critical Study of Reade's Fiction," *Publications of the Modern Language Association,* LXIII (1948), 686–695.

Burns, Wayne, "Charles Reade's *Christie Johnstone:* a Portrait of the Artist as a Young Pre-Raphaelite," in *From Jane Austen to Joseph Conrad* (Minneapolis, 1958), pp. 208–221.

Gettmann, Royal A., "The Serialization of Reade's *A Good Fight,"* *Nineteenth-Century Fiction,* VI (June, 1951), 21–32.

Haines, L. F., "Reade, Mill and Zola: a Study of the Character and Intention of Reade's Fiction," *Studies in Philology,* XL (1943), 463–480.

Howells, William Dean, *My Literary Passions,* New York, 1895, pp. 191–197.

Orwell, George, "Books in General," *The New Statesman,* XX (August 17, 1940), 162.

Sutcliffe, Emerson Grant, "The Stage in Reade's Novels," *Studies in Philology,* XXVII (1930), 654–688.

Sutcliffe, Emerson Grant, "Femina Vera in Reade's Novels," *Publications of the Modern Language Association,* XLVI (1931), 1260–1279.

Sutcliffe, Emerson Grant, "Plotting in Reade's Novels," *Publications of the Modern Language Association,* XLVII (1932), 834–863.

Sutcliffe, Emerson Grant, "Psychological Presentation in Reade's Novels," *Studies in Philology,* XXXVIII (1941), 521–542.

Sutcliffe, Emerson Grant, "Fact, Realism and Morality in Reade's Fiction," *Studies in Philology,* XLI (1944), 582–598.

Sutcliffe, Emerson Grant, "Reade in His Heroes," *Nineteenth-Century Fiction,* I (1946), 3–16.

Swinburne, A. C., *Miscellanies,* London, 1886, pp. 271–302.

HARPER'S MODERN CLASSICS

(Continued on next page)

HARPER'S MODERN CLASSICS (*Continued*)